Reader's Digest

CONDENSED BOOKS

THE READER'S DIGEST ASSOCIATION LIMITED
Berkeley Square House, Berkeley Square, London W1X 6AB
THE READER'S DIGEST ASSOCIATION
SOUTH AFRICA (PTY) LTD
Reader's Digest House, 130 Strand Street, Cape Town
Printed by BPCC Petty Ltd, Leeds
Bound by BPCC Hazell Books Ltd, Aylesbury
Original cover design by Jeffery Matthews FSIAD

For information as to ownership
of copyright in the material in this book see last page

CONDENSED BOOKS

TSUNAMI
Richard Martin Stern

PUBLISHED BY SECKER & WARBURG

THE CITY OF JOY
Dominique Lapierre

PUBLISHED BY CENTURY HUTCHINSON

SPEARHEAD
Peter Driscoll

PUBLISHED BY BANTAM

HUNTER'S MOON
Garry Kilworth

PUBLISHED BY UNWIN HYMAN

CONTENTS

TSUNAMI

Richard Martin Stern

Tsunami is the dreaded word for a killer wave that, fuelled by millions of tons of water, can travel at over six hundred miles per hour, and explode on shore to a height of over a hundred feet. If oceanographer Pete Williamson's calculations are correct, just such a force will soon hit Encino Beach, California, packed with people and boats. Is Pete's prediction accurate? And can he convince the sceptical townspeople in time?

High-impact suspense from the author of *Wildfire*.

page 9

THE CITY OF JOY

Dominique Lapierre

In Calcutta lies an overpopulated, disease-ridden slum known ironically as Anand Nagar, the City of Joy. To this place come two men: one, a priest seeking to share the lives of its people; the other, a peasant toiling between the shafts of a rickshaw to provide for his family. As each is absorbed into the community, he becomes part of the day-to-day heroism that transforms it from a place of despair to one of hope, even for its children.

A moving, true account by a distinguished author.

page 99

SPEARHEAD

Peter Driscoll

For twenty-five years Lincoln
Kumalo, a revered black nationalist
leader, has been a political prisoner in
South Africa. Now in failing health,
he is a severe embarrassment to the
government. As an audacious plot to
murder Kumalo is put into operation,
an ex-SAS major and a motley team of
supporters hatch an ingenious—and
highly dangerous—counter-plan.

An action-packed novel, as exciting
as it is topical, that enhances Peter
Driscoll's reputation as a master
thriller writer.

page 207

HUNTER'S MOON

Garry Kilworth

O-ha the vixen has lived in Trinity
Wood ever since leaving her parents.
Now she is fully grown, with a mate of
her own, awaiting her first litter of
cubs. Surrounded by the wood she
loves, she thinks her happiness can
never end. But every day the humans
are coming closer, with their
bulldozers churning up the earth and
their concrete mixers creating streets
and houses.

Garry Kilworth's thrilling and
powerful story skilfully dramatises the
threats to our vanishing countryside.

page 371

TSUNAMI

A CONDENSATION OF THE BOOK BY

Richard Martin Stern

ILLUSTRATED BY WALTER RANE

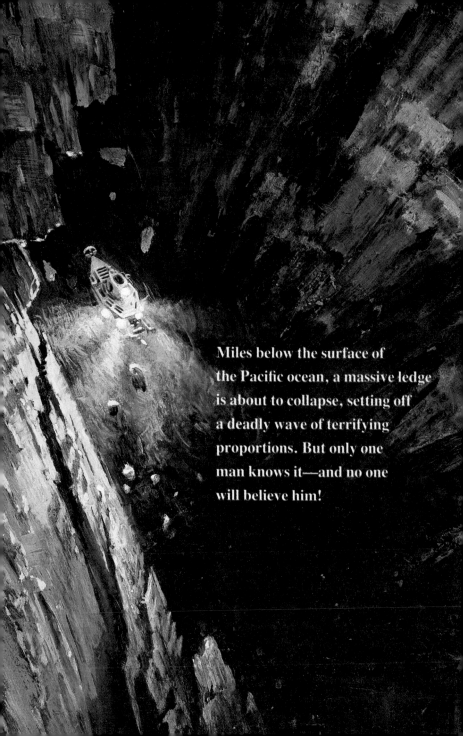

Miles below the surface of the Pacific ocean, a massive ledge is about to collapse, setting off a deadly wave of terrifying proportions. But only one man knows it—and no one will believe him!

Prologue

Even before they reached the seven-thousand-foot depth, the steadily decreasing sunlight had disappeared altogether, and outside the small portholes there was only total blackness.

The gauge for water temperature showed merely minor fluctuations in its inexorable drop towards near freezing. The pressure on the tiny submarine's hull would continue to build to almost one and a half tons per square inch, ample force to flatten the hulls of lesser vessels like so many beer cans.

The cramped and dimly lit interior was filled with instrumentation and controls, condemning the two men inside to limited movement. After a dive of several hours it would be almost unbearably confining.

Henry Larson, biologist, unshaven and wearing headphones, dressed like his companion in T-shirt, jeans and sneakers, said, 'Your second time down, right? I've pretty well lost count of mine, but it's still a little different from a trip to the corner grocery store.'

'A bit,' Pete said—Peter Wayne Williamson, PhD, geologist, senior fellow at the Encino Beach (California) Oceanographic Institute. He was experiencing the same sensations as during his first dive: his pulse rate had risen, he knew that his blood pressure would have increased, and, most markedly, he was aware of a heightened sense of alertness, as if an internal switch had been thrown the moment the water had risen above the portholes and the sky had disappeared.

'Three thousand metres,' Henry said. 'Still not much to see yet, but we might as well have some light anyway.' He flipped on the external floodlights to illuminate the monochromatic world beyond the portholes. 'Shark,' he said. 'See him? Big fellow. Fascinating swimmers.' The sleek vision was almost instantly gone beyond the floodlights' range, into the surrounding gloom.

Pete watched without comment. He glanced at the depth gauge. 'Four thousand metres,' he said, and did the multiplication in his head—about thirteen thousand feet, and steadily descending.

'There,' Henry said suddenly. 'See it? The escarpment?'

'I see it.'

Pete watched the dimly defined bulk of the submerged cliff come into view. They were descending into a massive canyon near the nineteenth parallel of the South Pacific, wide and deep enough to contain the Grand Canyon as a minor wrinkle, but still only a tiny part of the largest geological feature on earth—a submerged mountain range and rift system over forty thousand miles in length, extending into and through all the oceans of the world.

And of all of that, Pete was thinking, people had actually seen only forty miles or so, which was why he and Henry were making this dive, the seventh of the expedition's planned fifteen, funded by the Department of Defense and drawing upon the scientists of the nation's leading oceanographic institutes: Woods Hole, Scripps, Encino Beach. It was all part of the continuing effort to unlock the secrets of the earth's origins and to understand the undersea behaviour of the oceans and ocean currents.

'I'm curious,' Henry said. 'I know the official info, but I get the impression you're not just along for the joyride. Are you looking for something special?'

'Just rock. I'm a geologist, remember?'

'Geologists hunt for oil and minerals.'

'Some of us look at oceans too. Land *and* water.'

Pete stared at the canyon wall and at the same time brought into focus his memory of the way it had looked nineteen months ago. Yes, damn it, there were changes, as he had anticipated.

Special precision wide-angle cameras to take before and after pictures would have been infinitely better than memory. The close-up cameras the tiny submarine was equipped with were of no use at all for his purposes. So I do the best I can, Pete told himself. Probably no one will believe me anyway.

Almost fifteen thousand feet, and yes, there was the broad ledge Pete remembered, curving off into the murky distance beyond the range of the floodlights. He studied it carefully, searching for the telltale changes.

'I'm interested in beasties,' Henry said. 'There is animal life in these depths, even though it's hard to believe, considering the enormous pressures and the scarcity of food. The pressures are still greater down

10

on the bottom, but so is the food supply, and there is life galore.'

Pete knew that on the bottom of this great chasm there was indeed another world—of huge blood-red worms within forests of white tubes; of great clams related to, but far different from, those found in shallow mud flats on the earth's surface; of crablike creatures able to withstand the enormous pressures of the depths, unable to survive in less. More important to Pete were the areas where molten magma, the stuff of the earth's interior, oozed out through widening cracks in the seafloor to cool into strange formations, building surface crust similar to the landmasses upon which man dwells. There were also signs of the vast tectonic plates, sections of the earth's crust, some of which in a manner of speaking bore entire continents upon their backs. They were forever in motion, separating, colliding, altering the physical world we live in.

When they reached the bottom of the trench, Pete and Henry would busy themselves with the multitude of tasks assigned to this dive—sampling, measurement, observation, gathering. But Pete's interest right now was on the canyon walls that loomed closer on either side as the minisub descended into the gigantic V-shaped abyss.

'Approaching nine thousand metres,' Henry said. 'A fair piece down, no?'

A little further beneath the ocean's surface, Pete thought, than the summit of Mount Everest was above it. He was silent, his eyes still fixed upon the canyon walls, measuring the fresh visual data against his memory of the dive nineteen months before. He stored it in his mind for later consideration. But already the uneasiness had begun, based at last on more than purely statistical suspicion.

1

Astonishingly, in retrospect, it began as a day very much like any other, with a smog cloud already blurring the sharp outline of the ridge separating the valley from the Los Angeles basin itself.

Dan Garfield had the car radio tuned to the classical FM station now playing Mozart's Piano Concerto No. 19—flowing, effortless music that once upon a time he would have scorned as old-fashioned, out of step with the modern world. He had worn long hair then, and had been convinced that no one in the world could match his young intellectual capabilities. But you changed your tastes and your opinions, and were no longer the same person at forty-two that you had been at twenty.

The guard at the Garfield Associates electronics plant gate gave a quasi-military salute as Garfield passed through the raised barrier. He drove up the hedge-lined road straight to the central building, where he parked in the slot that bore his name.

The guard at the front door said, 'Good morning, Mr Garfield,' and the phrase was repeated by the receptionist inside, by two men stepping out of the elevator, and by the executive-suite receptionist on the third floor. In his inner office the always-efficient Helen was waiting with her usual smile and greeting. Then she was immediately down to business, reading from her ever-present notebook.

'Baker, the Plant Three manager, would like to see you. I have set the appointment tentatively at ten thirty.'

'Right,' Garfield said, wondering what bee was in Baker's bonnet now. 'What else?'

'At nine thirty,' Helen said, 'there is the engineering staff meeting, if you wish to attend?'

'Keep it open. What else?'

Helen's voice was toneless. 'Mr Case and Mr Carmichael would like to see you at nine. Mr Case said it was urgent.'

'It frequently is. I'll see them, of course.' He glanced at his watch. 'That's in fifteen minutes. Any mail?'

'On your desk,' Helen said, and turned away. At the door she paused and looked back. 'Your luncheon date with Miss Anderson is for noon. I have booked your usual table at Angelo's.'

All quite normal so far.

Paul Case and Walker Carmichael, Garfield's business partners, arrived precisely at nine. The punctuality, Garfield thought, would have been Paul's doing, his facts-and-figures mentality demanding precision. Walker, the salesman, marched to a less regulated drumbeat.

'Paul . . . Walker,' Garfield said, 'good morning. Sit down, please.' He watched Case close the door carefully and take his seat with his usual neat movements. Carmichael plumped into an overstuffed chair and looked uneasy. Garfield waited.

Case said slowly, 'The Atlas offer is still on the table, Dan.'

'We've already discussed that.'

Carmichael cleared his throat. 'They've sweetened the pot. By six and a half per cent.' He emphasised the figures.

'Which works out for each of us,' Case said, 'counting stock and stock options, very close to—'

'I'm not interested in the figures,' Garfield said. 'They're meaningless. We built this place from nothing, and each of us is already taking out more than he can ever spend.'

'The figures,' Case said, 'do not even include continuing royalties on your personal patents, Dan. You would be enormously wealthy. Enormously. We all would, as far as that goes.'

The trick, Garfield had long ago learned, was never to show your temper or your impatience. The politician's smile and quiet logic were the tools of persuasion. And if persuasion failed, there was always in the last resort a show of the authority that had become habitual over the years. 'We're all three still young,' Garfield said. 'And we're still growing. Our reputation, which is precisely what Atlas wants to buy, guarantees that we will continue to grow. And prosper.'

Carmichael, the salesman, said, 'How much is enough, Dan? There's a big, wide, wonderful world out there, and I, for one, want to enjoy it. All of it.' He hesitated.

'Go on, Walker,' Garfield said. 'Spell it out.'

'OK,' Carmichael said. 'I'm tired of this place. I want out. No more sales pitches, no more flying trips, no more haggling with gourd-headed bureaucrats. That's the bottom line, Dan.'

Garfield could recognise and face finality when he saw it. And he could make decisions on the spot. 'All right, Walker,' he said. 'If you've made up your mind—'

'I have.'

'Then Paul and I can buy you out. Our partnership agreement provides for that.'

Paul Case cleared his throat. 'Uh, negative, Dan,' he said. The office was suddenly still, the silence almost deafening. 'We have had legal advice, and there will be no difficulties.'

'Except me,' Garfield said. 'I won't go along, period.'

Paul Case stood up. 'You have no say, Dan. We have always deferred to your judgment up to now. But in this instance you are outvoted. We have instructed our attorneys to notify Atlas that its tender is accepted, and transfer of ownership will go forward. I believe there is nothing more to be said.'

He was gone, closing the door gently.

Carmichael heaved himself out of the large chair. 'Sorry about this, Dan,' he said. 'But their offer was too good to turn down.' He shook his head and produced a smile. 'You're going to be rolling in it, absolutely rolling. "Gotrocks" Garfield, that's you. Better try to get used to it.'

As simple, as unexpected and as devastating as that.

'THIS IS PURELY INFORMAL, a brainstorming session,' the Assistant Secretary said, looking round the table. 'The indications are that the French are planning another nuclear test in the South Pacific. What are we to make of that?'

The DOD—Department of Defense—man said, 'So what else is new? They've been doing it for years. It's a nuisance, but they give warning in the area, and the South Pacific is so big . . . They'll kill some fish, is all.'

The scientific adviser, whose name was Harry Saunders, said, 'Unless—' And then he stopped and shook his head. 'Will this be another fission test? Or is there a possibility of fusion?'

The Assistant Secretary said, 'Presently unclear. Is it important?'

'The difference,' Saunders said, 'is between kilotons—that is to say, thousands of tons of TNT—and megatons, millions of tons.'

The Assistant Secretary was looking at the scientific adviser. 'Give us a worst-case scenario. Are you thinking tidal wave?'

'Tsunami is the proper word,' Saunders said. 'Caused by some kind of seismic disturbance—an earthquake or volcanic explosion, that kind of thing. They can be devastating.'

'An example?'

'In nineteen sixty,' Saunders said, 'an earthquake on the coast of Chile sent out tsunamis that crossed the entire Pacific Ocean. On the way, those waves destroyed two square miles of downtown Hilo in Hawaii, and then continued their course to cause some three hundred and fifty million dollars' worth of damages in the harbours of Honshu and Hokkaido in Japan—travelling a total distance in excess of ten thousand miles.'

'And,' the DOD man said, 'you're thinking that a nuclear test in the South Pacific, especially a fusion test, could set off that kind of thing? Poppycock! We ran tests ourselves, and nothing happened.'

Harry Saunders disliked arguments or even theoretical discussions with laymen. They rarely led to anything but confusion. 'No doubt you're right,' he said. 'I was just giving examples.'

FOR THE FIRST TIME in his adult life Dan Garfield felt unable to cope with the situation. *Helpless* was the word that sounded in his mind like a drumbeat of doom.

Garfield had always prided himself on his logic and his knowledge of facts in governing his actions and his life. Now this smart fellow, Dan Garfield, clear-sighted, prescient, was suddenly and without warning blindsided, as they say in football, by his partners, two men he had always considered completely under his control. The shock still stunned him.

Everybody assumed that the sale was Garfield's idea, and the admiration expressed for his business acumen merely made matters worse. I am a sham, he told himself, but could not bring himself to tell anyone else, not even Maude Anderson. He had had his chance, and not taken it, that first day at lunch at Angelo's.

She had worn a dress of a particular shade of blue that accentuated the tone of her eyes and her even, glowing tan. 'You're preoccupied,' she said, and smiled. 'But then you usually are, except sometimes when I do think I get your whole attention.' The smile spread. 'But that's not in public.'

Usually he enjoyed vague references to their intimacy, but today it made him uncomfortable. Everything was suddenly changed. 'You've been away,' he said. 'I've missed you. Good trip?'

14

'Old friends. Tahoe. Some waterskiing, a job offer.' Her smile lit her eyes. 'But I like it here in the LA area better. And if I sell a house or two every now and again, I have all I need.' The smile disappeared. 'You *are* preoccupied, Dan. What is it?'

'Hunger. Shall we order?' And so the moment had passed, and had not returned.

Running into his old friend Dr Tom Winslow on the street almost immediately following the Atlas deal was sheer chance. Tom's eyes did not miss much. 'You look,' he said lightly, 'as if somebody just stole your candy.'

'I lost my taste for sweets years ago.'

'Then you're not sleeping well.' The tone turned serious. 'And from what I read in the financial pages, I don't wonder. Big negotiations. High finance. Clara tells me there is even a piece about you in *Time* making you out to be a genius.'

'If they say that,' Garfield said, 'they're a hundred and eighty degrees wrong.'

Tom glanced at his watch. 'How about a cup of coffee? My next patient isn't due for a half-hour.'

They found a relatively secluded booth in a nearby coffee shop. 'We go back how long?' Tom said. 'Twenty years?'

Almost exactly. Garfield had been a young PhD in electronics and Tom had just been finishing his residency in internal medicine when they met. 'About that,' Garfield said.

'You had big ideas, and I was going to cure the world's illnesses. Your ideas succeeded spectacularly, and I haven't even made a dent in all the bellyaches and ulcers man is prey to.' Tom was still studying Garfield, but his tone was almost casual. 'Clara's opening the house at the beach. She and Lucy are moving down for the summer. I'll get there mostly on weekends. Why don't you go down for a little rest and keep them company? Frankly, boy, you look as if you could use a change.'

'It shows?' Garfield tried to make it light.

'It does.' Tom stood up abruptly. 'Be right back,' he said, and was gone, walking purposefully. He was back in a few minutes, smiling as he slid into his seat again. 'All set. Clara's delighted. She's looking forward to having a man around the house.'

'Now, wait a minute. Maybe after she's settled in, a weekend when you go down, that kind of thing. But don't just dump me in her lap like this when she's busy.'

'I told you, she's delighted. And I'd say you need it bad, even if I don't know why.' Tom paused. 'Give me one good reason against.'

That was the trouble—he didn't have any reason against. Encino Beach would be a distraction from his bitter thoughts. He sat silent, tempted but reluctant.

'You can change light bulbs,' Tom said, 'and put that electronics expertise to work fixing the toaster.' He finished his coffee at a gulp and stood up. 'I told Clara you'd be down this afternoon. See you, boy,' he said, and was gone.

2

Once, Encino Beach had been just another seacoast harbour town south of Los Angeles, with a commercial fishing fleet, a boatyard, a single yacht club, and scattered cottages owned by visitors who enjoyed sailing or deep-water fishing. The harbour was natural, and protected against storms by a low, narrow peninsula. Later, stone jetties were added at the harbour entrance, extending the narrow channel for further protection.

After World War II, as southern California exploded in population and money became plentiful, larger and more expensive houses were built in all the areas fronting on or near to the harbour. On holidays and summer weekends the broad beach on the ocean side of the peninsula was filled with visitors, although serious surfers transported their boards to San Onofre or Malibu where, unlike calm Encino Beach, incoming swells piled up surf of sometimes ferocious size.

When the freeway came, it was built well inland on higher ground, bypassing Encino Beach and leaving the old, overburdened coast highway at near sea level to carry the coastal traffic. More and more, Encino Beach became a year-round residential area, a Los Angeles bedroom community where, during rush hours, community traffic moved bumper to bumper by fits and starts.

His Honor Jimmy Silva, Mayor of Encino Beach, was an insurance man by trade, a native son, product of three generations of local commercial fishermen. Now in his fifties, Silva was getting thick round the middle, something he attempted to conceal by wearing wildly patterned aloha shirts, their short sleeves amply displaying his hairy, brawny forearms.

He knew all the long-time locals and a good share of the regular visitors. He had known Joe Hines, Encino Beach harbourmaster, since youth. Joe Hines sat in Silva's office now, the door to the reception room closed.

'Too many people,' Joe was saying, 'too many boats, too much money floating around in the whole country, if you ask me.' He was tall and lean and weathered, once a prized crewman for big ocean-racing sailing yachts.

'More people,' Jimmy said, 'more money. Simple as that. You got to catch up.'

Joe was not to be diverted. 'Not an empty slip or an empty mooring

16

in the whole harbour. You want to buy a boat, first thing you better think is where you're going to keep it.'

'We're going to help solve that,' His Honor said, and took a rolled architect's drawing from a shelf beside his desk. It was a sketch plan of multiple houses, each one fronting on a canal, with its own slip and moored sailing or power yacht. Joe studied the plan carefully.

'Neat, huh?' His Honor said.

Joe's eyes were still on the sketch. 'And just where in hell are you figuring to put this?'

'Over in the back bay, where you and I used to go clamming on those mud flats.'

Joe looked up then. 'Dredge her out?'

'Dredge her out and build her up, solid landfill. If we had big tides to contend with, we might have problems.' The mayor shook his head. 'But we don't. A few feet, is all.'

'You in real estate now? I can't keep up with you. Says Insurance on the door.'

'Just spreading my bets,' said His Honor with a complacent grin.

Joe was studying the sketch again. 'Over fifty houses. That's going to take a lot of dredging and filling, and a whole lot of money.'

'Bond issue,' His Honor said. 'They're big now—municipal bonds, tax-free income, what they call tax shelters.'

Joe Hines sighed and stood up. 'All I got to say is, we already got too many boats in this harbour, and too many of them owned by landlubbers who don't know how to handle them. If we ever had to get all those boats out to sea—'

'Now, just why would we have to get all the boats out to sea?'

'Dunno,' Joe Hines said, glancing again at the drawing. He looked as if he wanted to spit. 'This is what you call progress?'

'That's the word,' His Honor said.

DAN GARFIELD TURNED OFF the causeway from the coast highway and drove slowly along Encino Beach's main street. Here at its beginning it offered a stunning view of the harbour, the bay flat and shining in the late afternoon sun, dotted with hundreds of pleasure boats. The moored sailing boats, Garfield noted, all pointed up the bay, their deep keels responding uniformly to the outgoing tidal current. The high-sided cabin cruisers were relatively unaffected, pointing whichever way wind currents swung them. The inexorable laws of physics, neat, predictable, determined their behaviour. Physics, science in general, constituted a world unlike that of humans, and one in which Garfield had always felt at home. By comparison, the totally unexpected behaviour of his partners was to him incomprehensible and aberrant.

Well, down here at Encino Beach maybe he could relax, recharge his exhausted batteries and somehow figure out how to regain the identity that he felt he had lost.

At the Winslows' house, Clara met him in cut-off jeans, sneakers and a short-sleeved blouse. She had always been a stunning woman, Garfield thought, and the years—she was now just forty—had, if anything, increased her attractiveness.

'Welcome, stranger,' she said. 'I could hardly believe it when Tom said you were coming.'

'You are good to take me in.'

'And Lucy is in a complete tizzy. You represent glamour.'

'Tinsel, nothing more. I'm simply one of the unemployed.'

'Good. Then Lucy and I can monopolise you.' Her eyes went beyond him. 'Here she is now.'

Garfield turned and stared. He had known Lucy since she was a baby, but not like this, suddenly blossomed at sixteen into rounded womanly curves, the awkwardness of adolescence entirely gone. He shook his head in wonder, conscious of Clara's amusement. 'I didn't expect this,' he said.

'Big deal,' Lucy said, 'It happens to all of us.' And then, suddenly shy, she added, 'Hi. We haven't seen you in a long time. You're famous now.'

Garfield hoped that his smile showed no embarrassment.

Clara said, 'You know where your room is, Dan. And you'll have time for a drink before dinner.'

When Garfield entered the kitchen after unpacking his bag, he found a visitor there. 'This is Pete Williamson,' Clara said. 'Pete's our nextdoor neighbour.'

A middle-sized, muscular, deeply tanned man, unshaven and wearing swimming trunks, a T-shirt and ragged sneakers, gripped Garfield's hand. His smile was friendly. 'Welcome to the beach.'

'Pete,' Lucy said, 'is an oceanographer at the Encino Beach Oceanographic Institute. He's just back from the bottom of the ocean, way out in the South Pacific. He brought me some coral.'

'Don't give away everything, Princess. That's just between us, remember?' Amused affection was plain.

Clara said, 'Why don't you two take your drinks out on the porch and leave Lucy and me to produce dinner. You'll stay, Pete?'

'With pleasure.'

The two men went out to sit on the porch in the fading light, looking over the bay, the boats, the houses jammed together. 'It grows on you,' Pete said, 'the place and the life.'

'I've known it for quite a while.'

Pete nodded. 'But knowing it and living in it are two different things. From what I read, you've been too busy for this relaxed life.'

True. And uncomfortably close to the bone. Garfield changed the subject. 'The bottom of the ocean, Lucy said. Hyperbole?'

Pete gave a quick grin. 'Not exactly. Minisub, diving out in the Pacific, thirty thousand feet down in one of the trenches.'

Garfield looked at the man with fresh interest. 'Doing what, if it isn't a secret?'

'Pursuing a pet theory. Long story.' Pete waved one hand in a vague gesture. 'An unpopular theory in some circles, including my own hierarchy. Oceanographers, most scientists, I guess, tend to be rather conservative.'

'And you're rocking the boat, making waves?'

'Something like that.'

'I'd like to hear your long story, if you're willing to tell it.'

'It's pretty far out. And what data I have are sketchy.'

Garfield sipped his drink. 'I'd still like to hear it.'

'Done,' Pete said. 'It'll be a pleasure to talk to somebody new. How about an oceanside walk tomorrow, say, about noon?'

'I can't think of anything I'd like better,' Garfield said, and suddenly realised that he meant it.

LUCY WAS IN THE KITCHEN when Garfield came down from his room the next morning. 'Mom's gone up to town,' Lucy said. 'I'm coping. What do you like for breakfast? Omelette? Bacon?'

'Sounds elegant,' Garfield said.

'Juice is in the refrigerator,' she said, busying herself at the stove. 'I read that story about you in *Time*. They say you're a genius.'

'I'm a fraud.' Strangely, he found no pain in the saying.

'Some fraud, raking in all that loot.' Lucy turned from the stove to study Garfield's face. 'I used to be scared of you, did you know that? Funny, I'm not any more.'

Garfield felt as if he had just been knighted.

He helped with the dishes after breakfast. That chore done, he headed for the local library, where he read Pete Williamson's monographs and papers. It was a quarter to twelve when he set out for their meeting. There were many questions in his mind.

Pete, dressed in faded jeans, T-shirt and the same ragged sneakers, was waiting on a bench facing the ocean. He was watching the lines of swells as they marched in, grew in height to become white-topped and then broke upon the sand in endless procession. Their effect was almost hypnotic, Garfield thought as he sat down on the bench. 'Good morning,' he said, and waited quietly.

Pete said, 'You still want to hear my far-out theories?'

'Very much.'

Pete nodded. 'OK. July twenty-fifth, nineteen sixty-three—ring any bells?'

Garfield closed his eyes. 'I had just finished my junior year at Cal

19

Tech. I had managed to grow a straggly beard.' He opened his eyes and smiled. 'The date has no connotations. Unless it had to do with electronics, I wouldn't even have noticed what was happening. My head was in the clouds.'

'The USA, Russia and Britain signed a treaty,' Pete said, 'banning all nuclear testing except underground. Only those three were signatories. France, for instance, has never felt bound by the treaty.'

'Hence their continued testing in the South Pacific?'

'You catch on quick.'

'I spent the morning in the library,' Garfield said. 'But I'm not sure I see the connection.'

Pete nodded. 'Without the data, you wouldn't. Before the treaty was signed we had geophysicists at Los Alamos, plotting and predicting the possible underwater effects of the testing we were planning. Big stuff, in the multimegaton range, also down in the South Pacific. When the treaty was signed that research stopped, but the collected and projected data were still available. You're with me so far?'

Garfield was silent. He merely nodded.

'When the French started testing,' Pete said, 'we warned them of some of the predicted results. But sometimes they don't listen, and as a result, one of the land sites they figured was safe is now eight feet under water.'

Garfield thought about it. 'I think I'm seeing at least the direction you're going, but—' He shook his head. 'Maybe it's best if you start at the beginning.'

'Right. A quick once-over.' Pete gestured at the shining ocean before them. 'The Pacific, seventy million square miles of it, one third of the earth's surface, the biggest and deepest of all the oceans. Those swells you see have come five, six thousand miles in lines that are usually so straight that the Polynesians used to navigate their big canoes hundreds of miles from island to island by steering at given angles to the lines of the swells.' He paused. 'So the ocean is predictable, no? Only it isn't. Not by a long shot.'

The man knew his subject and was able to explain it, Garfield thought as he listened.

'Counterclockwise from the top,' Pete said now, tracing a circle in the air as he spoke. 'Alaska and Russian Kamchatka to the north; Japan, Philippines, Indonesia to the west; Australia, New Zealand, Antarctica to the south; and to the east the coasts of South, Central and North America—that more or less defines the Pacific basin. Ringed with volcanoes and fracture zones, with more fracture zones on the sea bottom out in the middle where it's deepest. Called the Ring of Fire, the whole area. With reason. It's in flux, the whole thing.'

Garfield nodded in silence.

'As an example,' Pete said, 'the entire *cordillera*, the mountain

chain that runs from Alaska to the tip of South America, all of it is geologically young and in a sense still being formed. Which is why we get things like that Mexico earthquake a few years back, the Mount St Helens eruption, the San Andreas Fault here that one day will go into action. And on the other side of the ocean there's Krakatoa, which exploded back in eighteen eighty-three with the loudest bang ever heard by man. These are just a few examples, and they're all part of the same thing—the Ring of Fire.'

Garfield said, 'I gather from your papers that in your judgment a large movement is due in one of those mid-Pacific fracture zones. Maybe overdue.'

Pete Williamson spread his hands helplessly. 'I can't prove it. Nobody can. But I've gone back as far as any reports or even folk tales go concerning my particular mid-Pacific fracture zone. I've had an old chum up at Cal Tech set up computer models, and I wangled a ride on this last dive, which was in the same area where I dived nineteen months ago. In the meantime, we've had seismic disturbances in that area of the South Pacific. It's a restless planet we live on. Its

21

crust is always moving, twitching like a horse's skin in fly time. But I wanted to see for myself if I could detect any changes in nineteen months, right there.' He paused.

Garfield waited, impassive.

'All I have is visual evidence,' Pete said at last, 'but there have been changes. And according to my data, the seismic activity correlates with the known nuclear testing the French have carried out in the South Pacific. So what do we have?'

'I think I see it,' Garfield said, 'but go on.'

Pete drew a deep breath. 'Ever see what an avalanche can do? A big one? Trees, rocks, the surface structure itself gouged out as if by a giant bulldozer. Wet, unstable spring snow up near the top of a mountain begins to slide and gather material and momentum as it goes. And it can be started by a disturbance as minor as a gunshot, or even a sharp whistle.'

'And you think an explosion could trigger the same kind of thing under water?' Garfield said.

Pete was well into the subject now. 'That entire trench is a fracture zone. I could see cracks that run along a broad ledge at about the forty-five-hundred-metre depth. How far those cracks extend, I don't know. Our lights only reached so far. But the ledge extends for a hundred miles or so. It may all be unstable, like the wet snow on the mountain top. And then?' He was silent.

'You're talking tsunamis,' Garfield said slowly. 'I thought that might be it. What the newspapers call tidal waves, and aren't. Ocean waves caused by seismic movement—an earthquake, a volcanic explosion, whatever—waves that can travel up to six hundred miles an hour for great distances, waves of enormous energy involving millions of tons of water. They slow when they reach shallow water because of the drag of the bottom, and begin to build, like these breakers here. Tsunamis have reached heights of one hundred, two hundred feet.'

Pete said slowly, 'In one morning you did a lot of reading.'

'Yes. I'm good at that. And I remember what I read.' He said it without pretension, as if he were saying, Yes, I'm left-handed.

Pete said, 'Not all seismic disturbances, even underwater ones, cause tsunamis. There has to be vertical movement which causes displacement in the underwater mass, a disturbance producing maybe seven point five and up on the Richter scale.'

Garfield said, 'Isn't that exactly what you're talking about, if that ledge is unstable for its entire length? An underwater avalanche of that magnitude would displace an enormous amount of water mass, wouldn't it?'

'Yeah.' Pete was silent, staring out to sea. 'So you see how far out I am? Just because of what I've researched, deduced, and been able to check only visually, almost casually, as we descended.' He scooped up a handful of sand, then tossed it away in one violent motion.

'What if it were to happen—a huge underwater avalanche in your unstable area, an avalanche producing a Richter-scale reading of eight or even higher?'

'The International Tsunami Warning System, headquartered in Hawaii, would go into action, collecting data from reporting stations all round the Pacific basin. They'd pinpoint the epicentre and, if tsunamis were generated, predict their arrival times at various shore locations by measuring wave length—the distance between the crests of the swells—and speed.' Pete smiled almost sadly. 'But about all there would be to do when you got the warning would be to put out to sea if you had a boat, or head for high ground if you were on land.'

'Put out to sea?'

'The swells,' Pete said, 'travelling maybe at four hundred and fifty miles an hour, would be only two or three feet high. At sea you wouldn't even notice one passing under your hull. It's when they reach shallow water and start to build up, and all the water, hundreds of millions of tons of it, builds the slowing swell into a wave—that's what would do the damage. In seventeen hundred and three a single series of tsunami waves is thought to have killed a hundred thousand people in a bay on the Sanriku coast of Japan. The Japanese have records of tsunami disasters going back to the tenth century. In fact, the word itself is Japanese: it means "large waves in harbour". '

Garfield said, 'And here? Right here?'

'We have a wide continental shelf,' Pete said, 'that's the shallow part, before the bottom drops off into really deep water, and that should protect us pretty well.'

'*Should?*'

'Oh, hell,' Pete said in exasperation, 'we're not dealing with certainties. This kind of thing isn't like your electronic circuitry. You know precisely what will happen there. We don't.' He blew out his breath in a soundless whistle. 'Waves have periodicity. See those swells out there? They're almost as regular as clockbeats. We could have a storm, a big one, pushing shore water levels well above normal, *and* a spring tide—that's the highest tide of the month—at the same time, and if a tsunami swell coincided exactly with the periodicity of the storm waves, you'd get an amplification of forces.'

Garfield nodded. 'Wave reinforcement.'

'*If* it all worked out that way,' Pete continued, 'large tsunami waves, combining with high spring-tide surf and hurricane-caused waves, might very well roll over that continental-shelf protection. What even one such big, destructive wave would do on this low-lying California coast, with wall-to-wall people and cars and houses, and boats in the harbour all jammed together . . . It doesn't bear thinking about.'

Everything that had been said had led up to this moment and this inevitable conclusion, as, right from the start, Garfield had been reasonably certain it would.

'You're wrong, you know,' Garfield said. 'It *demands* thinking about.' The words carried the authority of incontrovertible fact.

Pete was silent for a long time, staring fixedly out to sea. 'OK,' he said at last, in an almost angry voice. He turned to look at Garfield. 'All I have is a wild theory based on some questionable data. You're the big-picture man, looking ahead and seeing possibilities. That piece in *Time* about you emphasised your vision. I—' He stopped and spread his hands. 'I'm just an oceanographer, not a mover and shaker. Sure, I have ideas, but that's all they amount to—ideas. And what is there to do about it anyway?'

'I don't know yet,' Garfield said. 'But you make a convincing case, and if it stands up to scrutiny, then you can't just ignore it. Neither can I, as far as that goes.' He was committing himself, he thought, and that had not been his purpose. Or had it? 'It's not my field, but facts are facts and logic is logic regardless of the subject matter.'

'My ideas,' Pete said, the anger no longer visible, 'run directly counter to conventional wisdom. Southern California has never, to anyone's knowledge, had tsunami damage, probably because of that wide continental shelf. Places like Japan, Chile, Hilo in Hawaii, and perhaps parts of Central America are far more likely to be devastated, if my theories are correct.'

'But in your worst-possible scenario,' Garfield said, 'we could have trouble here as well.'

Pete nodded. 'That's how I see it. So what do we do about it?'

'We scrutinise your data first.'

'We?'

'You have a printout of your computer models. Let me study it. I'm not exactly a stranger to data analysis, and you can provide the technical expertise I lack.'

'First, verification. Then what?'

'We decide what can be done. And do it.'

Pete shook his head in gathering wonder. 'Boy, you are something else! The man with all the answers.' He felt relief that at least he was no longer alone with his dark thoughts.

'Maybe I'm just the man with the questions,' said Garfield.

MAUDE ANDERSON HAD READ the *Time* story, too, with its detailed account of the sale of Garfield Associates to Atlas Telecommunications and its praise for Garfield's apparently calculated reluctance, which resulted in a far higher price than was originally offered. Then she thought back to that last lunch with Dan, whom she hadn't heard from since. She sat for a long time gazing out of the window of her apartment in the Westwood section of Los Angeles, her thoughts ranging from happiness for Dan to puzzlement over his long silence, and confusion concerning her own feelings.

She had no real claim on him, she told herself sternly. Their relationship had been without conditions, an adult association between a man and a woman, no more than that, which was precisely the way she had wanted it. Lunches at places like Angelo's, seats in a box at the Hollywood Bowl, a weekend in Hawaii, but no deep personal involvement. After her divorce it had taken her years to regain a sense of wholeness, and she was not about to jeopardise it again even with someone she liked as much as Dan Garfield.

But why had Dan suddenly dropped out of her life? Because he was now no longer merely well-off, but, if the *Time* article was to be believed, wealthy almost beyond comprehension? If that was it, she could not escape a feeling of resentment.

She was a direct, straightforward person, and her immediate impulse was to pick up the phone and demand an explanation, an impulse she quickly stifled. She had never pursued a man in her life, and she was not about to start now. So Dan could call or not, as he chose, and that was an end to it.

Then, at a party one night, her friends Jack and Betsy Barnes said that they were opening their Encino Beach house for the summer and why didn't she come down for a week or so?

'Love to,' she said, reflecting later that it could not have been sheer coincidence, but somehow had to have been ordained.

PETE WENT BACK to his office at the institute that afternoon after delivering the computer printout to Garfield. He stopped by habit at the seismograph room for a look at the revolving cylinder on which the mechanical pen traced a continuous line. There were the usual squiggles and minor irregularities; the line was never entirely smooth, because somewhere, at some magnitude, the earth's crust was always being disturbed, and the vibrations from those disturbances travelled through and round the earth in varying types of shock waves that registered on the seismograph.

He walked along the hall to his office and plumped down in his desk chair to stare at the huge wall map of the Pacific Ocean. There, in the vastness of the ocean, was where he had made both dives; he had marked the location carefully with a small *x*. The large-scale map, of course, told him nothing except relative location, but he had detailed bottom charts, the results of innumerable soundings made accurate by modern technology.

The ledge was there: the charts corroborated that. And it did extend for almost a hundred miles, about a hundred and sixty kilometres. How much of it was as apparently unstable as the tiny portion he had been able to study so briefly, he could not possibly say.

So face it, he told himself. The scenario Dan had manoeuvred him into describing was possible. And there was another possibility he had not even mentioned, and it could make the situation far worse. Tropical disturbances sometimes turned into full-fledged hurricanes, their paths totally unpredictable. In 1939 the fringe of a hurricane had caught this low-lying California coast, and waves had swept across the Encino Beach peninsula and into the harbour. Encino Beach was not wall-to-wall people then, and damage had not been great.

But suppose, just suppose, instead of a mere storm, a hurricane fringe were to coincide with tsunami waves emanating from that x marked on the wall map and speeding in all directions, as ripples spread in a pool. What would be the result then?

Sheer, utter and total disaster. Nothing less.

3

Jack and Betsy Barnes were in their late thirties, attractive, gregarious and, because of Jack's shrewd real-estate investments, wealthy.

They owned a home in the Brentwood section of Los Angeles, a waterfront house in Encino Beach and a half-share in a skiing condominium at Big Bear. At Encino Beach they kept a fifty-foot power cruiser on a mooring at the yacht club.

They knew Maude Anderson through her real-estate work. They were on their sun deck overlooking the bay, drinks at hand, when Maude arrived for her planned visit.

'Looking good, babe,' Jack said as he kissed her lightly in welcome. 'Get comfortable and join us. I'll build you a drink.'

It was Betsy who broached the subject later, in private on the beach. 'Your man's down here. Did you know that? Is that why you agreed to come down? Don't answer that.' Her mind rarely stayed on one subject long. 'New swimsuit?' Maude nodded, slightly embarrassed.

Betsy barrelled on. 'I've always thought one-piece could be far sexier than bikinis. All they do is display.' And again the change of pace. 'We're going out to dinner, hon. A new place Jack found.'

The new place was called Harbor Haven, and it featured, as Jack put it, 'Either blackened—that is, charred—seafood, or beef grilled over a mesquite-wood fire. They're the in things this week. Who knows what it'll be next week.'

In essence, Maude was thinking, Jack was expressing what non-southern Californians considered the basic criticism of the area: its constant change. She had heard it in the East long before she ever came to LA. Impermanence was the word. She wondered if the word applied to Dan Garfield as well.

'Pensive, aren't we, hon?' Betsy said. 'Have you heard from glamour boy at all since he won the jackpot?'

Maude smiled without answering.

'If and when you see him,' Jack said, 'you might tell him that I've got a couple of propositions that could interest him.'

Betsy said, 'You promised to lay off business while Maude's here.'

'Just a word and a hint.'

'I heard he's staying with the Winslows,' Betsy said. 'I was on the Arts Festival Committee last year with Clara Winslow, so we could ask them over for drinks or something.'

Maude felt naked, exposed, and shook her head in silence.

'Don't try to rush it, huh?' Betsy said. 'Probably you're right. Let's wait a couple of days and see what happens. If he catches sight of you in that swimsuit . . .'

Maybe coming down here was a mistake, Maude thought, but it was too late now to reconsider. 'I like this blackened fish,' she said, managing to smile.

THE ASSISTANT SECRETARY had the scientific adviser, Harry Saunders, alone in his office. 'Off the record,' the Assistant Secretary said, 'we've tried a little pressure, but our Gallic friends have politely told us to attend to our own problems. They intend to go ahead with their testing. Any suggestions?'

'I've given it some thought,' Saunders said. 'There's a man, an oceanographer, out on the Coast, at the Encino Beach Oceanographic Institute, who's written a paper. Fellow named Williamson. Well thought of, if a little far out. I might fly out there and have a talk with him. His ideas could give us ammunition.'

'You do think there's danger?'

'I don't know enough to have an opinion yet. Will the next test be fission or fusion? If it's fusion, how sure are they of their megaton range? Then, there's a lot more data that could be pertinent—time, weather, tides, bottom configuration.' He spread his hands. 'Not a simple equation.'

'And really none of our business,' the Assistant Secretary said. 'Unless something bad happens. Then Congress will want to know why we didn't foresee it.' He pushed back his chair and stood up, holding out his hand. 'Thanks for coming in. After you've talked with Williamson, be in touch, OK?'

OF THE SEVEN MEMBERS of the Encino Beach City Council, four were handpicked by His Honor Jimmy Silva. The remaining three were well-off residents who practised their professions—architecture, medicine and the law, respectively—in Los Angeles. In Jimmy's estimation, they were a pain in the neck.

In closed session the council heard Jimmy's explanation of the marina he had in mind for the back-bay mud flats. When he had finished he opened the floor to questions.

The architect said, 'Who's going to do the designs?'

'Big LA firm.' Jimmy named it. 'And they'll want consultation with somebody who knows the beach area. I gave them your name. I hope that was OK.' From the satisfied look on the architect's face, Jimmy thought, there would be no opposition from that direction.

It was the surgeon, who had considerable financial knowledge, who brought up the matter of funding.

'Glad you asked that,' Jimmy said. 'I went to a broker in town. Told me all about bond issues for municipal improvements. He worked up a little proposal for me, and I had copies made.' He passed them round. 'Take them home and see what you think. Me, I don't see any holes in it.'

'Only one more question,' the lawyer said. 'Assuming this goes ahead, who arranges acquisition of the land from the city and sells the houses? In other words, who makes the money? You?'

'Insurance is my thing,' Jimmy said. 'I'm no real-estate guy. And the way it's structured, the city doesn't sell the land, it leases it. It's a municipal project, and, sure, we pay commissions, but that's all.' He spread his big hands to show that he had nothing to conceal. Then, seeing there were no further questions, he adjourned the meeting.

The next day Jimmy had a visitor: Maude's host, Jack Barnes. 'You don't know me, Mr Silva,' Jack said, 'but—'

'Barnes, John T,' Jimmy said. 'Yacht club member. Waterfront house off Onyx. Real estate, aren't you? Sit down.'

Jack sat down and mentally revised his game plan, along with his opinion of ex-fishermen. 'I've heard about your planned development over in the back bay.'

'Word gets around, doesn't it?' Jimmy said.

'I've also heard,' Jack said, 'that you're going to lease, not sell, the land.' He nodded approval. 'That's smart. How long will the leases run?'

'Not decided yet,' Jimmy said. 'If you were selling the houses, what do you think would be a good lease span?'

Jack thought about it. 'Maybe forty years. To the people who'll be in the market for a house, forty years is more time than they'll figure they have to enjoy it.'

'You think good,' Jimmy said. 'Is that why you're here? You interested in being the one to handle the house sales?'

'It had entered my mind.'

'Your name was one that kept turning up,' Jimmy said.

Jack Barnes took a deep breath. He hoped he had figured it right. 'Of course,' he said, 'it would seem only fair that whoever thought this up in the first place and then went to a lot of work putting it together ought to get some benefit, don't you think?'

'You're talking about me? I'm an elected official, and I'm doing this for the good of Encino Beach.'

Jack nodded gravely. 'Of course. But you have put in a lot of your own time, maybe taken time from your insurance business, sacrificed business deals you might have followed up.'

Jimmy sighed. 'There is that, now that you mention it.'

'And so,' Jack said, 'I think you ought to derive some benefit. Maybe a half point of the commission from each house sold.'

Jimmy took his time. He said at last, 'I think maybe we can do business, Mr Barnes.'

PETE HAD A VISITOR that day in his office at the institute. It was Harry Saunders, the scientific adviser from Washington. After presenting his business card, Saunders sat down. His eye caught the large Pacific chart on the wall and the small x marked in the middle. 'That's your spot, isn't it?' he said, pointing. 'I hear some call that bit of the big formation Williamson's Trench.'

'The feeling is,' Pete said, 'that I'm so hipped on it, I can't think of anything else.'

Saunders smiled. 'I've heard rumours. And I've read several of your papers. I'd like to hear it first-hand, if you have the time.'

Pete went over his theory that nuclear testing in the Pacific was causing geological changes that could result in an underwater avalanche of devastating proportions.

'Of sufficient magnitude to cause a tsunami?' Saunders asked.

'That's my estimate.'

Saunders looked contemplative. 'Nasty things, tsunamis,' he said. 'Hawaii and Japan, of course, are always at risk when a large disturbance occurs almost anywhere in the Pacific basin. And in nineteen sixty-four, following the quake near Anchorage, Crescent City on the northern California coast was pretty well damaged.'

Saunders had done his homework, Pete thought, but then that was to be expected. Pete had heard of him, a topflight physicist on leave from the Massachusetts Institute of Technology to serve a stint in Washington. 'But,' Pete said, 'I imagine what you're really concerned about are military establishments out in the Pacific, yes?'

'Of course. Pearl Harbor, Subic Bay, others. With ships or aircraft the solutions are simple: the ships put out to sea and the aircraft fly to safer places once the tsunami alarm is sounded. Shore installations present greater problems.' He paused. 'You are thinking of other danger points as well?'

'As a matter of fact,' Pete said, 'we are. Right here, for one.'

Saunders raised his eyebrows. 'I hadn't known before that southern

California was prone to this kind of threat.'

It was a long shot, Pete admitted, requiring the combination of a heavy storm, even perhaps a hurricane fringe, high spring tides and tsunamis of considerable magnitude. 'But,' he finished, 'we're convinced it could happen.'

Saunders was smiling now. 'Murphy's Law,' he said. 'Whatever bad can happen, will happen. You make a strong case.' For a long moment he was deep in thought. He said at last, 'You use the word we? Other geophysicists share your view?'

'Negative,' Pete said. 'Just one other person so far, and he's not in the field. Fellow named Dan Garfield.' He watched Saunders's expression change. 'You know him?'

'I've met him. We sat on a board together a year or two back. A very good man indeed. How did he come into it?'

Pete explained.

'And Garfield is now scrutinising your data?'

Pete nodded.

Saunders stood up. 'I'd very much like to know his conclusions. The phone number on that card will reach me.' His handshake was firm, cordial. 'I appreciate your time,' he said, 'as well as your information. You will call?'

'That,' Pete said, 'goes without saying. I think we're going to need any help we can get.'

GARFIELD PUT DOWN the computer printout sheets and his pencil and leaned back in his chair to stare out at the bay. It was morning, and the breeze was just beginning to stir the flat water of the harbour. A sleek sailing boat under power came past the yacht club, made a slow turn round the moored fleet and headed for the harbour entrance and the open ocean.

Garfield watched it idly, two disparate thoughts struggling for dominance in his mind. The first concerned the computer data, the second, Maude Anderson.

He glanced at the computer sheets and smiled faintly. Only logic was required in order to reach a conclusion there. With Maude and himself, however, he was dealing with human intangibles, and the familiar tools of mathematics were of absolutely no use. I know things, he thought, not people.

Had he understood people better, he wondered, might he not have foreseen what he had come to think of as his partners' treachery? Foreseen it and headed it off? Had there been indications of their unhappiness that he had ignored until it was too late? He had thought that everything was running smoothly, and obviously he had been dead wrong. Logic and reason did not seem to apply to people—only to things.

So, all right, he told himself, it was my fault. So? Did that lessen the pain and the bitterness? Not a whit.

All of which took him a long way from his original problem, which was Maude. He glanced again at the computer sheets. These, at least, he could deal with. He heaved himself out of the chair and went into Tom Winslow's study to telephone.

Pete was in his office at the oceanographic institute. 'I've been through the printout,' Garfield said. 'We'd better have a talk.'

GARFIELD HAD THE COMPUTER SHEETS neatly stacked and his handwritten notes in order when Pete arrived at the Winslow house.

Pete said, 'Before we get into this, I had a visitor yesterday.' He held out the scientific adviser's card as he sat down.

'Harry Saunders is interested? Maybe that changes things.'

'Are you convinced of the danger?' Pete asked.

'Almost. Say on the order of eighty per cent.'

'So what do we do now?'

Garfield patted the pile of sheets. 'These are good as far as they go, but they don't go far enough. What we need is a deeper analysis, correlating, among other things, the changes you saw with known dates and data of the nuclear testing.'

Pete pursed his lips in a silent whistle. 'Shall we throw in the moon while we're wishing? You're talking about a complicated program and time on one of those monster supercomputers.'

'Harry Saunders could be the key. That's why I said he might make a difference. He's smart. He'll see the need. I'll talk to him and explain our problem.'

Pete seemed slightly uncomfortable. 'One more thing. I'm attached to the institute. I have a lot of leeway, but I am supposed to keep in touch, at least let them know from time to time what direction I'm working in. Howard Boggs—'

'Who's he?'

'My boss. The director. He likes to know what's going on.'

Garfield was thinking: he had gone this far, he might as well go the whole distance. 'Then we'll tell him,' he said, 'that the institute is about to receive a special grant to further your research.'

Pete blinked. 'You'll tell him that?'

'I don't think he'll argue,' Garfield said. 'You'll set up a meeting?'

Pete stood up. 'As soon as I get back to my office.' He glanced at Saunders's card on the table. 'You'd better keep that. See you.'

After he had gone, Garfield decided that a walk would be a good idea. He had been sitting too long. There was also the matter of manners; he was, after all, a houseguest.

He found Clara on her knees behind the house, setting out plants in a minuscule garden plot. She looked up when Garfield appeared, and held out her grubby hands for his inspection. 'I ought to wear gloves, but I've never been able to work in them.'

'I used to like getting my hands dirty just fussing with things.' Garfield found himself smiling in memory. 'Once, when I was a kid, I took the family TV apart and had it in pieces when my father came home and wanted to watch a ball game.' He shook his head. 'There was hell to pay.'

Clara patted the last plant into place. 'In all the time we've known each other,' she said, 'I don't think I've ever heard you speak of either your father or your mother.' She stood up, and they walked together into the house.

'Not much to tell,' Garfield said. 'Mother died of cancer when I was not quite sixteen.'

Clara began to scrub her hands at the sink. Her back was to him. 'You were at school?'

'Finishing my freshman year at Cal Tech.'

Younger than Lucy is now, Clara thought, and already a year in college, and his mother gone. 'I'm sorry.' She turned from the sink and dried her hands on a towel. 'And your father?'

'He had a reserve commission in the army. He volunteered for Vietnam. I don't think he could face things without her—my mother. His name is on that wall in Washington.'

'How old were you then?'

'Almost eighteen. I was all right. I had a scholarship and I was all wrapped up in my studies and experiments.' He made a small gesture of dismissal. 'I haven't been much of a houseguest.'

'You're not a guest, Dan. You're family.'

'I was thinking of a walk?'

'Am I included?'

'Definitely.'

The sea breeze was brisk now, and boats filled the lower basin of the harbour, heading for the ocean, multicoloured sails set in the bright sunlight. Garfield and Clara walked slowly along the narrow strip of sand at the bay's edge, then across the pen-insula to the sea.

'Maude Anderson's down here, you know. When did you see her last, Dan?' Clara said.

The day the roof fell in, he thought. 'Over a month ago.'

'You were seeing her fairly regularly, weren't you?'

'Yes.'

'Then, the inevitable question is, what happened?'

'I lost my faith in myself.'

Clara had stopped walking and was studying him carefully. 'There's a bench,' she said. 'Let's sit down.'

It was the same bench on which he and Pete had sat for their long talk, Garfield realised.

'Do you want to tell me about it, Dan?'

He nodded slowly. Once begun, the words came out in a flood. 'I didn't negotiate the sale of Garfield Associates. I lost it. Or maybe it's better to say it was taken away from me. By two partners I thought I had under control. My fault.'

'And you've been brooding about it ever since?'

'It's not something you forget.' He produced a wry smile. 'All I am now is rich. That's pretty funny, isn't it?'

'No. Sad. Is that why there's no room for Maude?'

'I hadn't thought of it that way.'

'Maybe you'd better, Dan. I don't think you've lost your faith. I think you've just lost some of the superficial confidence that went with the position you were in as head of a successful company. But

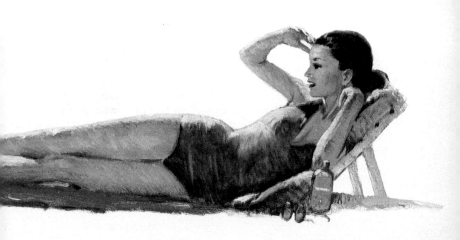

you haven't changed. I've watched you with Pete. You're still sure of yourself, just as you always have been.'

He smiled. 'Insufferable is what you mean.'

'No. Confident of your abilities. With ample reason.' She touched his arm gently. 'You haven't lost anything except the trappings of success, and they don't really count.'

'A good pep talk.'

Clara shook her head emphatically. 'I'm only speaking the truth. You don't need position to establish yourself as a person, Dan. You stand out all by yourself.' She stood up. 'Shall we go on with our walk?'

The breeze from the sea was refreshing. Garfield regarded Clara with open fondness. 'Tom and Lucy are lucky to have you.'

'I'm lucky to have them.' She paused. 'Lucy is smitten with you. I hope you realise that. You're role-perfect for the teenage idol—older, but not out of reach, attractive—'

'Wait just a minute.'

'You're also rich. And then there was that article in *Time*.'

'Just pure puffery.'

'What counts is appearances. Accept it. Everyone else does.'

They turned inland again, to the bay. The harbour was a moving panorama of shapes and colours. 'Tom will be down this weekend,' Clara said.

'You'll be glad to see him.'

Clara's smile was wistful. 'Yes. We don't have much time together. But I want him to see you too, and changed, Dan. He was worried.' Her hand touched his arm again with gentle pressure. 'Will you see Maude, talk to her? Please?'

'I've been trying to think what we might talk about.'

'You'll think of something. I'm sure of it.' She had stopped walking. 'Do it, Dan. She's staying with the Barneses in that brown-shingled house.' She pointed. 'I'll leave you now.'

Garfield stood indecisively, looking at the house. Clara had tricked him, he thought, but he felt no sense of resentment. He started towards the house, suddenly feeling foolish and awkward, like a young boy approaching his first date.

Maude was outside, sunning herself on the narrow stretch of sand between the walk and the water. Her eyes were closed, and for a moment Garfield stood silent, looking down at her.

She wore the brief one-piece swimsuit Betsy Barnes had admired. It clung to her body, intimately following each lovely curve.

'Do I pass inspection?' Maude said. Her eyes had opened, and she caught him momentarily off balance.

He gathered his composure. 'You always have.'

Maude hesitated. 'Long time, Dan.'

'Yes.'

'Sit down. The sand is soft.' She watched him lower himself to sit facing her. 'You've been busy,' Maude said. 'I read about it.'

'Something like that.' He was still uncertain, not at all in command of the situation and finding conversation difficult.

'You're a celebrity,' Maude said. 'Is that why you're down here—as escape?' She sat up suddenly. 'Strike that. It was a nosy question. Are you staying long?'

'It depends.' He was thinking of Pete and of Pete's boss, Howard Boggs, and of Harry Saunders in Washington.

'You're preoccupied again,' Maude said. 'Just as you were the last time I saw you.' Her smile was fond. 'It's good to see you, Dan. I've missed you and wondered why I hadn't seen you. But you've been busy, and maybe that explains it.'

'Not entirely.' It was the honest answer, and he wondered where he went from that point. 'I had a lot of thinking to do. I still have.' He heaved himself to a squatting position and straightened slowly. He watched her yet a moment more, trying to make up his mind. He said at last, 'Let's see how it works out.'

'Yes,' Maude said slowly. 'Let's see.' She watched him as he walked away. Tears were very close.

4

J. Howard Boggs, director of the oceanographic institute, was waiting in his office for Pete and Garfield the next morning. He rose to shake hands. 'I'm very pleased to meet you, Mr Garfield. I've heard a good deal about you. Dr Williamson—Pete—tells me you're interested in his research.'

'His research and his theories. I've seen his computer printouts, and I'd like to know more about them.'

Boggs's eyes turned shrewd. 'We have a number of very interesting and important projects aside from his,' he began.

'I'm sure. But at the moment I'm interested in what Pete is doing, and if I were to make a grant, I'd reserve the right to limit its application to that.'

Boggs said, 'May I ask what size grant you had in mind?'

'One hundred thousand dollars. More if necessary.'

Pete opened his mouth and shut it again. We do not fool around, he told himself. He looked at Boggs and waited.

'We could certainly use the money,' Boggs said. 'But to assign that much to a single, narrow field of research ...' He glanced at Pete, disapproval plain. 'We tend to frown on outright, selfish solicitation by our staff.'

'There was no solicitation,' Garfield said. 'The idea was entirely mine. I know a considerable amount about data analysis. And, as I said, I've studied the computer printouts and I think they're going in an interesting direction, but I don't believe they've gone quite far enough. What I want for my grant is for Pete's research data to be analysed as thoroughly as is possible, under his and my direction. It will cost the institute nothing beyond Pete's time.'

'And then?'

'When we have accomplished all that we think necessary, whatever funds remain will be turned over to your general fund to support other research.' He watched Boggs for a long time. 'Do we have a deal?'

Boggs slowly nodded. 'I see no objections. In your phrase, a deal, Mr Garfield.'

Pete and Garfield walked in silence down the hall to Pete's office. Pete dropped into his desk chair and shook his head. 'That,' he said, 'was quite a show. You don't pull your punches, do you? So now what?'

'I'll try Harry Saunders in Washington.'

'Here?'

'I think not,' Garfield said. 'We want that back at the house, in private.'

Pete stood up. 'OK. But first . . .' He walked to the window and drew the heavy curtains, shutting out all daylight. 'I want to show you something, a bit of amateur movie film I watch every now and again.'

He already had the screen set up and a loaded movie projector on a table. In the dimness of the darkened room he flipped a switch, and the film began. 'Here we go,' he said.

The picture that appeared showed a broad channel and, on one side, rising green hills. Pete said, 'This is one of those Aleutian towns with an unpronounceable name, too out of the way to make the news. The photographer took these from up behind the town, with a good camera on a tripod. He wanted film of a quaint little harbour with the tide coming in.' The projector whirred on, showing the flat water, no breath of breeze to disturb its surface. 'This,' Pete said, 'is what he got. Watch.'

Garfield stared unbelievingly as the water level suddenly began to drop, precisely as the level of the water in a basin drops when the plug is removed. 'You said the *in*coming tide.'

'Yep. Only it wasn't.'

Mud flats that had been hidden began to appear, as if the ground itself were rising.

'This was the warning,' Pete said. 'You can almost hear the sucking sound the outgoing water would make. Now, watch!'

The bottom of the channel was showing, almost all water drained away. Rocks long hidden appeared, along with bottom debris, some of it encrusted and unrecognisable. There was an entire boat frame, its naked ribs gaping obscenely.

And then, churning and frothing at the edges, the water swiftly rose again, covering the channel bottom, the rocks, the debris, the mud flats, filling the inlet to its normal depth and above, flooding the banks and rising still.

'Here it comes,' Pete said.

An incoming ocean swell filled the camera's frame from side to side, rising, building, propelling its force into the inlet's mouth. As it swept up-channel it grew in height, higher and higher, seemingly without end. Garfield held his breath, waiting for the swell to topple from its own weight, as breakers do on the beach, but instead it continued to grow into a monstrous, smooth, shiny entity charging directly at the camera's lens.

'Too much water behind it and within it for it to break,' Pete said. 'At this stage it's about thirty foot high and still growing. Now watch as it comes out of the channel into the harbour area. There's room for it to diminish and spread out, but it doesn't.'

Freed of the channel's constraint, able to spread its energy, the monster swell nonetheless retained its full shape and size.

There was only one boat in the harbour, Garfield noticed now, a trawler at anchor, one man on its deck. Onshore there was a single dock and a shedlike building, outside which men were standing, their backs to the camera, staring out to sea.

'Keep your eye on that trawler,' Pete said with rising excitement. 'And watch those men on the dock.'

The swell reached the trawler first. Smoothly and easily it lifted the boat higher and higher, until the anchor line was clearly visible for a moment before parting and whipping through the air like a thing alive. Still the trawler remained upright, continuing to rise to the very crest of the swell, where it hung, balanced, as the mass of water bore down upon the dock and the startled men outside the shed. They looked upwards to face the monster and hesitated, their bodies stiff with fright. Then they turned and fled in panic along the dock towards the shore.

'There are seven of them,' Pete said, his voice expressionless. 'Now there are six, four, two and then one. And there he goes.'

The men simply disappeared. One moment they were racing towards the camera; the next moment they were gone, and the smooth surface of the gigantic swell, still carrying the trawler on its crest, swept over the dock and onto the shore.

'At this point,' Pete said, 'I'd put the height of the swell at about fifty foot. With the entire inlet full of water behind it, you can only guess at its force.'

The picture on the screen died suddenly, and Pete switched off the projector. 'That,' he said, 'is a tsunami. The film ran out and the photographer didn't even notice. Can't say I blame him. That trawler, by the way, ended up a mile and a half into town. It must have been carried over half a dozen buildings. There were two men aboard. They weren't even scratched.'

Garfield was still staring at the blank screen, stunned. He said slowly, 'I've imagined what one of the waves would be like, but between imagining and seeing . . .' He shook his head.

'Yeah.' Pete was busy rewinding the film. 'That's why I run that every so often—to remind myself exactly what we're dealing with.' He walked to the window and threw open the curtains. 'Now, shall we go see if Saunders will give us a hand?'

Driving back to the Winslow house, Pete seemed compelled to talk. 'The first thing you think of,' he said, 'is some kind of defence. But there is no defence except being on high ground, or at sea, where the tsunamis pass in the form of harmless low swells.'

Garfield listened, unable to shake off the picture of that gigantic wave, smooth, swift and relentless.

'We know a great deal about tsunamis,' Pete went on, 'but we don't know the two most important things. The first, when a tsunami will be generated. The second, what to do if Murphy's Law applies and we get all the wrong factors of heavy storm and spring tide at the same time.'

'We'll work on that,' Garfield said, his voice definite, 'when we see where we stand. There is no point in raising fears before we're sure of our ground, or as sure as we can be.'

Clara was not at the Winslow house when they arrived, but Lucy was, curled up on a settee with a magazine. 'Hi,' she said, and was on her feet in one effortless motion. 'What's doing?' And she added without seeming to take a breath, 'They say the surf's up at Onofre.' She looked at Garfield. 'You a surfer?'

'Not since I was your age, or younger. I'm an old man, honey.'

'Phooey! Pete surfs. Lots do, even older than you.'

Pete said, 'We've got business, Princess. Sorry.'

He started to follow Garfield towards the study, but Lucy's voice stopped him. 'Todd's looking for you. You know, Todd Wilson. His family just got down for the summer.'

'What did he want?'

'He wouldn't tell me.'

'Male chauvinist pigs,' Pete said. 'That's what we all are.'

'You know what? You're right.' Lucy stuck out her tongue as the study door closed.

Garfield was already dialling the number on Saunders's card. In only moments Saunders came on the line. 'Dan, how are things?'

'I'm with Pete Williamson,' Garfield said.

'You've gone over his computer printout?'

'Carefully.'

'And?' The voice was sharp with interest.

'I told Pete I was eighty per cent convinced that there's an imminent danger. We want to dig deeper. With your help, on one of your big Department of Defense supercomputers.'

There was a short silence. 'Give me about fifteen, twenty minutes,' Saunders said. 'Stay by the phone. What's your number?' He listened, then his tone changed. 'It's good to know you're in on this, Dan. Frankly, there aren't too many whose word I'd take without going over the data myself. Somebody'll call shortly.'

Garfield hung up and leaned back in the chair. 'A few minutes,' he told Pete.

There was a new note of awe in Pete's voice. 'You have clout.'

'They have an interest, just as we do. That's all it is.'

The telephone call came in a little less than fifteen minutes. 'Mr Dan Garfield? My name is Robinson, Bert Robinson, I was told to call you.'

'You're the computer man?'

'That's me.'

'Where?' Garfield said. 'And when?' With the phone tucked between cheek and shoulder, he began to write quickly on his yellow pad. 'Pasadena. Two o'clock tomorrow. We'll be there.'

'I'll be waiting,' Robinson said.

As Garfield hung up, Pete rose from his chair. 'Now I can go surfing with the princess with a clear conscience. Want to come?'

'You know,' Garfield said, 'I think I do.'

PETE, LUCY AND GARFIELD drove down to San Onofre in Pete's convertible, Pete's and Lucy's surfboards in the back. Once there, Garfield was strictly a spectator, feeling very much out of place with his white skin among all the tanned bodies.

When they arrived back at the Winslow house in the late afternoon, Todd Wilson, a muscular young man with shaggy blond hair, greeted them. 'Hi, Dr Williamson. I wanted to talk to you.' And he added, suddenly unsure of himself, 'If that's OK, I mean?'

'Why, I think I can put up with it,' Pete said as he got out of the car. 'This is Daniel Garfield . . . Todd Wilson.'

The boy's eyes widened. 'I've read about you. I mean, I guess everybody has.'

'I hope not,' Garfield said easily.

And Pete said, 'What's on your mind, Todd?'

The boy took a deep breath. 'I'm majoring in geology at college, and we went on a kind of field trip, just sort of poking around.' He pointed towards the low hills inland. 'Back in there, maybe seven, eight miles onto the LaPorte property, we found rocks. Big ones. I couldn't lift a couple of them.'

'Outcroppings?'

'No.' The boy's headshake was emphatic. 'Loose. Just scattered around. But the funny thing is—' He stopped. 'I know it sounds far out, but they were the same kind of rock the point is composed of. Igneous, isn't it?'

Pete nodded.

'And the underlying rock where we found these boulders is all sedimentary—sandstone, I think.' He took a deep breath. 'So how could boulders that size get up there from the shore? They weren't there to build anything. And who'd go to the trouble of hauling them up there just for the fun of it?'

'Seven, eight miles from shore, you said?'

Todd nodded. 'Would you like to see them?'

'I would indeed.' Pete looked at Garfield and Lucy. 'Coming?'

They got back into Pete's car and drove off. The rocks were there, as Todd had said, boulder size, one or two of them weighing, Pete estimated, two hundred pounds or more.

'Where did they come from?' Todd said. 'I'd say the shore, but that doesn't make sense, does it?'

Pete looked around, estimating distance from the shore and height above sea level. Then he looked at the boy. 'You're a surfer. You know waves. What kind of a wave would it take to bring these rocks up here?'

'You're kidding! A wave big enough to move these would go right across the peninsula as if the land weren't even there. It would wipe out Encino Beach. You *are* kidding, aren't you?'

'Not kidding,' Pete said. 'Just speculating. Such waves are possible. I'll tell you about them on the way back.'

Later, sitting with Garfield on the Winslows' porch, Pete said, 'The accidental find of a kid who was curious.' He shook his head. 'Possible—I emphasise possible—indication that at some time this coast was hit by a tsunami. I can't think of any other explanation for those rocks.'

Garfield was thinking again of that monster tsunami sweeping towards the camera. 'Scary, isn't it?' he said.

BERT ROBINSON, THE COMPUTER MAN in Pasadena, wore a thick black beard and longish hair. He studied Pete's typed data, the computer printout pages, and Garfield's handwritten notes. When he had finished he looked at them both and smiled.

'I'm tempted to ask if you're joking,' he said, 'but from what Harry Saunders said, I know damn well you aren't. We don't play games on my big baby. Time on it is too important.' He stood up. 'OK, gents.

40

Give me a few days, a week at most, I'll have a program ready.'

Pete said, 'How long will it take on the computer when you've fed it in?'

'I'd guess about twelve minutes.'

Pete shook his head in disbelief.

Robinson said, 'I give baby the data and ask the questions, and baby gives out the answers almost before I'm finished. You'd like to be here? I'll give you ample warning of kickoff time.'

Pete was almost ebullient driving back to Encino Beach. 'The last thing I expected was cooperation at this level. You—'

'Harry Saunders came to see *you*,' Garfield said.

'But he only really perked up when I told him you were involved.' Pete glanced at Garfield's face. 'And I still don't know why you are.'

'I'm enjoying it,' Garfield said, and realised it was the truth.

Tom Winslow came down from LA late Friday afternoon. Despite the air conditioning in his car, he looked hot and tired as he walked into the house. 'Freeway traffic,' he said. 'Never mind. I can relax now.' He looked out at the bay. 'Tomorrow we can spend the whole day on the water—no phones, no medical crises.' He looked at Clara. 'OK?'

'Lovely,' she said. There was such a glow of happiness on her face that Garfield, watching them, felt a pang of envy.

Showered and refreshed, Tom came out on the porch a half-hour later. He sat down and studied Garfield. 'I hear you've been to San Onofre. Picked up a little colour instead of that prison pallor,' he said approvingly. 'But I understand you're involved with Pete Williamson already, in some kind of—what?'

'Pete has a theory that makes too much sense to ignore.' Garfield sketched in the major points of the potential tsunami threat. 'Briefly, that's where we are.'

Tom stared at the water, the moored boats. 'Hard to believe, but if you're convinced— '

'Almost convinced,' Garfield said. 'When we have the deeper analysis, I may lose all hesitation.'

The doctor nodded, but his thoughts seemed to be elsewhere. 'Clara tells me,' he said, without looking at Garfield, 'that Maude Anderson is down here too.'

'She is. I've seen her.'

'Clara and I are not matchmakers.' He faced Garfield. 'But we've known you for a long time, and it did seem that at last you had found somebody who lived up to your high standards.'

'You've turned shrink, have you?' Garfield was smiling. 'Or is it advice to the lovelorn?'

'Damn it, boy, you've been alone too long. I would have gone mad long ago if I hadn't had Clara. And Lucy. Everybody needs somebody.'

He too was smiling now. 'And you may quote me.'

'I'll give it due heed, Doctor.'

'Maude's a stunning woman. And bright.'

'Granted.'

'And, I think, in love with you. Clara thinks so too.'

'So I'm the problem? You may be right. Probably you are. So I'll just flounder around until I get the problem sorted out.'

'Are you even trying?'

'Right now, frankly,' Garfield said, 'I'm too wrapped up in Pete's theory for much of anything else.'

'You were too wrapped up in Garfield Associates too.'

The difference between what he was doing now and what he had spent his adult life doing, building Garfield Associates, suddenly seemed stark and clear. 'There is no comparison,' he said. 'This —what Pete has uncovered—is real. From this distance the other— inventing and manufacturing electronic gadgets—seems somehow artificial.'

'I'd say you've got religion bad.' The doctor stood up. 'And maybe that's good. Who knows? Let's join the ladies. I have trouble getting enough of them just during a weekend.'

5

THE Aleutian Islands chain sweeps in a great southwesterly arc fifteen hundred miles down into the North Pacific from the mainland of Alaska. Early on Saturday morning, July 12, three undersea earthquakes rocked the tip of the island chain. The largest of the three measured seven point seven on the Richter scale. Its epicentre was approximately ninety miles northeast of the island of Adak, about twelve hundred miles from Anchorage.

Walls were cracked and windows shattered by a tsunami at the naval air station on Adak, but the five thousand island residents, mostly navy personnel, had already been evacuated to high ground.

Seismographs round the world recorded the shocks, and the International Tsunami Warning System's headquarters at Ewa Beach, near Honolulu, Hawaii, issued a Pacific-wide tsunami warning. Officials in Alaska, Washington, Oregon, California and Hawaii immediately recommended evacuation of low-lying coastal areas.

'It's nonsense,' Peter Williamson said. 'An alert, maybe, but a warning, no. That's putting out the red flag, and I'll bet my shirt it isn't necessary. Earthquakes are common in the Aleutians, and this one isn't so big that it will raise that much hell.'

It was early evening, and Pete and Garfield were in the parking lot of The Dunes, a shorefront restaurant a little north of Encino Beach.

From within came sounds of voices, music, laughter.

'You think this will turn out to be a false alarm?' Garfield said.

'Definitely.'

Inside the restaurant, the head waiter said, 'If you want a window table, gents, they're all taken. Sorry.'

Pete said, 'Why the crowd? Far more than usual.'

'Haven't you heard, there's a tidal wave coming? People want to see it.'

'But the waves aren't supposed to come this far south,' Pete said. 'Only way up on the northern coast.'

'Well,' the head waiter said, 'people aren't sure the folks who predict these things know what they're talking about, and if there is anything to see, they want to watch it.'

Walking back to the car after dinner, Garfield said, 'Let's go down on the beach, see what's doing there.'

Pete walked to the edge of the parking lot. 'You can see from here,' he said. 'There're fires, people drinking beer, cooking hamburgers, waiting for the show.' There was disgust in his voice.

'The major problem,' Garfield said as they got into the car, 'is that once these people have been disappointed because there are no spectacular waves and no danger, they will pay little or no attention when the real waves actually have been generated. Agreed?'

'Yes,' Pete said. 'You're right, as usual.' He started the engine. 'I wonder how folks are behaving up north, and in Hawaii where there *are* going to be some waves.'

'We'll find out tomorrow,' Garfield said.

PACIFIC TIDAL WAVE A WASHOUT

Sunday, July 13

Thousands of Pacific-coast residents fled to higher ground after sirens and loudspeakers warned of a tidal wave triggered by yesterday's earthquakes off Adak Island in the Aleutian Islands, but the biggest wave was a human one.

A tsunami warning was posted, and about 21,000 people fled low-lying coastal areas in Hawaii, Alaska, Washington, Oregon, British Columbia and northern California. Many boats headed out to sea to ride out the waves. But there was a festive atmosphere in the emergency shelters, and several hundred evacuees who gathered in the Oahu, Hawaii, community of Ewa Beach threw a tailgate party to watch the waves come in.

Waves were less than 8 foot high in Hawaii, 2 to 3 foot in Washington and only 5.8 foot on Adak Island, closest to the epicentre. Japan's Central Meteorological Agency said a tsunami of 9 inches was observed there. No casualties were reported in any area.

It was the Monday morning following the tsunami warning.

After Tom Winslow had left to go back to LA, a telephone call caught Garfield in the kitchen in swimming trunks, just as he was about to go surfing with Lucy. 'For you,' Clara said, holding out the phone.

Harry Saunders was on the line. 'I thought you might want to know about our Gallic friends. Indications are that they're planning a test on or about the thirtieth of this month.'

Garfield was silent, eyes closed, concentrating.

'You still there?' said Saunders after a moment.

'Right here. I was calculating. That's full moon.'

'Is it?' Saunders's voice changed. 'Oh, I see. One of your factors, spring tide.'

'Exactly.'

'Well, there's more. We *know* very little, but we *infer* it may be H type.'

H type, hydrogen, fusion rather than fission.

'And I have something else you might also like to hear,' Saunders went on. 'I got it from one of the Los Alamos people who was there at our first H test. It seems that they'd greatly underestimated the megaton yield.'

'Possible similar uncertainty this time?'

'Exactly. We've hinted at the possibility of miscalculation, but they're not buying it. Thought you'd like to know.'

'I appreciate it.'

'*Ciao.*' The line went dead.

Garfield hung up slowly. 'I'm afraid,' he told Lucy, 'that we're going to have to postpone our surfing lesson. I'm sorry.'

Lucy hesitated, her smile uncertain. Clara watched in silence. 'That's OK,' Lucy said at last. She turned quickly away and was gone.

Garfield looked at Clara. 'That tore it.' He spread his hands. 'I didn't mean to—'

'Dan, it's not your fault. Go do whatever it is you have to do. Lucy will be all right, and there will be other times for you to indulge her.'

'I don't indulge her. I enjoy her company.'

Clara smiled brightly. 'You're beginning to relax, Dan,' she said. 'Just when I was beginning to despair of you.'

Pete sat at his desk and listened carefully to Garfield's account of Harry Saunders's phone call. 'So what have we got?' Pete said. 'Not only a test shot, but likely a big one, biggest yet, multimegaton range. We've got a date right smack on the full moon, highest tide of the month. All we're lacking is bad weather. What's the forecast?'

'That's over two weeks off,' Garfield said. 'Forecast has to be uncertain as of now.'

The phone on Pete's desk rang. He picked it up and listened for a moment. 'OK,' he said. 'Thanks. Will do.' He hung up and looked at Garfield. 'That was Robinson. He and his wizard computer are ready for us.'

THE FRENCH OCEANOGRAPHER said, 'We have had a warning from the Americans that our proposed test shot could have—dire is the word they use—consequences.'

'Nonsense,' the project director said. They were in his Paris office. 'America has been trying to stop us testing for years. A matter of jealousy. They must learn that when they snap their fingers, the world no longer obeys.'

'This is not a matter of political thinking.'

'No? Then?'

'A matter of geological results. Not certain. But possible, even probable.'

'A pretext.'

Inwardly the oceanographer sighed, but allowed nothing to show. 'There was, you will remember, a similar warning years ago. We discounted it and lost our atoll base as a result.'

'That was then. We are far better informed now.'

'But I don't like the . . . import of this new warning. That our testing has hastened certain submarine geological changes until the situation is now precarious. The fear is that our proposed test may trigger an underwater seismic disturbance of enormous proportions. The analogy is that of a cannon shot setting off a massive alpine avalanche. If the facts are as they represent them—'

'If! And how do we know that they are not bluffing?'

'We don't.'

'Then?'

'The only way to find out,' the oceanographer said, 'is to carry on with the test. And then we may find out too late.' He waited, knowing very well what the answer would be.

The director shook his head decisively. 'Boldness. We must be bold. We have set our course, and we must follow it to the letter. Is that clear?'

The oceanographer shrugged. He had done what he could. Further protest would only be futile. '*Naturellement*,' he said.

BERT ROBINSON, THE COMPUTER MAN, was waiting for Garfield and Pete in Pasadena. 'You said you wanted to watch the show. Not that there's much to see except printout sheets emerging.'

He turned to his keyboard, and his fingers busied themselves for a matter of seconds, no more. Almost immediately the swift, quiet hum of the printer began, and the first of a continuous flow of printout pages emerged and settled into neat folds in the receptacle. 'Baby already has the answers for us. He's way ahead of the printer,' Robinson said.

Pete watched in awe as the printer poured out an avalanche of paper. 'How fast—' he began.

'Does baby work?' Robinson said, and a smile appeared through his black beard. 'A few million calculations a second. A number of countries—Russia, for one—would give their eyeteeth for one of these.'

The printer stopped. Robinson glanced at the clock. 'Twelve minutes, seventeen seconds.' He picked up the pile of printout pages and held it out. 'Here you are. As promised.'

Pete studied Robinson's face. 'You know the results?'

'I've done some peeking, and some guesswork, yes.'

'And?'

'Good luck with whatever you're planning to do,' Robinson said. 'I don't know what else to say.'

'Maybe a prayer?' Garfield said.

IT BEGAN, AS TROPICAL disturbances do, as clusters of cumulonimbus clouds in the high, humid air over the sun-warmed waters of the Pacific. Summertime is the breeding season.

A drop in barometric pressure supplied the original impetus, and the clouds slowly began to gather and stir themselves almost lazily into a counterclockwise motion round a vaguely defined central vortex.

On the phone the National Weather Service meteorologist said, 'All I can tell you is that we have several tropical disturbances on the satellite photos right now, out in the Pacific, north of the equator. This time of year it would be unusual if we didn't.'

'And?' Pete said.

The meteorologist's voice was unconcerned. 'Any one of them could go either way: gather momentum and work itself into something big or just futz around until it runs out of steam and collapses as a system. But it's unlikely that one of them will achieve hurricane status.'

Pete had an unpleasant thought. 'You say there are several disturbances right now. What happens if they merge, become one big system?'

'Whoosh.' For the first time the meteorologist's voice showed emotion. 'Then you're talking about real trouble, friend.'

'You have my name and number,' Pete said. 'Call if there's any significant change.'

'We routinely notify your institute.'

'I mean a personal call,' Pete said. 'It could be important.'

'OK,' the meteorologist said. 'I'll see to it myself.'

GARFIELD GOT UP from the desk and stretched his arms wide to relieve some of the tension that had developed during his time of concentration over Robinson's computer printout sheets. Outside it was still broad daylight. Dusk would have been more appropriate, he decided, a fading day to match his sombre thoughts. He sat down again and reached for the telephone.

Across the country a familiar voice answered, 'Saunders.'

'Garfield here. I've been through Robinson's analysis. A first-rate job.' He paused. 'The conclusions are pretty much as we expected, although perhaps a bit more drastic. All merely probabilities, of course, but . . .'

Saunders said drily, 'Probabilities have a way of living up to expectations.'

Garfield continued. 'Sooner or later, and probably sooner, there is going to be a massive seismic disturbance in that area Pete Williamson has been studying. In short, an avalanche of enormous scope. Tsunamis are bound to be generated.'

'Emanating in all directions from the epicentre,' Saunders said. 'As we feared. We also have assessed the situation—a copy of the printout was transmitted to us simultaneously. We have already taken some precautions at what we consider our vulnerable spots. The target date, by the way, seems still to be the thirtieth, which, as you pointed out, is full moon and spring tide. Assuming a test yield in the multimegaton area, what is your educated guess? Do you think the projected avalanche, as you call it, will be triggered this time?'

'My guess is yes.'

'Thanks,' Saunders said. 'We'll crank that into the equation.'

Garfield said, 'You'll keep us posted if you turn anything up?'

'Will do. And if you have further thoughts, I'd like to hear them. *Ciao.*' Garfield hung up and again got out of the chair. A little exercise, he thought, at least a stretching of the legs. He walked out of the study and through the house.

It was good to stroll in the warm sun, feeling the freshness of the sea breeze, clean and salt-smelling. Sails were out in the harbour. They made pleasant, changing patterns against the wide sky and the backdrop of the houses crowded together along the shore. A peaceful, easygoing, laid-back locale, in its way epitomising the lifestyle of southern California.

'Hello, Dan.' It was Maude, in shorts that displayed her slim, tanned legs to advantage. 'I was just coming out of the house and saw you—oblivious as you walked along, probably on some important mission.' She was smiling.

Garfield shook his head. 'No mission. No responsibilities.'

'That I won't believe, Dan. Not now, not ever. I think you are the most responsible person I have ever known.'

47

'A damning accusation if ever I heard one.'

'Not meant.' She hesitated only a brief moment. 'Are you out for a walk? Want company?'

He put all thoughts of computer printout sheets, of Harry Saunders and of Pete behind him. Strangely, it was easy to do. 'I'd like that,' he said. 'Let's cross over to the ocean side of the peninsula. I've been cooped up and I want to look at infinity.'

The tide was coming in, succeeding breakers reaching further and further up the beach. They walked slowly, eyes on the water.

'There are rhythms,' Garfield said. 'You can feel them.'

'Yes.' Maude's voice was quiet.

'A kind of music, I suppose, if you could make it out.'

'Can't you hear it?' Maude looked at him in mild surprise.

'I can't say I ever have. Not really.'

'It's there.'

'Maybe you're right.' He was smiling. 'Or maybe we're talking about different things.'

'I think we frequently are, Dan.' She was silent for a few moments. 'So often you have been—how do I say it?—wrapped up in your world, what you were going to do, deciding whether it would work or not. Although I have an idea it always did work. You're used to success.'

'I've left that world.'

'I think you'll always carry your own world with you, Dan, wrapped round you like a cloak. It's something I'm not sure I've ever become used to. Or ever could.' The brilliant smile appeared briefly. 'The air down here, the . . . openness. They make it seem like the normal rules don't apply, so you can say things you wouldn't dream of saying in LA. Sorry.'

'Funny, I was feeling almost the same thing myself.'

'Were you? Now you're just being sweet, easy on me. Sometimes you are very considerate, did you know that?'

'Frankly, no. Mostly I've been told I'm self-centred, that I wear blinkers and that—'

'That you don't suffer fools gladly, which is definitely true.' Maude suddenly flung out one hand. 'Look at the pelicans!'

There were six pelicans, flying in rigid line ahead, no more than ten foot above the incoming swells. From time to time the leader ceased his wingbeats and glided easily for some distance before he resumed. In perfect sequence the trailing birds ceased and then resumed their wingbeats at precisely the same points, an airborne ballet. Maude clapped her hands in delight. 'You can hear the music now, can't you? You have to. It's choreographed, every movement planned to the beat. Beaks tucked in, shoulders held just so—that takes endless practice.'

Garfield shook his head slowly. He was almost laughing. 'You must be right. A-one, a-two, a-three?'

'Exactly.' Maude caught his arm impulsively. 'Maybe there's hope for you after all.'

They walked back to the bay side and stopped in front of the Barneses' house. 'I won't ask you in,' Maude said, 'Jack Barnes would probably try to get you to invest in some real-estate scheme. But I've enjoyed the walk, Dan.'

'So have I. Maybe we can do it again?'

'No, I'm afraid not. I'm going back up to LA. Back to work.'

Garfield was frowning. 'When did you decide that?'

'About ten minutes ago.'

'Am I the cause?'

'I don't think I want to answer that, Dan. Let's just leave it as it is.' Her smile was less than full. 'Maybe I can sell a house or two before the end of the month.'

The end of the month. Full moon. Nuclear test shot. The low-lying beach and peninsula so vulnerable. 'Maybe,' said Garfield, 'it's just as well if you do go back. I'll come up soon. Can I call you there?'

Maude hesitated. She seemed about to say something and then changed her mind. She nodded. 'Of course. Until then, Dan.' She was gone, up the path, up the steps, long, slim, tanned legs moving quickly, almost running.

#

Garfield sat down at the kitchen table in Pete's little house and said, 'I finished going over the printout, and the answer is as we expected.'

'It's certain?'

'As certain as it can be. The probabilities are overwhelming.' He told about his call to Saunders. 'I told him I think this test will kick off the whole disaster.'

Pete nodded. 'During his last dive, Henry Larson, the biologist, saw flaking from the cliff structure. That seems to clinch it. If you're satisfied with Robinson's analysis, then I'll go right along with you that this test shot, assuming it's a big one, will bring down that cliff. But how do we put out a Pacific-wide warning?'

'I had hoped,' Garfield said, 'that there would be time for you to pass the word in person. You have contacts, no? At the prime danger spots round the Pacific basin?'

'Pen pals, most of them, yes. Some I know.'

'Then get on the phone and lay your neck on the block with a flat-out prediction—big trouble ahead, timed to coincide with the spring tide. I understand that risking your reputation—'

'The hell with my reputation,' Pete said. 'It's what has to be done. But what about Boggs, my boss? We'll have to talk to him first, because I'll be, in a sense, involving the institute.'

'We'll do more than talk to him,' Garfield said. 'We'll lay the printout in his lap and let him draw his own conclusions.'

THE CLOUDS STIRRED counterclockwise round the central vortex of the tropical disturbance. By their motion, and with growing strength, they both defined and expanded the boundaries of that vortex. Condensation of moisture from the humid air rising and cooling within the core released enormous quantities of heat energy, which gradually turned the entire mass into a gigantic thermodynamic engine.

The resulting cloud crown spread outwards for tens and then hundreds of miles, blowing downwind. Within the growing monster intense line squalls, spiralling inwards, reached velocities upwards of a hundred miles per hour. Its irresistible strength consolidated, the entire system began to move northeastwards at an unhurried pace of about ten knots.

On the phone the weather service meteorologist told Pete, 'You asked to know if and when changes occurred. Well, they have, and what we've got now is a full-fledged hurricane, approximately a thousand miles off the coast of El Salvador. His name is Bob, and I must say he is a fine, healthy specimen.'

'Lovely,' Pete said.

'We're tracking Bob, of course,' the meteorologist said.

'And you're predicting he will go where?'

'No prediction. We follow hurricanes; we don't try to lead them. Like six-hundred-pound gorillas, they go where they want.'

'Could you make a guess at its northerly limit?'

'No. I can give you statistics and averages, none of which mean a thing. We have a hurricane on the loose, with winds in excess of a hundred miles per hour. At the moment it is moving northeastwards, as they tend to do. We're warning shipping, and any pleasure craft, but we're not issuing a shore alert yet.'

'You will,' Pete said. 'You will. I'd make book on it.'

JOE HINES LISTENED on the telephone without expression.

'Just an advisory, Joe,' the coastguard's voice said. 'They haven't even issued a shore alert yet. But we've got a hurricane named Bob possibly heading in our direction.'

'Every so often,' Joe said, 'you get a feeling . . .'

'This isn't by any means sure, Joe. It's just an advisory.'

'But the smell of trouble is in the wind. OK, thanks.'

Joe hung up and sat for a moment looking at the far wall.

The telephone rang again, and he snatched it up.

'Jimmy here,' His Honor's voice said. 'Get over to my office on the double. We got a date to see J. Howard Boggs at the oceanographic institute—me and you and Pete Williamson and that guy who was in *Time* magazine, Dan Garfield. They think the stuff's going to hit the fan any minute, and they want us to know about it. You—'

'Stop clicking your teeth,' Joe Hines said. 'I'm on my way.'

J. HOWARD BOGGS SAT behind his large desk. Garfield, Pete, Jimmy Silva and Joe Hines faced him in a semicircle. The pile of neatly stacked computer printout sheets lay on his desk.

Boggs said, 'Apparently what we have is an emergency situation. At least, it is so represented to me.' He looked at Garfield. 'Will you take over?'

'Pete first,' Garfield said.

Pete stood up and, using the wall map he had brought from his office, outlined his findings from his own two minisub dives and the report of flaking rock from the dive the previous week. Next, Garfield brought Boggs, Silva and Hines up to date on the nuclear test scheduled for the thirtieth. He ended by saying, 'The Department of Defense has accepted our conclusions and is taking steps to protect its installations from tsunamis that will be caused if the ledge does collapse from the force of the explosion. They are also noting that the date of the test shot is full moon, which means that in all the oceans of the world there will be the highest tide of the month.' He looked round. 'All clear so far?'

Joe Hines said, 'And now they're talking hurricane-force winds heading in this direction.' He shook his head. 'Troubles come in litters, like kittens.'

Pete said, 'I've set up to run some film I want you to see.' He walked to the table where the projector stood. 'Lights, Dan, please.' And as the room turned dark and the film began, he said, much as he had said before, to Dan, 'This was pure luck, an amateur photographer filming a picturesque harbour.'

They watched in strained silence as the film rolled. It ended suddenly, as it had before, and there was only the flapping sound of the film's loose end.

Pete said, 'Time for lights again.' His voice was not quite steady. 'That,' he told them all, 'is a tsunami. Any questions?'

Boggs cleared his throat quietly. 'Your thesis, I take it, is that if there is underwater geological change, specifically collapse of that ledge, tsunamis are bound to be generated?'

Pete confined himself to saying merely, 'Yes.'

'And further,' Boggs said, 'that with a combination of spring tide and hurricane-induced surf well above normal limits, the low-lying coastal area here is also in danger from those tsunamis?'

Pete nodded. 'Yes again.'

Boggs looked at Garfield. 'You concur?'

'Without hesitation.'

Boggs took his time. 'I am afraid,' he said, 'that I do too. I'll want to examine these printouts, of course, but the indications of trouble are too compelling to ignore.'

'Trouble, hell,' Joe Hines said. 'This here is disaster.' He looked at Jimmy Silva.

Jimmy stood up. 'Let's go,' he said. 'We got things to do.'

THERE WERE SEVENTEEN BOYS, ranging in age from sixteen to twenty, in Joe Hines's harbourmaster office. All bore the southern California trademark of a deep tan, and most had sunbleached hair. They stood silently in Joe's presence.

'Ain't one of you I haven't chewed out,' Joe said, 'for hotrodding in harbour or other shenanigans—some, I'll admit, I hadn't even thought of before you did them.'

There were universal smiles and a general sense of relaxation.

'How you managed to survive beats me,' Joe said. 'But you have, so far, and you've all turned out to be good seamen too. That's why I got you here this morning. Now, you all know about the big-wave warning we had, couple weeks ago. Pure bilge, wasn't it? Well, one of these days it's not going to be.'

He perched on a corner of his desk. 'We got hundreds of boats in this harbour. And there's only one way out—through the channel and between the jetties. Time comes—and it will—when we want to get as many boats out to sea as we can, we don't want some landlubber from town running his sixty-five-footer aground and blocking the channel for the rest. You all see that?'

A big, muscular twenty-year-old in droopy swimming trunks said, 'Why would we want to get the boats out to sea? It's safer in here if it comes to a blow.'

'Mostly you're right,' Joe said. 'Even in a good blow you're better off inside, maybe double up on your dock lines or ground tackle.' He paused. 'But if that warning couple weeks back had been real—one of them big waves coming from an earthquake somewhere—you'd have been far better off out at sea, well beyond the ten-fathom line. All you'd catch would be a swell, maybe three, four feet high, that wouldn't start building into something big until it got into shallow water.'

'Where do we come in?' the twenty-year-old asked.

'Every one of you has crewed aboard one of the big power cruisers we got here in harbour.' He reached back across the desk into the top drawer and brought out a paper. 'Got a list here. There's seventeen big power cruisers I'm worried about. The smallest is a fifty-footer, and a couple are sixty-five footers. They're all owned by weekenders, folks who don't know much about handling their boats. That's where you come in.'

'Doing what?'

'I got the keys to every one of them boats,' Joe said, 'I got the owners' permission, in writing. Just in case, I told them, to try to save their property if worst comes to worst.'

The big twenty-year-old said, 'Hey, you're quite an operator, Joe. I know some of those people who wouldn't trust anybody—'

'But who wouldn't like to lose their half-million-dollar boats either,' Joe said. 'They told me the keys were only for emergency use. I didn't tell them if that emergency comes along, I was going to turn their boats over to you to take out to sea and stay there until it's safe to come back in. But I am telling you.'

The office was suddenly very still.

Joe said, 'Anybody here think he can't handle it? You all grew up in boats. Command scare you?'

Sixteen-year-old Tommy Parks said, 'Joe—' He stopped. Although he could hold his own with every other youngster in the room at swimming, surfing or sailing, there remained the barrier of age to keep him on the outside, looking up with envy at the eighteen- and nineteen-year-olds.

Joe said, 'Your daddy sailed an eighty-five-foot motor sailer to Japan and back, ten, twelve thousand miles. You were aboard, and you stood your tricks at the wheel all by yourself out in the middle of the ocean, and you were responsible for the boat and seven people asleep below. You can't take a sixty-five-foot twin-screw cruiser like *Lubelle* down-channel and out to sea by yourself? You scared? You've crewed on her how many times?'

Tommy produced what he hoped was a confident smile. 'You put it like that, no, I'm not scared. Sure I can do it. Be fun.'

'That's what I thought,' Joe said. He looked round at them all. 'Maybe your owner will be aboard. If he is, you take the wheel anyway. He'll be glad to let you. If he isn't there, it's all yours. Just don't block that channel. Get out to sea and stand off until the radio says it's safe to come back in.' He paused. 'Could be you won't be able to come back in here. Can't say. If that's it, the radio'll tell you where to go.' He looked round the room again. What he saw satisfied him, and he nodded approvingly.

JIMMY SILVA WAS NOT wasting his time either. He had called an extraordinary meeting of the city council.

'We got a problem,' he told them. 'What I guess you call a dilemma. First thing, the marina project is out. Dead.'

The large room was still. 'A moment, please.' It was the lawyer.

'Precisely what are we to infer from that?'

'Simple,' Jimmy said. 'There ain't going to be no marina. Not now. And maybe not ever.'

'It is a unilateral decision?' Brown asked. 'I trust you have reasons.'

Jimmy did not have to close his eyes to see in memory the picture of that huge, smooth tsunami swell sweeping in towards the camera. 'Yep,' he said, 'I got reasons. In spades.' He sketched briefly that session in Howard Boggs's office. 'The people in Washington are convinced. Joe Hines is convinced. So am I.' He paused to let it all sink in.

'Now,' Jimmy continued, 'what we got to do is figure how we handle it. First off, I want emergency powers to handle the police and the fire people like I see fit. Then there's—'

'I would prefer,' the lawyer said, 'to dwell a little longer on the marina. We are committed, and I do not see that we can back out now. The reputation of Encino Beach is at stake.'

'Maybe you didn't hear me good,' Jimmy said. 'I'll admit the idea takes some getting used to, and I don't like it any better than you do, but what we're talking about ain't the reputation of Encino Beach. What we're talking about is something that maybe won't even leave enough of Encino Beach to have a reputation. What we're talking about is maybe a ruined harbour and no houses left on the peninsula, maybe the whole beach washed away. You got that?'

The council members sat in stunned silence.

'The marina's dead, like I said.' Jimmy's tone was implacable. 'Now let's get down to how we handle this situation, because whether we like it or not, we're responsible for making the decisions. That's what they elected us for. We got people to think about.'

WILBERT ELLIS, THE DIRECTOR of the County Office of Disaster Preparedness, was small and stocky, with a firm handshake. He led Pete and Garfield into his office and closed the door after them.

'If you've come about that tsunami warning that was issued earlier this month,' he said, 'I'll admit it right off: the National Weather Service was, shall we say, hasty in issuing that warning. But once it was issued, we had no option but to set our defence mechanisms in motion.' There was no mistaking the bitterness in his voice.

'We didn't come about the past,' Garfield said. He nodded towards Pete, who sketched in the background and the present situation. When Pete was done, Ellis let out his breath in a long sigh.

'This is not another San Andreas rift scare?' he said. 'It doesn't sound like it, but after that last foul-up I'm gun-shy.'

Garfield said, 'You're already aware of the hurricane threat. For the rest, you could check with the DOD. A man named Harry Saunders, scientific adviser. Or you could go over the computer printout sheets from the DOD's supercomputer in Pasadena.'

Ellis smiled ruefully. 'I withdraw my scepticism.' He hesitated. 'Until we have an actual warning, of course, we can do nothing officially except stand by.'

'If what we anticipate does take place,' Garfield said, 'Encino Beach may well be a prime danger area, because of its coastal configuration and bottom contours. That's not to say that other areas would not also be at risk. Much would depend on the fringe winds from the hurricane they're calling Bob or, heaven forbid, on the hurricane itself coming ashore.' He glanced at Pete for confirmation, then went on. 'So what we had in mind was some kind of coordination among the low-lying communities that might be affected, coordination that would best be set up in advance.'

Ellis was scribbling notes on a pad. He looked up and nodded. 'Good thinking,' he said. 'I'll get on to it immediately.'

Garfield said, 'Given the recent fiasco, will your disaster system respond again as it's supposed to?'

Ellis leaned back in his chair. 'We hope so. We think so. We have, of course, considered the possibility of a succession of disasters: earthquake, flood, fire, even the unthinkable, a nuclear explosion from whatever cause. And we realise that there could be a breakdown in communications. But the systems are programmed to function

automatically once warnings are issued.'

'Radio? TV?'

'All of that. And more. At need, loudspeakers, sirens, cruising patrol cars with bullhorns, deployed law-enforcement personnel, even the military. I don't want to boast, but it is likely that California leads the nation in disaster preparedness. But, frankly, this scenario you outline . . . will there be any warning?'

'At a minimum,' Pete said, 'three hours.'

'Is that enough time to set things in motion?' Garfield asked.

'From any Touch-Tone telephone,' Ellis said, 'I can set our defence mechanisms in operation. That is all it takes.' He hesitated, then opened a drawer and took out a card which he handed to Garfield. 'Normally we rely on our own warning channels. But a call from you to that number any time, day or night, and I will see to it that action is taken.'

GARFIELD WAS ON THE OCEAN side of the peninsula, on the same stone bench he had chosen before, gazing out at the vastness of the sea. The only sounds were the quiet thunder of the surf and the occasional scream of a gull. It was there that Lucy found him.

'Hi,' she said. 'I sort of thought I'd find you here. I've seen you on this bench before.' She sat down. 'This is your . . . kind of secret place?'

'I guess so. Everybody needs one, don't you think?'

Lucy smiled, pleased with his understanding. 'Where you can go,' she said, 'and think, all by yourself. I have one. I found it a few years ago. A cave, out on the point. It looks shallow, but it isn't, it goes back I don't know how far. When I sit just inside, nobody can see me except the seals in the water and maybe a gull or two.' Her face became serious. 'I've never told anybody before.'

'I'm honoured. And I will respect the confidence.'

'Do you want me to leave you alone so you can think?'

'Don't go. I enjoy your company.'

Lucy took a deep breath. 'Todd,' she said, 'keeps talking about those waves, whatever their name is.'

'Tsunamis.'

'Yeah. Well, all of a sudden geology's his thing, and he can't think about anything else.'

Garfield said cautiously, 'And your other friends?'

Lucy scuffed one bare foot on the scattered sand in front of the bench. 'I guess I don't have many friends. They—people—always want to know everything.'

Garfield hid his smile. 'I know the feeling.'

'You do?' There was genuine surprise behind the words. 'Do you sometimes have the feeling you'd like to . . . talk to somebody, really talk? I mean, let it all hang out? But you can't quite do it?' Her eyes searched his face.

'Welcome to the club,' Garfield said. 'I know that particular frustration well.'

'No wonder Mom and Dad have always thought you were so neat,' Lucy said suddenly, wearing a shy half-smile of embarrassment. 'So do I. You're easy to talk to. Most grown-ups aren't.'

'You flatter me.'

It was the full, brilliant smile now, lighting her face, her eyes. Lucy jumped up from the bench, all cares suddenly wiped away. 'I'll bet you can bear up under it,' she said, and was suddenly gone, almost running out of sheer ebullience.

MAYOR JIMMY SILVA had one more thing to do this day, and because it seemed to put the stamp of finality on predictions of disaster, he found it a distasteful task to perform. But he had always prided himself on his willingness to face facts. So he called real-estate operator Jack Barnes in Brentwood. Jack answered immediately.

'Jimmy here,' His Honor said. 'The whole damn project has blown up.'

There was a brief silence. 'Fill me in,' said Jack Barnes in a surprisingly mild tone. He was, and had always been, a gambler, and had long ago discovered that the wrong roll of the dice or turn of a card was not the end of the world. He listened carefully and in silence.

'How do you like the odds?' His Honor said in conclusion.

'I don't have any flood-damage insurance on my house,' Jack said. 'Can you write me some before news of all this breaks?'

Jimmy pursed his lips in admiration at this demonstration of practicality. 'I'll see what I can do.'

'On the other hand,' Jack Barnes said, 'I've had several offers for the place. Maybe I'd better take one of them. Yes,' he added shortly, 'forget the insurance. Now, about the boat . . . three hours' notice, huh? And out at sea will be safe? OK, we'll manage that. Thanks for the warning.'

Jack Barnes hung up and sat for some time, considering how to deal with this intelligence. The morality, or lack of it, of selling a house that was presumably doomed did not even occur to him. *Caveat emptor* was a principle established long before Jack Barnes came on the scene. He consulted his desk telephone file. Bert Flanagan first, he thought. He dialled the number.

Bert Flanagan was in his office and still interested in the Encino Beach house.

'There's a time factor,' Jack said. 'I want cash soon.'

'So, OK, we'll get on it right away. But are you willing to talk price in return for the hurry?'

Jack hesitated as long as he thought necessary for effect. 'OK, I'll talk price. But I won't give the place away. You understand that?'

'Of course,' Bert Flanagan said, and found it hard not to laugh aloud at his good fortune.

Jack Barnes hung up and leaned back in his chair, satisfied.

His next call was to the Encino Beach house. 'Betsy, hon,' Jack said, 'there'll be some people coming round to look the house over. Show them through. Tell them whatever they want to know.'

'Who are they?' Betsy demanded. 'And why are they coming?'

'We're selling the place, hon.'

There was a lengthy silence. Betsy said at last, 'Have you lost your mind? We like it here.'

'Have I ever steered us wrong? Answer me that.'

She sighed in resignation. 'I suppose you have reasons. You always do. It's just that I never know what they are.'

'That's my girl.'

'What about the boat? Are we selling that too?'

'It's just fine where it is, right on its yacht club mooring. And we can use it, just as we always have.'

There was more silence.

'Got it, hon?' Jack Barnes said.

'I guess so. You just bowled me over, that's all.' Betsy's voice changed suddenly. 'It's been a long time since I've felt like crying. But this—'

'OK. Tell you what you do. Get Maude Anderson down again to keep you company. How about that?'

'I don't think she'll want to come. She feels she struck out with Dan Garfield. I think he's crazy.'

'What if you tell her you need her?' Jack said.

There was a pause. 'Yes,' Betsy said, 'she'll come then.'

'That's my girl,' Jack said again. 'I'll either call or come down myself tonight. Bye now.'

Dr Tom Winslow came down to Encino Beach early on Saturday, July 26, for the start of his annual vacation.

'Sorry I couldn't make it last night,' he told Clara, 'but I had a patient in intensive care and I couldn't leave him.'

'What's his problem?' Long ago Clara had become accustomed to hearing about cases Tom could not shake from his mind.

Tom was already shucking off his city clothes. 'I don't know whether a heart attack, liver cirrhosis or lung cancer will get him first.'

Clara said, 'What can you do for him?'

Tom pulled on a pair of sailing shorts. 'Unless we put him in a straitjacket, gag him and strap him to the bed, there isn't much. He's used to having his own way, and he'll keep on smoking, drinking and eating too much no matter what I say.' Tom had his sailing sneakers on now, and he straightened up, smiling. 'But he's up there, and I'm down here, and the sun is shining, so I'm going to forget all about him, and all the others. I'm on vacation.'

'The trouble is,' Clara said, 'you never can completely forget. You're too conscientious, too caring.'

The doctor grinned. 'How about some breakfast?'

MAUDE ANDERSON and Betsy Barnes sat over coffee. Through the picture window they could look out over the bay.

'Bless you for coming down,' Betsy said. 'I slept better last night with you here. I'm not even embarrassed to admit it. Jack—' She shook her head. 'I don't know a thing about Jack's business. Real estate is an elastic term. For all I know, he may be peddling drugs.'

Maude smiled. 'There are wheelers and dealers, and there are good solid folks.' She lifted her slender shoulders and let them fall. 'All kinds. But for what it's worth, Jack's reputation is solid.'

Betsy set the coffee cup down carefully, her eyes avoiding Maude's. 'No rumours that he's . . . hard up?'

'None that I've heard.'

'You make me feel better, though I still don't know why we're selling this place.' Betsy looked around. Then she asked, 'Now, what about your man?'

'Dan?' Maude had thought of little else since going back up to LA. 'I think that's finished,' she said, and wondered if that was what she truly meant. She had been fond of Dan Garfield. She still was. In some ways he had always been unreachable, but maybe she had expected or hoped for the impossible. He had his world, just as she had hers, and was it logical at her age and his, or even likely, that those worlds could ever merge completely?

'Somebody else?' Betsy said.

'I don't think there's anyone.'

'Then it's not finished.' Betsy's voice was definite. 'Men can change their minds. They may think they know what they want, but most of them really don't. They have to be shown.'

'I'm not aggressive,' Maude said. 'I'd just make a fool of myself.'

'If you want him—and you do—then you have to go after him.'

'Betsy, please!'

Betsy picked up her coffee, looked at it, and set it down decisively. 'I won't have you pining away for nothing. You hear?'

THE WEATHER SERVICE meteorologist studied the computer-enhanced time-lapse satellite photos of hurricane Bob. Advance, retreat, advance again—all the time gathering strength. He reached for the telephone to call Pete Williamson.

When Pete was on the line, the meteorologist said, 'You asked for blow-by-blow coverage. Well, I'm looking at photos of Bob's latest antics. They don't tell me a thing except that he's big and dangerous and hasn't made his mind up what he wants to do. His position as of noon, our time, was a little more than three hundred miles west of Manzanillo, Mexico, and about the same distance south of the tip of Baja California.'

Pete got up from his desk and carried the phone over to the large wall map of the Pacific. He spanned the distance with his thumb and spread fingers. 'That puts its centre about eleven hundred to twelve hundred miles south of here,' he said.

'About that.'

'Maybe, just maybe,' Pete said, 'he'll behave himself and stay down there.'

The meteorologist chuckled. 'I sure wouldn't count on it. Bob could just as easily start north at a trot, and that would get him in your vicinity in two, three days, if that's what he finally decides. Although it hasn't happened often, a hurricane that far north.'

'I'll think positive,' Pete said. 'Thanks. Keep me posted, please.' He hung up and carried the phone back to his desk, where his list of places to call—places that had had tsunami damage in the past—was spread out. He began dialling.

IN HILO, HAWAII, Jerry Matsuo listened quietly on the phone. 'Fun and games, huh?' he said, after a time. 'There isn't anything we can do, of course, except watch for the warning. But thanks, Pete, anyway. When are you coming over? I'll show you some waves to ride that make Onofre look pretty pallid.'

'That,' Pete said, 'may be just what I'll need when all this is over.'

IN VALPARAISO, CHILE: 'Many thanks, Dr Williamson. We have a long coastline, as you know, and we are—how you say?—vulnerable. But rest assured that we will make all preparations in case of this thing happening, although I hope it will not.'

'I hope not too,' Pete said. 'This is one time when I wouldn't mind being wrong.'

IN HONSHU, JAPAN, Dr Kanuko, educated at the University of California at Berkeley, spoke in almost unaccented, idiomatic English. 'I'm afraid I understand too well, Dr Williamson. We Japanese grow up aware of the threat of earthquake and tsunami, as I am sure you know, and we do have our own preparations to prevent total disaster. I am in your debt for this early warning. I will be in touch with Hokkaido and other islands as well.'

'You'll have longer than the rest of us to get ready,' Pete said.

'The factor of distance, yes. We will have perhaps six hours of warning, as against your—what? About three?'

'And Hawaii will have less.'

'I am deeply grateful, Dr Williamson. Rest assured that we shall alert ourselves immediately.'

7

On Monday, July 28, Pete and Garfield sat in the office of Wilbert Ellis, director of the County Office of Disaster Preparedness, once again. With Ellis this time was a man named Heinz. 'Mr Heinz,' Ellis said, 'is attached to the state office. At my request he flew down this morning from Sacramento.' Ellis hesitated. 'I felt that this threat was more than a local matter.'

'Correct,' Pete said. 'I've talked with Hawaii, Japan, Chile, and a few other places, filling them in on the possibilities. I've stuck my neck way out.'

'You are that convinced?' Heinz sighed. 'I had hoped—never mind. We have to accept what is.'

'Hurricane Bob has started north,' Pete said. 'Weather service man called me only a few minutes ago. And that is bad news.'

'What do you suggest we do?' Heinz asked.

'Coordinate information among Mr Ellis's colleagues, for starters,' Garfield said promptly. 'The French test is scheduled only two days from now.'

Heinz nodded. 'We would like your thinking on another aspect. Do we pass the warning along quietly, or do we go public immediately in order to try to counteract the effect of that unfortunate tsunami warning a few weeks ago?'

Ellis said, 'I believe the question is already moot. My wife called me less than an hour ago to say that the cleaning woman had heard there was a real tidal wave threat this time, and did I know anything about it. In small communities word spreads fast.'

'A leak was probably inevitable,' Garfield said. 'What the general reaction will be is anybody's guess, but I should think the sensible course is to go public with all the facts.' He was watching Heinz's face. 'You disagree?'

'Our policy,' Heinz said, 'has always been on the side of caution against premature disclosure. I asked your opinion in the hope it would reinforce our thinking. I am sorry it does not.'

Garfield said slowly, 'I should have thought that the government would have learned by now that attempts to hide the facts are inevitably futile—Watergate, Iran arms sales . . .'

'What we have here, Mr Garfield,' Heinz said, 'are not facts, but

61

conjecture. *If* the test takes place, and *if* the geological results are as you predict, and *if* hurricane Bob does approach this southern California coast closely enough . . .'

Pete looked at Garfield. 'I think we're wasting our time here.'

'I'm afraid I have to agree,' Garfield said. He nodded to Ellis, to Heinz. 'Gentlemen.' He walked out with Pete.

'What now?' Pete said.

Garfield had already been thinking about it. 'What about the mayor?'

Pete began to smile. 'Jimmy's hell on wheels once he gets started. Good thinking. Jimmy Silva it is.'

THE MAYOR LEANED BACK in his chair and scowled at the ceiling. His first reaction was, 'Those damn bureaucrats.' He sat up straight. 'OK. What can we do? Joe Hines has kids lined up to take some of the bigger boats out to sea.' He explained Joe Hines's plan. 'The three hours' warning—that's enough time for them. But auto traffic is what we got to think about. You ever go to a Rose Bowl game and see how long it takes to get those cars out when the game's over?'

Garfield said approvingly, 'You've given this some thought.'

'Hell's fire,' Jimmy Silva said, 'I haven't been thinking of anything else. This is my town. I grew up here. I don't want anybody hurt. If I have to, I'll tell our police guys to block off the roads and keep everybody out, make all the traffic one way leaving the beach. I'd rather do what we can and maybe be wrong than not do a thing and get some folks hurt, maybe killed. You can rebuild a house, but except in the Bible, I never heard of bringing anybody back to life. Did you?'

THE WINSLOW HOUSE seemed unusually quiet when Garfield let himself in that evening. Both Winslow cars were in the small parking area, but no lights had been turned on, and as Garfield went from room to room it was evident that no one was at home, until Lucy burst in, excited and apologetic, her short hair dancing.

'Sorry I'm late.' Her voice was a mixture of worry and annoyance. 'I mean, Todd and I got to talking, or I'd have been here sooner. I'll bet you thought you'd been deserted.'

'I did wonder.'

'Mom and Dad are out in the boat. They sailed this afternoon. They'll be back tomorrow or maybe Wednesday—' She stopped, and her eyes searched Garfield's face. 'Why, what's wrong?'

'Nothing.' He added vaguely, 'Wednesday's the thirtieth.'

'Sure. Full moon too. Sailing in full moon's fun. They're not so old, Mom and Dad, and they don't get much time alone, you know? That's why I didn't sail with them. Mom said it was OK. You'd be here, so I wouldn't be all alone.'

62

'I think you are a very considerate daughter,' Garfield said.

Instantly she was off in another direction. 'Now, what's for dinner? Are you as starved as I am? Todd and I . . .' Her smile faded and her unhappiness was plain.

'Todd and you?'

Lucy was silent for a few moments. 'We had a fight,' she said at last. 'Guys make me mad sometimes, Todd especially.' She smiled sheepishly. 'And you know what? When I get mad, I get hungry. Crazy, isn't it?'

Garfield too was smiling. 'Maybe it's a good thing. Relieves tension. Would you like to go out to dinner?'

'No, thanks. If it's all right with you, I'll fix dinner here. I like to cook. How about that?'

'Wild,' said Garfield.

THE NEXT DAY, Tuesday, July 29, Garfield stopped at Pete's house just as Pete got off the phone to the meteorologist.

'Bob,' Pete said, 'is flexing his muscles and beginning to move north a little faster. All shipping off the Baja coast is being warned away. From Punta Eugenia, which sticks well out to the west, to Ensenada, less than a hundred miles south of the border, all shore localities are being alerted.'

'I think it's time you talked with Boggs again,' Garfield said. 'We'll want his backing when we talk to the papers.'

Pete's eyebrows rose. 'We're going all out with a warning?'

'Do you have an alternative? Ellis can't make a move until Heinz gives the nod, and we saw Heinz's reaction yesterday. We have to take matters into our own hands.'

Garfield's logic was impeccable, as always, Pete thought.

Garfield turned to leave. 'If you should want me, I'll be over on the ocean side. Maybe I'll think of other precautionary steps we might take.'

Outside, the sun had already burned away the morning mists, and the water of the bay lay flat and shining, no hint yet of a breeze yet from Bob's distant strength to disturb its surface.

All those boats in the harbour, Garfield thought as he walked, and all those people, with at most three hours' warning if the worst possible scenario did develop. And for the majority of the boats—millions of dollars' worth of pleasure craft—there was probably no hope. He was not a sailing man, but he was sure that only the most seaworthy boats, both power and sail, would be able to cope with the kind of seas hurricane Bob would be stirring up.

As he thought about this it occurred to him that he had never before in his life faced the kind of elemental threat that was now approaching. He had lived his life engrossed in matters—inventing electronic gadgetry and making money—that now were beginning to seem more and more inconsequential.

It was in this mood of introspection that he encountered Maude.

'Hello, Dan.' Her smile was tentative. 'Are you wondering why I'm here when I said I was going back to LA?' She studied him as they fell into step automatically. 'Or hadn't that thought or any other concerning me even occurred to you?'

'I'm sorry. I'm not sure exactly why, but I am truly sorry.'

'You see?' Maude said. 'You are basically a considerate person. I said that once before.'

'And I believe I rejected the concept.' The words were light, but his thoughts were brutally analytical. I was in no way considerate of others, he told himself, because I was wrapped up in my own ambitions to the exclusion of all else.

'You have always been a single-minded person, Dan. That I will grant. You could not have been so successful otherwise.'

'Maybe selfish is the better word?'

'Dan!' Her tone reprimanded him. 'A hair shirt does not become you. I have no idea what has been happening that has changed you, softened you. You were what you were, and I was fond of you both because of and despite it. But you are different now, and I'm not completely sure what I think. I will admit that in some ways I like the results.' She made an odd, swift gesture of dismissal. 'Dan, you do tempt me into saying things that would probably be best left unsaid.'

'I'm glad you said them.'

'Now you're being kind. And I'm not sure I can stand that.' She had stopped walking and turned to face him. 'You infuriate me sometimes, and I'm not sure why.'

He was suddenly relaxed. 'I'm beginning to understand that I infuriated a lot of people,' he said. 'But I'm not going to spend the rest of my life going around apologising to them.'

'Good.' Her smile took on a new, friendlier quality. 'Let's leave it like that. Agreed?' She held out her hand.

Garfield took it and shook it solemnly. 'Agreed.'

'Now,' Maude said, 'would you care to have me walk with you, or would you rather be alone?'

'I'd like your company. Maybe we'll see some more pelicans.'

They walked in companionable silence. From time to time Garfield found himself glancing at the ocean swells marching in to end their long journey on the white sands. Was it imagination, he asked himself, or was he seeing an increase in the size of the swells, caused, perhaps, by distant contact with hurricane Bob's peripheral winds?

'I came back down here,' Maude said without warning, as if explanation were required, 'because Betsy Barnes asked me to hold her hand. They are selling their house. Betsy has not the faintest idea why, and Jack won't tell her. It has upset her badly.'

'Is Jack Barnes a shrewd operator?' Garfield asked.

'Apparently. He is very successful in real estate.' Maude looked at Garfield's face. 'There was a point to that question?'

'Maybe.'

'I'm listening, Dan. If I can ease Betsy's mind in any way . . .'

'It's possible,' he said, 'that Barnes is selling while the selling is good. A shrewd operator would have had his ear to the ground.'

'Now you're talking in riddles.'

'It's a long story.'

'I'd like to hear it, Dan. Please.'

He was silent, hesitant. Then, why not? he asked himself. Others already know.

She listened quietly while he went through it all, chapter and verse, as they walked: nuclear testing, geological changes, careful analysis of all available data, predicted results, the spring tide and the approach of hurricane Bob. In the bright sunlight it all seemed unreal.

'The trouble is, it all adds up,' Garfield said. 'And it may be why Jack Barnes wants to sell his house.'

'Knowing—no, believing—that it could be destroyed?' Maude turned the matter over in her mind. 'Should I tell Betsy?'

'Up to you. She's *your* friend.'

'I'm asking you, Dan. I'm not sure I believe any of this. Really believe it, I mean. But telling Betsy—'

'What good would it do? And if it wouldn't do any good, then why do it?'

'Is logic all there is, Dan . . . the only consideration?'

'I'm not a philosopher. Sorry. But logic can be a most important consideration. That's why I suggest that you go back to Westwood.'

'And leave Betsy?'

'Is she your responsibility?'

'She's my friend. Isn't that the same thing?'

Beyond Maude, Garfield saw Pete coming towards them at a trot.

'I don't know the answers,' Garfield said. 'Maybe I've never really understood all the questions. Anyway, I'm afraid our tête-à-tête is finished. Sorry.' He hesitated, then turned from her as Pete pulled up, breathing deeply. 'Yes, Pete?'

'Conference,' Pete said. 'Boggs, Jimmy Silva, Joe Hines, Ellis, you and me. My car's just back there.' He jerked his head towards the shore road.

'I repeat,' Garfield said to Maude. 'I am sorry.'

CHAIRS HAD BEEN BROUGHT into Howard Boggs's office at the oceanographic institute and set in a rough semicircle.

'I have called this meeting,' Boggs began, 'because, unfortunately, matters seem to be coming to a head.' He tapped the pile of computer printout sheets on his desk and looked at Garfield. 'I don't know, Mr Garfield, if you are aware that the people in Washington have also seen this printout and that they concur with your opinions.'

Jimmy Silva growled, 'Get on with it. Washington can go to hell, for all I care. I'm worried about Encino Beach.'

'I take your point, Mr Mayor, but what Washington has set in motion will also affect Encino Beach.' Boggs paused briefly. 'Convinced of the threat—no, of the likelihood—that Dr Williamson's, Pete's, theories are correct, Washington has arranged aerial surveillance of the test site tomorrow, complete with photographs of the explosion itself. The surveillance will officially be accidental, to avoid ill feeling. And video coverage of likely danger spots—in Hawaii, in Chile, in Central America and elsewhere—has been arranged and will be broadcast via satellite in order that the severity of the tsunami may be judged accurately.'

'That means,' Garfield said, 'that an hour and a half, perhaps even two hours, before we are threatened here, we will know something of what we are up against.'

'Right,' Boggs said. 'In the meantime, the weather service and the air-force meteorologists have kept careful watch over hurricane Bob. As of thirty minutes ago, the centre of the storm was approximately seven hundred miles southwest of Encino Beach and moving north-eastwards at a speed of approximately twelve knots—fifteen miles an hour, more or less. The winds within the hurricane have reached velocities on the order of a hundred and twenty miles per hour. The seas in its path are tumultuous.'

'There's a word,' Joe Hines said.

Garfield looked at Ellis. 'Any official changes since we met Heinz?'

'None.' Ellis took a deep breath. 'I have agonised over this,' he said, 'and I am prepared on my own authority to issue a general warning whenever you gentlemen give the word. I cannot in conscience do less.'

Jimmy Silva broke into a smile. 'Gutsy,' he said. 'I like that. You ever get a ticket in Encino Beach, chum, you bring it to me. I'll tear it up and kick the cop who gave it to you.'

Garfield looked at Joe Hines. 'We know of your plan to send certain large boats to sea in the care of the local boys.' His tone indicated no reservations. 'Now, what about the small craft?'

Joe hesitated. 'Some'll do fine even in'—he glanced at Boggs—'tumultuous seas. Others . . .' He shook his head. 'They'd better stay in harbour and hope for the best.'

Boggs said, 'We are going to set up cameras on high ground, the bluff beyond the coast highway, with a good view of the peninsula and the channel, as well as the harbour and Encino Beach itself.'

Jimmy Silva said, 'I'll give you some police protection, keep the crowds away. We'll want a record of . . . what was. Anything else?'

Boggs looked round the room. He said quietly, 'I think that about covers it. Thank you, gentlemen. I will see that you are informed of any change in hurricane Bob's status. Pete and Mr Garfield, if you will stay for a few minutes?'

After Jimmy Silva, Joe Hines and Ellis had gone, Boggs said to Garfield and Pete, 'Do you have plans, gentlemen?'

Pete said, 'I want to watch the seismograph. My guess is it's going to jump off the paper when they shoot off the test. So I'll be here in the morning.'

Garfield said, 'I don't know my plans yet. I'll have to let you know. I'm going to be a very interested observer.'

He and Pete walked together out to Pete's car. Pete said, 'You're thinking of—what?'

'Clara and Tom are at sea. May be back today, maybe not until tomorrow.'

'Tom's a good sailor,' Pete said. 'He'll keep his scanner on, and he'll be monitoring Bob's progress on all frequencies. If there's a threat, he'll run for home pronto.' He was studying Garfield's face. 'The point is, will we want him to come in or stay at sea? Right?'

'Exactly.'

'Clara,' Pete said, 'will want to be with Lucy, and that means coming ashore. The trouble is that with what we're expecting, they'll be safer out there. *Westerly*'s a good, stout boat. I've sailed aboard her. If they head west, out of Bob's probable path, they should be all right. Think you can persuade him to stay at sea, with Lucy ashore?'

'I can try.'

'It would mean that somebody—you—would be taking responsibility for the girl. You realise that?'

He had already accepted it. 'Yes.'

Pete got into his car and closed the door. There he just sat, his hands on the wheel, his face thoughtful, while Garfield got in too. Pete turned to look at him, suddenly smiling. 'Did you have any idea what you were letting yourself in for when you came down here for—what? A rest? A change? Vacation?'

'All of the above,' Garfield said ruefully. 'And the answer is no, I didn't have any idea.'

AT DINNER WITH BETSY BARNES that evening, Maude Anderson was quiet.

'What's bothering you?' Betsy said. 'Something certainly seems to have gotten to you.'

'I ran into Dan Garfield.'

'And?'

'We walked and we talked,' Maude said. She wondered just how one could possibly express the confusion that was in her mind. There were too many factors. Dan, for one, and a changed Dan at that—a warmer, more sensitive man. And then there was Jack Barnes and his apparent lack of scruples, along with the threat of what Dan had described. How did one make sense out of all that?

'Men,' Betsy said. 'The trouble is that we can't get along without them. Are you going to see him again?'

'I don't know. We didn't talk about that.' It was then that Maude reached her decision. 'I'm going back to town tomorrow, Betsy. I think it's best.'

'Let him come to you?' Betsy thought about it. 'Maybe you're right. Sometimes running away until you finally catch him is the best system.'

'I'm not looking at it like that.'

'Anyway'—Betsy reached across the table to pat Maude's hand—'I appreciate your coming down to let me cry on your shoulder. I don't know what I'd have done without you.'

Just before sleep came that night, Maude thought back to that remark and felt as if she had betrayed her friend.

LUCY PUT TWO PLATES on the table. 'It's chicken Marengo,' she said, studying Garfield's face as he tasted the dish.

'It's delicious,' he said.

Her pleased smile was warming. But then it was suddenly gone. 'Todd and I had another fight this afternoon.'

'I'm sorry.'

'Why do guys think they have to pat you on the head and tell you it's only a movie, everything's going to be OK?'

'I don't know about that.'

'You don't do it. At least you haven't done it so far.'

'I'll try to be careful.' Garfield glanced at the kitchen clock. 'Do you think your folks are coming in tonight?'

'No. It's almost dark, and if he can avoid it, Dad doesn't like to have Mom try to pick up our mooring in the dark. I guess he's afraid she might fall overboard. Silly, but that's the way he is.'

'I find that rather admirable, as well as considerate.'

'Looking out for her, you mean? I guess so.'

It was after dinner, the dishes done, when the phone rang. 'I've got it,' Lucy called into the living room, and there was a long, scarcely audible conversation in the kitchen. Then Lucy appeared. 'I'm going out,' she said. 'With Todd.'

Despite himself, Garfield could not contain his surprise.

'So, OK,' Lucy said. 'We had a fight this afternoon. But that was then. OK?' The single word bristled with challenge.

'It's fine with me,' Garfield said, and hid his smile.

That night Garfield thought back to this episode just before he went off to sleep. No, he told himself, what he had said to Pete was the whole and simple truth: he had had no idea what he was letting himself in for when he allowed Tom to talk him into coming down to Encino Beach.

8

Wednesday, July 30. At breakfast Garfield said as casually as he could to Lucy, 'Your father has a radio transmitter here, doesn't he? Ship-to-shore?'

'In his study,' Lucy said. 'In the cabinet. Why?'

'Just wondered.'

Lucy put down her cereal spoon. Her eyes searched his face. 'You aren't telling me something,' she said. 'What is it?'

'We don't know anything yet.'

'But you have a good idea. What is it?'

Garfield tried evasion. 'You heard the weather report.'

Lucy nodded. 'Is the hurricane coming up here? Or is it those big waves again? Is that what it is? Is it?'

'It's only possible. We don't know yet.'

'You guys are all alike.' Her voice was overloud. 'You and Todd and . . . everybody. Last night—' She stopped, breathing hard, and angry tears ran down the sides of her nose. 'He still wouldn't tell me anything. Just like you. What gives you guys the right to think you can make all the decisions? I have feelings too.'

'Lucy—' Garfield began. It was too late.

She jumped up from the table, and her chair overturned with a crash. 'I'm sick and tired of being patted on the head and being treated like a baby by Todd, and now by you. And I won't sit here and take it any longer.' She was gone, almost running.

Garfield heard the outer door slam, and wondered what he was supposed to do now. He was still at the table when Pete walked in.

Pete surveyed the scene. Wordlessly he righted the overturned chair and sat down. 'Little problem with the princess?' he asked.

'Probably my fault.'

Pete nodded solemnly.

Garfield had a sip of coffee and set the cup down next to his unfinished breakfast. 'Tom and Clara didn't come in last night.'

'I know. I saw the empty mooring.' He paused. 'So what now? You can probably raise them on the ship-to-shore, try to persuade them to stay outside, head west. Bob's still coming this way. And he's picked up more speed.'

'I know.'

'Tell Clara you'll take care of the princess. Where is she, anyway?'

Garfield spread both hands. 'I don't know.'

'Well,' Pete said, 'I guess we can find her.' He looked at his watch and stood up. 'I'm going to the institute, the seismograph. Have you taken a look at the surf this morning?'

Garfield shook his head.

'It's high, and getting higher. We're already catching Bob's fringe force. High tide's in a little over three hours. If Bob keeps coming, it could be timed just right—or wrong—to coincide with what we're expecting.'

Garfield watched him quietly.

'Oh, yes,' Pete said. 'It's coming—worst possible scenario. I know it. I feel it right here.' He patted his stomach.

'I know.' Garfield stood up. 'I'll call Tom and Clara.'

After Pete had gone, Garfield went into the study. The transceiver was there, in its handsome cabinet. Garfield flipped on the power switch and saw the red signal light appear. He left the selector dial at the frequency at which it was set, adjusted the volume and, depressing the button, spoke into the hand microphone. 'Calling yacht *Westerly*. Repeat: calling yacht *Westerly*.'

He released the button and waited. There was no immediate response. He had expected none. He raised the microphone and repeated the call.

Tom Winslow's voice, distorted in transmission but nonetheless recognisable, said, 'Yacht *Westerly* here. Come in.'

'Home base,' Garfield said, knowing his own voice would also be recognised. 'Are you following weather reports?'

'Affirmative. Weather looks bad. We're coming in.'

'How much sailing time?'

'Depending on wind, four, five hours.'

Exactly the wrong timing, Garfield thought. About three hours to high tide, Pete had said, and if the test shot took place soon . . .

The telephone on the desk rang. Garfield spoke into the microphone. 'Stand by.' He put down the mike and reached for the phone.

Harry Saunders's voice said, 'They've fired it. And it was a big one. Bigger, I'm sure, than they expected. That's all I can tell you now.'

'Thanks,' Garfield said, hung up and jumped back to the transceiver. 'You're there, *Westerly*?'

'Right here. What's doing? Why—'

'I can't explain. You'll get radio warnings soon. Put out to sea. Head north and west, and *stay* out. There won't be any shelter here. Acknowledge.'

'Dan!' This was Clara's voice. 'What is happening?'

'What we feared. It's all but certain now. It's—'

'Is Lucy with you, Dan?'

70

Garfield took a
deep breath. 'Not at the
moment.'

'Then where is she?'

'I'll find her. You can
count on that.'

'Dan!'

Tom's voice again. 'We're coming in, Dan!'

'Damn it! Believe me,' he said into the mike. 'It's all coming together, those big waves. Three hours if we're lucky.'

Tom's voice was calm. 'You are sure, Dan? There will be no shelter inside? It *is* that bad.'

'No shelter. Devastation. Sorry, but that's it.'

'Roger. We will put out to sea, head northwest. Wish us—'

Clara's voice interrupted. 'Dan, promise me you will find Lucy, take care of her. Promise?'

'Promise.' Garfield closed his eyes. 'Good luck.'

'Thanks.' Tom's voice again. 'Over and out.'

AT AN ALTITUDE of thirty-eight thousand feet, miles distant from the site, the aircraft swung in a great circle at a steady cruising speed. The cloudless sky provided a clear view for the cameras, their lenses covered by heavy dark filters.

The crew of the aircraft too wore protective goggles, and before they left base their instructions had been definite and decisive. 'Do not, repeat, do *not* look directly at the blast. Its light will be more intense than that of the sun. Even through these lenses the retinas of your eyes can be permanently damaged.'

But with the first, sudden burst of light from the tiny atoll and the immediate, sure knowledge that the test shot had been fired, the

71

temptation to look directly at the scene was almost irresistible. The pilot said harshly into the intercom, 'Eyes away, unless you want to walk with a white cane the rest of your life.' And that message did get through.

Moments later, as the fireball began to develop to its eventual gigantic size, rising swiftly in the clear air, they did look, and then stared in wonder as the blast began to display its awesome might. The seas surrounding the atoll boiled and churned. An enormous mushroom-shaped cloud rose and spread with unbelievable speed, and within the gigantic fireball that was its centre, ignited gases boiled in a furnace of changing colours.

Great seas rocked the witnessing ships, and the thunder of the explosion stunned even those wearing protective earpads. Sound shock waves spread instantly in all directions, but with greater speed through water than through air. Along the ledge that Pete Williamson had studied from the minisub, cracks in the rock began to widen, and small pieces broke free to drift down into the abyss.

Suddenly, like an enormous building slowly absorbing the effect of dynamite charges exploded at its foundations, the entire ledge shuddered gently, hung poised for long moments, then ponderously separated from the parent structure and plunged into the depths.

Along almost a hundred miles of this gigantic submarine earth-fracture, hundreds of millions of tons of rock began their fall. Behaving like dominoes, they toppled in swift succession, accelerating as they dropped, suddenly and forcefully displacing the water in the depths and altering the shape and contours of the sea bottom itself on contact, by their bulk and weight.

On the surface, the ocean boiled and heaved as the energy from the disturbance beneath was transmitted upwards. Visible sea waves came into being directly above the underwater avalanche, their crests scores of miles apart, their surface height no more than two or three feet, but their speed well in excess of four hundred miles per hour.

The inexorable process had begun.

WITHIN MINUTES the seismic detectors linked to the Honolulu Observatory had fixed the epicentre of the quake. A tsunami watch was issued to the fourteen Pacific coastal and island nations and territories of the warning network. The watch was followed shortly by a tsunami warning, and the estimated time of arrival was quickly broadcast to each vulnerable Pacific locality

With an eight-point-seven Richter-scale reading for a seismic disturbance on the sea bottom, there was no doubt what was going to happen. All that was left was to find out how much damage was going to be done. And where.

IN THE COUNTY OFFICE of Disaster Preparedness in Encino Beach, Wilbert Ellis took a deep breath and, in as calm a voice as he could manage, issued the orders to his assistant.

'A countywide alert on LIFE,' he said. 'At once!' LIFE was the acronym for Lifesaving Information for Emergencies, copied from the system first established in California's San Diego County.

Special LIFE receivers around the county were immediately notified by Touch-Tone telephone signals: tone number one alerted police and fire dispatch; tone number two alerted radio and television stations; tone number three alerted key county officials; and tone number four alerted hospitals and schools. These signals were followed by voice messages giving particulars.

JIMMY SILVA HAD A CAPTAIN of the California Highway Patrol in his office. 'Most times you and me, we get along fine,' Jimmy was saying, 'and no reason we can't here too. You know your freeways like the back of your hand. I know Encino Beach and its roads and its people. Way I see it, you got two big problems and you handle them, and I'll handle my end down here. OK?'

The captain disliked being talked to like this by a beach civilian, even if he was a mayor, but he had his orders to cooperate, so he said merely, 'What do you see as my two problems?'

'First,' Jimmy said, 'there are going to be a lot of fools who'll head for the beaches to watch the fun. It always happens. A big storm, they come down to watch the waves. Park all the way out to the jetties. They do that this time and the starfish and the spiny lobsters are going to have a lot of dead meat to feed on.'

'What do you suggest?' the captain said.

'Shut off all roads coming down here except for folks who got business—a house, a boat, family to get out.'

The captain said neutrally,'And my second problem?'

'Coast highway's a deathtrap,' Jimmy said promptly. 'It runs only fifteen, twenty feet above mean high water. Them what's-its— soonamis—come in thirty, forty, fifty feet high with half the Pacific Ocean behind them, and they'll wipe out anything they hit. I mean, wipe it out—cars, houses, office buildings, people. You get the picture?'

I'm beginning to, the captain thought. There was something about Jimmy Silva in his aloha shirt, with his heavy, hairy forearms, an intensity in his voice and manner, that just made you believe him. The captain said nothing.

'I grew up here,' Jimmy said. 'I know every waterway and path and old road there is, not just the paved ones we use now. We got to get folks going uphill to the bluff just as fast as we can. I'll give you a couple of local cops who know the area as well as I do. They'll show you roads that can be opened and kept one way—up. Up where the ground is safe.' Jimmy faced the captain squarely. 'How about it? We going to get along?'

The captain nodded slowly and held out his hand. 'We'll get along, Mr Mayor,' he said with conviction.

DAN GARFIELD TELEPHONED Pete at the institute. 'You're busy, I know,' Garfield said, 'but have you any idea where Lucy might have gone when she left this morning?'

'Try the Wilsons,' Pete said. 'They'll know, if anybody does. Aside from that, you reached Tom and Clara?'

'They're putting out to sea. Northwest.'

'And you're left holding the baby? OK, I understand, but I don't have a clue. She could be anywhere, and we've got about two hours and twenty-five minutes, is all.'

'The Wilsons,' Garfield said. 'Thanks, Pete.' He hung up, found the Wilsons' phone number and dialled.

Mrs Wilson answered. 'No,' she said, 'Lucy isn't here. Todd has gone up to town, and she isn't with him. Have you heard the sirens? And the radio? Have you—'

'Yes,' Garfield said. How in the world did I ever get myself in this position? he asked himself.

'She is a very responsible child, Mr Garfield. She'll probably be back in a few minutes. She couldn't miss all the commotion, the sirens and all.'

He hung up. 'All right, know-it-all,' he said softly to himself, 'what do you do now?'

IT SEEMED TO JACK BARNES that just about every state highway patrol officer in California was out and active, and determined to keep him from reaching Encino Beach. The freeway had suddenly turned one way—in some places eight lanes of traffic heading inland—so Jack took the lesser streets and roads, weaving and dodging, sometimes ignoring traffic signals as he slowly but steadily worked his way south.

He had long since switched off the car radio, with its almost hysterical warnings, and switched on the cassette player. The orchestral sounds flowed over him unnoticed while he weighed the various factors he had to consider. The Encino Beach house was no longer his concern. Forget the house. He disliked driving his BMW into a danger zone, but the boat was far more valuable. He would leave the car at the yacht club and take the boat out to sea. If he lost the car, that was tough, but it was the only logical choice, and logic, practicality, played a large part in Jack's thinking. Betsy. He could take her with him aboard the boat, but that had two major drawbacks. First, it would mean leaving her BMW where it too could be lost. Second, although Betsy was pleasant company, she was not worth a damn aboard the boat. Jack would not put it past her to turn hysterical if they ran into rough seas. And so that choice too was clear.

He reached the coast highway at last and worked his way to the entrance to Encino Beach, where a local cop blocked his way.

'You're going the wrong way, buddy,' the cop said. 'We're evacuating—there's a tidal wave coming.'

'I've got a house down here and a boat on a mooring. I want to take the boat outside, where it's safe.'

'Rough out there. Storm warning's up.'

Jack nodded and said nothing.

'OK,' the cop said, following orders. 'It's your skin.' He stepped back from the car and waved it through. 'Good luck.'

Betsy was at the house, distraught. 'What's happening? Answer me that. Is this for real or just another false alarm? You told me to stay here, and you don't even look worried.'

'Nothing to worry about,' Jack said, glancing at his watch, 'for about two hours. By then you'll be back in Brentwood.'

'And where will you be? Here? What's going to become of this house? If we'd known this was going to—' She stopped in midsentence, and her eyes grew round. 'Is that why we're selling? Because you knew this would happen?'

'Never mind.' Jack's tone was calm. 'Let's just take it as it comes. We'll pack what valuables we can in your car and you head for Brentwood. I'm taking the boat out to sea.'

'That's crazy! There's a storm out there!' Betsy stamped her foot in frustration. 'Oh, damn. I wish Maude hadn't left. She'd help me talk some sense into you.'

'Now listen to me.' Jack's tone was low-pitched, commanding. 'We're going to pack what valuables we can and load them in your car, and you're heading for Brentwood. Have you got that?'

Betsy brushed her hair back, nodding slowly.

'That's my girl.' His tone was softer. 'And I'm taking *Spindrift* out to sea, where she'll be safe. I won't have her caught in harbour in the kind of mess we're going to get, any more than I'll have you caught here in this house. Is that clear?'

Betsy swallowed hard and nodded again.

'Then move it,' Jack said.

Still she hesitated. 'You—' She stopped and caught her lower lip between her teeth. 'Outside in this storm they're talking about—'

'*Spindrift* and I'll be fine, just fine. She's been in rough weather before. She loves it.'

MAUDE HAD LEFT THE FREEWAY and was driving east on Sunset Boulevard towards her apartment when she heard the emergency bulletin on her car radio: 'The tsunami is expected by approximately one thirty this afternoon Pacific Daylight Time. Well before then, seaside residents are urged to move inland to higher ground. Repeat: a tsunami, or tidal wave, warning is now in effect . . .'

There was more, but Maude heard none of it. Paramount in her mind was the thought that she had been both premature and foolish to leave Encino Beach in the first place. The decision had been pure vanity, no more than a reflexive retreat from possible humiliation if she stayed on. And what did that mere possibility amount to in the face of this threat of real and total disaster? She could play an active role or sit for ever on the sidelines; there were no other choices open to her.

At the first opportunity she made a U-turn and headed for the southbound freeway, driving faster than she usually did. She felt lighter and easier, yes, and freer than she had in a long, long time. It did not even occur to her to wonder why. At the junction with the Harbor Freeway a roadblock had been set up and she was shunted off to lesser roads, which she negotiated, heading ever south. By the time the same cop who had stopped Jack Barnes at the entrance to Encino Beach flagged her down, her mood was almost ebullient.

'Yes, Officer?' she said.

'We've closed off this area. There's a tidal wave warning—'

'I know. That is why I must go in.'

'Lady—'

'Officer.' Maude looked straight up at him, her eyes holding his. 'Have you ever been in love?' The words seemed to come out of their own accord and, once spoken, took on a life and a conviction of their own.

'I got a wife and three kids, lady—'

'That,' Maude said, 'was not what I asked.'

The cop scratched his chin. Maude watched him steadily. He began to smile. 'OK,' he said. 'I guess I see what you mean.' He stepped back from the car. 'Good luck.'

Maude too was smiling as she drove into Encino Beach.

9

In the Winslow house the phone rang, and Garfield jumped to answer it. It was Pete. 'We're getting video transmission by satellite from Hawaii,' Pete said. 'ETA there is in about twenty minutes. Saunders called. The wave has already hit a flyspeck island below the equator. It was big. Damn big. Over two hundred foot high. We'd like you here to watch Hawaii . . .' His voice trailed off.

'Yes,' Garfield said, 'but . . .' His anxiety had turned to anger now. Silly, childish behaviour, he was thinking. 'Lucy . . .'

'No word?' Pete said.

'None.'

'Why hasn't she heard the sirens, all the commotion? Where could she be and not hear?'

'Quite,' Garfield said.

'Look'—Pete's voice altered—'you can leave a note for her, damn it. She can read.'

'No. I have to find her.'

'OK. But keep an eye on the time. ETA here, one thirty-two. That's confirmed. And there won't be any appeal for leniency.'

Garfield hung up. All right. So where could Lucy be that she would not have heard the commotion? How about the beach? The wind and the surf making too much noise, how about that?

The telephone rang again and he snatched it. Maude's voice said, 'I thought you would be there. I hoped so.' In her tone there was no undercurrent of doubt or even of hesitation, which had not been true before. 'What are you going to do, Dan?'

There was comfort in the sound of her voice. 'Lucy is gone. The Winslows' daughter. They left her in my care—they're at sea. I don't know where she is, and I promised to find her.' And then, quickly, a new worry began to set in. 'Where are you? I thought—I hoped you were going home.'

'I did. Then I came back. I'm at the Barneses' house. Betsy is gone. So is her car. And I just saw Jack's boat, *Spindrift*, going down the channel. Jack was at the wheel.'

Garfield said, 'You shouldn't have come back. Haven't you—'

'I have heard the radio, Dan. I have heard the warnings.'

'The only sensible thing to do is leave.'

'But you are staying.'

'That's different. I have a reason.'

'So have I.'

Garfield frowned. 'I don't get it. What is your reason?'

'You. I'm coming over, Dan. I'll be there in a few moments.'

The line went dead.

Garfield hung up and sat motionless, staring at the wall, trying to unscramble his thoughts and feelings. Too many different emotions competed in a swirl of confusion. When the telephone rang again, he picked it up, wondering if Maude had changed her mind, astonished to find that he hoped she had not.

It was Todd Wilson, breathless. 'Mom said you called and asked if she knew where Lucy was. Where is she?'

'I don't know. She ran out at breakfast. She was angry.'

'Yeah, she's been that way recently. Where are her folks?'

'At sea, and not coming in. I persuaded them to stay outside.'

Todd said, 'What are you going to do?'

'There's only one thing to do—wait here, unless you can think of some place where she might be.'

'No.' The young voice was heavy with disappointment.

'Call me if you do.'

'Sure,' Todd said, and hung up.

From the doorway Maude said, 'Tell me about the girl, Dan.' She came in and sat down on a kitchen chair, as if they were simply picking up a conversation where they had left it. 'She's gone, you say, and you don't know where. Do you know why?'

'My fault, I suppose. I was so damn adult and male, she thought I was treating her like a child, which I was.'

Maude studied him quietly. 'The change in you is even more apparent, Dan. Or maybe I'm seeing things more clearly. Never mind. You have no idea where she might have gone?'

'She is probably somewhere where she wouldn't hear all the sirens, all the commotion. The beach maybe. It's most likely deserted, and the surf will be high and booming.'

'That's easily checked. Anywhere else?'

Garfield shook his head. 'I don't know.'

'Have you ever walked out on the jetty?' Maude asked. 'It's all huge rocks piled there as a breakwater. When you walk out, you leave the land behind you. There is just you and the huge rocks and the sea on both sides of you. It's frightening. And beautiful. Would she—'

Garfield shook his head again, more savagely this time. 'I hope not. There are storm waves and worse coming. They'll break right over the jetty.'

'Then you'd better go see, Dan.'

'Somebody has to be here.'

'I'll be here. Until you come back, I'll be here. That is final.'

In Director Boggs's office at the oceanographic institute a console television set was already turned on. 'We're about to watch Armageddon,' Pete said, as a colour picture of superb clarity showed the city of Hilo, Hawaii, the harbour almost deserted and the city streets themselves totally devoid of life. A smiling Oriental man appeared on the screen and said, 'Jerry Matsuo. I'll try to call the action. If Pete Williamson's watching, hi. ETA'—Jerry Matsuo paused—'is about eight minutes.'

Pete looked curiously at the TV console. 'You're taping this on the VCR?' he asked Boggs.

'Naturally. We shall want to study it.'

Jerry Matsuo said, 'It's beginning. See it? The harbour's draining.'

What he had watched so many times on his own film, impressive and even scary as it was, Pete was thinking, had affected only a small harbour in an obscure Aleutian fishing village. Hilo was a major city, open, vulnerable, helpless, with millions of dollars of property and thousands of lives involved.

On the screen, in perfect clarity, the water was rising now, swiftly, silently. The harbour bottom, which had been exposed, disappeared smoothly. A pier that only moments before had stood stark and gaunt on its pilings was now at water level and suddenly no longer visible. Still there was no sound but the faint whisper of Jerry Matsuo's breathing in his microphone.

The camera's focus shifted suddenly, reaching out beyond the harbour's entrance, and Jerry Matsuo's voice came again. 'There it comes! See it building?'

Only a faint line at first, the wave began to grow, its outline becoming plain. A swift swelling of water, it moved at incredible speed directly towards the camera. And with it came the first sound, a low-pitched, rumbling, distant roar, as if the earth itself and the waters it contained protested against confinement and demanded release.

'That headland,' Jerry Matsuo's voice said, no longer calm, no longer steady, 'is thirty feet above mean high water. And look! It's going under!' The gigantic wave was rearing itself within the harbour confines, bearing down swiftly upon the city. At its top the wave was breaking, unable to contain itself, but its body, high above the harbour shore, remained intact, hurtling down upon the land.

The shimmering green mass reached the shore and engulfed it. Its sound a hoarse bellow of rage, it flung itself upon a row of buildings lining the waterfront. The buildings disappeared and the wave swept on unchecked, meeting more solid opposition now in the form of masonry buildings that crumpled like matchboxes beneath the enormous weight and force of the water.

Jerry Matsuo's voice, shaking now, said, 'Worse, far worse than nineteen sixty! Incredible! Stop it, stop it!'

Gradually, its fury spent, the wave slowed, reached its furthest limit, then began its retreat, exposing the tangled mass of destruction its swift and merciless onslaught had caused.

Here a reinforced-concrete building was reduced to sodden rubble; there a pile of wreckage, twisted and nearly unrecognisable, was all that remained of an automobile. A single wall of another building miraculously remained standing, empty windows gaping like eyeholes in a skull, and then suddenly it too collapsed.

Boggs said in a hushed voice, 'I've seen this desolation before—in pictures of Hamburg and Dresden, Hiroshima and Nagasaki, after the bombings. God! I wouldn't have believed it.'

FROM THE ROCKY POINT to the jetty the beach was deserted. Garfield turned up the collar of his jacket as he walked, head bent, leaning slightly into the wind.

The waves were pounding now, and the sky had darkened, as if it were already evening. Formless cloud masses swirled, and here and there a rain squall roiled the tossing waters further. A bleak, almost frightening scene, Garfield thought. Obviously the girl was not here, and yet somehow he sensed that in her adolescent anger this would be precisely the kind of place she might choose, for it would match her mood.

He retraced his steps to the car, started the engine and drove slowly back along the peninsula to the Winslows' house.

He found Maude on the sheltered porch, studying the bay in its grey, tossing beauty. She seemed to know that Garfield was there before he spoke. 'No sign of Lucy?'

'None.' Garfield sat down in a wicker chair.

'I've been thinking,' Maude said. 'How well do you know the girl?'

'We get along. Or did.'

'She is how old? Sixteen? And you have talked, before this last disagreement?'

'Yes, of course we've talked. What are you getting at?'

'Quite simple. A sensitive girl that age, with a much older man who is not family—it's easier to talk to someone like that about little, personal things than to your mother or father. Think about it. Did she ever tell you anything about herself?'

'Absolutely inconsequential things.'

'Are you sure? When you were young, didn't you ever unburden yourself to someone who was handy at the moment, who maybe seemed very special?'

'I don't see what this gets us—'

'Perhaps not, but think about it anyway. You may know more about her than you realise.'

Garfield was frowning. Maude watched him quietly.

'Pete Williamson called from the institute,' she said after a moment. 'He told me what they had watched on television—devastation in Hawaii. Worse even than they'd feared.'

'Which means that the place for you is home.'

'I am staying here with you, Dan.' Her voice was definite.

Garfield sat wordless. Admit it, he told himself, you take comfort in her presence. You want her near you for as long as she can safely remain. He glanced at his watch. 'One thirty-two is the estimated time of arrival here,' he said at last. 'That is about one hour. If you stay, it is on one condition.'

'That is?'

'That when I say "go", you will.' He hesitated, but the words finally emerged without effort. 'Your safety is important to me.'

'I think,' Maude said slowly, 'that is the most wonderful thing anyone ever said to me. Thank you, Dan.'

'It's agreed?'

She could smile then. 'You must dot the *i*'s and cross the *t*'s, mustn't you?' Slowly she nodded. 'I agree.'

TOM WINSLOW, WITH CLARA at the wheel holding *Westerly* into the wind under power, had taken down the big jib, replaced it with a smaller one and roller-reefed the mainsail to about one half its area. With the yacht on a northwest course and under reduced sail, he was back at the wheel, satisfied that the boat was as ready as possible for whatever might come.

The wind had increased. The seas had lost their precise alignment and were beginning to break at their tops. Streaks of foam had appeared, spreading downwind, and spray was beginning to affect visibility. Clara sat huddled on the leeward seat, her face and hair shiny with spray, her eyes fixed on the tossing waters.

'Better go below and get into foul-weather gear.' Tom had to raise his voice against the sounds of wind and sea. 'No point sitting here in misery.'

'I can't help it.' Clara showed no expression. 'We ought to be with Lucy, wherever she is.' Reluctantly she went below.

Tom watched her. As a physician he was accustomed to talking out problems with patients, but he was not at all sure he could handle this one. His decision to put out further to sea had been logical, and urged by Dan Garfield. Still, how did one balance logic against parental affection?

Clara came up from below, wearing oilskins. In her hand she carried a large, steaming mug, which she held out to him. 'Hot soup,' she said. 'You can use it. It's cold out here.'

It was. It was also uncomfortable sailing. *Westerly* was a splendid sea boat, but the corkscrew gyrations she was now forced into demanded the helmsman's full attention and skill.

'We're stuck on this course,' Tom said. 'Bad as it is with the wind on our quarter in these seas, we still have to make some westing, or we'll be closing on a lee shore.'

'I understand.' No mention of Lucy, but obviously the unhappy worry would still remain.

'Yes, of course you do. I'm just talking to make sounds.' After a scalding mouthful of soup he said, 'Dan will see that she's all right. He promised.'

LUCY WAS MORE FRIGHTENED than she had ever been in her life. In her first anger with Garfield she had given no real heed to the possible danger of going to her secret place, where she could be alone and feel sorry for herself. Always before, making her way from this secluded spot had been easy enough. But the rocks were wet now, soaked with spray, and slippery. One false step in the climb to safety could be her last. Staying here was fast becoming nonsensical, but she lacked the courage to make the first move.

She shrank back as she watched the largest wave of a sequence gather itself in reaction to the bottom drag. Its crest, windblown, rose higher and higher as the mass swept towards shore, and Lucy could only watch it in frightened fascination, a sick feeling growing in her stomach. As it prepared to break, she closed her eyes against the imminent shock.

The wave crashed against the rocks with a booming sound that seemed to shake the earth. Its green water almost, but not quite, reached Lucy's level, and she was drenched by the spray it flung into her shelter.

She was gasping with cold and increased terror. She would die here, she was sure of it, and no one would ever know.

IO

It had happened all at once rather than gradually. For the rest of his life, sixteen-year-old Tommy Parks thought, he would remember the sudden realisation that he was doing everything right and was, in fact, enjoying himself immensely.

He had *Lubelle*, a sixty-five-foot, twin-screw, gasoline-powered yacht, headed into the mounting seas with just enough power in both engines to maintain steady but almost imperceptible forward progress. There was a rhythm that he could feel and thrill to, and there were infinite minor adjustments within each manoeuvre that his hands on the wheel seemed to accomplish almost automatically.

The seas were large, and the shriek of the wind was a banshee sound out of a nightmare. From time to time he sighted another sailing or powerboat, and even though he could not recognise any actual boat, let alone those on board, he nonetheless felt a kinship with them. Out here, alone, master of his own fate, he felt that all at once he was a full-fledged member of a bold fraternity of seafarers who were willing to dare the perils of the ocean while lesser folks cowered safely at home or fled to the hills.

When the radio scanner paused at one frequency long enough for him to hear, 'Calling yacht *Lubelle*, calling yacht *Lubelle*. Come in,' he pushed the button to hold on that wavelength, picked up the microphone and, with his eyes never leaving the seas, said, 'Yacht *Lubelle* here. Come in. Over.'

'How you doing?' Joe Hines's voice. 'Over.'

Tommy wore a huge grin. 'I'm having a blast. Over.'

'Don't get cocky, youngster. You got a big responsibility on your hands. That's the biggest thing afloat in the area. Over.'

The grin did not fade. 'Aye, aye, sir. Over.'

'Keep in touch on this frequency. Over.'

'Roger. Over and out.' Tommy hung up the microphone and, with both hands on the wheel, headed up as the next crest approached. His spirits soared with the rising bow.

TODD WILSON STOPPED the car behind the Winslows' house, switched off the engine and got out.

The kitchen door was unlocked, as always, and Todd went in. 'Lucy! Hey, anybody home?'

'In here.' It was Garfield's voice, from the study. Todd followed the sound. 'Come in,' Garfield said, and as if this were a cocktail party he added, 'Maude Anderson . . . Todd Wilson. Sit down, Todd. Do you know anything?' His voice was calm, but his eyes betrayed the strain he felt.

'No, sir.' Todd sat down. The prospect of never seeing Lucy again was growing in his mind like a painful tumour. 'I guess you don't either?'

Maude said, 'We've been trying to think. Perhaps you can help.'

'Sure. I mean, if I can.'

'Has she ever disappeared like this before?' Garfield asked.

A sudden wind gust rattled the windows, and the sirens wailed.

Todd said, 'She's funny sometimes. Girls are.' He caught himself quickly. 'I mean—'

'We know what you mean,' Maude said gently. 'And they are.'

Garfield said, 'She does go off by herself?' Something was tugging at his mind, and he could not put his finger on it. 'Where does she go?'

'She never tells me.'

Garfield said, looking at Maude, 'When you were a girl, did you have a special place where you could be alone?'

'Up in the attic. If I kept quiet, nobody knew where I was.'

Garfield let his breath out in a long sigh. 'Then I think I know where Lucy is: her secret place. She told me about it once.' He was looking at Todd now. 'Out on the point, in a kind of cave. Only the seals in the water could see her, she told me.' He looked at his watch. 'One thirty-two is the expected arrival time of the wave. Less than forty minutes.'

Todd was already on his feet. 'I've climbed around the rocks on the point. And I've dived for abalone there. I'll find her.'

'I'll go with you,' Garfield said. 'You have a car? Good. You drive. You know the way. I'll be out in a moment.'

Todd left. They heard the back door slam.

Garfield stood and held out both hands. Maude rose to take them.

'This,' Garfield said, his smile mocking his words, himself, 'as they say in films, is it.'

'I understand. I will wait—'

'No, you will not. You will take your car now and drive up to the bluff. Pete Williamson will be there with the cameras they are setting up. Stay with him and wait for me—us—there.'

'Dan—'

'You promised, remember? You agreed that when I told you, you would go. Unless you do—' He stopped at the sight of tears forming in her eyes.

'I will go, Dan.' She wiped the tears with the backs of her hands, and a tremulous smile appeared. 'Kiss me, Dan.' Her voice was soft, gentle.

It was not a long kiss, and when it was over, Garfield brushed her cheek with his fingertips. 'There will be another,' he said, 'when I join you on the bluff. That's a promise too.' He turned away and hurried out to the car.

BETSY BARNES PULLED into the driveway of the Brentwood house and then just sat there, her hands resting on the wheel, as she recalled that emotional scene in Encino Beach.

Jack would be safe. He had said that, and Betsy clung to his words. But what if he was not safe, out in what the radio called heavy storm seas? What then? The concept was too dreadful to think about.

She roused herself at last and with difficulty concentrated on carrying into the house the things she and Jack had packed into the car. Inside, she made no attempt to put the things away, but left them in a heap on the dining-room table. It was, she thought suddenly, a pitifully small and unimportant collection of items to represent her and Jack's life together: a picture of the two of them taken during an Acapulco vacation; her wedding sterling silver flatware; Jack's gold wristwatch, which he had given her for safekeeping when he went aboard *Spindrift*; the cup they had won at mixed doubles the year before at the yacht club; half a dozen jazz albums . . .

Tears were very close as she turned away and walked out to the large, immaculate kitchen. She made herself a cup of instant coffee and just sat, alone and miserable, with a growing feeling of emptiness.

JIMMY SILVA, STILL in his short-sleeved aloha shirt, impervious to the growing cold, sat in the right-hand seat of the black-and-white patrol car, window down and bullhorn ready in his hand. They drove slowly through the empty streets.

'We keep our eyes open for a sixteen-year-old girl,' Jimmy was saying, 'and for anybody else fool enough to hang around.'

The cop who was driving was named Connors, and his nervousness increased as he kept glancing at his wristwatch.

'We got plenty of time,' Jimmy Silva told him. 'The eggheads say one thirty-two, and they been right all along. At one twenty-two we start for the bluff, not before. Stop here.' He pointed at a lighted house window and raised the bullhorn. 'Hello! Anybody there?'

The door opened and a man appeared. 'Who's asking?'

'Me, Jimmy Silva.' He squinted in the gloom. 'That you, Hornby? What are you doing still here? Can't you hear the sirens?'

'I heard them. I heard them last time too, and nothing happened.'

'I'm going to tell you once,' Jimmy said, 'and after that, if I have to, I'm going to get out of this car and throw you in the back seat. You got that? You head for the bluff right now.'

'Now look, Jimmy—'

His Honor flung open his door and started to get out. Hornby threw up his hands and backed away hastily. 'OK, OK.'

'Get into your car and drive out of here,' Jimmy said. 'We'll wait to see you do.'

At the wheel Connors looked nervously at his watch again. It was eight minutes past the hour. Suppose the eggheads were wrong.

'OK,' Jimmy said as they heard a car engine start up. 'Let's move on. We still got plenty time.'

JOE HINES RELEASED the button on his microphone but left the transmitter power on as he looked round his office and, through the doorway at the partially empty anchorage.

He had called, one by one, all the boys he had sent to sea in large power cruisers. To a man, they were enjoying themselves, as he had privately guessed they would—each one in sole command of a magnificent power yacht, out in heavy seas that to their young tastes were more fun by far than moderate conditions. The experience beat surfing by a mile, one said.

Joe guessed he had done just about all that he could do. He glanced at the clock on the wall, which said ten minutes past the hour. Another ten minutes just to see if anybody called with a problem. Then he'd shut her down and head for high ground, though he'd a hell of a lot rather have been at sea himself.

WARY OF THE SAND that extended from the road out to the rocks of the point, Todd parked the car as close as he dared, shut off the engine and turned to Garfield. 'I've been thinking while I was driving,' he said. 'There are a lot of crevices, but I don't remember any place big enough for someone Lucy's size to hide in.'

'It's there,' Garfield said with conviction. 'It's got to be.' He had already opened his door, and the howling wind made his words hard to follow. 'Come on.'

Together, bent against the wind, they trotted out to the rocky extremity. To Todd, the seas seemed far more savage than any he could recall, shattering themselves against the solid promontory, throwing up heavy spray that filled the air.

As wave after wave crashed against the point Todd led the way almost to the edge. He peered over it and saw only sheer rock, with occasional shallow indentations and crevices. As he had said, nothing large enough to hide someone of Lucy's size. He looked at Garfield, who pointed left and right, sharp, commanding gestures, indicating that they were to separate. Todd nodded and started off, shouting 'Lucy,' as he went.

Wherever she was, he thought, as he made his way as fast as he dared, she would be cold and soaked and scared, as well she deserved to be if she had indeed come out here.

Todd reached the end, where the rocky point turned inland, away from the crashing seas. There he stopped and began to retrace his steps. They were running out of time. He looked up and saw Garfield, a hundred yards distant, staring down at the waves. Garfield made a beckoning gesture, and Todd broke into a careful trot.

He reached Garfield and looked down at the water, following Garfield's pointing finger. A seal had poked his head up through the turbulence and seemed to whuffle through extended whiskers as he looked around. A huge wave threatened, and only microseconds before it crashed against the rocks, the seal's head disappeared without seeming haste, to reappear only moments later, again looking round with casual interest.

All at once Todd understood. 'Of course,' he shouted into the wind. 'If she said they could see her . . .'

Garfield nodded and, turning to face inland, began to let himself down the rock face, searching for footholds. Todd followed with care. A slip and a fall here and either man would be finished, helpless against the smashing waves. As he clambered down, Todd raised his voice. 'Lucy, come out! Come out!'

Her head appeared, looking round timidly, questioningly. Then slowly her shoulders emerged from an opening in the rocks.

Her hair was plastered to her head and rivulets of water streamed down her cheeks. She stared imploringly at Todd. 'Come on,' Todd shouted. 'Come out of there. Move.'

But Garfield was shaking his head, glancing at his watch, his face almost angry as he motioned for Lucy to retreat into her shelter. 'Go back,' he shouted.

The girl hesitated, obviously uncertain, but there was that in Garfield's face and manner that made her obey. She disappeared from Todd's view, and Garfield followed. Todd went after them.

It was a small cave that seemed to have no rear wall. As Todd's eyes accustomed themselves to the near darkness he could see that the cave went back into the rock, how far he could not tell.

'We can't stay here,' Todd said.

'Look at your watch,' Garfield said. 'We have less time than it took us to get here from the house, and we'd still have to climb the bluff. We wouldn't have a chance. We have to stay here.' Lucy, shivering, looked from one to the other.

'We'll drown in here,' Todd said, 'like rats.'

'That depends on how deep this cave is and whether it narrows as it goes back in,' Garfield said. 'Move it, both of you!'

The cave made a bend, and another, as Garfield had guessed, narrowing as it went. At last they reached its end and crowded together in the darkness against the solid rear wall. Garfield's voice seemed to echo in the gloom.

'When the wave hits, it will compress the air in here. The air pressure just may be enough to save us by keeping the water out— the same principle as air trapped inside a sunken submarine. It's our only chance.'

Lucy made a small, whimpering sound. In the blackness Todd found her slim shoulders and drew her close. 'Easy,' he said. 'Easy. Let's hope he's right.'

Garfield was speaking again, slowly, distinctly, to avoid misunderstanding. 'The pressure is going to be intense. Keep your mouths open when it starts to build up, to help equalise the pressure inside and outside your head.' He was silent for a moment. 'Now,' he said, 'we just have to wait.'

ON THE BLUFF the TV cameras were in place and manned. Maude had joined Pete, who was standing near the edge with as good a view as possible in the rain squalls and blowing spray. To their right, in the far background, was the point, to their left were the jetties and the sand beach that had been built up south and east of them by the coastwise current.

Pete said, his voice raised above the sound of the wind, 'We're three hundred feet above mean high water here. That will be plenty, although I expect we'll catch some heavy spray when the tsunami hits.'

Howard Boggs joined them. 'You are still confident,' he asked Pete, 'that despite the broad continental shelf the tsunami wave will come ashore?'

Pete said, 'You can see what the breakers are doing to the shore outside right now. What do you think?'

Boggs said, 'I am afraid I am convinced. Your predictions have been right all along, and I have no reason to doubt the accuracy of this one.'

Maude, her eyes not leaving the point and the automobile parked on it, said, 'Dan and Todd and the girl ought to be here with us.'

Pete said gently, 'Don't wish for them to show up now. It's too late. They'd be caught in the open.'

Maude caught her lower lip between her teeth. She released it with an effort. 'Then where? How can they be safe?'

'I don't know,' Pete said. 'But if there is a place or a way, Dan'll find it, if anybody can. You can count on that.'

One of the technicians nearby, binoculars raised, said, 'I see a line, a swell. It's growing! Beyond the bell buoy! See it?'

Pete glanced at his watch. 'On time to the minute,' he said.

A cameraman said, 'I've got it, but it's moving towards us so fast I can hardly keep it in focus!'

Within only a brief moment the line, a fast-growing swell now, was

88

clearly visible even without binoculars. To Pete, the scene was familiar both from his own film and from the transmitted pictures he had seen of Hilo. The swell was curving inwards to conform with the bottom contours, concentrating its energy. It would reach the point first, Pete decided, and he wondered where Garfield was at that moment. He closed his eyes and hoped.

WITHIN THE DARK CAVE they could hear it: a deep, distant, low-pitched, angry, rumbling sound that reverberated within their small rock chamber and seemed to shake the earth itself.

'Here it comes,' Garfield said, determinedly calm. 'Remember, keep your mouths open. It might even help to shout.' After a momentary pause he added, 'Luck to us all.'

Lucy, still shivering, stood within the protective circle of Todd's arm, pressed tight against his strength, his solidity, trying to draw courage from his presence. 'Last night . . .' she began unsteadily.

'Forget last night.' Todd's voice was sharp. 'Just keep your mouth open. And when it comes, shout, like the man said.' His arm tightened round her shoulders. 'It's going to be all right. You hear?'

'I hear.' And Lucy closed her eyes, as if by the action she could shut out the terror she felt.

The pressure came first, with unbelievable speed and force, a blast of damp sea air heated faintly by compression. It seemed to explode against the rear wall of the small chamber and continued to build, stifling, throttling, overpowering the senses. The cave was filled with a roaring sound.

Garfield's mouth was open wide, and he shouted, trying to keep his nasal passages and eustachian tubes open to equalise the pressure that threatened to burst his eardrums. He felt dizzy, and he was aware that he was blacking out. The roaring sound grew in intensity, and heavy salt spray drenched him from head to toe. Or was it solid water? No matter. He tried to breathe, and could not.

The last thing he remembered was that at least Maude was safe.

II

Jimmy Silva had appeared at the top of the bluff, and with him Joe Hines. They stood silent, looking seaward. Because of the sheer drop on the ocean side of the point, they were unable to see the enormous swell as it met the rocks, but the solid sheet of water flung skyward at impact, high above the top of the rocks, told the story all too well.

They watched in near disbelief as that sheet of water, now reinforced from behind, crashed down on the top of the point. It caught up Todd's parked car, threw it high into the air and carried it forward across the land on the swell's crest, to slam it down finally into the waters of the bay, where it disappeared.

Pete said, 'Look at the channel! That incoming wave is thirty feet high and still building!'

'More like forty,' Joe Hines said. 'Houses there are sixty feet above high water.'

Jimmy Silva said, 'There go the first houses. See there, middle of the peninsula. And the wave isn't even slowing.'

It was not. The huge mass of solid water was sweeping across the peninsula, burying houses within its monstrous body, bringing the sea itself across the land until the ocean and the bay were one, the peninsula no longer visible.

Still the wave swept on, its top a dirty whitish-grey colour now, frothing as a breaker froths, neither slowing nor collapsing in the manner of surf, but continuing its relentless surge. It reached and engulfed the coast highway and slammed itself at last against the solid mass of the high bluff with a crash and a shock that could be both heard and felt by those above, as if there had been a massive underground explosion.

Solid water and spray flew high and fell like a cloudburst on the onlookers, leaving them drenched and stunned.

'We ought to get underwater pay,' one of the cameramen said, wiping his mouth with the back of his hand. No one even smiled.

Unbelievably, almost as rapidly as it had come, the water began to recede. The backwash uncovered the bay, the scattered and smashed boats torn from their moorings. It uncovered the peninsula, displaying the wreckage of the cheek-by-jowl houses, some shattered, some still partially standing in drunken attitudes, as if the slightest push would bring them crashing to the ground.

What remained of the beach on the ocean side of the peninsula was gradually visible again, but what had been smooth, plump contours were now gaunt, jagged stretches of rock, with the wreckage of houses, carried seaward by the backwash, strewn along the shore as far as one could see. The entire process had taken only a matter of a minute or so. And now all was changed.

The seas retained their stormy character; the wind still gusted in howling fury, still snatching spray from the wavetops. But the monster wave was suddenly gone, retreated back into its watery lair, its fury spent, and the scene, instead of turbulently chaotic, seemed by comparison almost peaceful.

Pete said to Maude in a voice that was not quite steady, 'Stay here.' He turned away.

Maude said, 'Where are you going?'

'I'm going looking. I don't know what I'm going to find, but I want to be alone when I find it.'

90

He trotted down the wet and muddy road towards what was left of the coast highway, a small, lonely figure. He reached the causeway and paused briefly to study it. It was a low concrete-and-steel structure leading from the mainland to the peninsula. It was designed to carry two lanes of automobile traffic in each direction. It seemed solid enough, but as Pete watched, one eight-foot section of two-lane roadway collapsed.

All at once he was running along the white line in the centre of the two remaining lanes. He reached the area where the other two lanes had collapsed, and increased his pace to a sprint. The roadway held. Ten strides beyond the danger area Pete slowed to a steady trot.

Through the town's devastation Pete jogged on, avoiding fallen debris, hurdling minor obstacles, past the edge of the town and on, as directly as the wreckage allowed, towards the point.

Here he passed the body of a dog, and there a baby's pram, happily empty, smashed almost beyond recognition. He glanced only once in the general direction of his own small house, saw total destruction and did not look again.

He had little hope that he would find anyone alive, but he did not slow his steady pace. He went out on what was left of the road Todd had driven along to the place where Todd's car had been parked when the wave caught it up, and there he paused to look around.

The top of the rocky point had been scoured clean of earth and vegetation. It was bare rock now, wet, shining, in places showing small rivulets of water, tiny streams flowing down the slope.

A place where only the seals could see her, Maude had reported from Garfield's explanation of Lucy's secret place. Pete knew the point as well as he knew his own living room. Without hesitation he trotted towards the area where the seals cavorted.

He reached it and looked down from the edge of the cliff. The seals were still there, apparently unharmed by the tsunami's enormous turbulence. But of a cave he could see no trace. There was nothing but rock and crashing water, howling wind until . . .

He saw movement. A hand emerged from the rock. It seemed to grope almost blindly for support, a man's hand, muscled, strong, a young hand.

'Todd,' Pete shouted. 'Todd, boy. Hang on.' And he let himself gingerly down the cliff's face, one foothold, one handhold at a time, ignoring the spray and the waves that seemed to be trying to reach him, until, stretching to his utmost, he could reach the hand and grasp it. 'Out,' he shouted. 'I've got you.'

Todd's head appeared. He was blinking hard, and his eyes did not seem to be quite in focus, but there was strength in the fingers that grasped Pete's wrist as Pete was grasping his, a double grip, more secure than a mere handshake.

Pete pulled, harder, but the boy's efforts resisted him. 'The others,' Todd said. 'They're here—Lucy, Garfield.'

'OK,' Pete said, and could not resist a triumphant smile. It was hard not to shout out in relief. 'You first. Find a secure position. Then pass the princess out. Then Garfield.'

SIXTEEN-YEAR-OLD TOMMY PARKS brought *Lubelle* into the Long Beach harbour with confident caution. He followed the harbourmaster's pilot boat into a designated anchorage, brought *Lubelle* to a stop precisely where ordered and, nimble as a squirrel, left the wheel and scuttled forward to let go the anchor.

Both engines secured, cabin and wheelhouse locked, sea bag over his shoulder, he dropped down into the shore boat for the short passage to the welcome-shed that had been set up.

To the coastguard officer keeping the log of arrivals Tommy said, 'Yacht *Lubelle*, Encino Beach Yacht Club, at anchor, safe and sound.' It was difficult to keep the pride out of his voice.

A large, bearded man wearing a worn blue uniform coat with four stripes on the sleeves said, 'Welcome ashore, Captain.' He took Tommy's hand in one huge paw.

It was hard for Tommy not to laugh aloud with joy.

THE YACHT *Westerly* put into Long Beach too. Tom Winslow, at the wheel, said, 'Easy. They said on the radio that she's fine.'

Clara said, 'There she is! See? On the float.'

'I see her,' Winslow said. He kept his voice carefully expressionless. 'And it looks as if she's all in one piece. Isn't that Todd with her?'

'You men,' Clara said. There were tears in her eyes. 'You have no feelings. None at all.' She was smiling fondly.

'That's us,' Tom said. 'No emotions at all.' He too was smiling. 'Let's get anchored and go ashore.'

IT WAS A COASTGUARD cutter that located what was left of the yacht *Spindrift*, whose owner was Jack Barnes. 'Just log the boat's name and number,' the coastguard skipper said.

'Somebody had to have been aboard,' the second-in-command said. 'Washed overboard.'

'They'll probably never find him,' the skipper said. 'It's a big ocean. Let's proceed. There'll be others. How many, nobody can guess. Our job is to find as many as we can.'

The second-in-command said, 'We may never know the count, you know that? Maybe some just put out to sea and nobody knew about it, so nobody misses them.'

'It's happened before,' the skipper said. 'No doubt it will happen again. Let's get under way.'

92

FIVE HOURS AFTER the tsunami reached Hawaii it had rolled its might down upon Kyushu, Shikoku, Honshu and Hokkaido. Of all the harbours on these four Japanese islands, Yokohama suffered the worst damage, which was duly recorded on videotape, a copy of which was sent to the Encino Beach Oceanographic Institute. Pete, Garfield and Howard Boggs watched in silence as the television in Boggs's office detailed the destruction.

'We fancy ourselves masters of our environment,' Pete said when the film was done. 'But against what happened in Hilo and here, as well as a hundred other places around the Pacific rim, we are totally helpless. Ironic, isn't it? We're just visitors on the skin of the planet, flies on a horse's back.' He was looking at Garfield. 'You're thinking what?'

'Why greater damage in some places than others?' Garfield said. 'Configuration of the land, bottom contours, ocean currents or prevailing winds—what are the factors involved?'

Boggs raised his eyebrows faintly. 'Is this mere idle curiosity, Mr Garfield?' he asked. 'Or is it deeper than that?'

'If we knew more,' Garfield said, 'might we not be able to issue more precise warnings, more specific predictions than simply time of arrival?'

'Sure we might,' Pete said. 'And more specific predictions would be valuable. No argument. But how do you gather the data on which to make the predictions?'

Boggs's eyes had not left Garfield's face.

'What we've just gone through,' Garfield said, 'happens how often? Once in a hundred years? Five hundred? A thousand? But the experience is fresh right now. There are eyewitnesses, films, tidal-gauge measurements, destruction that can be studied, analysed. It's all available now; in five, ten years it won't be.'

'So,' Pete said, irony plain, 'you're suggesting that somebody spend the next few years visiting all the sites, gathering the data and trying to make sense out of it?'

'Why not?' Garfield looked at Boggs. Wouldn't that be a worthy project?'

'I would think so,' Boggs said. 'But there is the matter of funding . . .'

Garfield's nod was solemn, his face expressionless. 'Yes, there is that.' He looked again at Pete. 'How about it? Care to do some travelling? The two of us?' He paused, thinking of Maude. 'Or maybe three of us?'

'What you're doing,' Pete said, 'is offering candy to a child, friend. If you're serious . . . are you?'

'I am. I'll fund the project.'

'Then sign me on,' Pete said, 'for the whole cruise.'

JIMMY SILVA AND JOE HINES flew over the entire Encino Beach area in a chopper. 'Bottom line,' Jimmy said, 'is that there ain't a whole hell of a lot left for me to be mayor of. And you'—he looked at Hines—'are a harbourmaster without much of a harbour.' Jimmy was resilient, and he had regained his sense of humour. 'But we'll rebuild her,' he continued. 'Bigger and better than before. You watch and see.'

MAUDE WAS AT HOME in her Westwood apartment when Garfield arrived. 'I've been waiting,' she said.

'I've been busy. Sorry.'

'I guessed that. And there have been telephone calls for you, people trying to reach you. The list is by the phone.'

Garfield picked it up and read from it. 'Walker Carmichael, Paul Case . . .' He put the list down. He was smiling. 'Names out of the past, out of another life. I'm finished with that.'

'Are you sure, Dan?' She watched him steadily.

Garfield sat down. 'I blacked out in that cave,' he said. 'I knew I was going to. I guess I was ready for it, or as ready as I could be. I was thinking of only one thing. Do you know what that was?'

She sat silent, waiting.

'You,' Garfield said. 'All the rest, including that past, is unimportant. I won't go back. Ever. I'm going forward into a new life.' He paused. 'Will you come with me?'

She could relax then, savouring the moment, a growing smile lighting her face, her eyes, bringing warmth into her mind. 'I will come with you,' she said, 'wherever you want to go.'

RICHARD MARTIN STERN

Thanks to Richard Martin Stern's zoom-lens style of fiction writing, Condensed Books readers have battled against forest fires in *Wildfire*, trekked through blizzards on a frigid mountain range in *Snowbound Six*, and fortified a bridge in the face of a fierce tornado in *The Big Bridge*. These adventures were set in Stern's home state of New Mexico, but the Californian location of *Tsunami* is just as familiar to him. Richard Martin Stern was born and brought up in California, and knows the state so well that years ago he invented his own
fictional town, Encino Beach, which he featured in numerous short stories before placing it centre stage in this novel.

Stern had his first personal brush with natural disaster fighting forest fires in the mountains above San Bernardino, in California. 'That was fifty-odd years ago,' he says, 'but I can assure you I haven't forgotten. I've seen some pretty terrifying flash floods too, both in California and New Mexico.'

How likely is his *Tsunami* scenario for the southern California coastline? 'Conventional wisdom says the area is practically immune to this kind of thing because of the broad continental shelf, but nobody can say for sure,' he tells us. 'So I've loaded the dice with the hurricane and the bomb test. Everything I put in the book, as nearly as I can determine, is possible, and if that is true, then all the elements could happen at once and result in a tsunami just as I described it.'

Though Richard Martin Stern specialises in bringing disaster to *our* doorsteps, he enjoys a relatively tranquil life at home in Santa Fe. In December 1987 he and his wife, Dorothy, celebrated their golden wedding anniversary.

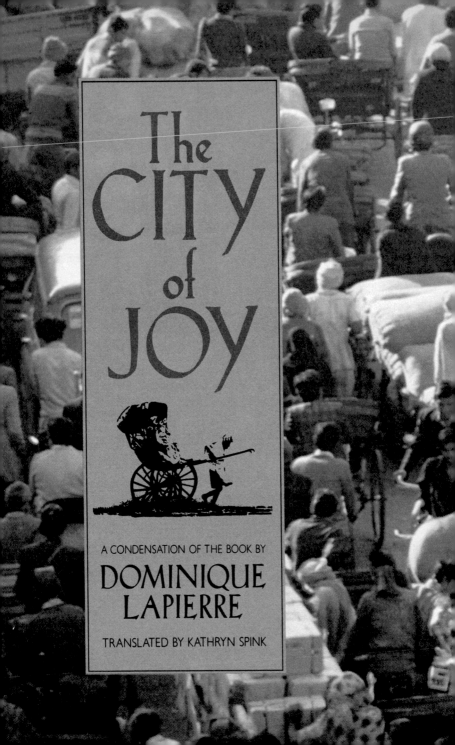

The
CITY
of
JOY

A CONDENSATION OF THE BOOK BY

DOMINIQUE
LAPIERRE

TRANSLATED BY KATHRYN SPINK

'I have never seen children more loved and appreciated than in the City of Joy.' *Dominique Lapierre*

One day in Calcutta, a rickshaw puller took best-selling author Dominique Lapierre to one of the poorest areas of this haunting city where over seventy thousand people live in an area three times the size of a football field. The district was Anand Nagar—the City of Joy—and going there would change the author's life for ever.

At the heart of this 'impoverished' community, Lapierre found more heroism, more love, more sharing, and ultimately, more happiness than in many cities of the affluent West. In order to convey the heroism of this remarkable place, he immersed himself in its awesome reality, learning first-hand what it was like to pull a rickshaw; to wash with a half litre of water; to survive on less than four pence a day.

Dominique Lapierre created *The City of Joy* from these unique experiences. It is an epic story about the soul of humanity . . . a hymn to life and a lesson in tenderness and hope for all people and all times.

1

He had the appearance of a Mogul warrior: a thick shock of curly hair, sideburns which met the drooping curve of his moustache, a strong, stocky torso, muscular arms and legs. Yet thirty-two-year-old Hasari Pal was merely a peasant, one of the five hundred or so million inhabitants of India who looked to the goddess Earth for their livelihood.

He had built his hut with mud walls and a thatched roof, a short distance from the village of Bankuli, West Bengal, a state in northeast India. His wife, Aloka, was a young woman with a clear complexion and the look of an angel. In one nostril she wore a gold ring, and her ankles were ornamented with bangles that tinkled as she walked. She had given Hasari three children: twelve-year-old Amrita had inherited her father's almond eyes and her mother's peach skin; ten-year-old Manooj and six-year-old Shambu were sturdy boys with black, tousled hair who would rather chase lizards round the pond than guide the buffalo into the family rice field. Hasari's father, Prodip, a gaunt man with a lined face, his mother Nalini, a bent old woman as wrinkled as a walnut, and his two younger brothers with their wives and children, all lived in Hasari's home.

A narrow verandah shaded by red and white bougainvilleas ran along two sides of Hasari's hut. Aloka was seated beneath the sloping porch roof, pedalling a rice husker, a kind of wooden seesaw with a pestle fixed to its end. Tick-tack, tick-tack, the pedal rose and fell as Amrita pushed new handfuls of grain under the pestle. The rice, removed from its husk, was picked up and sorted by her grandmother.

All round the hut golden rice plantations stretched as far as the eye could see, sprinkled with the dark green of mango orchards, the light green of palm tree clusters and the soft green of bamboo groves. Like sparkling lacework reflecting the blue of the sky, irrigation canals stitched the landscape tightly into squares. Footbridges formed delicate arabesques over pools covered with lotuses. Children with sticks drove great shining buffalo across the small dykes, stirring up ochre-coloured dust as they went. At the end of this stiflingly hot day, the sun was sinking below the horizon, birds cried joyously, and a welcome breeze was blowing in from the sea.

With the disappearance of the sun came the 'hour of the cow dust', when the cattle came back from their grazing and the men returned from the rice fields. Hasari Pal whistled as he ambled peaceably along, carrying his wooden plough over his shoulder. In the tamarinds a tribe of mynahs, India's sparrows, struck up a deafening concert. Two striped squirrels scampered about in the papaya, and herons and egrets made hastily for their nests. Gradually the high-pitched squeak of the cicadas faded away. There was a last tick-tack of the rice machine—then silence, a silence that was almost immediately broken as the frogs started up their chorus.

In less than five minutes, the tropical night had descended upon the land. As she did every evening, Aloka blew into a conch shell to greet the goddess of the night. The cow and goat were tied up in the shanty that served as a stable, and Hasari pulled a barbed gate across the entrance to the courtyard to keep out jackals and foxes.

While the women cooked the meal outside over a clay oven, Hasari and his two brothers sat beside their father on the verandah. The four rested silently, and Hasari's father fell into a reverie.

Prodip Pal couldn't remember how many generations of lotuses had bloomed in the pond since he was born. What he did remember, however, was that he had once been a prosperous peasant, with as many as six granaries and over three hectares of fertile land. He had been able to provide for the future of his sons and give his daughters generous dowries to procure them good husbands. For himself and his wife in their old age, he had kept the strip of land and the house he had inherited from his father. 'We will be able to live there in peace,' he had promised her, 'until the day when Yama, god of the dead, comes to claim us.'

But the old man had been wrong. The land had been given to his father years ago by a *zamindar*, a wealthy landowner, in recognition of his loyalty. One day this benefactor's heir laid claim to the land and the case came before the courts. The young *zamindar* bribed the judge, and Prodip Pal was obliged to abandon his land and his house. To pay the legal costs, he even had to sacrifice the dowry saved for his last daughter and the land of his two youngest sons.

Fortunately, his eldest son had been able to rescue the whole family by taking them under his roof. Hasari was a good son. He treated his father as if he were still the head of the family and the old man continued to enjoy those things which, for an Indian peasant, constitute wealth: a small rice granary, two cows and a buffalo, a piece of land, a little grain kept in reserve in earthenware jars in case of hard times, even a few rupees in a moneybox. The Pals might be poor, yet they were happy. The time for harvest always came, and with it the season of hope.

But more trials lay in store for Prodip Pal and his family. Their legal wrangles with the *zamindar* had left them with only one fifth of a hectare of good land, which produced about five hundred and forty-five kilos of rice, barely a quarter of what was necessary to feed the family. When they ran out of rice, they lived on the fruit from their three coconut trees and on vegetables that required very little irrigation, such as the 'serpent gourds'—a kind of cucumber that measures up to six feet in length—marrows, and giant radishes. The Pals had thus been able to survive for two years.

During the third year, however, disaster struck again. A parasite destroyed the rice crop in midgrowth. To overcome this catastrophe, Prodip Pal called on the *mahajan*, the village usurer, and by mortgaging the family field obtained a loan of two hundred kilos of rice, on condition that he would return three hundred after the first harvest.

By this time the cycle of poverty had begun to strangle the Pals. One of Hasari's brothers was forced to take a job as an agricultural labourer. Bad weather added to their plight. In April, a storm brought down all the mangoes and coconuts. Consequently they had to sell the buffalo and one cow, despite the fact that these were indispensable in the working season.

Then, weakened by lack of food, Hasari's younger brother fell ill. A doctor's fee and the cost of medicine could take several months' income, so, to save his brother, Hasari resorted to the only remaining course of action: he broke open his clay moneybox and went to the Brahmin, the village priest, begging him to celebrate a special *puja*, a ceremony of offering to the gods.

The boy regained sufficient strength to take part in another event that year which was to sink the family a little further into destitution: the marriage of his youngest sister. This involved a dowry, an ancient custom that had been officially abolished, but which still prevailed in practice. The small farmer with whom Hasari's father had negotiated the marriage of his last daughter had demanded one bicycle, two cotton loincloths, a transistor radio, and a few jewels for the young bride—all under the guise of a dowry. In total his requirements amounted to a good thousand rupees (about £60).

Furthermore, custom required that the girl's father alone should cover the cost of the ceremony, which meant finding another thousand rupees to feed the families and their guests, and buy presents for the officiating Brahmin. For these poor people it was a cruel bloodletting, but the marriage of a daughter is a sacred duty for a father. Once his last daughter had left home, the old man would have completed his task on earth.

Prodip Pal went back to the usurer for a new loan of two thousand rupees at sixty per cent annual interest. As collateral, he took with him his wife Nalini's jewels, his family's only remaining assets. They were part of her own dowry, but the old woman had little hope of seeing her jewels again—jewels that she had worn with such pride on feast days during the forty years of her life with Prodip Pal.

IT WAS THE MONTH of May, the very heart of the Bengali summer, and the air seemed to shimmer above the overheated countryside. The sky was gradually assuming the tints and shades of peacock feathers, and the Brahmin was predicting a year of exceptional riches, a year without drought or locusts or any other calamity.

The time to sow had come and Hasari, with his father and brothers, presented himself at the little altar by the banyan tree at the entrance to the fields. 'Gauri, I offer you this grain,' Prodip Pal recited, placing a grain of rice in front of the image of the wife of the god Shiva, protector of the peasants. 'Give us plenty of water and return it to us a hundredfold.'

Three days later, sure enough, a gentle rain came to soak the seedlings. Every morning Hasari went with his father and brothers to the edge of the field where they observed the growth of the soft, young green shoots with satisfaction. The beginning of the monsoon was predicted for Friday, June 12. Friday is not a very auspicious day in the Hindu calendar but it did not matter really: the monsoon was the monsoon, and its arrival every year was the gift of the gods to the people of India.

Everyone—men, women, children, even the animals—anxiously studied the sky. Friday, June 12 came and went, however, without a cloud, and throughout the days that followed the sky remained steely white. After a few weeks the rice shoots began to turn yellow. Hasari was forced to hire an irrigation pump at six rupees an hour, and for six hours its pulsating engine brought the lifeblood essential for growth to the shoots in the Pals' field. They regained their beautiful emerald colour and even grew ten centimetres.

The village elders delved deep into their memories in an attempt to remember when the monsoon had ever kept them waiting like this. One of them recalled that in the year Mahatma Gandhi died it had not arrived until July 2. In the year of the war with China it had hardly come at all.

Even the most optimistic began to worry. The Pals went with their neighbours to the Brahmin to ask him to celebrate a *puja* to induce the rain to come. The priest demanded twenty rupees and everyone borrowed more money from the *mahajan*. Then the Brahmin burned incense and intoned *mantras* in front of the statue of Ganesh, the god who brings good fortune, while the peasants listened respectfully.

But neither Ganesh nor any of the other gods heard their prayers and by the beginning of July the pond that served as the village water reserve was going dry. Finally, on July 23, they had to remove the fish which were floundering in the mud, and divide them among themselves.

In the Pals' field the luminous emerald green changed first to grey-green and then to yellow. The rice drooped, wilted, and finally died. That day, overwhelmed by the calamity, Hasari stood motionless at the edge of his field for hours. Before each strip of ground other despairing peasants remained through the night, their heads bowed in dejection.

At dawn, Hasari went home to sit on the verandah with his father and brothers. He heard his mother lifting the lids of the storage jars containing the rice on which the Pals had to survive until the next harvest. The old woman was trying to evaluate how long her family could hold out on their meagre reserves. Hasari already knew that there was only enough food for two months left, but his mother put the lids back on the jars and announced with apparent serenity, 'We have rice for a good four months. Afterwards, we'll have the vegetables.' Reassured, old and young went back to their chores. Only Hasari remained behind. He saw tears on his mother's cheeks, and his father moved to embrace his wife. 'Mother of my sons,' he said, 'we will both go without food so that the rice lasts longer. The children must not suffer.' She nodded in agreement.

Already, many villagers had nothing left. The first indication of this harsh reality was the disappearance from the village of the very poorest families—the Untouchables. This year, they knew there would be no rice to be gleaned from the fields, and so they had left for the great city of Calcutta, about sixty miles away. Next, it was the turn of the fathers and the eldest sons from homes where the earthenware jars were empty, and, finally, entire families began to take the road that led to the city.

The summer passed with hardly a single downpour, and once again it was time for winter sowing. But without water, there could be no sowing: no lentils, no sweet potatoes, no winter rice. By this time the Pals' remaining cow was nothing but skin and bone. One morning Hasari found her lying on her side, her tongue hanging out, and he realised that all the livestock would ultimately perish. Cattle merchants closed in like vultures from the surrounding towns, buying truckloads of cows for fifty rupees and buffalo for scarcely a hundred more.

November went by. With the loss of the cattle there was no more dung to serve as fuel for cooking, and no more milk. The children's stomachs swelled up like balloons, and several died.

At the beginning of January, the village wells began to run dry. The water was rationed to a bucketful per family per day, then half a bucket, then only one cup per person. Eventually, sentries armed with clubs had to be placed next to the only well that was not yet dry. By now the fields were nothing but a vast colourless expanse covered by a deep-cracked crust. Many of the trees were dead and the bushes had long since been scorched.

The Pals' resistance was coming to an end. One day Prodip Pal gathered his family round him. From a knotted corner of his *dhoti* he took five tightly rolled ten-rupee notes and two one-rupee coins and handed them

103

to Hasari. 'You, my eldest son, take this money and go with your wife and children to Calcutta. In the city you will find work. You will send us whatever you can. You are our only hope of not dying of starvation.'

Hasari stooped down and touched his father's feet. The small man laid his palm on his son's head, then on his shoulder, and gripped him tightly until Hasari stood up again. The women wept in silence.

Next morning, as the sun dawned pale on the horizon, Hasari and his family set off, without looking back at those who watched them go. Hasari walked ahead with Amrita, his daughter. Aloka, dressed in a green cotton sari, followed with their two young sons, Manooj and Shambu. Over his shoulder Hasari carried a cloth knapsack in which his wife had packed a few clothes for the family and the sandals Hasari had received as part of her dowry. It was the first time this peasant family had ever left their village and the two boys pranced for joy at the prospect of adventure. 'As for me, I was terribly frightened,' Hasari was to admit later, 'frightened of what lay in store for us.'

2

A few days after the departure of the Pal family for Calcutta, a young man got off the train at that city's Howrah Station. With his relaxed walk and manner, he looked very much like Jack Nicholson, the actor. He was dressed in jeans, an Indian shirt, and baseball boots. Only the black metal cross dangling on his chest proclaimed that this thirty-two-year-old Pole, Stephan Kovalski, was a priest.

For him, Calcutta was the culmination of a long journey that had begun in Krasnik, the Polish coal-mining city where he was born. The son and grandson of mining men, Stephan Kovalski had spent his early childhood in the gloomy environment of the pit into which his father used to descend each morning. He was five when his father moved his family to northern France, where coal miners' salaries were six or seven times higher than they were in Poland. In 1946 there was a long and bitter strike, and one evening an ambulance drew up outside the Kovalskis' home. Stephan's father was carried out of it, his head wrapped in bandages. In a violent confrontation between the miners and the police he had suffered burns to his face, and lost an eye.

The trauma of this experience so affected this quiet and profoundly religious man that when he recovered he rose up in rebellion against the suffering of the miners and was involved in a number of serious incidents. There was talk of industrial terrorism, and he was arrested. A few days later, the mayor came to inform Stephan's mother that her husband had hanged himself in his cell.

This suicide was a terrible shock for young Stephan. He stopped eating and shut himself away in his room for hours to meditate before a picture of the Sacred Shroud of Turin which his father had given him for his First Communion. Then one morning, as he kissed his mother goodbye before leaving for school, he made an announcement. 'Mother, I'm going to be a missionary.'

Stephan entered a small seminary in Belgium, where he spent three years. The religious instruction he received seemed to him far removed from everyday exigencies, but deeper study of the Gospel reinforced his desire to identify himself with the poor, to achieve by other means what his father had attempted to accomplish by violence. Later, at the Louvain seminary, Kovalski met the man who was to give a definitive direction to his journey. Padre Ignacio Fraile belonged to a Spanish order called the Fraternity of San Vincente, which gathered together priests and consecrated laymen who took vows of poverty, chastity, obedience and charity in order to 'seek out the poorest of the poor and the disinherited, to share their life, and to die with them'.

The day Stephan Kovalski was ordained a priest, he caught a train to spend a few hours with his mother. She was terminally ill, and before embracing her son for the last time, she gave him a black metal cross engraved with the dates of his birth and of his ordination. 'Never be parted from it, my son,' she said to him, clasping his hand. 'This cross will protect you wherever you go.'

Knowing that the poorest of the poor were to be found in the Third World, Stephan Kovalski had studied Spanish at the seminary, in the hope of being sent to the shantytowns of South America. Instead, however, it was to India that his fraternity assigned him. Impatient to leave, Stephan Kovalski applied to that country for a resident's visa. Month after month, for the next five years, the Indian authorities promised delivery of this essential document but, unlike a temporary visa, a resident's permit required the approval of the Ministry of Foreign Affairs in New Delhi. The inclusion of his status as a priest on Stephan's application was the root of the problem, because for some time India had been prohibiting foreign missionaries from entering its territory.

While awaiting his visa, Stephan Kovalski made his home in an immigrant slum near Paris where, true to the ideals of his fraternity, he shared everything: the exhausting work at wages below the legal minimum, the punishing mattresses of immigrants' hotels, the foul stews from barrack-room-style kitchens. He became successively a machine operator, fitter, turner, metal worker and storekeeper.

On the fifth anniversary of his ordination, Stephan decided the waiting had gone on long enough. With the approval of his superiors, he applied for a simple tourist visa and in the space reserved for profession he wrote 'skilled factory worker'. On the following day his passport was returned to him, complete with the precious visa. Although it authorised him to stay for only three months, once he was actually in India he would apply for permanent residence.

As soon as he got off the train in Calcutta, Stephan Kovalski called on the bishop, who lived in a beautiful colonial-style house surrounded by a vast garden. He was an Anglo-Indian of about fifty, with a white cassock, a purple skullcap, and a majestic manner.

'I have come to live with the poor,' the Polish priest said to him simply.

'You'll have no difficulty in finding them,' sighed the prelate. 'Alas, the poor are everywhere here.' He gave Stephan Kovalski a letter of introduction to the parish priest of a working-class district on the other side of the river.

With its two white towers and vividly coloured stained-glass windows, the church could be seen for some distance. Inside were elaborate statues of the saints, collection boxes, and fans suspended above the pews reserved for the faithful. Its name was like a challenge cast before the innumerable homeless people who lived on the surrounding pavements. It sprawled in luminous letters across the façade: Our Lady of the Loving Heart.

Father Alberto Cordeiro, the rector, was a Goan with carefully combed curly hair, round cheeks, and a paunch beneath an immaculate cassock. He looked more like a monsignor of the Roman Curia than a priest of the poor. An American car was parked in the courtyard of the church, and several Christian servants assured him the comfortable existence befitting a rector in charge of a large parish.

The sudden arrival of a foreign priest in jeans and baseball boots seemed to disconcert the ecclesiastic.

'Don't you wear a cassock?' he asked.

'It wasn't the most comfortable attire for travelling about your country, especially in the heat,' explained Stephan.

'Ah,' sighed the rector. 'You Westerners will always be respected. Your skin is white. Whereas for us Indian priests a cassock is both a symbol and a protection. In a country that recognises the sacred, it guarantees us a place apart.'

When he read the bishop's message, Father Cordeiro appeared aghast. 'You really want to go and live in a slum?'

'That's why I'm here.'

Such an idea had obviously never occurred to the good Father Cordeiro. But despite his very natural reservations, the rector proved to be most understanding. He entrusted Stephan to one of his assistants, who undertook to find him a room in the nearby slum of Anand Nagar, the 'City of Joy'.

In the 1960s, Calcutta was one of the most prosperous cities in Asia. Thanks to its harbour and its numerous industries, its metal foundries and pharmaceutical works, its flour mills and cotton factories, it boasted one of the highest average wages in India. One third of the country's imports and nearly half of its exports passed along the waters of the Hooghly, the branch of the Ganges on the banks of which the city had been founded three centuries earlier.

But Calcutta was also a refuge for six million starving people who, in the course of one generation, had arrived in the hope of feeding their families. The metropolis sat at the heart of one of the world's richest yet most unstable regions, an area of failing or devastating monsoons, of cyclones and apocalyptic earthquakes. The earthquake that shook Bihar on January 15, 1937, caused hundreds of thousands of deaths and sent entire villages fleeing towards Calcutta. Six years later a famine killed three and a half million people in Bengal alone, and created millions of refugees. In 1947, Indian independence and the partition of India and Pakistan cast upon Calcutta some four million Muslims and Hindus, fleeing from Bihar and East Pakistan. In 1965, a cyclone with the force of ten three-megaton H-bombs, capable of razing a city the size of New York, once more sent entire communities to Calcutta.

These successive waves of destitute people transformed Calcutta into an enormous concentration of humanity, and the city became one of the biggest urban disasters in the world, with indescribable chaos on the roads, a record accident rate, nightmarish traffic jams. Without adequate refuse collection, over eighteen hundred tons of rubbish accumulates daily in the streets, attracting swarms of flies, rats and cockroaches. In summer, it brings with it the risk of epidemics of cholera, hepatitis, encephalitis, typhoid and rabies.

Calcutta is an inhuman city where people can die on the pavements surrounded by apparent indifference. And to the hunger and the communal conflicts must also be added one of the world's most unbearable climates. For eight months of the year, torrid heat melts the asphalt on the roads and so expands the metal structure of the great Howrah Bridge that it measures well over a metre more by day than by night.

In Calcutta, three hundred thousand people live in the streets. Others crowd into the jumble of planks and daub that are its three thousand slums; these are inhabited almost exclusively by refugees from rural areas. Everything in these slums combines to drive their inhabitants to dejection and despair: chronic unemployment, appallingly low wages, child labour, debts that can never be redeemed, the mortgaging of personal possessions and their ultimate loss. Seven out of ten families survive on no more than one or two rupees a day, a sum that is not even sufficient to buy half a kilo of rice. There are no reserve food stocks and most residents must buy in minute quantities—one cent's worth of salt, two or three cents' worth of wood, one match. Privacy is unheard of, with ten or twelve people sharing a single room.

Yet the miracle of these concentration camps lies in the fact that the poverty and suffering is counterbalanced by other factors that allow their inhabitants not merely to remain fully human, but even to transcend their conditions and become models of humanity.

In these slums people actually put love and mutual support into practice. They know how to be tolerant of all creeds, how to give respect to a stranger, how to show charity towards beggars, cripples, lepers, and even the insane. Here the weak are helped, not trampled upon. Orphans are immediately adopted by their neighbours and old people cared for with reverence by their children.

Because so many of the occupants of these slums are former peasants, they reconstruct the life of their villages in their urban exile. It is perhaps an adapted and disfigured life, but it is nonetheless so valid that their poverty itself has become a form of culture. The poor of Calcutta share in a communal world and respect its social and religious values, maintaining their ancestral traditions and beliefs.

One of Calcutta's oldest slums is wedged between a railway embankment, the Calcutta–Delhi highway, and two factories. Out of either ignorance or defiance, the factory owner who had, at the beginning of the century, lodged his workers on this land, a reclaimed marsh, had christened the place Anand Nagar, 'City of Joy'. His factory has since closed its doors, but the original workers' estate expanded to become a veritable city within a city, with more than seventy thousand inhabitants concentrated in an area three times the size of a football field. Some ten thousand families split into groups divided geographically according to their various religions: sixty-three per cent are Muslims, thirty-seven per cent Hindus. Here and there are islands of Christians, Buddhists and Sikhs, as well as Jains, who wear masks over their mouths to avoid taking a life by accidentally swallowing an insect.

The City of Joy has the densest concentration of humanity on this planet—eighty thousand people per square kilometre. It is a place where there is not even one tree for every three thousand inhabitants, and almost no flowers, butterflies or birds, apart from vultures and crows. It is a place where children do not know what a bush, a forest or a pond is; where the air is so laden with carbon dioxide and sulphur that pollution kills at least one member of every family; a place where leprosy, tuberculosis, dysentery, and all the diseases of malnutrition until recently reduced life expectancy to one of the lowest in the world.

Like most slums, the City of Joy is generally shunned by other citizens of the city around it. Considered a dangerous neighbourhood, the haunt of Untouchables, pariahs, social rejects, it is a world apart, living apart from the world.

IT WAS FIVE O'CLOCK in the evening when Stephan Kovalski and his guide arrived at the entrance to the City of Joy. The red of the sinking sun was veiled in a shroud of greyish vapour. A smell of burning suffused the city, as everywhere *chulas*, small portable stoves, were lit to cook the evening meal. In the narrow alleyways the air was heavy with acrid fumes which burned the throat and lungs, and one sound was distinguishable above all others—the noise of the coughing that racked innumerable chests.

Forty-nine Nizamudhin Lane: the address was painted across two planks nailed together, which served as a door to a windowless hovel. The floor was beaten earth, and the sky could be seen through missing tiles on the roof. There was no furniture, no electricity, no running water. Near the door ran an open drain overflowing with nauseating black slime. On the left, a small platform built over the drain supported a tiny teashop under a bamboo roof.

The landlord of this hovel, a stout Bengali dressed in Western clothes, was believed to be one of the richest men in the slum. He owned a block of houses at the end of the alley, near the communal latrines and the well. Now, he had cups of tea with sweetened milk brought from the teashop.

'You're sure, Father, that this is where you want to live?' he asked, eyeing the priest incredulously.

'Quite sure,' said Stephan Kovalski. 'How much is the rent?'

'For you, it will be only twenty-five rupees a month. Payable in advance.'

'Twenty-five rupees!' Father Cordeiro's assistant exclaimed indignantly. 'For a miserable room without a window, that's highway robbery!'

'It'll do,' Stephan interrupted, reaching into his pocket. 'Here's three months' rent.'

Kovalski was to discover how privileged he was: his neighbours were living with ten or twelve other people in huts like this.

The deal concluded, Father Cordeiro's envoy lost no time in introducing the newcomer to the few Christians of the City of Joy. At first none of them would believe that the sahib in jeans was really a priest. But, when they realised that he was going to live among them, everyone wanted to help organise his household. Some offered a bucket, others a mat, an oil lamp, a blanket. That night he returned to his new home followed by an escort laden with gifts.

So began the first evening of his Indian life. 'It was already dark,' Kovalski wrote to one of the superiors of his order. 'I lit an oil lamp lent to me by one family, then unrolled the mat I had been given and sat on it with my back propped against the wall as I emptied my old knapsack. From it I took my razor, my shaving brush, toothbrush, the small box of medicines given to me by friends when I left, a change of underpants and shirt and my Jerusalem Bible; in other words, all my worldly possessions. Between the pages of the Bible was the photograph of the Sacred Shroud of Turin given to me by my father years ago. As I was pinning it to the wall, a little girl appeared on the threshold, barefoot and dressed in rags but with a flower in the end of her pigtail. She was carrying a bowl of rice and vegetables. She set it down in front of me, joined her hands in the Indian gesture of greeting, bowed her head, smiled, and ran away. I gave thanks to God for this apparition and for this meal provided by brothers unknown to me. Then I ate, as they do, with my fingers.'

Shortly after midnight, silence enveloped the City of Joy. Numb with fatigue and emotion, Stephan Kovalski folded his shirt and jeans to form a pillow, and stretched out on the narrow mat. After a last look at the Sacred Shroud, he blew out the lamp and closed his eyes with an inner peace such as he had not experienced since the day of his ordination five years earlier.

At once a frenzied chorus started up directly above his head. Striking a match, he discovered dozens of rats chasing one another about on the bamboo framing and rushing down the walls with a cacophony of shrill cries. Stephan leaped to his feet and tried to hit the intruders with his boots, but as fast as one group made off, others arrived through the holes in the roof until the sheer size of the invasion forced him to surrender. With determined resignation he lay down again, but almost immediately he felt something stirring on his scalp. Lighting the lamp once more, he shook his head until an enormous hairy centipede fell out of his hair. Fervent admirer of Mahatma Gandhi and his principle of nonviolence that he was, he nevertheless crushed the creature. Later he was to learn that it was a scolopendra, whose sting could be as venomous as a scorpion's.

For the second time he lay down again, but the City of Joy had further surprises in store. Indian mosquitoes have as a distinguishing characteristic the fact that they are minute, make very little noise, and tease one endlessly before making up their minds to bite. He recited a rosary in the hope of regaining some serenity.

3

After a morning of walking, several hours in a swaying bus, and a night in a packed third-class train compartment, Hasari Pal and his family arrived at Howrah Station. They were so stunned by the spectacle confronting them that at first they were unable to move. They found themselves engulfed in a tide of people going in all directions, of men bearing mountains of suitcases and packages, and vendors offering every conceivable sort of merchandise. Never had they seen such riches: pyramids of oranges, sandals, combs, scissors; piles of shawls, saris, *dhotis*, newspapers, and all kinds of food and drink. Shoeshiners, ear cleaners, cobblers, public scribes and astrologers were all there, offering their services.

For a while the Pals wandered about, dazed and dumbfounded, in the midst of the throng. They gazed curiously at a family who appeared to have taken up residence in a corner of the main concourse. Beside their carefully tied bundles they had set out their cooking utensils and a *chula*. They were peasants from the state of Bihar, driven to Calcutta by the drought, like the Pals, and they understood a little Bengali. They had been

110

living in the station for several weeks. Hasari questioned them about the possibility of finding work, but they themselves had found nothing yet and had been reduced to sending their children out on the streets to beg. The shame of it was written on their faces.

Hasari told them that he knew a young man from his village named Prem Kumar who was working in the market of the Bara Bazaar and that he was hoping to contact him. The Biharis suggested that Hasari leave his wife and children with them while he went to make enquiries. Comforted by the kindness of these strangers, Hasari bought some *samosas*, triangular fritters filled with minced meat or vegetables, which he shared with his new friends, Aloka, and his children. Then he plunged resolutely into the flood of travellers emerging from the railway station.

Outside, a cyclone of trucks, buses, taxis, handcarts, cycle rickshaws, motorbikes and bicycles swirled by in a kind of collective madness. A horde of pedlars surrounded Hasari with offers of ball-point pens, pastries, lottery tickets. Beggars besieged him. Lepers clung to his shirt. The tooting horns, the throbbing engines, buses' horns, cart bells, carriage bells, seemed to compete to see which could make the most noise. Hasari spotted an impassive policeman who was attempting to direct the traffic. He fought his way over to him to ask directions to the Bara Bazaar. The policeman waved in the direction of an entanglement of metal girders at the far end of the square. 'On the other side of the bridge!' he growled.

The Howrah Bridge is the only link between the twin cities of Calcutta and Howrah. It spans the Hooghly River and is undoubtedly the most congested bridge in the world. Over a million people, hundreds of thousands of vehicles, and herds of animals cross it every day. Hasari Pal was swept up in a stream of people who were pushing their way in different directions between two unbroken lines of vendors squatting behind their wares. In the six lanes of traffic, hundreds of vehicles were stuck in a gigantic bottleneck that stretched as far as the eye could see. People clung in clusters to the sides of the overloaded double-decker buses, which leaned over so far they seemed about to tip up at any moment.

On the other side of the bridge, where the traffic was even more congested, Hasari noticed a small cart on two wheels, transporting two passengers. Between the shafts there was a man. Good God, he thought, there are even human horses in Calcutta! He had just seen his first rickshaw. The nearer he drew to the bazaar, the more there were of these curious little vehicles lugging people or merchandise about.

All the cities of the former colonial world have banished rickshaws, one of the most degrading examples of man's exploitation of his fellow man, from their roads. All except Calcutta, where even today some hundred thousand human horses run more kilometres per day than are flown by the thirty Boeings and Airbuses of Indian Airlines, India's domestic airline. Each day, rickshaws transport more than one million passengers and no

111

In Calcutta, three hundred thousand people live in the streets. This family has set out its cooking utensils and *chula* — a portable stove — on the pavement.

More than one hundred people live in this cramped corner of the City of Joy, without running water or electricity.

The Howrah Bridge is the only link between the twin cities of Calcutta and Howrah. It spans the Hooghly River and is undoubtedly the most congested bridge in the world. Over a million people, hundreds of thousands of vehicles, and countless herds of animals cross it every day.

A boy showers himself, using a tin can.

One of many teahouses in Calcutta where sweet tea can be bought to quieten the pangs of hunger.

one would dream of relegating these anachronistic carriages to a museum, for in Calcutta human sweat provides the world's cheapest energy.

Invented in Japan at the end of the eighteenth century by a European missionary, rickshaws derive their name from the Japanese *jin riki shaw*, 'vehicle propelled by man'. The first rickshaws appeared in India around 1880 and it was not long before they became a common sight in Calcutta. For many peasant farmers who seek refuge there, rickshaws provide a means of earning a living.

Because no additional operating licences have been issued since 1949, there are officially fewer than ten thousand of them, but unofficial statistics suggest a figure five times larger, as four out of five rickshaws operate illegally. Each one of those fifty thousand provides a living for two pullers, who take turns between the shafts from one sunrise to the next. The sweat of those hundred thousand drudges feeds as many families, so it is estimated that over one million people look to the rickshaw for their daily bowl of rice.

WHEN HASARI REACHED the Bara Bazaar area, he saw a network of small streets, covered alleys and narrow passageways lined with hundreds of stalls, workshops and stores. He passed through an arcade where dozens of stalls sold nothing but perfume. Then he entered an alley where, amid the glitter of gold and small glassware, all he could see were jewellers. There were hundreds of them, lined up like prisoners behind the bars of the cages containing their treasures. Beyond this street lay the sari market, where women lingered over sumptuous displays, particularly in the shops that specialised in wedding saris dripping with gold and spangles.

Hasari questioned dozens of workmen and tradesmen, but only a miracle, he realised, could help him find Prem Kumar in such a seething mass. Nonetheless he continued his search until nightfall. Then, exhausted, he bought five bananas and asked the way back to the railway station. His children swooped on the bananas like starving sparrows and the whole family settled down to sleep on the station floor.

Next morning Hasari took his elder son, Manooj, with him and together they explored another section of the Bara Bazaar: first the metalworkers' and tinsmiths' corner, then the workshops where dozens of men and children spent their day rolling *bidis*, thin Indian cigarettes. Hasari described his friend to anyone who would listen, but it was like looking for a grain of rice in a bundle of straw.

After the third day of searching, with no money left to buy food, Hasari picked up all the peelings and scraps he could find in the bazaar before making his way back to the railway station. Then, that evening, overwhelmed with shame and despair, he and his wife sent their daughter, Amrita, and her two brothers to beg at the entrance to the station.

Utterly dejected, Hasari returned to the Bara Bazaar next morning. As he was passing a workshop where some workmen were loading iron bars

114

onto a handcart, one of the men suddenly began to cough up blood. He lay down on the ground, so pale that Hasari thought that he was surely dead. When the workshop owner came out, shouting because the bars had not yet left, Hasari rushed forward and offered to replace the ailing workman. The owner hesitated, but his delivery could not wait and he offered Hasari three rupees for the run.

Hasari braced himself with the other workmen to shift the heavy load. Their destination was a factory on the other side of the great bridge. The workmen fought like beasts to pull the load across the bridge and Hasari thought the blood vessels in his neck were going to burst. But halfway up the incline, their vehicle came to a standstill. A policeman came over and threatened the men with his stick because they were holding up the traffic. Finally one of the workmen bent down to put all his weight against one wheel and the others managed to drive the cart forward.

Exhausted, but proud of his first earnings, Hasari returned to the railway station that evening only to find that his wife and children had disappeared. After a long search he found them on an embankment behind the bus terminal. 'The police chased us out,' Aloka explained through her tears. 'They said if they ever saw us in the station again, they'd throw us into prison.'

The Pals had no idea where to go next. They crossed the great bridge and simply kept on walking until they reached the very heart of the city. Pitiful in her shabby peasant sari, Aloka carried her younger son in her arms and held her daughter by the hand. Manooj walked in front with his father. The pavement was littered with sleeping people, wrapped like corpses from head to toe in bits of grimy cloth. Finally, the Pals stopped to rest beside a family cooking *chapattis*—flat rounds of unleavened bread— on a portable stove. They too had left the countryside for the mirage of Calcutta. The mother offered the Pals a hot griddlecake and swept a patch of the pavement so that the newcomers could settle themselves next to them. The strangers' hospitality brought new hope to Hasari. At least his family would be safe in their company until he found work. But that afternoon he had learned a harsh lesson: 'Since men in this inhuman city die on the job, I'll be damned if I can't manage one day to replace one of the poor fellows.'

AT THAT TIME the City of Joy had only some ten wells and fountains for seventy thousand inhabitants. The fountain closest to Stephan Kovalski's room was near a buffalo shed at the end of his alleyway. By the time he got to it on his first morning in the slum, the neighbourhood was just waking up. Each dawn, people who had spent the night packed in a single rat-and-vermin-infested hovel seemed born again with the daylight.

Their daily resurrection began with a general process of purification. There, beside the sewer, the inhabitants of the City of Joy banished the miasma of the night with a meticulous toilet. Without revealing so much as a patch of nudity, the women managed to wash themselves all over, from their long hair to the soles of their feet. After that, they would comb and plait their hair with great care, sometimes decorating it with a fresh flower picked from God only knew where. At every water point, men showered themselves with tins. Boys cleaned their teeth with acacia twigs coated with ashes, and mothers deloused their children before vigorously soaping their little bodies.

When Stephan arrived, several dozen women and children were standing in line at the fountain, but its output was so feeble that it took for ever to fill a bucket. It didn't much matter—time was of no importance in Anand Nagar, and the fountain was an information centre. For Kovalski it was a marvellous opportunity to observe his neighbours.

A little girl came up to him, gave him a big smile, and with great authority took charge of his bucket. Placing a finger on his wrist, she said to him in English, 'You must be in a great hurry.'

'Why do you think that?' asked Kovalski.

'Because you have a watch.'

WHEN HE GOT BACK to his house with his water, the priest found several people outside his door. He recognised them as the occupants of the Christian compound to which Father Cordeiro's envoy had taken him on his first evening. A young woman offered him a *chapatti* and a small bottle.

'*Namaskar*, Father,' she said warmly. 'My name is Margareta. My neighbours and I thought that you might not have anything with which to celebrate Mass. Here is some bread and wine.'

Overwhelmed, Stephan Kovalski surveyed his visitors. They may not have anything to eat, but they've managed to get hold of bread and wine for the Eucharist, he thought.

'We have set up a table in our courtyard,' added the young woman with a conspiratorial smile.

'Let's go,' said Kovalski, his face showing his joy.

These people belonged to the families who formed a tiny island of Christians in the midst of the seventy thousand Muslims and Hindus in the City of Joy. Although they too were poor, they were for several reasons slightly less destitute than the rest of the population. First, they were a small minority—and the smaller the number of people, the easier it is to provide aid for the least fortunate. Also, their religion did not teach them to resign themselves to their fate. For the Hindus, misfortune was the result of actions carried out in previous lives; this *karma* must be accepted so that one may be reborn under more auspicious circumstances. The Christians were free to improve their lot as best they could.

The families about to assist at Kovalski's first Mass in Anand Nagar numbered about twenty people in all, mostly women with babies, and a few old men. Nearly all the heads of families were at work, an indication that this compound was privileged, for others were full of the unemployed.

What the priest encountered on entering the Christian compound would remain for ever engraved upon his memory. They had covered a plank supported on two crates with a square of spotless cotton and placed a candle at each corner. A bowl and cup served as paten and ciborium. A wooden crucifix and a garland of yellow marigolds completed the decoration of this improvised altar erected in the centre of the courtyard.

For a while Stephan Kovalski stood and gathered his thoughts, meditating upon the miracle that he was about to accomplish against a backdrop of smoking *chulas*, ragged clothes drying on rooftops, children in tatters chasing one another about in the gutters, and all the uproar of horns, singing, shouting, and compound life in general. In his hands, a piece of *chapatti*—so like the unleavened bread Christ Himself had broken at His last supper—was about to evoke the Creator who was the origin of all things. In the midst of these suffering and despised people, he sensed all that would be unique about this sharing of bread.

As Kovalski was celebrating his Mass, three stray dogs scampered across the courtyard in hot pursuit of a rat almost as big as they were. The scene was so commonplace that no one paid any attention to it. A balloon seller who passed by during the reading of the Gospel did, on the other hand, attract a few glances. As the multicoloured clusters disappeared into the distance, Kovalski's voice rose resonantly above the assembled heads. The priest had carefully chosen the Gospel for the message of good news it conveyed. Looking with love upon the emaciated faces before him, he repeated the words of Jesus Christ: '"Blessed are the poor in spirit, for theirs is the Kingdom of Heaven. Blessed are those who mourn, for they shall be comforted. Blessed are those who hunger and thirst for righteousness, for they shall be satisfied."'

After a silence, he held out his arms and gazed intently at each of his new brothers and sisters. Then, letting Christ speak through his voice, he proclaimed, 'Peace be with you, for you are the light of the world.'

ON HIS WAY BACK from the Christian compound, the Polish priest felt a distinct reserve on the part of his non-Christian neighbours. Women pulled their saris over their faces; children scurried away like rabbits. The vermin were the only ones who did not ostracise him. Like the rats and mosquitoes of the night, the flies now danced attendance on him. There were hundreds of them. Green, grey, big, tiny—they moved about in squadrons, getting into his ears, nostrils, eyes, and down his throat with each bite of food. When he slapped at them they moved on a few centimetres to inflict their torture on another part of his anatomy.

When Stephan returned to his room, Father Cordeiro's envoy was waiting for him, concerned about how the Pole had survived his first hours in the slum.

'Father Cordeiro has asked me to tell you that there is a comfortable

117

room for you at the presbytery,' he said. 'That wouldn't prevent you from spending as much time here as you liked. I beg you to accept it. This is no place for a priest.'

Finally, realising that his entreaties were falling on deaf ears, the envoy shook his head sadly and took out of a bag two large books that Father Cordeiro had asked him to pass on to Kovalski. One was a Bengali grammar; the other was an edition of the Gospel in Hindi. The Pole received the gifts with delight. He knew that they would be indispensable in helping him to break down the wall of silence that isolated him in his new existence.

AFTER ANOTHER DAY spent roaming the Bara Bazaar, Hasari Pal returned in the evening with only two newspaper cones full of *muri*, rice roasted in hot sand, which the poor eat as a last resort to stem their hunger. The dried grains were hard and had to be chewed for a long time, prolonging the illusion of actually getting one's teeth into something.

Parents and children chewed for a while in silence. 'There you are. That's for you,' said Hasari, happily giving the remainder of his own share to his younger son, who was looking at him longingly.

Aloka observed her husband's gesture with an aching heart. Among India's poor, food was always given in priority to those who could work and provide for the family's needs. Hasari had lost a lot of weight since their arrival in Calcutta. Two deep lines had carved themselves beneath his moustache, and his dark, shining hair had turned grey above his ears. How he has aged! she thought, as she watched him stretch out for the night on the bare asphalt. She thought of the first time she had seen him, so handsome under the canopy erected for their marriage in front of her family hut. He had been wearing a new white tunic and a saffron-coloured turban. Aloka had been only fifteen and he barely three years older. She remembered her terror when her mother and aunts left her alone with him after the ceremony. Their union had been arranged by their parents and they had not met before the wedding. He had gazed at her intently and said, 'You are very beautiful. I hope you will be happy to have me as your husband.' She had merely smiled in response, because it was not decent for a new bride to speak freely to her husband on their wedding day.

That day the father of my children looked as strong and solid as the great banyan tree at the entrance to our village, Aloka reflected. And now he seemed so fragile, curled up on his patch of pavement.

4

On the morning of their sixth day in Calcutta, Hasari left with Manooj and Amrita for the Bara Bazaar. The market was always overflowing with so many goods that there was invariably some rotted food to be gleaned from its refuse heaps, and that morning Hasari left his children to forage among them while he once more scoured the bazaar. He offered his services to dozens of traders and several times he even followed overloaded carts in the faint hope that if one of the workmen keeled over with exhaustion, he might take his place. Finally, with his belly screaming with hunger and his heart heavy with despair, Hasari collapsed against a wall. Suddenly, through his dizziness, he heard a voice. 'Would you like to earn a few rupees?'

The small man in spectacles looked more like a bureaucrat than a tradesman. Hasari stared at him in astonishment and nodded.

'All you have to do is come with me. I'll take you somewhere where they'll take a little of your blood and give you thirty rupees for it. That's fifteen for me and fifteen for you.'

'Thirty rupees for my blood!' repeated Hasari, stunned. 'Who would want to take blood from a poor man like me and on top of that give me thirty rupees?'

'Blood is blood!' replied the man. 'Whether it comes from a *marwari* loaded with money or from someone like you, it's still blood.'

With an effort, Hasari got to his feet, sent the children back to Aloka, and followed the stranger.

For every transaction or service provided in Calcutta, there is a swarm of parasitical middlemen to take their cut. The man with the glasses was a procurer for one of the numerous private blood banks that flourish in Calcutta. He prowled around the entrances to work sites, factories, markets, anywhere he knew he would find men at the end of their resources, ready to agree to anything for a few rupees.

The blood needed in the hospitals and clinics of a metropolis like Calcutta amounts to tens of thousands of litres a year. Since the official blood banks are incapable of meeting such a demand, private entrepreneurs take advantage of the opportunity. All they have to do is obtain the complicity of a doctor, lay a request before the Health Department in his name, rent premises, buy a refrigerator, a few syringes, pipettes and bottles, and engage a lab assistant. The result is a roaring trade with an annual turnover in excess of ten million rupees, about £600,000.

Hasari followed his bespectacled 'benefactor' through the streets of the business quarter until they reached a blood dispensary set up in an old garage. Hasari and the procurer had just reached its door when they were accosted by a man with a mouth reddened from chewing betel. 'Are you coming for blood?' he asked in a low voice.

When the procurer nodded, the stranger said with a wink, 'Then follow me. I know another place where they pay forty rupees. Five for me, the rest for you two. Agreed?'

This man was another cog in the wheel and was procuring for a rival blood bank down the street. The ten additional rupees it offered had nothing to do with generosity. It simply meant that it took three hundred

119

cc's from its donors, instead of the usual two hundred and fifty. However, it did add a royal bonus for a man with an empty stomach: a banana and three glucose biscuits.

Hasari was invited to sit down on a stool, and a male lab assistant knotted a tourniquet round his biceps, while another stuck a needle into a vein. Hasari watched the red liquid rise in the bottle. Was it the sight of his own blood, the idea that he was being emptied like a water vendor's bottle, or was it his lack of food? Hasari's vision blurred and he started to sweat thick beads of perspiration, despite the fact that he was shivering with cold. The voices of the lab people seemed to reach him from another planet, through a strange clamouring of bells. Then everything went blank.

The attendants did not even interrupt their work. Every day they saw men weakened by deprivation faint as they sold their blood.

When Hasari opened his eyes again, he saw a dreamlike vision: one of the men in white overalls was offering him a banana.

'There you are, little girl,' the lab assistant mocked him gently. Then he took a receipt book out of his pocket and asked, 'What's your name?' He scribbled a few words, tore off the sheet, and told Hasari in a peremptory tone to sign it. Hasari made an X and pocketed the forty rupees under the covetous gaze of the two intermediaries. The money would be divided up outside. What Hasari did not know was that he had put his signature to a receipt for forty-five rupees, not forty. The lab assistants, too, were taking their commission.

Light-headed and reeling, Hasari took hours to find the piece of pavement where his wife and children were waiting for him. Of the seventeen and a half rupees that the procurers had left him, he had decided to spend five on celebrating with his family the joy of actually having earned some money. He bought half a kilo of delicious Bengali nougat and some *mansours*, yellow pastries made out of chickpea flour and sweetened milk. He also picked up enough paper cones of *muri*, the roasted rice that crunched between the teeth, for the neighbours on the pavement to share in his good fortune.

THE SALE OF BLOOD enabled the Pal family to hold out for four days. During that time they lived on bananas and whatever the two eldest children gleaned from the Bara Bazaar, while their father was out looking for work. The last few paisas of the last rupee were spent on four cow-dung cakes for boiling up a stew of scraps and peelings on the neighbours' *chula*. When, finally, there was nothing left, Hasari made a heroic decision. He would sell some more of his blood.

From a medical point of view, this was madness, but many men in the depths of despair turned up at the blood banks every week; indeed, one out of four donors, a medical report showed, had a haemoglobin level of less than half the acceptable minimum. These men did not generally live long: they would be found dead of anaemia in some street, or on a bed in Mother Teresa's home for the dying.

That day a crowd was waiting at the door of the blood bank when Hasari arrived. A group of procurers for rival banks had assembled there, trying to divert some of the clientele towards their own employers. Hasari was immediately accosted by a man with two gold front teeth. 'Forty rupees,' whispered the man with the air of a prostitute lowering her price. 'Thirty for you, ten for me.'

Thirty rupees! That's almost double what I got last time, Hasari thought. He did not realise that in Calcutta the price of blood varied from day to day. The difference in fee stemmed from the ability of the middlemen to assess the naiveté of their prey and hence to fleece them with greater or lesser success. At first glance, the man with the gold teeth had registered the small red mark on Hasari's arm marking him as a professional donor.

The Paradise Blood Bank was aptly named. Decorated in pink and furnished with comfortable seats, it was housed in an outbuilding of one of the most modern and expensive clinics in Calcutta, and was used exclusively by wealthy businessmen and their families. The nurse in immaculate white who was in charge of admitting donors grimaced at Hasari's pathetic appearance. She made him sit down on a chair with a reclining back. Then, much to Hasari's amazement, she only pricked his index finger, making a drop of blood fall onto a glass plate. But the man with the gold teeth realised all too well what was happening. 'The woman is sabotaging me,' he grumbled.

He had guessed correctly. A minute later the young woman informed him politely that his client's blood did not meet with the requirements of the dispensary. The reason given would have precluded the majority of the inhabitants of Calcutta's slums: a subnormal haemoglobin level.

The blow was a harsh one for Hasari. Back in the street, he pleaded with the procurer, 'Don't you know anywhere else? I don't even have a coin to buy a banana for my children.'

The man laid a friendly hand on his shoulder. 'For the moment, what you've got in your veins is water, my friend. But come with me: I'll give you a present.' He took Hasari to the nearest drugstore, where he bought a bottle of pills. It was unlikely that the chemists in the Swiss laboratory that manufactured the ferrous-sulfate tablets had foreseen the use the desperate people of the Third World would make of their product.

'Take three a day and come back here in exactly seven days,' said the procurer, handing Hasari the bottle. Then, suddenly menacing, he added, 'Mind you turn up or that junk in your veins may well flow free of charge.'

LESS THAN TWENTY-FOUR hours later, the procurer was surprised to see Hasari Pal walking resolutely in his direction.

'Hello, old friend!' Hasari called out cheerfully.

'What's got into you?' the man with the gold teeth said, surprised. 'Have you won first prize in a lottery?'

'I think I've found a job, so I've come to give you back your pills. Here, you can let someone else benefit from them.'

Fortune did indeed seem to be smiling at last on Hasari. He had once more gone to take up his stand near one of the workshops on the outskirts of the Bara Bazaar—the same spot where he had earned five rupees by standing in for the workman who had fainted. This time, two men were in the process of loading metal springs onto a handcart, when one of them tripped over a stone and dropped a spring on his foot, crushing it. The man cried out with pain and Hasari rushed to his rescue. Tearing a strip from his cotton loincloth, he knotted it round the foot to stop the bleeding.

In Calcutta, an ambulance was rarely available, so all the owner of the workshop could do was call a rickshaw. Obviously furious at the incident, he took several five-rupee notes out of his belt, put one into the hand of the injured man and gave a second to the rickshaw puller. Seeing Hasari lift the workman into the carriage, he entrusted two more to him. 'Keep one for yourself. The other is to grease the palm of the attendant at the hospital entrance.'

Hasari Pal's hesitation in climbing into the rickshaw intrigued the puller.

'Haven't you ever sat in a rickshaw before?'

'No,' admitted Hasari, perching himself timidly next to the injured man.

The puller braced himself against the shafts and the rickshaw moved forward with a jolt. The puller's greying hair and stooped shoulders indicated that he was no longer young, but with rickshaw pullers, physical appearance bore little relationship to age. People grew old very rapidly pulling such machines.

'You're not from round here?' the man asked Hasari when he had picked up a little speed.

'No, I'm from Bankuli.'

'Bankuli!' repeated the rickshaw puller, slowing down sharply. 'But that's only thirty kilometres from my home!'

Hasari would have liked to leap out and hug him, but he made an effort to conceal his joy for the sake of the wounded man, who was groaning with every bump. The puller, who introduced himself as Ram Chander, began charging towards the hospital as fast as his bandy legs would carry him. At unpredictable intervals, however, he would have to throw himself backwards in a desperate effort to avoid a bus or truck cutting across his path.

Calcutta's general hospital was a city in itself, a collection of dilapidated buildings linked by endless corridors and courtyards in which entire families squatted. A crowd of people milled round the emergency door, with a great deal of shouting and arguing. Women carried babies so weak they didn't even cry any more, and from time to time a stretcher was carried past with a corpse being borne to a funeral pyre.

Hasari slipped the five-rupee note given to him by the workshop owner into the attendant's hand. The bribe paid off. Instead of sending them away as he did most of the other people, he allowed them to carry the wounded workman into a room inside. There, the two men laid him down on a stretcher still stained with the blood of the previous patient. A penetrating smell of disinfectant pervaded the room.

'He'll have to have surgery,' the nurse said after a cursory examination, 'so there's no point in your waiting. Someone can pick him up in a couple of days.'

Outside, Hasari and Ram Chander retrieved the rickshaw from the hospital courtyard and walked down the street together in silence. When they arrived at a crossroads where a policeman was directing traffic, Ram took a coin out of his shirt and put it in the policeman's hand as he passed.

'It saves all sorts of trouble,' he explained with a grin. 'Especially when you don't have a licence to operate your rickshaw.' Then, sliding his palms along the shafts, he asked, 'How would you like to pull one of these contraptions?'

The idea seemed as ridiculous to Hasari as if he had been asked if he would like to fly a plane, but he was touched by the interest the rickshaw puller was showing in him. 'Any kind of job would suit me,' he replied.

'Try it,' said Ram Chander, pulling up sharply and stepping out of the shafts. 'Stand between the shafts and jerk your back to get the wheels rolling.'

Hasari did as he was told and was surprised by the sheer weight of the carriage. 'At first, it takes the strength of a buffalo! With passengers on board, you might be pulling a good one hundred and thirty-five kilos,' Ram said. 'And once it's moving, it runs as if it has a life of its own. It's quite a trick to pull up suddenly in an emergency.'

Ram showed Hasari an area on the shafts where the paint had worn off. 'The main thing is to find the right balance for the weight you're carrying. You have to put your hands on exactly this spot.'

After he handed the shafts of the rickshaw back to its owner, Hasari mopped his forehead with a tail of his *longhi*. The effort had exhausted him.

'We should celebrate your initiation!' Ram exclaimed. 'Let's go and have a glass of *bangla*. I know a place that isn't too expensive.'

But Hasari seemed unenthusiastic as he pulled out the five-rupee note given to him by the workshop owner. 'My wife and children haven't had anything to eat,' he said. 'I must take something back.'

'No problem! It's on me,' Ram assured him.

They plunged into an area of old buildings with decaying façades and narrow alleyways, packed with people at the windows and in the streets. Music blared from loudspeakers. Laundry was drying on the edge of the roofs, and buffalo, cows, dogs, chickens and pigs roamed about among

123

children who were playing with paper kites. Above, dots of every conceivable colour flew through the sky; in Calcutta, kites were favourite toys, as if somehow those scraps of paper soaring high above the rooftops carried the children's dreams of escaping their prison of mud, fumes and poverty.

In a corner behind a palisade of planks, the owner of the bar, a man in a dirty vest, sat beneath a tiled porch roof. Ram Chander directed Hasari to a bench at one end of the only table. The place reeked of alcohol. The owner clapped his hands, and immediately a boy appeared with two glasses and a bottle that had neither label nor cork. It was full of a greyish acrid-smelling liquid in which floated small white flakes. Chander carefully counted out fourteen one-rupee notes and handed them to the proprietor. Then Chander filled Hasari's glass with the concoction. In silence, the two men clinked glasses and swallowed a mouthful. 'There's nothing like *bangla* for putting a tiger in your tank!' exclaimed Ram Chander, paraphrasing an advertisement that had once covered the walls of Calcutta.

'That's true!' said Hasari Pal. He grimaced and rubbed his stomach. 'Except that this particular tiger rumbles a bit inside you.'

That it 'rumbled' was not surprising—the concoction was one of the most lethal mixtures ever brewed by man. It came from a village situated on the fringes of Calcutta's garbage dump, where, throughout the year, all kinds of refuse, animal entrails and cane juice were fermented for a month in large jars. In India, noxious alcohol like this claims as many victims every year as malaria. It has only one virtue and that is its price.

When the two friends left the bar, Ram Chander was hailed by a fat elderly woman dressed in the white sari of a widow. Hasari helped her climb into the rickshaw and Ram set off at a trot. As he watched them pulling away, Hasari couldn't help thinking how lucky his new friend was. At least he can look other people in the eye. He has a job. He has his dignity. Whereas I'm just like the mangy dogs that roam the streets. I don't exist.

Before the two men parted, Ram had promised to introduce Hasari to the rickshaw owner's representative the next day. 'Meet me at the Park Circus esplanade,' Ram said. 'With a little bit of luck and a generous tip, he might just find you an old heap to pull.'

Hasari had difficulty believing in anything so wonderful, but the *bangla* had given him wings. He wandered about for a long time before finding his family.

EVERY NIGHT at about eleven o'clock, it would start up again. First came the sobbing, then the groans. Gradually they increased in intensity, cascading through the dividing wall. A ten-year-old Muslim boy was dying of osteotuberculosis in the hovel next door to Stephan Kovalski. His name was Sabia.

During the first few evenings the priest had succumbed to cowardice. He had stopped his ears with cotton so that he could not hear. 'I was like Job on the brink of revolt,' he wrote to his superior. 'Who could dare say to this child, "Rejoice, you who weep today, for joy shall be yours tomorrow"?'

It was several nights before the priest could bring himself to listen to Sabia's cries—and several more before he could listen to them not only with his ears but also with his heart. He was torn between his faith and his very human feeling of revolt. Had he any right to be happy, to sing praises to God, while that intolerable torment was going on right next to him? Night after night when his young neighbour began to groan again, Kovalski's eyes turned in the darkness towards the picture of the Sacred Shroud, and he prayed until the groans were still.

Sabia's illness grew worse and the sounds of his agony increased. Since his illness was incurable, Stephan Kovalski felt that the suffering child should at least be able to die in peace. One morning the priest caught the bus to the nearest hospital.

'I need a syringe and a dose of morphine. It's very urgent,' he said to the nurse in charge of the hospital pharmacy, handing her thirty rupees.

But Stephan met with some hostile gazes when he stopped outside Sabia's hovel. There were many in the area who mistrusted the priest. Why did this infidel want to visit the little Muslim who was dying? Was he going to try to convert the boy? Tell him that Allah was not the true God? Nevertheless, Sabia's mother welcomed him with a warm smile. She invited the priest to come in and sent her eldest daughter to fetch him a cup of tea from the old Hindu.

Sabia was lying on a mattress of rags, his arms crossed, his skin pitted with sores. As Stephan drew near to him, the boy opened his eyes and his gaze lit up with a spark of joy. Stephan was totally overwhelmed. How could so much serenity radiate from that tortured little body? Stephan's fingers tightened on the vial of morphine.

'Salaam, Sabia,' he murmured, smiling.

'Salaam, *Daddah*,' responded the child cheerfully. 'What have you got in your hand? Sweets?'

Startled, Stephan dropped the vial and it shattered as it fell. But Sabia had no need of morphine. His face radiated peace. Mutilated as the child was, he remained undefeated. He has just given me the most precious gift of all, Stephan thought: a secret reason never to despair, a light in the darkness. How many brothers and sisters of light like Sabia did he have in this place of suffering? Hundreds, perhaps thousands. Every morning, after celebrating the Eucharist, he would visit some of them with the small amount of assistance he could give them: a little food, some medicine, or simply the comfort of his presence.

Nothing raised his spirits more than his visits to a blind leper woman who lived next to the railway lines. This woman too, plunged as she was into unutterable stages of decay, radiated serenity. She would spend entire days in prayer, curled up in a corner of her hovel without lighting or ventilation. As if her blindness were not enough, leprosy had reduced her hands to stumps. But round this Christian woman had been woven one of those networks of mutual help and friendship that transformed the City of Joy into a privileged place. Such help was all the more remarkable because her neighbours were all Hindus, a fact that would normally have prevented them from touching anyone suffering from leprosy, or even from entering her house. Yet, every day, the neighbours took turns bringing the woman a dish of rice and vegetables, helping her wash, doing her housework. The slum, so inhuman in other respects, gave her something which no Western hospital could have provided: the gift of love.

Some sixth sense always alerted the woman to Kovalski's arrival. As soon as she felt him approaching, she would smooth down her hair with what was left of her hands and rearrange a tattered cushion for her visitor. As soon as he was settled beside her, she would touch the priest's face as if to sense the life in it.

'Father, I wish the good Lord would come and fetch me. Why won't you ask Him to?'

'If the good Lord keeps you with us, it's because He still needs you here,' the priest replied. Then he told her about his visits to young Sabia. She listened with her sightless eyes fixed upon him.

'Tell him that I shall pray for him.' Stephan searched in his knapsack for the clean handkerchief in which he had carefully wrapped a piece of *chapatti* consecrated during his morning Mass. After he had given her Communion, the woman's face was radiant with joy. When Kovalski rose to go, she lifted up her rosary in a gesture of salutation and offering.

'Be sure to tell those who are suffering that I am praying for them,' she said.

That evening Stephan Kovalski wrote in his diary: 'That poor woman knows that her suffering is not useless. I affirm that God wants to use her suffering to help others to endure theirs. That is why my prayer for this poor woman must not be one of sadness. Every time I leave the hovel where she lives, I come away revitalised. How can one despair in this slum of Anand Nagar? In truth, this place deserves its name, City of Joy.'

5

When Hasari Pal turned up at the Park Circus esplanade as agreed, Ram Chander, the rickshaw puller, was not there. Hasari decided to wait. But when Ram Chander arrived in the early afternoon, without his carriage, he looked dejected.

'They've taken my rickshaw,' he growled. 'Last night, just after dark, a cop stopped me because I had forgotten to take my lamp with me that morning. He suggested the usual arrangement.'

'The usual arrangement?' asked Hasari.

'Yes, of course! "Give me fifteen rupees," he said, "or I'll arrest you." When I told him I didn't have that kind of money, he took me to the police station, and they confiscated my rickshaw. To top it off, they ordered me to appear in police court tomorrow. They're going to hit me with a fine of at least thirty rupees.' Ram took a long puff on the cigarette he held cupped in the hollow of his hands. 'Let's go and get something to eat,' he said. 'Even the worst troubles look better on a full stomach.'

He took Hasari to a cheap restaurant consisting of a small low room with five marble-topped tables. The owner presided bare-chested over the cooking pots. On the ceiling an antiquated fan showed signs of increasing fatigue with every turn of its blades. There was a strong smell of frying oil.

A young boy brought the two friends each a plate of rice and a bowl of *dal*—boiled lentils. They poured the soup over the rice, then ate in silence. It was a real feast for Hasari, his first proper meal since he had arrived in Calcutta.

By the time they had finished, Ram Chander's optimism had been restored and the two men set off to visit Musafir Prasad, representative of the largest rickshaw owner in Calcutta.

After twenty years of toiling between the shafts of a rickshaw, Prasad had moved up to the area where the money was made. At forty-eight, the peasant from Bihar had become a boss. Beneath his black wavy hair, shiny with mustard oil, his brain functioned like a computer. He managed an operation of three hundred and forty-six rickshaws and the seven hundred odd human horses who pulled them; and he did so with neither pencil nor paper, for the very good reason that he could not read or write. He was responsible for collecting daily hiring fees from the rickshaw pullers. Whether it was forty-four degrees in the shade or a monsoon was raging, he would cover tens of kilometres a day on his squeaking bicycle, making contact with each of his pullers.

To do his job properly, Prasad needed a heart of stone. When he claimed the five-rupee hiring fee, he knew that on some days many of the men would have to go without food to pay him. Every day pullers collapsed in the street, and each time one of them couldn't get back on his feet, Prasad had to look for a replacement. There was no shortage of candidates, but the owner always made him go to a great deal of trouble to choose the right pullers, to find out about their background, because the thought of strikes, blackmail and threats was a constant nightmare to him. 'Musafir, I don't want any worms in my guava,' he would say repeatedly to Prasad. Rickshaw pullers now had their own unions and people were saying the pullers should be given the ownership of their vehicle.

Musafir was resting in the shade and pondering this situation when he saw Ram Chander approaching him with a thin, diffident-looking companion. Musafir already knew that the night before, Chander's carriage had been picked up by the police for having no light, which was only a pretext for a bribe in a city where the vast majority of trucks and cars operate without lights. Now Ram had two ten-rupee notes in his hand, but he wasn't offering them to Musafir to get his rickshaw out of the pound. Instead, he wanted the boss to take on his friend, Hasari. 'Sardarji, I'd like to introduce a compatriot of mine,' he said. 'He comes from my district. I and my family have known his clan for generations. He is a brave and honest worker. For the love of our Mother Kali, give him one of your rickshaws to pull!'

Musafir took the two notes, then examined the man who hung back behind Ram. Although he was very thin, his shoulders and arms looked solid. Musafir asked him to lift his *longhi* so he could check the condition of his legs and thighs. Finally, he weighed the pros and cons before responding to the eager expectation of the two Bengalis. Then he said, 'You're in luck. One of my men died last night near Bhowanipur market.'

HASARI PAL STOOD and gazed at the rickshaw before him, as if it were the god Ganesh in person—Ganesh, the benefactor of the poor, who brought good fortune and removed obstacles. He approached the vehicle with awe and rubbed the shafts, then touched his heart and his forehead with his hand.

'It's a gift from the gods,' he said to Ram Chander. And yet it was just a run-down old jalopy, without even a licence to operate. Paint was peeling off it in strips, straw stuffing was leaking from holes in the seat, and the rubber tyres were so worn that the wood showed through them. On the back of the carriage a metal plate bore the number 1 and three number 9s. It didn't matter that the number was an invented one, made up of figures that in the Hindu calendar augur well.

Hasari took his place between the shafts, raised them respectfully, and placed his fingers on the worn spot vacated only hours earlier by the hands of the poor fellow to whom the number 1999 had certainly not brought good fortune. He threw his hips forward and heard the wheels creak, and the sound was as reassuring as that of a millstone grinding rice. How could Hasari fail to believe in the benediction of the gods?

Ram gave Hasari a quick run-down on the tricks of the trade. 'You'll get all sorts of people,' he said. 'Some will make you run and some will tell you to take your time. Others will try and knock a few paisas off the fare. But if you're lucky enough to pick up a foreigner, you can ask for more money.' He warned him against customers who gave drivers the slip without paying when they reached their destination. 'And lay in a stock of mustard oil to massage your body,' he advised. 'For the first few days, your thighs, arms and back will feel as if every policeman in Calcutta had broken his *lathi* on you.'

'Then I found myself alone,' Hasari told Aloka later. 'Alone with this strange vehicle in the middle of an unknown city. I was terrified. I didn't think I would ever find my way through those confusing streets or manage to slide between the trucks, buses and cars.'

As Ram had instructed him, he pulled the rickshaw to Park Circus, a very busy junction, to wait for his first client. There were numerous workshops and schools there, as well as a large market frequented by housewives from wealthy neighbourhoods. A long string of rickshaws was permanently parked at this privileged place.

But the line shortened swiftly and as Hasari's turn approached, he felt his heart pounding in his chest. The prospect of plunging into the traffic with the dilapidated rickshaw paralysed his arms and legs. To give himself strength he bought a glass of sugar-cane juice for twenty-five paisas. As the pure sugar content sent a blast of warmth from his stomach to his thighs, he felt he could have pulled the rickshaw up the highest peak of the Himalayas.

Then, as if in a dream, he heard a voice. 'Rickshaw wallah!' A young girl with two long plaits and wearing the white blouse and navy-blue skirt of the uniform of a nearby school, was clambering into his rickshaw. She asked Hasari to take her home, then, realising that he had no idea where she lived, she gave him directions.

Hasari would never forget those first moments when he found himself in the middle of traffic. He felt like a man who had thrown himself into the water to get away from wild beasts, only to find himself surrounded by a herd of crocodiles. Bus and truck drivers seemed to derive malignant satisfaction from terrorising rickshaws, charging them like wild bulls amid the noise of their horns and engines. Hasari was so terrified that he moved forward at a walk, concentrating simply on keeping the vehicle balanced while crossing bumpy thoroughfares, ditches, holes and ruts, open drains and tramlines. But Hasari felt that Ganesh was watching over him during that first run. The god steered him through the obstacles and brought him to the girl's house safe and sound.

'How much do I owe you?' she asked as she stepped out of the rickshaw.

Hasari hadn't the faintest idea. 'Give me whatever you think is fair,' he said.

She looked in her purse. 'There's three rupees. That's more than the usual price, but I hope it brings you luck.'

Hasari took the notes, thanking her effusively. He felt a sudden surge of hope, a conviction that by working hard he could actually achieve what his family needed from him.

He couldn't wait to present the money from that first job to his wife and children immediately. He made for the nearest vendor selling fritters and then started to run, with the bag of fritters as his only passenger, for the pavement where his family was camping. His arrival attracted a crowd as the news that a pavement dweller had actually become a rickshaw wallah spread from one end of the street to the other. Men felt the weight of the shafts, and women looked at Hasari with admiration and envy. To these people who, like the Pals, had left their rice fields, Hasari was living proof that there was always hope.

Hasari decided to devote part of his earnings to the purchase of one accessory that is the emblem of all rickshaw pullers: a bell that the pullers jangle against a rickshaw shaft to attract clients. Hasari bought his first bell for two rupees from a puller in Park Circus. It had a fine leather strap which he fastened to his index finger. With such a jewel on his hand, how could he not believe in the generosity of his *karma*?

It did not take long for disenchantment to set in. Next morning when he woke, his arms, legs and back hurt so much that he could barely stand. Ram had warned him—you don't turn into a human horse overnight, even if you are of good peasant stock. The effort of pulling, the rough jolts, the acrobatics to keep the rickshaw balanced, all gave the body a brutal shock, especially when a man has barely eaten for months.

Although Hasari followed Ram's advice to massage himself from head to toe with mustard oil, he was totally incapable of taking up the shafts of his rickshaw. He could have wept. He entrusted the vehicle to Aloka and dragged himself off to the Park Circus stand, absolutely set on giving the five rupees for the day's rental to Musafir Prasad. It was a matter of life and death: thousands of other starving peasants were waiting to get their hands on his rickshaw.

At Park Circus he ran into Ram, who had just got his rickshaw back after his clash with the police. He laughed when he saw Hasari shuffling along, bent over like an old man.

'You haven't seen anything yet!' he jeered. 'Before three months are up you'll be coughing red too.'

And that was how Hasari discovered that his friend, who always seemed so hearty, had diseased lungs.

'Are you taking any medicine for it?'

Ram looked at Hasari in surprise. 'You must be joking! You've seen the queues at the dispensary. You get there at dawn and by evening you're still there. You're better off treating yourself to a nice bit of *pan* every now and then so that when you cough, you don't know whether it's blood or *betel*. That way you don't worry so much.'

A MUSLIM FAMILY of six—three children and three adults—occupied the hovel behind Stephan Kovalski's room. Mehboub, the head of the family, was a wiry, muscular little man in his thirties with a lively, determined expression beneath his shaggy eyebrows and a forehead half concealed by a thick shock of curly hair. Though his wife, Selima, was several months pregnant, she was constantly on the go, sweeping, cleaning pots and pans, preparing meals or doing the laundry. Mehboub's mother, an old woman who was almost blind, lived with them, and Nasir, the only son, aged ten, was employed in a small workshop. One of his sisters went to the Koranic school. The youngest, only three years old, scampered about the alleyway. The family was comparatively well-off. For thirteen years Mehboub had worked as a day labourer in a naval yard in East Calcutta.

At first Stephan's relations with these neighbours had been confined to the exchange of a polite 'Salaam' each morning and evening. Evidently this Muslim family (and they were not the only ones) disapproved of the intrusion of a foreign Catholic priest into their neighbourhood.

It took an unfortunate incident to break the ice. One evening Mehboub came home from work looking totally dejected. The shipyard had just laid off its entire work force. It was a practice that had started with the introduction of a law forcing employers to pay their workers on a permanent contract basis after several months of regular work. The unions had joined management in opposing the law: management fought it because increasing the number of workers paid on a monthly basis would reinforce the strength of the unions, and the unions because they were composed of workers paid by the month and eager to keep this advantage to themselves. Everyone conspired to get around the law, and to avoid having to give labour contracts people were laid off periodically, then rehired. So thousands of men never knew whether or not their jobs would be waiting for them on the following day, and after many years of employment, when it was no longer possible to put off giving an employee a contract, he was simply laid off permanently. This was what had just happened to Mehboub.

Before Kovalski's eyes, Mehboub began to waste away. His stomach racked with hunger, he walked many kilometres each day round the industrial suburbs of Calcutta, in search of any available way of earning a crust of bread. The six members of his family had to survive on the twenty rupees that Nasir earned each month in a sweatshop. There, for twelve hours a day, the boy dipped the clips for ball-point pens into a chrome bath, inhaling toxic vapours all day from the metal electrolysis.

Kovalski wanted to help the family, but without falling into the trap of becoming a foreign Santa Claus. One morning, as he was cooking rice on his paraffin stove, he burned his hand, and he used his clumsiness as a pretext to ask Selima, Mehboub's wife, if she would prepare his meals. In payment, he offered her three rupees (20p) a day, a princely sum by slum standards, and he insisted that Selima cook exactly the same food for him as she did for her family. For Stephan it was actually an opportunity to experience something on which he had set his heart. How could he share faithfully the living conditions of his brothers in the City of Joy without knowing the hunger that conditioned every instant of their lives?

Next day at noon, one of Selima's daughters brought him a plate with his food for the day: a ladle of rice, a little cabbage and turnip, and some *dal*—the lentils which often provided the poor of India with their only protein. With his European appetite, the Pole prepared to gulp his meal down in two minutes. But Selima had remained true to the Indian tradition which required that all food is afire with chillies and other incendiary spices. Stephan had to absorb each mouthful slowly and cautiously. Later, he would learn the reason for this culinary practice: because it releases perspiration, stimulates circulation and accelerates assimilation of food, chilli is a means of duping the hunger of millions of undernourished people. And hot spices make it possible to swallow even rotten food!

Stephan put up with his new diet bravely for the first two days. When he felt hunger pangs, he would drink a cup of sweet tea from the old Hindu's shop across the way. On the third day, however, violent cramps began to gnaw at his stomach, accompanied by dizziness and icy sweats, and throughout the next day and the days that followed it, his hunger gave him no respite. He tried to pray but his spirit seemed as empty as his stomach. He was humiliated at finding himself reduced to a limp rag while his neighbours managed to pull carts or carry loads more fit for beasts of burden on far fewer calories. After a few days, however, the sensation of hunger faded as if by magic. His body had adapted. Not only did he no longer suffer, he even experienced a sense of well-being.

It was then that he made a fatal mistake. When a visitor from France took him a Camembert cheese, he offered the delicacy to his neighbours. Mehboub would accept only on condition that his friend shared in the treat and the result was disastrous. The food awoke Stephan's appetite uncontrollably, and the nausea, cramps and attacks of sweating reappeared with such increased vigour that he lost more weight. He had difficulty standing upright for half an hour. He suffered from hallucinations, and nightmares haunted his sleep. By physically living the curse of hunger for himself, Stephan Kovalski had joined the majority of the occupants of Anand Nagar.

But he knew the exact range of his experience, and its limitations. He was like those volunteers in survival training who know that they will be rescued after a certain amount of time. Unlike the truly poor, Kovalski knew that if his hunger exceeded bearable limits, he had only to make one gesture to eat as much as he wanted.

Mehboub and the occupants of the City of Joy suffered the anguish of those who have no hope of rescue. Yet not a single complaint ever issued from Mehboub's mouth. He allowed his despair to show only when his youngest daughter cried with hunger. Then he would take her in his arms and go into the neighbouring courtyard to beg a piece of *chapatti*. A poor person would never close his door on him. That was the law of the slum.

HE'S GOING TO DIE right here in the street, Hasari thought with horror. His friend Ram Chander's chest was distended, as he desperately tried to gulp in air. His face had turned yellow, and his mouth gaped like that of a drowning man. A sudden coughing fit convulsed him and he began to spit blood. Hasari helped him onto the seat of his rickshaw and offered to take him home, but Ram shook his head. 'It's only a damned cold,' he said. 'It'll pass.'

That year the Bengali winter was murderous. Winds from the Himalayas had brought down the thermometer to minus ten degrees Celsius, a temperature that was devastating for a population used to baking in an oven for eight months of the year. For the rickshaw pullers it was particularly harsh. Alternating as they did between the sweatbath of a run and the cold of prolonged waiting, their undernourished bodies had little resistance. Many of them died.

Ram had become Hasari's best friend. They spent hours sitting side by side at the corner of Park Circus and talking. Ram's dream was to go back to his village one day and open a grocery shop. 'Just to sit there all day, without having to run around,' he would say, imagining his future paradise. He pictured himself enthroned in his shop, and all round him piles of vegetables, sacks overflowing with *dal* and rice, intoxicatingly aromatic spices, biscuits and bars of soap.

Before this dream could be realised, however, Ram Chander had a promise to keep. He had to reimburse the *mahajan* in his village for the loan he had taken out to pay for his father's funeral rites. Otherwise the family field, which had served as collateral, would be lost for ever.

The five-year term on his debt was due to expire in a few weeks, so despite the rapid deterioration of his health, Ram went on working.

One morning Hasari ran into him outside the post office in Park Street where Ram had come to mail his monthly money order. The sheer bulk of the package of notes he pulled out of his *longhi* amazed Hasari.

'I swear you've robbed the Bank of India!' he exclaimed.

'No,' replied Ram with unusual gravity, 'but this month I've got to send them everything. Otherwise our field will be lost.'

Sending them everything meant that for the past month he had cut his own food down to starvation rations: two or three *chapattis* and a cup of tea or a glass of sugar-cane juice a day.

AS SOON AS HE SAW the neighbour's boy running towards him, Hasari somehow knew. The news spread quickly round all the main rickshaw stations in the area and soon about thirty pullers had assembled in the little shed where Ram Chander lived. He was lying on the plank that had served as his bed for the five years he had spent in Calcutta. His shock of grey hair was like a halo round his head and his lips were shaped into one of his familiar mischievous grins. He looked as if he were enjoying the joke he had just played on his friends. According to the labourer who shared his lodgings, Ram had had several very violent bouts of coughing and had even vomited blood the night before. Then he had gone to sleep, and never woken up again.

It was left to his friends to carry out the funeral rites, and they took up a collection among themselves. Ram's neighbours also wanted to contribute, for Ram had been much loved in the neighbourhood.

Hasari went to the market with three other pullers to buy the items for the funeral rites: the litter to transport the body to the cremation grounds, incense sticks, four and a half metres of white linen, garlands of white jasmine and a clay pot with which to pour water from the Ganges into the mouth and over the head of the deceased.

The rickshaw pullers washed Ram and wrapped him in the linen shroud so that only his face and the tips of his feet were visible. Then they lifted him onto the litter. He was amazingly light, even for a rickshaw puller. Recently he had been obliged to turn down passengers who were too fat.

It took the group over an hour to cross the city with Ram's body. They sang hymns along the way. At the *ghat*—the cremation grounds—pyres were burning and several corpses waited on litters. The foreman in charge belonged to the Dom caste, the caste which specialises in the cremation of the dead, and before he allowed the pullers to cremate Ram, he demanded a hundred and twenty rupees for wood. (Wood for a cremation is very expensive, so indigents and those without families are simply thrown into the river without being burned.)

Hasari went down to the river to fill the clay pot with water and each puller let a few drops fall onto Ram's lips. The Brahmin attendant recited the ritual *mantras*, then they placed the body on the pyre and covered it with sticks of wood.

As the final moment drew near, Hasari felt his throat tighten. Images flooded through his mind: his first meeting with Ram when they took the injured worker to the hospital, the bottle of *bangla* they drank together afterwards, their visit to the rickshaw owner's representative. Ram had been like a father to him and now, without him, Hasari felt like an orphan.

Since Ram had no family in Calcutta, the Brahmin asked Hasari to light the pyre and complete the ritual. As he did so, Hasari wished Ram a good journey and that he might be reborn with a better *karma*: in the body of a *zamindar*, for example, or that of a rickshaw owner. When only ashes were left, the group went down to the Hooghly River and scattered them on the current so that they would be borne away on the great Ganges to the eternity of the oceans.

There remained just one last rite. To conclude that sad day the pullers went to one of the numerous dives that were open day and night in the vicinity of the cremation *ghats* and ordered plenty of bottles of *bangla* and a feast of curd, rice, *dal* and pastries—a rich man's feast in honour of a poor man's death.

FOR TWO DAYS, in the Muslim quarter of the City of Joy, the women had been unpacking the festive clothes they had so religiously preserved. The men had strung garlands of multicoloured streamers across the alleyways. Electricians had installed loudspeakers and strings of coloured light bulbs. Their poverty and anguish forgotten, the fifty thousand Muslims in the slum were preparing to celebrate one of the most important events in the calendar—the birth of the prophet Muhammad.

The poor adorned themselves for the occasion like princes. Hindu women assisted their Muslim neighbours in cooking the traditional feasts. Others, armed with combs, flowers and ribbons, helped with hairdos. Others brought saffron, carmine and henna to embellish their friends' faces and arms with skilful motifs. The children were made particularly elegant. With their eyes accentuated with great rings of kohl, their skinny bodies draped in shiny silk tunics and muslin veils, and their feet tucked into Turkish slippers, they looked as if they had just stepped out of *A Thousand and One Nights*.

A joyful crowd filled the square in front of the Jama Masjid, the City of Joy's main mosque, and then moved off in a parade headed by a blind mullah, a venerable patriarch in a white silk turban. Above their heads fluttered a multitude of green-and-white flags, red banners marked with the crescent of Islam, and streamers decorated with verses from the Koran and the golden cupolas of the sacred mosques in Jerusalem, Medina and Mecca— symbols that illuminated their decaying surroundings with faith and dreams.

Blaring from a motorcycle sidecar equipped with a loudspeaker, a litany of canticles was taken up by thousands of voices. Every two minutes the mullah stopped, took the microphone, and chanted invocations to the faithful. Soon the cortege extended for more than a kilometre and a half, a prodigious stream of colour flowing between the walls of the hovels and suffusing the slum with light, noise and religious fervour.

From the doorway of his hovel, Kovalski watched with amazement as the procession passed by. The pinks, blues and golds of the girls' costumes, and the boys' embroidered muslin shirts and braided toques, were an enchanting medley of colour. How, he wondered, could so much beauty spring out of so wretched a place? The sight of the children was particularly compelling. 'Thank you, Lord, for having given these people so much strength to believe in you and love you,' the priest murmured softly to himself, overwhelmed.

Suddenly, he heard someone calling him. It was Sabia's mother. 'Big Brother Stephan,' she said, 'Sabia was very fond of you and I would like you to bless my son before he is taken away.' The boy had died at the very moment the procession of the Prophet was passing the hovel that had sheltered his agony.

Even in her pain, Sabia's mother retained her extraordinary dignity as she cleared a way for Stephan between a crowd of mourning women. He found the child swathed in a white shroud, a garland of yellow marigolds on his chest. His eyes were closed and his face had relaxed into an expression of utter peace. With his thumb, Stephan Kovalski traced the sign of the cross on the boy's forehead. 'Goodbye, my glorious little brother,' he whispered.

'Kites were favourite toys, as if somehow those scraps of paper soaring high above the rooftops carried the children's dreams of escaping their prison of mud, fumes and poverty.'

Rickshaws were invented in Japan at the end of the eighteenth century by a European missionary. They derive their name from the Japanese *jin riki shaw*, 'vehicles propelled by man'. The first rickshaws appeared in India around 1880 and it was not long before they became a common sight in Calcutta.

'Marvellous children of the City of Joy. Their freedom from care, their zest for life, their magical smiles and dark faces set off by luminous gazes coloured the entire world in which they lived with beauty.'

A street herbalist sets up his dispensary.

6

The death of young Sabia changed the attitude of Stephan's neighbours. Even the most mistrustful now greeted the priest with 'Salaam, Father!' The children squabbled over who would carry his bucket on the way to the fountain.

Another event completed the transformation. A few doors away from Stephan's room lived Banno, a girl of fifteen who had been blinded by an infection. Her eyes were so painful that she cursed the world and everything in it. Finally, her mother came and stood before Stephan Kovalski, her hands joined together in supplication.

'For the love of God, do something for my daughter,' she implored.

The only drugs Stephan had were a few aspirin tablets, some vitamins, and a stray tube of some sort of ointment. In desperation, he decided to apply a little of the ointment to the girl's eyes. Three days later the infection had vanished, and by the end of the week young Banno had recovered her sight. The news spread like wildfire. 'There's a white wizard in the neighbourhood!'

The incident earned Stephan not only acceptance in the slum but a degree of notoriety which he could well have done without. Dozens of the sick and ailing made their way to 49 Nizamudhin Lane. He was forced to seek out more medicines, and his room became a haven for people in the direst straits. 'Jesus of Anand Nagar, every day I try to share in the plight of the poor,' Kovalski wrote in the notebook he used as a diary. 'I am only a poor sinner like all the rest and sometimes I am crushed or despised like my brothers here. But no one can take away the joy that fills me, because you are truly present, here in the depths of this wretched slum.'

Suddenly, Kovalski found himself credited with any good thing that happened in the community, like the decision of the Calcutta government to dig ten new wells, or the exceptionally mild winter. For the impoverished occupants of his neighbourhood, Stephan became the ultimate intercessor, one who could do anything because of his white skin, the cross that he wore on his chest, and his wallet which, for people with nothing, must have seemed as fat as that of a millionaire.

The notoriety exasperated Kovalski. He did not want to be Santa Claus, a welfare department, nor Divine Providence. All he wanted was to be a poor man among the poor. His ambition was to give these people faith in themselves, so that they would feel less abandoned and want to undertake actions to improve their own lot.

One evening some of his neighbours walked into his room led by Margareta, the young widow who had brought Stephan the bread for his first Mass.

'Stephan, Big Brother,' she declared, 'we want to discuss how we can do something useful for the people here.'

Then she introduced a young Hindu couple, an Anglo-Indian Christian, a Muslim labourer, and an Assamese girl in her twenties—six poor people who wanted to restore their own dignity and build something together.

Shanta and Ashish Ghosh, the Hindu couple, were attractive and bright. With her red cotton veil and smooth clear skin, Shanta looked like a Renaissance madonna. She was the eldest daughter of a poverty-stricken peasant. Her husband, Ashish, a gentle, bearded young man with curly hair, was one of the eleven children of an agricultural labourer. The couple were unique in that they had married for love. Their defiance of tradition had caused such a scandal that they had been forced to flee their village and seek refuge in Calcutta.

After starving for nearly a year, Ashish had found a job as a teacher's assistant in one of Mother Teresa's training centres for handicapped children. Shanta taught in the Howrah area. After the birth of their first child they had found their El Dorado: a room in a Hindu compound in Anand Nagar. In the slum, the Ghoshes were privileged people, which made their readiness to serve others all the more remarkable.

The Anglo-Indian they brought with them, grandly named Aristotle John, was a small man with a sad face and a worried air. He worked as a switchman on the railway. The fifty-two-year-old Muslim, Saladdin, had a short moustache and wore an embroidered skullcap on his head. He had been in the slum the longest of the group. After escaping the massacres during Partition, he had shared a hovel for twenty years with three mullahs for whom he acted as cook.

To build something together! In this 'gulag' where seventy thousand people fought each day for survival, where hundreds of people still died each year of tuberculosis, leprosy, dysentery, and all the diseases caused by malnutrition. In this environment so polluted that thousands never reached the age of forty, there was everything to build: a dispensary and a leprosy clinic were needed; a home for malnourished children; drinking-water fountains; more latrines and sewers. The urgent requirements were countless.

'I suggest we each make an individual survey,' said Kovalski, 'to determine our brothers' most immediate problems.'

The results came in three days later. They were identical. The sustenance the slum people sought was not for their children's frail bodies, but for their minds. All six surveys revealed that the most urgent demand was for a night school where children employed in the workshops, stores and teashops could learn to read and write.

Kovalski gave Margareta the task of inviting the families concerned to find a hut to serve as a classroom, and he offered to share in the remuneration of two teachers. He had achieved his main objective. The people of Anand Nagar were taking charge of their own lives.

Anyone could attend the meetings of the committee, and soon the news spread: 'There are actually people willing to listen to the poor.' Stephan christened his little team the Listening Committee for Mutual Aid. It, too, was a revelation: people discovered that there were others even worse off than themselves.

The priest made it a rule that each meeting should begin with a reading from the Gospel. Hindus, Muslims, Christians, all men of goodwill could understand the link between the message of the Gospel and their lives of suffering, between the person of Christ and those who had taken it upon themselves to continue His work.

No one seemed to feel this link with greater intensity than the young Assamese girl who had come that first evening to offer her services to Kovalski. With her plait hanging down her back, her slanted eyes and pink cheeks, she looked like a little Chinese doll. Her name was Bandona, which means 'praise God'.

Her father was a peasant who had worked a small terraced plot, painfully wrested from the hillside in the shadow of the foothills of the great Himalaya mountain range. Entrepreneurs from Calcutta began cutting the wooded jungles and the peasants were compelled to venture further and further afield to find wood to cook their food. Since the vegetation no longer had time to recover before the monsoon came, erosion ravaged the soil, and in a matter of years the whole region had become a desert. For those who lived there, there was no alternative but to leave the land for the city which had ruined them.

Bandona was four years old when her family set out for Calcutta. They were lucky enough to find a room in Anand Nagar. Five years later her father died of tuberculosis. Her mother had brought up her four children by retrieving metal from the rubbish heaps and selling it to a dealer. At the age of twelve Bandona started work in a shop that turned out parts for trucks. From then on she was her family's only support, for her mother, too, was struck down with tuberculosis. Bandona left home at five in the morning and rarely got back before ten o'clock at night. Sometimes she would not come home at all: power cuts often forced her to sleep at the foot of her machine so that when the electricity was restored she could make up the time lost. She earned four rupees a day, which barely enabled her to pay the rent and guarantee her mother and brothers a bowl of rice or two *chapattis* a day.

Now some donations from Europe, channelled through Stephan, made it possible for Bandona to leave the workshop and work full-time for the Listening Committee for Mutual Aid. No one had a better understanding of sharing and of dialogue, of respect for other people's faiths, than Bandona. Her extraordinary capacity to communicate opened all doors to her. Two or three times a week, she would accompany sick and dying people to the hospitals, steering them through the terrifying traffic and guiding them through corridors and packed waiting rooms. In such institutions, an indigent person without an escort had almost no chance of actually reaching an examination room. And even if he did, he could not explain what was wrong or understand the treatment he should follow because, nine times out of ten, he couldn't speak the particular dialect of Bengali the doctor spoke. Demanding, storming doors, forcing entry, Bandona fought like a wild animal to have her sick people treated like human beings.

In a few weeks the girl became the strength and heart of the Listening Committee. Her memory was a card index of all the miseries in the slum, but it was the quality of her smile, her love, that earned her the title, '*Anand Nagar ka Swarga Dug*'—the 'Angel of the City of Joy'.

One evening, returning from a trip to a hospital, Bandona burst into Stephan's room to tell him that a doctor had diagnosed a fatal skin disease on a pregnant woman. Only a serum made in England could possibly save her.

'Stephan *Daddah*,' she pleaded, 'please have the medicine sent over immediately. Otherwise that woman and her baby will die.'

The next day Kovalski went to the post office and sent a telegram to the head of his fraternity. With luck the serum would arrive in a week and, sure enough, a week later Stephan received a slip from the Calcutta customs asking him to come and pick up a parcel.

That was the beginning of an odyssey he would not soon forget.

THE CALCUTTA CUSTOMS OFFICE, a crumbling old building, was a shrine to bureaucracy. Brandishing the slip for his parcel of medicine, Stephan swept into the first office, then stopped in his tracks, transfixed. Before him was a battlefield of ancient tables and shelves, sagging beneath mountains of dogeared files and yellowing paperwork tied vaguely together with bits of string.There were piles of ledgers, all of which appeared to have been chewed by rats and termites, and some of which looked as if they dated back to the previous century. Even the cracked concrete of the floor was strewn with papers.

A dozen officials were seated in the middle of this chaos, beneath a battery of fans which kept sending the papers into a whirl of confusion. While some scrambled to catch documents as if they were chasing butterflies, others jabbed a single finger at antique typewriters, pausing after each letter to verify that they had actually managed to hit the right key. Some were reading newspapers or sipping tea. Others were asleep, their heads on the papers that covered their desks.

The entrance of a foreigner aroused only slight interest, but eventually a little man with bare feet passed by, carrying a teapot. He jerked his chin in the direction of an official who was typing with one finger. Stepping gingerly round stacks of files, the priest made his way over to him and handed him the slip he had received in the mail. The official examined it at length, and then enquired, 'Do you like your tea with or without milk?'

'With,' replied Kovalski, somewhat taken aback.

The man rang a bell and a shadow emerged from among the mountains of files. The official ordered tea for the priest, then consulted his watch. 'It's nearly lunchtime, Mr Kovalski. Afterwards, it'll be a bit late to find your file before the office closes. Please come back tomorrow morning.'

'But it's a very urgent consignment of medicine,' protested the priest. 'For someone who could die without it.'

The official assumed a compassionate air. 'Drink your tea. We'll do everything we can to find your parcel as quickly as possible.' With these words, he got up and left.

Next morning at exactly ten o'clock, the time when all administrative offices in India open, Kovalski was back. Some thirty people were already waiting. Just before he reached the head of the queue, he saw the same official get up and leave for lunch, just as he had done on the previous day. Kovalski rushed after him. Still with the same courtesy, the man pointed to his watch with a grave expression: it was midday. Stephan pleaded with him; the official remained inflexible. Stephan decided to stay and wait, but the official never reappeared.

As luck would have it, the next day was Saturday. On Monday, after three more hours of waiting in line, Stephan found himself once more before the same official.

'Good morning, Father!' he cried in a friendly way. 'Do you like your tea with or without milk?'

But this time he actually got up and headed for a metal cabinet. He strained at the handle, and when the door finally did turn on its hinges, the cabinet expelled an avalanche of files, ledgers and notebooks, almost burying the unfortunate official. Had there not been a life at stake, Stephan would have burst out laughing.

The official began to thumb through the pages of several of the ledgers, and suddenly Kovalski saw his finger stop. He leaned forward and read his name. This discovery propelled the official in the direction of another sea of papers. With the dexterity of a pearl fisher, he took out a yellow-covered file on which again Kovalski deciphered his name. But then, as if exhausted by the effort of his find, the official straightened up, consulted his watch, and sighed. 'Father, we'll continue after lunch.'

That afternoon the man looked more forbidding. 'The information in the ledger does not correspond to that on your slip,' he announced. 'It'll have to be verified in another ledger.'

Two more days passed. No one could find the correct ledger. On the eighth day, the official demanded forty rupees from the priest to assign two more employees to search for the right references. Two more weeks went by. After six weeks had elapsed, Stephan had given up all hope. Then he received a further notice in the mail, inviting him urgently to come and clear his parcel. By some miracle Bandona's sick woman was still alive, so Stephan set out.

The same official received Stephan with all the transports of affection befitting an old friend. He asked for another thirty rupees for revenue stamps, then told Stephan to fill in a series of forms to establish how much duty he was to pay. The final sum was three hundred and sixty-five rupees—three or four times the value of the medicines.

Clasping his precious receipt to his chest, Kovalski accompanied the official down two floors to a storeroom where mountains of parcels and crates were piled high on shelves. The official asked a uniformed customs officer to fetch the package of medicine. Moments later, Stephan at last saw the precious object, a box no bigger than two packets of cigarettes. It was like a mirage, the promise of a miracle. He held out his hand for it.

'I'm sorry, Father,' apologised the uniformed customs officer, studying the label. 'But I can't let you have this.' He pointed to a door with a sign: GOODS INCINERATOR.

'The date for your medicine expired three days ago,' he explained, heading for the incinerator. 'We're obliged to destroy it. That's an international regulation.'

The official, who until now had remained silent, grabbed the tail of the man's shirt. 'This Father is a holy man,' he protested. 'He works for the poor. He needs that medicine to save the life of an Indian woman. You must give it to him.'

The uniformed customs officer surveyed Stephan's patched shirt.

'You work for the poor?' he repeated respectfully. Stephan nodded. Then he watched as the customs officer crossed out the word 'expired'.

'Father, don't tell anybody about this. May God bless you.'

But despite the medicine, Bandona's protégée died. She was twenty-eight years old, a widow, and she left four orphans. However, in an Indian slum, such a qualification didn't really apply to any child. When parents died they didn't leave orphans behind: other members of the family or, in the absence of any relatives, neighbours would adopt them at once.

The young woman's death was very quickly forgotten. That was another characteristic of the slum. No matter what happened, life went on with an energy and vigour that was constantly renewed.

IT WAS WHEN HE RETURNED home that morning from the customs office that Stephan Kovalski heard the news. Selima, the pregnant wife of his neighbour Mehboub, had disappeared.

The young woman had been discreetly approached by Mumtaz Bibi, one of her neighbours, three days earlier at the fountain. Her face pockmarked from smallpox, this portly woman was something of a mystery figure. Although her husband was only a simple factory worker, she lived in the alley's only brick house and from her ceiling hung a rare and wondrous ornament: an electric light bulb. It was said, too, that she owned a number of rooms in the surrounding area, yet no one knew exactly where her money came from.

'Stop off at my house on your way home from the fountain,' she had said to Selima. 'I have an interesting proposition for you.'

Selima did as she was asked. The young woman had become little more than a shadow since her husband had lost his job. Her beautiful face was haggard, and she, who had always borne herself with such dignity in her worn sari, now walked like an old woman. Only her taut belly remained unaffected, and she carried it with pride, for it meant that she was pregnant with her fourth child.

Mumtaz Bibi had prepared two small cups of tea with milk. She motioned for her visitor to sit down.

'Are you set on keeping that?' she asked, pointing at Selima's belly. 'If you'd agree to sell it to me, I could make you a good deal.'

'You want me to sell you my future child?' stammered Selima, flabbergasted.

'Not your child,' the fat woman corrected her, 'only what you've got inside you at the moment. And for a good price: two thousand rupees.'

The opulent Mumtaz was carrying on the very latest of Calcutta's clandestine professions: the sale of human embryos. The mainsprings of the industry were a network of foreign buyers who scoured the Third World in order to supply international laboratories and institutes for genetic research. They used the embryos either for scientific work or in the manufacture of rejuvenating beauty products for a clientele of privileged people. The demand had produced a lucrative trade in Calcutta.

Mumtaz assumed a maternal tone. 'Think hard about it, little one. You already have three children. Your husband's out of work and your family doesn't eat every day. This is perhaps not the time to add another mouth to your household. Whereas, you know, with two thousand rupees you can fill plenty of plates with rice.'

Poor Selima knew that only too well. Finding just a few peelings and scraps to put on her family's plates was her daily torture.

'But what will my husband say when I come home with two thousand rupees and nothing in my...?'

The dowager gave her a sly smile. 'I'll give you the two thousand rupees in small instalments. Your husband won't need to know how you lost it, and you'll be able to buy something to feed your family every day.'

ALL DAY AND ALL NIGHT Selima was haunted by that visit. Everything inside her seemed to protest against the horrible exchange. She could never agree to what amounted to murder, not even for two thousand rupees. But then there were other voices that haunted Selima in the night, the familiar voices of her three small children crying with hunger. At dawn she made her decision.

It was all fixed for two days later. The place into which Mumtaz and the middleman took Selima had few pretensions to the title of clinic. It consisted of a single room divided in two by a curtain. One half served as a reception and treatment area, the other as an operating room. The surgical equipment was basic: a metal table, a fluorescent light, one bottle of alcohol and one of ether on a shelf. There was no oxygen and no reserve supply of blood.

Nauseated by the smell of ether from the floor and walls, Selima sank down on a stool beside the table. The act that she was bracing herself to have performed seemed to her progressively more monstrous, yet she approached it with resignation. 'This evening my children will be able to eat,' she kept telling herself.

The surgeon called for the operation was a man in his fifties with a receding hairline and large hairy ears. He asked Selima to lie down on the table and examined her attentively. Behind him, the middleman was growing impatient. 'What are you waiting for, Doctor?' he said.

The surgeon opened his bag, slipped on a gown, soaked a large piece of cotton wool in ether and placed it over Selima's nose and mouth, then took up his scalpel. Twenty minutes later, mopping up with gauze compresses the blood flowing from the uterus, he placed the embryo in the hands of the middleman. It would have been a boy.

It was after he had cut the umbilical cord that disaster struck. A reddish bubbling issued from Selima's womb. The surgeon tried to compress the lower abdomen with a very tight bandage. Then he felt for the abdominal aorta and pressed with all his might in an attempt to stop the haemorrhage. But without a massive dose of coagulants, his efforts were in vain. He tried to find Selima's pulse, but it was almost imperceptible. At that point, he heard a door bang behind him and turned round. The middleman had left with the embryo, followed by Mumtaz Bibi. The surgeon spread the dying woman's old sari over her, then took off his blood-soaked gown and folded it carefully. He arranged his instruments in his surgical case, and he too left.

Selima remained alone until the sole employee of the 'clinic' arrived, a stunted little man with bushy eyebrows and a hooked nose. He knew a useful address where they cut up unidentified corpses to recover the skeletons for export.

7

From the outside nothing distinguished the little colony by the railway lines from other quarters in the slum. The same compounds in a square round a courtyard were to be found there, with the same sort of laundry drying on the roofs and the same open drains. But this was a very special ghetto, for it was here that the City of Joy's six hundred lepers lived.

One of the lepers, Anouar, had no legs and propelled himself around on a wooden platform with wheels. He had reached the advanced stages of his illness and was going through utter torment. There was nothing more that could be done for him since the disease had reached his nerves. When the pain became too intolerable he would have himself carried to

145

Nizamudhin Lane, where Kovalski would give him a shot of morphine.

Although the lepers were free to go about the slum, an unspoken code forbade them to enter the compounds of the healthy. By entering Stephan Kovalski's room, Anouar had broken the rule, and the infraction could have cost him his life. There had already been several lynchings in the slum. Though they would give alms to lepers to improve their own *karma*, most Indians looked upon leprosy as a curse of the gods.

One day when Stephan encountered Anouar in an alleyway, the leper looked unusually preoccupied.

'What's wrong, Anouar?' Stephan asked.

'I'm fine, Stephan *Daddah*. But my neighbour, Saïd, is not too good. You ought to come and see him. He's so ill he can't eat or sleep.'

Stephan Kovalski promised to come that afternoon.

What Stephan discovered was not so much a leper colony as a chamber of horrors. Were those skeletons, consumed with gangrene, really human beings? Saïd, Anouar's friend, a man of barely forty, was left with no hands and no feet. Leprosy had also eroded his nose and eaten away his eyebrows. But when Anouar performed the introductions, Saïd turned his blind face towards the priest and Stephan detected a smile on it.

'Stephan, Big Brother, I'm fine,' he assured him. 'You shouldn't have taken the trouble to visit me.'

Examining Saïd's arm, Stephan realised that it was gangrenous and that Saïd was beyond all treatment. He filled a syringe with morphine and found a vein beneath the hard, cracked skin. He could do nothing more.

Nearby, a woman was stretched out on a rough bed with a baby boy lying next to her. Kovalski bent over and picked up the child. He was amazed at the force with which the boy's sturdy little hand gripped his finger. 'He's going to be a big fellow,' he promised the mother. The leper woman turned away and Kovalski thought he had hurt her. An interminable moment passed as she made no move to take back her son. She was crying. Finally, she pushed away the sheet and held out her mutilated arms. Kovalski placed the child carefully at her side. Then, joining his hands in the Indian gesture of salutation, he left without a word.

Outside, a crowd of cripples, blind men and amputees waited to receive a blessing from the 'Big Brother' who had dared to enter their ghetto. Afterwards, Anouar led Stephan to a compound where leper musicians performed a concert for him on flutes and drums. Everywhere he went in the leper colony, people came out of their hovels. His visit was turning into a fête. Anouar led the way, propelling himself along on his platform with great pride at acting as guide for his 'Big Brother Stephan'.

'Stephan *Daddah*, come and sit over here,' he ordered at last, gesturing towards a mat of jute sacks that a woman had just unrolled for him in one of the courtyards. Several lepers scrambled to settle themselves next to him. That was when he realised that he was being invited for a meal.

Kovalski thought he had come to terms with everything about poverty, yet he admitted later that he felt revolted by the idea of sharing food with these, the most bruised of his brothers. What a long way I still have to go! he thought. He hid his uneasiness as best he could and soon the warmth of the lepers' hospitality dispelled it. Women brought bowls of steaming rice and vegetable curry, and the meal began. Kovalski did his utmost to forget the fingerless hands battling with balls of rice. His hosts seemed overwhelmed with gratitude. They were pariahs among the pariahs, and never before had a foreigner shared their food.

Kovalski was aware that leprosy was not a fatal disease, that, while it could not be cured, it was quite easily controlled provided it was treated in time. It was that day, confronted by the sight of so much mutilation, that he made his decision. He would set up a leprosy dispensary in the City of Joy, a clinic with people who knew how to handle the disease.

Next day Stephan Kovalski climbed aboard the bus that went across the Hooghly. He was going to the south of Calcutta to lay his plans before the only person in the city who could help him to implement them.

LIKE A FLOWER straining towards the sun, the sugarloaf-shaped dome of the temple of Kali rises from a confusion of alleyways, houses and stores. This high place of Hinduism, built near a branch of the Ganges, is the most frequented shrine in Calcutta. Day and night, crowds of the faithful swarm inside and around its grey walls. It is also one of the most congested places in the overpopulated city. Hundreds of shops surround the temple and numerous funeral corteges wend their way between the cows, the dogs, the children playing in the street, and the flocks of faithful worshippers. At the temple of Kali, the most vibrant life goes hand in hand with death.

Round the corner from the temple stands a long, low structure with windows covered by plaster latticework. There is no door in the imposing sculpted entrance. Anyone can enter at any time. A wooden board announces in English and Bengali: THE PLACE OF THE PURE HEART—HOME FOR DYING DESTITUTES.

Stephan Kovalski mounted the few steps and went into the building. An indefinable smell which even disinfectants could not obscure floated in the air. Once his eyes had grown accustomed to the dimness, he made out three rows of litters with thin green mattresses. Shadowy shapes moved silently between the rows. On the beds lay the fleshless bodies of men stretched out in various postures of agony. In a second room, rows of similar beds were occupied by women. On the wall was the framed text of a Hindu poem:

> If you have two pieces of bread,
> Give one to the poor,
> Sell the other,
> And buy hyacinths
> To feed your soul.

What struck Kovalski immediately was the serenity of the place. There was no horror here. No longer were the wretched people who had come to this place alone and destitute. They had found love and peace.

The one hundred and ten occupants of the Place of the Pure Heart owed that peace to the staunch little woman in a white cotton sari whom Stephan Kovalski spotted leaning over a dying man at the far end of the room. The entire world was beginning to recognise the name of this saint who picked up abandoned children and dying destitutes from the streets of Calcutta. She was Mother Teresa.

AGNES BOJAXHIU was born in Skopje, Yugoslavia, of Albanian parents. Her father was a prosperous merchant. She was attracted to the life of a missionary in India at a very early age. At eighteen, taking the name of Teresa in memory of a French saint, the Little Flower of Lisieux, she entered the Missionary Order of the Loreto Sisters and on January 20, 1931, she stepped off a steamship onto the quay at Calcutta. For sixteen years she taught geography to the daughters of well-to-do British and Bengali society in one of the most prestigious convents in Calcutta. One day in 1946, however, during a train journey to Darjeeling, a town on the slopes of the Himalayas, she heard a voice. God was asking her to leave the comfort of her convent, to go and live among the poorest of the poor. Having first obtained permission from the Pope, she began to wear a plain white cotton sari, and founded a new religious order whose vocation was to relieve the misery of the most neglected of mankind.

The home for the dying which Kovalski had just entered was born out of a particularly moving encounter experienced one evening by Mother Teresa.

It was in June 1952. The monsoon cataracts were beating down upon Calcutta with a noise that seemed to herald the destruction of the world. A white figure, stooping under the deluge, was skirting the walls of the Medical College Hospital. Suddenly she stumbled over something stretched out on the ground. She stopped, and discovered an old woman lying in a pool of water, hardly breathing. Her toes had been gnawed to the bone by rats. Mother Teresa scooped the woman into her arms and ran to the hospital. But when she went into a reception room and deposited the dying woman on a stretcher, an attendant intervened.

'Take that woman away immediately!' he ordered. 'There's nothing we can do for her.'

Mother Teresa picked up the dying woman and set off again at a run. She knew another hospital, not far away. However, the woman's body stiffened in her arms and she realised it was too late. Putting down her burden, she closed the dead woman's eyes and made the sign of the cross, as she prayed beside her in the rain.

The next day, she went to the town hall and besieged its municipal offices. This stubborn European nun in a white cotton sari was so persistent that one of the mayor's deputies finally agreed to see her. 'It's a disgrace that people in this city are forced to die in the streets,' she declared. 'Give me a house where we can help the dying to appear before God in dignity and love.'

A week later the municipality placed at her disposal a former rest house for Hindu pilgrims, next to the great Kali temple. At first, the intrusion of a nun adorned with a crucifix into a neighbourhood consecrated to the worship of Kali provoked only curiosity. Gradually, however, orthodox Hindus became indignant. Word spread that Mother Teresa and her Sisters were there to convert the dying to Christianity. Incidents broke out. One day a shower of stones and bricks rained down upon an ambulance bringing a dying patient to the home. Mother Teresa dropped to her knees before the demonstrators.

'Kill me!' she cried in Bengali, her arms outstretched in a gesture of crucifixion. 'And I'll be in heaven all the sooner!'

Impressed, the rabble withdrew, but the harassment continued. Delegations from the neighbourhood presented themselves at police headquarters to demand that the 'foreign nun' be expelled. The chief of police promised to satisfy their demands but insisted upon first making his own enquiries. At the home for the dying he found Mother Teresa kneeling at the bedside of a man who had just been picked up off the street, a skeletal figure lying in a state of indescribable filth, his legs swollen with purulent sores. Dear God, he wondered, how ever can she put up with that? Mother Teresa cleansed the horrible wounds, applied antibiotic dressings, and promised the suffering man that he had nothing to fear, that he was loved. Her face was bathed in an extraordinary serenity and the chief of police found himself strangely moved.

'Would you like me to show you round?' she asked him.

'No, Mother,' he replied. 'That won't be necessary.'

As he emerged from the building, the neighbourhood's young fanatics were waiting for him on the steps.

'I promised you that I would expel this foreign woman,' he told them. 'And I will keep my promise. But not before you persuade your mothers and sisters to come here and do what she is doing.'

But the battle was not yet won. During the days that followed, troublemakers continued to throw stones. Then one morning Mother Teresa noticed a cluster of people outside the Kali temple. As she approached them she saw a man stretched out on the ground, a Brahmin of the temple. No one dared touch him: they knew he was suffering from cholera. She bent over, took the Brahmin in her arms, and carried him to the home for the dying. Day and night she nursed him, and eventually he recovered. One day he was to exclaim, 'For thirty years I have worshipped a Kali of stone. But here is the real Kali, a Kali of flesh and blood.'

Never again were stones thrown at the little Sisters in the white saris.

Caring for the dying destitute, however, was only a first step for

Mother Teresa. The living too needed care, among them the newborn babies who might be found in the morning on a rubbish heap, in a gutter, or in the doorway of a church. On February 15, 1953, Shishu Bhavan, the Children's Home, welcomed its first guest, a premature baby wrapped in a piece of newspaper, picked up from the pavement. He weighed less than three pounds and had not even the strength to suck at the bottle Mother Teresa gave him. The nun persisted, feeding him through a nasal tube, and won her first victory in this new haven of love and compassion.

Soon several dozen babies were packed into cots and playpens, with five or six more arriving every day. Her Sisters were worried. How was she going to care for so many people? Together with the occupants of the home for the dying, there were now several hundred mouths to feed. Mother Teresa's response was a luminous smile. 'The Lord will provide!' And the Lord did provide. Gifts poured in. Rich families sent their chauffeurs with cars full of rice, vegetables, fish.

Mother Teresa also constructed, on land lent by the railway company, a building of rough bricks and corrugated iron, in which she soon harboured hundreds of lepers, bringing them dressings, medicines and words of comfort each day. Next, she dispatched commando groups of Indian Sisters into the city with mobile clinics. Several small white vans bearing the emblem of the Missionaries of Charity patrolled the enormous city to bring treatment into the most neglected areas. It was one of these vehicles that Stephan Kovalski wanted to bring into Anand Nagar. Even better, he hoped two or three of Mother Teresa's Sisters would come to assist him in the running of the little leper clinic he planned to set up in the City of Joy.

He made his way between the rows of bodies and approached the kneeling figure. The nun was bathing the wounds of a young man who was so thin that he looked like one of the living dead in a concentration camp. Sensing a presence behind her, Mother Teresa stood up. She noticed the cross on Stephan's chest.

'Hello, Father,' she said. 'What can I do for you?'

Stephan Kovalski felt awkward. He had just interrupted a unique conversation. The eyes of the dying man seemed to be imploring Mother Teresa to bend over him once more. The priest introduced himself.

'I think I've heard people talk about you,' she said warmly.

'I've come to ask for your help, Mother.'

'My help?' She pointed towards the ceiling. 'It's God's help you want to ask for, Father. I am nothing at all.'

At that point a young American in jeans came over, carrying a towel. Mother Teresa handed him her washbowl and cloth and gestured towards the dying man. 'Love him,' she said. 'Love him with all your might.' Then she steered Stephan Kovalski towards a table and bench, where she listened as the Pole outlined his plan.

'Very good, Father, very good,' she commented in her picturesque accent, a mixture of Slavonic and Bengali. 'You are doing God's work. All right, Father, I'll send you three Sisters who are used to caring for lepers.'

A young Sister came over and spoke to Mother Teresa in a low voice. Her presence was needed elsewhere.

'Goodbye, Father,' she said. 'Come and say Mass for us one of these mornings.'

Stephan was overwhelmed. 'Bless you, Calcutta, for in your wretchedness you have given birth to saints.'

WITH ITS HANDLEBARS BRISTLING with headlights and horns, its thick wheels painted green and red, its tank a gleaming streak of silver, and its seat covered with panther skin, the motorbike was straight out of Hollywood. Dressed in leather trousers and a silk shirt, its owner roared through the muddy alleyways of the City of Joy. He was a strapping fellow in dark glasses who dispensed waves and smiles like a campaigning politician. His name was Ashoka, and he was the eldest son and first lieutenant of the local mafia boss.

Despite a population of more than seventy thousand, the City of Joy had no mayor, no police force, no legal authority of any kind. This gap had, however, been promptly filled by Kartik Baba the mafia godfather, who reigned supreme, directing affairs, extorting, arbitrating. A Hindu, with thick-lensed glasses, Baba lived with his sons and his wives in a modern four-storey house built on the edge of the slum on the other side of the main Calcutta–Delhi highway. He was about sixty and the name Kartik Baba had been given to him by his father as a tribute to the son of Shiva, god of war.

Practically all the clandestine drinking dens in the slum were his property. It was he who controlled all the drug traffic and local prostitution, and he was the largest real-estate owner in Anand Nagar. He had exercised great wisdom in choosing his tenants. Instead of refugee families, he much preferred cows and buffalo. Most of the cattle sheds, harbouring some eight and a half thousand head of cattle in the slum, belonged to him. This animal population, with its stench, its clouds of flies, and the river of liquid manure it discharged into the drains each day, went back to the days when, for reasons of hygiene, the municipality had banished cattle sheds from the centre of Calcutta. The animals had been rehoused in the City of Joy and other similar slums. The godfather had been one of the principal beneficiaries of this operation. It was more advantageous to house a cow than a family of nine people. As he himself said, 'For the same rent and the same amount of space, there are no complaints and no demands.'

Everyone knew that the godfather had plenty of other sources of revenue. Above all, he had one from which he derived considerable benefit: he exploited the lepers of Anand Nagar.

Not content merely to collect rent for their miserable shacks, he forced the leper beggars to pay him a daily tax of one or two rupees in exchange for his 'protection' and a place on the pavement at Howrah Station. Substantial political backing was necessary for the godfather actually to implement this, but rumour had it that he was a generous contributor to the coffers of the party in power, for which he also acted as a diligent electoral agent. Ballot papers in the City of Joy, even those held between wasted stumps, formed part of his trafficking. Strangely, the residents were not unhappy with this state of affairs. Since there was no other uncontested body of authority in the slum, they had frequent recourse to the godfather.

The presence of the godfather's son's motorbike outside Stephan's door one morning caused an enormous sensation in Nizamudhin Lane. Rumours flew: 'The godfather's picking a quarrel with Big Brother Stephan. The godfather wants to turn him out...'

However, this anxiety appeared unjustified. After prostrating himself respectfully before the priest, the godfather's messenger said, 'My father has asked me to deliver an invitation to you. He would like to discuss a small matter. Something quite insignificant...'

Stephan knew that nothing was 'insignificant' to the godfather, and that it was useless to stall.

'Fair enough,' he said. 'I'll follow you.'

Ashoka waved his large, hairy hands. 'No no! My father doesn't see people at just any time of day! He'll be expecting you tomorrow at ten o'clock. I'll come and get you.'

The following morning, the heir to the throne picked up Kovalski and the two men crossed the City of Joy on the bulky motorbike with all its sirens wailing. Stephan found the experience somewhat comical: he could imagine Father Cordeiro's expression if he could see him now.

The godfather's house was palatial. Outside the door three large American cars were parked, complete with radio antennae and protective screens at the windows. There were several motorbikes of the kind the police use to escort heads of state. Inside, the hall opened into a large room furnished with oriental rugs and comfortable cushions. A small altar with the images of numerous gods adorned one corner of the room. Sticks of burning incense exuded a heady fragrance.

The godfather was seated on a carved wooden throne inlaid with mother-of-pearl and ivory. He was wearing a white cap and a black velvet waistcoat over a long white cotton shirt. Tinted glasses with very thick lenses concealed his eyes but his reactions could be discerned by the puckering of his bushy eyebrows.

Ashoka motioned to Kovalski to sit on a cushion placed in front of his father, and left. Turbaned servants brought tea, iced lemonade, and a plate of pastries.

'Welcome to this house, Father,' the godfather said in a ceremonious and slightly hollow voice, 'and consider it your own. It is a very great honour to make your acquaintance.' One of the servants proffered a tray of cigars tied together in a bundle. The mafia boss untied the cord and offered a cigar to the priest, who declined it. The godfather took his time lighting his own.

'It has been reported to me,' he said, 'that you have made an application—I can't actually believe it!—for Indian citizenship.'

'You are very well informed,' the priest said.

The godfather chuckled and settled himself comfortably in his chair. 'If by any chance the response to your request is delayed, do let me know. I have connections.'

'Thank you, but I put my trust in the Lord.'

The godfather had difficulty believing what he had just heard: was it possible that this man was refusing his support?

'Father,' he said, 'I have heard some strange rumours. It would seem that you intend to create a leper hospital in the slum. Is that right?'

'"Leper hospital" is a very grand expression. It will be more of a dispensary to treat the worst cases. I've asked Mother Teresa for the help of two or three of her Sisters.'

The godfather surveyed the priest sternly. 'You know that no one can concern himself with the lepers in this slum without my authorisation.'

'In that case, what is keeping you from helping them yourself? Your assistance would be most welcome.'

The godfather's eyebrows puckered above his thick glasses. 'The lepers in the City of Joy have been under my protection for twelve years, and it's probably the best thing that has ever happened to them. Without me the other inhabitants would have thrown them out long ago.' He leaned forward with an air of complicity. 'My dear Father, have you asked yourself how the people next door to your dispensary will react when your lepers start to show up?'

'I have faith in the compassion of my brothers,' Kovalski said.

'Compassion? You holy men are always talking about compassion! All you'll get by way of compassion is a riot. They'll set fire to your dispensary and lynch your lepers!' The godfather took a long draw on his cigar. Then he said, 'I can see only one way for you to avoid all these problems. You will have to subscribe to a protection contract.'

'A protection contract?'

'It will cost you a mere three thousand rupees a month. Our rates are usually much higher, but you are a man of God and in India we respect what is sacred.' Without waiting for any reply, he clapped his hands and Ashoka came hurrying in.

'The Father and I have come to an amicable agreement,' the godfather announced with evident satisfaction. 'The two of you can agree on the terms and conditions.'

The godfather was an aristocrat. He did not concern himself with details.

THAT EVENING THE FOUNDERS of the Listening Committee for Mutual Aid met in Stephan's room to discuss the godfather's ultimatum.

'The godfather's family is all-powerful,' declared Saladdin, the old Muslim. 'We'll just have to pay.'

'All the same, three thousand rupees for the right to take care of a few lepers is exorbitant.' Margareta was indignant.

'Is it the sum that bothers you,' asked the priest, 'or the principle?'

She seemed surprised. 'Why, the sum of course!'

All the others shared Saladdin's view; all, that is, but Bandona. 'May God damn this demon!' she exclaimed. 'To give him one single rupee would be to betray the cause of all the poor.'

Her words mobilised Stephan. 'Bandona is right!' he cried. 'We must fight, resist him. We will show our people that they are no longer alone. It's now or never.'

Early next morning, Ashoka's giant motorbike halted outside Stephan's room. As his father had ordered, Ashoka had come to discuss the payment terms for the 'contract'. The meeting, however, lasted only a few minutes, just long enough for the priest to communicate his refusal to the young ruffian. It was the first defiance ever laid before the authority of the all-powerful head of the mafia in the City of Joy.

One week later the little dispensary was ready to receive the first lepers. Bandona and a number of volunteers set out to bring back the six urgent cases Kovalski wanted to hospitalise first, while he himself went to Mother Teresa's to collect the three Sisters who were to nurse them.

Bandona's group had hardly reached the square on which the great mosque stood, when they were intercepted by a commando group of young thugs, armed with sticks and iron bars.

'No one's going any further!' shouted the leader, a pimply adolescent whose front teeth were missing.

Bandona tried to move forward but an avalanche of blows stopped her. At the same moment Stephan arrived from the other end of the slum, accompanied by the three nuns. A second gang had begun using iron bars and pickaxes to ransack the old school that was to serve as the leper clinic. Terrified, the neighbourhood shopkeepers hastily barricaded their shop windows. When the destruction of the dispensary was complete, a third gang appeared carrying explosives. The street emptied in a flash and a series of detonations shook the entire neighbourhood, echoing far beyond the boundaries of the City of Joy.

At Stephan's side, Mother Teresa's Sisters began to recite the rosary aloud. Stephan led them into Margareta's compound, entrusted them to her protection, then ran in the direction of the explosions. When he heard someone call his name, he stopped and turned round to find that Margareta was hurrying after him.

'Stephan, Big Brother,' she pleaded. 'For the love of God, don't go any nearer! They'll kill you!'

154

As they stood there, a crowd of demonstrators turned in from the road that skirted the slum, bearing banners with slogans in Hindu and English: 'No leper hospital in Anand Nagar!' A man with a megaphone marched in front chanting other slogans that the horde behind him picked up: 'No lepers here! Father Sahib go home!' These were not neighbourhood people. Calcutta has the largest reserve of paid demonstrators in the world. Any political party or organisation can rent a thousand of them, at five or six rupees per head per day.

As soon as he spotted the emblem of Indira Gandhi's party on the demonstrators' banners, the local Communist Party representative ran as fast as his crippled leg would allow to alert a few comrades. In less than an hour, the Anand Nagar Communists had mounted a counter-demonstration. Now, nothing could contain the fury of the men and women stampeding through the slum. There was a savage clash under a deluge of tiles, bricks and Molotov cocktails thrown from the rooftops. Caught up in it, Stephan and Margareta found themselves in the thick of the throng. Stephan saw before him the bleeding face of his father on the evening when police and striking miners had battled near the coalpits. But this confrontation was even more vicious.

Dozens of wounded fell on all sides. Kovalski saw a child of four or five pick up one of the projectiles lying beside a drain. The device exploded, tearing off his hand.

A few seconds later, the priest saw an iron bar flash above Margareta's head. He had just time to throw himself in front of her and deflect the blow. Already another assailant was bearing down on them with a knife. At the instant the man was about to strike, Kovalski saw someone seize his attacker by the collar and hurl him back. He recognised Mehboub, his former neighbour. Following Selima's death, the Muslim had entrusted his elderly mother and his children to the care of his son, Nasir, and disappeared. Now he had surfaced here as a henchman of the godfather.

Suddenly, Kovalski saw the thickset silhouette and dark glasses of Ashoka, the godfather's eldest son. He was issuing orders, and the attack stopped short as if at the wave of a magic wand. The combatants put up their arms, turned on their heels and walked away. In minutes the groans of the wounded, the bricks and debris cluttering the road, and the acrid smell of smoke were the only signs that a battle had just taken place.

Stephan Kovalski had been given due notice: no one in the City of Joy could defy the godfather with impunity.

8

Fifty thousand bombs dropped on each of the fifty thousand rickshaws in Calcutta could not have caused more of an uproar. The rickshaw owners had just announced that they were going to increase the daily rent paid by the pullers from five rupees to seven, starting the next day.

For the pullers it was the worst blow inflicted by the rickshaw owners since the confrontations of 1948, when the owners had demanded that every vehicle bring in two sets of fees, one for daytime use and the other for night-time. This had caused the first strike, which had ended with victory for the human horses and the formation of the Rickshaw Workers' Union, affiliated to the Indian trade unions.

This new and exorbitant increase in rent was hitting the pullers with tremendous force, and so it was that from street to street, from square to square, the city began to resound with a strange concert. Tap, tap, tap— the haunting, angry sound of bells struck against the wood of rickshaw shafts.

'Some men have knives to defend themselves, or guns,' Hasari Pal told Aloka later that day. 'All we had was a ball of copper the size of a betel nut. But that little bell was the voice of the rickshaws of Calcutta—our voice. And our voice must have made a real din, because the owners' representatives moved in quickly to explain why their bosses had decided to raise the rent. Shouting above the sound of the bells, Musafir, my owner's representative, challenged me. "Do you know, Hasari, how much it costs nowadays to change the spoke in a wheel or put on a new hood?" he said.

'An argument started, but as everyone was shouting at the same time it was impossible to make yourself heard. Then Golam Rassoul, the secretary of our union, arrived and the noise stopped. Despite his small build—he looked like a sparrow that had fallen out of its nest—he confronted the whole line of owners' representatives. "Go and tell your bosses to cancel their rent increase. Otherwise there won't be a single rickshaw left on the streets of Calcutta."'

It was a call to strike. The representatives disappeared to report to their owners. Pullers came running with their rickshaws from every corner of the city and soon the Park Circus esplanade was so packed with people that trams and buses couldn't get through. A few police vans showed up and tried to get the traffic moving again, but they could do little in the face of such an enormous crowd.

The unhappy look of the representatives when they came back told the strikers the bad news: the owners were sticking to the increase. Rassoul stood up on a rickshaw with a loudspeaker and spoke to the crowd. He said that many of them had lost their land, and that if the hope of earning a living by pulling their rickshaws was taken away, there would be nothing left for them to do but die. He pointed out that they were numerous and strong enough to make the owners back off. And he concluded by asking those in favour of an unlimited strike to put up their hands.

The pullers looked at one another in silence, wondering who among them could face a single day without the means of earning his living. Does a bird saw through the branch he's sitting on? They knew they could be reduced to skeletons before the owners lost a single roll off their paunches. And yet they had no real choice. A fellow next to Hasari, known as Scarface, put up his hand. He had been so named because a blow from a policeman had smashed his cheek in. He coughed like Ram Chander, and Hasari, watching him, thought that strike or no strike would make very little difference to this man. But after that, other hands went up. And more. Finally, one by one, all the hands went up, including Hasari's.

Then an overwhelming feeling of revenge came over the pullers and they began to move in procession towards Chowringhee Road. They were suddenly the masters, those pullers of men, the ones whom taxi, bus and truck drivers insulted, the ones whom the cops tormented and beat, the ones whom passengers were always trying to cheat out of a few paisas. Not a single vehicle could pass through the city centre any more, blocked as it was by fifty thousand or more rickshaws.

The union leaders distributed posters all along the route, announcing that the rickshaw pullers of Calcutta were rejecting the new increase in rents. Passers-by watched in astonishment. Never before had they seen so many rickshaws at once.

The throng of pullers walked, chanting slogans and jangling their bells. It was as if they were drunk. They shouted without thinking. They shouted because they were all poor men who had come together, to shout together.

Their destination was the Sahid Minar, a column on the Maidan that soars so high that it seems to pierce the clouds. At the base of the column was a platform decorated with red flags. Abdul Rahman, the president of the union, arrived. He was a plump little man and some of the strikers thought that he couldn't have pulled many rickshaws, unless of course it was during some other life. A dozen men cleared a way through the people, and he waved his hand as he passed. On his fingers several gold rings with enormous jewels glinted in the sunlight. He too climbed onto the platform, but when he spoke Hasari couldn't follow what he was saying very well because he spoke mainly in Hindi. However, Hasari managed to make out that the president was telling them that the bosses were inflicting starvation on them, that they were building their own futures out of the pullers' sweat and blood, and that this would go on just as long as the government refused to expropriate the carriages and give them to the people who actually had to pull them.

After Abdul Rahman, the representatives from other unions all spoke. However, it was not long before the pullers realised that the speeches were doing nothing more than preventing them from earning their living that day and that the next day would be the same. They were asking themselves just how long they could hold out. At the end of all the speechmaking, Abdul Rahman asked them to sing the workers' song with him. Hasari had never heard of such a song, but the people on the platform began it and thousands of voices joined in. Hasari's friends told him that it was the song of workers all over the world. It was called 'The Internationale'.

THE STRIKE HAD PARALYSED Calcutta's most popular means of transport. But a strike is a rich man's weapon. The finest resolutions don't last long when your belly is gripped with hunger cramps, and the rickshaw owners knew that only too well. After only two days some pullers picked up their shafts again. Others followed, and soon all the pullers were back on the road chasing after clients, even doing bargain-rate runs to get something to eat right away. And they were forced to pay the new rent.

'Despite all their speeches, their promises and their red flags, we were snared like pigeons in glue,' Hasari Pal said, after the elections that brought the Left to power in Bengal. The new government quickly passed a law that obliged the courts to order not only the seizure of rickshaws operating without official permission, but their actual destruction.

Among the pullers there were several theories to explain this law having been passed. The man they called Scarface believed that if the government officials wanted to burn all unlicensed rickshaws it was because the officials themselves did not want competition. He had learned that several of them had their own rickshaws to exploit. On the other hand, Golam Rassoul, the union secretary, claimed that the people responsible for the persecution were the city officials who felt that rickshaws had no place in the Calcutta of the future. Their Calcutta would be one of machines, not human horses. Five thousand more taxis and buses would be better for everybody than the sweat of a hundred thousand workers.

For whatever reason, the law was implemented and unauthorised rickshaws were confiscated. No puller dared use the main avenues where there were traffic policemen. Other policemen began to check on them at the stands.

'Let me see your licence,' an officer would say to the first puller in line.

'I haven't got a licence,' the puller had always apologised in the past, taking a few rupees out of the folds of his *longhi*. But now, the policeman would pretend not to see the notes, for he was under stricter orders. Soon, outside all the police stations were long snaking lines of rickshaws stacked up against each other, their wheels shackled with chains. But as long as they were there, there was still the hope that one day they would be restored to those for whom they provided a livelihood. Even that hope was soon crushed.

As the law required, the courts ordered the destruction of the confiscated rickshaws. One evening they were all loaded onto municipal rubbish carts and taken to an unknown destination. Rassoul followed the trucks and soon the pullers learned that their rickshaws had been taken to the city's public dump, probably to be burned.

It took less than an hour for the pullers to assemble in a major demonstration. Led by Scarface and the union staff, the column set out on a march to the dump, shouting, 'Our rickshaws are our rice!' As they advanced, other workers joined them: in Calcutta, demonstrating helped one to forget an empty stomach.

They marched for miles, through the outermost suburbs of the city, until finally they reached an enormous mound of putrescent garbage on which dozens of trucks and bulldozers moved about in a cloud of nauseating dust. Flocks of vultures and crows circled above the dump. There were so many of them that the sky was as black as a monsoon day.

The confiscated rickshaws were on the far side of the dump, in a long snake of wheels and shafts slotted into one another. Hasari wondered how God could have allowed them, the poor men's only means of putting rice into their families' mouths, to end up like this.

What happened next was to remain the most terrible sight of Hasari's life. Behind the rickshaws were concealed three police vans. When the procession spilled onto the dump, the policemen, a special antiriot unit with helmets, guns and shields, surged out of their vehicles to block their way. They had been ordered to drive back the demonstrators and carry out the total destruction of all the rickshaws.

Rassoul shouted through the loudspeaker that the rickshaw pullers had come to oppose this destruction. Some of the policemen advanced, brandishing their guns, but not a single puller faltered. Suddenly, one of the policemen lit a torch and plunged it into the body of a rickshaw, right in the middle of the line. The flames immediately set the hood and seat ablaze, then spread to the next vehicle. After one stunned second, the people in the front ranks of the procession hurled themselves at the wall of policemen, trying to push the burning vehicles away, to save the others. But the police formed an impenetrable wall.

At that, Scarface, who had been marching beside Hasari, let out a great shout. He managed to hoist himself up onto a comrade's shoulders, then he stood up and leaped clean over the wall of policemen. The demonstrators saw him launch himself onto the line of burning carriages, trying to topple them into the ravine that encircled the dump.

It was a mad thing to do and the policemen only watched in astonishment. A scream went up from the blazing mass of rickshaws. Hasari saw Scarface's arm and hand reach out to grasp one of the shafts. Then smoke enveloped the scene and the smell of burning flesh mingled with the stench of the dump.

Silence fell over the scene. All that could be heard was the crackling of the flames as they consumed the rickshaws. Officialdom had won.

When the fire at last died down, Hasari found an empty jar on the dump. With it, he collected a few of Scarface's ashes from the cinders. He and his comrades would scatter them on the waters of the Hooghly, which flowed into the sacred River Ganges.

HASARI PAL RETURNED to the rigours of his life as a human horse. The situation on the streets of Calcutta seemed to grow worse daily. Bottlenecks immobilised traffic more and more frequently, and at times advancing just one step was a major feat. Everywhere swarms of

This family have managed to find a doorway as their residence.

Pulling a rickshaw in the congested streets of Calcutta can be a very dangerous occupation.

'With its handlebars bristling with headlights and horns...Ashoka's motorbike was straight out of Hollywood.'

Mother Teresa and her Sisters of Charity, in their white saris, bring aid and love to the destitute people of Calcutta.

'Rag-pickers from the City of Joy scrabbled, located, sorted and stowed away their booty as fast as they could. Bottles, parts of cooking utensils and crockery, broken tools, old tubes of toothpaste, run-down batteries, empty tins and scraps of clothing and food all went into their baskets.'

pedestrians competed with rickshaws for a share of asphalt in streets disrupted by frequent burst water pipes or drains. Things seemed to crack and crumble a little more each day. There were clients too, who pricked Hasari in the stomach with the point of a knife and demanded the day's takings; drunkards who paid with their fists; elegant memsahibs who cheated him out of a few paisas.

Taxi drivers were also a real problem, most of them with no sympathy whatsoever for the human horses. Riding along like rajahs in their black-and-yellow chariots, they never missed an opportunity to assert their superiority. One day, in a traffic jam, one of them nudged Hasari and his rickshaw into a gutter. And then something amazing occurred. The driver, a small, bald man with a scar round his neck, actually stopped to apologise. He too, it seemed, was a Bengali, and he helped Hasari extricate his rickshaw from the gutter and even suggested sharing a bottle of *bangla* with him.

The taxi driver was named Manik Roy. He had been a bus driver, until one night a gang of thieves had stopped him on the road. They made him and his passengers get out, relieved them of their possessions, then slit their throats. By some miracle, Manik had been found alive the following day, but as a reminder of that night he bore an impressive scar on his neck and was nicknamed Chomotkar, which means literally, 'Son of Miracle'.

In Hasari's eyes that man was to become the 'son of miracle', indeed, but for quite another reason. One morning, on his way back to Park Circus, Hasari heard a squeal of tyres as a taxi stopped beside him. It was Son of Miracle.

'Just the person I was looking for!' he called out. 'I've got great news for you, but first you'll have to buy me a drink.'

He swept Hasari into an alley where he knew a clandestine drinking den. There he ordered two bottles of *bangla*. After his first glass his eyes began to sparkle.

'One of my neighbours, Ashish Ghosh, is leaving Calcutta and going back to his village,' he said. 'So his room will be free. It's a solidly built room, with a real roof, walls and a door. I thought of you right away!'

That day Hasari asked the clerk in the post office to add a short message for his father to the money order he sent each month. He wrote, 'We are well. I am earning my living as a rickshaw puller.' Then he hurried back to the pavement where he was still camping with Aloka and his children to announce the good news that they had found a place in a slum.

ASHISH AND SHANTA GHOSH, the young Hindu couple on Stephan's committee, visited him one evening to announce some news. 'We've decided to leave the slum and go back to our village,' said the young man.

From beneath her red veil, Shanta watched for the priest's reaction.

Dear God, thought Stephan, this is the happiest news I've heard since I came to the City of Joy. If people actually start going back to their villages, we're saved!

'For three years now we've been saving up paisa after paisa,' Shanta said. 'And we've been able to buy some good land near our village.'

'We're going to have a big pool dug out in the middle, to breed fish,' Ashish explained.

'And the water will let us irrigate our land so we will have a second harvest in the dry season,' added Shanta.

Stephan could not conceal his joy. He was witnessing a kind of miracle, the miracle of which thousands of people compelled to take refuge in Calcutta dreamed.

'Above all,' Ashish said, 'we want our return to bring something to the people of our village. The Bengal earth could yield three harvests if it were properly irrigated. I shall try and form a cooperative.'

'And I shall start a craft workshop for the women.' Shanta's dark eyes glowed.

'May God bless you,' the priest said at last. 'For once, light and hope will spring forth from a slum.'

'KEEP OUR LEAVING a secret?' exclaimed Ashish Ghosh. 'In an ants' nest where everyone spends his time spying on everyone else? You know it's impossible!'

Son of Miracle nodded his head. The taxi driver knew very well that his young neighbour was right. The slum was a cauldron in which people simmered together. Every activity of life, even the most intimate, took place here with the full knowledge of everybody else. Nevertheless, he had hoped that the fact of a vacancy could be kept secret until he had had time to negotiate with the landlord for Hasari Pal. He might as well have tried to prevent the day from dawning!

The impending departure of the Ghoshes soon became the sole topic of general conversation. So many aspiring successors to the hovel crowded round the Ghoshes' door that the landlord himself, a corpulent Bengali, turned up unexpectedly. Even the foulest hovel in the City of Joy had a legitimate owner. Some of them even had four, one for each wall.

The fact that the landlord had appeared in person did not bode well at all, Son of Miracle knew. Sure enough, it was not long before the owner informed him that instead of thirty rupees a month, the room would cost the next tenant sixty, an outrageous price for one room with no electricity and no windows. Sixty rupees were, of course, quite beyond the miserable means of a rickshaw puller.

Son of Miracle would not admit defeat. 'We must get the godfather to help,' he told Hasari Pal. 'He's the only one who can cut down that pirate's demands.'

'Do you really think the godfather would put himself out over so trivial a matter?' asked Hasari.

'Of course he will! Doesn't he call himself the protector of widows and orphans, the guru of the poor?'

Son of Miracle requested an audience with the godfather, and two days later an envoy came to fetch him. He underwent the same ritual as had Kovalski. When the godfather's eldest son appeared to conduct the visitor into the vast reception room, Son of Miracle stared, wide-eyed with wonder. The godfather sat enthroned at the far end of the room on his inlaid armchair. His dark glasses and heavy jowls gave him the air of an ageing toad. Without a word, he jerked his chin towards the taxi driver to indicate that he was ready to listen.

Son of Miracle presented his request eloquently. After a very few minutes the godfather raised his fat, hairy hand. He signalled to his son to approach the throne and whispered to him the price of his intervention. Protector of the poor or not, the godfather is like a racehorse: he doesn't run without his oats, thought the taxi driver as he counted out the sum demanded.

ON THE MORNING of the Ghoshes' departure, the landlord burst into the compound accompanied by half a dozen thugs. He carried an enormous padlock to secure the door of the vacant hovel, and was about to use it when Ashoka arrived at the head of a gang armed with clubs. Pushing the owner and his guards aside, they stationed themselves in front of the hut. Fighting broke out between the groups, and women fled, screaming. Roof tiles began to fly, followed by pails and bricks.

At this point the godfather made his appearance. Dressed in an immaculate white *dhoti* and gilded sandals, carrying an ivory-handled cane, he was flanked by two bodyguards. The fighting stopped instantly. The godfather advanced towards the landlord, entrusted his cane to one of his guards, raised both his hands to the level of his face and joined them in a gesture of salutation.

Then, taking back his cane, he pointed the tip of it at the large black padlock the landlord was gripping. With a small movement of his head, he ordered one of his guards to take possession of it. The landlord bade the godfather a respectful farewell and withdrew with what was left of his escort. The godfather then made a tour of the compound to savour his power, caressed the cheeks of a number of children in their mothers' arms, and departed.

Son of Miracle was exultant. He had lived up to his name. It was true that the price of the godfather's intervention had been very high but the result was well worth the sacrifice. His friend Hasari would at last be able to escape the degradation of the pavement and settle with his family in a compound in Son of Miracle's own neighbourhood: a four-star compound where the houses were built of mud and bricks, and topped with proper roofs. Even better, Hasari's home carried the bonus of an authentic white-skinned holy man as an immediate neighbour.

THE PALS LEFT THEIR PAVEMENT discreetly, under cover of night. No sooner had they piled their meagre possessions into the rickshaw and turned the corner of the street than a new refugee family moved in to take their place.

Son of Miracle was waiting for Hasari and his family at the entrance to their new home. The residents of the compound immediately formed a circle round the somewhat dazed newcomers and the taxi driver made the introductions. He had bought several bottles of *bangla*, and glasses circulated from hand to hand. The unofficial head of the compound pronounced a few words of welcome and clinked glasses with Hasari, who was overwhelmed by the warmth of the reception.

Stephan Kovalski joined in this little celebration. The Pals would now be among his nearest neighbours, and his stomach had survived so many onslaughts it could certainly put up with a few mouthfuls of alcoholic poison. Not everyone, however, had his powers of endurance. Stephan saw Hasari's pupils dilate suddenly. Before anyone had time to react, the rickshaw puller staggered and fell to the ground, where he was shaken by convulsions. Stephan fell on his knees and raised the sick man's head. A reddish froth appeared at the corners of Hasari's mouth. The residents of the compound realised then that it was not the *bangla* that was making their new neighbour ill. He had the red fever—tuberculosis.

THAT EVENING, as the sun's disc was vanishing beyond the mantle of smoke that imprisoned the slum, the sound of a horn tore the priest away from his meditation before the picture of the Sacred Shroud. As soon as Hasari had regained consciousness, he had decided to honour his new dwelling with a *puja*. He had placed incense sticks in the hinges of the door and in the four corners of the room. Then, as thousands of millions of Indians had done each evening since the dawn of history, he blew into a conch to draw down upon himself and his family 'the beneficent spirits of the night'. Stephan prayed with a particular fervour that this cry might be heard. But for some time the gods of the slum had seemed to be suffering from a cruel deafness.

That year, summer struck like a bolt of lightning. In a matter of seconds, night fell in the middle of the day. Panicking, the slum dwellers rushed out of their compounds and into the alleys. From his doorway, where he was sorting medicines, Stephan saw an atmospheric disturbance such as he had never seen before. A wall of suspended particles of yellow sand was bearing down upon the slum with lightning speed. There was no time to take shelter before the tornado devastated everything in its path, tearing off the roofs of houses and throwing their occupants to the ground. The

165

slum was immediately covered with a shroud of yellow dust. Then a succession of flashes lit the darkness, and a bombardment of hailstones was followed by a torrential downpour.

When the sun finally came out again, the thermometer rose from fifteen to forty degrees Celsius, and the seventy thousand inhabitants of the City of Joy realised that the short winter truce was over. The blazing inferno of summer was with them once more.

Summer inflicts unimaginable suffering upon the occupants of this part of the world. In the windowless hovels crammed with up to fifteen people, in the tiny compounds scorched for twelve hours a day by the sun, in the narrow alleys where there is not the slightest breath of air, the summer months are as much a form of torture as hunger itself.

In the avenues of Calcutta, policemen directing traffic are equipped with linen parasols, attached to their belts in order to leave their hands free. Other people shelter themselves beneath umbrellas, briefcases, newspapers, books, or the tails of their saris or *dhotis* raised over their heads. The furnace-like heat is accompanied by humidity that often reaches 100 per cent. The least movement—a few steps, going up a staircase—drenches people in perspiration. The asphalt on the streets becomes liquefied tar which scorches strips of flesh from the soles of bare feet.

Pulling a rickshaw on this fiery carpet was an act of pure heroism, and to protect his feet, already ulcerated and burned, Hasari Pal, for the first time in his life, put on the beautiful pair of sandals he had received as part of his wife's dowry. They parted company with his feet on the first patch of burning asphalt, sucked off by melting tar.

For six days the inhabitants of the City of Joy held out; then they began to die. With lungs burned by the torrid air and bodies dried of all substance, a host of babies, and those who suffered from tuberculosis and asthma, were the first to succumb. The members of Stephan's committee ran from one end of the slum to another to help the most desperate cases.

Strangely enough, it was the priest who, though used to a more temperate climate, seemed best able to resist the rigours of the blazing heat. With his burning-hot metal crucifix dancing on his bare chest, his waist and thighs swathed in a cotton *longhi* and his head covered with an old straw hat, he looked like a convict from Devil's Island.

On the tenth day, the thermometer at the old Hindu's teashop reached forty-two degrees Celsius. So numerous were the victims of sunstroke and dehydration that the alleys were strewn with people incapable of even standing up. The perpetual dampness helped spread a series of malaria, cholera and typhoid epidemics that decimated families. But it was gastroenteritis that claimed the most victims. It could kill a man in less than twenty-four hours.

Then, because of the lack of dressings and antibiotics, outbreaks of boils, carbuncles, and a fungus disease called mycosis hit the slum. The bodies of Mehboub's children became open sores, and Mehboub himself,

166

who had returned home, fell victim to a painful outbreak of carbuncles which the priest had to lance with a penknife.

One morning, as Kovalski was shaving, the mirror cast a shock back at him. His skin had assumed a waxlike hue. It was stretched over his bones like a piece of old, shining oilcloth. His cheeks were deep-sunken and two heavy furrows had appeared round his mouth.

Several weeks later, Kovalski felt under his armpits and on his stomach the beginnings of an intense itch that within a few hours extended to every part of his body. He could not resist scratching himself and soon he was covered with sores. Suffocating with heat and drained of all strength, he remained prostrate in his room. However, a slum is not like a Western city where a man can disappear or even die without his neighbour noticing. The first person to be perturbed by Kovalski's failure to emerge from his room was Nasir, Mehboub's young son. He ran to inform Bandona and in a matter of minutes the whole neighbourhood knew that Big Brother Stephan was sick.

Only a place where men live in such close contact with death could offer so many examples of love and solidarity, thought the priest, on seeing Surya, the old Hindu from across the way, coming into his hut with a pot of tea and a plate of biscuits. A few moments later Sabia's mother brought in a bowl of 'ladies' fingers', green vegetables that look like large beans. Bandona arrived next and she diagnosed the ailment at a glance: the Pole was being devoured by tiny mites called *acari*, which produce a painful skin disease which was ravaging the slum.

'Big Brother Stephan,' clucked Bandona, 'you've got scabies!'

At the end of April the thermometer rose several more degrees, and with this new assault a sound that usually formed part of the background to life in the City of Joy was silenced. The only birds in the slum, the crows, ceased to caw. Some days later, their corpses were found on the roofs and in the compounds: thin traces of blood trickled from their beaks. The heat had burst their lungs.

Then the month of May ended with a terrible premonsoon storm, during which the level of the drains and the latrines rose by more than half a metre in one night. The corpses of dogs, rats, scorpions and thousands of cockroaches began to float around in the foul sludge. Naturally the floodwater invaded most of the hovels, transforming them into cesspools.

Yet, in the very midst of the horror, there was always some kind of miracle to be found. The one which Stephan Kovalski experienced in the depths of his hut on that Whit Sunday took the form of 'a little girl in a white dress, with a red flower in her hair, who picked her way through all the horror with the regal air of a queen'.

THE CITY OF MIAMI, Florida, lies approximately eight thousand miles west of Calcutta. In reality, however, the gulf separating these two cities would be better measured in light-years. Certainly, Miami possesses slums almost as poverty-stricken as those of Calcutta, but it also harbours islands of wealth and luxury beyond the wildest imaginings of most inhabitants of Calcutta. One of them is King Estates, a vast, elegant marina nestled among palm trees and clusters of jacaranda, a haven for multimillionaires. Most houses have swimming pools, tennis courts and private docks from which cabin cruisers and yachts ride the bright blue sea. Several properties have heliports, others polo fields with stables to accommodate several dozen horses.

One of King Estates' most distinguished residents was Arthur Loeb, a well-known surgeon. His Mexican hacienda with its luminous white walls, its colonnaded patios and its fountains, was among the development's showpieces. A giant of a man, his red hair barely flecked by grey, Loeb ran a luxurious Bel Air clinic where he treated diseases of the respiratory system with techniques that were at the cutting edge of medical science.

Loeb had a twenty-five-year-old son, Max, who was, like his father, a redheaded giant covered in freckles. Max was about to receive his degree from the Tulane University medical school in New Orleans. In two years, after he had completed his internship, he intended to specialise in thoracic surgery. He was a source of enormous pride to his father and his decision to specialise in chest surgery seemed to promise that Loeb's Bel Air clinic would one day pass into his hands. Until, that is, Max delivered some startling news to his unsuspecting father as they walked side by side one sunny spring morning.

'Dad, I'm leaving the country.'

Arthur Loeb turned to face his son. 'What do you mean, you're leaving the country?'

'I'm going to India for a year.'

'What about your internship?'

'I've asked for a deferment.' Max tried to remain calm. 'I need a change of air ... and I want to be of service to someone.'

'What do you mean "you want to be of service"?'

'Just that. To help people who need help.' Max knew he couldn't beat around the bush any longer. 'I've been invited to work in a dispensary in Calcutta,' he said.

The word Calcutta stunned Arthur Loeb. 'Calcutta! Of all places, Calcutta!' he repeated, shaking his head. 'Is that the best place you can find to exercise your talents? And do you really think that the medical establishment is going to keep a place warm for you until you get back?'

Max made no reply.

'Does your mother know?'

'Yes.'

'And she approves?'

'Not exactly ... but in the end, she seemed to understand.'

'And Sylvia?'

Sylvia Paine was Max's fiancée, a beautiful, tall blonde girl of twenty-three. Her parents owned the property next to the Loebs in King Estates.

'Yes, she knows,' replied Max.

'And what does she think of this idea?'

'She suggested she come with me!'

SIX WEEKS AFTER that conversation, Max Loeb flew to Calcutta. On his last evening in Miami he took Sylvia to dinner at The Versailles, a fashionable restaurant in Boca Raton. There, he ordered a bottle of Bollinger and Sylvia proposed a toast to the success of his mission and his earliest possible return. She was wearing a low-cut pink linen dress with a simple string of pearls round her neck. Her hair, caught up in a chignon, set off her neck and the superb bearing of her head. Max could not take his eyes off her.

'You're so beautiful,' he said. 'How am I going to manage without you?'

'Oh, you'll find plenty of beautiful Indian girls. I hear they even know how to prepare special drinks that make you fall madly in love with them.'

Max thought of the slum Stephan Kovalski had described in his letter, but the idea of arousing Sylvia's jealousy was not altogether unpleasant. He had said nothing to his fiancée of the deeper reasons for his decision: there were some actions in life, he thought, that did not call for explanation. But now, on this last evening, he decided to admit the truth. 'Just in case anything should happen to me, I want you to know that I'm not going off on a whim,' he said.

He told Sylvia how, one day in the Tulane library, he had come across a photograph of a child on the cover of a magazine published in Canada by a humanitarian organisation. The child was a little Indian boy of five or six, and he was sitting in front of the crumbling wall of a house in Calcutta. What struck Max was the boy's smile, a tranquil, luminous smile which revealed four shining teeth. He was completely naked and in his arms he was clutching a baby, only a few days old and wrapped in pieces of rag.

'He was holding it with so much pride,' Max said, 'with such an obvious sense of his responsibilities, that for several minutes I couldn't take my eyes off him. He was from the "City of Joy", and the baby in his arms was his little brother. The journalist who took the photograph wrote in his article about his visit to the slum and his encounter with a "white apostle" who had come to live among the world's most underprivileged people. The white apostle was Stephan Kovalski. In answer to one of the journalist's questions, Kovalski had expressed the wish that someone with advanced medical training would come to Anand Nagar for a year to help him to organise proper medical services for the slum.

'I wrote to him,' concluded Max. 'And he replied that he would expect me as soon as possible.'

A SHARP DECELERATION thrust Max backwards in his seat. The wing of the Boeing had just tipped towards the ground, revealing an enormous city traversed by a brownish-coloured river, a city with contours rendered indistinct by the shroud of smoke that blanketed its entanglement of roofs. As the flight attendant announced that the aircraft was about to land in Calcutta, Max made out the Gothic bell tower of a cathedral, the stands of a racecourse, and red double-decker buses moving along an avenue. Finally, the Boeing levelled off and landed.

As soon as the door was opened, the heat surged into the plane. 'I felt as if I was being hit by a blast from a giant hair dryer,' Max wrote to Sylvia. 'For a moment I found myself struggling to catch my breath. Then, when I got out onto the gangway, I was blinded by the fierce reflection and had to hang on to a rail.'

Moments later, in the confusion of the arrivals terminal, Max spotted a garland of yellow flowers held aloft. It was Stephan Kovalski, brandishing a welcoming garland in traditional Indian style. The two men recognised each other instinctively. Their greetings were effusive but brief.

'I suggest I take you to the Grand,' said Stephan as they climbed into a taxi. 'That's the local luxury hotel. I've never actually set foot inside it but I imagine it's a more suitable place than the City of Joy for a first encounter with the realities of this city.'

The young American was perspiring more and more heavily. He knew the priest was right: it would make sense to acclimatise himself rather than go straight from a millionaire's playground in Miami to the depths of hell. But after a moment's hesitation, he turned abruptly to his companion. 'I'd rather come with you to Anand Nagar,' he said.

An hour later, the new friends were facing each other across a table, in the flickering light of one of the slum's eating places.

'Buffalo stew?' asked the American, daunted by the look of the strange mixture one of the young waiters had placed before him.

'Not real "stew",' Stephan corrected, mopping greedily at his plate. 'Just the sauce. There isn't any meat in it. But the bones, skin and marrow have been so well simmered that it's full of protein. And for thirty paisas you can hardly expect duck pâté, can you?'

Max made a face that spoke eloquently of his repugnance.

'I think you should realise that we were lucky to get a table,' added Stephan, eager to portray his slum in the best possible light. 'This is actually the Maxim's of the neighbourhood!'

Twenty or so other customers were eating their meals amid a din of voices. They were all factory workers without families. The establishment belonged to a baldheaded Muslim named Nasser, who presided over his steaming cauldron like a Buddha behind an incense burner. He oversaw a dozen employees. Five of them were slum children, the eldest no more than eight years old. They worked from seven in the morning till midnight for their food and a monthly salary of ten rupees. Barefoot, dressed in rags, they ran to fill buckets at the well, wash the tables, chase the flies away, and serve the meals. Three other workers, in charge of cleaning the vegetables, were mentally deficient. Nasser had picked them up when they were begging on the Great Trunk Road.

Stephan wondered what effect the surroundings were having on this American who had just landed from a different world. He knew from experience that it would be a long and difficult adjustment for the young doctor. But an event was to take place that first evening which would plunge Max Loeb into the very heart of his new surroundings. Stephan had just ordered his companion an Indian dessert when a small man burst into the restaurant, threw himself at Kovalski's feet and spoke to him urgently in Bengali, his hands joined in a gesture of supplication. Max noticed that several fingers were missing from both his hands.

'How much do you know about obstetrics?' Stephan asked, getting quickly to his feet.

Max shrugged. 'Only what I learned at medical school ... not much.'

'It's got to be better than nothing. It seems our friends here have a little surprise to welcome you. They want to give you a brand-new baby!'

Wading up to their calves in sludge, Kovalski and Loeb moved cautiously behind the messenger. From time to time they stumbled on something soft—the carcass of a dog or a rat. Darkness falls early in the tropics and the night was black as ink.

'Duck!' Stephan called, saving Max from cracking his skull against a fat bamboo beam. He added, 'You have to get used to bending down around here ... At least it's good for your humility!'

Max bent again to enter a courtyard full of people. They were chattering noisily, but the arrival of the two foreigners brought instant silence. By the flickering light of a candle, the American made out noseless faces and the stumps of limbs moving about like those of marionettes, and realised that he was in the leper quarter of Anand Nagar. A grey-haired old man led the two men towards a small room from which feeble groans were issuing. Someone brought a candle and Stephan recognised a pale face with deep-sunken eyes.

'Meeta!' he exclaimed, astonished.

Meeta was the youngest daughter of a refugee potter from East Pakistan. At the age of sixteen, when her parents were about to arrange for her marriage, the girl had discovered a small whitish patch on her right cheek that was insensitive to the touch. After weeks of hesitation, she went to the hospital. The verdict was immediate: it was a patch of leprosy. As far as her parents were concerned, God had cursed their daughter. They banished her from the family hut.

Reduced to begging round the train station, Meeta was picked up by a procurer, who sold her to a brothel in Calcutta. When the proprietor discovered that his new girl was a leper, he beat her and threw her out. She was picked up half dead by some rag-pickers and taken to Mother Teresa's home. The Sisters nursed her back to health and afterwards she once more took up begging near Howrah Station. It was there that Anouar, Kovalski's leper friend, had found her. He became her protector, and one year later, he married her.

The young woman looked exhausted. She opened her eyes with difficulty, but when she saw Stephan's turned-up nose and the familiar forehead with its receding hairline above her, her mouth formed a faint smile. 'Stephan, Big Brother,' she sighed feebly.

She reached out for him, as Max started a hurried examination.

'We'll have to move quickly!' the American declared a few minutes later. 'If not, they've both had it!' He had discovered that the baby was wedged halfway out of the uterus. 'Have you got anything to strengthen her heart?'

Kovalski foraged in the bag that was his constant companion, and in which he always carried a few emergency medicines. He took out a bottle. 'I've got some Coramine.'

Max grimaced. 'Nothing stronger? An intravenous cardiac stimulant?'

The question seemed so incongruous to the priest that, despite the circumstances, he could not help laughing.

'What do you think I am, a Miami drugstore?'

The American apologised with a slightly forced smile, and Stephan asked for a cup of water into which he poured the medicine. Kneeling at the bedside of the young leper woman, he supported her head and helped her to drink slowly.

'Tell her to start pushing again, as hard as possible,' Max ordered.

Kovalski translated this and Meeta contracted her body, panting with effort. Tears of pain rolled down her cheeks.

'No, not like that! She's got to push *down*. Tell her to take a deep breath first and then push hard as she breathes out. Hurry!'

The temperature was at least forty-four degrees inside the hut. Max mopped his face and neck. A rancid taste rose in his throat. Was it the heat, the buffalo stew, or the sight of all those mutilated bodies? He was gripped by a terrible desire to vomit. Seeing him turn white as a sheet, Stephan emptied the remainder of the Coramine into the cup from which Meeta had been drinking.

'Get this down you, quickly!'

Max stared at him. 'Are you out of your mind?'

'You can't catch her sort of leprosy. It's not contagious.'

Max raised the cup to his lips, closed his eyes, and drank the contents down in a gulp. He felt better. Bending over to examine the woman more closely, he could see that the child was positioned the wrong way. There was only one way of saving it: he would have to turn it.

'Do you think it's still alive?' Stephan asked.

'I can't tell without a stethoscope.' Max put his ear to Meeta's stomach, then straightened up with an expression of disappointment.

'Can't hear a heartbeat! But I can't be sure, since it's turned the wrong way. Tell her to push harder!'

The Coramine was taking effect; Meeta's contractions were coming with increased vigour.

'Go round the other side,' Max said to Kovalski. 'While I try to turn the baby, you massage her stomach to help the downward motion.'

As soon as Stephan was in position, the doctor slid his hand in behind the baby's neck. Meeta groaned. Max's hand had just reached the baby's shoulder when two balls of fur brushed against his head and landed on Meeta's stomach. In the framing of the hovel's roof, some rats had taken shelter from the heatwave. They were as large as cats. In his astonishment, Max withdrew his hand. Was it his abrupt movement or the shock of the creatures' landing? One thing was certain: the baby's body righted itself.

'Push, push!' cried Max. Ten seconds later, a magnificent boy weighing at least six pounds emerged into his hands. Max lifted him up like a trophy. The baby's mouth opened to let out a cry that raised an amazing echo in the courtyard of the compound. One of the women tied off the cord with a piece of jute. Another brought a basin to wash the child.

Since no Brahmin priest would enter a leper compound, the honour of undertaking the first rite that follows the birth of a child fell to Stephan Kovalski. He felt someone touching his feet and, looking down, saw Anouar, who had just entered the room on his wooden platform. The leper raised his stumps to his forehead as a mark of respect.

'Stephan, Big Brother, you've given me a son. A son!' he exulted. Paralysed with anxiety, Meeta's husband had kept out of the way until this triumphal moment. Now, he brought a bowlful of rice grains as an offering to the priest. 'Put the rice next to my boy,' he said, 'that the gods may grant him a long and prosperous life.'

In his first letter to Sylvia, Max Loeb described the demonstrations of joy that followed. 'All the lepers joined in the celebration. Withered hands flung themselves round my neck. Pitted faces embraced me. Cripples clapped their crutches together like drumsticks. "*Daddah*, Big Brother, God bless you!" the people cried. Children brought biscuits and sweets. Stephan seemed completely at home. He grasped the fingerless hands held out to him, while I confined myself to joining mine together in the beautiful gesture of greeting that I had seen people use at the airport. And the cries of that newborn baby filled the night—my first night in Calcutta.'

10

'It's not exactly the Miami Hilton,' Stephan apologised, 'but just keep telling yourself that people here live twelve to fifteen to a room half as large as this.'

Max grimaced as he inspected the room Stephan had found for him in the very heart of the City of Joy. Yet, compared to many others, it was a princely lodging, complete with a cupboard, a table, two stools, and on the wall a calendar depicting a fine, chubby baby. It even boasted a window opening onto the alleyway, and its floor was raised so that it was, in theory at least, protected from the monsoon floods.

Bandona arrived and Max was charmed by the oriental beauty of the young Assamese girl.

'Welcome to Anand Nagar, Doctor,' she said shyly, offering the American a bouquet of jasmine.

Max breathed in the strong scent of the flowers and for a second he forgot his surroundings, the noise, and the smoke from the *chulas* which was stinging his eyes. He was transported thousands of kilometres away. The perfume was identical to that of the tuberoses which in springtime swathed the terrace of his home in Florida.

It took Bandona only a few minutes to make the American's room more welcoming. Moving as noiselessly as a cat, she unrolled a mat, lit several oil lamps and some incense sticks, and put the flowers in a copper pot on the table. Then she looked up at the ceiling.

'And you up there, I'm ordering you to let the doctor sleep! He's come from the other end of the world and he's very tired.'

That was how Max discovered that he was, in fact, to share his room. He heard a croaking noise and Bandona laid a hand on his arm with an expression of joy.

'Listen, Doctor,' she urged, cocking her head. 'It's the *tchik-tchiki*. He's greeting you.'

Max looked up at the roof and saw a green lizard looking solemnly down at him.

'That's the best omen you could have,' announced the young woman. 'You will live for a thousand years!'

MAX LOEB'S ROOM became the City of Joy's first clinic. From seven in the morning till ten at night this single room was to become waiting room, consulting room, nursing ward and operating theatre combined, a room full of suffering and hope for the slum dwellers.

Max's table and bed were used for both examination and treatment. There was no steriliser and the only instruments were a few tweezers and scalpels. There was a fairly good stock of bandages, gauze and cotton wool, and Stephan had passed on to Max a gift from one of his sponsors: several boxes of sterilised compresses for the treatment of burns. The priest had spent three agonising days arguing with customs officials before obtaining their release *without* paying four hundred rupees in duty and bribes.

It was medicines that Max lacked most. All he had was a small amount of sulphone for the lepers, ryfomicine for tuberculosis patients, quinine for malaria, some ointments for skin diseases, and a few vitamins for those children who were suffering most acutely from malnutrition. Finally, there were about ten antibiotic capsules for cases of infection.

Stephan asked Bandona to assist Max. Only someone as shrewd as the young Assamese girl could sift out those who were really sick from those who just wanted to visit the 'big daktar' from America, and sort out the emergency cases, the chronically ill and the incurable.

A tidal wave descended on the clinic. Mothers thronged through the door with children covered in boils, abscesses, anthrax, scabies, sick from every possible disease caused by the heat and the staphylococci which ran rampant about the City of Joy. At least two out of three children suffered from gastroenteritis and parasites. What a training it was for a young doctor in dealing with many diseases that were virtually unknown in the West! Without the aid of Bandona, Max would never have been able even to identify them.

'You see those chalky traces on the pupils, Big Brother Max,' she would say, showing him the eyes of a small child. 'That's a sign of xerophthalmia. In a year this poor child will be blind. They don't know that where you come from.'

Max Loeb was out of his depth, submerged, drowned. Nothing he had learned had prepared him for the Third World at its worst. During the first week, he examined and treated as best he could close to five hundred sick people. Symptoms such as yellow eyes, chronic weight loss, painfully swollen ganglions in the throat corresponded with nothing he had experienced. Yet these were the symptoms of the most widespread and fatal disease in India: tuberculosis, the feared red fever.

But there were some comic interludes, like the man who turned up with a prescription that was several years old, which said that as the patient was suffering from terminal cancer, he should take six aspirin tablets a day. Or another man who arrived bearing, with as much solemnity as if transporting a sacred picture of the god Shiva, an X-ray of his lungs that was at least twenty years old.

But it was the tragic cases that predominated. One day a little girl was brought in atrociously burned. A locomotive had released its steam when she was picking up bits of coal along the railway. Most unbearable of all for Max was the sight of malnourished babies with their inflated stomachs, tiny monstrosities placed on his table by their supplicant mothers. At a year or eighteen months they weighed less than nine pounds, and with this degree of malnutrition the majority of their brains' grey cells had probably been destroyed. Even if Max managed to pull them through, they would probably be profoundly retarded.

On Max's second day at the clinic, a young Muslim woman in a black tunic and veil placed a baby wrapped in rags on Max's table. She fixed the doctor with a wild look, unfastened her tunic, bared her chest, and cupped her breasts in her hands.

'They're dry!' she exclaimed. 'Dry! Dry!'

Then she caught sight of the calendar hanging on the wall with the picture of the chubby baby. She picked up her pathetically thin child and thrust him into Max's arms. 'Take him!' she wailed. 'Take him to your country! Save him!'

Max Loeb was sure that for the rest of his life he would see the distress burning in the eyes of the mothers of the City of Joy, as they impotently witnessed their children's agony.

That very evening, Calcutta provided Max Loeb with yet another unforgettable memory. 'CALCUTTA DOCTORS BRING A TEST-TUBE BABY INTO THE WORLD' announced a huge headline in a local newspaper.

THE 'LEPER BUS' was the nickname Stephan had given the ambulance that Mother Teresa sent him every Wednesday, with three of her Sisters. Having been unable to open his leper clinic, this was the only means he had for caring for the worst cases. To avoid any further confrontation with the godfather and his hoodlums, he parked the ambulance in the avenue leading to the railway station, well outside the boundaries of the City of Joy.

Those three Sisters of Mother Teresa were like orchids scattered over putrefaction. The eldest, a tall girl with very clear skin, beautiful in her white sari with a blue border, was not yet twenty-five. Her name was Gabrielle. An Indian from Mauritius, she spoke the picturesque, lilting French of that island. Swallowing her r's, she had nicknamed Kovalski 'Dotteu Stef'. The priest could not help laughing each time she called him.

One morning, there was, as always, a massive rush as soon as the Sisters' small red-and-white van appeared in the avenue. Clinging to their crutches, to their crates on wheels, or dragging themselves along on planks, the lepers swarmed round the three folding tables the Sisters set up on the pavement. One table was used for the distribution of medicines, another for injections, and a third for dressing wounds and for amputations. Gently but firmly, Sister Gabrielle guided the crowd of cripples into a fairly orderly line. By the time Max and Stephan arrived, the line stretched back more than twenty yards.

Armed with a pair of forceps and a saw, Max cut and trimmed dead flesh amid a sticky swirl of flies and sudden dust squalls. In the overpowering heat his sweat streamed down over the wounds. Sister Gabrielle acted as anaesthetist. She had nothing to relieve the pain of certain amputations, no morphine, no curare. She had only her love. Max would never forget the sight of the Indian girl taking a leper in her arms, pressing him to her and humming him a lullaby as Max cut off his leg.

Max had been operating for three hours when two lepers deposited on his table a bearded crippled man whom Kovalski recognised immediately. 'Max, it's Anouar!' he shouted. 'Anouar, whose wife gave birth the evening you arrived.'

The leper's eyes were closed and he was speaking incoherently. Max had great difficulty finding his pulse.

'Gangrene,' said Stephan, examining the dirty, malodorous dressing round Anouar's forearm. Helped by Sister Gabrielle, the two men carefully undid the bandage. Anouar seemed to be unconscious. When they got down to the bare flesh, Anouar's rotten arm, the crowd of faces round him, the penetrating whistle of passing buses, Stephan's voice, all suddenly toppled into a dizzy maelstrom of colours and sounds in Max's head. Then, all at once, everything went blank. Max had fainted.

Leaving Anouar in the care of another Sister, Gabrielle and Kovalski picked up the young man and laid him in the ambulance. When the American finally opened his eyes, he was amazed to find Gabrielle and Stephan bending over him.

'Where am I?' he asked.

'On a pavement in Calcutta, in the middle of cutting off leprous arms and legs,' Kovalski replied sharply, a little annoyed by the incident. But immediately he was angry with himself for his impatience. 'It's nothing, old friend. Just a little fatigue from the heat.'

Within five minutes, Max took up his forceps and his saw once again, to amputate Anouar's gangrenous arm. When he reached the bone just below the shoulder joint, he felt his legs sinking again but he clenched his fingers on the instrument and pressed with all his might. To avoid thinking, feeling, seeing, he talked to himself. 'Sylvia, Sylvia, I love you,' he repeated as his hands accelerated mechanically back and forth.

THE PULLER WITH WHOM Hasari shared his vehicle was a young Muslim with fuzzy hair. His name was Ramatullah, and round his neck hung a miniature Koran on a small chain. He worked from four until midnight, and sometimes even later if he could find passengers. In order to save as much money as possible for his family, he slept on his carriage, his head and legs dangling over either side of the shafts. It was not very comfortable, but at least no one could steal the rickshaw while he slept.

Ramatullah was a good friend to Hasari and ever since he had seen him coughing blood, he had been concerned. If Hasari did not turn up in the morning on time, he would run all the way to Harrington Street to collect the two children his friend was supposed to take to school every day. He knew that to lose a 'contract' like that, so sought after by the other pullers, would have been a catastrophe. In the afternoons he would show up a little earlier to save Hasari the fatigue of a last run, and each time he did so, he gave the sick man the money he had earned in his place.

One morning when Ramatullah passed the rickshaw to Hasari he searched his friend's face with compassion.

'You're as green as an underripe lemon,' the young man said. 'You ought to see a doctor at once. Go on, get in the rickshaw. Today, you are the first *marwari* of the morning!'

'A featherweight *marwari!* You're in luck,' observed Hasari, settling himself on the seat.

Ten minutes later, the Muslim helped his Hindu friend into the cramped clinic of a specialist. Two other patients were already waiting on a bench. The doctor, a fat, bald man in an impeccable white *dhoti*, was seated at the rear of the room in an armchair, as if giving an audience. Dozens of jars and bottles full of herbs and powders were displayed on shelves that ran round the room. After each consultation the doctor would get up, select several jars, then sit at a table behind a set of scales. After weighing each ingredient carefully, he made up his different prescriptions.

When it was Hasari's turn, the physician studied him with a sceptical air and scratched his bald head. 'It began with a feeling of utter fatigue and an aching in my bones,' Hasari told him. 'I thought that it was probably old age creeping up early, as it does with many rickshaw pullers. Then I began to feel a strange warmth in my chest. Even when I was standing still, waiting for a fare, I was bathed in perspiration from head to toe. I thought perhaps I'd caught malaria. A friend of mine brought me some malaria pills and I swallowed two or three a day. But I went on sweating like a pig and every breath I took was painful. Each time I took on a customer, I had to stop every two or three minutes to get my breath back.

'One day I saw myself in a shop window and I had a real shock. For a second I asked myself who this old man was, with his hollow cheeks and his white hair. Suddenly I saw the image of my father on the morning he blessed me before I left for Calcutta.

'I began to feel an irritation at the base of my throat that set off uncontrollable coughing fits. One day when I had just picked up a *marwari*, something wedged itself in my chest. I collapsed onto my knees. The *marwari* was a kind man. Instead of calling another rickshaw, he hit me on the back to help me get my breath back. Then I felt something hot gurgle into my mouth. I spat it out. The *marwari* grimaced when he saw that it was blood. Handing me a five-rupee note, he transferred his packages to another rickshaw.

'My wife burst into sobs when I told her about that. She ordered me to see a healer immediately.'

The doctor lifted down ten jars from his shelves. It took him a long time to work out his different prescriptions. In payment he asked for twenty rupees, which was considerably more expensive than a street healer would have been. But Ramatullah assured Hasari that there could be nothing better than the drugs of this man of science for getting rid of the red fever. Two of his friends had been cured by him.

THERE WAS NO DOUBT in Max Loeb's mind: the incredible vision was an effect of the heat. I'm delirious, he thought to himself. He put down his scalpel and rubbed his eyes but the vision was still there, planted in the middle of the alleyway.

'Dad!' he finally yelled.

The tall figure with the russet hair was indeed Arthur Loeb, although with his trousers rolled up to his knees, the surgeon looked more like a shrimp fisherman. For a moment father and son stood facing each other, speechless, then Arthur held out his arms and Max rushed into them. The sight of the two sahibs embracing each other provoked much hilarity amongst the crowd that thronged round the door.

'Is that your hospital?' asked Arthur Loeb at last, pointing to the mud-walled room.

Max nodded, and they laughed together, but Arthur Loeb's features became set as he gazed at the pitted faces, the skeletal babies in their mothers' arms, the protruding chests of tuberculosis sufferers.

'The lame, the sick and the dying . . .' he muttered.

'My reception committee,' Max said. 'If you'd warned me in advance, I would have provided dancing girls, garlands of flowers and a welcoming *tilak*.'

'Welcoming *tilak*?'

'That's the red dot they put on your forehead. It's known as the third eye and it enables you to see the truth beyond appearances.'

'What I can see here is staggering enough,' Arthur said. 'Isn't there a happier place to celebrate our reunion?'

'What would you say to a Punjabi dinner tonight? The best restaurant is right in your hotel—I take it you are staying at the Grand Hotel?'

Arthur nodded.

'I'll meet you at eight o'clock at the Tandoori restaurant there.' Max pointed to the line of sick and crippled people. 'And tomorrow, you can come and give me a hand! Respiratory illnesses are your specialty, aren't they? Well, you are going to have fun!'

Like all up-to-date places in Calcutta, the Tandoori restaurant was equipped with air conditioning and it felt like an icebox. However, the turbaned head waiter dug out a magnum of Dom Perignon which quickly relaxed the two men.

Arthur raised his glass. 'To your speedy return home, Max!'

Max clinked glasses with his father. 'First, let's drink to your discovery of Calcutta!'

They drank several mouthfuls, then Arthur said, 'What a shock that was this afternoon.'

'And yet you didn't really see anything tragic.'

The surgeon looked incredulous. 'Do you mean there's worse?'

'It must be hard to imagine after a paradise like Miami,' said Max, thinking of his father's luxurious clinic. 'In fact, no one can really have any idea of the way millions of people here live without actually sharing their lives, like the Polish priest I told you about in my letters. And me, to a lesser extent.'

Arthur listened with a mixture of respect and astonishment. When he was younger, Max had had a morbid fear of dirt. At high school, his mania for washing had earned him the nickname of 'Supersuds'. Later, at medical school, his obsessive fear of vermin had occasioned many practical jokes, like leaving a colony of cockroaches in his bed. The gods of the City of Joy had metamorphosed his son.

'Didn't you want to run away when you first landed in this cesspool?' he asked.

'Sure I did,' Max replied. 'Especially since Stephan, the sadist, had a surprise in store for my arrival: one of his leper friends in labour. You should have seen my face!'

The waiters brought several dishes laden with aromatic mountains of orange-coloured pieces of chicken and mutton. Arthur Loeb grimaced.

'Don't worry. That colour is typical of dishes from the Punjab,' explained Max. 'The meat is macerated in yoghurt and spices. Then it's coated with a kind of chilli paste which gives it that distinctive colour. After that, it is baked in a *tandoor*, a special clay oven. Have a taste, it's marvellous.'

Arthur took a bite, but almost immediately Max saw his father's cheeks turn crimson. He stammered a few words and Max finally understood that the poor man was asking for some champagne to put out the fire in his mouth. He quickly filled his father's glass and ordered some *nan*, the delicious oven-baked bread that is ideal for soothing burning palates. Arthur chewed his way through several pieces in silence, then suddenly looked up.

'Supposing I were to buy your City of Joy?'

Max nearly swallowed a chicken bone.

'You mean buy the slum?'

'We could put together a group of benefactors, then raze it to the ground, rebuild it with running water, drains and electricity. And give the residents their homes as a present. What do you say to that, my boy?'

Max smiled. He could just imagine the expressions on the faces of the government *babus* when they learned that some American sahibs wanted to buy up one of Calcutta's slums. 'Dad, it's a brilliant idea,' he said at last. 'The only trouble is that we're in Calcutta, not in South Miami or the Bronx. I'm afraid a project like that would be difficult to implement over here.'

'If you're willing to pay the price, you can implement anything,' replied Arthur, slightly irritated.

'I'm sure you're right. It's just that over here, money isn't enough. All kinds of other considerations come into play. For one thing, no foreigner is allowed to purchase real estate. It's an old Indian law.'

Arthur swept away the objection with a wave of his hand. 'I'd use Indian front men. The end result would be the same.'

But Max had another, more serious objection. Since immersing himself in the poverty of the City of Joy, Max had been forced to revise a fair

180

number of his theories on how the problems of the poor should be resolved.

'When I arrived in the slum,' he told his father, 'one of the first thoughts Stephan shared with me came from a Brazilian archbishop struggling shoulder to shoulder with the poor in the *favelas*. According to him, our help serves only to make people more dependent unless it is supported by actions designed to wipe out the actual roots of poverty.'

'Does that mean that it's no use taking these people out of their hovels and setting them up in new housing?'

Max nodded his head sadly. 'I've even come to learn the validity of a strange reality here,' he said. 'In a slum, an exploiter is better than a Santa Claus . . .' Confronted by his father's stupefied expression, he went on to explain, 'An exploiter forces you to react, whereas a Santa Claus immobilises you.'

IT TOOK THE SURGEON from Miami several days to understand exactly what Max meant. Every morning he climbed into a taxi and went to join his son in his clinic. With an infallible eye, Bandona directed the most serious cases to him, many of them patients in the terminal stages of tuberculosis. In all his career he had never seen such impaired respiratory systems. As far as Loeb was concerned, these people were already dead. But he was wrong. These walking dead were really alive. They jostled one another, argued and joked. In the City of Joy, the life force always seemed to prevail over death.

Above all, this daily plunge into the very depths of an Indian slum enabled Arthur to understand better what form of help would be most effective. 'I had been prepared to give a million dollars to buy a whole slum and build it anew,' he said after he returned to Miami, 'when in fact the urgent need was for a ration of milk to be distributed to rickety babies whose fontanelles were still open, for inoculations for high-risk people, for thousands of tuberculosis sufferers to be rescued from fatal pollution.' The experience made him appreciate a fundamental truth: it's at grass-roots level that gestures of solidarity are really noticed and appreciated. A simple smile can have as much value as all the dollars in the world.

THE STIFLING HEAT of the premonsoon weeks made sleep inside the slum houses impossible, and there were too many members of the Pal family to lie down outside their own hovel. So Big Brother Stephan invited Hasari and his eldest son to share the small verandah outside his room.

Stephan would never forget the first night he spent lying beside his neighbour, not only because with each breath Hasari's lungs sounded like a blacksmith's forge, but also because of the confidences he was to hear.

Hardly had the priest lain down when Hasari turned to him. 'Don't go to sleep yet, Big Brother,' he entreated. 'I need to talk to you.'

Kovalski had heard appeals of that kind many times, often from complete strangers. 'I'm listening, my brother,' he said warmly.

Hasari hesitated. 'I know that my *chakra* will soon cease to turn for this life,' he finally declared.

The priest knew well the meaning of those words. Hasari was sensing his impending death. He protested, but only as a matter of form. He knew that neither Max nor anybody else could save Hasari.

'I am not afraid of death,' Hasari continued. 'I've had such a tough time since I left my village that I am almost sure ...' Again he hesitated. 'Almost sure that now my *karma* is less heavy and will have me born again into a better incarnation.'

Kovalski had often discerned this hope in the confidences of the slum people he had helped to die. It seemed to give them serenity. Tonight, however, it was of other things that Hasari Pal wanted to talk. 'Big Brother,' he went on, propping himself up on his elbows, 'I do not want to die before I've ...' He stopped, shaken by a fit of coughing, then went on, 'Big Brother, I cannot die before I've found a husband for my daughter, Amrita.'

For an Indian father, there was no more powerful obsession than that of marrying off his daughter. Amrita was only thirteen years old, but from her earliest years her mother had steadily prepared her for the most important occasion of her life: her marriage. For one day that event would transform a child of poverty into the subject of all conversation in the small world of the poor around her. Like all Indian parents, the Pals knew that they would be judged by the way in which their daughter conducted herself in her husband's house, and, as her role would always be one of submission, Amrita had been trained to renounce all personal inclinations and even childish play in order to serve her parents and brothers, something she had always done with a smile. From infancy, she had accepted the Indian idea of marriage, a concept that now made Hasari say to Stephan, 'My daughter does not belong to me. She has only been lent to me by God until she marries. She belongs to the man who will be her husband.'

Indian custom generally requires that a girl should be married well before puberty, hence the 'child marriages' that seem so barbaric to Westerners. However, in such cases the wedding is merely a ceremony. The real marriage takes place only after the girl's first menstrual period. Then the father of the bride goes to the father of the groom and informs him that his daughter is now capable of bearing a child. A more definitive ceremony is held and it is then that the girl leaves her parents' home to live with the young man to whom she has been 'married' for years.

The daughter of a poor rickshaw puller not being a particularly desirable match, Amrita had not been married before her first period. Now, in order to fulfil his duty, Amrita's father had to resolve a very crucial problem. Like millions of other Indian fathers, Hasari had to put together a dowry. Although Indira Gandhi actually outlawed this ancestral custom, its tyranny continues in modern India.

'I can't give my daughter to a man who is paralysed or blind or a leper!' the rickshaw puller lamented to Kovalski. Only such outcasts would agree to take a girl in marriage without a dowry.

Hasari had made endless calculations, but he always came back to the same unhappy conclusion: he had to amass two thousand rupees before the very humblest of young men would accept his daughter. Two thousand rupees! That meant a whole year of running between the shafts of his rickshaw. 'But when you cough red,' he told Stephan, 'you watch the sun rise each morning and wonder whether you'll see it set.'

After that conversation, Stephan took Hasari to Max, who treated him with antibiotics and vitamins. At first, the effect on a system totally unaccustomed to medicines was spectacular. The attacks of coughing became less frequent and Hasari recovered enough strength to start pulling his carriage again. But even that was not enough to guarantee the indispensable two thousand rupees.

It was then that fortune intervened in the form of another encounter with one of the middlemen who prowled the streets of Calcutta. Hasari had just set down two women and their heavy suitcases outside the SAS airline agency when he was struck by an attack of coughing so violent that two other pullers ran over to help him lie down on the seat of his carriage.

Suddenly a face pockmarked from smallpox appeared above Hasari's. The eyes were full of sympathy.

'Well now, my friend,' volunteered the stranger, 'you don't look too well.'

This overture comforted Hasari. There were not many people who treated you like a 'friend' in this inhuman city. He wiped his bloodied mouth with a corner of his vest.

'It must be really tough pulling one of those carriages when you're coughing your head off!' continued the stranger. 'What would you say if I were to offer you as much money as you earn in two months sweating between your shafts, without your having to do anything?'

'As much money as . . .' stammered Hasari, at a loss for words. 'I would say that you were the god Hanuman in person.' But then he remembered the middleman who had accosted him in the Bara Bazaar when he first arrived in Calcutta. 'If it's my blood you're after, you're on the wrong track,' he announced sadly. 'It's no good.'

'It's not your blood I'm after. It's your bones.'

'My bones?' Hasari's expression of horror brought a smile to the procurer's face.

'You come with me to my boss,' he explained calmly. 'He'll buy your bones for five hundred rupees. When you kick off he'll collect your body and take your skeleton.'

This man was one of the links in a trade that makes India the prime exporter of human bones in the world. Each year, some twenty thousand

Women go about their daily chores, washing a baby and cooking, while a man sleeps on a *charpoy*. This has been raised on bricks to protect the family and their possessions in a monsoon.

During a monsoon, rickshaws were the only form of urban transport. But conditions were harsh and dangerous, as objects were obscured by the floods, and the rickshaw pullers' feet became covered in ulcerated wounds. But the real danger lay in the constant swing between the heat of a run and the chill of standing waiting for a fare. Many died from pneumonia.

Rickshaw pullers grow old rapidly. This puller is less than fifty years old. His baby son represents his only wealth and his hope for the future.

complete skeletons and tens of thousands of different bones leave India's airports and seaports, carefully packed and destined for medical schools in the United States, Europe, Japan and Australia. This lucrative business brings in approximately one and a half million dollars a year and its centre is Calcutta. The principal exporters—eight in number—all have warehouses and are registered with the local customs headquarters.

The fact that Calcutta was the hub of this unusual activity had nothing to do with the mortality rate in its slums. Rather, it was due to the presence in the city of a community of Doms, an extremely low caste destined from birth to take care of the dead. The Doms usually lived near the funeral pyres of the Hooghly, cemeteries and hospital morgues, and it was they who provided the exporters with most of their macabre merchandise in a variety of ways: primarily by picking up the bones and corpses cast up on the banks of the Hooghly. In the cremation area they would intercept families too poor to pay for the services of a priest. The Doms would offer to undertake the funeral rites themselves for a lower price. The families never knew that their relatives' remains were cut up in a nearby hut and their bones sold to an exporter. Hospital mortuaries were another reliable source for the Doms. From the morgue alone, more than twenty-five hundred unclaimed bodies fell into their hands each year.

Then there was the method of buying a man while he was still walking about, in order to secure the right to dispose of his bones when he died. In this way the traffickers accumulated stock, for there was certainly no shortage of poor and terminally ill people in Calcutta.

'Five hundred rupees!' The sum tumbled about in Hasari's head like the balls in a lottery barrel. The middleman had not been mistaken. He could spot his prey at a glance. The streets were full of poor devils coughing their lungs up, but not all of them could provide the necessary guarantees. For the purchase of a man to be a solid venture, he must have a family, an employer—in other words an identity and an address. How else could his body be retrieved after his death?

'Well, friend, do you agree?'

Hasari looked into the pockmarked face awaiting his response. He remained silent, but the middleman showed no sign of impatience. He was used to this. Even a man with his back against the wall doesn't sell his body just like that.

'FIVE HUNDRED RUPEES, no less! What do you say to that?' Hasari was still marvelling to Ramatullah at the astonishing offer he had just received. He had asked the middleman for time to think it over until the next day.

Because Ramatullah was a Muslim, the idea of bodily mutilation after death was repugnant to him. His religion even forbade the donation of organs to science, and the few Indian eye banks had not one single Muslim on their files. Nevertheless the sum was so considerable that Ramatullah could not fail to be dazzled by it.

'Hasari, you've got to do it,' he said eventually. 'Your gods will forgive you. They know you've got to get your daughter married.'

But the Hindu faith required that, for the soul to transmigrate into another form after death, the body must first be destroyed and reduced to ashes by the fire that purifies all. Hasari resolved to confide in Father Stephan.

Living in the poverty of a slum had led Stephan to accept occasional compromises between the ideals of faith and the imperatives of survival. 'I think you should take this opportunity to further the completion of your mission here below,' he finally told Hasari reluctantly.

THE MIDDLEMAN KNOCKED several times at the door of the warehouse and soon a face appeared in the half-open door. The middleman indicated Hasari.

'I'm bringing a client,' he announced.

The door opened wide and the porter motioned the two men inside. The smell that hit them was a suffocating stench of the kind that tears at the throat. For a moment Hasari wavered in his resolve, but his companion pushed him forward.

Hasari had just entered a place such as only the imagination of a Dante or a Dürer could have conceived, an incredible catacomb in which dozens of skeletons of all different sizes were ranged upright along the walls like a supermarket display. Rows of tables and shelves were covered with thousands of skulls, spinal columns, ribs, sacra, coccyges. Every skeleton, indeed every bone, bore a label on which the price was marked in US dollars. An adult skeleton for demonstration purposes, with movable bones and metal articulation, was worth between two hundred and thirty and three hundred and fifty dollars, according to its size. A complete thorax might cost forty dollars, a skull six.

The company maintained a team of specialists—bone extractors, painters and sculptors. They were crouched among the mountains of human remains, scraping, decorticating, assembling and decorating. Sometimes real works of art emerged from their hands, like the collection of articulated skulls with movable teeth and jaws that could be dismantled which had been ordered by the dental faculty of a large American university.

In an office at the far end of the warehouse, Hasari and the middleman found the man who negotiated the purchase of 'living' skeletons. Dressed in white overalls, he presided over a dusty table heaped with files and a collection of paperweights made out of the skulls of newborn babies.

The man examined Hasari closely. The puller's bony chest and prominent vertebrae reassured him that it would not be unduly long before what was left of this individual enriched the stocks. He gave the middleman a satisfied wink, then drew up a formal purchase agreement.

Hasari was entitled to a first payment of one hundred and fifty rupees. He was informed that the balance would be paid as soon as his health showed signs of final deterioration.

11

Because of the appalling heat, the inhabitants of Calcutta look forward to the monsoon just as eagerly as the country dwellers.

It was late afternoon when Hasari Pal saw the first drops of water fall. As soon as they hit the asphalt, the heat caused them to evaporate instantly. To a former peasant, banished for ever from his land by drought, that first drop of water was like manna from the heavens, proof that the gods could still weep for the plight of mankind.

That first monsoon downpour was exceptionally violent. The water battered the ground with the sound of drums beaten by a million fingers. Swiftly, Hasari put up the hood of his rickshaw, then gave himself up to the sheer joy of being soaked by the flood as a breath of air blew through the warm shower, bringing with it a touch of coolness.

Instead of seeking shelter, people rushed out into the rain. Naked children danced and laughed and performed somersaults. Women allowed themselves to be drenched until their saris clung to their bodies like the thin bark of bamboo canes. Trees that had looked like dusty old men grew shiny with freshness and youth.

In the slum Max could hardly believe his eyes. 'A whole race of people who only a second earlier had seemed half-dead had just been resurrected in a fantastic explosion of happiness, exuberance, and life,' he wrote to Sylvia. At the end of his alleyway, he saw a tall figure with white skin. A part of the celebrations, Kovalski was dancing unrestrainedly in a circle with other residents of the City of Joy. On his streaming chest his metal cross jumped about as if to beat out the time. 'He looked like the god Neptune under the waters of some celestial spring!' wrote Max.

FOR THREE DAYS the deluge continued, a deluge such as Bengal had not known for several years. But soon, from one compound to the next in Anand Nagar, there rang out the word that had haunted the memory of India for as long as the monsoon had existed. '*Barha!*'—'Flood!' The initial jubilation was succeeded by a frantic hunt for umbrellas, bits of canvas, cardboard, anything that might serve to patch up the roofs and hold back the water streaming into the huts.

The water welled up from out of the ground, too, for the slum was built on marshland. People used bricks to raise the *charpoys*, the frame-and-rope beds, in their hovels to shelter their children and their few possessions. To save Max's medicine chest, Bandona suspended a sheet from the four corners of his room to form an improvised hammock.

The lapping of the water rose above the general commotion and voices assumed a distinctive resonance as they echoed across the sheet of water. Hunger was soon added to discomfort, for with the cow-dung cakes reduced to sponges, the women could no longer cook. And the rain continued to fall, the water level to rise.

The rest of Calcutta was experiencing a similar nightmare. Thousands of residents had been compelled to flee the city or take refuge on the rooftops. The downpour had flooded the transformers and the entire city was plunged into darkness. No trains could reach the stations. Traffic on the roads had come to a standstill and supplies had begun to run out. To the delight of the rickshaw pullers, there was no longer any other form of urban transport.

Hasari, thinking of Amrita's dowry, was ecstatic. All of a sudden rickshaw pullers were no longer despised, insulted animals whom people cheated once they reached their destination. Now they offered two, three, even four times the usual price to be able to sit on the drenched seat of the only boats still afloat in the sea of Calcutta.

The shortest of trips made Hasari a small fortune. Yet how much suffering it cost him! Obscured by the floods, every obstacle became a trap. Sweating in the downpour without ever being able to dry off aggravated his condition. Steeped in the water, many of his colleagues contracted skin diseases and their feet became covered with ulcerated wounds. But the real danger lay in the constant swing between heat and chill. A number of Hasari's colleagues succumbed quickly to pneumonia in that monsoon.

When Hasari showed Son of Miracle the proceeds from his first two days in the monsoon, the taxi driver, condemned to unemployment by the flood, let out a hoot of admiration. 'Hasari,' he cried, 'that's not water pouring from the sky, it's gold nuggets!'

The rickshaw puller's joy was to be short-lived. When he arrived at the Park Circus stand next day to pick up his rickshaw, he looked around for Ramatullah. 'Your pal is dead, Hasari,' one of the pullers told him. 'He fell down a manhole. That's the third man to drown since yesterday. Apparently some *babu*'s given the order to take off all the drain covers so that the water can flow away.'

STEPHAN CALLED HIS COMMITTEE together: help had to be organised urgently. They met in Max's room. In the gloomy atmosphere they could hear only the beating of the rain, the lapping of the water, and the piercing cries of the rats as they fled from their lairs.

'Big Brother Stephan, panic has broken out,' announced the old man, Saladdin. 'At least five hundred people have taken refuge in the great mosque.' The rumour was spreading that, eroded by the water, hundreds of hovels were collapsing all over the slum. The Jama Masjid, the only building with several storeys, stood above the flood.

'And this is only the beginning,' said Margareta, whose soaked sari was clinging to her. 'Apparently the Ganges is overflowing its banks.'

'That's enough bad news!' interrupted Aristotle John, the Anglo-Indian. 'We're not here to whine, but to decide how we can help.'

'Aristotle John is right!' said Kovalski, whose sneakers, full of water, were sending up a steady flow of bubbles.

In the silence that ensued, each one considered the enormity of the task. Max was the first to speak.

'We ought to vaccinate people quickly against cholera and typhoid ... There's a risk of epidemics ...'

'Shouldn't we start by organising emergency provisions for the refugees?' suggested Saladdin. 'Thousands of people are going to find themselves without food and water.'

'Big Brother Stephan, our first priority must be the old and infirm who have stayed in their homes,' Bandona said gently but firmly. 'Many of them will drown if someone doesn't go and find them.'

No one perceived priorities better than Bandona. But her remark reminded Stephan of something even more urgent.

'The lepers!' he exclaimed. 'I'll go to them with Aristotle John and Margareta. You three look for the sick and elderly,' he directed Bandona, Max and Saladdin. 'We'll all meet at the Jama Masjid!'

The little leper colony, since it was below the level of the railway lines, was completely flooded, but not a single inhabitant had left. The parents had put their children on the roofs and the relatively able-bodied had piled *charpoys* one on top of another for the sick. Stephan found Anouar, who had survived the amputation of his arm, perched on one of these improvised pyramids, half immersed in water. He was smiling.

'Anouar, old friend, I've been looking for you,' said the priest breathlessly.

'But why? This isn't the first time the monsoon has got our feet wet!'

'The rain is still falling,' Stephan said, amazed at the leper's stoical, almost cheerful attitude. 'You could all be drowned.'

Even as he spoke, Stephan became fully aware of the difficulty of the situation. How could he hope to evacuate these people when he himself and his companions had several times nearly fallen into the eddies of dark water as they made their way to the leper colony?

Stephan knew he must get reinforcements, but how? Then he saw before him the image of a man with small cruel eyes and the fat jowls of a pleasure-seeker.

He called out to Margareta and Aristotle John. 'I'm going to see the godfather. He's the only one who can help us get them out of here.'

With its four storeys of solid masonry, the godfather's house rose like a fortress out of the floodwaters. Lit by a powerful generator, it illuminated the waves that beat against its walls. Inside, seemingly insensible to what was going on outside, the godfather remained as impassive as ever, enthroned in his ivory-inlaid chair.

'Good evening, Father,' he said in his hissing voice. 'What kindly breeze brings you here in weather like this?'

'The lepers,' replied Stephan.

'Them again?' said the godfather. His forehead puckered. 'It would seem that it's always to the lepers that I owe the honour of an encounter with you. What is it this time?'

'They will probably all drown if they're not evacuated at once. We need men and a boat immediately.'

Whether out of the fear of losing a solid source of income, or an unexpected surge of humanity, the City of Joy's godfather suddenly reacted spectacularly. He rose and clapped his hands, and Ashoka, the little thug with the big motorbike, rushed in. There was a whispered conference, then other members of the family appeared. Less than ten minutes later, a boat set out with Stephan, Ashoka and a team of family members on board.

As the first strokes of the oars bore the vessel away into shadows, Kovalski heard the godfather's voice again. Turning, he saw the squat little man framed in a lighted window. He would never forget the words he heard ring out across the swirling water.

'Ashoka,' the godfather shouted at the top of his lungs, 'bring all the lepers back here! Tonight, our house is for the wretched ones.'

AN HOUR LATER, the arrival of the first boatload of lepers at the godfather's house was the occasion for deeds that even a heart as full of love as Stephan's could not have imagined. He saw Ashoka take Anouar in his arms and carry him carefully to the *charpoy* in his own room. He saw the women of the house strip off their beautiful muslin veils to rub down naked children shivering with cold. He saw the godfather's wife, a plump matron, her arms jingling with bracelets, bring them a cooking pot full of rice and meat. And he saw a sight that would obliterate for ever the spectacle of the Molotov cocktails exploding outside his small leper clinic: the godfather himself reaching out his gold-ringed fingers to receive the castaways, helping them to disembark, drying their mutilated limbs, and serving them tea and pastries.

ALL THROUGH THE NIGHT Max accompanied Bandona on her rescue operations, holding his medicine chest above the floodwaters. The head and heart of the Assamese girl contained a complete list of all the most serious distress cases in the slum. With the help of a team of young men, she and Max waded from one hovel to the next, rescuing blind and paralysed people, bedridden patients with tuberculosis, beggars, and even a madwoman. Only once did they arrive too late. When they entered the hovel occupied by the old blind leper woman to whom Stephan took Communion every week, they found her wasted body afloat in her widow's garments. Her rosary was twined about her wrist and her

191

mutilated face looked unaccountably serene.

'Her torment is over now,' Bandona murmured as she helped Max hoist the body onto a ledge. 'The God she called upon has taken her to be with Him.'

IN THE IMMEDIACY of the flood, all the people of the City of Joy had become brothers. Muslim families took Hindus into their homes, young people nearly drowned carrying the elderly on their shoulders, rickshaw pullers transported the sick free of charge in vehicles that were three-quarters submerged.

But the torment of the flood victims of Calcutta was to continue for days. As Max had feared, cholera and typhoid broke out. Paradoxically, with all that liquid around, there was not a drop of drinking water. People hung up rags and umbrellas to collect a little rain, but some had to drink the polluted water that engulfed them. The food situation was desperate, despite the fact that teams of rescue volunteers were working miracles. Saladdin had managed to find a boat and two large pots. Paddling as hard as his strength would permit, the old man did the rounds of the restaurants, to fill his pots with rice and wheat flour which he took to the people marooned in the mosque.

The strangest thing about this cataclysm was that life still went on much as before. At the corner of a submerged alleyway, Kovalski remained rooted to the spot, confronted by a group of children up to their shoulders in water, laughing and splashing before a tiny platform on which an old man was selling little plastic cars and dolls, oblivious to the rain.

'Marvellous children of the City of Joy,' Kovalski wrote in his diary. 'Little innocent beings nourished on poverty, in whom the life force never ceased to flourish. Their freedom from care, their zest for life, their magical smiles and dark faces set off by a luminous gaze coloured the entire world in which they lived with beauty. If the adults here managed to retain some spark of hope, was it not because of the children, because of their dazzling freshness, because of the earnestness of their games? Without them the slums would have been nothing but prisons. It was they who managed to turn these places of distress into places of joy.'

For eight days and eight nights the anger of the heavens remained unrelenting. Then gradually it began to wane, although it was more than a month before the floods retreated altogether. Slowly, Calcutta began to hope again.

When the water subsided, the City of Joy was nothing but a polluted marsh. Stinking mud covered everything, interspersed with the decaying carcasses of dogs, cats, rats and even humans.

By the time Stephan, concealed behind a two-week beard and covered with dirt, finally returned to his compound, all the other occupants had already moved back and were busy clearing up after the inundation. In his absence his neighbours had washed, scrubbed and completely repainted his hovel! Before the picture of the Sacred Shroud a pattern of *rangoli*, the attractive auspicious motifs traced on the ground in coloured powder, paid homage to Stephan's God.

12

In his obsession to put together the money for his daughter's dowry, Hasari calculated his assets over and over again. 'If I add the five hundred rupees of my bones to the eight hundred I earned during the monsoon, and if on top of that Shambu could bring back two or three hundred rupees from rag-picking, that makes ... that makes ... that makes close to two thousand rupees!' Hasari could already see the Brahmin binding his daughter's hand to that of her husband.

Every morning, Nissar, a twelve-year-old boy with a harelip, would set off from the slum to pick rags from the city dump. He knew where all the most profitable spots were and he agreed to take Shambu, Hasari's son, with him. At the first light of dawn, he led Shambu and four other slum children to the mouth of the great Howrah Bridge. Pointing to one of the overloaded buses, he directed Shambu to hang on to the rear bumper. Every day tens of thousands of people made use of Calcutta's public transport in this way. In the hellish traffic, balancing on the bumpers was a dangerous acrobatic feat and nearly every week someone was crushed by the wheels of a truck or electrocuted by a tram.

When the bus emerged from the last suburb east of the city, the road ran across a flat expanse of marshy land. There, the six children let themselves drop onto the asphalt. With an old jute sack slung over one shoulder, Nissar led the group to the dump. In addition to the vultures and the cows that grazed on the refuse, large numbers of men, women and children were already at work on the huge mound.

Nissar stopped short of the approach ramp used by the dump trucks. 'We'll have to be quick,' he said. 'It's the hotels and hospitals day.'

Once a week the municipal rubbish lorries brought the refuse from these establishments, and their arrival always produced a frantic onslaught. Real treasure often lay concealed in their loads, the kind that represented top value on the dumping-ground exchange: flasks, bandages, syringes, scraps of food.

'You, Shambu,' ordered Nissar, pointing to a ditch, 'park yourself there. As soon as you see a bit of red rag in the window of a truck, whistle to let me know. That means it's coming from a hospital or a hotel.' He took a five-rupee note out of his belt. 'I'll run over to the truck waving this note. The driver will slow down to grab it and we'll all jump onto the back. The driver will make for a far corner of the dump and ditch his load as quickly as possible. Then we'll really have to move quickly before the others get there.'

They hurried into position to wait for the first truck. One yellow truck arrived, then another, then a third. Nobody moved. Hasari's son watched the spectacle around him with fascination. A crowd of barefoot women and children were scouring the hill of refuse with baskets in one hand and long spikes in the other. To protect themselves against the sun and the dust the women and girls had covered their heads and faces with colourful pieces of cloth, which gave them the air of harem princesses. The boys, with their felt caps full of holes, and worn-out shoes that were far too big for them, all looked like Charlie Chaplin in his early films.

Shambu saw a vulture bear down like a torpedo on a small boy, to snatch the piece of meat he had just found. Even pigs, cows, goats, stray dogs and, at night, hyenas and jackals had made their homes on the dump, as did hosts of other small creatures and insects.

The arrival of each vehicle unleashed a frenzy of activity as everyone scrambled after it. Flurried searching went on around the bulldozers which worked at levelling the mountains of refuse. Children slipped without hesitation under these mastodons to be the first to explore the manna turned over by their steel scoops. How many had perished, suffocated by their solid bulk or crushed by their caterpillar bands? Shambu felt a cold sweat break out on his back.

Then a fourth truck appeared and Shambu's heart began to pound: he saw the red flag in its window. Stuffing his fingers into his mouth, he whistled as arranged. Nissar loomed up in a cloud of dust and jumped onto the running board to hand over his five-rupee note. The driver braked, and with the agility of lizards the six little rag-pickers from the City of Joy climbed aboard the truck.

The driver accelerated to climb the access slope, but then, instead of heading towards the bulldozers, he veered off in the opposite direction. This was part of the deal. Nissar and his band would have ten minutes in which to forage alone.

The truck pulled up sharply. The six boys leaped down and watched it unload its avalanche of garbage. Then they scrabbled, located, sorted and stowed their booty away as fast as they could. Bottles, parts of cooking utensils and crockery, broken tools, old tubes of toothpaste, run-down batteries, empty tins and scraps of clothing all went into their baskets. They knew only too well that they had to move on before the furious crowd of other rag-pickers fell upon them.

Caught up in the fever of the search, Shambu sank his spike into the stinking mass for one last time, and suddenly let out a cry. Something glinted in the garbage. He thought it was a coin and reached for it in a frenzy. What he grasped was a bracelet—and on the bracelet was a watch.

HASARI PAL TOOK THE WATCH in his hands and lifted it to his ear with as much respect as if he were offering it to some deity. The voices around him in the compound fell silent. For several seconds Hasari remained immobile, incapable of uttering a word, as if transfigured by the treasure that ticked in unison with the beating of his heart. Tears obscured his vision. I shall be able to die in peace, he thought. Thanks to this watch and to the five hundred rupees for my bones, my daughter will have a good husband.

FORTY-THREE-YEAR-OLD Hari Giri, a pale little man, was the neighbourhood *pujari*, the Hindu priest. One evening he paid Hasari Pal a visit to ask him the time and date of his daughter's birth. 'I shall be back soon with some good news for you,' he assured him.

A few days later he returned.

'Your daughter's horoscope and caste are in perfect harmony with those of a boy with whom I am acquainted,' he announced triumphantly to Hasari and Aloka. 'The family concerned are *kumhars* (potters). They have two potteries not far away and are highly respectable people.' Then, addressing himself exclusively to Hasari, he added, 'The boy's father would like to meet you very soon.'

Profoundly moved, Hasari prostrated himself on the ground before the Brahmin. No self-respecting *pujari* would be satisfied with mere gratitude, however. Holding out his hand, he claimed an advance on his fee.

This visit marked the beginning of a tragicomedy in which Stephan played a leading role. Although it is customary for the long and detailed negotiations that precede a marriage to be conducted in public in the middle of the courtyard, the two parties often prefer a more discreet place when it comes to the discussion of financial matters.

'My room is always at everyone's disposal,' the priest had said. So it was there, in front of the Sacred Shroud, that the two parties met. 'The parties' did not include either Amrita or her prospective husband: they would not meet until the evening of their nuptials. Rather, it meant the father of the prospective groom, Hasari, the Brahmin, and Stephan.

'My son is an exceptional boy,' the father, a large, surly man, said firmly. 'And I want his wife to be no less so.'

'My daughter is as exceptional as your son,' retorted Hasari, not wishing to be outdone.

'If she is such a jewel, you will no doubt have anticipated giving her a generous dowry,' said the father of the boy.

'I have anticipated doing my duty,' assured Hasari.

'Well, let's see then,' said the father, lighting up a *bidi*.

An Indian bride's dowry is made up of two parts: her trousseau and personal jewels that remain, in principle, her property, and the gifts she will take to her new family. Hasari's list included two cotton saris, two bodices, a shawl, various household utensils and a few imitation jewels and ornaments. The presents for the groom's family were two *dhotis*, as many vests, and a *punjabi*, the long tunic that buttons up to the neck and goes down to the knees. It was truly a poor man's dowry, but it represented so many trips through the waters of the monsoon, such deprivation, so many sacrifices, that the rickshaw puller felt he was giving away his own flesh and blood.

The boy's father raised his eyebrows. After a silence, he enquired, 'Is that all?'

Hasari shook his head sadly. 'My daughter's qualities will make up for what is lacking.'

'Maybe,' growled the boy's father, 'but one or two toe rings would not be superfluous. Also a gold brooch. As for the gifts for my family ...'

The Brahmin interrupted to declare, 'Before continuing your bartering, I would appreciate it if you could come to an agreement on the price of my services.'

'I had thought two *dhotis* for you and a sari for your wife,' replied Hasari.

'Two *dhotis* and a sari!' The *pujari* guffawed. 'You must be joking!'

Stephan saw great beads of sweat break out on Hasari's forehead. Dear Lord, he thought, they're going to fleece him down to the very last hair.

The discussion went on for a good two hours, but nothing was achieved; both parties maintained their positions. Marriage negotiations were traditionally very long-winded affairs.

The second meeting took place three days later in the same place. Hasari was having more and more difficulty in breathing. His coughing fits, initially suppressed by Max's emergency treatment, had started again. Haunted by the fear of dying before he had fulfilled his duty, he was ready to concede to any demands.

This time it was the *pujari* who opened fire, but his claims were so excessive that, for once, the two fathers were in agreement. They rejected them unanimously.

'In that case, I shall withdraw,' threatened the Brahmin.

'That's too bad. We shall just have to find another *pujari*,' responded Hasari.

The Brahmin burst out laughing. 'The horoscopes are in my possession! No one will ever agree to take my place!'

They had reached an impasse. Suffering from a surge of fever, Hasari had begun to shake. The *pujari* went through the motions of getting up to leave, but Hasari caught his wrist. 'Stay!' he begged.

'Only if you pay me a hundred rupees at once.'

The fathers exchanged helpless glances. After a few seconds' hesitation they each foraged in the waistbands of their *longhis*.

'There you are!' Hasari said tartly, tossing a bundle at the little man. The negotiations began again.

No king's marriage could have been more keenly debated than this proposed union of two waifs in a slum. It took no fewer than eight sessions to settle the question of the dowry, while crises of weeping alternated with threats, broken off by reconciliations. There was always some new demand. One day the boy's father suddenly added a bicycle; next day he wanted a transistor radio; the next, an additional *dhoti*.

This marathon of bargaining completely exhausted Hasari. One morning when he had just collected his rickshaw, he felt the ground dissolve beneath his feet. Then everything went blank, an immense dark blank.

When Hasari opened his eyes, he recognised the face of Musafir looming over him. He was doing his rounds, collecting the rickshaw fees.

'Hey there, fellow, have you drunk a bit too much *bangla*?' Musafir asked in a friendly way.

Hasari indicated his chest. 'No, I think my motor is giving out.'

Musafir was suddenly on the alert. 'Hasari, if your motor's really giving out, you're going to have to hand in your machine. You know how the old man is always saying, "I want buffalo between my shafts, not baby goats."'

Hasari nodded. There was neither sadness nor revolt in his expression, only resignation. He thought of Ram Chander and of all those whom he had seen die in the arms of their rickshaws, their strength sapped by the climate, by hunger, and by their superhuman efforts. He looked with tenderness upon his old rickshaw, the two great wheels, the black bodywork, and the shafts, those instruments of torture between which he had suffered so much. How many thousands of kilometres had his naked feet travelled on the molten asphalt of this mirage city? He did not know. He knew only that every step had been an act of will to induce the *chakra* of his destiny to complete just one more turn. And now, that *chakra* was going to stop, once and for all.

He looked up at Musafir. 'Take your rickshaw back,' he said. 'It will make someone happy.'

He got to his feet again and for one last time pulled rickshaw No 1999 back to the stand on Park Circus. While he was saying goodbye to his friends, Hasari saw Musafir call out to one of a group of young men waiting on the edge of the pavement. They were all refugees, part of the latest exodus that had emptied the drought-ravaged countryside. All of them longed to harness themselves to a rickshaw. Hasari went over to the one the representative had chosen and smiled at him. Then he took the small copper bell from his finger.

'Take this bell, son,' he said, jangling it against a shaft. 'It will be your talisman to keep you safe from danger.'

Before going home, Hasari called at the skeleton warehouse where he claimed the second part of the proceeds from the sale of his bones. The cashier examined him with care and, judging that his decline was well under way, agreed to a further payment.

It took three more days of heated arguing before everyone agreed upon Amrita's dowry. As tradition required, the bargain was sealed with a special ceremony in the Pals' compound, with all the other residents as witnesses. Coconuts, incense and a carpet of banana leaves were laid on the ground to enable the *pujari* to carry out the various rites and pronounce the *mantras* for the occasion. Hasari announced that he was giving his daughter away in marriage and enumerated the list of goods that would constitute her dowry. Much to Stephan's fury, this provoked a further outburst from the groom's family. Suddenly they demanded proof of the cost of the jewels, protested that the wedding sari wasn't beautiful enough, and announced that the transistor radio they had received was pathetic. Each recrimination took away a little more of the small amount of breath left in Hasari's chest.

On the eve of the wedding, yet a new drama erupted. The groom's father and uncles and a group of his friends burst into the compound to check the preparations for the event.

'There will be at least a hundred of us,' declared the father. 'And we want to be sure there will be enough to eat.'

Stephan saw Hasari start. 'A hundred?' he protested. 'But we agreed that there wouldn't be more than fifty of you.'

A loud argument followed, to the amusement of the entire compound. The visitors dissected the menu, demanding that a vegetable be added here, a fruit or pastry there. His back to the wall, Hasari finally said, 'Agreed, if you reduce the number of guests by twenty.'

'Twenty? Never! By twelve and not one more.'

'All right, twelve,' sighed Hasari. But his problems were not yet over. For astrological reasons, Indian weddings nearly always take place in the middle of the night. 'Where's the generator?' asked the groom's father. 'A wedding without lots of lights is not a proper wedding.'

Once more, Hasari felt the ground dissolve beneath his feet. Faces, walls, sounds, all swam together in a haze, and he groaned, 'I'm not going to make it. They're going to do me out of Amrita's marriage.' Yet this time the groom's father was justified. For the millions of slum people condemned by a lack of electricity to live in perpetual obscurity, there could be no celebration without lights. But Hasari shook his head sadly, showing them his empty palms. He had taken the two rings and the small pendant that had formed part of his wife's dowry, plus the watch his son Shambu had found among the refuse, to the usurer. He had killed himself working. He had sold his bones. He had exceeded the possible. Yet now he must submit to the supreme humiliation.

'If you persist in these demands,' he said, pausing frequently to regain his breath, 'there is only one solution: we shall have to cancel the wedding. I have no more money.'

So less than fourteen hours before the ceremony, they had reached an impasse. For the first time Hasari appeared resigned to the collapse of negotiations. Appalled, Stephan decided to intervene.

'I know a compound not very far away where they have electricity,' he said. 'A cable could easily be led off it to here. With four or five lamps, there would be plenty of light.'

For the rest of his life Stephan would remember the gratitude on Hasari's face.

But the battle was still not won. Less than seven hours before the ceremony, a new crisis erupted. This time Hasari himself was responsible. He enquired of the groom's father as to the manner in which the groom would arrive at the ceremony. Even in this slum of mud and pestilence, such a journey was usually undertaken on a horse, caparisoned with gold and velvet.

'In a rickshaw,' replied the father.

Stephan thought Hasari was going to choke. 'My daughter will never marry a man who comes to her wedding in a rickshaw,' he thundered. 'I demand a taxi.'

Providence was once more to call upon Son of Miracle. Informed of the latest point of difference between the two families, the taxi driver was quick to offer his car to transport the cortege.

And so, a few hours later, Hasari at last witnessed the marvellous sight towards which all his travail had been directed.

'Look, Big Brother Stephan, how beautiful my daughter is!' he murmured ecstatically. Amrita was swathed in a scarlet sari sprinkled with golden stars. Her head bowed, her face concealed behind a muslin veil, her toes, ankles and wrists sparkling with the jewellery that was her dowry, she was led by her mother to the rice-straw mat placed in the courtyard, just in front of the little brazier in which the sacred and eternal flame burned. His lips parted in a smile that rose from the very depths of his soul, Hasari rejoiced in the magical scene that wiped out so many nightmare images: Amrita crying with cold and hunger in the winter nights on the city pavement, foraging through the refuse from the Grand Hotel, begging in the Chowringhee arcades ... This was a moment of triumph, of apotheosis, of final revenge on a cruel *karma*.

A brass band burst into sound, accompanied by singing and shouting. Preceded by a troupe of dancers, the groom's procession made a grand entry into the courtyard. With his cardboard diadem encrusted with bits of coloured glass, the groom looked like a maharajah surrounded by his courtiers. Before taking up his position, he had to submit to the ritual of *parda*, the imposition of a veil, so that his betrothed could not see his face before the moment prescribed in the liturgy. The *pujari* motioned to him to sit beside Amrita.

So began the interminable and picturesque ritual of a Hindu wedding ceremony.

The gathering noticed that the best man's place, to the right of the bride, was still vacant. Hasari had offered this privileged place to his brother in poverty, the man of God who, with Son of Miracle, had been his providence, his friend, his confidant. But Stephan had not been able to occupy the place. At the very moment the groom made his entrance, a brutal series of convulsions had shaken Hasari's chest and the priest had

199

hastily carried him into his own room. The eyes and mouth that only a moment previously had been exultant with joy had closed in an expression of intense pain. When the convulsions stopped, Hasari's body remained stiff and motionless. His lips were completely blue, a clear indication of respiratory failure.

Putting all his weight on Hasari's chest, Stephan started to massage it vigorously. The sternum and ribs creaked under the pressure of his fingers. Soaking his beautiful white best man's *punjabi* with perspiration, the priest worked with all his might and, miracle of miracles, a very feeble, almost imperceptible breath quivered through the fleshless form.

Stephan wrote of the events that followed in a letter to the superior of his order. 'Hasari opened his eyes. He was breathing very faintly and he seemed to be straining to hear the voices and music of the festivities. He smiled weakly at the joyous commotion, then looked at me with eyes that were full of supplication. "Big Brother, Big Brother," he repeated, then murmured some words in Bengali. I realised he was asking me to take care of his wife and sons, and I tried to reassure him.

'With his hands, Hasari indicated that he wanted to leave the compound so as not to disrupt the celebrations. Quietly, Son of Miracle and I removed him to a room in another compound. After that, it all happened very quickly. Hasari was shaken by a violent attack and shortly afterwards his chest caved in with a rattle. It was all over. I closed his eyes and recited the prayer for the dead.'

Less than an hour later, a series of heavy knocks shook the door to the room where Son of Miracle and Stephan were watching over the mortal remains of their friend, now enveloped in a white *khadi* shroud and adorned with a garland of marigolds. The taxi driver went to open it. In the shadows he could just make out two dark-skinned faces.

'We're the Doms,' announced one of them. 'The deceased was under contract. We've come to collect his body.'

13

'Brothers, sisters, listen!' Stephan Kovalski pointed towards the ringing bells and then closed his eyes to absorb fully the crystalline notes that came cascading across the fume-laden sky. 'Christ our Saviour is born,' announced the peal from the illuminated church of Our Lady of the Loving Heart. It was midnight on Christmas Eve.

At that instant, from one end of the immense metropolis to the other, different chimes sounded out the same news. Despite the fact that Christians represented a small minority in Calcutta, the birth of Jesus was celebrated with as much display as that of Krishna, Muhammad or Buddha. Christmas was only one of approximately twenty official religious festivals marked by a general holiday in a city where such a miscellany of faiths and such devotion to God prevailed.

Filled with decorations, the church looked, in the darkness, like a maharajah's palace on a coronation night. In the courtyard, only a few metres from the pavements where thousands of homeless people slept huddled in the bitter cold, an enormous crèche with life-size figures showed the birth of the Messiah in the straw of a Bethlehem stable. Women in magnificent saris, their heads covered with embroidered veils, and men and children dressed like princes filled the vast nave, which was adorned with banners and garlands.

Suddenly a burst of firecrackers shook the night. To the accompaniment of the organ, the congregation joined in singing a hymn celebrating the advent of the holy infant. The rector, Alberto Cordeiro, the priest who had once tried to dissuade Kovalski from going to live among the poor of the City of Joy, looked more opulent than ever in his red silk vestments. He made his entrance escorted by a double row of choirboys, moving ceremonially through the nave towards the altar.

Deep in the alleyways of the City of Joy there were garlands of lights and streamers on the Christian homes. Loudspeakers sounded with carols and hymns. 'So much celebration among so much poverty,' marvelled Max Loeb, who attended midnight Mass for the first time in his life. For the Christians of the City of Joy, however, it was the luminous star poised on the end of a bamboo cane above Kovalski's hovel that was the most beautiful symbol of that magical night. Surya, the old Hindu from the teashop, and Saladdin, the Muslim, had hoisted the emblem into the sky over the City of Joy, as if to say to the despairing people of the slum, 'Be not afraid. You are not alone. On this night when the God of the Christians was born, there is already a saviour among us.'

That night the 'saviour' was celebrating the mystery of the Eucharist for some fifty worshippers who had assembled in Margareta's compound. And, listening to the carols that filled the night, one conviction impressed itself upon Stephan more forcefully than ever: nowhere was the message of a God who was made man to save humanity more alive than in this slum. The City of Joy and Bethlehem were one and the same place. Before lifting to the heavens the fragment of unleavened bread, the priest felt the need to speak a few words:

'It is easy for any man to recognise and glorify the riches of the world,' he said, seeking out faces in the shadows. 'But only a poor man can know the riches of poverty. Only a poor man can know the riches of suffering. And because it is the poor who know such riches, it is they who are able to stand against the wretchedness of the world, against injustice, against the suffering of the innocent,' he continued. 'If Christ chose to be born among the poor, it was because He wanted the poor to teach the world the good news of His message, the good news of His love for mankind.

'Brothers and sisters of the City of Joy, it is you who are the bearers of that flame of hope. I can promise you that the day will come when the tiger shall lie down with the young child, and the cobra will sleep with the dove, and all the peoples of all the nations will be as brothers and sisters.'

SEVERAL WEEKS LATER, Aloka, Hasari Pal's widow, brought Stephan Kovalski a brown envelope covered with official stamps.

'Big Brother Stephan, a registered letter arrived for you this morning,' she announced.

Kovalski saw immediately that it came from the Home Ministry. His heart pounding, he opened it. Dear God, he thought, the government is kicking me out. Anxiously he scanned the words, then reread them several times to be sure of their meaning.

'The Government of India hereby grants the said Stephan Kovalski the certificate of . . .' The letter went on to declare that after he had pledged his loyalty at the time appointed and according to the regulations prescribed by the law, he would be entitled to all the privileges, prerogatives and rights and would be subject to all the obligations, duties and responsibilities of an Indian citizen.

'An Indian citizen,' stammered Stephan. All at once it was as if the very heart of the slum were beating in his chest. He leaned against the wall and closed his eyes. When he opened them again, he grasped the cross he wore round his neck and gazed at the two dates his mother had had inscribed upon it: his birth and his ordination. His vision dimmed by tears of happiness, he considered the little blank space that remained. This very day he would add the date of his final entry into the great family of his Indian brothers, for this was the third most important day of his life.

DOMINIQUE LAPIERRE

For years, Dominique Lapierre enjoyed all the perks of a career as a world-renowned journalist and author—first-class travel, a comfortable home in the south of France, two swimming pools. As an editor with *Paris Match*, Lapierre covered the international scene for fifteen years, interviewing some of the most prominent men and women of our time. With American journalist Larry Collins, he co-authored a number of important bestsellers, including *Is Paris Burning?* and *O Jerusalem*. When *Freedom at Midnight*, their epic account of the events leading up to Indian independence, was published in 1976, critics hailed it as a masterpiece.

Then, in 1980, Lapierre travelled with his wife, also named Dominique, to India to donate royalties from *Freedom at Midnight* to the poor. He met people like Mother Teresa and Stephan Kovalski and discovered that the seemingly inhumane city of Calcutta had the magical power to create heroes and saints.

Intrigued, he returned to Calcutta in 1981 and took up residence in Anand Nagar where he lived for three years—the most moving experience of his life. 'I pulled rickshaws—including Hasari's—rolled *bidis*, cooked on a *chula*. Above all, I learned to thank God for the smallest blessing, to be unafraid of death, never to despair.'

Living conditions in the slum have improved enormously in the past few years. Funding from European, North American and the Bengal and Calcutta governments has helped create training centres for adolescents, medical clinics and soup kitchens. Today Bandona, Margareta and Aristotle John, along with some two hundred Indian social workers, nurses, doctors and foreign volunteers, form the mainspring of an extensive network of mutual help and education.

Lapierre himself has received over forty thousand letters in response to *The City of Joy*, many of them containing gifts of money, bonds or jewellery for the poor of Anand Nagar. With those donations and half of his royalties from the book, he and his wife founded an association called Action Aid for Lepers' Children of Calcutta. The group has five thousand members throughout Europe and the United States, and supports a home for two hundred and fifty children in Calcutta.

SPEARHEAD

A CONDENSATION OF THE BOOK BY

Peter Driscoll

ILLUSTRATED BY JACK McCARTHY

Mass meetings testify to the indestructible popularity of Lincoln Kumalo, the black nationalist leader who has languished for twenty-five years in a South African prison cell, known only as prisoner 4008. Now, Kumalo is seriously ill and the government is faced with a grave dilemma: they cannot release him unconditionally and yet they dread the consequences should he die in custody.

As elements within the Intelligence Service devise a cunning plot to rid themselves of Kumalo once and for all, their plans are overheard by a prison inmate, who bravely smuggles to Kumalo's followers a cryptic message which ends, 'Who shall deliver him?'

Within hours, the search is on for a man with the necessary experience and expertise—a man who will welcome a challenge where all the odds are stacked against him.

Prologue

The cemetery stood on high ground, a forest of gravestones and small marble crosses close to the summit of a windswept hill, and the townships were visible on all sides around it. Row after row, block after block, the tiny, identical, iron-roofed houses stretched away in the midmorning light to a dim horizon. Here and there stood a few sickly-looking bluegum trees or a patch of veld blackened by winter burning, but otherwise it was a landscape almost without features.

The funeral procession had been in view all the way from the church, a dark river of people twisting its way up towards the hill, and now they were close enough for the policemen and soldiers blocking the road to hear the sounds they made. Banners swayed above them in the thin winter sunshine, the brilliant colours of the People's Congress standing out against the drabness of the backdrop.

'God bless Africa,' said Corporal Frank Rendle.

'And all who sail in her,' said Nicky Flynn.

It was an old joke, and neither of them laughed. Rendle swigged reflectively at the litre bottle of Coke laced with brandy and passed it to Nicky Flynn, then leaned against the dusty side of the Saracen armoured personnel carrier and tipped back his visored riot helmet. He was a big, brawny young man with a nonchalant, self-contained air.

Nicky Flynn, the lance corporal of the squad, was less composed. He drank quickly, then picked up his rifle and glanced along the slope at the police Land-Rover and the three Hippo riot trucks that straddled the road. A couple of dozen cops were perched on top of them, protected by their twelve-foot sides of armoured steel, pump guns and gas at the ready.

'Remember the rule,' Rendle told Flynn. 'We're keeping out of this. If the Boers want any zapping done, let them do it themselves.'

You could smell the hatred in the air. The procession moved closer, the hearse groaning along in bottom gear. Among the banners there were placards, most of them blownup photographs of the same man. It was always the same picture, with no need of a caption or slogan. The photograph explained itself, for it was this man's wife they were burying.

It was the squad's principle to avoid trouble. They were an ill-assorted mob with an easy coherence long established: Brakpan, the Saracen's driver, Lightning, their gangling radio operator, Carver and Fish, Blikkies Steyn and Younis the Greek. Back in Angola they'd been in a real war together, and this stuff, by comparison, was a dirty joke. They had only turned up at the funeral by chance. Their radio hardly ever worked, the result of some undetectable tampering by Lightning, and the Saracen was like a gypsy caravan in which they wandered more or less at will. There'd never been much love lost between cops and troopies—especially since the police had failed to impose order on the townships and the army had been drawn reluctantly into the turmoil. It wasn't what these national servicemen had been trained for, and mostly it wasn't to their taste.

Beside one of the Hippos, a red-faced little police major was fiddling with a megaphone. The procession had halted, a hundred yards short of the police line. The singing died away.

'Attention! Attention!' The major addressed them through his bullhorn. 'This is an illegal gathering in terms of the Emergency Regulations. You are not, repeat not, permitted to use a funeral for the purposes of a political demonstration ...' His voice echoed back tinnily from the rooftops. 'The coffin and the clergy and the immediate family of the deceased may enter the cemetery. The rest of you have two minutes to disperse peacefully or force will be used ...'

'Whyn't they just let them bury the old cow and be done with it?' Lightning wondered plaintively. Nobody answered him. Tension seemed to make the air shimmer between the opposing sides now, the cops watching from the high battlements of their trucks, the mourners massed beneath the silently accusing photographs.

For a minute, neither side seemed sure what to do. Then a group of three or four people detached themselves from the crowd and began to walk towards the police, a deputation led by a priest. At the same time one of the Hippos eased its way forward.

ALEX MZANDWILE DUMA, lingering near the centre of the crowd, sensed there was going to be trouble. The presence of the Boers was a provocation in itself. You would think they'd have more sense than to interfere on such an emotionally charged occasion as the burial of Elizabeth Kumalo.

He kept to the middle of the procession and out of view. Comrade

Duma, as he was known to some, was an officer of the outlawed People's Congress, a veteran of guerrilla training across the border, and for that reason a marked man. Only the size and anonymity of the crowd protected him; only allegiance to Nandi Kumalo's father and the memory of her mother had coaxed him out onto the streets at all.

The Hippo stopped twenty yards short of the crowd. A half-brick went sailing out, arced over the heads of the priest and his deputation and clattered harmlessly off the side of the truck. A couple more stones were flung. Duma caught a glimpse of the priest turning to face the procession, mouthing some unheard appeal, and for a few moments nothing more happened. The disorder might have ended there, but suddenly one of the policemen sprang to his feet and fired a gas grenade. The shell struck the ground in front of the delegation and engulfed them in tear gas.

There was always a thin line between defiance and fury, and it was crossed in a second. A great roar of anger went up round Duma. The priest and his companions reeled aside, coughing and sobbing. Women and older people fled from the vapour, but young men were already gathering stones and hurling them at the truck. More gas grenades were lobbed; screams were interspersed by the sharper bark of shotguns as the police began blasting at the scattered groups of stone-throwers.

All the while Duma was being carried along by a solid mass of men who were eager to join the battle. He tried to push against them, to wriggle out sideways, but was thrust steadily forward. He saw the first Hippo moving again, ploughing its way through the crowd and bearing down on him like an ocean liner.

RENDLE'S SQUAD had a panoramic view of the riot from their vantage point on the hill. They were still gathered round the Saracen, watching, when the little police major marched angrily over from his Land-Rover.

He stood weighing Rendle up for a second. 'Listen to me, Corporal. Here in the townships you army blokes take your orders from us. So you'll go down there and help pick up the agitators among that mob. Any Kaffir who looks like a stone-thrower, you pull him in. Got it?'

The policeman strutted off. Rendle jerked his head resignedly at the others and within seconds they had all piled into the Saracen—Brakpan and Lightning in the two front seats of the cab, Rendle in the turret behind them, the other five in the rear. The Rolls-Royce engine coughed throatily into life, and Brakpan gunned the vehicle down the slope—an ugly, snub-nosed, ten-ton monster for which they had all developed a perverse affection. 'Where to?' Brakpan yelled at Rendle.

'Oh, we'll look busy for a bit and then buzz off.'

Rendle had spoken. It was Rendle who had taught them not to buck the system but to use it; Rendle, the busted-down helicopter pilot, who knew it made more sense quietly to ignore orders than to disobey them; Rendle the leader of an undeclared but permanent state of mutiny.

NOW DUMA SAW that one of the riot trucks had swung round behind him, cutting off his retreat. There was open ground ahead, and it was only fifty yards to the nearest houses. There the streets would swallow him up, but to reach them he would have to cross a gap between another Hippo and a prowling Saracen armoured car. He knew he would be horribly exposed, but anything was better than waiting here.

He braced himself to run, then felt a hand seize his arm. He snatched it away and turned in panic to see Nandi behind him: Nandi Kumalo in her black mourning dress, a black straw hat askew on her head.

'What do you want?' he demanded fiercely.

She shook her head. Clearly she didn't know what she wanted. Her mother's death, and now the shambles of the funeral, had confused her beyond any logic. 'Get lost, Nandi! Don't draw attention to me.' He thrust her away from him and ran.

He raced diagonally away from the road, towards the nearest houses. He was only yards from the entrance to a lane when he felt a kind of sharp tug at his left shoulder and was lifted off his feet by some unseen force. The crash of the pump gun reached him as he hit the ground. He got to his hands and knees, crawled a few yards into the lane and collapsed. All he could think, before a dim shadow spread over his consciousness, was that he'd been a fool.

THE SARACEN HAD MADE a wide circle round the stranded hearse, its wheels crunching over the debris of rioting: stones, tear-gas shells and abandoned placards. The shooting stopped, and across the open space half a dozen wounded youths were being herded to the trucks.

From the turret Rendle caught a movement to his right and saw a woman in a black dress running towards an alleyway between some houses. Just inside it she stopped and bent over a figure lying on the ground. For no reason he could think of, Rendle yelled to Brakpan to follow her.

In a few seconds the vehicle pulled across the entrance to the alley, blocking it. The woman was kneeling now beside the prone figure of a young man. She looked up in fright as Rendle called down to her.

'Is he dead?'

She shook her head. 'Badly hurt. Let him go. He'll be all right.'

Rendle dropped to the ground and went over to the injured man. The left shoulder of his jacket had been torn off by birdshot, and his left arm and back were soaked in blood. He seemed unconscious.

'Just let him go,' the woman repeated. She was young, with strong Zulu features, and quite attractive. 'I don't think those Boer police know he's here,' she said. 'They don't have to know, do they? It will go badly with him if they take him.'

'Who is he? What's he done?'

'His name is Duma. He's my friend. He's done nothing that I would call a crime, but they will beat him and torture him all the same.'

Rendle shrugged. 'He needs patching up. He needs a doctor.'

'Then will you help him?' she asked quietly. 'Take him out of here?'

Carver, Fish and Nicky Flynn had spilled out of the Saracen. They had heard the question as well and they stared at Rendle, who looked back down the lane, with the glint of amusement in his eyes that was always his response to a challenge. It could be done, of course; the police had either missed Duma or assumed the soldiers were picking him up.

Rendle took a decision. 'Get him into the wagon,' he said to the others, and to her, 'This conversation never happened, right? As far as you're concerned we just took him away. Where does he live?'

'Everywhere. Nowhere. You know Dr Sithole's clinic in Meadowlands? They'll take care of him and ask no questions.'

Only Nicky Flynn demurred. Nicky worried at times about the way they carried on. 'We're supposed to take him in, Frank. That major said—'

'He said to pick them up. He didn't say what to do with them.'

Carver and Fish staggered with the wounded man to the Saracen, manoeuvred him through the doors and onto one of the rows of seats that faced each other along the sides. The three men hopped in after him. The young black woman stood by the doors.

'Thank you.' She gave the soldiers one of those sudden, wide, natural African smiles that banish any thought of mistrust. 'Our people will remember you for this.'

'I'd rather they didn't, frankly.' Rendle slammed the doors and shouted instructions to Brakpan, and a moment later they were moving. The policemen standing by their Hippos glanced at them casually as they turned northwards, and the major watched their departure with only brief puzzlement. Bloody soldiers were worse than useless out here, he thought.

Chapter One

The commandant's chauffeur stopped the car in front of the prison's main entrance. He got out at once to open the rear door, but Dr Louis Rose had already alighted and was striding towards the great steel gates, leaving little Dr Els to scramble out and hurry after him. Their arrival had been observed through a television scanner, and the narrow door set in one gate swung open to admit them.

Dr Rose was tall and distinguished, carrying a black medical bag in one hand and an expensive calfskin briefcase in the other. He drummed his fingers on the reception counter and studied his drab surroundings with disfavour while Els, the harassed prison medical officer, spoke to the men in Afrikaans and a telephone call was made. Finally the sergeant in charge put down the phone and said, 'We'll take you up right away, gentlemen.'

The hospital was in a new wing connected to the main prison block.

Access to it was up some stairs, through a maze of passageways and a series of steel doors. Not for nothing was Pollsmoor Prison considered the most secure in the country.

Finally, glass doors opened into a well-lit lobby and, apart from the bars on the windows, a more conventional hospital atmosphere.

A gate was unlocked to give access to two more flights of stairs. Outside a door at the very end of yet another corridor a warder was posted. He knocked on it at their approach, and another man examined them through a peephole before letting them in.

The object of all this attentive isolation was sitting up in a high hospital bed that looked too small for him, smiling a welcome.

Thirty years of medical practice had trained Dr Rose never to show surprise. Yet even this professional conditioning could hardly prevent his gaping in astonishment. He turned to Els. 'You might have warned me.'

'I did say it was highly confidential,' the little man muttered.

WHEN THEY RETURNED to the hospital lobby half an hour later, three men were lined up formally to greet them in Dr Els's office. Els made the introductions: the prison commandant, a Mr van Straaten and a Colonel Prinsloo. Rose shook hands briskly with each of them.

'We're grateful to you for coming all this way, Doctor, and at such short notice.' That was van Straaten, a slight, dapper man of forty, with gold-framed glasses and a grey suit. 'I trust everything has gone smoothly?'

'Thank you.' Rose made it clear that he was not interested in small talk. 'I have to say I find all this subterfuge a little distasteful . . .'

'But perhaps now that you've seen the patient you can understand why. He is, after all, a security prisoner . . .'

'Or what some of us would call a political prisoner.'

Van Straaten winced slightly. 'Please try to understand, Dr Rose. His health is of great concern to us. Dr Els recommended calling you in because you're the best in your field. Depending on your diagnosis, decisions may have to be taken at the highest level. In the meantime we can take no risks. His daughter will call on Tuesday, for example. That's why you were asked not even to reveal your identity to him.'

Colonel Prinsloo, a tall, dyspeptic-looking man in his fifties, spoke in Afrikaans to van Straaten. The younger man in turn looked at Dr Rose.

'Well, Doctor,' he said. 'If you'll let us have your diagnosis?'

Rose glanced questioningly at Els. Medical protocol required him to report to the colleague who had consulted him, not to these laymen. 'Go ahead, go ahead,' Els said hastily, and the visitor unclipped his briefcase and began to spread out X-ray plates and dossiers on the desk.

His examination had only confirmed the conclusions he had reached by studying the plates and medical notes he had been sent. It had been a very conscientious examination all the same. Although they had not said much to each other, the doctor had been aware at once of an extraordinary magnetism in his patient's personality: a quality of easy authority, inner strength and absolute conviction. Like every legendary figure, the man had always seemed more a myth than a live human being. His was a name uttered with reverence by millions of people, by no means all of them black. He was the very embodiment of the struggle for racial justice; he had been in jail for twenty-five years, and he was perhaps the world's most famous prisoner. Yet the man had an illness that was real enough, and Rose was going to tell his captors with a vengeance. He was contemptuous of these people: they were frightened of Lincoln Kumalo, deep down, but they were even more frightened of his dying on them, from neglect or incompetence. He understood now that they wanted him, Dr Louis Rose, not just because he was the country's leading urologist but also to show that their own hands were clean.

'Very well. Now that I've seen Mr Kumalo—'

'Please . . .' The interruption came from Prinsloo. 'Not the name, if you please. Officially he's still anonymous.'

'Now that I've seen this anonymous patient, then,' said Rose with sarcastic emphasis, 'I have found nothing to contradict the opinion I formed after my first scrutiny of the X-rays. Without doubt he is suffering from cancer of the prostate gland. He's going to need surgery.' He spoke now without looking at Dr Els. 'Frankly, I'm surprised that it wasn't diagnosed sooner.'

PHINEAS MOLEFE was four foot nine inches tall, weighed slightly less than one hundred pounds, and had long ago learned that the key to his survival lay in giving no offence. In his four years in Pollsmoor, Phineas had also learned to keep his own counsel: he had not forgotten that it was only the stupidity of an accomplice that had landed him here in the first place, and that otherwise he might still be creaming off fifty rands a week from the takings of the dairy in Salt River where he had once worked as a clerk.

Because he gave no trouble and did what he was told, Phineas had been made a trusty. He had worked quietly and efficiently as a clerk in the dispensary for three years now, and was as inconspicuous as the low stool on which he squatted behind the counter. But in his spare moments Phineas counted off the months and days to his release, and knew exactly what he would do when it came. He was going to go north to join the liberation army of the People's Congress.

This morning, to all appearances daydreaming as usual, Phineas listened with slightly more than his usual idle interest to the drone of voices from next door. A quirk in the way the rooms had been rearranged along the corridor gave him this opportunity to eavesdrop. Through the thin partition he could often hear Dr Els talking on the telephone, or holding discussions with his staff. These were usually incomprehensible to Phineas, but he was bored enough much of the time to find almost any distraction welcome.

DR ELS TOOK OUT CIGARETTES, offered them round and was refused. The commandant, whose presence had been purely ceremonial, had excused himself and left. Van Straaten and Prinsloo were giving Dr Rose their full attention.

'The symptoms were first investigated six weeks ago,' said Rose. He picked up two X-ray plates and indicated each in turn. 'Now, when we look at the pictures taken last week, we see that the tumour has grown quite substantially. It was at this stage that Dr Els sought my opinion.' He paused. 'At present it is a matter of concern rather than alarm. It's not yet close to spreading to other organs, and that's where the real danger lies.'

'What can be done about it?' van Straaten asked.

'The treatment is surgical removal of the gland, though that depends very much on the general condition of the patient. Assessing that was the main purpose of my examination, and I can tell you now that he's in superb shape. He has the constitution of a man twenty years younger.'

'You'll operate, then?'

'Yes, but not immediately. With a tumour, my approach is to begin with a course of hormone treatment which will reduce the size of the carcinoma while also preventing its spread. That, in turn, will minimise the trauma of surgery. In a man of his age, which I understand is sixty-eight, the healing process is slow, no matter how fit he may be. I would say four to six weeks from now, depending on the success of the hormone tablets. In fact, if we set a date now for about six weeks hence, I'll guarantee that he'll be in the best possible condition to undergo surgery.' He consulted his diary. 'December the sixteenth would be ideal.'

Van Straaten looked pained, as though he felt he was being hurried. 'As I mentioned, Dr Rose, this has to have approval higher up.'

'Then get it quickly. You can't play politics with this man's life. Within four months or so his condition might be quite irreversible.'

The bluntness of this statement reduced them to silence, giving Rose the opportunity to follow through. 'Another thing. I understand that this hospital isn't equipped for major surgery. You may know that my clinic near Johannesburg specialises in these disorders. That is where I propose to operate.'

Colonel Prinsloo began to protest at once, but van Straaten put a restraining hand on his arm. 'Is that really necessary, Doctor? Surely there are quite adequate facilities here in Cape Town?'

'Of course. But if you intend to let me have full control, then this is the only way I can exercise it. I have a reputation to protect, after all.'

'The security problems—' Prinsloo began.

'Will be your concern, Colonel. And you'll have plenty of time before the sixteenth to solve them.' Van Straaten did not seem put out. 'If that's what you require, Doctor, then I have little doubt that the relevant persons in government will approve. However, this does make the matter of secrecy even more vital.'

Van Straaten took a folded sheet of paper from his pocket, opened it out and placed it on the desk. Rose picked it up. It was a printed form, headed *Act 16 of 1956: The Official Secrets Act (As Amended)*.

'Quite ridiculous!' Rose was scornful. 'My dealings with this patient are covered by my medical confidentiality. What if I refuse to sign?'

'Then, regrettably, the matter will end here and now.' Van Straaten's small brown eyes were suddenly sharp behind his glasses. 'The security laws in any case require you to forget everything you have seen and heard in here. We'll find someone else.'

'Perhaps I should have asked,' said Rose, 'exactly who you mean by *we*.'

'Ah. I thought you might have guessed that, Doctor. Colonel Prinsloo is an officer of the Security Police, entrusted with special responsibility for this prisoner. And I have the privilege to be Deputy Director of the National Intelligence Service.'

PHINEAS MOLEFE SAW DR ELS and one of his visitors leaving the hospital. Phineas was carrying a tray from the kitchen and he stepped nimbly aside to let them pass. Dr Els didn't notice him and he was quite happy to seem insignificant.

He went into the dispensary, still mulling over what he had learned in the past forty minutes. He had heard the conversation next door only in snatches, and not a lot of it made sense. But one thing was certain: it was Kumalo, the greatest of the Leaders, whom they had been discussing. Many of the words had been incomprehensible, and Phineas was only just beginning to get the drift of it when the pharmacist sent him out to fetch his morning coffee. Now he carried the coffee and biscuits to his boss in the room at the rear of the dispensary, and returned with his own tin mug of tea and hunk of brown bread to the counter.

Voices drifted through from Dr Els's office once again.

'There's a wonderful opportunity here, Prinsloo, if we're up to grabbing it. The first opportunity we've ever had of solving this whole problem without getting mud on our faces. It's going to need permission from the top, friends at court, but after what I've heard this morning I know it can be done.'

The voices became low and incomprehensible. Then he heard a coarse laugh and the other voice said quite clearly, 'We had a much simpler way of doing this sort of thing in the old days. It was called "Shot while trying to escape".'

'Phineas! You're asleep again, my boy.'

The pharmacist was standing in the doorway of the back room, and Phineas realised that it was not the first time he had been called. The voices next door went silent. Phineas quickly collected himself and followed the pharmacist back to the dispensary.

Phineas's day continued in its humdrum way: requisitions for drugs were brought to his counter; he took these to the pharmacist, and when the orders were made up he took them back. He recorded each order in the daybook and filed a copy of the requisition.

He carried out these functions automatically, his mind in a turmoil of doubt and confusion, for he had understood enough of the words that had been spoken to grasp that he had eavesdropped on a ghastly secret. He wished he could seek advice, confide in someone about the things he had heard. But there was no one. The Leaders were inaccessible. As for his fellow *mugus* in Cell Block C, they were thieves and violent criminals, for the most part stupid and not to be trusted.

Phineas took no risks and asked no favours. It had not, for instance, escaped the notice of the others in his cell block that he was sitting on a gold mine in this job: a handful of pills could have bought him anything from extra food to a month's supply of cigarettes, but he had resisted all pressures. He knew that once he began there would be no stopping.

All of which made it difficult to know what to do. That he had to do something seemed beyond question. If he could talk to no one in here about it, perhaps he could get a message out—but to whom? The Leader's daughter? He had heard them mention that she was to visit him next Tuesday. But Phineas could not possibly gain access to her. Besides, what could such a message actually convey? The only real fact at his disposal was the date, a day which had a significance of its own and on which a terrible thing was planned. Of the thing itself he had no knowledge.

A warning. That was all the message needed to contain. If a warning reached the right people, they would know how to act upon it. If it was intercepted, however, that would only make matters worse. The thing was to conceal its origins yet somehow show that it was authentic.

He pondered over these problems until late afternoon. His final job of the day was to file the drug prescription dockets. This had always seemed a pointless task: the dockets were seldom if ever needed again and thrown out at six-monthly intervals. There was one that was difficult to read, written in the shapeless scrawl of Dr Els, a prescription for a substance Phineas had never heard of. Stilboestrol? *Stilboestrol 3mg x 30*, it said: thirty tablets of three milligrams each. It carried today's date, November the second, and Dr Els's signature, and ...

Phineas stared at the docket as though hypnotised. Against the printed notation that said *Name of Patient*, Dr Els had written: *Prisoner 4008*.

At once everything seemed to fall into place. Everyone in here knew who Prisoner 4008 was. Presumably those outside—or those who mattered anyway—would recognise the number as well. This was a prescription for the drug the Leader was to have. This bit of paper could make the message authentic.

Down the corridors, warders began yelling for the trusties and orderlies to form up for the march back to their sections and cell blocks. Hastily Phineas stuck the docket into the file: he could retrieve it whenever he wanted. Now he could see a solution to his problem. Now he could plan.

AT THE WESTERN EDGE of the great sprawl of townships known collectively as Soweto, the road back to the military camp at Lenz led past a number of small farms. Down a track between two of these, in a fold among the mealie fields, Rendle's squad had discovered a small irrigation dam half full after the heavy spring rains, and this afternoon they swam in it. They stripped off their uniforms and wallowed and wrestled in the shallows.

Their banter was cruel but essentially good-natured, in the way of people who have nothing left to hide from each other. Their time in the bush together had exposed all their strengths and weaknesses. Only Rendle maintained a certain aloofness, and only Nicky Flynn was serious—or conventional—enough to flinch at their crudeness.

Nicky had had enough horseplay after a few minutes, and he left the water and sat naked on the rear deck of the armoured car, letting the late-afternoon sunshine dry him off as he watched the antics of the others.

Back in the rookie camp, the Afrikaner instructors had had a name for people like them. They were *kakdroogmakers*. Troublemakers. Each of them had brought his own kind of trouble with him from home, and they had drifted together the way dissenters paradoxically will, defying the rules imposed on them but creating a set of their own.

Nicky turned to pick his clothes from among the jumble of uniforms in the back of the wagon and saw a solitary black man approaching, dressed in jeans and a dark T-shirt and carrying a plastic shopping bag. He stopped a few feet away from the Saracen and smiled. 'Hello. You remember me?'

He didn't. The newcomer reached into his plastic bag and, mysteriously, took out a bottle of brandy. He tossed it to Nicky.

'I owe you that, white boy. Remember now?'

Now Nicky recognised him. 'Hey! Alex Duma? From that funeral?'

Duma was still smiling. 'I've seen you guys here before. I was waiting for a chance to show my thanks.'

Nicky would certainly not have recognised Duma if he had passed him on a township street. He was affable and self-possessed, quite different from the frightened animal they had helped on that day back in August. 'You get yourself patched up?' Nicky asked.

'Sure. Got a souvenir to show for it, though.' Duma pulled up the left sleeve of his T-shirt to expose the upper arm and shoulder. Against his brown skin was a rash of darker spots where the flesh was peppered with the tiny craters of birdshot. 'Soweto confetti,' he said with a grin. 'Almost like a war medal these days. You going back to your camp now?'

'In a few minutes.'

Nicky set the bottle down and began to get dressed. Duma, clearly in no hurry to go anywhere, sat down on the ground and watched the others horsing around in the water. He knew he was safe enough out here, away from the townships. Sometimes he came out to these fields and just lay about for a while, soaking up the sun. That was how he had spotted and recognised this Saracen truck and its crew, a fortnight ago.

'You guys don't take your work too seriously, ha?'

'We try to avoid aggro, that's all.' Nicky finished dressing and sat down beside him. 'We mark time. We take any fun we can find.'

'It would be good if there were more like you. Why should you do the Boers' work for them? Apartheid is finished. Why should we fight over the mistakes old men have made? What's in it for you?'

Nicky didn't reply. Watching the others beginning to leave the water and drift back to the Saracen, he knew it was a question they all asked themselves from time to time. Even Carver and Fish, whose thoughts rarely stretched beyond motorbikes and fighting. Even Brakpan, whose passion for driving fast cars—other people's fast cars—had had him in and out of reformatories from the age of fifteen.

They came back to the wagon and gathered in a naked, dripping circle round their visitor. All of them remembered Duma, once he had reintroduced himself. The incident in August had stuck in their memories.

Rendle, the last to arrive, glanced suspiciously at the brandy bottle now being handed round.

'Just returning a favour, Corporal,' said the black man with a grin. 'Showing that someone appreciates you, ha? Your job must be frustrating. The people may be afraid of your guns, but they have no respect for you. It's the People's Congress they look up to.'

'You reckon,' said Rendle neutrally. He took a drink from the bottle and passed it on. 'But what's the choice? The People's Congress isn't all sweetness and light. There've been bombs in supermarkets, people burned to death with rubber tyres round their necks.'

'The Congress doesn't approve of such things,' Duma said. 'But there are times when people take matters into their own hands. Excesses are committed in every war. They don't alter the basic justice of our cause.'

'Well, we prefer to stay neutral.'

'Nobody can be neutral in a struggle like this! Some day you'll have to make a choice between them and us.'

Halfway through dressing, several of the soldiers glanced at each other in silence. Duma knew he had struck a chord familiar to at least some of them, but it was Rendle who said, unexpectedly, 'There is a third choice, and that's just to get out. Leave the country legally and quietly, leave all this behind. That's what I'm planning to do.'

'You serious, Frank?' That was Carver, surprised. 'You going to take the chicken run?'

'There's nothing chicken about wanting to live your own life. If you guys had any sense you'd think about it too.' Rendle sounded faintly irritated. He was fully dressed now and he glanced at his watch. 'Time to go.' To Duma he said, 'If you came here to indoctrinate us, you're wasting your time.'

'Oh, I don't know. I'm just talking loosely. I really came only to thank you. Maybe I'll see you again, white boys.'

'Maybe.' Rendle gave him a curious look. The brandy bottle was in his hand again after doing another round, and he tossed it to Duma. 'Thanks,' he said.

The soldiers gathered their weapons and piled quickly into the Saracen. As it swung back onto the track, Duma stood up and waved. He drank the remaining brandy and threw the bottle away among the mealies. That had been a good investment, he thought. He had a feeling that these white boys were all drifting. With the right inducement they might be very useful.

JUDITH ROSE GOT BACK from the clinic to find that her father was already home from his trip. Thank God she'd remembered at the last minute to send the driver to the airport; otherwise she'd have got another of those pained little lectures about inefficiency. Louis Rose had just had his evening swim—thirty vigorous lengths of the twelve-metre pool, never more, never less—and was coming in from the terrace in his bathing trunks, rubbing himself dry.

She gave him a perfunctory kiss on the cheek. 'How was Cape Town?'

'I didn't see much of it.'

'What does it take to make Dr Rose travel fifteen hundred kilometres to see a patient? Must be somebody pretty special.'

'Special enough.'

'Give us a clue. A cabinet minister? An oil sheik?'

'You know my patients are my own affair, Jude. Why don't you go for a swim? It would put colour in your cheeks.'

She made a face at his retreating back as he padded off through the big drawing room. Even without meaning to, he could always find a way of criticising her. It really was time she got off her backside and found a place of her own to live.

Judith went to the drinks tray, poured herself a stiff Scotch and slumped into an armchair, staring out at the view across the garden through the open french windows. Her mother, in a straw hat and armed with a trowel, was discussing something with the gardener beside her fearsomely disciplined border of flowering shrubs. Hell! There was something degrading, at the age of twenty-seven, in living with your parents and working for your father. It was eighteen months now since she'd started doing the silly little job as an administrative assistant at the Woodvale Clinic, and sheer inertia had prevented her from moving on.

She stood up, poured another whisky and wandered with it out onto the terrace. Her mother had gone indoors, but the gardener was still out there, setting the sprinkler going. There was much that was seductive about this life, though others had rejected it long ago. Uncle Joshua, for instance— not really her uncle but her father's cousin and her godfather. She'd been only eleven when Joshua had slipped out of the country, and she wasn't old enough to understand the circumstances: the denial of a passport, the several arrests, the twilight world of the banning order. He had always seemed more fun than her father—more relaxed, less aloof—and even today it was difficult to think of him as a revolutionary. The Joshua Rosenblatt mentioned sometimes as one of the few white men prominent in the liberation movement seemed quite a different person from her Uncle Josh, the difference in their surnames merely reinforcing the impression. He had explained once that he'd reverted to using the family's original name not because he wanted to make anything of being a Jew, merely because it seemed less affected.

When she returned to the drawing room she found her father scanning a medical journal. She went to the drinks tray and poured another Scotch.

'Is that your second or your third?' her father suddenly asked.

Judith stood with the decanter still poised over her glass. 'I haven't been counting. Have you?'

'Of course not. I just can't help noticing that you're drinking rather more these days.'

'Are you talking from a medical or a moral point of view?'

'A medical one, naturally. It's a habit that becomes hard to break.'

Judith slammed down the glass and marched back out to the terrace. Standing there, staring out at the darkening garden, she felt tears of frustration pricking at her eyes but forced them back. Tomorrow, without fail, she would start hunting for a flat. And maybe she'd write to Uncle Joshua too.

Chapter Two

The weekly meeting of the State Security Council had been in progress for half an hour before Deputy Minister Frans Hoeksma was called in. Knowing his item was fifth on the agenda, he had arranged to be notified in his own office just before he was needed. It didn't do one's standing any good to be seen waiting about like a petitioner.

He was aware, as he entered, of the critical scrutiny of the dozen older men grouped round the table. Beside the President himself, eight of the others were politicians, and like all of their profession they were wary of young lions in their midst. When Hoeksma had been persuaded to give up a professorship in economics at Stellenbosch University to stand in a safe National Party seat three years ago, it had been on the understanding that early promotion would follow. What he had to say here this morning might well make a critical difference to his career.

He stopped just inside the door as it closed behind him, inclining his head slightly towards the head of the table.

'Mr President. Gentlemen. Good morning.' There were a few murmured replies. The President himself merely glanced up at him and continued a quiet conversation with the Minister of Justice on his left.

Hoeksma walked briskly to the vacant chair beside his own minister and sat down. He took out his folder and waited, attentive and respectful.

The President faced the table, commanding their attention. He was a heavy-featured man who didn't smile easily.

'Item five on the agenda,' he said. 'Subject: Lincoln Kumalo.'

Hoeksma cleared his throat. For the past two years the matter of Kumalo had been on the agenda at least once a month. At the first such meeting he had been asked to take personal control of the case, to report, to recommend, and—by implication—to find a solution.

The plain fact was that the government was in a gigantic dilemma over Kumalo. When they had put him in jail all those years ago it had been fairly safe to assume that he would soon be forgotten, a black rabble-rouser who had broken the law and paid the price. In fact, precisely the opposite had happened: Kumalo had become famous. In prison he was an embarrassment; out of it, he would be dangerous. Nobody knew what the hell to do with him, and the buck had been passed to Hoeksma.

They had also given him a brilliant assistant named Tertius van Straaten. Like Hoeksma himself, van Straaten was a fashionable young academic plucked from Stellenbosch to be made Deputy Director of the National Intelligence Service.

'Deputy Minister Hoeksma,' said the President, 'will update us.'

'Thank you, sir.' He paused. 'First, the matter of Kumalo's health. I am assuming you have all received a copy of the report prepared yesterday by my office.' Several of them nodded. 'Then you'll understand that it's necessary for him to have an operation soon: not a risky procedure, I gather, but a fairly major one. I believe you'll appreciate that it's important to demonstrate to the world that Kumalo is being treated humanely and is receiving the best possible medical care. The specialist we have engaged insists on performing this procedure at his clinic near Johannesburg. I think we should go along with that proposal.'

'The security problems . . .' He had been waiting for the first objection, and it came from the Commissioner of Police.

'They are in capable hands,' said Hoeksma, 'and I think are thoroughly outweighed by the advantages of doing this as openly as possible. Kumalo's daughter and his lawyer will of course have to be informed that an operation is pending, but there's no reason why the date and place of the operation shouldn't be kept secret until the last minute. There is another reason, which I'll come to later, for asking you to agree to this. But now I would like to address some of the wider issues which it raises.'

He had their full attention.

'As you know, gentlemen, Lincoln Kumalo has been in jail now for twenty-five years. And, as I hardly need to point out, we have been under considerable pressure, both domestically and internationally, to release him. All the same, he was sentenced to life imprisonment— '

'I think we all know the background, Frans,' his own minister interrupted, a trifly edgily.

'What I'm getting at is this. The whole political climate has changed since those days, when acts of political violence were the exception rather than the rule. There were no Arab terrorists blowing up planes then. There were no bombs exploding in the streets of London or Paris. Today, in comparison with others on the international scene, Kumalo is a moderate. And every day of his detention he becomes that much more of a living martyr.'

'If we let him out unconditionally we'll have a revolution on our hands,' said the Minister of Defence.

'And you think a revolution hasn't already begun?' He spoke harshly. 'Out in the townships they believe they are part of a revolution, and Kumalo is their hero. He has their support, almost unanimously.'

'You seem to be making an excellent case for keeping him where he is,' the Commissioner of Police put in drily.

'No. What I'm saying is that his importance as a symbol cannot be overstressed. But there's another side to that coin: without the symbol, this revolution would lose much of its coherence. We are engaged on our own programme of racial reforms, which in time we hope will cut the ground from under the more radical black elements. We need to buy that time, gentlemen, and in order to do so we've always known that Kumalo would have to be removed from the equation.

'Up to now our strategy has been to effect his release upon certain conditions—to let him go while seeing to it that he is politically neutralised. He has seen through that, and rejected it. That has left us with two alternatives: to keep him in prison indefinitely or to release him on his own terms and face the consequences. In view of the situation that has arisen over his health, I believe we now have a third choice.'

He paused again, a little theatrically, glancing round the table at their heavy, serious faces. He had primed them well, he thought.

'We have an opportunity here,' he said, 'through a set of circumstances that will never arise again, to achieve exactly what we want without appearing to influence events at all. The key to this enterprise is to let him think he has beaten us. In a roundabout way, of course: it shouldn't be made to look too easy. Anything that happened after that would be coincidental, outside our control.'

'How do you persuade him that he's won?' asked the Commissioner of Police suspiciously.

'We don't have to. We have only to convince a few others, beginning with his daughter.'

IT WAS ON THAT SAME FRIDAY afternoon that Phineas Molefe put his plan into effect.

In the outer room in which he worked was a metal cupboard containing minor medical accessories. At one o'clock the pharmacist went to lunch, locking the door of the back room as usual. Left to himself for half an hour, Phineas went to the bottom shelf of the cupboard and pulled out a box of empty tablet phials, small brown plastic tubes with snap-on lids that were used by the hundred every week. From the half-empty box he took a small phial, two inches long by half an inch across. Then he went to the cabinet where the prescription dockets were filed and took out the one that Dr Els had made out for Prisoner 4008 two days ago. He folded it, and rolled it into a cylinder of just the right size to go into the phial. He capped the phial and slipped it into the pocket of his prison blouse.

Back at the store cupboard, he opened a jar of Vaseline and skimmed a good-sized blob of the jelly off the top. Then, with the Vaseline concealed in his fist, he left the dispensary and went to the lavatory.

There are few places to hide things in a prison, and none that are totally secure, but for a couple of hours this would have to do. Standing on the lavatory seat, Phineas was just tall enough to lift the lid off the old iron cistern. He scraped the Vaseline off his hand onto the inside edge of the metal, above the waterline. He dropped the phial into the cistern and left it to float there. He replaced the heavy lid, flushed the lavatory, washed his hands and returned to the dispensary.

The next stage would be much trickier. Although Phineas never spent more than a few minutes in the back room with the pharmacist where the controlled drugs were kept, he knew the exact location of almost every type of drug in the place. He also knew there were ninety-four five-milligram Dexedrine tablets on a shelf just inside the room to the right. The number hadn't changed for several months.

Dexedrine was an 'upper', an amphetamine, still used to treat certain forms of epilepsy but otherwise rarely prescribed nowadays because of its addictive properties. The chances that a few of these tablets would be missed were remote, at least until next month's stocktaking.

Phineas worked on as usual through the afternoon. One of his daily chores was to sweep out the dispensary, and at a quarter to four he was wielding the broom awkwardly in the narrow space when, with a clumsy swing of the handle, he swept a dozen plastic jars off the shelf beside him.

The containers were unbreakable. They simply clattered and bounced all over the floor, the pills inside them rolling noisily about. '*Phineas, joy kakhandige doos,*' the pharmacist swore at him mechanically. '*Verskoon, baas, verskoon,*' Phineas pleaded, abandoning the broom, going through a pantomime of apology, and gathering up the jars. On his hands and knees in front of the table, he was below the line of his boss's sight. It took only two or three seconds to unscrew the top of the Dexedrine jar and spill a few of the tiny white tablets into his hand. He transferred them swiftly to the pocket of his blouse, replaced the lid of the container and stood up.

He put the Dexedrine container and the others neatly back where they belonged; then he resumed his sweeping. The pharmacist, counting out some capsules, had long ago lost interest in him.

At five to four Phineas asked to visit the lavatory before his return to the cell blocks. Locked into the cubicle, he retrieved the tablet phial from the cistern. Hastily he transferred the amphetamines one by one from his pocket into the tube. He replaced the snap-on lid, sealing the tablets in together with the prescription docket. Then he got the blob of Vaseline down from the tank and smeared it evenly all over the phial. He pulled down his shorts and with care inserted the tube into his rectum.

He fastened his shorts, flushed the lavatory, and joined the march back to the cells. Now he had a way to authenticate his message, and the means to pay for sending it out. It remained to select a messenger.

BECAUSE THEY WERE NOT POLITICAL, or 'security' prisoners, the forty or so inmates of Cell Block C, Black Male, were permitted an hour each evening for free association. This meant that before lock-up time they were allowed to wander in and out of the four large cells that made up the block and to mingle in the corridor that connected them. This was the high point of the day, when gossip was exchanged, friendships were formed and enmities were sharpened. There was also frantic trading in prison commodities: tobacco for chocolate, soap for jam, sugar for thread.

As well as leafing through the Gideon Bible, and copying from it with a chewed pencil-stub onto the small yellow sheet of prescription paper, Phineas had done much preparation for the next stage of his plan. By subtle questioning he had learned the routines of the gangs who laboured outdoors in the prison grounds, for he needed not only a messenger but one who could be guaranteed to be in the right place at the right time; a man, as well, who could be trusted not to talk foolishly afterwards. Now he made his way to the cell at the end of the corridor, stood in the doorway and called to a man who lay on his bunk in the corner.

'Bobbejaan!'

The man sat up, blinking at him. Phineas beckoned, and he got off the bunk and shuffled out, frowning. Bobbejaan in fact looked more like a gorilla than the baboon after which he had been nicknamed. His shaven head rested on a neck so short and thick it was almost invisible. His body was barrel-shaped, two hundred pounds of sheer gristle, and his hands could have strangled an ox. Everyone was wary of him, even the warders.

'I greet you, Bobbejaan. Are you well?'

'I'm well, little Phineas.' They spoke in Sotho, their mutual language, not much understood by the other prisoners, who were mostly Xhosas.

'There's something I want you to do for me, Bobbejaan. I'll pay you well for it, provided it remains a secret between us.'

'What thing is this, little brother?'

'I'll give you this, now, to show that I trust you.' He opened his palm to show a crumpled toothpaste tube. 'There are forty pills in here, Bobbejaan. Forty Dexies.'

'*Forty?*'

'And forty more when you've done what I ask. As long as you're careful what you do with them.'

Phineas had been rather alarmed, when he counted them, to find he had stolen eighty-one of the amphetamines. This number would buy Bobbejaan an untold amount of smuggled *dagga*.

Bobbejaan's gaze had brightened with astonishment. 'What is this thing you want?' he asked.

Five minutes later the deal was struck. Bobbejaan took the toothpaste tube and the innocuous tablet phial with its bit of paper inside; he had his instructions, though he was ignorant of their purpose.

'One other thing,' said Phineas sternly. 'There are important people that we do this for. If you fail, or if you only pretend to do what I ask, they will know. It will go badly for you.'

Bobbejaan seemed impressed at this bit of bluff. As for Phineas, he went back to his cell satisfied. He had done what he could for the Leader. Now he could only mark time before retribution came.

THE SITTING ROOM of the top-floor suite in the President Hotel in Cape Town was dominated by a vast picture window. The view over Table Bay was splendid, and dead in the middle of it was the dark hump of Robben Island, where Lincoln Kumalo had spent the first twenty years of his imprisonment. The fact that they had chosen this as a meeting place seemed to confirm something Nandi had always thought about Afrikaners: they had no sense of irony. And, as if to reinforce the point, Colonel Prinsloo was present.

Prinsloo had haunted her childhood like a bogeyman. It was he who had been responsible for enforcing her mother's various banning orders, and now here he was again, in the company of little Mr Hoeksma. Luckily, Prinsloo seemed no more talkative than she was, and all the conversation had been between Hoeksma and her lawyer Ibrahim Khan. But what was its purpose?

'Of course,' Deputy Minister Hoeksma was saying, 'I have never had the privilege of meeting Lincoln Kumalo, but speaking in a personal capacity, I have to say that it's a matter of profound regret that a man of such brilliance should languish in prison.'

'Then, why not just let him out?' demanded Ibrahim.

'If it were left to me . . .' Hoeksma made a helpless gesture. 'The political reality is that he's made it very difficult for us.'

'The way he sees it is that you've made it impossible for him.'

'There were conditions, of course. There had to be conditions.'

In a different frame of mind Nandi might have found the contrast between Hoeksma and Prinsloo comical, the one small and plump, the other tall and lean. Hoeksma had been at pains to welcome them, and he was an unlikely-looking antagonist. Prinsloo, on the other hand, was one of those lanky, narrow, taciturn Afrikaners with coarse features and angry eyes. Again she wondered what he was doing here.

'Mr Kumalo,' said Hoeksma judiciously, 'has always rejected our conditions. But he has never really said what he found wrong with them.'

'What was wrong was that you tried to impose conditions at all. His position remains what it always has been: either he comes out as a completely free man or he stays where he is.'

Hoeksma sighed. 'You know, I believe there is always some middle ground between two points of view. There is always something, no matter how small, on which opponents can agree: a starting point.' He turned to Nandi. 'You're due to visit him tomorrow, Miss Kumalo, not so? Would you convey a message to him?'

Was this where the conversation had been leading? She said stiffly, 'If you think I have any influence over him, you're wrong.'

'I don't think that. But personal circumstances are involved, and the message might be better received from his closest relative than through official channels.' Hoeksma leaned forward, straining to show his sincerity. 'What I am saying must not go beyond the four of us in this room—unless you agree to convey it to your father. Is that acceptable?'

She glanced at Ibrahim and got an encouraging nod. 'All right.'

'You know that his health has been causing some concern?'

'We know that he has prostate trouble,' Ibrahim answered for her. 'I've tried to get more details from the prison authorities and met with a good deal of obstruction.'

'The diagnosis was only confirmed a few days ago. The position is that he has a tumour ... Please don't let it frighten you. It's not as serious as it may sound. It's a small tumour, it's been detected in good time and it will be operated on before the end of the year. There's every reason to believe he'll make a full recovery. That's as much as he knows at present, and as much as I'm at liberty to tell you.'

'That's ridiculous!' Ibrahim protested. 'You're going to carry out an operation on him in secret?'

'There are questions of security involved,' Hoeksma said, with a glance at Prinsloo. 'And you should know, Mr Khan, that since all prisoners are the legal responsibility of the government no permission is required from their relatives for any medical procedure.'

'But ...'

'Please, let's not get sidetracked. What I have to say is this. After the operation there will be a convalescent period. In similar circumstances in the past, where a prisoner has served the bulk of a long sentence, consideration has sometimes been given to his release on medical, or humanitarian, grounds.'

Nandi gave Ibrahim Khan a startled look. It was he who was the quicker on the uptake. 'What are you saying? Unconditional release by another name?'

'Please don't put words into my mouth, Mr Khan. I'm saying that a discharge on medical grounds could, subject to certain understandings, solve the dilemma for both of us: a medical discharge, nothing more nor less. We'd want no talk of an unconditional release.'

'But that would be a condition in itself,' Ibrahim objected. 'It would save face for you, and for that reason I can't see him agreeing to it.'

'Ib, surely . . . ' Nandi stifled her words at a look from Ibrahim.

Hoeksma continued, 'All we ask for now is an agreement in principle that he would not say no if he were officially offered a discharge after his operation. In due course we could come to a wink-and-nod arrangement permitting him to engage in any political activity that was within the law.'

Prinsloo stirred his long frame on the sofa. 'All that interests me is the security of this country. Lincoln Kumalo has come to seem a safer bet than the crowd who run his Congress from Lusaka. The external leadership of such a movement is always more extreme than those on the ground.'

He lapsed disconcertingly back into silence, almost as though his speech had been a set piece, rehearsed for the occasion. Hoeksma took up what seemed to be the thread of his argument. 'We want your father's co-operation, Miss Kumalo. We're no longer asking him to compromise. Is it worth years more of wrangling over his future for the sake of one small concession? I ask you to put it to him as a human being: Does he want to breathe free air again? Will you ask him that?'

She nodded numbly. 'I'll ask,' she said.

Three minutes later they were leaving the hotel. In the lift on the way down they did not speak, but in the darkness of the car park Ibrahim seized her arm. 'We're going to get him out, Nandi!'

'But you said he would refuse . . .'

'Of course he'll refuse. Why should he agree? Don't you see? They've played their last card, and it's a loser. Once he says no to this they'll have nothing more to offer!'

'They can always keep him in jail,' she said pragmatically.

'They didn't even threaten that! They've made up their minds. They've decided that Lincoln Kumalo is more trouble in prison than out of it. I'm certain of it. They're going to let him go.'

ChapterThree

The following day, Tuesday, Ibrahim Khan's Mercedes was admitted through the first of Pollsmoor's security barriers. At the next one, guarding the inner precincts, he had to turn into the visitors' car park and leave Nandi to walk on alone to the big stone gateway.

It was an improbable prison: the main building looked like a great country house. It was only when you drew closer that you saw the bars on the windows and the machine-gun positions on the roof.

227

In the office beside the gates she went through the rigmarole of recording her name and address and being issued with a visitor's tag. A white wardress examined the contents of her handbag and gave her a brisk body-search before escorting her through more control posts until they stepped into the familiar passageway that led to the visiting area. The door slid shut behind them. At the end of the passage she was admitted to a bare, narrow room, divided down the middle by a counter with a partition of thick bulletproof glass rising to the ceiling. Half a dozen chairs were drawn up to face the counter. To allow conversation, a telephone handset was placed in front of each chair, connected to another behind the glass. It was assumed that everything said would be recorded.

She was the only visitor, and there was only one prisoner sitting behind the barrier, with a single warder for an escort. Lincoln Kumalo rose to greet his daughter. Nandi was always surprised to rediscover what a big man her father was. Well over six foot tall, deep-chested and wide-shouldered, he dwarfed the white warder who stood behind him. A century ago he would have been a splendid Zulu warrior. In his sixties he still had an aura of physical power that was undoubtedly part of his magnetism.

He gave her a grin of delight. She stumbled forward and they mimed a kiss through the glass. She sat down hastily, fumbled for the telephone receiver. And then, suddenly, she found herself with nothing to say. Tears welled from her eyes. All she could think was: I am not worthy.

OUTSIDE, IN THE CAR PARK, Ibrahim Khan supposed that he ought to be enjoying the fresh air. He wandered restlessly round the small enclosure in the sharp spring sunshine, smoking and glancing every few minutes at his watch. Ibrahim had never been much good at waiting.

While he paced the car park, Ibrahim had been idly watching a gang of black convicts moving towards the fence across the nearest of the vegetable plots, half a dozen of them in the charge of a single white warder; low-security prisoners, no doubt. They were planting potatoes.

Ibrahim turned away, glancing at the sinister bulk of the prison. He checked his watch again. Nandi's visit would be halfway through.

'Mister!'

The voice came from behind him. Not quite a whisper, low but clear, a bass African voice raised just loud enough to draw his attention. He turned in surprise and saw that one convict had moved ahead of the others and was only twenty feet away, leaning on his spade. He stood facing Ibrahim but kept glancing back at the warder dawdling behind them.

'Mister! Come to the wire.'

The man spoke in the same level tone, suppressing urgency beneath his words. He had a shaven head, a heavy, simian face and a stocky, powerful body. As Ibrahim stared at him, he left his spade and trotted quickly towards the fence.

'Mister!' He called openly and loudly now. 'You got cigarettes, mister?' He reached the barbed wire and thrust his hands out, in a begging attitude. 'Mister, you got cigarette for a poor *mugu*?' He glanced round at the warder, loping down the furrow now, pulling the truncheon off his belt.

'*Kom weg van daai draad, Bobbejaan! Weg!*'

Ibrahim regained his presence of mind. He hastily pulled out his packet of twenty Rothmans and began to tip cigarettes into his palm.

'The packet, man, the packet!' the convict hissed. The warder was almost on top of him now, roaring and swearing. Bewildered, Ibrahim thrust the whole thing at him, spilling cigarettes on the ground, spotting as he did so a little brown plastic tube in the man's hand. He slipped the tube into the flip-top box and closed it just as the warder swung his truncheon and fetched him a crack on the side of the head.

'*Jou moer, Bobbejaan!*'

The prisoner lurched back from the fence, dropping the packet. The warder grabbed him by the shirt collar and hit him again.

'He was only asking for cigarettes,' Ibrahim protested.

'It's not allowed.' The warder glared at him through the wires. 'It's not allowed, and he knows it.'

'He asked me for cigarettes. I didn't see any harm in giving him a few.'

'He'll be put on a charge for talking to you. We could charge you as well. What are you doing here?'

'I gave a lift to a visitor.' Ibrahim had all his wits about him now. Although his instinct was to quarrel, he said humbly, 'I didn't know about your regulations. I'm sorry.'

'All right, forget it this time. But remember it well for the future. Go and wait in your car. That way you'll keep out of trouble.'

The man picked up the Rothmans packet and passed it through the wire. Ibrahim took it with a suitable show of gratitude. The prison officer turned and herded the convicts away from the fence, the big man called Bobbejaan shambling off among them without looking back.

Back in his car, he sat for five minutes doing absolutely nothing. He had to consider the possibility that someone might be watching him.

Finally he could resist no longer. He took the Rothmans packet from his pocket, removed a cigarette and lit it. Keeping the packet well below the level of the dashboard, he took out the little plastic tube that the convict had inserted in it, flipped off the lid of the tube and teased out the slip of yellow paper rolled up inside.

The message had been written in pencil on the back of a small official form of some kind, in the bold capitals of a not over-literate hand: AS THE LORD GOD IS MY WITNESS THIS THING IS TRUE. AND ALL THE PEOPLE SHALL SAY AMEN (Deuteronomy, 27:24). BY THE RIVER OF NCOME THE APPOINTED TIME, AND THE DESERT SHALL REJOICE AND BLOSSOM (Isaiah, 35:1). WHO SHALL DELIVER HIM? (Romans, 7:24).

He read it through half a dozen times. Had the whole charade been for the sake of these... absurd religious ravings? Yet someone had put considerable thought into the means of delivering the message. There could be a subtle mind at work here. What if the writer *wanted* this to sound like the harmless rantings of a religious lunatic, just in case it fell into the wrong hands?

It was only as he was refolding the slip of paper that he thought to glance at its reverse side. It was a printed form bearing the coat of arms of the prison service. It seemed to be a carbon copy of a doctor's prescription. It bore several lines of hasty scribbling, only one of which was easily legible. Opposite *Name of Patient*, it said *Prisoner 4008*.

'YOU'VE GOT FIVE MORE MINUTES,' the warder said behind her.

Nandi scarcely heard him. All her concentration was on the figure behind the glass, on the voice that came to her through the telephone. She had told him about her mother's funeral, circumspectly describing the way the police had broken up the procession. He told her about his health and the visit of the anonymous specialist, the hormone treatment, and the prospect of an operation. This led them, with time running out, to the matter of Hoeksma's offer. He shook his head sadly.

'It has to be no, Nandi. I'm sorry.'

'I'm only their messenger. Ibrahim warned me what to expect.'

'I've had twenty-five years to think, sweetheart. I've anticipated every option they could offer me, and there's only one I could accept.'

'Unconditional release? Those very words? They've gone as far as they can without actually using them.'

'There are no degrees in a thing like this.' He grinned at her. 'It's like chastity. You either are a virgin or you aren't.'

His flippancy slightly annoyed her. 'Ib seems to think—'

'I think I know what Ib is thinking.'

'Do you agree with him?'

'One more minute,' the warder called out.

'I'll tell you this, Nandi, Ib can afford to hope on my behalf. Hope doesn't cost him anything. In this place, it's a dangerous commodity. I'd prefer to wait and see.'

'And if Ib is wrong? Then it could be another five years, or ten ...'

'Yes, by then it could be too late,' he said. 'Too late for me, perhaps, but not for millions of others.'

'Time up now, please.'

'Oh, Daddy ...' Nandi was stricken suddenly by despair.

'I love you, Nandi. I know you're brave, Nandi. You don't need to convince me.'

'Say your goodbyes now,' the warder urged them, not unkindly. Inside the glass cage the other guard was moving the switch that controlled the telephone. Kumalo mouthed another kiss to her through the glass, and he was smiling as the warder touched her elbow and turned her away.

HOEKSMA, WHEN THEY MET HIM an hour later in the same suite at the President Hotel, seemed more resigned than actively disappointed.

'Mr Khan, you heard the terms of the offer. It is now withdrawn.'

'And will not be renewed?'

'Certainly not. The matter is closed. Now, if you'll excuse me ...'

Once again they left the hotel. There was an hour and a half to go before Nandi's train left for Johannesburg, where she lived, and she assumed they would stop at Ibrahim's office. Instead they set off up the mountainside and through the white suburb of Oranjezicht.

Eventually Ibrahim stopped the Mercedes and got out, slamming the door. He walked to the edge of the road, turned and beckoned. For a moment she'd almost forgotten the possibility of bugs in the car.

She slipped out of the Mercedes, joined him, and stood staring in silence over the city a thousand feet below. Ibrahim smiled at her and fiddled with his cigarette packet. He took out a brown plastic tube and handed it to her. 'Tell me what you make of that.'

Nandi plucked the message out of the phial and read it. He told her to look at the back as well. Finally she said, 'What *is* this?'

He told her briefly of his encounter with the convict at Pollsmoor. 'I know it reads like rubbish, but I'm sure it has a hidden meaning. What convinced me was the paper it's written on. A prescription form, obviously from the prison hospital, with Lincoln's prison number on it.'

'You don't think it's the prescription itself that's significant?'

'Ah! A good notion, but I think you're being over-subtle. It's dated November the second, last Wednesday. Presumably this is the hormone they've started him on. No, I go for the number as the clue.'

'It tells us this is a message about my father. Is that right?'

'Yes. That's why it was given to me. But God knows what it means.'

They began to stroll along the road, Nandi still studying the paper. 'We'd need a Bible to look up these references, for a start,' she said.

'Perhaps we're overlooking another possibility.'

'That it's a plant?' Nandi was quick to grasp his meaning. 'But it would be a very uncertain way of sending a false message.'

'True.'

A grey squirrel hopped out from among the pines and sat watching them. Lost for any means of making sense of the message, they fell back to speculating on who might have sent it.

'I can't see that prisoner Bobbejaan as the originator. He didn't look the subtle type.'

'What about the prescription form? Who would have access to such a thing? Someone who works in the hospital?'

'And who knows Lincoln is sick. Perhaps that's all he was trying to tell me, not realising that I knew already. *As the Lord God is my witness this thing is true.*' Ibrahim had taken the paper back and was reading from it aloud. '*And all the people shall say Amen. By the river of Ncome the*

appointed time... That one struck me as really nonsensical.'

'Ncome?' Nandi grabbed the message from him and studied it again. When she looked up at him there was a triumphant gleam in her eyes. 'Ncome! I knew there was something familiar about it. The battle in eighteen thirty-eight, in which the Zulu nation was finally defeated by the Boers!'

'Wasn't that the Battle of Blood River?'

'The Boers only gave it that name afterwards, because the water ran red with Zulu blood. Before then the river was known as the Ncome.'

Ibrahim was nonplussed. 'Why should I be expected to know that?'

'Not you, Ibrahim.'

The penny dropped. 'You think the message is for *you?*'

'Of course it is! One thing we haven't asked ourselves is how its originator knew you would be there this morning, in the prison car park. The answer is, he didn't. But he knew somehow that *I'd* be visiting.'

'And so Bobbejaan saw us arrive together, perhaps, but couldn't get close enough to the fence at the right time. So he gave it to me. All right, I'll buy that; but what more does it tell us?'

' "*By the river of Ncome the appointed time,*" ' she quoted again. 'It sounds like a rendezvous of some kind. But why "time" and not "place"?'

Before he could answer she had turned and begun to walk briskly back towards the car, leaving him to hurry after her.

'What's the rush? We've got plenty of time.'

'I want to get hold of a Bible, of course. To study on the train.'

In the car on the way down Ibrahim ventured a small theory of his own.

'You know there is a rendezvous at Blood River every year? It's December the sixteenth, the anniversary of the battle. It's the day the Afrikaners commemorate their victory. Do you think that could be your appointed time?'

NANDI SAT STARING out at the dark wasteland of the Great Karroo. An angry red sun had set behind the mountains as the engine strained up the final gradient onto the great African plateau; after that the train had gathered speed and now it thundered steadily over flat semidesert country, its carriages rocking with a gentle hypnotic motion.

Without being asked, the Coloured conductor had given her a couchette compartment to herself; it was part of the silent conspiracy of sympathy that surrounded her name. She supposed she ought to feel guilty about accepting it, but found herself glad of the privacy.

She turned from the window to the folding table in front of her and addressed herself to the puzzle again: the message from Pollsmoor, the scrawled pages of notes she had made, the Pocket Oxford edition of the King James Bible bought on the way to the station.

The opening sentence—*As the Lord God is my witness this thing is true*— was biblical in style, but did not appear to refer to a particular passage.

The other three quotations had been easy to look up. Each was part of an incomplete verse. Set out in full, the verses read:

Cursed be he that smiteth his neighbour secretly. And all the people shall say Amen.

Deuteronomy

The wilderness and the solitary place shall be glad for them; and the desert shall rejoice, and blossom as the rose.

Isaiah

O wretched man that I am! Who shall deliver me from the body of this death?

Romans

It had struck her that the significance of each sentence might lie in the part of the verse that had been left out, along with the substitution of *Ncome* for *Babylon* in the other, distorted, quotation. The message then might read:

This thing is true:
Cursed be he that smiteth his neighbour secretly;
December 16th;
The wilderness and the solitary place shall be glad for them . . . as the rose.
O wretched man that I am . . . the body of this death.

She pondered the fact that in the final quotation he had changed Who shall deliver *me*? to Who shall deliver *him*? In the other place where he had misquoted the Bible, substituting *Ncome* for Babylon, it had been done deliberately. The same was probably true here. With two references to death, she had no doubt now that the writer was trying to warn her of some danger. He was also making it clear that it was not he who was being threatened but somebody else. *Him.* Who else but Prisoner 4008? And what was the danger? Death.

Nandi sighed. The whole thing could still mean anything or nothing. The only thing she had resembling a positive clue was the one that Ibrahim had given her, about the date. Was something that involved her father due to happen on that day, *the appointed time?*

December the sixteenth was thirty-eight days away.

She pulled down the window blind and began preparing for bed. What all this needed was a fresh pair of eyes. Perhaps she would ask Alex Duma for help. For all he was a hothead, he was intelligent. Duma had the right contacts to take the puzzle one stage further.

WHEN HE HAD NOTHING better to do, Virgil would hang about the Woodvale Clinic's reception area trying to chat up Yvonne. Virgil was one of the security guards, an overweight young English immigrant with an overeager smile. He was leaning over the reception counter when Judith returned from the city that Thursday afternoon.

'Three o'clock,' he said, ostentatiously checking his watch. 'Long lunch, eh? All right for some people, isn't it?'

She ignored him. 'I got it!' she said triumphantly to Yvonne.

'The flat? Hooray!'

'The one I told you about, over in Northcliff. Furnished, as well. I've got it on a year's lease. I can move in on the first of next month.'

'Congratulations.'

She went round the corner and into the admin office. She settled at her desk, opened her handbag and briefly inspected her make-up in a tiny mirror. She heard Virgil droning on outside as she sorted through a pile of mail, but by the time she had finished he had gone.

'What was he on about?' Judith asked as she handed Yvonne her post.

'There've been two government officials looking the place over. They're in with your father now. Virgil maintains they're from the Security Police.'

Judith snorted. 'Conspiracy theories. He's a real Boy Scout.'

'Actually, they were behaving a bit oddly. They went through the buildings thoroughly and they've been checking the personnel files.'

Judith looked at her blankly. 'How do you know?'

'I'll show you,' said Yvonne with a secretive smile. 'Strictly between us.'

The Coloured girl led her back into the office, to the computer terminal. She switched it on, tapped into the system, pressed a couple of keys and the screen produced an alphabetical list of the clinic's staff.

'You know how this works?' she asked. Judith shook her head. 'The personnel records are held in your father's private file, accessed by his personal password. It's the computer equivalent of keeping them in a safe with a combination lock. But he's been making hard copies on the printer in his office—obviously for his two visitors to look at.'

'Does this mean we have access to the files?'

'Well, we could have, just for as long as this stays on the screen. I'm sure he'll be deleting it shortly.'

'Go on, let's have a peep at our own.'

Yvonne looked uncomfortable. 'I said we could, not that we should.'

'It's regarded as a civil right in some countries. Go on!'

Reluctantly Yvonne pecked at the keys, lining the cursor up against Judith's name and pressing the READ button. A page in document form, like a completed questionnaire, flashed up on the screen. Judith read through it. It was all very ordinary and impersonal: date of birth, education, previous experience and so on. At the bottom of Judith's file were two brief lines:

> SECURITY RATING: Negative
> ACCESS TO INDUNA PROJECT: Nil.

She could hardly believe her eyes. 'A *security* rating?'

'Keep your voice down,' Yvonne hissed.

'Like hell I will! I'm going to demand an explanation!'

'You can't ...'

'I sure can. What's more, I'm going to confront him with the evidence before he can get rid of it.'

She leaned across the panic-stricken Yvonne and attacked the keyboard. In a few seconds the printer had copied the document. Judith ripped it off the machine and stalked down the corridor towards her father's office. She was halfway there when the door opened and he led his two visitors out.

She halted in front of them, no longer quite certain of herself. Both the men were tall and had unmistakable Afrikaner features.

Her father looked displeased to see her, raising an enquiring eyebrow.

'What is it, Judith?'

'I need to see you,' she said tersely.

'You'll have to hang on a minute, while I see these gentlemen out ...'

'No, no, we'll leave you here,' said the taller of the two politely. He was looking at Judith with speculative interest and suddenly he thrust out a powerful paw, introducing himself in the abrupt Afrikaner way.

'Prinsloo,' he said. She shook his hand numbly.

'Booysen,' said the other man, also offering his hand. Neither of them gave any further explanation of himself.

'My daughter Judith,' said Dr Rose rather grimly. He seemed anxious not to prolong the conversation, and the man called Prinsloo took his cue.

'We'll be off, then, Doctor. We'll be in touch. Goodbye, Miss Rose.'

Prinsloo and Booysen marched away. 'Come in,' Dr Rose said ungraciously, and she followed him into the office. By the time he had closed the door she had regained her anger and she thrust the computer printout at him.

He glanced through it, flinched and looked up at her.

'What's the meaning of this, Judith? You've been tampering with confidential records!'

'I think it's you who owe me an explanation, Daddy. Security rating? Induna Project? What sort of sinister nonsense is this?'

'Now, look here, Judith. . .' He was trying to be stern but he was also on the defensive. 'You may find this hard to take, but I'm not in a position to answer any of your questions yet.'

'Well, if you can't tell me, they will have to. They can't have left yet.'

She turned towards the door, but he put a restraining hand on her arm. 'Don't do that, Judith. You could get me into trouble.'

She swung round to face him. 'Trouble? You?' she said incredulously. Then she realised that perhaps Virgil had been making sense for once. 'Were those men from the Security Police?'

'Colonel Prinsloo and Major Booysen,' he muttered.

'What the hell did they want with you?'

Spearhead

'They were making a routine security check on the staff. I agreed to it, and I can promise you there was nothing conspiratorial about it.'

Even he did not seem convinced by this bland assurance. Judith could sense that he was uncomfortable. There was much that was arrogant about her father but he would never arbitrarily refuse to discuss anything. Now he tried to sound reasonable. 'Listen, Judith, I don't like this part of it any more than you do. But the fact is that I've taken on a particularly sensitive job for those people and I'm not allowed to discuss it with anybody. Since you've stumbled on one aspect of it, though, I can only take you so far into my confidence as to warn you not to let it go any further. Will you promise to be satisfied with that?'

IT WAS LATE the following night before Nandi and Duma finally admitted defeat. For more than four hours they had racked their brains over the message, sitting at the kitchen table in her little house in the Orlando section of Soweto. Still they had got no further with the mystery.

'I don't know.' For perhaps the hundredth time Duma scraped back his chair, stood up and prowled round the room. He was dressed in a leather jacket and dark suede trousers, the original Black Panther. 'Maybe there is no mystery, Nandi. Maybe it's just a hoax.'

She nodded. She was grateful to Duma tonight, though she did not always welcome his nocturnal appearances on her doorstep. There were informers about; social calls from a wanted militant would not go unnoticed for ever. Besides, whatever work it was that Duma did for the Congress, he clearly didn't keep the same arduous hours she did, trailing lifelines to the old and destitute of Soweto six days a week. He wanted to talk the nights away; she wanted to sleep. 'Yes, it could be a hoax, Duma. Some elaborate joke by the police. There's just something about it that has the ring of genuine urgency to me.'

'So what are we left with, Nandi? A warning of some unspecified danger to your father possibly occurring on the sixteenth of December.'

Nandi smiled, partly to disguise a yawn. 'Ibrahim Khan thinks they're going to let him out, you know. Unconditionally.'

'*What?* You didn't tell me that.'

'Perhaps because I'm reluctant to believe it myself. It would be odd if it happened on December the sixteenth, wouldn't it? Yes, Ib is convinced they're going to release him after his operation.'

Duma ceased slinking up and down the kitchen and gestured at the pages of notes that smothered the table. 'You know what I think you should do? Give all this stuff to me. Let me send it to our friends in Zambia, see if they can make any better sense of it.'

'In Lusaka? What help could they be?'

'Who knows? They have other sources of information.'

She shrugged. She couldn't see much point in the idea, but she was too tired to argue. She stood up, yawning openly this time. Duma gathered the notes, folded them and stuffed them inside his jacket. Nandi turned off the gas lamp before cautiously opening the kitchen door. The township night was silent but for the distant howling of dogs.

'Will you be all right out there?'

He grinned. 'I am a fish in a sea of men.' He trotted across her back yard and in a moment was absorbed by the darkness.

Chapter Four

Joshua Rosenblatt looked up from his typewriter, grateful for a distraction. The first tentative cloudburst of the rainy season had blotted the dust on the window of the motel chalet, and through it he saw Harry Makibani's old Toyota enter the driveway. At the gate a Congress sentry, disguised as a Zambian militiaman, had stopped the car and then waved it through. Bouncing on worn springs, it came to a stop outside what had once been the motel's reception office. Harry levered out his bulk and the morose figure of J.K.Govender came to meet him. They disappeared into the office and Joshua addressed himself again to the Olivetti.

Chapter Three, he had typed. *The Evolution of the People's Congress.* And that was all. With only an hour before they had to leave for the airport, he didn't know why he was bothering. He had often been tempted to abandon this project, but for several reasons felt he couldn't. There was the advance already paid by his publishers in London and, more seriously, he wanted to explain the aims of the Congress in a way that would capture the understanding and sympathy of Western readers. He wanted to explain that it was not a bloodthirsty terrorist organisation, but a national movement that was more than seventy years old, that had resorted to armed resistance only when every peaceful avenue had been closed to it. In a sense he wanted also to vindicate himself, as the only white man to reach a prominent position in the movement: its treasurer.

He abandoned his typewriter, stood up and walked to the window at the rear of the chalet. It was vastly inefficient that the Congress executive should have to keep moving like this, but it was the result of lessons learned over the years. They paid only fleeting visits to the movement's headquarters, an office in Lusaka where a bomb had been planted just five months ago. There'd been other headquarters, and other bombs.

He returned to his desk but did not sit down. What was he trying to say? For most of its long history the People's Congress had conducted a peaceful struggle on behalf of South Africa's disenfranchised black majority. Only in the late 1950s, when a young lawyer called Lincoln Kumalo became its president, did the Congress become more militant.

In 1960 the movement was outlawed. Those of its leaders who escaped arrest either went underground or fled abroad. Since then, the development of the Congress, from a mildly subversive organisation to a revolutionary movement that had won a degree of international respect, had been a long and sometimes painful process. The Western powers distrusted them because they accepted some grudging aid from the Russians. Their hosts, the Zambians, treated them at times like embarrassing relatives that custom obliged them to welcome.

Joshua caught a movement in the window. Harry Makibani was bustling across the motel courtyard towards his room. Coming to check that he was ready for the trip, Joshua supposed. It wasn't a journey that he relished: twelve hours or so to Algiers in some bone-shaking military aircraft, in order to attend the Conference of Non-Aligned Nations, where the People's Congress would have observer status.

Harry Makibani appeared in the doorway. Harry was their public affairs officer, an energetic man who moved as though he were always trying to work off his excess weight. 'Josh! Before we go . . . something's come up. Something we ought to talk about.'

Harry was not alone. J.K.Govender, the Congress secretary, a doctrinaire Indian, had followed him across the courtyard and now slithered past Harry into the room. Just behind him came Lawrence Gumbi, a tall and taciturn black man who headed the armed wing of the Congress, five thousand well-trained men.

'Pahlani is just coming,' Harry said. 'He's on the phone to London.'

That would make five of them. Joshua said, 'What the hell is up?'

'We've had a message. It's about Lincoln.'

Lincoln. In any gathering of this group there was always, metaphorically, an empty place. Lincoln Kumalo, their president, hovered like Banquo's ghost at the head of their table. It was Kumalo who gave them coherence; their squabbles seemed petty beside what he had endured.

'It's like this,' said Harry. 'I've just picked up a file of dispatches that got into town from Jo'burg this morning. There's one from a comrade called Duma. Dated Friday, so it's only two days old. Duma is close to Lincoln's daughter and he says she's got hold of some notion that they may be going to release him soon.'

Nobody spoke for several seconds. Joshua felt a thrill of apprehension and sensed the same feeling ripple through the others.

J.K.Govender broke the silence. 'Just whose notion is this?'

'It comes from his lawyer, Ibrahim Khan. It's only conjecture so far, but nobody is closer to the situation than he is.'

'Ibrahim Khan,' said J.K. with disapproval, 'has never been one of us. And Nandi Kumalo isn't a Congress activist either.'

That was J.K. for you, Joshua thought.

'Look,' said Harry in exasperation, 'she sees her first duty as being to her father. Just like Khan. Not everyone is born to be a political animal. The point is, coming from sources like this, the story can't be treated as just another rumour.'

'What about this Duma fellow?' asked Lawrence Gumbi.

'I know him well. He is a little excitable but dependable also. He went through one of your own training courses.'

'So supposing there is something to all this,' Joshua interrupted, conscious that time was running out, 'what can we actually do about it?'

'Start making contingency plans,' Harry said. 'If they really are thinking of letting Lincoln out unconditionally, then they must soon start talking to the movement that he leads.'

'All this on the basis of one man's conjecture?' J.K. was about to launch into a new argument when the door opened and Godfrey Pahlani entered. The acting president of the Congress was a dapper, dignified figure with a crop of white hair and glasses with thin gold rims.

'I was filling them in,' said Harry, 'on this story about Lincoln.'

'Yes. I've been talking to Moses Mohaila in London. He's heard nothing.'

The idea that the Congress representative in Britain might know something they didn't was by no means absurd. London was a major listening-post for all kinds of news from South Africa.

'There's something else we ought to discuss,' Harry said. 'While Ibrahim Khan and Nandi Kumalo were visiting Pollsmoor last week, some kind of garbled message was smuggled out to them. It doesn't make a lot of sense, but she seems to think it was a warning of some kind. Some danger to Lincoln. Duma has sent us a lot of notes, asked if we can figure them out. There's nothing specific about the message except, maybe, a date: December the sixteenth.'

'The anniversary of Blood River,' Pahlani mused. 'Well, we can talk about that later. Right now we have a plane to catch.'

As the others filed out of the room Joshua pulled the beginning of Chapter Three out of the typewriter, stared at it wistfully and then tossed it into the wastebin. The book would never get written.

IN ALGIERS, EARLY the following Saturday evening, Joshua was passing through the lounge of the Aletti Hotel when he spotted Harry Makibani sitting glumly on his own in a corner.

Joshua went over to him. 'How are things, Harry?'

'Could be better. Not enough for me to do.'

Joshua pulled a chair up to Harry's table. 'Where are the others?'

'Around and about. Up at the *gabfest*, probably. Not my idea of a Saturday evening's entertainment.'

Joshua smiled ruefully. It was true that the debates of the Non-Aligned Conference frequently degenerated into a series of squabbles. But for the South African People's Congress the main reason for being here was to lobby for funds from sympathetic governments, and in this respect Joshua had had a rewarding week. Most of his business had been done in private meetings away from the main conference, and he had come away with promises of just over seven million dollars in immediate aid.

While Joshua went round with the begging bowl, Govender and Pahlani had sat stiffly through the debates, Gumbi had vanished on mysterious missions involving the supply of arms, and Harry had put in token appearances at the conference.

'I've had time to think, Josh,' the black man said, 'and I'm worried. We haven't discussed the message that was sent out of Pollsmoor. I've been breaking my skull over it, but I've got no further. I don't know how much it matters, I just think we're letting people down by not even trying.' Harry glanced at his watch. 'Listen, why don't we have dinner together and talk some more? I've found a place where you can get a decent bottle of wine. Meet you down here. Twenty minutes?'

They stood up and went to the reception desk. With his room key Joshua was handed a letter, postmarked London, from his publisher.

Up in his room, Joshua delayed opening the letter until he'd had a quick shower. He was a little nervous. Perhaps his long-suffering publisher was about to become less tolerant.

The envelope was bulky, and when he opened it he understood why. Besides a brief covering note on his publisher's stationery it contained another letter, sealed in an airmail envelope with just his name, and the heavily underlined instruction, *To be forwarded urgently. Private and Confidential.*

Joshua tore open the second envelope and extracted several sheets of writing paper. There was no address at the head of the letter, just a date: November 11. That was eight days ago:

Dear Joshua,
I don't know when, where or even whether this will reach you, but I have to write in the hope that it will find you somehow, and soon.

It must be ages—3 or 4 years?—since I last heard from you, and even longer since I wrote to thank you for the birthday cards you sent. Ungrateful cow. Nowadays I'd rather forget my birthdays. You had such a lot of addresses over the years that I lost track, and now I can't find the last one you gave me.

As it is, I feel I'm firing this off into a vacuum. I recall you saying you had a commission to write a book. I remembered the publishers' name and got their address from the flyleaf of one of their titles.

Why I'm writing is this. Daddy has got himself involved in something sinister. He's going to operate on someone in secret, at the behest of the Security Police. I discovered something about this by accident and confronted him with it. He told me just that. You know how they ill-treat people, how they take them into custody and make them just disappear. The point is that I believe he's letting them use him—his position, his reputation—to do their dirty work for them. I think in a way he sees this himself, but believes he's in control.

What I want to ask is whether you could find a way to expose this somehow, before it's too late. There's nobody here I could risk approaching. I don't know the name of the patient (or victim) but they've got a code-nàme for this project. It is INDUNA.

I do feel vaguely disloyal. I don't see eye to eye with Daddy about many things but I hate to think of his integrity being compromised. Mummy of course is oblivious to everything but her dahlias ...

'*INDUNA*,' SAID HARRY half an hour later, taking a gulp of wine. He had read Judith's letter three times. 'An *induna* was the leader of an *impi*, a Zulu regiment, back in the old days. Apt enough. Tell me who she is again.'

'My cousin's daughter. Judith Rose. Actually she always called me "uncle".' They sat in a crowded restaurant in what had once been the elegant Rue d'Isly in French colonial times. 'You didn't know I had a cousin in Jo'burg? Louis is a specialist in urinary diseases. He's also the owner of a small private hospital called the Woodvale Clinic. A fat cat, in other words, and a liberal up to a point.

'Our fathers were the Rosenblatt brothers, Abie and David. They grew up in Frankfurt, but went to Johannesburg together as young men in the nineteen twenties. They were both tailors. They set up shop and came to be known as the Rose brothers. There were some social advantages to not being too obviously Jewish in Jo'burg in those days. Well, Abie's wife had one son, Louis, and I was David's boy. There were no other children.

'The families were pretty close, as you can imagine. Our fathers had prospered. We were both sent to a rather posh school. I can't say I distinguished myself there, but Louis was a high achiever. He did brilliantly at medical school, while I sort of blundered into accountancy.

'Well, he became Dr Louis Rose. I reverted to plain Mr Rosenblatt. I think Louis was always driven by a need to escape from his background, while I tended to backslide into mine. I always got on well with his family. Especially Judith. I gather she hasn't really settled down to anything much since she left school, and it seems from this letter that she's been working lately in her old man's exclusive clinic. Well, that's the background. The letter explains itself.'

Harry sighed, sat back and looked at Joshua.

'Yes, Josh. It does explain itself. It also explains the message from Pollsmoor.' He took the sheaf of notes from his pocket and flattened them on the table beside the letter. 'All these biblical quotations. Nandi Kumalo was on the right track, but she hadn't a hope of figuring them out without more information. Look here. It's this middle sentence that made the least sense of all.' He quoted, ' "The wilderness and the solitary place shall be glad for them; and the desert shall rejoice, and blossom as the rose." Isn't it obvious?'

'Not to me, I'm afraid.'

'*As the rose*, Josh. Just put a capital *r* on that and you have the name of

242

your esteemed cousin. Dr Rose.' He watched Joshua's face with satisfaction. 'You want more proof? Cut out this middle bit about the desert rejoicing, and the key words you are left with are "wilderness—solitary place—rose". For "wilderness" read wood, for "solitary place" read vale. Vale of Tears, and all that. The Woodvale Clinic.'

Joshua was incredulous. 'You're saying Louis is going to operate there, on Lincoln Kumalo?'

'And on December the sixteenth.'

'All right. Assuming you are correct, does it change anything?'

'Of course it does. We must now take the whole thing very seriously indeed. Your little Judith lady is quite right: there is something sinister going on. Whoever sent this obviously believes that Lincoln is in some danger, Josh. And it's got to be stopped.'

'What do you mean, stopped?'

'*Who shall deliver him*, Josh?' Harry spoke with sudden solemnity. 'You and me, Josh, that's who. We're the only ones who know, and we're going to keep it to ourselves. We're going to find out what's going on down there, Josh, and we're going to stop it. If necessary, we're going to get Kumalo out!'

He fell silent as a waiter appeared and removed their plates. Two crème caramels were placed in front of them. Harry tucked in to his with relish.

'You're not making sense, Harry. Even if such a thing were possible, the rest of the executive would have to agree—'

'Forget them!' Harry waved his spoon carelessly. 'They'd hum and they'd haw, they'd raise objections. Besides ...' He became confiding. 'You and I know quite well that there are people in our movement who pay lip service to the idea of having Lincoln back as our leader, while all the time they know that he'd threaten their own positions. He's safer where he is, as far as they're concerned.'

Joshua shrugged uncomfortably. 'All this is highly hypothetical.'

'Maybe. But a lot could be hanging on it. December the sixteenth is less than a month away. What we need is our own man in there. Yes, that's it—somebody who knows what he's doing, who can find out what's going on and act on it if necessary. A complete outsider, in fact, who'd report directly to us.'

'Come off it, Harry.'

'You're not taking me seriously!' the black man snapped. 'We're in the business of revolutionary politics—a thing you perhaps forget when you're buried in your account books. I'm talking about a professional operation, possibly a military one, and we need a skilled professional to take charge of it. Though I don't like to admit it, he'll probably have to be a white man. Someone for whom money is an inducement but not the decisive factor. Someone who's actually willing to take our side.'

'Assuming you could find such a paragon, he'd still have to be paid,' Joshua pointed out.

'We've got money,' Harry said. 'We've got seven million dollars.'

'You know that isn't ours to play with.'

'We wouldn't be playing with it. We'd be investing it.' Harry gave a sudden mischievous grin. 'Just you and me, Josh. A small private investment. Now, this money we've just been pledged, how soon will it be paid? What are the mechanics?'

Joshua felt he was on safe ground. 'Well, as you know, we keep our main holding account at the Union Banque Suisse in Zurich. I'm making arrangements with each of the contributing governments to pick up the cheques at their embassies in Bern. I'll deposit them at once.'

'What's to stop you depositing some of that money in a new account, a different bank?'

'There's no earthly reason to do that, Harry.'

'Stop thinking like an accountant, Josh. Can you or can't you?'

'I could, but only with the agreement of the full executive committee.'

'But, as you well know, it's you who handles these things on a day-to-day basis. All the executive needs to know is that we've decided to establish a relationship with a second bank, to diversify our investments. It's not as though we'd be stealing the cash,' he added soothingly. 'And by the time the executive finds out . . . well, they may have no choice but to consider it money well spent. The thing is, I can't go to this man empty-handed. I've got to have something to put up front.'

'This man? You talk as though you'd already chosen him.'

'As a matter of fact,' said Harry, 'I think I have.'

Chapter Five

A dozen times that Tuesday the labrador bitch had flushed pheasants from the long wet grass, but Patrick Marriner had taken the trouble to shoot only twice, bagging a fat hen each time. There was no point in killing more than could be eaten.

Marriner always enjoyed these three-mile tramps round the perimeter of his farm, in this hilly south Cork country. They gave him a reassuring sense of possession. For a man who had rarely been settled in one place for more than a year or two, there was still enough novelty in the idea of his owning this land to please him. Ownership being, of course, a relative term: the farm was still heavily mortgaged.

Patrick Marriner had also discovered that farming wasn't quite the time-consuming business that everyone made it out to be. After a couple of years of really backbreaking work, he had found that the system functioned smoothly enough to require supervision rather than actual labour on his part. Especially at this time of year, with the mature bullocks sold, the hay cut and stored, and the silage made.

He saw a car approaching the house when he was still two hundred yards short of it. It was a newish, red Ford Fiesta, one that he didn't recognise. He felt automatically for the spare shotgun cartridges in the pocket of his Barbour jacket, then told himself he was being ridiculous. If trouble ever came to Ballygarron, it would not arrive in broad daylight.

The Fiesta drove onto the gravelled forecourt, disappearing from Marriner's view. He walked on, ordering the bitch to heel. He had a lean but muscular six-foot frame and a rangy outdoor look that made him seem younger than his age, which was forty-three. His colouring was tawny in the permanent way of fair-skinned people who have spent years in hot climates.

In the yard behind the kitchen he leaned his shotgun against the wall and stripped off his gumboots and jacket. Mary O'Leary, his housekeeper, came to the door. 'There's a man wanting to see you, Major. A Mr . . . Mac-something. I've put him in the library.'

'Thank you.' He handed her his game bag with the pheasants in it. 'Hang these for me, will you? Oh, and did the man say what he wanted?'

'No. He . . .' There was an odd note of curiosity in her voice, but she stopped herself and disappeared into the house. Marriner followed her, pausing beside the door to slip on his shoes.

Ballygarron House had been in his family since the early eighteen hundreds, and was still much as his uncle had left it, a bachelor establishment for the past forty years, stuffed with heavy old furniture and gloomy paintings. Uncle Ham had been emphatically a gentleman first and a farmer second. Only the loyalty and hard work of Mick O'Leary had saved Ballygarron from bankruptcy years before Uncle Ham succumbed to a long-standing liver complaint, leaving the estate and its debts to his nephew. Marriner's first inclination had been to sell the farm for whatever it would fetch, but then he reconsidered. Although he had no sentimental attachment to the place, it seemed a pity to surrender it. Then, as he was nearing forty, facing up to the reality of a failed marriage and wondering whether twenty years in the SAS wasn't long enough, he had resigned his commission and decided to make a go of Ballygarron.

He walked from the kitchen, down the long faded hallway to the library. His visitor was standing by one of the bookshelves, paging through an old leatherbound volume he had picked out. He looked up and beamed with pleasure, and Marriner had to hide his surprise.

Mr Mac-something was black.

He wore a grey three-piece suit and his face was familiar from somewhere. Marriner could get no nearer than that.

'Major Marriner!' The man's smile was vivid. He snapped the book shut. 'Please forgive the intrusion. I meant to phone first, but on impulse I decided just to turn up. We have met, but there's no reason why you should remember. It was at Beira, in Mozambique—oh, seventy-eight or nine? Makibani. Harry Makibani.'

He stuck out a hand and Marriner shook it. Recognition came. Beira had been a hotbed of intrigue in those days. The Marxist government of Mozambique had given refuge there to the Rhodesian liberation movement, ZANU, then still engaged in its bush war against the white rebel regime across the border. Harry Makibani, as a fraternal delegate from the South African People's Congress, had been a frequent visitor to ZANU's headquarters.

'I do remember. It's a surprise to see you, all the same. You aren't living here now, surely?'

'No, no, just visiting. Still in Lusaka, still in the same business.'

'Sit down. Some coffee? Or maybe it's time for a drink?'

Makibani glanced appreciatively at the bottles arrayed on a table in the corner. 'It *is* time for a drink,' he said firmly. 'Cork Dry Gin? I think I should give that a try. With tonic.'

To forestall questions while Marriner mixed their drinks, Harry said, 'I was a little surprised to learn that you were living here. With the trouble in Northern Ireland, an ex-British Army officer . . . couldn't you be at risk?'

'From the IRA? It's a slight possibility, but only from those who don't know my history. I'm Irish, you see. Anglo-Irish. My grandfather was shot by the Black and Tans. Right in front of this house, actually.' Marriner handed him his drink. 'Well, cheers.'

Harry took a hefty swallow of gin and they sat down, facing each other, in a pair of leather armchairs. Marriner's silence was a tacit invitation to his visitor to state his business, but Harry wasn't quite ready for that yet. 'Major Marriner—'

'Do call me Patrick.'

'All right. Patrick.' Harry smiled. 'Patrick, I can't say I know you well, but I think you're the sort of man who would appreciate frankness. And the truth is, I went to some trouble to locate you.'

'I had worked that out already,' Marriner said coolly.

'When I was visiting London a few years ago I saw your name in a newspaper, mentioning that you'd resigned your army commission to take up farming in Ireland. The only thing that made it newsworthy was that you'd recently been decorated for heroism in the Falklands campaign.'

Marriner nodded. Harry went on: 'Three days ago I happened to remember that newspaper item. I came back to London to try to find you. I didn't want to go through official channels, so it was a matter of hunting through telephone directories and voters' lists. I located you, and had a few discreet enquiries made. Without, of course, revealing why.'

Marriner was amused. Harry was about the least likely private detective he could imagine. 'Well, you haven't told me why yet.'

'Patrick, you've spent quite a large part of your military career doing cloak-and-dagger jobs of one kind or another. You were brought up in Southern Africa, and your soldiering took you back there quite a lot. That means you know it from the inside. I think you also have sympathy for its problems. That's quite a unique combination of qualities.'

Marriner looked at him curiously. 'You make me sound like a colonial romantic. Well, it's true that in some ways I feel more at home out there than anywhere else.'

'That's good, Patrick. I want to know if you'd consider going back there for a short while? And doing a job for us?'

'For the People's Congress? What kind of job?'

'Just the kind you're equipped for. Covert intelligence, and quite possibly a rescue mission. I won't beat about the bush: at best it will be tricky, at worst it will be bloody dangerous. It's also extremely urgent.'

For all his cheeriness, Harry Makibani could be businesslike and even forceful. Marriner found himself readjusting his defences.

'I know that your first inclination will be to back off,' Harry said, 'so I'll tell you straight away that the money will be good. It could be spectacular, in fact. Do I need to add that this is entirely between us?' Marriner shook his head. 'Very good. You're not married, Patrick?'

'No.'

'So you have nobody you have to give an account of yourself to? I mean, if you went away for three or four weeks at fairly short notice?'

'Now hang on, Harry.' The man needed firm handling. 'Do you imagine this farm runs itself?'

'Of course not. But, unlike some of my more idealistic friends in the Congress, I have great faith in the power of money to solve problems. However, all I want to know now is whether you could manage a short trip to Zurich in the next couple of days? No strings attached.'

'Why Zurich?' Marriner asked suspiciously.

'Because that's where the money is, Patrick. That's where we'll take it a stage further, and ask you to say yes or no. We'll pay all your expenses, naturally, but also we don't expect you to give us your time for nothing. There'll be—what shall we call it?—a consultancy fee. And also a sign of our good faith. How does five thousand pounds sound?'

It sounded good. 'How would it be paid?' he asked.

'I have a cash cheque already made out, Patrick.'

'That was jumping the gun a bit, wasn't it?'

'I don't have time to mess around. I told you it was urgent.'

He made a decision. 'All right,' he said. 'I'll fly to Zurich and talk to you, but I won't decide until then whether to cash the cheque or not. I want to know more about this first.'

Harry looked pleased with himself. 'Well, now that's out of the way,' he said, 'there are one or two things I can tell you.'

THE SWISSAIR FLIGHT touched down at Zurich-Kloten airport at eleven o'clock, and Marriner was clear of Customs and Immigration fifteen minutes later. He took a taxi into the city, marvelling like any first-time visitor at its impossibly beautiful lakeside setting.

The Meilenhof Hotel, arranged by Harry, turned out to be a modestly elegant little building tucked away in a side street. The room to which he was shown was chintzy and restful, an impression disrupted the moment he had dumped his bag on the bed by the ringing of the telephone.

'Patrick?' It was Harry, of course. 'Did everything go smoothly? That's good. Whenever you're ready, leave the hotel, turn left and take the first turning left. There's a little pub called The Aurora about halfway up the street. We'll meet you there.'

He didn't hurry. Faintly irritated by Harry's hustling tone, he unpacked his bag, freshened up and changed before leaving the hotel.

The Aurora was three minutes' walk away, a place of heavy oak beams and latticed windows. Its interior was gloomy and quiet, and Marriner saw Harry at once, at a corner table in the company of a white man.

'Patrick! Good to see you!' Harry beamed. 'Patrick, I want you to meet Joshua Rosenblatt, the treasurer of the People's Congress. Josh, this is Major Marriner.'

Rosenblatt stood up and offered his hand. He was balding and his features were unremarkable, vaguely Jewish. 'I'm glad to meet you.' His accent was South African. 'Harry's told me a good deal about you.'

Harry bustled about them. 'Patrick, sit down. What will you drink? Josh, more coffee? *Bitte ein Bier, zwei Kaffees*,' he called in an atrocious accent to an approaching waiter. 'Now,' he said, settling in his chair, 'I suggest we get our business out of the way first, then have an early lunch in this place. That will leave us plenty of time to go to the bank.'

'You're three jumps ahead of me again,' Marriner said firmly. He turned to Rosenblatt. 'I hope it's been made clear that nothing is agreed.'

Rosenblatt nodded uncomfortably. 'Of course. I must tell you quite honestly that I'm in some doubt myself about the wisdom of this scheme.'

'Accountants never make good gamblers,' Harry said dismissively. 'This is a gamble, I'll admit, but in my opinion the odds are acceptable. Do you feel any better about the idea now, Patrick?'

'There's a hell of a lot more I want to know first. About your own security to begin with. How many people are in on this?'

'There are just the two of us, and one other. He is Moses Mohaila, the Congress representative in London. He had to know for procedural reasons that I won't bore you with, but I can assure you he's trustworthy.'

'Only three of you? Does that mean that your full leadership isn't aware of this plan?'

It was Harry's turn to look uneasy. 'It happens that Josh and I are the only ones with the information, and we've decided to keep it that way for now. After all, the security of the Congress may not be watertight. However, since Josh and I also have control of the money, the decisions are ours to make.'

They fell silent as the waiter arrived with the beer and coffee. This was not a good beginning, Marriner thought. He had the distinct impression that this was all Harry's show and that Rosenblatt—and he himself, for that matter—were being dragged along in his wake. It had been the name of Lincoln Kumalo that had come as the real shock of Harry's visit to Ballygarron. Up till then he'd merely received a scrappy but not unconvincing word-picture of an anonymous black political figure under threat, a need to find out more, the possible necessity of springing the man from a hospital bed. It was when Harry let slip the name that the whole scenario seemed to become absurd.

'Patrick, I'd better mention that there are rumours going round that Kumalo is to be released soon. You're bound to hear them yourself sooner or later. I can only say that we have no way of knowing whether there's any substance to the story. In fact, one piece of information we have suggests precisely the opposite: that they're going to kill him. In which case the rumours have been started as a blind.'

Harry paused to let this sink in. 'As I explained, Patrick, we want you initially to check out this information. On the other hand, it will be necessary to make plans from the start for getting him out of that clinic, and out of the country. Such plans can always be called off, but they certainly can't be cobbled together at the last minute.'

'Three weeks is almost no time as it is,' Marriner said. 'Have you any idea of the complexity of such a project? Perhaps the SAS could pull off a stunt like that, but you're asking a freelance like me to arrange it.'

'Try to look on the positive side. This clinic is a soft target—much softer, anyway, than Pollsmoor Prison. You'll also have the advantage of surprise. The South Africans don't know there's been a leak.'

'What makes you so sure?'

'The nature of the information we have makes it impossible for them to know.' Harry lifted his glass. 'The People's Congress is sometimes called the spear of the revolution. You can be our spearhead, Patrick!'

'All right. Supposing for a moment that it was feasible. I would need all kinds of back-up facilities. Communications, weapons, supplies, possibly a plane to fly him out of the country, which in turn means a pilot. Above all I would need a team of trustworthy and experienced men.'

'I was coming to that,' Harry said. 'In their own army there are many disaffected men. We keep a lookout for them, as a source of possible sympathy to our cause, young white men, conscripted against their will, who don't like what they are made to do. They are armed, and they often have combat experience.'

'What am I supposed to do? Advertise for some in the papers?'

'Of course not.' Harry ignored the sarcasm. 'One of our comrades out there is aware of a particular group. He would be in touch with you when you arrived. It will be a matter of making your own assessment, Patrick.'

'How about financing all this?' said Marriner, still sceptical. 'Do you realise how much it's going to cost?'

'Your department, Josh,' said Harry.

Rosenblatt adjusted his glasses. 'All the arrangements must be made here in Switzerland, partly because there are no exchange-control problems, partly because their banking system is efficient and confidential. I would propose opening a current account in your name into which the initial deposit would be made. You've had an advance of five thousand pounds, we would add forty-five thousand to that on your acceptance.'

'That's fifty grand just for saying yes,' Harry elaborated. 'Just for going out and looking around. Guaranteed. Unconditional.'

'In addition, should the project be successfully completed, we would deposit another two hundred thousand pounds in your account.'

'That's a straight quarter of a million. And the whole thing can be arranged this afternoon,' Harry said triumphantly.

Marriner leaned back in his chair. A quarter of a million pounds. The figure was almost meaningless to him.

'As well as that,' said Harry by way of encouragement, 'you'll be able to draw on a separate million to cover the cost of the operation. You'll have to open a bank account over there, Patrick, and send to Josh for money as and when it's needed.'

'How do I explain an influx of money on that sort of scale?'

'Who will you have to explain to? It's your own money. It could be an inheritance or something, that you're planning to invest out there. In fact . . .' An idea came to Harry, and he grinned. 'We were having trouble thinking of a cover story for you. Well, here it is. You're a farmer. Why don't you let it be known that you've decided to buy a farm? That will explain your presence there. It will also account for the money.'

Marriner considered. This at least wasn't a bad notion. It wasn't implausible that a man who'd spent half his life in Africa should have a hankering to go back there and take up something he was familiar with.

BY HALF PAST ONE everything was settled. In spite of his misgivings, Marriner had come to the simple conclusion that he would be a fool to turn the offer down. Nothing of the sort would ever come his way again. Fifty thousand pounds would pay off the debts at Ballygarron. With the other two hundred thousand . . . But he refused to think about that. The money was in proportion to the risk.

At two o'clock they took a taxi to the Handelsbank Bauer, and opened two accounts. Into the first Rosenblatt deposited a cheque for forty-five thousand pounds drawn on a sterling account at the Union Banque Suisse. Into the second he transferred one million pounds from an account he had already opened with the Handelsbank Bauer.

Their day's business was not yet over. From the bank they took another cab into the Unterstrass district, to the north, where Rosenblatt had rented a service flat. They sat down round the table in the small dining-alcove and began to talk.

They talked for two and a half hours, covering everything that had happened, or as much as they knew had happened, since the day Nandi

Kumalo had received the message from Pollsmoor. If one thing was clear to Marriner at the end, it was that the girl Judith Rose held the key to one large part of the puzzle. 'She's obviously as nervous as hell,' he said, 'and she'll have no reason whatever to trust me.'

Rosenblatt got up and went to a suitcase, and removed an old leather-bound photograph album. From a page in the middle he carefully loosened a picture and handed it over. 'She'll know this can only have come from me. It's nine or ten years old, but it's the most recent I have.'

It was a black and white portrait, showing a girl in her late teens with short curly dark hair. There was an inscription on the back, in the same writing as that in the letter. *To Joshua*, it said. *Me facing up to my matric exams. Nil desperandum. Love, Judith.*

Marriner nodded. 'That should do nicely.'

From earlier events they moved on to future ones. There was no point in trying to make plans for the springing of Kumalo from the clinic, since that was something Marriner would have to work out on the ground. There was, however, the equally vital question of getting him out of the country afterwards. Here, Harry had been doing his homework.

'Personally, I wouldn't consider any option except flying. The moment the stuff hits the fan, the ground is going to be crawling with police and troops. Kumalo is sixty-eight years old and not in the best of health. Not up to an arduous journey or a long period in hiding, anyway.'

Harry spread a map of Southern Africa on the table. 'Look, the two nearest borders are those of Botswana in the west, Mozambique in the east. Botswana is closer but its government is edgy about its relationship with South Africa. Mozambique is a much better bet. It is hostile to South Africa. It will welcome Lincoln Kumalo as an honoured guest.'

Marriner had been studying the map with interest. 'Overflying Swaziland *en route* to Mozambique would cut down on the time spent in South African air space.' Swaziland was entirely surrounded by South Africa except for a shared a border of perhaps sixty or seventy miles with Mozambique.

'Swaziland is almost totally dependent on South Africa,' Rosenblatt objected. 'Its king is an autocratic ruler who is not friendly to us.'

'We're not going to ask for his help, Josh. We're just going to take a quick hop over his territory.' Marriner was tracing a line with his finger eastwards across the map. 'Once we've crossed Swaziland, we're over southern Mozambique. I visited that area once. It's pretty wild, very few roads. I doubt if there's even an airstrip.'

'I'll check it out for you. I'll be flying back to Lusaka this weekend, but of course we will stay in touch. Which brings us to the question of communications.'

It appeared that while Harry planned to return to Zambia, Rosenblatt was to stay in Zurich. His flat would serve as a link between Marriner and Harry, for it would be far too risky to attempt to communicate directly between Johannesburg and Lusaka. As an added precaution, they would use a telephone scrambler.

Darkness had fallen, creeping through the gloomy little flat, by the time they had said all that seemed to need saying. They wished Marriner good luck, and he left the flat carrying his dubious souvenirs: the telephone scrambler and the photograph of Judith Rose. Back in his hotel room he telephoned Swissair reservations. He had decided on a change in his itinerary. He needed a few hours in London. There were some cards in this game he wanted to deal for himself.

Chapter Six

Marriner phoned Fred Dyce as soon as he arrived at Heathrow Airport, and luckily found him at home. They had been at Michaelhouse School in Natal together, had bumped into each other again in Zambia a dozen years ago and remained in touch. Dyce had made a good career for himself in London as a freelance journalist of mildly left-wing views, a specialist on Southern African affairs. He agreed to meet Marriner for a drink at El Vino in Fleet Street.

Once they were settled Marriner said he wanted some advice. He was thinking of going back to South Africa, possibly to take up farming. He wondered what Dyce, as a close observer of the scene out there, thought of the country's future.

'Buying a farm?' the journalist replied. 'Well, you're a braver man than I am, Patrick. Nobody is investing money there these days. On the other hand, if you're prepared to take a gamble, I suppose you could get a pretty good deal. The price of land is depressed at the moment, I gather. In ten years' time, say, you might either sell it for a fortune or find it's quite worthless, depending on how the wind blows.'

Marriner was glad to find his cover story was not greeted with complete incredulity, and the conversation quite naturally led on to the People's Congress and Lincoln Kumalo.

'In a way, Kumalo holds the key to the country's future,' Dyce said. 'From the government's point of view, a time must eventually come when letting him go will seem a lesser evil than keeping him locked up. What's really interesting is what that would do to the Congress leadership.'

'How so?'

'Like all those African liberation movements, it has dissension at the top. While they all agree on the need to overthrow the system, they differ quite fundamentally over what to put in its place. There are extreme left-wingers among its leaders—men like J.K.Govender and Lawrence Gumbi—and it's their influence that would wane if Kumalo were free.'

'And who would stand to benefit?'

'The moderates. People like Harry Makibani. Kumalo himself is a social democrat. If he came out and took charge, there would certainly be a shakeup. Perhaps that's what the government is gambling on: Kumalo as a moderating influence.' Dyce glanced at his watch. 'God, I'm late already. Well, good luck, Patrick. Invite me to your farm some day.'

'After the Revolution,' Marriner said with a grin.

From the wine bar Marriner took a taxi to the South African Airways office in Regent Street, and booked a flight to Johannesburg for Sunday evening, leaving the return date open. Then he went to South Africa House where he talked with a pleasant sandy-haired young man from the commercial section. There was no point in having a cover story unless you could make it stand up. No, the official said, he was not aware of any restrictions on foreigners buying or leasing land in South Africa. And yes, any amount of capital could be imported for such a purpose.

THE WEEKEND WAS PREDICTABLY hectic. Although this was a slack period on the farm, there suddenly seemed to be a least hundred jobs that needed doing, and even more to be planned for during his absence.

On Sunday Jenny Swanson brought over a picnic lunch, which they shared in the kitchen once he had finished packing. When Patrick had first come to south Cork, and before he had even met Jenny, he had heard her described as The Merry Widow. It wasn't that she was promiscuous; her vivacious nature was simply mistaken for availability. Jenny was rather amused at her own reputation, but her conscience was clear. She had loved her husband, but she had been only thirty at the time of his death in a car crash, and she wasn't going to spend the rest of her life grieving for him. That he had left her extremely well off was beside the point. She managed her four hundred acres with an effortless efficiency that still allowed her time to ride to hounds, play tennis, collect paintings and indulge her passion for interior decorating. She had style and she had energy. It had seemed almost inevitable that she and Marriner should drift together.

'You really ought to get that moulding restored,' she said, looking round the room.

'Maybe I will fix it up,' he said. 'The trouble with this house is that renovating one part would make all the rest look twice as shabby. What if I were to give you a free hand with the house? I mean, invited you in to do whatever you thought it needed. Within financial reason, of course,' he added quickly. 'What would it cost?'

'Oh, well, you'd want the floorboards sanded and polished. New wallpaper and paint throughout. Some plasterwork and some other small repairs, inevitably. I suppose three or four thousand.'

'I know these things always cost more than one expects.'

'Not with me in charge. You aren't actually serious, are you?'

'I'd pay you for it, of course. As I'll be away for a few weeks it would be a good opportunity to get it done.' For the first time Marriner looked at the cheque for five thousand pounds that Harry Makibani had given him last week. It was, as Harry had said, made out for cash and therefore anonymous. 'Better pop this in your own account,' he said to Jenny, 'and draw on it when you need to.'

She slipped the cheque into her handbag. 'All right. Is there anywhere I can reach you out there? There will be things we'll have to discuss.'

Marriner hesitated. He did have the name of a hotel in Johannesburg to which Harry had directed him. There was no need to make a secret of it, but something cautioned him against being so specific. As far as Jenny or anyone else knew, he was still just on his way to Africa 'on business'.

'I don't know when I'll be in touch, frankly,' he said. 'I'm not really sure of my movements yet.'

At five o'clock she drove him to Cork airport for his connecting flight to London. He felt vaguely guilty towards her as she kissed him goodbye. Sitting back in the steeply climbing Boeing 737 it was with a sense of ignoble relief that he looked down on the dwindling scattered lights of the south Irish coast.

It was only when he stepped aboard the SAA jumbo jet at Heathrow and heard the familiar South African accents around him that he began to have any real sense of foreboding.

AT ABOUT THE TIME Marriner's plane was lumbering into the dark autumn skies over London, six thousand miles away in the beautiful Eerste River Valley, inland from Cape Town, Deputy Minister Frans Hoeksma's open-air party was just getting into full swing.

His house was a gracious white-gabled Cape Dutch mansion that had been in his family for four generations, and the guests had been invited to arrive before sunset, the better to appreciate the spectacular view of the distant purple mass of the Franschhoek Mountains.

There were eighty people present, just enough to fill the gardens without making them seem crowded. They amounted to a fair cross-section of the Cape Afrikaner elite. The only ones significantly out of place were Colonel Prinsloo and Dr Els. They watched with a pretence of distant amusement the younger people who cavorted in the swimming pool before dinner. Els seemed a little overawed by it all and was drinking too fast, while Prinsloo found himself disguising a certain rebellious anger. He had nothing in common with any of these people, and knew he would never have been invited for his own sake.

Els had glimpsed Tertius van Straaten across the lawn earlier on, but he had disappeared by the time dinner arrived: skewers of barbecued lamb marinated in a spicy Malay sauce, together with T-bone and fillet steaks, baked potatoes and heaped platefuls of salads, all washed down with excellent wine. A deep, warm darkness enclosed the floodlit gardens. Eventually the shadow of their host moved across the grass to fall on Prinsloo and Els where they sat. 'Gentlemen. I've been neglecting you. Shall we have our chat now?'

The inside of the house still held some of the heat of the day. From the front door a wide, stone-flagged hall led past the main living rooms to a small room which served Hoeksma as a private office.

Van Straaten was already in the room. When Hoeksma had shut and locked the door he waved them into chairs round a small table. Four balloon glasses and a brandy bottle were on the table. Hoeksma poured them all a good measure, then took up his own glass and swirled the cognac in it with his plump, delicate hand. He had greeted Dr Els briefly on his arrival, but now he took serious notice of him for the first time.

'Doctor, I understand that you may be in a position to help us on a rather delicate matter of some importance to our national security. I understand also that you have some objection to the part you have been asked to play in this. Now, I haven't asked you here to put pressure on you, Doctor, merely to try to emphasise the importance of what we're asking. It seems to me that you are a true Afrikaner, that you're a man who might be able to see the cause of this nation as more important than any narrower loyalty.'

'Loyalty to my medical ethics, you mean. I don't see why I should have to make such a choice.'

'But you make choices all the time, Dr Els.' Hoeksma moved into what sounded like a well-rehearsed argument. 'Every doctor does. What happens, for instance, when there's a disaster and the emergency services can't cope with all the casualties? Some have to be left to die in order that others may be helped—for the greatest good of the greatest number.'

'It's a false comparison,' said Els, rather surprised at his own nerve. 'I can't stop this going ahead. I just don't want to be part of it.'

'I'm trying to make you see that there are wider considerations, Doctor. Do you know that forty thousand children die every day in Black Africa? Every day. And why do they die? Because they live in countries that can't afford to feed them. It's because we don't want this country to become like that, Doctor, that I'm putting this to you. It's because we want the time to make peaceful and orderly progress, without pressure or interference.'

'If I thought you could guarantee that ...'

'Of course we can't,' said van Straaten. 'We can only tell you it's the best hope we've got.'

Els took a defiant swallow of brandy. 'Supposing I say no? Supposing I say to hell with you and walk out of here and tell the whole story. Maybe to the foreign press.'

'But what story, Doctor?' Van Straaten's chilly, meticulous tone didn't change. 'There are three witnesses here, including a deputy minister, who will deny everything you say. It's true that you could cause some inconvenience, but another way would be found to complete our project, Doctor. A way that would not depend on you. Nobody is indispensable.'

Els stared at each of them in turn. Hoeksma looked regretful. Van Straaten blandly sipped cognac, and Prinsloo wore a cynical smile.

It was Hoeksma who broke the brief silence. 'I suggest you go back to the party for a while, Dr Els. Think over what has been said. And then let us know.' He unlocked the door and Dr Els left. When he rejoined the others at the table Hoeksma allowed himself a small, satisfied smile.

'I believe he will see the sense in cooperating.' He poured them all more brandy. 'Dr Rose has agreed to have Els present at the operation?'

'Under protest,' said Prinsloo. 'I gather it's all right as long as he doesn't touch anything.' He grinned. 'A bit of a prima donna, is Dr Rose.'

'But he's cooperating?'

'Oh, yes. He's a devil for efficiency. He's devised a whole computer program to cover his arrangements, reorganising the routine of the clinic. No, I don't think we have to worry about Dr Rose, though I did have reservations about that old family connection of his. His cousin, Rosenblatt.'

'Well, there seems to be no harm in that. It helps to establish his credentials. A man who has a relative who's active in the Congress: there could be no better proof of his independence from us.'

'There is a daughter, Judith,' Prinsloo said, 'who used to be tied up with the radical student movement. She doesn't seem to have been very active politically, though. The only thing that bothered me slightly is that she actually has a job in her old man's clinic.'

'You consider her a security risk?' van Straaten asked.

'I don't think so,' said Prinsloo after a few moments' reflection. 'She'll probably get an inkling sooner or later that something is going on, but nobody will really know anything until the last minute.'

THE TERMINAL BUILDING at Johannesburg was vast, functional and uncrowded. It was eight o'clock in the morning and the thin Highveld air was already warmed by the sun. At Passport Control a man in summer whites carefully studied Marriner's entry card. 'You're a farmer, Mr Marriner? Your passport says you're an army officer.'

'I used to be. Nowadays I run a farm.'

The official made a note on the card. ' "Length of stay: six weeks. Purpose of visit: business," ' he read out. He glanced up. 'That's rather a long business trip.'

'I may be buying some land here. I need time to look round.'

The lie tripped easily off his tongue now. The man looked impressed. 'Buying land? Well, good luck,' he said. He stamped the passport, snapped it shut and handed it back. He even managed a small smile.

Marriner collected his baggage and took it as a good omen when he passed through the green Customs channel without being stopped, thus facing no awkward questions about the telephone scrambler. As he walked towards the taxi rank he stopped deliberately and took several deep breaths of the familiar, intoxicating air of Africa.

The Windsor Hotel was a pleasantly old-fashioned place in the heart of the city. There were potted palms in the lobby, a marble-topped reception desk, and mulligatawny soup on the menu pinned beside it.

Yes, said the woman at the desk, they had a room.

His room was on the third floor and of an impressive size, sharing the threadbare elegance of the rest of the building. Besides the big double bed and other standard furnishings, it easily accommodated a sofa and a pair of armchairs. He unpacked his bags and went down for breakfast.

When he had eaten his bacon and eggs Marriner still felt restless. He'd had only a few hours' sleep on the plane but he wasn't tired enough for bed yet. He was, as Harry had advised, going to lie low for a couple of days; but there was no harm in getting a few necessary and innocuous tasks out of the way.

He handed in his key and left the hotel. The streets were much as he remembered them, noisier and more crowded if anything, but the big difference was the presence of black people in far greater preponderance than he had known before. Whatever their political and economic disadvantages might be, there was a new assertiveness about them. On the yellow T-shirt of a youth wired into a Walkman he noticed the legend *Free Kumalo*.

The western end of Fox Street was at the heart of the financial district. Here a slender skyscraper housed the headquarters of the Standard Bank of South Africa. At the reception desk Marriner stated his business and was led to the office of Mr Jepson of the foreign department.

Jepson was a cheery, ruddy-faced, outgoing man. His accent was South African but his speech was peppered with outdated English jargon. 'Just got in from Blighty, Mr Marriner? Years since I was over there. Well, you just visiting, or planning to peg out your tent here?'

Marriner explained that he was thinking of buying a farm, that he had money in Switzerland that he could send for if and when he found what he was looking for. He had the equivalent of several thousand rands with him at present, and was interested in opening a current account.

'No problem at all, old boy. Never turn away anyone with a spot of the ready. Of course the best cattle country is well north of here, but if you wanted to start in a more modest way, there are a lot of small farms for sale to the northwest, over towards the Magaliesberg. You might even talk one of the owners into leasing it for a while.'

Half an hour later Marriner left the bank equipped with an account number, a chequebook and a promise that a cheque card would be forwarded to him within a couple of days.

What he needed was a car. He found a hire firm a few blocks away in Main Street, and chose an inconspicuous grey Ford Orion. There was one form to fill in, requiring little more than his name, address and signature, for insurance purposes. The man barely glanced at the details and didn't even ask to see his driver's licence. He drove off into the chaotic city traffic, heading back to The Windsor.

Over lunch, he paged through copies of the *Farmers Weekly* he had bought, studying the farms for sale and noting the names of the agents who advertised them. At half-past two he returned to his room, and by three o'clock he was catching up on his sleep.

THE NEXT MORNING, refreshed and rested, he set off early to go exploring.

He drove northwards onto the motorway that led to Pretoria. The route took him past miles and miles of leafy white suburbs before opening out into bare veld surmounted by woody ridges. It seemed hardly any time before he was nearing Pretoria, its appearance marked by the vast granite monolith of the Voortrekker Monument. Soon after that he found a turning leading west towards Brits and Hartbeespoort, two of the several little settlements scattered about among the hills of the Magaliesberg, the area Jepson had been talking about yesterday.

From the beginning he had known that if it did become necessary to spring Kumalo from the Woodvale Clinic, then he would need a secure base from which to mount the operation, and possibly to use as a temporary refuge afterwards. The base would have to be somewhere secluded, but within a reasonable distance from the clinic.

He hadn't the remotest hope, of course, of buying a farm in the time available, which was now only eighteen days. Buying land in any country was a complicated business involving lawyers, the transfer of deeds and the registration of ownership. Renting a farm, on the other hand, ought to be a much simpler business. Provided he could find one that was suitable, and even that was asking a lot in so short a time.

The day grew hotter as he meandered along the country roads, not quite certain what he was looking for but sure that he would know when he found it. He drove back towards Johannesburg by a circuitous route, reaching the village of Muldersdrift, on its outer northwest fringe, at four o'clock. He had seen a dozen or so promising properties with FOR SALE notices at their gates, and half of these had been advertised by the firm of Labuschagne & Son, of Muldersdrift.

Mr Labuschagne junior turned out to be a pleasant, urbane young man who offered Marriner tea. 'Mostly the people who are buying up these small places are weekend farmers,' he said. 'Replacing the old fellows who can't make a living out of them any longer. The weekenders keep a few cattle, maybe some chickens or ducks, and have a boy to look after them. No, if you want real farming, Mr Marriner, you'll have to go out a good fifty kilometres or so. We have some good sizable places on our books ...'

'I'm not sure I'm ready for that big a risk,' Marriner said. 'I want to take it slowly, learn from my mistakes. That's why it struck me as ideal to try out one of these small places for a while. Perhaps get a lease for six months or a year, with an option to buy as a further incentive.'

Labuschagne looked doubtful. 'These vendors are usually looking for hard cash. On the other hand, it's just possible that one of them might agree to some leasing arrangement. It will take a while, of course. A lot of them aren't on the phone. It will mean my writing to them, or calling in when I have the time.'

Marriner finished his tea. He could understand the agent's lack of enthusiasm: a deal like this was probably more trouble than it was worth. He said, 'Do you mind telling me what your commission is?'

'I take ten per cent of the first year's rent from the lessor.'

'What if I threw in another ten per cent from my side? Plus a bonus of five hundred rands if you come up with the right place inside a week?'

Labuschagne was taken aback. 'You *are* in a hurry, aren't you?'

'Staying in a hotel is costing a fortune. The money is well worth it if I can get settled quickly.'

'Some of the houses on these farms may not be up to your standards of comfort.'

'Oh, I've been known to rough it before.'

Considerably more animated, Labuschagne stood up and shook hands. 'That's a deal, then. I'll get to work on it at once.'

Marriner left the office after arranging that the agent would telephone him at the hotel as soon as he had some prospects lined up. He was beginning, like Harry, to acquire some faith in the power of money.

ON HIS THIRD MORNING in Johannesburg, Marriner decided to address himself to the problem of approaching Judith Rose. What he'd accomplished so far had been useful groundwork, no more. Harry's contacts in the People's Congress had made no attempt to get in touch with him; he presumed they were avoiding him deliberately for a while.

Once again he drove northwards onto the Pretoria motorway. He had the photograph Rosenblatt had given him in the glove box of the car, but it was out of the question for him to approach Judith Rose directly. She might suspect a trick. For the moment it would be enough to locate her.

He left the motorway at the Edenburg junction, and turned onto a narrow road that led north to Woodvale. A few hundred yards down the lane he stopped, backed into a driveway and waited for a couple of minutes, pretending to study his map. When he was satisfied that he wasn't being tailed, he drove on.

He passed a discreet little pair of gateposts made of pale yellow brick, and only at the last moment caught sight of a brass plate that said WOODVALE CLINIC. PRIVATE PROPERTY. In spite of this warning the gate was open and unguarded. He drove slowly through.

Inside, a drive curved round a wide expanse of lawn and past a group of single-storey buildings, pleasingly modern and functional in style. The buildings took up only a small portion of the land, which must have run to four or five acres and was tastefully planted with clumps of shady trees. A few of the clinic's patients strolled about or sat on benches.

He drove cautiously on. No one was likely to query his presence unless he entered one of the buildings—like all hospitals, this one must have a constant stream of people entering and leaving its grounds.

The clinic was impressive. It had tranquillity and it had seclusion. The land sloped gently down from west to east, overlooking a landscape of small vegetable farms. Beyond that was the wide slash of the Johannesburg–Pretoria motorway. Pine trees had been planted all round the perimeter to mask the less appealing sight of an eight-foot boundary fence of steel mesh. This, however, was more a deterrent than an actual barrier. When it came to safeguarding Kumalo here, the real security of the place would lie in its isolation, the ability to seal it off discreetly.

The driveway meandered across the grounds and doubled back on itself near the southern perimeter. Marriner swung the car round, stopped for a minute and studied the view of the clinic from this new angle.

'Are you visiting a patient, sir?'

The voice was startlingly close. It came from a young white man in a security guard's uniform, bent beside the car.

'Sorry. Did I give you a turn?' The man was apologetic but slightly wary. 'It's just that you seemed to be waiting for someone.'

'No . . . No. I took a wrong turning. I drove in here by mistake.'

'Oh. Yeah. That can happen,' the guard conceded. He was a lumpish young fellow with a brass pin on his shirt which identified him by the improbable name of Virgil. 'Where was it you were looking for?'

By some miracle a name seen on a gatepost five minutes ago came back to him. 'Bracken,' he said. 'A house called Bracken.'

'Down the road a bit. On the right.' Virgil stepped back, inviting him to move off.

Marriner started the car and drove off the way he had come. In the mirror he saw the guard standing straddle-legged in the middle of the driveway, watching his departure, and he cursed his own foolishness. He had drawn attention to himself, and for no good reason at all.

Distracted, he made a genuine wrong turning. Instead of staying on the main route he found himself bumping along a potholed side road across a patch of rubble-strewn veld. Ahead, to his surprise, he saw the unmistakable low smoky sprawl of a black township. Curiosity pushed him on a little further, until he could read a sign he had spotted by the side of the road. *Alexandra Township*, it said, *No Unauthorised Entry*; and to reinforce the point a police and army roadblock had been set up a hundred yards ahead.

He remembered the name. Alexandra was the only one of Johannesburg's townships not neatly segregated off into the satellite city of Soweto to the southwest. It was about as different as was possible from the tranquil affluence of Woodvale, only a few minutes' drive away.

Marriner stopped the car well before the roadblock, turned round and headed back to the motorway. He could do without having to explain himself twice in one morning.

Chapter Seven

The London office of the People's Congress occupied one of a row of drab three-storey Victorian houses just off the Chalk Farm Road. Like its counterpart in Lusaka, it had suffered its share of destructive attention. Three years ago, a bomb had blown out the windows of the information office on the ground floor; more recently, the offices had twice been broken into. No one was ever arrested for these crimes, though it was not difficult to guess that the South African National Intelligence Service had inspired them. But if the intention of the bombing was to intimidate the eight employees of the office, the motive for the burglaries was harder to fathom. They could not have expected to discover much. Like all revolutionary organisations, the Congress maintained a strict division between its political branch, which functioned openly under the direction of Moses Mohaila, a former schoolteacher, and its activist military wing whose operations were conducted in the strictest secrecy.

Jasper Darries left the office at midday that Wednesday on his regular weekly errand to the printer's shop in the Fulham Palace Road to deliver copy for the Congress's London newsletter. Given the time spent waiting for Tube trains and buses, it was usually three o'clock, sometimes later, before he got back to the office.

Half an hour could easily go unaccounted for in such a period. Half an hour was all the time he ever gave his Controller—an agent of the South African intelligence service—and he had never pressed for more. From the beginning Jasper had set his own terms. He would meet them only during working hours, and only when he himself judged it to be safe. That way, he had held them at arm's length, had kept them from invading his private life. Soon he would qualify for British citizenship, and then he would no longer need a work permit. Then, in turn, he could kiss both the Congress and the Controller goodbye. Although he had worked conscientiously for both, because that was in his nature, he had not the slightest interest either in promoting revolution or in fighting it. Jasper was interested only in making his own way in the world. He had a bank deposit account with forty-five thousand pounds in it, and in another year it would be close to sixty thousand. That was when he planned to drop out of sight. Leave London altogether, settle down in some provincial city and start his own business. And until then he was content to be just what he appeared: a rather diffident young Coloured man of modest attainments.

He reached the printer's shop at a few minutes to one. There were no problems with the material he had brought, and Jasper had left the premises again by a quarter past. A little way down the Fulham Palace Road he bought a copy of the *Evening Standard*, and entered the saloon bar of The King's Arms. He bought a half of Guinness and found a seat. The place was as crowded as usual, and Jasper didn't bother trying to spot the lookout man. The *Standard* was the signal. If he was carrying one, the meeting would go ahead. If not, it would be cancelled.

After exactly ten minutes, Jasper left the pub by a side entrance which gave onto a long deserted mews. A Volkswagen van was parked five yards round the next corner. It opened its sliding door as Jasper approached and within a few seconds had swallowed him in from the pavement and was driving off towards Chelsea.

There was a hardboard partition between the front and rear of the van, so Jasper never got more than a glimpse of the driver and the lookout man. The man he knew only as the Controller sat on one of the bench seats in the back, huddled in a quilted anorak with a hood. Presumably he missed the South African sun.

The Controller grinned at him. '*Alles reg*, Jasper?'

'Everything's OK.'

The Controller reached into a cupboard beside him, produced a bottle of Scotch and two plastic tumblers. '*Gesondheid*,' he said. They drank. They were on friendly terms, as friendly as it was possible to be in the circumstances. 'Have you got any paperwork for me?'

'No. Nothing worth taking. Nothing I could risk copying.'

The Controller looked disappointed. He liked things on paper, presumably because they proved he was doing his job. From the pocket of his anorak he took a small cassette recorder, placed it on the table and pressed the RECORD button. 'All right. Tell me your news.'

'Well, Harry Makibani is still in Europe, I don't know where at the moment. On the twenty-second he went to Ireland for two days. Later he went to Switzerland. As you know, they have their bank accounts there.'

'Why Ireland?'

'I have no idea. One thing I have since discovered is that he took a cheque for five thousand pounds with him. It was a cash cheque, drawn on a small account that the Congress finance committee keeps. The money had to be telegraphed from Zurich, from the Handelsbank Bauer.'

The Controller gave a low whistle. 'Does that suggest anything to you, Jasper?'

'Nothing. The Congress has sympathisers in Ireland but, if anything, the money should come from them to us.'

'Have they ever had dealings with the IRA?'

'Not that I've ever heard. And I find it hard to imagine such a thing.'

'I would love to find out where that cheque went to, Jasper.' The idea of establishing some link between the Congress and the IRA had taken root in his mind. If such a thing could be proved, it would do much damage to the respectable image the Congress was seeking to cultivate with Western governments. 'Can you do that for me?'

'I doubt it. Wait a minute. Let me think.'

Jasper knew that most banks these days no longer enclosed paid and cancelled cheques with the statements they sent out to their customers, unless they were specially requested. There was nothing to stop him, over the phone, requesting that cheque back on behalf of Moses Mohaila. It would be posted to the Congress office and, as long as he knew when to expect it, he could be sure of intercepting it before it reached Mohaila himself.

'I'll try,' he said. 'If I can get hold of it, I'll bring it next Wednesday.'

The Controller didn't answer. Something else seemed to be bothering him. 'You mentioned the name of a Swiss bank. Bauer, was it? Spell that.' Jasper spelled it out for the tape recorder. 'But don't they keep their money in the Union Banque Suisse?'

'Not all of it, any longer. I know a little about that, too, but I hardly thought it was worth mentioning.'

'It's not for you to decide what's important,' the Controller said. 'It's not for me, either.'

They talked on for another fifteen minutes while the van threaded its way from Chelsea to Knightsbridge, into Piccadilly and down the Haymarket. They finally dropped Jasper a hundred yards from the Embankment station, which allowed him to catch a Northern Line train straight back to Camden Town. Today he was back in the office before three o'clock.

HOUGHTON DRIVE: a long, tree-lined avenue bisecting the priciest residential land in the country. By seven thirty that Thursday morning Marriner was parked fifty yards down the road from the gates of the Roses' home. By daylight he felt uncomfortably exposed, but he'd been gripped by desperation when he realised that today was December the first. There were only fifteen days to go and, risk or no risk, he was going to have to make contact with Judith Rose.

There was one means of waylaying her, and that was to arrange a small car crash. Hardly the happiest way to make her acquaintance, but it would have the merit of seeming accidental.

At ten to eight a Jaguar nosed its way out of the gates, swung right and accelerated past him, heading north. Marriner got a glimpse of Dr Rose as he passed: a patrician profile, a head of wavy grey hair. It was another half an hour before he saw a sporty red Opel Manta appear at the entrance with its right indicator going. He started his engine and watched in his mirror as the driver waited for a gap in the traffic. Finally she turned. Again, he caught only a profile view of the driver as the car sped past, but it was Judith all right: the same strong serious face that was in the photograph. He waited a few seconds more, giving another car time to get between them before beginning to follow her.

She drove fast and aggressively, so that he had to overtake the intervening car in order to keep her in sight. Where the road divided at the far end of Houghton Drive she was held up by a traffic light, and he coasted in slowly behind her. Now, before she bore right to head for

Pretoria, was the time for a little accident. Just the slightest of bumps, hop out of the car, sorry, no harm done... But as he inched the Orion up behind her the lights changed to green and she raced off.

She didn't take the right fork. Without a signal, she turned left. Wherever she was going, it wasn't to the clinic. Bewildered, but determined not to lose her, he pushed the Orion as hard as it would go.

THE HOUSE WHICH Deputy Minister Hoeksma maintained in Pretoria was not on the scale of his mansion in the Cape, but was discreetly impressive in its own way, a white clapboard affair complete with pool and tennis court. Hoeksma and his wife had only just come off the court when van Straaten arrived, and were red-faced and panting from their exertions. Hoeksma led his unexpected visitor back into the garden, to some chairs in the shade of a mulberry tree. 'What's on your mind, Tertius?'

'I do apologise for turning up unexpectedly, Minister, but I wanted a word in private. This is something a little outside Prinsloo's ... scope. It may or may not have something to do with the Induna project.'

'Then why are you bothering me with it, Tertius?'

'Minister, if you'll just bear with me ... As you must be aware, my service keeps track as closely as possible of the activities of the People's Congress overseas. I learned this morning that within days of seven million dollars in aid having been pledged to them by a number of the so-called non-aligned nations, they had opened a new bank account with the Handelsbank Bauer in Switzerland. Already a small sum has been filtered through a bank in London to someone in Ireland, but what concerns me much more is the possibility that some of it, possibly a lot of it, may find its way here.'

They were interrupted by the arrival of the houseboy, wheeling a trolley of drinks across the lawn. When he had parked it at Hoeksma's elbow and departed, van Straaten continued.

'The money *might* be earmarked for some subversive purpose here. There are many ways of bringing it in, but the best method is to do it officially, through a bank. The details of all foreign-currency transactions are passed on in due course to the South African Reserve Bank.'

'That's how they keep track of our foreign reserves.' Hoeksma stood up and busied himself with the drinks. 'I'm having whisky and soda. Same for you? I don't quite see what help you expect from me, Tertius.'

'The thing is, Minister, it's quite possible to trace the source of any money that's imported, but usually only after the event. Now, I want to speed up the procedure a bit. All it would take is one key person in the right department to tip us off the moment they were notified of any transfer of funds from the Handelsbank Bauer. There can't be many transfers from such a small bank. Could you have a word with the Minister of Finance?'

'All right, Tertius, I'll see what I can do. I hope you're not letting this little matter distract you from our other business.'

'It's because it *was* distracting me that I want it put in hand. Nothing may come of it, but at least I'll have taken precautions.'

'Where did you come by this information, anyway?'

'Oh, just a source.' Van Straaten gave him a tight little smile that told him that there were some things that couldn't be mentioned, even to Deputy Minister Hoeksma.

THE MOMENT HE ENTERED the room Phineas Molefe knew things were about to go very badly for him. He had known all along roughly what to expect, of course. Today was the first of the month: stocktaking day. And the young man from the Central Pharmaceutical Stores wore the grim, almost sorrowful expression that white men took on when you had outraged them beyond anger. All he could do was begin by protesting his innocence, then later tell the clerk and the pharmacist part of the truth. They believed things if you made them hard work for them.

For a minute neither of the men spoke. Then the pharmacist said, 'Phineas, *kom hierso.*'

'*My baas?*'

Phineas went round the counter to where the dispensary records were spread out on the table: the stock sheets, the drugs register.

'There's something missing, Phineas.'

'*My baas?*'

'Missing. Tablets. Amphetamines. *Verstaan?*'

Phineas gave the sort of dumb, uncomprehending look that was expected of him. But it was the storeman who spoke next. 'There are eighty-one Dexedrine tablets missing. What happened to them, Phineas?'

He puckered his brow in thought. 'I don't know, *my baas.*'

'Of course you do. I'm giving you the chance to come clean.'

'I know nothing.'

'Right. The security officer will have to take this over. There's another thing,' the storeman said. 'While I was cross-checking the prescriptions, I found one of the dockets missing.'

'One of the dockets?' Now the pharmacist seemed to be playing dumb. 'Does it matter?'

'I think this one might. It was a prescription for Stilboestrol hormone tablets. They were for Prisoner 4008.'

The pharmacist glanced at Phineas, then back at the stores officer. 'What are you saying? That the docket was stolen, too?'

'All I'm saying is that you've got two discrepancies in your records. Are you going to call the security officer, or shall I?'

THE OPEL MANTA cut a zigzagging trail across the northern suburbs of Johannesburg. After twenty minutes or so, however, it set course along a fast dual carriageway that seemed to be taking it towards a high rocky hill.

Northcliff, it was signposted. The highway petered out soon, giving way to a two-lane road that rounded the base of the hill and then began to climb it. There was little other traffic here, and Marriner followed more cautiously, the red car disappearing from his view for a few seconds at a time as it took the bends between stylish houses and apartment blocks. Somewhere near the top, Marriner realised that the Opel had been out of sight for almost a minute. Then, suddenly, he found himself at the top. Somewhere along the road Judith Rose had turned off, and he'd lost her.

Cursing, he stopped the car and thought for a minute. An open, straightforward approach was the only one left to him. He decided to go searching for her, and turned the Orion. Many of the houses lay in hollows, or behind outcrops of rock, and were hidden from the road. He began methodically driving into each entrance he came to, backing out once he had established that Judith Rose's red car wasn't present. Guard dogs ran out to bark at him. Mystified servants stared from verandahs. He was entering perhaps his eighth tortuous driveway—this one leading to a small block of flats—when he had to brake sharply for a car coming out. They stopped bumper to bumper, and the other vehicle was the red Opel.

He leaped out of the Orion. Unexpectedly, Judith Rose had got out of her car just as quickly and stood next to it.

'You bastard!' she shouted.

He flinched. He realised she was very angry. 'I'm sorry,' he said. 'I didn't mean to scare you. I have to talk to you.'

'You don't scare me, mister. If you've come here to intimidate me, then you might as well give up. I don't intimidate easily.'

'I don't think you understand ...'

'I understand perfectly well. Do you think I didn't hear about your visit to the clinic yesterday? Do you think I didn't see you this morning, waiting to follow me? I thought I'd managed to lose you up here, but obviously you're determined to hound me. Well, I can't stop you people wasting your time, but I'd prefer it if you didn't waste mine. Will you please get that car out of my way?'

Realisation hit him. 'You think I'm a policeman?' he said.

'For heaven's sake, stop playing games!'

'I had a reason for following you. We have to talk. I'm not what you take me for. Just give me a moment.'

She had no choice but to wait while he went to his car. He took the photograph from the glove box, went back to Judith Rose, and held the picture out to her. She took it and stared at it uncomprehendingly.

'Turn it over,' he said. She did so, and he saw the shock start into her face. He explained quickly, 'Joshua Rosenblatt gave me that, just last week. It's to prove that I've come from him. He wanted me to contact you, about the letter you sent him. I've got to discuss it with you.'

She looked up at him. 'Who are you?' she said.

'Patrick Marriner. The name won't mean anything to you. But I've seen your letter. I've come specially from Europe to talk to you about it.'

'You could still be from the Security Police. You could have stolen this.'

'I've got a phone number for Joshua, in Europe. I'd like you to talk to him yourself and verify who I am.'

She looked past him, at the road. 'Listen, I've got to go. I can't stand here talking. Will you please move your car if I promise to think about it?'

'No,' he said bluntly. 'I haven't time to wait while you think.'

Judith bit her lip and took a decision. 'You know Eloff Street Extension, on the south side of town? There's a café called Choy's, about halfway down on the left. Meet me there at seven tonight.'

'Right.' He turned away at once and went back to the Orion. When he'd reversed a few yards he watched her start her car with a jerk and race it out through the opening and down the hill. Marriner turned the car and headed back towards the city, this time making no attempt to tail her.

At the Windsor Hotel there was a message asking him to phone Mr Labuschagne at the estate agency. He went at once to the public telephone off the lobby. Outside calls from his room would be logged and charged to his account, and were therefore traceable.

Labuschagne told him he had found four farmers who were willing to consider renting out their farms if the price was right. He'd made tentative arrangements to look them over on Saturday. Marriner told him that would be fine. Pondering his progress over the past four days, however, he didn't seem to have got all that far. There were still several vital things missing from the equation, not least of which was the failure of the Congress to get in touch with him.

IT WAS WORSE than Phineas had feared. He had been locked in a windowless cell and left alone. Nobody had beaten him. Nobody had even shouted at him.

It was bad enough that the Dexedrine tablets had been missed, but that was something he had been resigned to, something that could be explained as an ordinary theft. It had never entered his calculations, however, that the absence of the prescription docket would be noticed at the same time.

He also had deep doubts whether what he had done had made any sense, or done any good. He knew from Bobbejaan that his message had been delivered to the Leader's lawyer—but had it merely been laughed at and thrown away? There was no possible way of telling.

A key grated in the lock, the door swung open. A white man in civilian clothes came in, smiling as if he were greeting an old friend. Most men seemed big to Phineas, but not all of them were threatening. This man was both. He had cropped, grey-blond hair, and a brutal face with a massive jaw and watery, slightly bulging blue eyes. He said nothing until the warder who had admitted him had relocked the door.

'Phineas Molefe?' he asked unnecessarily. 'I am Major Booysen.' He surprised Phineas by speaking in English, a courtesy that Afrikaners rarely extended to Blacks. Such politeness was dangerous. 'I think you know why I am here, Phineas.'

'I stole some pills, sir.'

'You stole some pills, *ja*. Who did you pass them on to?'

'Nobody, sir.'

'Did you need to buy a favour from somebody?'

'No. I took them, sir. Swallowed them.'

'You swallowed eighty-one amphetamines?'

'It was nearly a month ago. I took two, three, every day.'

The major sighed and leaned back against the wall of the cell. 'OK. Let's forget the tablets for now. I don't give a damn about the tablets. I want the truth about that prescription docket, Phineas.'

Phineas summed up a look of dumb helplessness. 'The other *baas* spoke of a docket. I don't know what he means. Sometimes there is no docket. Sometimes one goes missing. Those files are not important.'

'Are you trying to tell me you don't know who Prisoner 4008 is?'

'Yes, sir. I don't know, sir.'

'You can tell me the truth now, Phineas, or we can do it the hard way.'

'God's truth, I know nothing.'

'OK.' Major Booysen stood up abruptly. 'You're going to come with me, for a little drive to a place we've got downtown. It's a place people go into with sins on their souls, Phineas, and come out pure and shining. Believe me, I know.' He turned and hammered on the door to be let out.

A DIM NEON SIGN identified Choy's Café as a pair of greasy shop windows set among factory buildings. It seemed an odd place for Judith to have chosen for a rendezvous, but he'd been aware since this morning that he was dealing with a rather odd lady.

He parked his car and went in, carrying the telephone scrambler in its little black case. The café was long and narrow, with a glass-topped counter down one side manned by an elderly Chinese in a grubby apron. Township jazz blared from a big portable stereo. There were four Chinese playing mah-jong at one table, several of the others were occupied by Africans engaged in animated conversation. In a corner, Judith sat alone.

He went over to her. She pointed to the chair opposite her, and he sat down. 'What the hell is this place?' He had to raise his voice to be heard over the music. 'It's not exactly private.'

'It's safe enough. Choy greases the right palms and the police keep away. It was the place to come to when I was a student. Very radical chic, don't you think?'

A Chinese girl in a waitress's overall came and stood attentively by their table. 'I'm going to eat,' Judith said. 'Are you hungry? You can have chicken with noodles, or chicken with fried rice, or just chicken. And whisky or beer to drink.'

'Whisky. And chicken with noodles.'

'The same for me.' When the girl had left, Judith rested her chin on her hands and looked at him. 'Well, Mr . . . Marriner? You want to talk, and I want you off my back. Go ahead.'

'I'd prefer you to start by speaking to Joshua, getting him to vouch for me. Is there a phone here we could use?'

'Do you really expect me to say yes to that? I'm not going to walk into some sort of set-up.'

'How else can I convince you to trust me?'

'It'll be uphill work. Virgil told me about you snooping around the clinic yesterday. He was sure you were a policeman.'

'Virgil.' He remembered the security guard. 'Well, Virgil was wrong.'

'That's why I was so annoyed when you turned up at my flat.'

'Your flat?' He was puzzled. Then the penny dropped. 'You're moving house? To that place in Northcliff?'

'I went to sign the lease this morning. It's all mine now.'

'I can only give you my word that—' He was interrupted by the waitress, who placed on the table two large tumblers half-full of neat Scotch.

'They cater for man-sized thirsts here,' Judith said, catching his look. 'Cheers.'

Since he had first caught sight of her that morning he hadn't once seen a smile on her face. Now it was there. 'You were saying?' she asked.

'All right, here it is. Your letter to Joshua said that your father is going to operate on someone at the request of the Security Police. We believe that that someone is Lincoln Kumalo. And from a separate source, the Congress has received information suggesting that the authorities may use this as an opportunity to get rid of Kumalo. How, where and when, we have no clear idea. I'm here to rescue him if necessary.'

Judith held her glass poised in front of her mouth, which opened in astonishment. '*Rescue* him? You've been sent to—'

'Shut up,' he said softly, with more menace than he'd intended. 'Think about it. It makes sense. There are rumours going around that he's soon to be released. If enough people start believing them, if the conviction grows among his supporters that the government has finally seen the light and is prepared to let him go, then anything that happens to him after that will seem like an unfortunate accident. Particularly if the authorities can show that their hands are completely clean.'

She leaned far back in her chair, as if to create a distance between them. 'Mr Marriner . . . why are you trying to involve me in this?'

'You already are involved. You can't undo what you've told Joshua. But all I need is to know more about the arrangements for this operation: when Kumalo is due at the clinic, where he'll be kept, what sort of security there'll be. More particularly, the exact timing of the operation itself. He'll have to be snatched beforehand, otherwise he'll be immobilised.'

'You will still have a sick man on your hands.'

'I gather he has a prostate condition, which isn't acute. He could have

the surgery once he was safely out of the country.'

The waitress arrived with a bowl of steaming noodles and another of chicken. She set out two smaller bowls and two pairs of chopsticks. They helped themselves to the food and ate for a minute in silence.

'It strikes me,' said Judith finally, 'that there's a much simpler way out of this. I have a lot of disagreements with my father, but I don't doubt his integrity as a doctor. If he found out about your suspicions, he would refuse to operate and that would be that.'

'No. If they really want to eliminate Kumalo, they'll find another way. At least we have some prior knowledge of this plan. It's the only chance we may ever have of saving him.'

'*We?* You're taking my complicity rather for granted, aren't you? Anyway, what evidence can you show me that this plot actually exists?'

'Not very much, at the moment,' he admitted. 'But I've got to plan as though it were definite. There are only fifteen days left. Will you at least talk to Joshua?'

She nodded resignedly. 'For old times' sake, yes. I promise nothing more than that. Not from here, either. I know of a better place.'

He followed her Opel through the city centre, over the Johann Rissik Bridge and into the car park beside the South African Airways terminal, and they went into the building. It was a good choice: a big concourse, not crowded, just busy enough for them to be inconspicuous. The row of open telephone cubicles was deserted, and they chose one at the end. Judith stood behind him, shielding him from view, as he took the scrambler out of its box and stood it on a small shelf beside the phone. He placed the receiver into the AX cradle, lifted the portable receiver and got a dialling tone from it, slightly muffled. He fed in several one-rand coins, and dialled the Zurich number Rosenblatt had given him. It rang only once before it was answered. Immediately he got a piercing howl of static in his ear. Within a few seconds it stopped and he heard Rosenblatt's voice, slightly distorted. 'Patrick? How are you getting on?'

'Not bad.' He tried to imagine Rosenblatt surrounded by snowy Alps. 'I have nothing definite to tell you yet, but I have Judith here. She'd like to talk to you.'

He turned, thrust the receiver at her and stepped out of the cubicle.

He heard her say hello and then he strolled away, watching from across the terminal until she put down the phone. When he returned he found her pale cheeks faintly flushed with excitement.

'The same old Josh! Same voice, same expressions, everything!'

Marriner put a finger to his lips. 'Well, did he give me the OK?' He packed away the scrambler.

'Oh, he confirmed who you were. And he asked me to give you whatever help I could.' She paused. 'I'm not sure how much that is.'

They began to walk towards the exit.

'All that information you want. I'm sure my father has it, but it's stored

272

in a computer file to which only he has access. Also there's a good chance the information leak will be traced back to me. It's all very well for you, skipping the country with Kumalo, but I'll still be here. You're asking me to put my head on a block, Mr Marriner.'

'There may be a way of covering for you, laying some false clues.'

She turned and faced him squarely in the doorway of the terminal. 'Look, I'm not unwilling to help. But I'd like to be sure it isn't all for nothing. A lot of what you've told me seems to be guesswork. If I knew for certain that I was helping Kumalo ...'

'Then that would make a difference?' He knew this wasn't the moment to push her. 'All right. Let's think about that.'

They made arrangements for staying in touch. Then, out in the car park, they shook hands with a rather awkward formality and she zoomed off into the night.

BY THE TIME Marriner had driven back to De Villiers Street, parked the car and walked to the hotel, it was after ten o'clock. He took the lift up to the third floor and walked to the end of the wide, deserted corridor. He put his key in the lock, turned it and opened the door.

He groped for the light switch on the wall to his left. Before he had found it something was clamped hard over his left wrist, pinning it to the wall. Another hand took hold of his arm, yanking him into the room, propelling him forward so that he lost his balance and fell, pitching head-first onto the bed. The telephone scrambler flew out of his grasp. The door was slammed behind him, and all light was blotted out.

Chapter Eight

Marriner rolled off the mattress. He heard his attacker come after him, lunging at the spot where he'd fallen, and missing. Marriner sprang to his feet, ready for another charge. But now, with his night vision improving, he could see that his attacker was staying crouched on the floor, a dim silhouette against the white paintwork of the door. He stepped forward, and then heard the sharp snap of a gun being cocked. He froze.

'Stay where you are, white boss.'

Marriner had had no time yet to be afraid, but now he felt his scalp prickle. Suddenly the overhead light came on. Marriner shielded his eyes and blinked. When he lowered his hand he saw a young black man, his hand on the light switch, wearing the khaki drill uniform of a hotel floor boy, with one sleeve pulled loose at the shoulder where Marriner had torn it. He had a heavy automatic pistol pointed straight at Marriner's middle. The room had been ransacked.

'Put your hands on your head,' he said.

'If it's money you're looking for ...'

'I think you know very well it isn't,' said the man with the gun. He came over, stepped behind Marriner and went through his pockets, removing his wallet, passport, some traveller's cheques, his notebook and a few other scraps of paper. He took them to the dressing table and flipped through them with his free hand, taking his eyes off Marriner for only a second at a time. Finally he gave the white man his full attention. He had thick hair, prominent cheekbones and a narrow jaw. At a guess he was twenty-five, and his eyes seemed prematurely knowing and bitter.

'Your name is Patrick Marriner?' he demanded.

'That's what all that paperwork says, doesn't it?'

'I am asking the questions. Tell me your address and phone number.'

Marriner recited them.

'You had a visitor from Africa recently. What car did he drive?'

Marriner hesitated. 'A red Ford Fiesta.'

'You later met in Switzerland. Where?'

'A place called the Aurora Bar, in Zurich. Would you like to know what we had for lunch?'

The young man ignored the sarcasm. 'All right. I think we can take it that you are who you say you are. But that still leaves other questions to be answered.'

Marriner felt anger building up inside him. 'Answer a question for me. You've known all along where I'm staying. I've been waiting for you to approach me. You could have done it days ago. Why was all this necessary? And why the gun?'

Now the young man seemed to watch him uncertainly. 'All right. I'll explain,' he said grudgingly. 'We had better sit down.'

Marriner lowered his arms and sat in the chair indicated by the other man with a flick of his gun.

'I will introduce myself.' The young man pulled a stool out from the dressing table and perched on it, letting the pistol dangle between his knees. 'I am Comrade Duma. I am the one who sent the message to Lusaka. As a result, Makibani has sent you here and asked me to give you all possible help. That is all very well, and I accept what Makibani says, that white men are needed for this task. But people in Lusaka cannot tell us how to fight our battles down here. We make our own decisions, because often our lives depend on them being the right decisions.'

'I've always known I would have to have your help.'

'You need it more than you realise.' He paused. 'This evening some information reached me from Cape Town. A prisoner named Phineas Molefe was taken out of Pollsmoor today for questioning by the Security Police. Why, what for, we have no idea. We have never heard of the man. The interesting thing is that he is employed in the prison dispensary.'

Marriner said, 'The prescription? The message? You think he sent it, and that they've caught him?'

'Maybe. There is no way of knowing. If it's him, the Security Police will not be long in getting the truth out of him. It struck me as a strange coincidence that this should happen almost as soon as you arrived in the country.' Duma raised the gun a fraction. 'It could have been that you were someone they had planted on us. In that case, I would have blown you away.'

THE ROOM WAS LARGE and bare, perhaps twenty feet square. It had no windows, but strips of neon set in the ceiling gave an even spread of hard white light. When Phineas came round he was sitting propped against the wall. Major Booysen was bending over him with his mad eyes bulging. He held a tin mug to Phineas's lips, and he gulped weakly at the water.

For seven hours Phineas had been standing on two bricks lying end-to-end on their sides. At first this had seemed easy, but then the narrow sides of the bricks had begun to bite into the soft flesh of his insteps; finally he had lost his balance and blacked out.

'Still sticking to your story, Phineas? All right, we're used to that. We're going to give you a little time in your cell to think it over now. Time for food and time for thought, but not for sleep. No sleep allowed here. And when you come back the questions are going to start all over again, understand?' He said to the other two, '*Vat hom.*'

Captain Kriek and Warrant Officer Willemse lifted Phineas easily between them, and carried him from the room.

'IT'S QUITE SIMPLE,' Duma said. 'If they are questioning this Phineas about the message, then it's a sign that they are taking it seriously.'

'It's also a sign that the message is authentic. But what if they make him talk ...'

'Oh, they will make him talk. Then the trail will lead to Kumalo's lawyer, and then to his daughter, and then perhaps to me. But that is where it will stop, because they won't find me.'

Marriner wondered how Duma could be so sure of this, but he kept the thought to himself. 'They will still know that there's been a leak of some kind,' he pointed out. 'They will be on their guard. Now I know where Kumalo is going to be, and roughly when, I'm hoping for more specific information. In the meantime I need to talk to these white soldiers you think may come in with us. How soon can you contact them?'

'Maybe tomorrow.'

'And what makes you believe they would help us?'

'Disenchantment is one motive. Money would be another.'

'Then tell them there's good money in it. Don't say anything specific about the job.'

Duma nodded and stood up. 'All right, Major.' He lifted the jacket of his uniform and shoved the heavy pistol into the waistband of his trousers, covering it with the jacket flap. He went to the door, opened it carefully and peered out. Then he was gone, closing the door gently behind him.

BECAUSE THEIR WORKING HOURS tended to vary, several employees of the People's Congress in London, including Jasper Darries, had their own keys to the front door.

For the past two mornings Jasper had made a point of being the first to arrive. This Friday he found the letter he had been expecting on top of the pile on the doormat: an envelope marked *National Westminster Bank* and addressed to Moses Mohaila. He placed the rest of the mail on the receptionist's desk and carried the letter up to his office.

He opened the envelope and took out the paid cheque he had requested on the telephone, using Mohaila's name. He merely glanced at it, confirming that it was the right one, before slipping it into his jacket pocket.

He went to the phone, dialled a number, let it ring twice and cut it off. He dialled again, left it to ring twice more and then replaced the receiver. After twenty seconds his own telephone rang twice in its turn and then stopped. That was confirmation that his message was received and understood; no conversation, hence no danger of its being intercepted.

Towards nine o'clock the rest of the staff began to drift into the office, among them Mohaila himself.

Long ago Jasper Darries had established a pattern of making brief departures from the office to visit the local branch library, where he would do research for articles in the Congress newsletter. Hence, nobody raised an eyebrow this morning when he announced where he was going.

The library was just a few minutes' walk away. When he got there the reference section was all but deserted. He took two books and carried them to a table. One was a volume of the *Encyclopaedia Britannica* which he had a genuine excuse to consult; the other he had calculated to be the least-used book in the library, a leatherbound edition of Hain's one-volume Persian–English dictionary, published in 1953.

He opened the dictionary. At the back, the long narrow slit he had made with a razor blade down the edge of the binding was barely noticeable, but when he prised its edges apart he opened up a pocket between the binding and the endpaper that was just big enough to conceal the cheque in.

He replaced the books in their correct positions on the shelves.

HANNES KOEKEMOER, Jasper's Controller, collected the cheque from the dead-letter drop exactly forty minutes later. He did not examine it until he was safely settled in his office in South Africa House.

The cheque was as Jasper had described it, payable to cash for five thousand pounds sterling, and carrying two signatures. One was certainly Moses Mohaila's, the other might have been Harry Makibani's. It had been written on the twenty-first of November; it carried a cashier's stamp dated the twenty-eighth and a final PAID stamp from the National Westminster. The cheque had been cashed—or more likely deposited, given its size—at the Bank of Ireland, Bandon, County Cork.

He turned it over. Now, here was an unexpected bonus. A signature on

the back of the cheque, bold but practically illegible. *J. Swa*—? *J. Swe*—?
He'd have to try to trace that signature.

He was still staring at the cheque when the commercial section's junior
officer came in to retrieve a file. Koekemoer showed it to him.

'Bandon?' The sandy-haired man looked puzzled. 'That rings a bell.'

'Yes?' Koekemoer was interested in things that rang bells.

'I can't place it.' The young man shook his sandy head. 'Someone I've
met in the last week or two. Maybe it'll come back.'

'I'd be extremely grateful if it did,' Koekemoer said.

WEST OF JOHANNESBURG, old mine workings were spread across the veld
like the aftermath of some geological disaster. These had been among the
earliest of the city's big gold mines, but they had been worked out years
ago.

It was up the side of one of the spoil dumps that Marriner found himself
climbing in Duma's wake, towards lunchtime on Friday.

They had left the Orion at the edge of a bluegum plantation and walked
along a steep track that ran along the side of the dump. Near the top,
Duma put a restraining hand on Marriner's arm and gave a low whistle. A
moment later a bronzed young white man appeared from behind the ridge.
He was bare-chested, but wore brown army trousers and boots, and was
holding an R4 self-loading rifle loosely at his side.

'Peace, Mr Carver,' said Duma.

Carver studied Marriner curiously before turning and vanishing over
the ridge. They followed.

Behind the top of the dump the ground sloped down to a basin of
powdery earth. Invisible from anywhere but the air, it was an almost
perfect refuge. A camouflaged Saracen armoured personnel carrier was
parked close to one side of the basin, and close to it seven more soldiers sat
or lay with their shirts off, sunbathing. Something was cooking over a fire,
and the area was littered with beer cans. As Marriner followed Carver and
Duma down the slope, he felt like a visitor to a bandit encampment.

Duma made a nervous announcement. 'Well, white boys, did you think
I was lying to you? This is the man. This is Major Marriner.'

None of them looked impressed. Marriner matched their silence with
his own. Finally it was Carver who was embarrassed into speaking up.
'Duma didn't tell us anything about you, sir. What kind of major are you?'

'Were. British Parachute Regiment. What outfit are you?'

'How about you explain what brings you here first, Major?' That was a
dark, heavily built young man who was idly shuffling a pack of cards.

'Later. I'd like to know who I'm talking to.'

'Listen, white boys, cut it out, will you?' The black man was growing
angry. 'This is no way to treat a man who has come to offer you a deal.' He
looked at Marriner and pointed to a man at the back of the group. 'Talk to
him. Rendle. He's supposed to be in charge of them.'

This man hadn't yet spoken. Now he stood up unhurriedly, strongly built in the rangy South African way, older than the others, tougher and more intelligent. He shook hands with Marriner. He addressed him as an equal. 'Yeah, I'm Frank Rendle. We're Fourth Armoured Infantry, based at Lenz camp. That's to say, we go back there when we have to. At the moment we're taking a break. We take a lot of breaks.'

Marriner glanced at the Saracen. It had a 7.62-millimetre machine gun mounted in front of its turret, and the crew's personal weapons were stacked against its side, a row of semiautomatic rifles and an Uzi gun.

'Aren't you in contact with your base?'

'Not very often. Lightning bends the radio. He's our electrical wizard.' Rendle indicated a lanky youth grinning up at them from the sand. 'We arrange it so that most of the time nobody knows where we are. Our job is township patrols. We put in an appearance now and then, but we don't get involved in any aggro. That's not what we joined the army for.'

'Who joined the army?' said another scrawny lad indignantly. 'We just got put into it!'

'All right, Brakpan, we got put into it.'

'Well, hell, it makes a difference. Don't give this man the wrong impression. We didn't all use to be hot-shot chopper pilots!'

'Shut up, Brakpan.' Rendle spoke with a quiet, commanding menace. He walked to where a couple of six-packs of beer were stacked in the shade of the Saracen. He tossed a can each to Marriner and Duma. 'Well,' he said, 'that's our story. What's yours, Major?'

'Did I hear right? You flew helicopters?'

'It's no secret,' said the corporal with a shrug. 'I used to be a lieutenant in the air force. Could have been a major myself if they hadn't thrown me out. Used to fly Alouettes, Puma gunships. Now all I do is ride herd on this wagonload of monkeys.'

Marriner took a decision. 'Can I talk to you alone?' he asked.

Rendle nodded. Duma said, 'Now, wait a minute. I'm not just the boy who carries messages between you two white bosses.'

'You'll get your look in, Duma. Just hold on.'

They strolled out together towards the centre of the sandy basin. From his own army experience Marriner knew that troublesome soldiers would often turn their rejection of higher authority into a perverse loyalty towards one of their own. It was why insubordinate privates sometimes made the best NCOs. Rendle had given shape to this bunch of malcontents, and they looked up to him. Rendle, he had quickly recognised, was the key to one whole part of this enterprise.

'What did Duma tell you about me?' he asked.

'Just that you were looking for some guys to do a job. That there was good money in it.'

'Do you know anything about Duma? Who his connections are?'

'I don't want to know, but I can guess.'

'Then maybe you've also guessed something about the general nature of this job. I'm talking about putting a big cat among a lot of fat pigeons, Corporal. Does that idea made you nervous?'

Rendle suddenly grinned, and Marriner knew the question had been unnecessary. 'All right. What about the rest of them?'

'They're all fed up, if that's what you mean.'

'When this is all over, you'll very likely have to skip the country, never set foot here again.'

Oddly, Rendle showed no surprise. He took a thoughtful sip of beer. 'I was planning to leave anyway. I've had it with this country. It would be nice to have some money to go with. The others have probably never thought about leaving, but if the idea looked attractive enough they might buy it. There's not a lot to keep them here.'

'And they all have combat experience?'

'Sure have. We were over in South West Africa together, mixing it with the SWAPO guerrillas. We got into Angola, too. Night ambushes, pathfinder patrols, we even took part in some commando raids. Yeah, the boys are good, and some of them have their own specialities. Brakpan is like a Formula One racing driver, Lightning is radio and electrics. Blikkies Steyn is a natural bush fighter. Carver and Fish prefer it at close quarters, on the streets.' Rendle paused. 'Just tell me this. Does this job of yours involve wasting anybody?'

'Not if it can be helped. Quite the opposite, in fact. I want someone rescued and taken over the border.'

They stood facing each other under the searing sun. 'Quite a tall order,' Rendle said. 'I suppose this is the right time to ask about money.'

'I can rustle up eight hundred thousand pounds sterling between you. That's a hundred thousand each, enough to give you a new start.'

Rendle looked impressed. 'That will get the boys interested. The next question is: When do we see it?'

'I haven't worked that out yet. At the moment it's in Switzerland.'

'Not much point in bringing it here, then, is there? We'd never get it out again. On the other hand, you can't expect the guys to go into this just on the basis of a promise. We'd need some kind of guarantee.'

'I'm sure we can work something out. But there isn't a lot of time. The job has to take place two weeks from today, and it will need careful planning. That means giving me quite a lot of your time. Can you manage that?' Rendle nodded. 'And on the day itself . . . well, I suppose you're just going to have to disappear the way you have today.'

'Should be no problem.'

Marriner paused. 'There's something I'm curious about. Why were you busted out of the air force?'

Rendle gave him a long, penetrating stare. 'Were you ever given an order you knew you couldn't even pretend to obey, Major? Something you knew you'd never get off your conscience if you did?'

279

'Not really,' Marriner said.

'Well, it happened to me. But it's a long story. It'll keep. I'm just glad you didn't lay any speeches on me about the difficulty of betraying my country. As far as I'm concerned, my country betrayed me.'

Marriner nodded, feeling more reassured than ever by Rendle. The young man's chilly blue eyes were deceptive, masking a degree of aggression and even anger.

They turned and began to walk back across the burning sand. 'All right, Major,' Rendle said decisively. 'It's on. As far as I'm concerned, it's on. Just give me a couple of days to convince the others.'

THE YOUNG CONSULAR ASSISTANT looked in at Hannes Koekemoer's office at two o'clock.

'By the way, sir,' he said. 'You remember me telling you that the name of that place was familiar? Bandon?'

'What about it?' said Koekemoer.

'I've just remembered. About a fortnight ago we had a visitor who came from there. Bandon: the address was on the card he filled in. He was enquiring about buying some farmland. It seemed a coincidence.'

Koekemoer leaned back in his chair. 'What was this man's name?'

'I don't remember offhand. It will be on the file. Seaman? Sailor? Something to do with the sea. No—Marriner.'

'Come in here, son.' Koekemoer flattened his palms on the desk and gave the young man an intimidating stare. 'Come in. Sit down. Tell me everything you remember about this man Marriner. Start right now.'

Chapter Nine

In spite of his protests to the contrary, young Mr Labuschagne was showing signs of impatience. They had called at three farms during the course of that Saturday morning, and after each visit Marriner had made the sort of noncommittal noises that to any estate agent signify a transparent lack of interest. 'I'm not quite sure what you *are* looking for,' Labuschagne complained at one point, and Marriner couldn't enlighten him. He was supposed to be looking over the land, but his eye was really on the farmhouses. He needed a secluded one, and the tendency in these hilly parts was to build close to the summits of the *koppies*, so that in spite of their love of privacy the farmers were more or less in sight of each other. But he wasn't able to tell Labuschagne that.

Their next appointment was at a farm a couple of miles south of the Hartbeespoort Dam. 'It belongs to an old man who's a bit of a, what do you say? A recluse,' Labuschagne explained as they approached it. 'The government is buying him out, and he has to move by next September. In the meantime, it's possible that he'd consider letting it.'

A little way down the road they rounded a bend and a vast and strange structure loomed suddenly ahead of them among the hills. It was about a mile long, a long, low, concrete building without windows, with a tall, tapering smokestack rising from it like a warning finger, faintly sinister in its stark modern functionalism.

'What's that?' Marriner asked.

'Pelindaba,' said Labuschagne shortly. 'The Pelindaba nuclear reactor.'

He took a turn to the left and they were driving straight towards the building. Marriner saw with dismay a security gate ahead, a checkpoint with armed guards, a high barbed-wire fence snaking off into the bush. A notice said *South African Atomic Energy Board. No Unauthorised Entry.*

Just before the gate Labuschagne took another turning, this time down a bumpy unpaved track to the right. From behind the fence a couple of uniformed guards watched them pass. 'This old fellow, Meiring, is having his land expropriated by the atomic energy people,' Labuschagne said. 'They're expanding their facilities here, and they've already got him practically surrounded.'

Through the fence, Marriner could see that the area round the reactor had been cleared of bush. More guards patrolled the grounds, there were two or three army vehicles parked close to the building. After a quarter of a mile or so the track veered away from the fence and began to descend to a sagging fence and a rusted iron gate held closed by a loop of wire. A wooden sign gave the name of the property: Rietvlei.

Marriner got out, opened the gate for the car and closed it once Labuschagne had bumped over the cattle grid just inside. Suddenly they were in thick virgin bush and tall savannah grass, hidden from the tidy parkland that surrounded the reactor. The only human imprint here was the track, twisting its way down into deeper bush.

After half a mile or so they came upon the house. It was a ramshackle wood and iron building at the end of the track, backing onto the hillside and shaded, in fact almost camouflaged, by mimosa trees. A stream ran beside the house and two rusty Chevrolets from the 1950s stood on blocks on either side of it. Stacked around them was a collection of bald tyres, wooden cartwheels, oil drums and rotting lumber.

The farm, if it really could be called that, lay somnolent in the damp heat of the valley, utterly isolated, tucked into the folds of the hills.

It was perfect.

No, it wasn't. The nuclear reactor and the security that surrounded it were alarmingly close. In spite of that, Marriner knew he hadn't a hope of finding anywhere as suitable as this in the thirteen days he had left.

They got out of the car. The deep silence of the valley was broken by the squeak of an unoiled door. The hermit had emerged and was watching them from the *stoep* of his house, shading his eyes against the glare.

'*Namiddag, meneer!*' Labuschagne called as they approached. The old man did not reply. He was tall and gaunt, possibly seventy years old, but still strong and fit-looking. He wore a trilby hat, a checked cotton shirt and bib-fronted overalls. Labuschagne stopped a dozen feet from the end of the *stoep* and told the man what Marriner was looking for.

Old Meiring listened and nodded and spoke a few sentences, and Labuschagne translated for Marriner. 'He's interested in letting the place, but he needs time to think about it. He'd have to go and stay with his sister in Pretoria. He'd like to buy another bit of land but he can't afford to. The government is only paying him eight thousand rands for this land.'

Marriner nodded. He was going to have to risk sounding pushy. 'What if I paid him in advance, a full ten months' rent up to next September? Would that make up what he needs to buy another place?'

The agent gave him a look. 'You're actually interested in this land?'

'I could be. I'd like to look it over.'

Labuschagne translated again, and Meiring studied Marriner curiously, rubbing the week's growth of beard that stubbled his chin.

'He wants to know first how much you might offer.'

'How about a thousand a month?'

These words Meiring understood. He gave a slow grin. Labuschagne stifled his surprise. 'He'd be getting a good deal, Mr Marriner. If you don't mind my asking, what has this place got that those others haven't?'

'Peace and quiet.' He waved around him. 'Charm.'

Twenty minutes later they were on their way back to the office at Muldersdrift with the deal agreed. One week from today, on December the tenth, Marriner would hand Meiring a cheque for ten thousand rands, and take over Rietvlei farm. That would leave him another six days to get everything and everyone else ready.

HE WAS BACK at the Windsor Hotel by half-past four. He went to his room, collected the scrambler phone and went out again, to the telephone booths at the railway station down the road. He was through on the scrambled line to Joshua Rosenblatt's number in Zurich within a minute.

He told the Congress treasurer of the progress he had made so far, and then explained his needs. He wanted fifteen thousand rands cabled to him at once, care of the Standard Bank. That was to cover the rental of the farm and Labuschagne's commission and bonus, plus a couple of thousand for further contingencies. He said he also wanted a new account opened at the Handelsbank Bauer, this time in the name of Frank Rendle, and he wanted eight hundred thousand pounds deposited in it.

'Patrick, that is eighty per cent of our entire contingency fund!'

'It's what the money is there for, isn't it? Get Harry to OK it, if you insist. All I need is a piece of paper, a receipt from the bank, with Rendle's name on it. It's a token of my good faith.'

'Well, all right,' said Rosenblatt reluctantly. 'But I can't do any of this till Monday.'

'As long as you can arrange it first thing, the money ought to be here by

Wednesday. There's also no time to airmail the receipt, so you'd better send it by courier, care of a man called Jepson at the head office of the Standard Bank. I'll alert him that it's coming.'

The pips began to sound on the phone, and he put down the receiver. He disconnected the scrambler, packed it away and left the station. Back at the hotel, he found himself once again at a loose end. So he went downstairs to the call box and dialled Judith Rose's new flat.

FOR SOME REASON they had allowed Phineas to sleep. Maybe it was because they were exhausted themselves: all three interrogators— Booysen, Kriek and Willemse—had grown grey-faced and haggard as they continued with their questioning. Maybe it was because even when he did try to answer he was no longer making sense.

He woke from a period of intense oblivion and found himself on the bunk in his cell, riven and shivering. His arms and legs felt feeble and useless, and he could hardly move at all without some part of him shrieking in pain. Yet his mind was oddly clear and sharp, even analytical. Sleep had swept away his confusion. He knew now that he would never last out. He knew what had to be done.

They came for him half an hour later, Willemse and Kriek, surprised to find him awake and sitting up. There was a strange glazed look to his eyes, as though their arrival had only half-aroused him from some reverie. They eased him to his feet, supporting him on either side, and took him in a stiff cramped walk out of the cell. They turned into the corridor leading to the interrogation room. The full-length window at the end was a pale rectangle of light, showing it was still daytime. With ten feet to go, he halted for a rest. The white men waited tentatively on each side of him.

With all the strength in his arms, Phineas thrust them both away from him, pushing them aside, knocking them slightly off balance. Free of their grasp he ran forward, hearing their shouts of alarm, feeling himself lurch and stumble as he struggled to gather speed, needing all the momentum his slight frame could gather. He heard them come charging after him, catching up with him as he covered the last couple of yards and then launched himself, head first, at the window.

It was made of toughened glass, but he went through it in a clean dive that took him several feet clear of the building, out into a blur of swirling sky, before he dropped like a stone from the height of thirteen storeys into the gutter at the feet of a horrified group of pedestrians.

COLONEL PRINSLOO hadn't been surprised to find van Straaten in Hoeksma's office, sipping whisky like an old college friend. Maybe that's what he was. Still, there were things you learned on the streets that Stellenbosch could never teach you, and one was not to be squeamish. He'd spared them none of the details of Phineas Molefe's death. He'd told them the story just as it had reached him from Cape Town.

Hoeksma, white-faced, needed another drink. Invited to help himself, Prinsloo poured an enormous neat brandy.

Van Straaten had recovered some of his composure. 'Why weren't we told when this prisoner was taken from Pollsmoor?'

'There was nothing to tell, sir. All Major Booysen knew at that stage was that the prescription docket was missing. The suspicion was that this Phineas had probably used it to smuggle a message out, a warning. The point was to establish whether he ever succeeded. The longer he went on denying it, of course, the more obvious it was that he was lying.'

'Why was that?' Hoeksma asked. 'If he knew nothing, he'd have had nothing to tell.'

'It doesn't work that way, sir,' said Prinsloo confidently. 'After a while, a man who's got nothing to hide starts making up stories, telling you what he thinks you want to hear.'

Hoeksma said, 'So we're talking seriously about the possibility of a leakage of information on the Induna project?'

'That could be the case.'

'To the People's Congress?'

'I can't think who else would be worth telling.'

'Are you sure we're not exaggerating this?' van Straaten said. 'What can one little hospital clerk really have found out, after all? Does all of this actually change anything?'

'Maybe not,' said Prinsloo. 'The first thing is to assess the damage. As for finding out whether a message ever got out of the prison, we are back where we started, except that we now have forty prisoners to question instead of one.' He threw back his drink. 'Well, gentlemen, unless there are any more questions, I'll be off.'

They watched the colonel leave with an odd sense of relief. If they thought him crude, they also found him intimidating.

'If the Congress has somehow got wind of the Induna project,' said van Straaten when Prinsloo was safely out of the way, 'you do realise how serious the consequences could be?'

'Of course I do, Tertius, but it's all hypothetical. I see no reason to change our minds. Induna goes ahead in thirteen days' time.'

'LET ME DRIVE,' Marriner said.

'No, I'm fine.'

Judith was just tight enough to resent the suggestion that she was anything but absolutely sober. She nudged the bumper of the car behind her as she manoeuvred out of the parking space. Concentrating fiercely, she swung out into the Saturday-night traffic.

'Watch it,' he cautioned nervously.

'Relax, Patrick. God is on my side tonight.'

Patrick. Well, that was an improvement on 'Mr Marriner', which she had persisted in calling him for the first half of the evening. She had insisted on going back to Choy's. It was safe, she said. This time they had eaten Choy's chicken with glutinous fried rice. It surprised him to see such a pale skinny woman eat with such gusto: three helpings, washed down with beer. Then, after a couple of Scotches, she'd become provocative.

'I hope you don't think I'm going to change my mind about helping you. I still don't see how I can.'

'I wasn't going to say a word about it. I just felt like some company, all right? It's Saturday night. I was free, and so were you. I thought we might have some civilised conversation.'

'I'm sorry.' She surprised him by sounding genuinely contrite. 'I'm afraid I haven't got the measure of you. All the nice men I knew have left the country. The others are creeps.'

After that they had managed to talk more easily.

Judith drove in silence, watching her coordination, and brought the car to a jerky halt outside the Windsor Hotel. She turned to look at him. 'Well, thank you for dinner.'

'I really don't think you should drive all that way home, you know. Why don't you come in and have some coffee, at least?'

'Ho ho ho.' Her sarcasm was automatic. 'That's an old line, isn't it?'

'I won't be making any passes at you in a hotel lounge. I'm trying to sober you up, not seduce you.'

'How disappointing.'

'Come and have coffee,' he said.

'All right.'

He opened the car door and she followed him into the hotel.

The lobby was quiet, but there were still a few couples in the lounge. Marriner approached the receptionist. 'We'd like some coffee.'

'Yes, sir. Take a seat in the lounge.'

Marriner turned to Judith and saw to his surprise Frank Rendle walking through the door.

The corporal was dressed in civvies, pale blue slacks, white shoes and a tight navy shirt that emphasised his muscular arms and shoulders. Seeing Marriner and the girl together, he halted and stared.

'Hello, Major,' he said.

'Well . . . hello.' The confusion was mutual. 'What are you doing here?'

'Sorry. I suppose I should have phoned.' Rendle's cool blue eyes flickered uncertainly over Judith. 'It's just that I've got a message for you.'

An introduction seemed to be necessary, but Judith didn't wait, announcing her name and sticking out a hand. The corporal shook it. 'Frank Rendle,' he said without elaborating, and then rather pointedly, to Marriner, 'It won't take a minute.'

'I get it. Men's talk.' She gave the newcomer a slightly sardonic look. 'I'll go and wait in the lounge.'

Rendle watched her with some suspicion until she'd disappeared.

'You're right,' Marriner said. 'You shouldn't have just turned up.'

'I was waiting for you. I stay at a friend's place quite close to here when I've got leave. It seemed safer than phoning.'

'Come and sit down.'

They sat in a couple of armchairs in a corner of the lobby. 'Is that woman in this with us? You didn't mention that you were involved with anyone. I hope it doesn't complicate things.'

'I'm not involved with her, I simply need her help. Now, what's your news?'

'Well, I've talked the boys round. Nicky Flynn was the only difficult one, as I expected. I had to promise him something in writing.'

'I'm taking care of that. It should be here in a couple of days.'

'OK. Then, if it's still on, we're with you.'

'It's on all right. But before we go any further I need your help across a couple of hurdles. Are there any computer freaks in your crowd?'

'Lightning knows quite a lot about them. At least, he's always boasting that a computer is nothing but a glorified bunch of light switches.'

'Then maybe we can give him a chance to prove it. Another thing: speed and surprise are absolutely vital to this operation. The way I saw it originally was to recruit a pilot to get us out in a charter plane. Then I realised we already had a pilot. All we need is something for you to fly.'

As THEY SIPPED their coffee a few minutes later Judith asked Marriner, 'What's the name of that hunk again?'

'Rendle. Frank Rendle.'

'Do you like him?'

He caught her note of deliberate casualness. 'Sure I do. Why?'

'I didn't think he liked me.'

'He didn't want to talk in front of you. That's understandable. He's risking even more than you and I are. That is, if you come in with us.'

'Do you still need my help?'

'It's going to be vital.'

'All right. Then you've got it.' The coffee had sobered her up, but the evening's drinking had made her yawn.

As she rose to leave Marriner looked up at her and said, 'Good. Well, that hunk ... that hunk is going to steal a helicopter for us.'

Chapter Ten

Koekemoer's report from London had been relayed to van Straaten at his home just before midnight. He at once put a request through to the Immigration Department, and when he reached his office in the Union Buildings first thing that Monday morning the details he had asked for lay on his desk. Patrick Marriner, British citizen. Occupation given as farmer, but described in his passport as an army officer. Arrived Jan Smuts

286

Airport 28 November. Address in South Africa, c/o The Windsor Hotel, Johannesburg.

Superficially, there was nothing to get excited about. Marriner's motive for visiting the country seemed legitimate and he had presented himself quite openly at the consulate-general in search of information, which was hardly the action of a man with something to hide.

Unless, of course, that was precisely what he wanted them to think.

There remained the unexplained payment of Congress money into the bank account in Ireland. And in van Straaten's mind a niggling worry was still lodged about the new Congress bank account in Zurich and what they intended to use it for.

Strictly speaking, this should now be a matter for the Security Police. However, van Straaten distrusted their ham-fisted approach, personified by Colonel Prinsloo. It wouldn't be beyond them to barge straight in on Marriner and take him off for questioning, thus scaring off whoever he might be dealing with as well as drawing a lot of flak from the British Embassy. A subtler strategy was called for. Van Straaten buzzed the duty officer, gave him the names of two of his most trusted younger subordinates and asked him to call them in.

'YOU'VE FOUND YOURSELF a farm, then?' said Mr Jepson cheerily.

'Just a place I'm renting for a few months, while I go on looking round.'

'Whereabouts? Did you try the Magaliesberg, as I suggested?'

'Out that way,' said Marriner vaguely. He had been open enough up to now, but the time had come to start covering his tracks.

'Do you want me to have your account transferred? We have a couple of branches in that area.'

'No, thank you. I'll leave it here for now. What concerns me more is what's happened to that letter.' The money from the Handelsbank Bauer had reached the Standard Bank that Tuesday morning, but the receipt from Switzerland confirming the transfer of eight hundred thousand pounds to an account in the name of Frank Rendle had still not turned up. It should certainly have arrived by now.

'Can't help you there, old boy,' said Jepson. 'All I can suggest is you chase them up from the other end. Anyway, I'll be on the blower to you the minute it arrives.'

Outside the bank, Rendle and the man he called Lightning were waiting in his car. He had picked them up, dressed in civilian clothes, at the dump that morning. He explained about the letter from Zurich, and Rendle said, 'No sweat. We've still got another nine days.'

Marriner drove to the city centre, parking close to a big radio and television store called Polliack's to which Lightning directed him. They entered the shop and went straight up to the first floor, where two-way radios, Citizen's Band systems and car telephones were displayed.

A young salesman sidled up. 'Can I help you, gentlemen?'

'Show us the best FM two-way you've got,' Lightning demanded. 'We're thinking of going into the security business.'

The salesman produced a heavy solid base-station unit and one of the hand-held transceivers that went with it. 'This is American. It's a Johnson 541 with a built-in scrambler. It'll work equally well in or out of a vehicle.'

Lightning was studying the set and nodding. 'Two-fifty to two-eighty megahertz. Two hundred kilohertz band-width. That looks good.'

'Of course, you need a licence to operate this, and a frequency allocation.'

'We'll sort that out.'

'How much?' Marriner asked.

'I'll have to check. We don't sell one of these every day.'

The salesman retired. Lightning said, 'Is there a nice high spot on that farm where we could site this thing safely? With a power supply?'

'Hell, no,' Marriner said, remembering Rietvlei Farm in its deep valley. 'It doesn't even have electricity.'

'We'll need somewhere else, then. Somewhere pretty high up. We need a range of thirty, maybe forty kilometres.'

Marriner thought for a moment. 'What about Northcliff?'

'Perfect. It's the highest point for a long way round here, and nicely at the centre of the operation. You've got somewhere there we could stow this safely?'

'I think I might have. Rendle has met its tenant.'

The salesman returned to tell them that the price of the base unit plus four portable transceivers would be two thousand rands. Marriner gave him a deposit, with a promise to pay the balance when they picked up the equipment on Friday.

As they left the shop, Rendle gave him a significant glance. 'You're asking her for some pretty heavy involvement, aren't you? You expect her to cooperate?'

'I hope she will. I don't want to ask too much of her at once. It's enough for now that she's agreed to let us have a go at that computer.'

COLONEL PRINSLOO'S PLANE arrived in Cape Town at a quarter to two that afternoon, and he reached the Security Police headquarters just after three. He took the special lift that carried him straight up to the thirteenth floor, and in Major Booysen's office found a small apprehensive group awaiting him: Booysen himself, Willemse and Kriek.

It was four days now since Phineas Molefe had flung himself from the window. Booysen accepted the responsibility. He shook his head and said it had been an awful mess.

'Yes,' said Prinsloo with feeling, 'it was a mess. But it's behind you now, and what I want to know is what you're doing to make up for it.'

Booysen explained that the forty men who had shared Phineas Molefe's cell block had all been removed to Roeland Street police station for questioning. All of them had made brief preliminary statements; all had denied any knowledge of the Dexedrine tablets, or the prescription dockets. 'So now we must start squeezing them. It's a hell of a job, Colonel. If we could just have some more men ...'

'More men, more wagging tongues. No. There has got to be some way of narrowing down the field of suspects. Was Molefe specially friendly with any of these forty?'

'We've tried checking that,' said Kriek. 'No one will admit to knowing him well.'

'I wonder whether we shouldn't approach it from another direction,' Willemse ventured. 'If we start by assuming a message *was* smuggled out of the prison, it had to be given to someone at a particular time and place. It seems to me we should see if the warders remember anything.'

'All right, Willemse. Take charge of it yourself,' said Prinsloo. 'Now, let's go over to Roeland Street. I'd like to get a look at this lot for myself.'

AT TWENTY TO SIX on Thursday evening Dr Rose stuck his head round the door of the Woodvale Clinic's administrative office and was surprised to find Judith still at her desk. She was typing some account entries into the computer.

'Not going home yet?'

'Not for an hour or two. I want to get these out of the way.'

'Well. Good. Don't overdo it.' Things had gone better between them recently, he thought, ever since she had moved out of the house. 'Oh, and if you ever feel like popping home for a drink or a meal ... your mother would be glad to see you.'

She gave him a neutral look. 'Thank you. I will.'

'Well, I'll be off, then. Good night.'

From the window she watched her father heading for the car park. As soon as his car had pulled out of the gates she went to the phone. When Marriner answered from a call box down the road she said simply, 'He's gone. You can come now,' and put down the receiver. Then she left the office and went in search of Virgil, the security man.

She found him strolling along the path from the Substance Abuse Unit.

'Two men are coming to do some work in the office this evening, Virgil, and they'd like to be left alone. Men from the government, like before.'

'Ah, them,' he said knowingly. 'What do they want here, anyway?'

'I know as little as you do. I suggest we both just keep clear of them.'

She returned to the office in time to see Marriner's car draw up in the car park. Virgil was watching as Marriner and another man approached the building, and she went out to meet them.

'In here,' she said without preamble. She led them to her own office and locked the door behind them. Marriner's companion was a gawky young man in a suit, obviously borrowed. He grinned at her amiably. Marriner introduced him as Lightning.

'How long is this going to take?' she asked.

'All depends. Let's get a look at the system.'

Judith led him to her terminal and switched it on. She began to explain what she knew of the computer's operations, but Lightning cut her short. 'I know. It's basically a row of lockers, and you all have keys to your own. But your old man's got a private locker all to himself, and it's the key to that we're looking for. OK. Show me how you get into the system.'

She sat at her desk and typed out her initials, JRO, and her six-letter password. They appeared on the status line at the foot of the screen, beneath the general directory. 'G-E-R-A-L-D.' Lightning read out the password. 'Why Gerald?'

'It's the name of one of my brothers,' she said neutrally.

'That's what most people do: choose a password that means something to them. OK. With six letters you've got a choice of something like eighty million possible combinations. So we'll have to find a bypass.'

'What's that?' asked Marriner.

'A way of bypassing the security has to be built into a system like this. Somebody has to be able to override the program in case the person with the master password gets run over by a bus.'

'And you think you can do that?'

'If I can get a look at the Central Processing Unit. Where is it?'

'Through here, I think,' said Judith.

She led them to what had been a storeroom near the end of the corridor. A steel cabinet hummed gently against the back wall.

'This is the thing's brain,' Lightning said. 'It's really only a big pinball machine. It can't think for itself, and it can be fooled. Nobody's going to notice if I put it out of action for an hour or two, are they?'

'I suppose not,' said Judith dubiously. 'As long as you don't lose anything that's stored on it.'

They left him, returned to the office and sat facing each other across Judith's desk. 'Where did you find him?' she said.

'He's one of Rendle's chaps. He's got a pass for the evening, but I have to have him back at the barracks by eleven.'

She was too tense to make any small talk, much less discuss anything serious. Once in a while Lightning would come back, work briefly at the terminal, and then return to the processing unit. An hour passed. Judith went to the kitchen and returned with three cups of coffee on a tray. Marriner carried one to the storeroom, where the sight of the processing unit alarmed him. Lightning had practically disembowelled it. Trays of silicon chips lay exposed and bunches of wire trailed out of them.

'Are you sure you know what you're doing?'

'Just about,' the young man said. 'Just about ready to give it a try.'

They returned to the office together. Lightning sat at the computer terminal and began to tap a series of instructions into it. Night had almost fallen, and Judith switched on the overhead fluorescent lighting.

'Got it!' Lightning sat back and gazed triumphantly at the screen. 'That's *it!* That's the override code. I found it by stripping everything else out of it. I fooled it into revealing its biggest secret!'

'And now?' asked Judith.

'Now all I have to do is restore the programs, and we're into them all as deep as you want to go.'

He vanished down the hall towards the storeroom again. Twenty minutes later he returned, typed the code into the system, and immediately the screen was filled with figures and letters. Opposite Dr Louis Rose's name they read: LRO-CLINIC.

'Dead simple, huh?' said Lightning, flushed by his achievement. 'Your old man's password is CLINIC.'

'Let's see what's in his file,' Marriner said anxiously.

Lightning keyed in the letters and the password. This time he got the headings of all the items Dr Rose had chosen to keep for his private scrutiny. The one at the top bore the title INDUNA. Lightning pressed some more keys and a page appeared headed *Induna Project, Page One of Fifteen*. It was the beginning of a carefully plotted schedule: dates, times, names . . . Marriner stared at it in fascination: it was far more than he had been counting on.

Lightning pressed the SEND button and the printer in the corner began to chatter. 'Don't forget to erase the print record,' Judith said. She was extremely nervous now, and for that matter so was Marriner. His hands shook as he tore the pages off the printer. Finally Lightning switched off the terminal and trotted back to the storeroom to check that he had left nothing amiss with the processing unit.

Marriner stacked the fifteen pages of printout, folded them and put them in his jacket pocket. Then he faced Judith.

'I hope you know how much I appreciate this. You've been marvellous.'

She was not susceptible to praise tonight. She said, 'I hope you appreciate the risk I'm taking.'

'I do. Believe me.' He kissed her cheek. 'This stuff is going to make a real difference, you know.'

A minute later they were ready to leave. Judith would hang about for half an hour in order to avoid the appearance of any connection with them.

Marriner got Lightning back to his barracks by ten o'clock, and was home in his room at The Windsor by eleven. He spread the computer printouts across his bed and read carefully through them. He began making notes. Planning was something he had always enjoyed. Deploying men and resources to the best possible advantage was an intellectual challenge.

The sun was well up before he had finished, and there were still many details to be filled in. There were also more things to do before he could consider sleep. At seven thirty he set off for Northcliff, reaching Judith's flat in time to catch her before she left for work. He found her mood just as brittle as it had been last night.

He tried to speak soothingly to her. 'I'm sorry, Judith. Believe me, I didn't intend to present you with a *fait accompli* like this. I was going to ask you yesterday. Too much else got in the way. I suddenly realised the radio transceiver had to be picked up today, and I'll have nowhere else to keep it.'

'You've taken advantage of me,' she said tonelessly.

'No, Judith, I think you knew what you were taking on. What would you have said if I *had* asked you in advance? Yes or no?'

She shrugged.

'Listen, Judith. Everything has changed. You're going to have to leave the country. You'll have to come with us. You can't just sit around afterwards pretending to be innocent. I've worked out a way of getting you out. What's left for you here, anyway? Hadn't you thought about leaving yourself?'

'That would have been my own choice,' she said with a little more spirit. 'Now you're forcing it on me.'

'You were the one who sent that letter. That's how it all got started.'

'I hate the idea of betraying my father.'

'If he has the integrity you claim he has, then he'll come to understand that you've done the right thing by helping Kumalo. Now I'm going to ask you to do two other things. Small things.'

She gave a weary sigh. 'What are they?'

'Tomorrow we're all going to meet out at the farm. In the afternoon Rendle has arranged to pay a visit to his old air base near Pretoria. I'd like you to drive him there. The other thing is that I'm going to have to become a patient at the Woodvale Clinic. I want you to help me arrange it.'

Chapter Eleven

'You're quite certain this is the one?' demanded Colonel Prinsloo.

The warder from Pollsmoor stiffened. 'Absolutely, sir. There aren't two like him in the whole place. Strong as an ox. Quiet, but dangerous.'

'Well done,' said Prinsloo with a sigh, not to the warder but to Warrant Officer Willemse. It was Willemse's patient legwork, and not the snarling inquisitions of Booysen and Kriek, that had finally yielded results, prising out of this young idiot the hazy recollection of an incident that had occurred early in November. It was the kind of thing that could happen once or twice a week, some *mugu* working in the fields who had spotted somebody outside the fence and tried to cadge something off him.

They stood watching the prisoner now with a certain awe as he was led out of the cell. Booysen snapped a handcuff to each of his wrists and fastened them to his own and to Kriek's: there would be no more mistakes.

The man was built like a tank, the turret of his head turning slowly on his mighty shoulders as he studied his captors.

'You won't frighten this one,' Prinsloo said thoughtfully. 'There's only one way to handle him, and this time I want no mistakes.'

'PELINDABA?' CORPORAL RENDLE spoke the name like an African curse. 'Are you serious, Major?'

They had just turned off the main road, and the pale ominous shape of the nuclear reactor lay straight ahead. In the back seat Lightning, Carver and Fish had suddenly stopped horsing around and fallen silent.

'Of course I'm serious. The farm is just behind it, but it's well out of sight.' Marriner glanced at Rendle beside him. 'Anything wrong?'

'Major . . . Pelindaba is one of the most sensitive places in the country. They say it's where we make our nuclear weapons.'

Marriner's hands went rigid on the steering wheel. He knew of the rumours that South Africa had its own nuclear arsenal, but he had never thought to connect them with this place. Of all the strokes of bad luck he could imagine, this was possibly the worst. No, not bad luck: carelessness. The heavy security surrounding the place should have alerted him.

The entrance to the plant lay just ahead. It was time to put a bold face on it, he thought. He stopped the car beside the gate. Judith and the rest of Rendle's squad drew up behind him in the red Opel and he signalled to her to stay where she was. Two men in dark blue uniforms, one of them cradling a machine pistol, emerged from the gatehouse as he approached.

'Good morning,' he said breezily. 'I thought I'd introduce myself, just in case you wondered. I'm the new tenant of the farm down there.'

He handed over his passport which the men examined in silence. It seemed to reassure them. He explained that some friends were helping him move in. In fact they were going to have a bit of a housewarming party. 'If you feel like a beer when you come off duty, you're welcome to join us,' he added. The men thanked him noncommittally, but by the time he turned back to the car he was sure he had won their grudging confidence.

'You think that was wise?' Rendle asked.

'Better than leaving them to wonder. They're employed by the Atomic Energy Board, and the left hand of government very rarely knows what the right hand is doing. Besides, there could be certain advantages in this place. Who expects a criminal to hide in a police station?'

When the little convoy reached the farmhouse they found old Meiring ready to leave, his possessions heaped on the back of a pick-up truck. Labuschagne from the estate agency was there as well. An impromptu party started up, with Rendle passing beer cans round and the old man joining Marriner in a toast to their respective futures. The formalities took only a minute: Marriner and Meiring both signed two copies of the lease, and the new tenant handed over a bank draft to the old man and another to Labuschagne. Eventually the pick-up rattled away, followed by Labuschagne's car, and Marriner and his guests were alone.

They helped him carry his supplies into the rickety farmhouse. He had checked out of the hotel first thing that morning. Besides his luggage he'd brought with him gas lamps, a camp bed, a sleeping-bag purchased from a camping supply shop, and a box of basic provisions. Other, less innocent, items he'd bring here over the next few days. Meanwhile this would be Marriner's home until he could get himself admitted to the clinic.

When everything was stowed away they went outside and sat in the shade of a mimosa and he began to address them.

'We haven't got a lot of time. Frank and Judith have to leave after lunch, so I want everything to be as clear as possible before then. I'm going to tell you my plan, and then we'll discuss it.

'Phase One. We are going to take Lincoln Kumalo out of that clinic and make him disappear. We're going to bring him here by road, and for a short distance on foot. Maximum time allowed: one hour. I will be in charge of Phase One.

'Phase Two. We will transfer Kumalo to a helicopter waiting here for him. We will fly him due east, to the closest possible point on the border, overflying Swaziland and landing at a designated point in southern Mozambique. Maximum time allowed: two hours. Frank Rendle will be in charge of Phase Two.

'Phase Three. At our landing point in Mozambique we will be met by representatives of the People's Congress, who will escort us to a safe hiding-place and in due course make arrangements for us to leave the country. Phase Three will be in the hands of the Congress and the Mozambique government, and I don't expect to have any details until our arrival.' Marriner paused. 'Any questions?'

THE MANAGER OF THE WINDSOR HOTEL was trying to be cooperative, but could scarcely disguise his impatience. He had an unusually busy Saturday afternoon ahead: a wedding reception in the ballroom and a coachload of German tourists arriving any minute. The two young men had approached him circumspectly, but he didn't like their manner. When they'd learned that the guest they were interested in had checked out that morning they had become almost accusatory.

'So he left no forwarding address? Isn't that unusual?'

'By no means. As you see, we have his home address in Ireland in the register. Any mail would be sent on to him there.'

'And you say you never saw him yourself?'

'I may have. I may not have. Look, I've had a hundred and twenty guests in here on any one night in the past two weeks. As far as I'm concerned this Mr Marriner was just a name and a room number.'

'He paid in cash, I notice.' One of the men was studying a duplicate of the receipted bill. 'A businessman would be more inclined to use a credit card, surely? I also see that he made no telephone calls from his room.'

'You expect me to account for a thing like that?'

'No, sir. I'm really just thinking aloud. It seems to me that Mr Marriner was very careful to keep himself to himself.'

The manager rolled his eyes. 'What is it you want this man for, anyway?'

'I'm afraid that's a matter of state security.'

FROM TIME TO TIME, Colonel Prinsloo strolled into the interrogation room to see how they were getting on. He didn't like to stay long, because even he couldn't stomach what was going on in there.

This time, five hours after the interrogation had begun, the sight of Bobbejaan gave Prinsloo a fright. In their own way the three interrogators were also close to the end of their endurance.

He left the room and found that Willemse had followed him out. The young man was so drawn and pale he looked in danger of being sick. Prinsloo rounded sharply on him. 'Well?'

'I've had enough of this, sir. It's not what I joined the police for.'

'I've got news for you, Willemse. It's not what *I* joined for, either.'

'Then, perhaps you'll understand,' said the other man, 'if I ask to be excused from any more of this. I'm thinking of resigning, in fact.'

'You can do whatever you like when all this is over. Send your resignation direct to Hoeksma, for all I care. But you try backing out on me now, Willemse, and I'll have you in that room yourself!'

IT WAS ONLY MIDAFTERNOON when Nandi Kumalo was startled by Duma's familiar knock on the back door of her house in the Orlando section of Soweto. With a puzzled frown she put aside the copy of the *British Journal of Guidance and Counselling* she had been reading. It was one of a batch of professional publications that had arrived that morning, the envelope ripped open for inspection and resealed with deliberate clumsiness by the Security Police, just to let her know they hadn't forgotten her.

As soon as Duma slipped through the door she was certain that something was wrong. He refused her offer of a chair and began his familiar routine of pacing about the kitchen.

'Nandi, they've found something out. My informer at the hotel told me that Major Marriner left this morning, and a few hours later they turned up looking for him. And now I have no way of reaching him, till we meet on Monday. Perhaps they will have picked him up by then. The damned man has been keeping me in the dark.'

Nandi pulled a chair out from the kitchen table and sat down. Over the past month, while she continued to work at her usual strenuous pace, her moods had gone through bewildering swings. It had been impossible to ignore the increasing rumours of her father's impending release, and her own growing conviction that he was in mortal danger. Even when Duma had told her of the arrival of this man Marriner, her responses had been contradictory: on the one hand the news raised a new hope, on the other it made the threat to Lincoln Kumalo seem that much more serious.

'Duma, listen to me.' She grabbed his arm and steered him round the table, forcing him to sit down and face her. 'I am tired of this uncertainty. Just what is it they are going to do?'

'Marriner knows where Lincoln is going to be. Marriner and these white boys are going to get him out. At least, that is their plan. They've still told me nothing more. But there is sense in what this Marriner says, about everybody needing to know only so much.'

'Ha! I am only his daughter, and so I need to know nothing, is that right? And what about him? Do you realise that the one person who is totally unaware of any of this is my father himself? I can't stand the idea that he is facing all this in ignorance. I can't let it happen that way!'

He looked at her sharply. 'You're not thinking of getting involved yourself, I hope.'

'I don't know what I'm thinking.'

Duma sighed. 'Maybe I will find out more on Monday,' he said. 'That is, if they haven't already caught Marriner by then.'

FRANK RENDLE had suddenly become talkative.

'I was in Angola, flying one of those Puma gunships you saw back there. Well, one morning my crew and I got orders to zap a village about forty kilometres behind the Angolan lines. They said it was a SWAPO guerrilla base-camp, and we were supposed to give it the works: rockets, napalm, the lot. The funny thing was, I'd overflown that village the day before on a patrol, and it was full of women and kids.

'Well, that's what I told them back at base, but they insisted there were guerrillas there, that they kept the women and kids there as a cover and I was to zap the lot of them. So I just refused to go. Is all this boring you?'

'Not at all,' said Judith. She was driving him past the perimeter fence of the Zwartkop Air Station near Pretoria.

'In the air force you don't say no to an order. There was a quick court-martial and a dishonourable discharge. My record didn't exempt me from regular national service, so it was back to square-bashing and then back to Angola. I learned a new way of surviving, and I pulled my squad through without losing any of them. Ever since then we've stayed out of trouble.'

Zwartkop was only one part of a very large military complex set among the bush-speckled hills just south of Pretoria. The complex itself was crossed by public roads; getting into any one of the bases, however, required either official permission or the pulling of strings.

Rendle's friend was waiting to meet them in the public car park of the big army hospital. His name was Captain Cross, his nickname was Jumper and he was a pilot with 19 Squadron. He greeted Rendle enthusiastically, they got into Jumper's car, and he drove them back to the air station. At the gate, he presented his ID to the guard and formally vouched for his guests, who were made to sign a visitors' book and given passes. Then they were on a road skirting the airfield.

Judith was secretly amused at her role as Rendle's girlfriend, going on a double date with his old air force pal and his girl. It would seem far more natural, he had explained, than for him to turn up on his own and pump the information he needed out of Jumper Cross. Jumper was a decent guy, she gathered, who shared Rendle's dislike of the gung ho, super-patriotic types in the squadron and had privately sympathised with him over the stand he had taken in Angola.

At the single quarters, which resembled a modern block of flats, they went straight up to Jumper's room and sat drinking beer on the balcony.

'So you're still driving the Pumas, Jumper?' Rendle asked.

'Yeah, *driving* is right. Excursion trips, tactical exercises, that sort of thing. And you? Still cruising the townships?'

Rendle steered the talk back to helicopters, and Jumper needed little encouragement. Flying was his passion. Although he apologised to Judith once in a while and tried to include her in more general conversation, within a minute or two he was always back to shop-talk, information about the flying routines of the squadron, its operational readiness, its strengths and weaknesses. Jumper seemed quite unaware that he was being indiscreet. When darkness had begun to fall over the airfield and the perimeter lights suddenly came on, he leaped to his feet.

'Heavens! My girl will be waiting. She'll be mad at me as it is when I have to tell her about next weekend.'

'What about it?' Rendle asked casually.

'The long weekend, you know? We were going to start out early on Friday and head for one of those resorts in the Drakensberg, but now I've been told I'm on duty. The Day of the Covenant: big military parade in Pretoria, big gathering of the faithful at the Voortrekker Monument, aerial flypasts and all that stuff. You haven't heard about it?'

'No,' said Rendle numbly.

'Oh, well, it's strictly an occasion for Boer drum-banging as far as I'm concerned. Reliving the Battle of Blood River and impressing our black citizens with how tough we are.'

COLONEL PRINSLOO WAS DOZING uncomfortably behind the desk of his makeshift office in the Securitas Building when the telephone rang late that night. A bleary glance at his watch told him the time was ten to eleven.

The caller was Major Booysen. There was no triumph in his voice as he said what he had to, barely even a sense of relief.

'What made him talk?' Prinsloo queried.

'Nothing in particular. He just suddenly decided he'd had enough.'

'So he gave the message to Ibrahim Khan?'

'Yes. But it was meant for Kumalo's daughter. He says he doesn't know what was in the message, and I'm inclined to believe that.'

Prinsloo spoke wearily. 'So at last we know where we stand. There was a leak, and we know where it went to. We don't know what the message said, but presumably Phineas Molefe had found out enough to justify the risk of sending it out. It reached Ibrahim Khan, and we must assume it was passed on to Nandi Kumalo. Next question: how much further did it get?'

'Next step: pick them both up and ask them,' said Booysen.

'Don't be dumb,' Prinsloo said irritably. 'You might as well send a telegram to the Congress telling them what we know.'

JUMPER CROSS HAD WARNED them that the disco would be pretty dire. Actually it wasn't all that bad, Judith considered. It had good music and lighting, but it would have been more enjoyable if she and Rendle hadn't been there under false pretences. Jumper's girlfriend, who was a nurse at the army hospital, turned out to be good company and she and Judith had talked a lot, leaving Rendle to continue quietly prising information out of his friend. They had danced a bit, and had a couple of drinks, and now at a quarter to twelve they were getting ready to leave. Jumper's girl had just gone to powder her nose when Rendle leaned across to him and said, 'You know, I would love to see how one of those new machines handles. The modified Pumas you're flying now? How about taking me up in one?'

'Not much chance, Frank. No tourists allowed.'

'I wasn't thinking of doing it officially, just hitching a ride. Next Friday, say, during this flying-circus act you were telling me about. It wouldn't be like going on a real operation. Nobody would need to know.'

'Hell, Frank, I'd be grounded if I got caught. You know the rules.'

'Well enough to know when they can be broken. It's just a bit of a lark, Jumper, but it would mean a lot to me.'

'Well, I don't know . . .' Judith could see that Jumper was in a quandary. He'd enjoyed his reunion with Rendle, he'd even talked about their meeting again next weekend, and now he didn't want to disappoint him. 'Others would have to see you. The ground crew, my own gunner—'

'I'd be logged in as extra crew, properly kitted out and everything. I know the drill, after all.'

'I suppose it might work,' Jumper conceded reluctantly.

MARRINER DROVE BACK to Johannesburg on Monday morning. His first stop was at an isolated call box in the northern suburbs, where he put through a call on the scrambler to Zurich. Joshua Rosenblatt had been in regular contact with Harry Makibani in Lusaka, and he reported that the plans for their reception in Mozambique were well in hand.

Rosenblatt told him something else. The letter confirming the transfer of funds into Frank Rendle's account at the Handelsbank Bauer had not been sent by courier after all, but had been accidentally airmailed to Marriner care of the Standard Bank.

Damn it, he thought. The letter was unimportant in itself, since Rendle was willing to take his word for it that the money was there. What bothered him about the letter was that it was dangerous. He unhooked the scrambler, dialled the number of the Standard Bank and told Jepson what had happened. Jepson said nothing had yet arrived, but of course he would continue to keep an eye open. 'Surely there's somewhere I can phone you, old boy?' he said.

'No. I don't have a telephone now. I'll ring you again.'

Resuming his journey into the city, he had plenty of other things to mull over. The arrangements for the three phases of the job were all, theoretically at least, now in place, but this left open the question of creating a diversion, something that would be vital to the success of Phase One. It would have to be a large and serious diversion, something to give scope to the talents of Comrade Duma.

IT WAS SIX HUNDRED MILES from the South African border at Beitbridge to the frontier between Zimbabwe and Zambia, and normally the young Congress courier reckoned to drive it in twelve hours. The rainy season had now set in, however, forcing him to reduce his speed. Even so, he reached the Congress headquarters in Lusaka at the appointed time of ten o'clock. The offices occupied a rambling collection of single-storey buildings in an alley off Cairo Road, with a protective presence of Zambian policemen at either end, and he had to be frisked for weapons before he was allowed in.

Almost always it was Harry Makibani who received him here, so he was surprised this morning to be met by a leaner and dourer man whom he knew as Lawrence Gumbi, the head of the Congress military wing.

Gumbi took the parcel of dispatches, thanked the courier perfunctorily, then walked through to an empty office at the back, where he sat down and began to examine the two or three dozen letters contained in the package. Many were addressed to him, but one envelope had Harry Makibani's name on it, and was undoubtedly from his young protégé Comrade Duma. Without hesitation Gumbi tore the envelope open. Harry had been playing games with the rest of the executive for far too long now. He was always receiving these private messages from Duma and he was forever on the phone to Rosenblatt, who himself should have been back from Zurich at least a week ago. Between them they were up to something, and Gumbi had no doubt that it concerned the conflicting rumours over Lincoln Kumalo. It was high time Harry was put back in his place.

'YOU'RE TELLING ME you've known this since Saturday, Duma?'

'What could I do about it? I didn't know where the hell you were.'

'If I'd left the hotel a few hours later . . . if I'd gone back there today, they'd have pulled me in! How did they know, Duma?'

The young man shrugged. Studied indifference was his pose today, though he hadn't been able to disguise his relief when Marriner turned up for their meeting at the dump. 'Maybe you have done something careless, Major. How can I tell? But now you must consider yourself a wanted man. Where does that leave the rest of us?'

'But wanted for what?' Marriner stared out over the wilderness of the old mine workings. 'I'm sure I've done nothing since I arrived here to attract their attention.'

Duma frowned. 'If you'd been around, I could have told you something else. I heard from Cape Town yesterday that after Phineas Molefe died the Security Police took away everyone in his cell block for questioning.'

'So they're still chasing the source of that message. That's even more of an indication that there's a limit to what they know.' Marriner wondered whether he was clutching at straws. 'Obviously they have found out something to interest them in me, but that doesn't necessarily mean they've connected me with Kumalo. We've got to carry on as though this hadn't happened. I'm ready to tell you more now, Duma. I'm ready to tell you how you can help.'

The young man was looking at him strangely. 'You mean that, Major?'

'Of course I mean it,' he said, puzzled. 'Isn't that what you wanted?'

'It's not that. I was half expecting you to say you were pulling out. Running away.'

Marriner gave a grim little laugh. 'There doesn't seem to be anywhere for me to run now, does there?'

Chapter Twelve

Besides being in charge of the Substance Abuse Unit at Woodvale, Dr Clooney was also in private practice as a psychiatrist. In this capacity he was in attendance at his rooms in Jeppe Street three mornings a week.

Twenty years of specialising in the treatment of alcoholics had given Dr Clooney much insight into their patterns of behaviour. While he was always sympathetic to their problems he had learned to be wary of their motives. Superficially Mr Davis, who had walked in on him without an appointment, seemed extremely fit and healthy, clear of eye and steady of hand. He had not been referred to the psychiatrist by his GP, which would have been the normal practice, for the simple reason that he didn't have one. He said he had come as a contract engineer to South Africa a couple of years ago and had never needed to consult a doctor in that time.

'But you say you had treatment in England? Where was that?'

Mr Davis rattled off the names of several hospitals in London.

'And it's five years since you had a drink?'

'Until three days ago. There was no particular reason: it just seemed more important to have a drink than not to have one. Once I started I could feel the old pattern reasserting itself.'

'Well, you obviously have a good understanding of your problem. I'm going to start by giving you a prescription for Antabuse tablets—'

'Look, I've been through all this before, Doctor, and I know the score. I'm frightened of going on a prolonged bout, and what I need is a week or two of medical supervision. I understand you're connected with the Woodvale Clinic.'

'It would certainly do you no harm to go in there.' Dr Clooney raised an eyebrow. 'You do have some idea of their fees, though?'

'I think so.'

'Well, I do know there are beds available. I can arrange for you to be admitted tomorrow, if that's what you really want. Who recommended you to me, by the way?'

Mr Davis smiled. 'I think it was someone I met in a bar,' he said.

Twenty minutes later Marriner was on his way back to Rietvlei Farm, as satisfied as he could afford to be with his morning's work.

THERE WAS LITTLE TRAFFIC on the long, monotonous road through the sodden forest and scrub east of Lusaka, but even so dusk was falling by the time Harry Makibani reached the turn-off, an unmarked road that twisted through the bush to the south. Several times his wheels spun and the Toyota slid sideways on patches of mud. At the end of the track he came to a fence and a gate of barbed wire, where two sentries armed with Kalashnikovs took a good look at him before waving him through.

It was Gumbi who had called the emergency meeting of the executive. Until five years ago the camp had been a mission school and its inoffensive appearance had been preserved as far as possible, particularly from the air. The parade ground was still carefully marked out as a soccer pitch, for which it was also used. The buildings, however, now housed nearly five hundred guerrilla recruits of the People's Congress.

When Harry arrived they were at their evening meal, gathered at the long tables under a shelter beside the cookhouse. He parked his car beside the main office and climbed the steps onto the porch.

This was a brick bungalow, with a row of interlinking offices in which the camp's administrative staff worked. At the far end was a conference room, and it was here that he found Gumbi, Godfrey Pahlani and J.K.Govender awaiting him. Clearly this was to be more in the nature of an inquisition than a meeting. Harry was ready for it.

'Good evening,' he said.

Only Pahlani acknowledged the greeting, with a slight nod. The others watched him as he pulled the single empty chair up to the table, sat on it and leaned forward on his elbows, deliberately diminishing the formality they were trying to create. 'Anybody got a beer?' he asked.

'This isn't a party,' Pahlani said. He had a heap of papers in front of him, with the letter that Gumbi had intercepted that morning on top of them. He slapped it with the back of his hand and said, 'We want to know just what the hell has been going on, Harry.'

'I think you know almost as much as I do now. We're getting Lincoln out. By this time on Friday we should all be reunited. Doesn't that please any of you? You don't look very pleased.'

'Just try not to be facetious, will you? Why was this kept from us?'

'I was intending to tell you tomorrow. You would have had to know by then anyway, since the formal request for help from the Mozambique government must come from the full executive. Everything else is already in place. All the preparatory work is done.'

'Harry, I don't think you realise the seriousness of your position,' Pahlani said sternly. 'You've committed a breach of Congress discipline. You've undertaken this adventure, you and Rosenblatt, without any authorisation from the executive. You've committed a million pounds of our money to it without authority. You expect us to accept this?'

'Frankly, Godfrey, I'm not terribly fussed what you think of it. The bottom line is that Lincoln is coming back to us, and if it had been left to you it wouldn't be happening.'

'You talk as though it were already accomplished. It could still go wrong.'

'Nothing will stop Marriner going ahead now. Nothing except treachery, that is. I was just coming to that.' He gestured at the letter. As you can see from what Comrade Duma has to say, there has to be an informer somewhere in the movement. Someone has fingered our friend Major Marriner. It can't have been anyone here in Zambia, because none of you knew about him until today. Keeping you in the dark has therefore been doubly useful. You're all in the clear, my friends.'

'It's very kind of you to say so, I'm sure,' said Pahlani, 'but—'

'The leak can only have come from London. Mohaila is investigating, to see how bad the damage is. I don't believe it can be too serious, because even Mohaila knows none of the details. As long as Marriner keeps his head down—'

'Harry, all this is beside the point,' snapped J.K. Govender. 'You don't make Congress policy. We do. We have a constitution, a book of rules, and we abide by them. It's called collective responsibility.'

'This is hardly an issue of procedure, is it? There's only one question to answer, and that is: do you want Lincoln Kumalo back or don't you?'

He met their eyes, each in turn, challenging them. Gumbi held his gaze, while Pahlani and Govender glanced uneasily at each other. He had them cornered, he knew, but he didn't care for Gumbi's silence.

'Of course we are not saying no,' Pahlani muttered. 'What we do not like is having a gun held to our heads, Harry. We've decided that you are going to face a disciplinary tribunal. It will be convened next week, once this business is over. In the meantime we are placing you under arrest.'

Harry heard the door open and glanced round. As if at some secret signal, four men came lumbering into the room, two of them carrying machine pistols. They stood in a row against the rear wall, awaiting orders. 'Lincoln won't put up with this,' he said defiantly.

'That all depends on whether Lincoln makes it, doesn't it?'

It was still Pahlani who spoke, but somehow Harry recognised Gumbi's thoughts behind the words. He stared hard at Gumbi, as though to provoke a reaction out of him. 'I think I see what's behind this now. You don't want Lincoln back, do you? You're scared of having him take over. You're jealous enough to actually sabotage this operation, just as long as none of you has to take the blame.'

Suddenly Lawrence Gumbi stood up, leaned across the table, bringing his face threateningly close to Harry's.

'Listen to me, Harry. I speak for myself now. I am not scared of Lincoln Kumalo. He will come back, and he will take his place among us as an equal. The question of leadership can then be democratically decided. I am the one who has built up the forces of our armed struggle, and I intend to remain in charge of them. In that capacity, it is I who will be in control of the third phase of this project. It is I who will receive Kumalo when he crosses the border. It will be a homecoming, not a coronation.'

He gestured at the men to take Harry away.

COLONEL PRINSLOO seemed to have brought a new kind of anger back with him from Cape Town. In the quietly elegant surroundings of Hoeksma's office, the anger went on radiating out of him. After reading the newly opened file van Straaten had sent for, he stood up and tossed it contemptuously on the desk.

'You're telling me you've been sitting on this for eight days?' he asked van Straaten.

'Hardly sitting on it. We took action at once and we've drawn a blank. That's why I'm passing it on to you.'

'Can you tell me why you didn't do that right away, sir?'

'Because I wanted it handled delicately. You were in Cape Town. Your hands were full overseeing the security aspects of the Induna Project, and there's still nothing to connect this man Marriner to it.'

'Nothing?' Prinsloo gave a derisive snort. 'Haven't you heard of circumstantial evidence? Here you've got a former British Army special operations man with an African background and a strong likelihood that he's been taking money from the People's Congress. He turns up soon after a leakage of information on this project, at least as far as Nandi Kumalo, and then he mysteriously disappears. You call that nothing?'

'I call it suspicious, but not conclusive,' said van Straaten. 'And it's surely a long way from knowing what the Congress intends to do about it. You haven't considered interrogating Nandi?'

'No.'

'You surprise me.'

Prinsloo gave him a condescending look. 'Pulling in Kumalo's daughter

303

is quite a different proposition from questioning a couple of dumb *mugus*, sir. That's not to say we are overlooking her. It will take only one move on her part to establish the link. If these people are planning something, then I want them flushed out, not scared off. That's why I wish I had known earlier about this man Marriner.'

'The connection is still not there. There's nothing to justify turning the country upside down to find him.'

'Gentlemen . . .' Hoeksma intervened a trifle nervously. 'I think you are both getting slightly sidetracked. We have less than two days to go, and important things still to discuss. I suggest you sort out this difficulty later. Meanwhile, let it be clearly understood that nothing is going to stop this project going ahead.'

To Hoeksma's relief Prinsloo sat down again, and they both gave him their attention. This was to be their final meeting before the events of Friday. 'We now have our final timetables,' he said, 'and I would like us to run through them together, comparing. Tertius, will you begin?'

'Certainly.' It was van Straaten's office which had supplied the master schedules. Each of them had one in front of him, and no other copies existed. 'We have of course received Dr Rose's timetable for the medical procedures, and have integrated those into our own. We start at six o'clock tomorrow evening, Thursday, when Kumalo will first be informed that his operation is to go ahead. An hour later he will be transported by helicopter direct from Pollsmoor to Ysterplaat Air Station. A Merlin jet transport plane fitted as an ambulance will fly him up here to Waterkloof Air Base. Dr Els will be accompanying him all the way.'

'Are you happy with your end of things so far?' Hoeksma said tactfully to Prinsloo.

'Most of this stage is in the hands of the air force, whose crews have been told only as much as they need to know. There will be armed guards on board the aircraft, of course.'

'For the next stage, he will be transferred to a joint police–military road convoy,' van Straaten continued. 'Time of arrival at the clinic: eleven pm.'

'By then our ground security forces will have established themselves at the clinic by arrangement with Dr Rose,' said Prinsloo.

'What about the other patients?' Hoeksma asked. 'And the staff at the clinic? How much are they going to know?'

'As little as possible. There are few night nurses on duty at that time, and the patients will be confined to their wards. A whole wing is being cleared to accommodate Kumalo and his guards. The whole thing—the official story, at least—will be public knowledge by Friday afternoon, anyway.'

'All right. Let's go back to Kumalo's arrival, then. Once he's settled in, Dr Rose goes home for the night. Dr Els is being quartered in the clinic, and you and your men are effectively in control of the place for the next six hours or so, correct?'

'Until Rose and his team arrive to conduct the operation.'

'Very well.' Hoeksma leaned back in his chair. 'Exactly what happens during those six hours is something that only the three of us and Dr Els will ever know about. We should never discuss it again, even—'

Suddenly the intercom on Hoeksma's desk buzzed and he snapped down the reply switch. 'I told you I wasn't to be disturbed!'

'I'm sorry, sir. It's a call for Mr van Straaten. They say it's urgent.'

Hoeksma gestured resignedly at van Straaten, who rose from his chair and picked up the telephone. He listened for a minute, giving monosyllabic replies, then put down the receiver.

'You talked about getting results, Prinsloo. Well, I've got a lead to the Handelsbank Bauer.' He explained quickly the connection between the Congress and the Zurich bank, and then turned to Hoeksma. 'You remember the man in the Reserve Bank? The one instructed to keep us posted on foreign-exchange returns? Well, he's just found one from the Handelsbank Bauer. A transfer made on the seventh of this month—when was that, just a week ago?—for fifteen thousand rands, to the Standard Bank in Johannesburg. It's got to mean something.'

'Who was it payable to?' Prinsloo asked.

'They don't get that information, but of course the Standard Bank will know.' Van Straaten reached for the phone again, then remembered something. 'Wednesday. The banks will have closed at one o'clock.'

Prinsloo's grin was sardonic. 'Closed to the public, maybe. Not to us.'

IT WAS JUDITH who had checked Marriner in at the clinic the previous afternoon, and it was she who stood behind the reception desk now, giving him a polite smile. 'Going out, Mr Davis?'

'Just for a couple of hours. That's all right, isn't it?'

'Of course. We just like it if you let us know. Oh, I think there's a message for you.' She reached into the rack behind her and handed him an envelope. 'Will you be here for dinner?'

'I'm not sure yet.'

'It doesn't matter. We do like you to make sure of being back by ten o'clock though. Thank you, Mr Davis.'

He tucked the envelope into his pocket, left the office and headed for the Ford Orion in the car park. The sense of freedom enjoyed by all the patients in the Substance Abuse Unit was scarcely an illusion. Apart from receiving a visit from Dr Clooney first thing each morning, and attending a group therapy session before lunch, they could do what they pleased with their time. The only thing on which there was gentle insistence was that they be present at ten o'clock at night to be given their various medications before retiring.

All of which suited Marriner just fine. He had spent most of yesterday with Rendle's squad at the dump, staking out a full-scale plan of the clinic with lengths of tape on its flat surface and practising the tactics to be used in the attack. He had also found time to buy some special clothing and equipment. Today he would give them their final briefing, and then all of them would lie low for the next twenty-four hours.

On the quiet road that led south from Woodvale he stopped the car, checked his watch, then took the walkie-talkie from the glove box, switched it on and spoke into it.

'Unit one to four. Receiving?'

'Unit four speaking, *my baas*.' Duma, the cheeky bastard, was holed up somewhere in Soweto, his voice clear enough and unscrambled through the base unit that Judith had left switched on in her flat.

'Don't fool around, number four. I'll call you again at plus-twelve hours.' He snapped off the set, reassured to know the system was working over a wide area.

He drove on. He joined the Pretoria motorway at the Edenburg junction, then cut off it again a couple of miles north, onto the old and almost disused two-lane road that had once linked the two cities and now served only to connect a number of small farming centres. A few hundred yards along it stood an abandoned petrol station, its custom and its pumps long ago dried up. He turned off and drove round to the rear of the building. It was Rendle who had picked this place as the final staging point for the Saracen's crew, and Marriner could see that it was ideally positioned. Invisible from the road, it looked out across the river to the wooded and secluded terrain south of the clinic.

At the back of the building was a wide opening into what had once been a service bay. The Saracen was backed in there. Rendle and his squad were sprawling about it in their usual indolent way.

Marriner stepped out of the car. 'All OK?'

'OK,' said Rendle. 'But we've got to be quick. We're way out of our usual territory here.'

'I'll only be a few minutes. I like the view from here.' They turned and stared out over the valley. 'Have you checked out the best approach?' It was Brakpan, the Saracen's driver, to whom Marriner spoke now.

'Yeah, Major. There's a shallow spot where the river widens out a couple of hundred metres to the south. We can cross it there, no problem, then head straight uphill. No cover on the eastern side, so we go for the fence on the south.'

'Right.' Marriner turned to the others. 'I'll concentrate on the south fence from the inside, then. Just as soon as I know how the guards are positioned, I'll tell you the best time and place to take them out. That and cutting the fence will have to be done in the dark.'

'It's going to look a bit strange, isn't it?' said Nicky Flynn. 'I mean, this monster trundling around the veld in broad daylight?'

'Not necessarily. There's going to be a heavy security presence at the clinic, and to any ordinary soldier you're just going to look part of it. By then yours will have different markings, anyway. You got the right paint?' he asked Rendle.

'Yep. And new army number plates. Nicked them from an old ambulance that's headed for the scrapyard. Nobody will miss them.'

'Good. Then, let's just run briefly through your schedules again. Starting at six thirty tomorrow evening, when Blikkies Steyn goes AWOL from the barracks. You're sure that will work out all right, Blikkies?'

'No roll call until they're formed up to move out at two in the morning,' said the young Afrikaner. 'All they can do then is notify the military police, and by then I'll be hiding out on the farm.'

Confirmation had come through yesterday that Rendle's squad and vehicle were among the detachment from the 4th Armoured Infantry Battalion being sent to Pretoria to take part in the ceremonies. This would cost them the freedom they normally enjoyed, and it was certain that their absence would be discovered quickly. On the other hand, providing they could slip out of the convoy *en route*, they would have the advantage of being able to hide up within a short distance of the clinic. 'It does mean the wagon will be missing for five whole hours,' Rendle said.

'They'll have a lot on their minds. We'll just have to hope they won't look for you too hard. By then you'll have other things to worry about, Corporal. Around three o'clock you'll pick up Judith's car. Here is her spare set of keys.' He handed Rendle an envelope. 'I gather you've made your own arrangements with her about the gear you'll be needing.'

Rendle gave him a look. 'That's right. It seemed simpler to fix it between us. Now, how about the equipment you promised?'

Marriner went to his car and opened the boot. Besides twenty spikeboards that he had made up earlier, at Rietvlei, there were torches, two gas-lamps, two pairs of powerful wirecutters, several lengths of quarter-inch nylon rope and half a dozen rolls of plastic insulating tape. They dumped the lot in the petrol station and in exchange Rendle produced an airline bag containing six tear-gas grenades from the Saracen's inventory, as well as four smoke grenades that he had managed to draw from the stores. Marriner inspected them, then zipped up the bag and put it in the boot.

'It doesn't seem like much, does it?' Rendle said. 'Not for what you have to do.'

'Let me worry about that. You just deliver that helicopter on time.'

'There's one other thing ...' Nicky Flynn said tentatively. 'That letter from the bank in Zurich, confirming that the money is in Frank's name. It still hasn't turned up?'

'No. It hasn't. I'll give it one last try tomorrow, but I think you'll just have to take my word that it's there.'

'We'd better go,' said Rendle.

Brakpan had already returned to the Saracen, and now its huge engine grumbled into life and he eased it out of the service bay. With some difficulty they hauled down the rusted roller door and padlocked it.

Marriner shook hands with each of the soldiers in turn. He felt

something in the nature of a speech was called for, but knew there was never anything to say at times like these.

'Good luck,' was all he could manage. 'See you all on Friday.'

'Good luck, Major.'

They climbed into the vehicle, and with a single wave from Rendle in the turret it disappeared round the corner. Marriner checked his watch. He would give them a five-minute start, then head for his final rendezvous with Duma at the dump before returning to the clinic.

WHEN HE HEARD his name called over the public address system at the Wanderers cricket ground, Mr Jepson of the Standard Bank felt disbelief and guilt in equal measure. He disbelieved because he was certain no one knew he was here, yet he was conscience-stricken because somebody obviously did.

Could it be his wife? Or the office? No, surely not them. He'd been certain he would never be missed on a Wednesday afternoon, what with the bank being closed to the public. He stood up and threaded his way along the row of seats, his apprehension growing.

The two men who waited by the information desk seemed instantly out of place. They looked like people who had had a tiring day's work and resented anyone who hadn't.

'Mr Jepson?' The taller one gave Jepson a momentary view of a plastic card encased in a leather folder. 'I am Colonel Prinsloo of the Security Police. This is Warrant Officer Willemse. We have some questions to ask you. We've had quite some trouble finding you, Mr Jepson.'

'Security Police? What on earth do you want with me?'

'Nothing to do with you personally, sir,' said the man called Willemse, with rather more grace than his superior. He took Jepson's arm and led him away from the desk. 'Your general manager put us on to you. It's about a sum of money that was transferred from the Handelsbank Bauer in Switzerland just a week ago, and converted to South African currency by your department. We need to know where it went.'

'Handelsbank Bauer? I don't ...' Jepson recollected himself. 'Look here, old boy, there's the question of confidentiality involved. I can't just go telling you our customers' business.'

'We do have statutory powers in these matters.'

Jepson shook his head in sorry wonder. 'All right. As far as I know we have only one customer who receives money from that source. His name is Patrick Marriner.'

Colonel Prinsloo gave Willemse a long, significant glance. 'And where can we find this Mr Marriner?'

'Well, that I don't know exactly. He's moved out to the Magaliesberg somewhere, but I don't have an address. What's he been up to?'

'I think we'll go back to your office,' said Prinsloo, steering him away, 'and have a good long talk.'

Chapter Thirteen

Mr Jepson was far from happy. If yesterday's experience had made him feel like a schoolboy caught playing truant, today he had more the sensation of being a suspect in a major crime. Two policemen had been waiting for him when he arrived at work and now Warrant Officer Willemse lounged in the chair across from his desk, reading *Die Transvaler*, while a technician fiddled about with a tape recorder plugged into Jepson's phone, two extension lines, and a radiotelephone with an open link to the main Johannesburg exchange.

When his secretary came in with tea she also brought his mail. He glanced through it while he stirred his tea: some news bulletins from the finance houses, the monthly report of the Reserve Bank—and an airmail letter addressed to Mr Patrick Marriner, c/o Mr Jepson. When he turned it over he saw the sender's address printed on the back: Handelsbank Bauer, 8022 Zurich.

Jepson held up the letter. 'It's the one he's been expecting.' He glanced at the date on the envelope. 'December the sixth. Held up by the Christmas rush.'

Willemse had his hand out for the letter and tore it open, extracting a single piece of paper. It was a printed form with details handwritten into it. Willemse studied it for some time, before suddenly making sense of what he saw. 'Ever heard of someone called Frank Rendle?'

'No.'

Warrant Officer Willemse nodded grimly, as though that was no more than he had expected.

'FRANK RENDLE.' Tertius van Straaten was repeating the name blankly five minutes later. 'Who the devil can he be?'

'Well, if the People's Congress are paying him eight hundred thousand pounds, I'm ready to bet it's not for supplying them with paperclips,' said Colonel Prinsloo. 'No, I've no idea who he is, but he's got to be in this job with Marriner.'

'What makes you so certain it involves Kumalo?'

'What else can you imagine them paying money like that for? And just at this time? Taken in conjunction with the leak from Pollsmoor, and with Marriner's arrival here . . . I'm telling you, Mr van Straaten, they're going to try something while Kumalo is out of that prison. And if they have some idea of our real intentions they're going to have to do it before the operation tomorrow morning. That gives us just twenty-two hours to find them. The important thing is to catch these people: that way there's a chance that nobody will be any the wiser about our plans. Come over here and let me show you what we're doing.'

Prinsloo pointed at a large-scale map that had been pinned to the wall.

'Here is the Magaliesberg region, three thousand square kilometres of pretty rough country. There are hundreds of little farms, some of them so hidden away that even the locals couldn't direct you to them. Now, we're only going on what Marriner told this man at the bank, Jepson, about moving out there, and Marriner sounds smart enough to have been deliberately misleading him. On the other hand, somewhere like this could be ideal for his purposes. I've sent thirty of my men there, to look around and ask questions. If we can locate Marriner's place, we'll mount surveillance on it before deciding on the next step. No sense in having a couple of country coppers walk in there and get their heads shot off.'

'Jepson said he thought Marriner had *rented* a farm,' said van Straaten. 'Would he have done that through an estate agent?'

'We're checking on that as well.' The colonel turned away from the map. 'Now, what do we do about this character Rendle? Another foreign mercenary? Rendle doesn't have to be his real name, of course, but since it's all we've got to go on I'd suggest you get your fellows to check the immigration records for the past couple of months. If he's South African, his ID should be on the Population Registrar's file. Takes hours to dig anything out of those people, but we might just get lucky.'

MARRINER DID NOT LEAVE the clinic until nearly four o'clock that afternoon, and then only to find a telephone box a healthy distance away, in the suburb of Rosebank. He fitted the scrambler to the phone before dialling the Zurich number, and Rosenblatt answered promptly.

'Patrick, I have your final instructions from Lusaka, and they're very simple. Once you reach Mozambique you simply keep flying due east until you reach the coast. You use the Ponta do Ouro lighthouse as your marker, turn north for one kilometre and land in a clearing where you'll see a group of white rondavels. It's apparently an abandoned holiday resort of some kind. You'll be met there and escorted north.'

'Ponta do Ouro? That's pretty close to South African territory, isn't it? Why not further north? Further inland?'

'I don't know, Patrick. It's got something to do with the condition of the roads at this time of year, I think.'

'All right. Ponta do Ouro it is. I hope Harry knows what he's doing.'

'I didn't speak to Harry. Lawrence Gumbi has made the arrangements. Harry's been put under restraint of some kind. Gumbi has taken charge.'

'Restraint? In God's name, what's going on among you people?'

'Well, we did railroad the rest of the executive into this, and I never expected them to like it. It needn't change any of your plans. Just be careful. Good luck.'

Marriner put down the phone with a feeling of utter unreality. As though delivering Kumalo and nine other people to Mozambique wasn't going to be difficult enough, the idea that they might not be welcome when they arrived was too grotesque to contemplate.

He had one more call to make, a mere chore, a minor distraction. He disconnected the scrambler and dialled the Standard Bank.

Mr Jepson sounded oddly flustered. 'Mr Marriner! Ah, good. Very good to hear from you. I do believe I've got something for you here at last.'

'Is it a letter?'

'It is. Now, what have I done with it? Could you hold on a moment?'

Marriner waited. Some indistinct clunking and shuffling noises went on as though drawers were being searched. It must have been a good minute before Jepson said, 'Sorry about this, old boy. Got it somewhere. You settled down now? You never did tell me where you were living.'

Marriner was growing impatient. 'Just tell me if the letter was from Switzerland. That's all I need to know.'

'Ah, here it is. Yes, Zurich. The Handelsbank Bauer. Got here this morning. Do you want to come and collect it now?'

'Isn't the bank closed at this hour?'

'Closed to the public, but we can always let you in by the staff entrance. I'll take you out for a drink. Hear how you're getting on.'

Now Marriner knew something was definitely wrong. He didn't speak for several seconds, and there was a heavy silence from the other end.

'I'm in no hurry,' he said. 'Keep the letter. I'll call you.'

'I can always have it delivered, if you'll tell me where you are.'

'There's no hurry.' Marriner put down the receiver. He snatched up the box with the scrambler unit in it and pushed open the door of the phone booth. It was all he could do to prevent himself running to his car. He started the engine and made a wild U-turn into the northbound traffic. What could have gone wrong now? It wasn't Jepson's probing questions that had alerted him so much as the strained cajolery of his manner. The man wasn't much of an actor. Somebody had been using Jepson, and they'd put a trace on the call. Somebody? Who else but the Security Police? Had the letter from Zurich really arrived, or was that merely a ploy to get him to the bank? If it had, it would have Frank Rendle's name on it. How long would it take them to trace Rendle?

As he drove back towards the clinic he found that a strange sort of fatalism had possessed him. What he had started now was unstoppable.

IN JEPSON'S OFFICE the police technician still had his earphones on, but he was shaking his head at Warrant Officer Willemse.

'If only you'd kept him talking for another thirty seconds, Mr Jepson,' Willemse said. 'I'm afraid he caught on, and we lost the trace.'

'Sorry.' Jepson was secretly relieved. He had been a reluctant participant in this, and it had probably showed.

The technician took the headset off. He said, 'All they can tell us is it was a local call, made from the four-four-two exchange area. That covers quite a big chunk of the northern suburbs.'

'So he was calling from Johannesburg? Well, that's something.'

312

WHEN HE GOT BACK to the clinic, Marriner noticed a big motor caravan standing in the car park, close to the administrative building, a military command vehicle thinly disguised with a new coat of dark blue paint. Bristling with radio and radiotelephone antennae, it was in effect a mobile communications centre that would house a miniature operations room and sleeping quarters. It looked out of place among the dozen or so smart private cars, which included Judith's Opel and her father's Jaguar.

He opened the boot of his own car and took out two small pieces of luggage: the airline bag Rendle had given him yesterday and a holdall he had picked up from Duma last evening. As he closed the lid he saw Virgil, the security man, sidling over. 'Help you with those, Mr Davis?'

'No, thanks, I'm fine.' He shouldered the bags and the security man strolled beside him. Marriner had come to recognise Virgil as a lonely young man who lived in something of a fantasy world. Since his arrival as a patient in the clinic, Virgil had been more convinced than ever that this mysterious Mr Davis was acting in some undercover capacity. It suited Marriner to play along with this game.

At the entrance to the Substance Abuse Unit, he turned to face Virgil. 'Are you on duty all night?'

'Sure am.'

'Well, I think you may be seeing a few things happen. No doubt you'll be told something official later. Just between us, everything is not going to be quite the way it looks. I may be needing your help.'

'You've got it, Mr Davis!'

Marriner entered the building. Thick, coffee-coloured Wilton carpeting covered the floors. The nurse on duty in the lobby sat at a simple walnut desk surrounded by brilliantly flowering plants. Marriner's room was at the end of the corridor on the right. It had windows facing east and south, which gave him a view over the valley in one direction and the lawns sloping down to the water garden in the other, with the main building of the clinic only just visible off to one side. It might have been a comfortable hotel room anywhere, with the single exception that its door could not be locked. Alcoholic patients could be trusted only so far.

He placed the airline bag containing the tear-gas and smoke grenades on the top shelf of the wardrobe among his other luggage. Then he unzipped the holdall which Duma had given him, and took out the gun.

It was a Czech-made 7.65-millimetre Skorpion machine pistol. In the bag with it were a short leather sling and four loaded twenty-round box magazines. It was a versatile weapon and as accurate as any of its kind. He fitted the sling and one of the magazines, but kept the metal stock folded forward over the barrel. This way, the gun was only slightly longer and heavier than an ordinary pistol, and almost as easy to conceal.

He slid the gun and the spare magazines deep under his mattress, where his radio transceiver was already concealed.

IN DR ROSE'S OFFICE, Colonel Prinsloo quickly scanned the list of names.

'Are all these people known to you personally?'

'Either to me or to Dr Clooney.'

'And their backgrounds are . . . how shall I say? Respectable?'

Louis Rose sighed. 'What I know about them is their medical histories, Colonel. But if you're looking for an average profile of my patients, I would describe them as white, middle-aged to elderly, and wealthy. They're paying upwards of four hundred rands a day to be here, and they're not paying to be treated like inmates of some internment camp.'

'Yes. All right. I get the picture.'

Prinsloo irritably folded up the list and put it in his pocket. These remaining patients were a source of annoyance to him. There were sixteen of them left now that one wing had been cleared for Kumalo, and Dr Rose had insisted that they were not to be inconvenienced. The possibility that the Congress had managed to infiltrate the clinic had not escaped Prinsloo, and for that reason he had arranged for the vetting of its staff. The patients were a different matter. This group of well-heeled alcoholics and recuperating invalids constituted a gap in the security net he was tightening about the place.

Well, he would have to rely on Rose's assurances. He said, 'Just as long as they understand that there will be certain restrictions . . . '

He left the office. On the way out he caught Rose's daughter avoiding his eye as she stood with the Coloured receptionist Yvonne behind the reception desk. A hostile one, he had always felt, but too scared actually to make any trouble. Just outside the building he met an earnest army major who had just completed his inspection of the perimeter. The major would be in charge of the detachment of troops appointed to guard the place, a hundred and fifty men in all, quartered under canvas in a field half a mile down the road. Half of these men would be on sentry duty at any one time, together with a Security Police detachment and a squad of elite anti-terrorist commandos. A hundred and ten men would surround Kumalo day and night. In addition, barriers would be set up on all roads approaching the clinic and pickets would be posted in the surrounding veld. It was a textbook operation. But maybe this man Marriner had read the textbooks too.

AMONG THE TASK FORCE of Security Police detectives who had spread out into the Magaliesberg, two had been detailed to make enquiries at estate agents' offices. They had called at Labuschagne & Son in Muldersdrift shortly after lunch and found that young Mr Labuschagne was out showing a property to a client. When they returned just before five o'clock they were confronted by a locked door and a notice announcing that the office had closed early for the holiday weekend.

'Do we forget about it?' asked Constable Smit.

'I don't think Colonel Prinsloo would like us to forget about it,' said

Sergeant Brink. 'We've been running around since seven this morning and come up with nothing. Colonel Prinsloo does not like negative information. This Labuschagne has got to live somewhere. Let's go and find him.'

THERE WAS NOTHING to stop Rifleman Blikkies Steyn applying for an evening pass and strolling out of the front gates of the Lenz army camp after supper, but he didn't want the time of his departure to be remembered. Instead, he walked to the boundary fence, to a point hidden behind a stores building. He tossed his kitbag over the wire and followed it, scaling the eight foot of barbed wire with a natural agility reinforced by his tough training. He dropped to the ground, retrieved the kitbag and moved quickly into the cover of an adjacent field of ripe mealies. In a small clearing among them he changed into the clothes he had brought in the bag: safari tunic, shorts, long socks and polished shoes. Dressed like that, he knew, he would have no difficulty in hitching a lift.

He stuffed his army boots, shirt and trousers into the kitbag, being careful not to cut himself on the razor-sharp panga that it concealed.

THEY HAD BROUGHT a wheelchair to his cell, but Kumalo refused it. From the way he strode down the long corridors of the prison you might almost imagine he owned the place. He had shown no surprise when Dr Els had given him an hour's notice of their departure; he had merely asked what he needed to bring, and now he was dressed for the journey in the plain white shirt and fawn slacks they had given him, and carried his own small suitcase.

Only when the western gate was finally swung open and he stepped outside did Kumalo pause, breathing deeply in the warm, fresh air. The sun had sunk behind the sharp spine of the Cape mountains, leaving a soft iridescent light over farmlands rich with summer greenery. Obviously Kumalo's senses were assailed by all this; he looked almost giddy.

'Are you all right?' Dr Els asked.

'I'm all right.'

They set off again, round a corner of the building to the helicopter pad where the Super Frelon stood. A mobile stairway had been wheeled up to the cabin door. Kumalo shrugged off Dr Els's offer of help.

'Take it easy,' Els cautioned him. 'You're supposed to get all the rest you can. They want you good and fresh for the morning.'

They were met by a flight sergeant who pointed them to two seats facing the door. Twenty soldiers and policemen were harnessed into seats down either side of the narrow gloomy cabin, craning their necks for a look at Kumalo as he sat down and the flight sergeant strapped him in.

'Well, where are we off to? It can hardly be a secret any longer.'

'Ysterplaat Air Station,' said Els. 'And from there to Johannesburg.'

The airman slid the cabin door shut and fastened it, then scrambled forward into the cockpit. A moment later the main rotor began to spin, its dull churning sound rising to a high-pitched whine. Dr Els had never flown in a helicopter before, but the nervous knot in his stomach had little to do with any fear of flying. He dreaded the thought of what was to happen tomorrow. It wasn't that Els couldn't accept the necessity of the thing: he was an Afrikaner, and the survival of his tribe could almost be said to be at stake here. He simply wished he did not have to be a part of it.

The helicopter began to rise. They were on their way.

SEVEN O'CLOCK was the most popular time for dinner at the clinic. When Dr Rose entered the dining room at ten minutes past the hour he found ten or eleven of the remaining sixteen patients present, the others being either confined to bed or out for the evening.

Heads turned at his arrival. Louis Rose smiled greetings as he passed the dozen small tables and turned to face them from one end of the room.

'Good evening. Please don't let me interrupt your meal. I just have a brief announcement to make. We're expecting a rather important new patient later tonight. Important enough to need a number of bodyguards. I simply want to set your minds at rest, because you'll notice a certain amount of security force activity about the place. I would like you to remain in your own rooms as always, from ten o'clock onwards.

'Tomorrow you may use the facilities of the clinic as usual, and you may come and go as you please. However, you will find that there are guards on the gate who may want to confirm your identity. These people are under orders to treat you with courtesy and respect, and I ask you in turn to co-operate with them. If you have any complaints at all, please do not hesitate to bring them to my attention. Do you have any questions?'

'Only one,' said Mr Ahlers, who was sharing a table with Marriner. 'Who's the big news?'

'Ah, that's something I'm afraid I can't disclose at the moment.'

Rose apologised again for the interruption and departed, leaving a subdued murmur of speculation behind him. Marriner attended to his dinner. He had no idea when his next meal would be and he needed all the energy he could get. He drank three cups of strong coffee, listening the while to some risqué stories from Mr Ahlers, and then went back to his room. Judith joined him there a minute later.

'Here.' She produced a big Chubb deadlock key from her handbag. 'That's the master key that will open the outer doors to all the buildings, including the back entrance to the operating theatre.' She was brisk and impersonal, and now handed him a small phial of tablets. 'These are Benzedrine. Take a couple if you feel sleepy. They'll keep you alert. I have to leave now. I'll drop my car in town. I'll switch on the transmitter at midnight. Is there anything else I should do?'

'Yes, Judith. You could talk to me not as though you were leaving messages on an answering machine. How are you feeling?'

'All right.' She looked anything but all right, her face paler than ever, dark rings under her eyes and her mouth drawn into a colourless little line. 'I'm afraid of losing my nerve. I feel sick all the time.'

'That's natural enough. Try to eat. Get whatever rest you can. Tomorrow all you have to do is be in the right place at the right time. You haven't picked up any clues about what they really intend to do?'

She shook her head. 'It's not just the mechanical details. I can handle those. To you this is a job, but to me it's still kind of... treachery, I suppose.' She seemed to want to say something more, but couldn't find the words. 'Good night, Patrick. Good luck.'

IMMIGRATION CONTROL had been quick to respond to the request from the National Intelligence Service. By lunchtime that day they had been able to report that no one by the name of Rendle had entered or left the country during the past six months. This news did not surprise Colonel Prinsloo. He had better hopes of the office of the Population Register in the Department of the Interior.

It had been just before five o'clock that afternoon, therefore, before they came up with a likely prospect: a Francis James Rendle, in his mid-twenties, with an address at the holiday resort of Port Shepstone on the Natal south coast. It seemed an odd spot for the man they were seeking, but Prinsloo had immediately ordered two officers to be dispatched from Security Police headquarters to follow up the lead.

Finally, at eight o'clock, the men put in their report, speaking to Prinsloo direct on the radiotelephone in his caravan behind the clinic. They had found the address, they told him, but they had not found Francis James Rendle. They had been directed instead to a small tourist hotel that was run by his father. They were estranged from each other, and hadn't been in touch for several years. The last thing the father had heard of him was a story about his being kicked out of the air force and being made to do his national service in the army.

'What do you make of that?' Prinsloo demanded when he had put down the phone. 'He's in the army! For all we know he could be one of the guards coming into this place a couple of hours from now.'

'Not too likely,' said Warrant Officer Willemse. 'They're a company that just got back from South West Africa. They knew nothing about this assignment until this morning.'

'OK, then, he's somewhere else, and that could be even more worrying. Now, I suppose, we have to get the Defence Department to check *their* records. More bloody red tape!'

While Willemse got on the phone, Prinsloo stepped outside. Night had only just fully fallen, one of those luminous starry Highveld nights that made the shadows move if you looked at them for too long. He still had no reason to believe that anything could go wrong. Experience had taught him to put faith in the feelings in his bones, however, and what they were telling him was that someone out there was planning to outwit him.

Chapter Fourteen

At a couple of minutes to eleven Marriner heard the arrival of the convoy, which comprised an armoured car at each end, with four police cars and a truckload of soldiers sandwiching the van. They entered the clinic with only a low growling of powerful engines and then a quiet opening and shutting of vehicle doors, a flurry concentrated round ward A, the one they had cleared for Kumalo. Once he heard the clear tones of Dr Rose calling out something about a blood-pressure gauge. Presumably the patient was being examined before being settled down for the night.

After a few minutes he lay back on his bed in the dark. Luckily there had been several patients still up and about half an hour ago, when the first shift of guards had arrived to seal the clinic, so he'd been able to observe them through the windows of the reading room. He estimated their numbers at between seventy and eighty, and he knew there would also be a substantial guard in and around Kumalo's ward.

Reassuringly, he had not heard the sound of any dogs: there were difficulties about employing dogs in unfamiliar territory, where everyone was a stranger and every scent was new. The luminous dial of his watch told him, unbelievably, that it was still only a quarter-past eleven.

WHEN JUDITH PARKED her red Opel in Gold Street she saw that the taxi she had ordered was already waiting twenty yards ahead, opposite the Village Main Hotel. She got out and locked the door. It was a bit like abandoning a much-loved pet. She walked to the hotel entrance, paused in the light there for a few moments, then left the building and crossed the street to the taxi, making it look as though she'd just come out of the hotel.

When she reached her flat at ten to twelve, she prepared a pot of strong coffee, then went through to the living room and phoned the same taxi firm, ordering a car to collect her at six thirty in the morning. All her actions seemed mechanical now. She went to her bedroom and dithered over what clothes she should wear tomorrow. Still undecided, she returned to the living room.

She stared at the radio base unit on the sideboard, then checked her watch. At exactly half a minute to twelve she walked over and switched it on. It made a brief buzzing sound as it warmed up, then settled down to a low hum. A few moments after midnight it crackled into life, and suddenly Marriner's voice filled the room.

'Unit One to base,' he said. 'Are you there? Over.'

She turned down the volume knob, pressed the transmit button and said breathlessly into the microphone, 'Here!'

'Very good. Thank you.' His voice was as impersonal as an airport announcer's. 'Unit Two, come in, please.'

'UNIT TWO. We're OK.'

Rendle stood in the shadow of the squad's own eight-bed hut, speaking down into the walkie-talkie concealed beneath his combat jacket. Across the road, in the vehicle park, the armoured convoy that would leave for Pretoria in two hours' time stood gleaming under the floodlights. The camp was alive with activity so nobody was taking any notice of him.

'That's good. Unit Three?'

'YEAH. THREE HERE.'

The squad were officially snatching a few hours' sleep before they set off, but each driver was responsible for seeing to his vehicle, which had given Brakpan the excuse to lurk in the rear of the Saracen.

'Right. Unit Four, can you hear me?'

'UNIT FOUR. I hear you.'

In a corrugated-iron shanty in Alexandra township, Duma sat at a table surrounded by half a dozen young black men. They were very serious young men. All of them were soldiers of the People's Congress; all of them were wanted, as he was, and would be putting their lives on the line tomorrow on the say-so of that anonymous voice. Marriner should be grateful for such unquestioning trust.

'Unit Four, OK. Stand by.'

'UNIT FIVE? Are you in place?'

'Unit Five, yes.'

Blikkies Steyn's place was lying flat on his stomach beneath the thorn bushes at Rietvlei Farm, on a slight rise close to the river and fifty yards from the house. He had made it here before eleven o'clock, creeping through the bush along the riverbank, keeping well clear of the guards who prowled the perimeter of the nuclear reactor. From this spot he could observe all the likely approaches to the farm, especially the track leading down from the reactor.

'ALL RIGHT,' said Marriner quietly into his radio. 'Everybody's in place. We switch off now and keep radio silence until minus five hours. In case of emergency, but *only* emergency, I will try to switch on for one minute only every half-hour, on the half-hour. If you don't get me, try half an hour later. All clear, I hope. Over and out.'

He turned off his set and breathed a grateful sigh. He was glad above all that Blikkies Steyn had made it to the farm. Everything there was evidently normal. Ever since he'd spoken to Jepson he had been worried that they might trace him to the farm. The Magaliesberg was a big area, but they would sooner or later track him down there.

A few minutes earlier he had heard the night nurse moving down the corridor, quietly opening the doors to check on her patients. Once she was satisfied that everyone had settled down, she would stay at her post in the lobby for the rest of the night.

Outside, after the brief activity surrounding Kumalo's arrival, the rest of the clinic had quietened down too. It was time for Marriner to go on the prowl.

He had already changed into a dark sweatshirt, black lightweight corduroy trousers and plain grey running-shoes. Now he pulled on black cotton gloves and a knitted balaclava, leaving the smallest possible area of skin exposed to reflect the starlight. He went to the east-facing window, already half-open, and carefully eased it wider. Then he stood beside it, waiting for Virgil's arrival.

He had kept track of the security man's patrolling patterns and knew that he passed by this end of the building every twenty minutes or so. This time he was right on cue. Earlier, Virgil had shown a brisk sense of purpose, anticipating some important role for himself in these goings-on; now he moved in a disconsolate slouch, entirely excluded from the arrangements.

The young man paused at the corner of the building and then passed out of sight. Marriner waited for only a few seconds more before he swung his legs over the windowsill and dropped swiftly to the ground.

He was at the base of a deep triangle of shadow thrown from the building by the main outdoor lights. Beyond it he could just make out the two nearest sentries, pale against the background of pine trunks that obstructed the view of the fence. They met, they turned, they sauntered past, while Marriner counted. Thirty seconds until they both reached the end of their beat and turned again. Thirty seconds with their backs to each other, but say twenty to be safe.

PRINSLOO AND ELS had been waiting for Dr Rose in the reception area. When he eventually turned up he was obviously in a hurry to leave, and he showed them out and locked the front door of the building behind him.

'Well, that's it for now. The patient is settled and in good shape for the operation. From what I've seen of the latest X-rays the hormones have considerably reduced the tumour, so I see no reason to expect any complications. My surgical team and I will be here at seven thirty. Are your quarters comfortable, Els?'

'Yes, they're fine, thank you.' Els had been given a room at the end of the ward that accommodated Kumalo and his guards. Prinsloo would be sleeping in his caravan, if he slept at all.

'I'll say good night, then. Just try to remember that I want the routine of the clinic disrupted as little as possible.'

Rose walked off towards the car park. The other two watched him leave. Prinsloo said, 'You can have the stuff you need any time you want.'

'Not yet. I want to be certain everything is quiet.'

They parted and went their separate ways across the grounds. When he reached the caravan, Prinsloo found Willemse just finishing a conversation on the radiophone.

'Got something out of the army at last, Colonel. There's a Corporal F. J. Rendle with the Fourth Armoured Infantry Battalion, based out at Lenz, about forty kilometres from here. He sounds like the one we want.'

'Just a corporal?'

'He used to be an air force pilot. Got discharged, just as his father said. Something to do with refusing a combat mission in Angola.'

'Ah, now that makes more sense. A bad apple, Willemse. You'd better get out there, boy. Ask the military police to detain him till you arrive.'

As Willemse left the caravan, Prinsloo grabbed the telephone. Those lazy bastards who were supposed to be searching the Magaliesberg had come up with absolutely nothing. He checked his watch: twenty to one.

IN THEIR TEAMS of two and three, the detectives had drifted back during the late evening to the headquarters set up for them in the small town of Brits. They had put their best endeavours into the search for Marriner, whatever Colonel Prinsloo might think. They had traversed the hills by car and on foot, they had visited a couple of hundred farms, they had questioned the owners of little wayside shops and garages, but they had found no one who remembered seeing a foreigner of Marriner's description.

Towards the end of the evening a crowd of them drifted over to the Brits Hotel to catch the bar before it closed. A group of safari-suited farmers sat at another table, talking in loud, confident voices.

At one o'clock Constable Smit sat nursing his fifth glass of brandy. As the youngest of the security policemen he felt slightly left out of the boozy reminiscences of the older men and had tuned himself in idly to the conversation across the room. This was of no interest to him either, until the mention of the name Labuschagne made him sit up and pay attention.

Smit nudged the arm of Sergeant Brink beside him.

'...en hy bring die Engelsman saam met hom wat'n plaas soek...'

Brink and Smit stood up together. Twice this evening they had called at the bachelor cottage where the estate agent Labuschagne lived, both times getting no answer at the door. It hadn't seemed to matter much, it was one more dead end among many, but here now was someone talking about him, and about an Englishman looking for a farm.

'Excuse me.' Sergeant Brink reduced the farmers to silence. 'Did you say something about Labuschagne? The estate agent? From Muldersdrift?'

'Fanie Labuschagne, that's right.' The man who'd been doing the talking looked at the ID card Brink flashed at him. 'What about him?'

'We can't find him. He's not at home.'

The farmers looked at each other incredulously. 'Of course he's not,' said one of them. 'He spends his weekends down at the dam.'

WHEN THE ROLL CALL was taken at one thirty, prior to the departure of the armoured-vehicle convoy from Lenz, the absence of Blikkies Steyn was treated only as mildly puzzling. He was considered a conscientious soldier; there had to be some explanation. Corporal Rendle suggested to the lieutenant who commanded their troop that Blikkies might have taken an evening pass at the last minute. He might have had an accident or been delayed outside the camp. Hadn't they better check with the police and hospitals? The lieutenant thought that sounded a bit drastic. Rifleman Steyn would be logged as AWOL until he turned up with some account of himself, and in the meantime there were other things to think about.

Five minutes later the squad were taken off guard when two red-capped military police staff sergeants appeared in the doorway of their hut.

'Corporal, come with us.'

Rendle straightened up from where he'd been bending at the foot of his bed. 'I think you're mistaken. If you're looking for Rifleman Steyn, he still isn't here.'

'No, Corporal. We want you. You're under arrest.'

Rendle stood at the end of the short aisle between the beds. His face was blank, and there was nothing in his demeanour to suggest anything but puzzlement. Confident of their authority, the two MPs moved forward.

It was only when they came fully into the room that they sensed the threat that surrounded them. Younis the Greek slammed the door shut, and Carver and Fish took the MPs from behind, clamping their hands over their mouths and ramming bayonets against their ribs.

'I still think you're making a mistake,' said Rendle.

JUST BEFORE TWO O'CLOCK Marriner returned to his room. Instead of climbing back in he waited for Virgil to appear, and when the security man came round the corner he gave a low hiss.

'Hey!' Virgil started. 'Who's that?'

'Me. Keep your voice down.'

Virgil came uncertainly towards him. 'Mr Davis! What are you doing out here?'

'What do you suppose, Virgil? Keeping an eye on things. It's called counterintelligence. Making sure that everyone is reliable. Nobody knows what I'm here for, except the top brass. And now you, of course.'

Virgil gave a satisfied sigh. Everything he had ever thought about Marriner was justified. 'What do you want me to do?'

'Just carry on as you are. I may have other instructions later.'

'Right you are, Mr Davis.'

Virgil shuffled away, and Marriner climbed through the window.

OUTSIDE THE GATE of the Lenz military camp, Warrant Officer Willemse had to pull off the road to let a convoy of armoured vehicles by, great ugly shapes looming at him out of the dark behind their blazing headlights. The boom of the gate came down behind them, and Willemse had to get out of his car and show his ID to the sentries. He explained that the duty officer of 15 Provost Company of the military police was expecting him. When the corporal in charge had telephoned ahead and got no reply, he escorted the visitor to the office himself.

It wasn't until twenty past two that they found the two staff sergeants strapped down to a pair of barrack-room beds in the dark, with their mouths stuffed full of army-issue khaki underpants.

IT HAD TAKEN AN HOUR to drive from Brits and then hunt along the shores of the lake for the spot where Fanie Labuschagne had pitched his tent. It took another few minutes to rouse him from sleep, and it was two thirty when three cars packed with detectives drove him up to the gates of the Pelindaba nuclear reactor.

'My God,' said Sergeant Brink softly as the headlights picked out the barbed-wire fence, and the guardhouse. 'This is about the last place on earth we would have come looking.'

Their arrival caused some alarm on the reactor site, and now there were a dozen guards gathered round the gate, telling their stories. What emerged was confirmation that Marriner had taken up residence on the farm: he had even shown his passport to identify himself. He had spent last weekend there with a crowd of younger people, but nobody had seen him since Tuesday.

Sergeant Brink got some idea of the layout of the farm from the guards. To surround the place completely would take many more men than he had with him, but it seemed imperative to look it over at once. He ordered one carload of men back to the road to check out the approach up the river, and another group to fan out along the fence dividing the farm from the reactor. When they had all moved off he pulled the snub-nosed Smith & Wesson revolver from his armpit holster and said to Constable Smit, 'Come. You and I are going for a walk.'

FOR TONIGHT'S PURPOSES Lightning had fixed the Saracen's radio so that it could both receive and transmit. At around two thirty the routine hubbub of traffic between the convoy and the base at Lenz had suddenly died down. When he reported in he was told abruptly to maintain position at the rear of the convoy.

'Something's up!' he yelled back to Rendle in the turret. 'What the hell has gone wrong? Why did they come looking for you, Frank?'

'No way of knowing.' Rendle glanced at his watch. 'No way of finding out, either, not until the next commercial break.'

They were moving round the southern fringe of Johannesburg now, nearing the place where he would have to leave them.

'Here you go, Frank!' Brakpan shouted.

He saw the motorway exit just ahead. The vehicle was beginning to slow, Brakpan gradually easing off the accelerator, not wanting to fall too far behind the rest of the convoy. Rendle scrambled out of the turret, clutching the duffle bag that contained his Uzi gun and his walkie-talkie, balancing on the roof and bracing himself for the leap to the ground. The vehicle jerked, knocking him off balance. Instead of jumping he went over the side in an uncoordinated sprawl, arms and legs flailing, letting go of the bag. He managed to land on his feet and roll with the impact but felt his right ankle twist beneath him as he fell. He heard a crunching sound as the vehicle passed by, a sound he could not identify. He scrambled to his knees, but when he tried to stand the ankle gave under him. He crawled in a panic for the edge of the motorway. Headlights picked him out as he reached up to cling to the metal crash barrier, and a car went roaring by. He saw its wheels pass either side of a dark flat object lying in the road.

It was the duffle bag. The Saracen had driven over it.

Hugging the crash barrier, Rendle hauled himself to his feet. His right foot was a mass of pain, but he guessed that the ankle was no more than badly sprained and he gritted his teeth and forced himself to put some weight on it. The ankle was a handicap, but not an immobilising one. The duffle bag was a different matter. Another car went by, its lights pinning him to the barrier again. He had to get off this road!

He let go of his support and hobbled to the centre of the motorway. He seized the bag and stumbled back with it just in time to avoid another car. Then he began limping along the roadside towards the exit.

In a couple of minutes he had made it down to the darkened streets of the Village Main area and found Judith's car. Rendle opened the boot and checked that the suitcase and flying bag were there with his two changes of clothes, his helmet tucked separately into one corner. Then he unlocked the driver's door and slid behind the wheel. He opened the duffle bag.

It was every bit as bad as he had feared. The Saracen's wheels had crushed the radio beyond any hope of repair. They had left the body of the submachine-gun intact but had squashed the metal pistol grip and the loaded magazine it held, rendering the weapon all but useless.

He found three or four shells that remained undamaged and slipped them into the pocket of his combat jacket. He shoved the bag, the gun and the ruined walkie-talkie under the passenger seat and drove off. His ankle was now painfully swollen inside his boot, making it clumsy to operate the car pedals. He might be able to bluff his way through the few minutes in which he would need the gun, but without the radio he would be out of contact with Marriner and the rest of them until the very moment of the rendezvous at the farm. At least there was still time to warn them of this, with a phone call to Judith, but it left no margin for error.

BLIKKIES HEARD THE MEN approaching up the riverbed long before he caught sight of them, three or four men moving with a strained attempt at silence. Soon he heard the others, too, coming stealthily down the track

324

towards the farmhouse, and after a while he spotted them, two dark figures outlined against the reflected starlight behind them. Blikkies felt his heartbeat quicken but he knew he was safe where he lay, screened by an impenetrable thicket of thorns. He heard the other men passing behind him now, just a few yards away, and then saw them move round the open space to join up with the other two.

More men emerged from the bush on the hillside to make about a dozen in all, spreading out now to surround the old shack at close range. Four of them sneaked up to the porch, and a few seconds later there was a sudden barrage of noise: the splintering of wood as the flimsy door was smashed down, threatening shouts, feet pounding on the floorboards. Torches were turned on and the men began chattering excitedly in Afrikaans as the tension ebbed. Blikkies might have found the whole thing amusing if it hadn't been for the terrible knowledge that somehow they had found out about the farm. He was sure Marriner had left no clues behind him as to the purpose for which the farm was being used, but having discovered his hide-out they were unlikely to go away and leave it.

Blikkies allowed himself a glance at his watch. It was a quarter to three. One of the men was reporting in on a hand-held radio now, and the volume of its talkback discouraged him from any temptation to use his own. He had time in hand. He could only wait and see what happened.

THE CONVOY HAD JUST PASSED the twenty-kilometre mark north of Johannesburg when Nicky Flynn in the turret spotted a string of headlights behind them, moving at well over the speed limit.

'Behind us!' he yelled down into the cab. 'Cops, I think.'

Brakpan glanced in his wing mirror. Beside him Lightning said nervously, 'What you going to do, man?'

'We'll wait and see. Play it by ear.'

The radio from Lenz had been ominously silent for the past ten minutes. They'd known that the column would be stopped—it was only a matter of where and when. Their hide-out was only three miles ahead, reached via the next exit but one from the motorway.

Nicky Flynn gripped the coaming of the turret and watched the lights approaching. There were three cars led by two motorbikes. Within a minute they had him fixed with their headlights, and now the cars reduced their speed and kept a hundred yards behind while the two motorcyclists roared past the Saracen to the head of the convoy. They were military policemen, their white gauntlets flapping as they signalled to the leading vehicle.

The convoy began to slow. At the same time two of the cars crept up behind the Saracen, the other swinging out into the centre lane, drawing slowly level with it. 'They're going to box us in,' said Lightning.

Brakpan shifted down through the gears. He'd been sticking close to the Saracen in front of them, but now he applied the brakes and dropped back a little. He glanced in the mirror again. The cars were close enough to be identifiable as police Chevrolets.

'Huh! Tin cans!' he said contemptuously.

The rest of the column halted, and he brought the Saracen to a stop, leaving a ten-yard gap between it and the next vehicle. In the rear of the wagon, Carver, Fish and Younis could only wait in a tense silence.

Brakpan gave Lightning a grin, then shouted to Nicky, 'Get your head down if you don't want to lose it! We're going to burn these bastards!'

Nicky ducked into his seat beneath the turret. Just as the doors of the cars burst open and cops with guns in their hands came swarming out, Brakpan engaged first gear and drove forward, halting just a few inches short of the Saracen in front. In one fluid movement he double-declutched and changed gear again, reversing now, gathering speed over the ten-yard gap as the police scattered in sudden alarm.

The flat armoured rear of the Saracen smashed into the front of the leading Chevrolet, crushing its light bodywork like tinfoil before it ploughed into the car behind it. With terrible shrieks from the tearing metal, Brakpan went on bulldozing them backwards for several yards before rocking the wagon to a halt. In an instant he was in forward gear again, swinging out into the centre lane, clipping the other car aside like a toy and charging past the rest of the convoy.

There were a couple of bursts of wild gunfire from behind them, and they heard the thud of bullets flattening against the armoured rear doors. Inside the vehicle, the two collisions had been felt as no more than sharp jolts. Brakpan raced past the astonished MPs at the front of the column, pushing the Saracen up to its top speed of forty-five miles an hour.

At that moment they heard the overlapping wails of a pair of sirens starting up as the MPs began to give chase on their motorbikes. Brakpan reached the next motorway exit in a couple of minutes, and flung the Saracen down the ramp, slowing it marginally on the secondary west-bound road, looking for a suitable point to leave it. They were in a pocket of sleeping suburbia just here, but soon it gave onto a tract of open veld, grassy and rocky, shining palely under the starlight. Brakpan swung off the road and then they were bumping up a slope over broken ground where no ordinary vehicle could possibly follow, leaving the lamps of the motorbikes flashing impotently behind them.

Brakpan switched off the Saracen's lights and guided it by the glow of the stars. The vehicle was at home out here.

MARRINER FINALLY TOOK two Benzedrine tablets at twenty-five past three, having caught himself falling into a doze. He had thought he was too worried for sleep. Neither Rendle nor Blikkies had responded to his scheduled radio call at three o'clock, and from the squad he had got an excited account of an attempt to arrest Rendle. At least the squad were all right. They'd been approaching their hideout at the time of the call, and he guessed they were safely tucked away there now. It meant, however, that only Duma's plans and his own seemed to have proceeded without mishap.

Of the two who had failed to report, he wasn't sure which concerned him more. Probably Blikkies. It was clear that Rendle had been traced through the letter to the bank, but luckily he had got away with his squad from the camp. If Rendle didn't call in at four, that would be the time to start worrying. As for Blikkies . . . well, he'd come through good and clear at midnight, so perhaps something had gone wrong at the farm.

He ceased his musing with a start and looked at his watch. It was within a few seconds of three thirty, time to switch on for any emergency calls there might be. He groped for his walkie-talkie, clicked it on and almost immediately heard the crackle that signified a transmission beginning.

'Patrick?'

It was the one voice he had not expected to hear. He pressed the transmitter button.

'Not my name. Please,' he whispered urgently. 'Over.'

'Sorry,' she said. 'Listen. I've had a call from Fr—from Unit Two. He's had an accident. His radio was smashed, and his gun. He's going ahead as planned, but you won't be able to contact each other. He'll try to phone me later but he can't promise. Did you get all that? Over.'

His mouth had gone dry. 'Listen to me. It's just possible that we may have to change the rendezvous. I can't make a decision until I know more. Did he say when he would try to call?'

'No. Just if and when he can get to a phone. Over.'

'OK.' There seemed nothing else to say. 'Keep in touch.'

He waited for another minute in case there were any more calls, then turned his own set off. He lay down. It seemed as though all the underpinnings of his careful plan were being knocked away, one by one.

LIKE A FIERCE DOG that had been lying in wait for the first passer-by, Colonel Prinsloo turned his anger on Willemse the moment he returned to the caravan. 'Oh, this is bloody wonderful, isn't it? We've lost Marriner, we've lost Rendle, and now we've got a maverick armoured car roaming the countryside! Tell me, Willemse: are they smart or are we just stupid?'

These questions did not seem to require an answer. The two radio technicians cowered in their alcove at the rear of the tiny ops room, and now one of them said tentatively, 'I've got Sergeant Brink at the farmhouse for you again.'

Prinsloo seized the headset he was offered. 'Yes, Brink! Yes, you bloody well stay where you are. I want you and Smit to keep to the house and the rest of your men to stay right back, at a discreet distance. You understand the word *discreet*? Good. I want Marriner to walk in there suspecting nothing, and I want him picked up, together with anyone who's with him. Alive, got it? Yes?'

There was a tap on the door and the army major entered, giving Prinsloo a new focus for his displeasure.

'Well, are your people going to give me the extra men I want?'

'I'm afraid they're making difficulties, sir. A lot of units have been drafted over to Pretoria for this show in a few hours' time.'

'What are you lot, soldiers or parade-ground puppets?' Prinsloo sneered. 'All right. I'm not so sure now that extra men are the answer anyway. What I want are some antitank weapons round this perimeter.'

The major blinked. 'Antitank weapons? Isn't that a bit extreme?'

'I'm feeling a bit extreme, Major.'

FOUR O'CLOCK. No word came from Blikkies, and there was no more news from Judith. Duma reported that he was OK, and the Saracen crew were safe in the disused garage and awaiting their orders.

'Right,' Marriner whispered into his radio. 'The guards are being changed now. We let them settle in, and we make our move at four twenty. There's one stationary picket at the southeast corner, about forty yards out from the fence. You'll have to take him first, then move along the southern fence to where we've agreed to meet. Got all that? Over.'

'Got it. Out.' It was Carver who spoke, Carver who would be in charge of the little patrol about to set off from the petrol station. Marriner switched off his walkie-talkie, took out the machine pistol, and went to the open window. When he was sure there was nobody near the building he lifted his legs over the sill and dropped once again to the ground.

RENDLE HAD DRIVEN Judith's Opel by a roundabout route towards Pretoria. He had a good deal of time to kill before he turned up at the base. As he drew near the city he noticed an unusual amount of traffic, crowds of pilgrims flocking to the Voortrekker Monument for the Day of the Covenant celebrations. Happy enough to be taken for just one more of them, he joined the stream of traffic, turned off with it onto the spur road leading to the shrine itself, and pulled in behind a station wagon from which a family laden with camping equipment were extricating themselves. After locking the car, he tagged on to the crowds moving towards the monument and the vast amphitheatre where the *volk* were gathering. The pain in his ankle had died down though he still walked with a limp. The air was cool, and he shivered slightly in the casual slacks and sports shirt that Judith had packed for him, his discarded army fatigues stuffed with the rest of his gear into the boot of the Opel.

THE PICKET OUT by the clinic fence had settled himself comfortably on a flat rock overlooking the valley. His gaze was naturally drawn to the moving lights of cars on the distant motorway, so that when he looked back over the empty grey-black terrain in between he had to blink once or twice to get it into focus. This was also his first shift of guard duty, and he'd been out here only twenty minutes, so he wasn't yet used to the small night noises of the veld.

Carver rose from a yard behind him. He jammed one hand over the sentry's mouth. The other went under his armpit and seized his right hand and the rifle stock, pinning them to his chest. Carver pulled the man against him in a tight bear hug, containing his struggling limbs, as Fish stood up from the boulders and came at a light run up the slope. He hit the soldier with the butt of his revolver, at the base of the skull just below the edge of his beret, and he sagged forward in Carver's arms.

Younis and Nicky Flynn rose from among the rocks and picked their way forward. They took the unconscious soldier between them, under the arms and by the ankles, and began to carry him carefully down the hillside.

It took five minutes to reach the little staging area they had chosen beside the Jukskei River, hidden in the deep shadow of its high bushy banks. Lightning was waiting for them there. The man was beginning to groan as they laid him down on a patch of sand, so they quickly gagged him with insulating tape and then tied him with lengths of nylon rope. Younis took off the knitted fisherman's cap he wore and replaced it with the sentry's black beret with its distinctive regimental badge. Otherwise they were identically dressed. Lightning stayed to guard the prisoner while Younis and Nicky set off in different directions up the slope.

When Younis got back to the soldier's perch, Carver and Fish had already moved off on their next job. Younis picked up the carbineer's rifle and took over his position on picket duty. Nicky, meanwhile, was making his way along the hillside to the south, keeping well back from the fence.

TIME SPENT ON RECONNAISSANCE is never wasted. Thus went one of the little maxims that had been drummed into Marriner as a cadet at Sandhurst, and he had since had more opportunities than most to prove its validity. During the hour and a half in which he'd sneaked about the grounds earlier in the night, he had absorbed a good deal of information. The wing which had been cleared for Kumalo was a self-contained building, connected by an enclosed walkway to the operating theatre. The wing was heavily guarded, inside and out, and quite impenetrable.

The one place to which no guards would be permitted access was the operating theatre. According to Dr Rose's schedule, Kumalo would be wheeled there at precisely eight o'clock in the morning. Guards would of course surround the building, but the only people within it would be the patient, Dr Rose, his anaesthetist and pathologist, a government doctor named Els, a theatre sister and two nurses.

On average, there was one sentry every twenty yards round the perimeter, each pair patrolling an overlapping beat of forty yards or so. None was therefore out of sight of any other for more than a few seconds at a time. On one beat along the southern fence, however, a thick clump of ornamental bamboo grew at one end and at the other end lay a gully, about twelve feet wide and eight deep, by which the little stream entered the grounds. The sentries on the far side of the bamboo could not see those on this side of it, and those to the east of the gully did not overlap with those to its west. The two soldiers who patrolled this stretch were, therefore, more vulnerable than any of the others.

Marriner was squatting in the gully when Carver and Fish arrived, belly-crawling up to the fence from the patch of woodland that adjoined it, and gave him a thumbs-up sign. He returned it.

Carver wriggled through a gap in the fencing, and then Fish, and together the three of them crawled downstream until they were in line with the guards. Marriner worked his way a little further on, to where the bank wasn't so high and he had a view of both the sentries. They met halfway and crossed, exchanging some murmured remark. Marriner unslung the machine pistol from his shoulder and clipped on the silencer.

The man approaching the gully stopped and turned, looking back along the perimeter towards his companion. Marriner's gaze followed his. The other sentry was facing away from him but he wasn't moving. He was taking a pee. Marriner raised his hand and signalled frantically to Carver and Fish.

They sprang out of the gully together, and took the nearer guard from behind, struggled for a moment on the edge of the bank before plunging down it with only a faint scraping and a slight splash.

At once Marriner was on his feet and stepping into the open. He stood on the very spot from which the sentry had vanished. He held the machine pistol with its long silencer pointed upwards from his shoulder, so that from a distance it would look like a rifle. Then he began to stroll towards the other guard.

The man was zipping up his trousers as he swung round and ambled forward. Marriner kept in the shadow of the pines as they approached each other. The gap closed and still the man gave no sign of seeing anything amiss about his fellow sentry. He spat casually off to his left. And then, incredibly, they were walking by each other with only five feet between them, the man muttering something, Marriner grunting in reply.

He stopped walking. He turned swiftly, gripping the gun by its barrel and swinging it. At the last instant the guard sensed something and began to turn his head, but the heavy stock of the gun cracked him behind the neck and he dropped like a stone.

In a few moments Fish had arrived and they were dragging the sentry in among the pines, and through the hole in the fence. They took him fifty yards into the woods, where Nicky Flynn waited to take charge of him.

They separated, Marriner leaving the gully to circle back towards his room. He could congratulate himself on a successful half-hour's work. He had two men inside the grounds now, and had neutralised the most important lookout position. The preparations around the clinic were well in hand, but what the hell was going on everywhere else?

FISH AND CARVER, wearing the berets of the sentries and carrying their rifles, resumed patrolling in their place. Once Marriner was on his way, Carver slipped over the fence and took out his wire-cutters. He paced out a distance of ten feet. At either end of this he reached up and snipped through the tough supporting wire at the top. Then he worked his way down the mesh, cutting two strands out of every three on each side, leaving the fence strong enough to remain standing but weak enough for the Saracen to smash through with ease.

DR ELS HAD BEEN PUTTING OFF what he had to do for as long as possible, but now he knew he could delay no further. He got out of bed and pulled on a track suit, remembering to clip to his collar the identity tag that would be needed from now on for everyone permitted within the inner security ring that surrounded Kumalo. He felt foolish in the track suit, since he never took any exercise, but it would explain his moving about so early.

He left his room. The air was filled with the stale smell of cigarettes. Men of the police antiterrorist squad sat lolling back in chairs, cradling submachine guns, just outside his door and halfway down the corridor opposite the room in which Kumalo slept. They gave him jocular greetings. 'Jogging, Doctor? Man, you are keen!'

More guards were seated around the lobby, the night nurse at her desk doing her best to ignore them, and when Els stepped out through the glass doors he saw another dozen slouching shadows against the lighted walls of the building.

The air was cool and bracing. Above the open veld to the east there was just the faintest tinge of grey in the sky as he set off at a brisk trot. Once he was past the dining room he was out of sight of the main buildings, and there he turned right and headed for Prinsloo's caravan.

Chapter Fifteen

Five o'clock. For the first time in two and a half hours, Blikkies Steyn considered it safe to use his radio. After the detectives had broken into the farmhouse they had carried out a cursory search of the surroundings by torchlight, but hadn't come remotely close to his hiding place. Finally, after receiving orders on the radio, most of them had scattered in different directions, leaving just two of them inside the house.

Blikkies could have left at that point, sneaked back down the river, put in a call to Marriner and warned him to forget about the rendezvous at the farm. There seemed a chance, however, that the police would give up their vigil at daybreak, so he had decided to wait.

He had backed his way out of the thorn bushes and set off round the farm, moving with infinite patience, establishing how many cops there were and the exact position of each. He had crept through the bush behind the house, getting close to its thin wooden walls and listening for half an hour to the desultory conversation of the two inside, and the radio messages that went back and forth. Finally, he had returned to his hiding place, collected his walkie-talkie and his panga, and moved a quarter of a mile down the river to be certain he was out of earshot.

He turned the volume down low before switching on the set.

'Unit Five,' he whispered.

'Five! Where've you been, for God's sake?'

Blikkies told Marriner what had happened. There were twelve policemen stationed round the farmhouse and they had orders to stay put indefinitely and to close their net round Marriner or anyone else who showed up. Even more ominously, there seemed to be reinforcements waiting nearby and capable of reaching the farm within ten minutes. It would be madness, he concluded, to bring Kumalo or the helicopter here.

There was silence before Marriner spoke. 'We may have no alternative,' he said. 'Unless I can get a message to Frank, he'll be heading straight there.' He explained that Rendle was unreachable on the radio. 'Is there anything you can do at your end? Anything to distract them?'

Blikkies thumbed the edge of his panga. He glanced up at where the sky was beginning to lighten against the broken outline of the hills. 'Maybe there is something,' he said. 'I'll come back to you.'

'UNIT FOUR?'

'Yes, Four here,' said Duma rather perfunctorily. He could do without these anxious hourly checkups. All night the comrades had been back and forth among the houses of Alexandra, exhorting the people to turn out early on the streets, supervising the making of placards. Others had stockpiled petrol bombs at strategic locations around the township.

'Listen,' Duma said into the walkie-talkie, 'you can take it that everything is OK unless you hear otherwise, all right?'

'Fine. I'll try not to bother you again. Good luck.'

UNIT THREE did not respond.

Brakpan sat rigid with fear behind the steering wheel, listening to the dogs that whimpered on the other side of the steel roller door of the service bay, and to the sharp commands of their handlers. Brakpan knew nothing about dogs. He could only rely on the assurances of Carver that the petrol splashed liberally about the ground outside would deaden their sense of smell. Although the fumes would no longer be noticeable to humans, enough of them lingered close to the ground to cover any human scent.

Thus the theory. In practice he had no way of guessing what the dogs and the men might have discovered, but he heard them circle the building once and then return to the steel door. One of them gave it a kick, and then the padlock was rattled in its staples.

There were three or four men to judge by the voices he could hear. He couldn't catch any of their words, but at a guess they were debating the merits of breaking into the building.

The voices stopped. He heard footfalls on the tarred surface outside, moving away. When he next heard a dog yap it was some distance from the building. After a minute there was no noise at all, and he sagged forward over the wheel in relief. The men had departed. There was work for him, now that dawn was starting to filter through the skylight. There was a new serial number to be painted on the side of the Saracen, there were new number plates to be fitted, there were the spikeboards to load into it. It was only when he had climbed out of the wagon and reached for a spikeboard that he realised how badly his hands were trembling.

THE TWO OBSERVERS on the Soweto rooftop were about to pack it in for the night when the one with the binoculars nudged the photographer and pointed. A car was drawing up outside Nandi Kumalo's house.

'Kaffir taxi,' said the photographer. 'Can you see the number?'

The taxi sign on the car's roof wasn't lit. The driver got out and began to walk up the short pathway to the house but was met halfway by a hurrying unmistakable figure in a dark blazer and skirt.

The photographer's camera motor whirred. The other man pressed his transmitter button. 'Can you copy this, base? Nandi Kumalo is leaving her house in a black Plymouth taxi, registration number TJ 183-986. Message timed at oh-five-three-two.'

They saw Nandi climb into the seat beside the driver, clutching a shopping bag. The doors slammed and the taxi drove past the watchers' house and vanished round the next corner.

'Thank you,' said the man at base. 'Which way is she going?'

'Eastwards. Not in the direction of her office.'

'Very good. I'll pass that on.'

SIX O'CLOCK.

Brakpan had checked in. Blikkies hadn't, but that didn't worry him. Rendle hadn't, and that did.

Marriner had used the hour for a bath and a shave, dressing carefully in a pair of denim slacks and a matching jacket. Now he strolled out of the wing, stood on the steps and inhaled the sharp morning air. A blazing sun was already making its heat felt. Marriner went in search of Virgil, whom he found drinking tea on a little patio behind the dining room.

'There's something I need to check out over at the main buildings, Virgil. I don't want those guards giving me a hard time. Will you come with me and help make it official-looking?'

They set off together, walking past the reception area and skirting round A wing, where the slouching police observed their progress idly but did not challenge them. Virgil's uniform had done the trick. The operating theatre lay just to the southwest. Its main entrance was via a glassed-in walkway from the administrative block. At the rear of the building there was another entrance, a pair of large double doors which Marriner knew opened into a corridor leading round three sides of the theatre itself. He stopped outside these doors and looked around.

Marriner brought out the master key Judith had given him. 'I'm going in for a look round, Virgil. I want you to stay on the lookout here.'

For the first time a look of misgiving crossed the young man's plump, innocent features. 'What d'you want in there?'

'I can only tell you this much. That VIP who came in last night is having an operation this morning. With all these strange people running about it's important to guard against interference, sabotage.'

This argument appealed to Virgil. He said, 'OK. You know you can't go into the theatre itself? It's what they call super-sterile.'

'I'll just poke about the adjacent areas.'

He turned the key and swung one of the doors open. He stepped into a small, white-tiled vestibule with corridors leading off to either side. No one was due here until seven thirty, according to Dr Rose's schedule. Marriner closed the door and relocked it. He moved to the left and turned down a short passageway with a door to either side.

Neither of the rooms was locked. The one against the outer wall contained the theatre's air-conditioning plant. The one across the corridor had sealed windows that looked into the darkened theatre itself. Packed with monitoring equipment, it had interconnecting airtight doors, through which equipment would be passed during operations.

He went back to the vestibule and down the passage. The place that interested him here was the sterile-supply room, where everything that entered the theatre was first rendered aseptic in autoclaves fed with high-pressure steam. Here, too, there was a window looking into the theatre, and a pair of self-sealing doors.

The geography of the place was all just as Judith had described it. Further along this corridor there was access to the main entrance, but he knew he need look no further. He was about to leave the supply room when a movement caught his eye behind the window, and he froze.

Someone was inside the operating theatre.

The room was a dim cavern surmounted by a dome. Some natural light entered the dome through narrow windows at its base, but all that could be seen in the theatre were the dark shapes of the equipment round the operating table. A blurred figure wearing a billowing garment had crossed the room, and now it moved again, bending beside the equipment for a minute. Then it straightened up and paused, as though listening.

Marriner stood in the dark and waited. He had a deep, compelling sense of disquiet. This person had obviously entered the building before he had. He supposed he or she might just be a nurse preparing equipment for the operation, but why go about it so furtively? Had Marriner unwittingly got it right when he'd spoken to Virgil about interference and sabotage?

He watched the figure finally open the doors and leave. Through the window of the room across the theatre he caught sight of it once more as the outer door was opened. It was a smallish man, dressed correctly for the sterile surroundings in a dark surgical gown, cap and face-mask. He closed the door behind him and left.

A sudden strange feeling of inadequacy took hold of Marriner. He needed time to think about this. He had to get out of here before anyone else arrived. He opened the door of the supply room and stepped out into the corridor, just as the other man came round the corner.

They saw each other at the same moment. Marriner walked forward. The other man stepped back a pace, staring at him. Belatedly he decided to challenge Marriner. 'What are you doing here?'

'I was about to ask you the same question.'

'I'm a doctor.'

'What a coincidence. I'm a patient.'

'Look, I don't know how you got here, but it's strictly forbidden ...'

'I suppose that's why you were sneaking around in the dark.'

Marriner stood close to him now and saw he was wearing a track suit with a name-tag on its collar. It said: DR J.H.ELS.

'I couldn't find the light switches. I had some equipment to check.' Els sounded very anxious, but he tried to assert some professional authority. 'I don't need to explain myself to you, whoever you are. Now, if you'll excuse me ...' He tried to push past, but Marriner put a hand out against the wall and stopped him. He remembered Els's name.

'I want to know exactly what you were doing in that operating theatre.'

'It's none of your business. Now let me out, please, or I'll call for those police out there.'

'I don't think you ought to do that, Doctor.'

'Are you threatening me?' Els demanded.

'Not in the way you imagine. What if I told Dr Rose you'd been tampering with the equipment in there?' He watched the reaction on Els's face. 'What if I told him you were going to kill Lincoln Kumalo?'

The doctor's jaw worked convulsively. There was no indignant denial, no more bluster. He couldn't hold Marriner's look and he glanced away. Finally he said, 'Who are you? How do you know about Kumalo?'

'I'm afraid the word got out. You've been sent to kill Kumalo, and I've been sent to stop you.'

'It's too late to stop anything now.'

'I don't know about that, Doctor. All I've got to do is keep you here till Rose arrives, and tell him what I saw.'

Els sighed heavily. His expression was still scared, but there was also something like relief in it. 'Are you saying other people know about this? Kumalo's people?'

'Not the details. But, yes, they know.'

'Then it can't possibly work now. They wouldn't want me to go ahead now.' Els spoke in a rush. 'Everything depended on secrecy. I never wanted any part of it, but they threatened to ruin me.'

'Who are *they*, Doctor?'

'No, no, I can't tell you that.' Els brought himself up short. 'Look, I still don't know who you are, what you want.'

Marriner pulled away from him and leaned back against the wall. 'Let's tell each other exactly what we're both doing in a place like this, Doctor. Let's start with you.' He looked at his watch. 'And let's make it quick.'

IN HIS CARAVAN, Colonel Prinsloo was mystified.

Two surveillance teams were following Nandi Kumalo's taxi as it left Soweto, and their reports were making no sense.

'First of all she goes to that Coloured township, Coronationville,' he told Willemse, 'and picks up a young unidentified female waiting for her on a street corner. Then they drive into a white area, the northern suburbs, and now they're heading for . . . it looks like Northcliff. What the hell takes her to a place like Northcliff?'

'It could all be quite innocuous,' Willemse ventured. It was his private opinion that Prinsloo was slightly obsessed with Nandi Kumalo, unable to believe that her father's revolutionary blood didn't run in her veins.

'Innocuous? Yes, maybe, Willemse, maybe,' he conceded. 'The only thing is, I've known her for twenty years, off and on, and I've somehow always had the feeling that she was too good to be true.'

EVER SINCE DAYBREAK the people had been drifting from the ramshackle houses of Alexandra, along its rutted streets towards a wide rectangle of baked earth that was known as Freedom Square. They had been told that this was to be a kind of counterdemonstration, a rejoinder to the celebrations in which the Boers indulged themselves on this anniversary.

From a fortified police station just outside the township a van, escorted by a truckload of troops, set out to investigate. At the edge of Alexandra they found the road blocked by a crude barricade of timber and old tyres, which was set alight as they approached, and young men emerged from the shanties to pelt the vehicles with stones.

A hundred yards behind the barrier, Duma sat in the sidecar of a motorbike, watching the vehicles back off and hearing the loud squawking of their radios. They were sending for reinforcements. They would find out soon what Alexandra was like when it was angry. He clapped the rider of the bike on the shoulder and they drove off.

JUDITH KNEW SHE HAD DRUNK one Scotch too many.

She wasn't drunk; the whisky seemed merely to have spread a faint layer of confusion over her anxiety, so that when she heard the taxi draw up she thought in a panic that her watch had stopped. A glance at the kitchen clock told her it was only six twenty, so the taxi she had ordered was early.

Well, it would have to wait. She couldn't leave for the clinic too soon. She went out on the balcony of the flat to call down to the driver, and was further muddled when she saw a black face behind the wheel. It wasn't the cab she had ordered, but a township taxi designated for the use of blacks, and now two women were getting out of it and looking up at her.

One was an African woman she didn't know, wearing a business-like tailored maroon blazer and white blouse. The other was Yvonne, the receptionist at the clinic, morning-fresh in a loose sleeveless dress. 'Sorry to disturb you, Judith,' she called. 'Can we come in for a minute?'

'No, no, wait there!' Judith said, remembering with alarm the radio transceiver that glared from the sideboard. 'I'll come down.'

In her empty hallway, the telephone began to ring.

RENDLE TRIED THE NUMBER again, in case he had dialled it wrongly the first time, but once more it rang and rang. After a minute he slammed down the receiver in frustration and left the phone booth.

He sat in the Opel for a minute, thinking. Judith must have left early for the clinic: it was the only possible explanation. Admittedly he had cut things a bit fine. He'd had trouble getting his car out of its parking place near the monument, and then he'd been held up by the military traffic flowing towards Pretoria.

He set off on an aimless crawl around the suburbs, with an hour still to kill and anxiety gnawing at him. He would have to try phoning her later, at the clinic, but if he couldn't make contact he would just have to carry on as arranged.

SEVEN O'CLOCK.

Blikkies called in. Brakpan called in. Marriner told Blikkies he had given up hope of hearing from Rendle now, and that he'd better go ahead and do what he had to do at the farm. For Brakpan he had disturbing news as well: on his way back to the operating theatre he had seen objects being unloaded in the car park which he'd identified as antitank missile launchers. Marriner switched off his radio, left his hiding place in the air-conditioning room and returned to Dr Els in the sterile-supply area.

Els looked both saddened and unburdened, like someone who had just signed a confession after lengthy questioning. 'I don't suppose you've got a cigarette?' he said.

'Afraid not. But it's safe for you to leave now. Won't you be missed?'

'Not yet. They left me to handle this on my own. I was the only one who could do it, and they'll be taking my word that it's been done.'

Marriner nodded. He, too, had to take Els's word for it that he'd undone the damage in the operating theatre. He had no way of checking. The small gas cylinder and its pressure gauges, which lay on the counter beside him, looked identical to the ones Els had replaced on the anaesthesia machine. He thought he knew enough now, however, to trust

Dr Els. He was a man who had kept some moral courage alive beneath layers of guilt and frustration.

'Who supplied you with that stuff?' Marriner asked.

'I've said, I won't tell you any names. The gauges are standard, and I suppose they were doctored by the security people's technicians. I gather the carbon-monoxide mixture was supplied by some state-owned company.' Els patted the cylinder. 'It's a sneaky killer. It prevents oxygen reaching the organs that need it, and the brain is particularly vulnerable. Oxygen starvation will cause global cerebral damage within two minutes.'

The plan, as Els had outlined it, had had a horrible simplicity. Under the normal preoperative procedure, the anaesthetist would give Kumalo his premedication injection about half an hour before surgery began, to make him drowsy and relaxed. Then, in the anaesthetic room, he would be injected with the short-acting barbiturate sodium pentothal, to produce general anaesthesia. On the operating table this in turn would be controlled through a respirator supplying him with a carefully balanced mixture of oxygen, halothane and nitrous dioxide, all drawn from separate cylinders attached to the machine.

It was the third cylinder that Els had switched. Instead of pure nitrous dioxide, the new container held just enough of it to produce its characteristic sweetish smell, but was otherwise filled with poisonous, odourless carbon monoxide. At the same time he had replaced both the gauges of the oxygen supply—the one fitted to the cylinder valve and the one at the head of the tube leading into the patient's windpipe—with gauges that gave false readings. Instead of the standard thirty per cent of oxygen in the mixture, Kumalo would actually be receiving less than half of that.

'Then, why bother with the carbon monoxide?' Marriner had asked. 'Why not just deprive him of oxygen?'

'Because that would be noticed too quickly. Remember, he would have been cut open by this time. A straightforward lack of oxygen shows itself in the blood, which becomes bluer and darker. Carbon monoxide, on the other hand, turns it a very bright red. Between the two, it would balance out to roughly its normal colour. There are other safeguards, of course: the heart rate would increase and the blood pressure would start to fall, but by then he would already be beyond help. Before any remedial action could be taken he would almost certainly be in a coma.'

That had been the intention, baldly stated: not to kill Kumalo, but to damage his brain beyond repair, to turn him into a vegetable. The carbon monoxide would disappear from his system within an hour or two, and there would be no autopsy to discover its presence.

'And you really believed you would get away with that?'

'I was quite certain of it. The point is, it would look like a simple case of anoxia. An accident of this sort does happen once in a while, and it's always due to negligence in monitoring the oxygen supply. I would have replaced the real nitrous-dioxide cylinder later in the morning. There would be an enquiry, naturally, and Dr Rose and his colleagues would be hauled up before the Medical Association, but they would be looking for a malfunction in the oxygen and the answer would be right there, in the faulty gauges. Why look any further? It would go down as an extremely unfortunate accident on the part of a medical team . . .'

'And the government could throw up their hands in horror? And say how awful, particularly since we were just about to release him?'

'I don't know how much the government as a whole knows about it.'

'But they'd be winning at both ends, wouldn't they? They'd be able to let Kumalo go, to live whatever sort of life was left to him, knowing he was no longer a danger to them. Above all, they'd be able to say with their hands on their hearts it wasn't their fault.'

Els shrugged. 'Look, I'd better go. You think you can cover for me?'

'I'll do my best. If this thing comes off, then what happens or doesn't happen in here is going to be the least of anyone's worries.'

'I suppose I should wish you good luck.'

Marriner saw him to the back door. Virgil was no longer about. Virgil had finally gone home, rather reluctantly, after performing one more escort duty to and from Marriner's room. Now Marriner was alone in the theatre buildings, with his radio and his gun and his smoke and gas grenades, all packed into the airline bag. He had chosen the air-conditioning plant as his hiding place. Now he settled down there to wait.

'WELL, WELL, WELL,' said Prinsloo. 'Now what did I tell you?'

His moods had become alarmingly variable, and after coming off the radio phone again he was on a sudden upswing.

'Little Miss Kumalo is now heading in this direction, and who has she got in that Kaffir taxi with her but little Miss Rose?'

'The doctor's daughter?' Willemse said incredulously.

'The same. I must have underestimated that little bitch. But now do you see what this means, Willemse? This is the clincher. This connects Nandi directly with the clinic. Something is going to happen, and they're both in on it. The two of them, Marriner, Rendle . . . we don't need to chase them any longer, man. They're all going to come to us!'

The warrant officer looked thoughtful. 'Tell me how you see the connection between these two women.'

'Nothing direct. Not at first anyway. It all began with Nandi, or at least with the message from the prison. She passed it on to the Congress, and they roped Dr Rose's daughter in to help them. Not difficult, considering her relationship to Joshua Rosenblatt.'

'There's only one reason why they could have wanted her help, Colonel: to find out more about the set-up here. It means they may have detailed knowledge, and they may have had it for some time.'

'All right, infiltration; we've been through all that,' Prinsloo said. 'We've vetted the staff, we're checking the visitors. The patients are lushes or geriatrics, sometimes both. Dr Rose has OK'd them all.'

'But you haven't seen them yourself?'

'Rose is sensitive about keeping them undisturbed. I didn't force it.'

'Things may be different now. Would you mind if I wandered around, had a look at them?'

'If it makes you feel any better. I've got a list of their names here somewhere. Just go about it quietly, you hear?'

AT THE NORTHERN END of the road that ran through Woodvale stood a post office and a small grocery store. Here the Plymouth taxi stopped and Judith and Nandi Kumalo got out.

Judith had cancelled her own taxi and travelled with Nandi. There hadn't been much they'd been able to say in the presence of the driver, however, and now she asked the question that had been nagging her all the way from Northcliff.

'Why do you feel you have to do this?'

'I want to be with my father,' Nandi said simply. 'Whatever happens, I've decided that's where I belong. I want to be part of his struggle.'

'You could leave later, join him abroad. They wouldn't stop you.'

'There's a chance he may not make it. In which case I would never see him alive again. I hope your friend Marriner will understand.'

'I won't see him until . . . well, until it happens. I'll do what I can. You wait here.'

'I'm sorry to impose on you. Thank you.'

If anyone had imposed on her it was Yvonne, she thought, and yet she couldn't be angry with Yvonne either. Yvonne had made the introductions in the forecourt at Northcliff and then set off for home, intending to call in sick, stay clear of the clinic, avoid any hint of involvement. 'I'm a comrade,' she had said unselfconsciously. 'No, I wouldn't have expected you to guess. As Duma says, we have people everywhere.'

Duma was only a name to Judith. Duma was the one that Frank said liked to play games. It transpired that he had approached Yvonne on Monday night, in her parents' home in Coronationville. He had just learned where Kumalo would be, and he had asked her to see to it that Nandi was taken along when her father was brought out. Yvonne had apologised to Judith for the lack of a warning: 'I thought it would scare you off, frankly.'

Judith left Nandi and began trudging up the road. She had about a quarter of a mile to walk to the clinic, and just ahead she could see the roadblock that had been set up, a striped boom flanked by police vans and guarded by soldiers.

DUMA WAS EXHILARATED. Bumped about in the sidecar of the motorbike, touring the outskirts of Alexandra, he felt like a general inspecting his troops. As the bike rocked him round Freedom Square he had a great sense of oneness with the thousands of people who had gathered there.

He hopped out of the sidecar as the bike came to a halt, and strode to the platform set up on the west side of the square. Several of the comrades waited nervously there. Soon the Hippos and armoured cars would come in; it was important to get the people moving before they were surrounded.

He stepped onto the platform and faced them. An expectant hush fell. Few in the crowd knew who this young man was, but they recognised something in his bearing that told them he would speak with authority.

'Comrades!' There was no loudspeaker and he had to bellow. 'I wish there could be a gathering like this in every township today! I wish we could show the white people that we have a history, too. Today is the anniversary of the Battle of Blood River. Every time the Boers commemorate it, what they are celebrating is not their victory but our humiliation. They think they killed our pride, but that is one thing that will never die!'

A low murmur of assent came from the crowd. Behind them he saw the first vehicles of a police convoy nosing cautiously round a barricade.

'Listen! I have an important message from the People's Congress. At this moment Lincoln Kumalo is less than six kilometres from here. He has been brought out of prison, but not so that he can be freed. The government have brought him out to kill him!'

A collective gasp turned within seconds to an angry roar. Duma quietened the crowd. 'We of the Congress know this. Lincoln Kumalo has been brought to a clinic where there is a conspiracy to dispose of him. Can we let that happen?'

'No, no!' they shouted, and pressed around the platform, sticks and clenched fists held aloft.

'Then let's go and show them that we know what they're trying to do!' he yelled, drawing his pistol. 'Let's go and stop them!'

Duma stepped off the platform. The crowd made way for him and then closed in round him, letting him lead them. They began to chant in unison, 'Kumalo, Kumalo!' as they headed in a wide, ragged column along the road, making for the Woodvale Clinic.

RENDLE REACHED THE GATES of the Zwartkop Air Station at precisely seven thirty and found Jumper Cross already waiting for him. Jumper was nervy and agitated. He said brusquely, 'Let's get a move on. We're wanted out there at eight.'

They went into the guardhouse to arrange a pass for Rendle. The MP on duty gave them an odd look. Who the hell had visitors at this time of the morning?

Rendle followed Jumper's car and parked beside it outside the single quarters. He collected his flight bag and helmet from the boot, as well as the duffle bag, and on his way through the lobby he said, 'I've got to make a phone call.'

'Later. I don't want anyone recognising you. Let's get kitted up first.'

PRINSLOO LEFT HIS CARAVAN to meet Judith Rose as she approached the gates. Ten minutes ago the surveillance teams had reported that the Plymouth taxi had dropped both its passengers down the road. Nandi Kumalo had stayed hanging about there and he'd told them to keep watching her; she could be dealt with later. Judith had headed for the clinic. Now Prinsloo stood at the entrance to the car park and stopped Judith with a look.

'Miss Rose. You're going to tell me exactly what's going on here.'

She stared at him. 'I'm afraid I don't understand,' she said.

'I have no time to play games. What is going to happen?' He got no answer. He said, 'Where are Marriner and Rendle? I want to know, now.'

The two names seemed to strike her like blows. She was about to say something but then a car swung in behind her and stopped, and a voice said angrily, 'Colonel Prinsloo!'

He turned to see Dr Rose climbing out of his Jaguar. 'Colonel Prinsloo, just what do you suppose you're up to?'

'I'm afraid I have some questions to ask your daughter.'

'I don't mean that! I'm talking about these rocket-launchers or whatever they are that you've got spread about the place. No sooner is my back turned than you've transformed my clinic into a war zone. I insist you remove them at once.'

'You don't understand, sir,' said Prinsloo. 'There's been a serious security leak and your daughter here is involved. I was about to ask her—' But he was interrupted again, this time by one of the technicians from the caravan. 'Colonel, you're needed at once!'

His tone was so insistent that Prinsloo let himself be drawn aside. The man whispered urgently in Afrikaans. 'They say there's a huge crowd of Blacks coming this way from Alexandra. They seem to know Kumalo is here.'

'Is *that* what it's all about?' Prinsloo breathed. He sprinted away across the car park.

Louis Rose was staring at his daughter. She was shaky, speechless. 'What have you been up to now, Judith? What on earth is going on here?'

'It's a complicated story,' she said, after a moment. 'And it's twenty to eight. Aren't you running late?'

'I suppose I am.' He paused. 'I never did think that chap had any sense of proportion.' He set off towards reception, Judith behind him.

WILLEMSE HAD NOSED his way unobtrusively round the clinic. He had accounted for fifteen of the sixteen patients in residence. Only a man called Davis seemed to be missing.

Willemse returned to the Substance Abuse Unit, walked down the corridor to Davis's room at the end, and knocked on the door. When he got no reply he went in. He looked round the room, glanced into the bathroom and then quickly began opening drawers and cupboards.

He found a set of car keys, but otherwise no personal effects whatever. In the wardrobe were summerweight clothes, all with the labels of European manufacturers. One that said *Alan Best Menswear, Cork*.

Cork? Ireland.

He spotted a small heap of soiled clothes and picked through them. He pulled out a pair of black cotton gloves and a black woollen balaclava cap.

'IT'S TOO LATE, Frank. I can't reach him now. The police have found the farm, but we have no choice but to go there. Frank?'

'Yes?'

'Look after yourself.'

'You too.'

Judith replaced the phone in its cradle and stood staring numbly out of the office window. She wished she could be twenty miles away, protected by Frank Rendle's arrogance and tough certainty.

RENDLE PUT DOWN the phone in the crew room and strapped on his flying helmet, while Jumper Cross fretted beside him. In their one-piece suits they hurried out, the last ones to leave, across the apron towards where the big Puma helicopters were parked, some with their rotor blades already turning. Rendle's transformation from civilian visitor to crewman had been easy to make. He was so obviously a part of the scene here that no one even wondered why he was still carrying his duffle bag.

IT HAD TAKEN WILLEMSE several minutes to find the new security man who had come on duty, and as they crossed the car park together they saw four army trucks pull up, troops leaping over their tailboards and hurrying towards the eastern perimeter. Some kind of flap was on. Willemse ignored them and led the guard to the rear doors of the operating theatre. He glanced at his watch: eight minutes to eight.

He entered the little vestibule, removing his pistol from its shoulder holster. No one was in sight, but he could hear women's voices. The theatre was being prepared for the operation.

Marriner had to be in here somewhere. It was the only place he had not already checked, and the only logical place for him to be. He entered the corridor to the left, rounded a corner and saw a closed door on each side, the passageway reaching a dead end beyond. Suddenly he heard a muffled voice from behind him.

It was a voice that he recognised, the voice he had heard on the phone in Jepson's office yesterday. It was Marriner. The hair prickled on the back of his neck as he stepped across the corridor and listened at the door.

'WATCH OUT FOR THOSE Entac missile launchers, Brakpan. They'll be positioned some way back from the fence. I'm hoping Carver and Fish will take them out, but they may need some help from you. OK, now go!'

Brakpan laid the walkie-talkie on the seat beside him. The Saracen's engine was already warmed up and rumbling, filling the service bay with choking fumes, and now he eased his foot off the clutch and moved the wagon forward. Its front bumper pushed against the roller door, stretching it. With a groan the door collapsed in folds over the front of the Saracen, which rolled over it as it nosed through the doorway. Brakpan paused. Ahead of him he could see the crowd from Alexandra moving over the veld like a great swarm of black ants; beyond them a couple of other Saracens and two or three Hippos were churning dust as they raced to catch up. Brakpan gunned his engine and swung to the left, heading down the slope.

PRINSLOO SHOUTED A CURSE at van Straaten, then slammed the radiotelephone receiver down. He glared at the army major.

'Get one of your trucks round the front. I'm going to get Kumalo out.'

'My men can hold off that crowd, Colonel ...'

'You may care to bet on that, but I don't. I'm acting on my own authority, and I'm telling you to get it done.'

The major backed hastily away and hurried off. Prinsloo followed him down the steps of the caravan and strode towards the main buildings. So this was how it would end, he thought, in a bloody shambles. And what of the fine pair of minds that had created all this, Hoeksma and van Straaten? Hoeksma was unobtainable, on his way to the ceremonies at the monument, and van Straaten had simply copped out, a quivering bundle of nerves, refusing to make a decision, passing the buck. So much for those clowns. Well, Kumalo dead was better than Kumalo free. Shot while trying to escape: the time-worn exculpation.

WILLEMSE HAD MADE a mistake. He knew it in the instant between flinging the door open and going into the room in a crouch, but by then he was too late to stop himself.

After the glare of fluorescent lighting everywhere else in the building, the dark sucked him in and he was surrounded by half-seen objects, swinging his pistol in an arc, and Marriner had two or three seconds to prepare himself. He fired twice with the machine pistol, the silenced shots making two quick coughing noises. From ten feet away, with the policeman outlined against the light from the doorway, he could hardly have missed. One shot caught Willemse in the right side of the chest, the next hit him in the shoulder, throwing him backwards.

Marriner stepped over to the man. He was clutching his chest, breathing in ragged gasps. The pistol had fallen out of his hand, and Marriner kicked it across the floor. It was three minutes to eight. He picked up his bagful of grenades and strode out of the room, closing the door behind him.

A man in a white laboratory coat stood in the opposite doorway. A nurse was hurrying towards him from the vestibule. They both

344

stopped, aghast, as he pointed the gun at them in turn.

'Stand still,' he said, as calmly as he could. 'Now, turn that way. Walk ahead of me. I mean walk, not run.'

They obeyed, and he followed them at a distance of eight feet. Keeping command, staying in absolute control, was everything. They crossed the vestibule and went down the next corridor. He herded them into the sterile-supply room and shut the door. He glanced through the window into the theatre, where several members of the surgical team had already assembled.

The woman and the man were watching him intently. He waved at the airtight door leading into the theatre.

'Stand facing that way. We're going in there, one by one.'

He motioned with the gun. The first went through the door and the other quickly followed, Marriner bringing up the rear. As he entered the cool silence of the theatre and levelled the gun, the anonymous gowned figures were already backing away, their eyes, above their masks, widening with shock.

Chapter Sixteen

Eight o'clock.

In the scrub room Dr Rose put out his hands for the rubber gloves that a nurse held ready for him, newly cut from their wrapping. As he was drawing them on, the door swung violently open and Colonel Prinsloo marched in.

'Doctor, I want your patient out of here. Now!'

'Are you mad?' Rose demanded. 'What are you doing in here?' Out in the corridor Rose could see Lincoln Kumalo being wheeled from the anaesthetic area to the theatre.

'Didn't you hear me? Kumalo is coming with me. There will be no operation.'

'This is preposterous! He's already under anaesthetic.'

'Doctor, your clinic is about to be attacked by a mob. Either you get Kumalo out of that theatre or I will. Bring him round to the reception area. There'll be a truck waiting.'

Prinsloo strode away. Dr Rose looked at the nurses and got sympathetic shrugs of the shoulders. He left the scrub room and walked to the main doors of the theatre. He pushed them open, entered, and stopped.

He could not believe what his eyes told him. The patient was not on the operating table, but still lay on the trolley which had brought him in, unconscious from the sodium pentothal injection. The tube which the anaesthetist had passed through his mouth into his trachea had been removed. The theatre staff were not gathered round the table where they should have been, but were lined up against the wall, together with

another nurse and a technician, faced by a man with a gun. He appeared to have been waiting for Rose.

'Over there, please, with the others. I'm not going to harm anyone, just so long as you do everything you're told.'

Dr Rose stood his ground. He said, 'What is the meaning of this?'

'The meaning of this, Dr Rose, is that I'm taking Kumalo away from here. I wouldn't be doing it unless it was for his own good.'

Rose took a step forward, anger still masking his fear, but stopped when the man swivelled the weapon towards him. The man was unnervingly well-spoken and intelligent, yet there was a menace about him that suggested he meant exactly what he said.

'I repeat, Dr Rose, stand over there. We have a few minutes to wait, and I want you all to remain very calm.'

THE MARCHERS WERE CLOSE to the riverbed when Brakpan cut across their path. A couple of young men broke ranks to hurl petrol bombs at the Saracen, but they fell hopelessly short, exploding with gushes of orange flame in the grass. At the head of the procession Duma halted for a moment to wave.

Where the river reached its shallowest point Brakpan took the vehicle across, axle-deep in water, before beginning the climb up the opposite slope. Lightning, abandoning his prisoners, had already made his way along the bank, and Brakpan slowed to take him on board.

Up the slope, Younis had also left his position, and they picked him up on the move. Then Nicky Flynn, darting from his cover at the edge of the wood, jumped on board as well and manned the machine gun.

The wood was an old pine plantation that had run wild, and the Saracen ploughed easily through it. As Nicky directed Brakpan towards the weakened section of fence, they saw Carver signalling behind it, lining them up.

INSIDE THE PERIMETER all the reinforcements had been deployed along the eastern fence, directly facing the marchers. The rest of the guards were looking in the same direction. The antitank crews had stayed where they were, however, six pairs of men crouched over the Entac launchers, each with a wire-guided missile that could pierce the thickest armour. Fish had been watching the nearest two teams, positioned thirty yards inside the southern fence, and knew that they were the greatest danger.

As Carver began signalling, Fish saw the soldiers stiffen. They had spotted the Saracen moving towards the fence, and they were turning the launcher towards it. Fish aimed his rifle and shot the gunner in the head just as the Saracen tore through the fence, Carver still urging it forward. The number-two man on the launcher looked up, startled, then stood and raised his hands in premature surrender. Fish's gaze was on the second crew now, but Brakpan had already seen them and charged down on the launcher just as its tube was pointed towards him. One of the gunners managed to roll aside; the other screamed as the Saracen's wheels crushed his legs. Brakpan halted, letting Carver and Fish scramble in, then headed back to the operating theatre.

The diversion had cost them a precious twenty seconds' worth of surprise. The antiterrorist police who guarded the theatre were alerted now, and closed in round the building, taking cover behind its corners, knowing better than to waste ammunition by shooting at the Saracen. It had only one vulnerable spot, and that was the man exposed in the turret.

Nicky Flynn had almost forgotten the machine gun in his hands. Now he began firing blindly at the police, forcing their heads down.

IN THE RECEPTION AREA, Prinsloo had been waiting impatiently for Kumalo to be brought out, when he heard the shooting. Behind him Judith stood tensely by the desk. He could see nothing from where he stood and after a few moments he left the building and made for the nearest corner.

In utter disbelief he saw a Saracen armoured car, with different markings from the one that had gone missing, slew to a halt. As he watched, it reversed into the rear doors of the operating theatre, wedging its rear end solidly in the opening. The vehicle's front visor-flaps were down. It seemed to have no human dimension apart from the head of a turret gunner, now swivelling his weapon.

Prinsloo ducked back behind the wall. He shouted to the soldiers on the waiting truck to follow him and raced back towards the operating theatre. He didn't notice that Judith had vanished.

WITHIN MOMENTS of hearing the doors break down, Carver, Fish and Younis had leaped from the Saracen into the vestibule of the building. Jammed into the doorway, the vehicle made an impregnable shield against any attack from outside. They raced down the corridor to the right, through the sterile-supply room and into the operating theatre.

One of the nurses lined up against the wall began screaming. Fish and Carver immediately ran to Kumalo's trolley and started to wheel it towards the exit. Younis, covering the main doors, almost opened fire when Judith came through, checking himself at the last instant.

Marriner, still holding his gun on the theatre staff, saw Dr Rose give a start as his daughter moved self-protectively to Marriner's side. For the first time he seemed to recognise Marriner. 'Aren't you a patient here? Davis? What is this insanity, Judith?'

'You'd better ask him,' she said, pointing to Dr Els at the end of the row. 'I'm sure he knows all about it.' She was breathing fast. 'They're the ones who are insane. They were going to kill Kumalo!'

'Worse,' said Marriner. 'They were going to turn him into a vegetable.'

Dr Rose turned to stare at Els. Now Marriner had to recollect himself:

the trolley had vanished through the exit and it was time to follow.

'Go, Judith!' he said, giving her a push, and she ran out without hesitation. 'The rest of you can start moving out as soon as we've gone.'

Younis was backing away from the main doors. Marriner reached into the airline bag, and tossed a gas grenade across the room. They fled into the corridor just as the acrid smoke began to engulf the theatre.

In the vestibule, Carver and Fish were already heaving Kumalo's recumbent form towards the Saracen. In the turret Nicky Flynn was firing short bursts at anyone who poked a head round a corner. Marriner tossed another gas shell down the right-hand corridor to halt any pursuit from that direction, then scrambled into the vehicle after Younis and Judith. He slammed the doors behind them and yelled at Brakpan, 'Go!'

The Saracen lurched free of the opening and turned into the driveway, heading for the gates. As it did so, a police sniper stepped out of cover beside the theatre building. He took careful aim at the retreating back of Nicky Flynn's head. He fired.

Inside the wagon they heard a soft thump from the turret, and then Nicky dropped through it and off the seat, flopping into the aisle beside Kumalo, dead before he hit the floor.

PRINSLOO, AT THE HEAD of the party of troops, pushed open the doors of the theatre, and fell back, met by an almost solid wall of tear gas. He tried the corridor at the side, and found that filled with gas as well. The only way out now was back through the reception area, and by the time he got there the Saracen was a distant dark blob at the far end of the drive. Off to his right the shattered doors of the theatre were gushing gas into the sunshine and the surgical team were stumbling out through it.

The army major appeared, looking panic-stricken. Prinsloo had forgotten about the major and the crowd beyond the fence.

'I think we need you down there, sir. They're getting close. If we have to open fire, you should be the one to give the order.'

More buck-passing, he thought grimly, but this time he would have none of it. 'Just do whatever you have to,' he said. 'My advice is to tell them that Kumalo has escaped. Show them they're wasting their time.'

Prinsloo stalked away. He had other things to think about. He had to look ahead. He wondered idly what had become of Willemse.

THE SARACEN CRASHED easily through the roadblock just north of the clinic, sending police and soldiers scattering. Inside the vehicle there was disorder; five passengers on the seats in the rear, Kumalo unconscious and Nicky lying dead beside him. Judith was staring in disbelief at his body. Now she looked up at Marriner.

'We have to stop along here. We have to pick up Nandi Kumalo.'

'*What?*'

'His daughter. She came to me this morning, asking for help. She wants to go with him. Your friend Duma arranged it.'

'Bloody Duma! Does he think this is a refugee service?' But he knew he could not refuse to take Kumalo's daughter.

THE AEROSPATIALE SA330 PUMA was designed as a fast transport helicopter. In its configuration as a gunship, the South African XTP model had a sliding door on its port side, a 20-millimetre cannon pod, and a swivel seat for its operator. It was this seat that Rendle occupied, several feet behind the cockpit section where Jumper Cross sat beside the weapons systems officer. For the purposes of this aerial display none of the choppers of 19 Squadron was carrying any ammunition.

Jumper had taken off at exactly eight o'clock, part of a flight of six. First they headed northeast to circle the Voortrekker Monument and the vast crowd gathered round it. Now they were over the suburbs of Pretoria, preparing for a run down Church Street in advance of the army parade.

Unnoticed by the others, Rendle unstrapped his seatbelt and eased himself out of the swivel chair. He pulled the damaged Uzi gun out of the duffle bag beside him and crawled forward. With his free hand he reached between the two cockpit seats and yanked out the leads that connected the VHF radio to the headsets built into the crew's helmets. Even as Jumper turned a startled face towards him, Rendle jammed the muzzle of his Uzi into the back of the gunner's neck. The man went rigid in his seat.

'Sorry, Jumper. I'm taking over now.'

'Frank! Have you gone berserk?'

'Never saner, Jumper!' They had to shout at each other over the scream of the turbine engines. 'You do exactly what I tell you now, or this guy gets it in the head!'

'I don't believe you, Frank!'

'You'd better start trying. No more games. I'm deadly serious. I want you to keep formation until I tell you otherwise.'

For the first time Jumper got a proper look at the Uzi.

'Hey, that gun is wrecked! You can't frighten me with that!'

'It's got one round up the spout, Jumper, and I'm betting on it firing. Are you prepared to bet against it?'

Jumper turned back to face the front. 'I don't know what you're up to, Frank,' he muttered, 'but you're a lousy ungrateful bastard!'

MENACING THOUGH THE CROWD still appeared from behind the fence, it had lost some of its tight coherence. A hundred riflemen faced them from beyond the wire mesh, and although a massed charge would no doubt have broken it down and carried them into the clinic, this would have required a desperation that the crowd did not possess. Instead they stopped twenty yards short of the fence, beginning a deep-voiced chant: 'Ku-*ma*-lo! Ku-*ma*-lo!'

The government Saracens and Hippos had eventually caught up with the marchers. Content to flank them for a while, the drivers now seized the chance to move into the gap between the fence and the front row of people.

Suddenly a ripple of excitement started, spreading rapidly through the ranks of people. Somehow a message had slipped through the fence: Kumalo had escaped from the clinic. Kumalo was free!

What had been a latently hostile crowd was transformed in moments into a festive, emotional one, singing, stamping and even beginning to dance. A Very pistol cracked, and tear gas began to mushroom at the furthest edge of the crowd. Even this did not dampen their mood, and as they fell back they were laughing and crying at once. Other shots followed, indistinguishable from the bangs of the gas pistols, and for an instant Duma thought someone had struck him in panic, or kicked him. But a paralysing numbness began to spread through him, shooting up into his skull and down his spine, and now he knew with a dreadful certainty what had caused it. He thought of Nandi reunited with her father. He thought how ridiculous it was to die now. His mind spiralled down a dark vortex, and he fell over slowly, rolling onto his side.

IT WAS DR ELS who found Warrant Officer Willemse.

Els had been the last to flee from the operating theatre ahead of the gas fumes, and as he groped his way with streaming eyes down the corridor he had an overwhelming, illogical urge to hide himself away. Instead of following the others out of the building he opened the door to the air-conditioning plant. The door seemed pretty airtight. As he closed it behind him he heard stertorous breathing in the room, over the hum of the machinery. He turned on the light and saw the policeman lying on his back, a pale frothy blood bubbling from his mouth, the certain sign of a lung wound; and at a guess there was a bullet buried in his shoulder as well. They would have a patient for their operating theatre after all.

MARRINER TOSSED a smoke grenade out of the Saracen and watched the grey cloud envelop the road behind them. They took another corner, at an alarming tilt, and suddenly the wail of pursuing sirens ceased. For the moment Brakpan was holding the wagon on its maximum speed, but it wasn't half what a motorbike or car would make. For that reason they had planned this course along a succession of country roads, where overtaking was impossible and pursuit could be hampered.

He turned to glance at Nandi and Lincoln Kumalo.

The young woman had nodded a breathless greeting to Judith and the others when she'd scrambled aboard, but now she knelt beside her father on the narrow deck, listening to his shallow breathing.

'Is he all right? Really all right?'

'You mustn't worry,' Judith told her. 'Sodium pentothal wears off quickly. He'll be confused for a while, but he'll be fine.'

She spoke with an assurance that Marriner wished he could share. Now

351

that they actually had Kumalo with them he seemed a terrifying responsibility.

From behind them they heard a fresh scream of sirens. Marriner picked up the first of the spikeboards and, holding one rear door of the Saracen slightly open, dropped it out onto the road, ready to shred the tyres of anything that followed. They had to expect further roadblocks ahead, but with luck there would not have been time to set up any with enough strength to halt the Saracen. There might well be aircraft observing their movements, too, which was why he had planned a period of invisibility between ditching the Saracen and boarding their own chopper.

All that depended on what was happening at the farm.

He picked up his walkie-talkie. 'Unit Five. Do you hear me?'

Blikkies Steyn did not reply.

BLIKKIES SAT PERFECTLY STILL in the thick bush on the slope thirty feet behind the farmhouse. After all the hours of waiting and observing, it was time to make his move.

He stood up. Holding his panga and his radio in one hand and his kitbag in the other, he began to pick his way carefully down the slope.

Ever since the police had settled themselves in around the farm, he had known that the key to outwitting them lay in controlling the house. It was the two cops in there, Brink and Smit, who were in contact with their base and gave orders to the others. Blikkies would have to enter the house from behind, since the front was overlooked by other men across the clearing. He would have to act swiftly and silently.

Keeping to the cover of the bushes, he moved up to the rear wall, pressed himself against it, and loosened the drawstrings of his kitbag. He opened it just wide enough to encourage the snake lying coiled in the bottom of the tough canvas bag to slither out.

It was a real beauty of a snake, a puff-adder which he had caught an hour ago when it emerged from its hole to bask in the early sun. As its head emerged from the bag now he caught it in the same way, pinning it by the neck with the flat of his panga blade, then grasping it tightly behind the head between thumb and forefinger. The snake hissed, and its five-foot-long, grey-brown body swelled with anger. He stood up, shaking it loose as it tried to coil round his arm. He peeped into the room again and saw the men still seated at the front window facing away from him. He reached in, holding the puff-adder head-down, and let it fall silently to the floor.

Blikkies moved to the other window and hoisted himself quickly through into the bedroom. He knew more or less what the snake would do, and more or less how the men would respond. Most people had a quite irrational fear of snakes. Not even a puff-adder would attack a.man unprovoked—but try telling that to someone trapped in a room with one.

He did not have long to wait. He heard a chair scrape sharply on the floorboards and then overturn, a muffled curse, a shout of alarm. Sergeant

Brink backed hastily into the bedroom, and Blikkies stepped from behind the door and struck him with the panga. Before he had hit the floor Blikkies was through the door, raising the panga again. Smit backed off but it caught him on the side of the neck. He clutched his neck and fell on top of the snake, which darted its head forward and struck him twice on the arm, through the fabric of his shirt.

Blikkies sat down in the chair vacated by Brink, reached for his radio and switched it on.

'YOU MUST KNOW this is crazy, Frank. Being off the air ... everybody will already know something is wrong.' Jumper Cross had been flying in sullen silence, woodenly obeying Rendle's orders.

They had crossed the centre of Pretoria and now they were drawing level with the small hill surmounted by a water tower which was their marker for a turn to the south.

'No news is good news, Jumper. Do it now! Turn south!'

As they came level with the water tower the lead helicopter banked and headed into the turn. Instead of following, Jumper eased the control column forward and suddenly throttled up, losing height and gaining speed simultaneously.

'Down some more, Jumper! Do it like you meant it!'

The Puma dropped again, to a hundred and then to fifty feet, and now it was racing over the low suburban sprawl at a hundred and thirty knots, a huge shadow charging ahead of it. The rest of the six-chopper flight was long since lost to view.

Jumper was right, of course. Ground Control at Zwartkop would have been concerned at the loss of radio contact, but by now they would be in a panic. They would be doing everything they could to keep track of the helicopter by its radar signal. On the other hand, they weren't going to shoot an expensive chopper down until they had a good reason.

In a dizzying minute or two they had left the suburbs behind and now they were out in the scrubby bush that stretched westwards towards the Magaliesberg. There was no chance of hitting power lines or television aerials out here, and Jumper, now in a rashly defiant mood, took the chopper down to fifteen feet, as far under the radar as possible.

Soon Rendle would be able to see the Pelindaba smokestack that was the marker for their landing.

ALL THE WAY past the straggling outskirts of Johannesburg and into open country the Saracen had stuck to the narrowest roads, with jolting overland short cuts, and had shaken off all pursuit. For the final leg to the farm, however, there was no avoiding the major national road running westwards from Pretoria to Hartbeespoort. It was about a mile along this stretch that they encountered the roadblock.

Younis, now in the turret, saw it first, and Brakpan slowed the vehicle for a couple of seconds while he sized it up, then charged confidently forward again. It was an adequate roadblock for all normal purposes: two police vans standing across the outside lanes and three cars parked at staggered intervals beyond. It would stop almost anything except ten tons of armoured steel bearing down on it at forty-five miles per hour.

Brakpan went for the gap between the vans. The right edge of the Saracen's reinforced-steel bumper caught the front of one van, slamming it out of the way. He slowed momentarily to gear down, then smashed into the first of the patrol cars broadside-on, overturning it and sending it tumbling along the road. He drove in a straight line between the next two cars, knocking them easily aside. Then the road was clear ahead except for a single policeman who had broken from cover and was deftly flinging a spiked chain across in front of them.

Brakpan was going too fast to stop. All six of the Saracen's wheels went over the spikes, and at once the tyres began to soften.

In its glowing interior, Lincoln Kumalo sat in the centre of a row of seats, supported on one side by Nandi, on the other by Carver. He was still very drowsy from the anaesthetic, but he knew enough to understand what was going on. 'Trouble?' he murmured.

'No trouble,' said Carver, gripping his arm. 'We got run-flat tyres. They'll slow us down, but they'll take us a long way yet.'

'We also got a busted radiator,' Brakpan called from the front, 'and that *is* trouble.'

Marriner, sitting opposite Kumalo, looked up in alarm. One of the collisions at the roadblock must have dented the armoured grille sufficiently to hole the radiator, and steam was gushing from the Saracen's nose. It had also lost speed. 'How much further?' he called to Brakpan.

'Three, four k's. I guess we can just about make it.'

Marriner's watch said ten to nine. They were just nicely inside their schedule. He picked up his walkie-talkie and spoke briefly to Blikkies again and then addressed the others.

'Listen, everybody. They're waiting for us at the farm, but Blikkies is in charge there now and he's going to draw them off. It means we have to make a diversion as well. We're going through the back door.'

'What back door?' Judith asked.

'We're going in through the nuclear reactor plant.'

'I'M ASKING YOU for the last time, Smit. *Where is Brink?*'

'To tell you the truth, sir . . .' Blikkies hesitated. 'It's like this. He's got a bad case of the runs. He keeps having to go out back. It's kind of embarrassing for him.'

There was a brief suspicious silence from Colonel Prinsloo. Then he barked, 'I'll give him the runs when I get hold of him! Now listen; this can't wait. The missing helicopter has definitely been hijacked by this man Rendle. The helicopter and the Saracen are both heading straight towards

354

you. You men are not equipped to stop the Saracen: that can be dealt with by the reinforcements who are about to surround the farm, but you must stop that helicopter at all costs. It must not be allowed to rendezvous with the people from the Saracen. Got it?'

'Got it, Colonel.'

'Inform me of every development. Out.'

Blikkies sat and stared for a few moments across the room, at the snake still watching him from one corner and the bodies of Smith and Brink lying in the other.

Blikkies was quite enjoying himself. He had realised early on that this radio with its two independent channels was the essential link between Prinsloo and the detectives out here on the ground. Neither side could communicate directly with the other, so Blikkies could give contradictory information to each without the other being any the wiser.

Prinsloo was still buying his act. The cops staked out in the bush had bought it as well, though he'd confined himself to two brief conversations with them, relaying fictitious orders from Brink to stay put. Now the deception would be put to its ultimate test. He pressed the button that linked him to the detectives on the second channel of the radio.

He heard the same babble of complaints and questions he had heard earlier. How much longer would they be stuck out here? When would they get some food? Why couldn't they talk to Brink?

Blikkies spoke up. 'I told you, Brink has the runs. He's not well. If you'll all just listen, I'll tell you the good news. Orders from Colonel Prinsloo. There's apparently no chance of anybody showing up here for several hours yet, so we're pulling out now.'

'About time,' said someone.

'A helicopter is coming in with fresh men. You can ignore it. Just make your ways separately to the riverbank and move down to the road. You'll be met there. Go now, and go quietly!'

'What about Brink?' asked another voice.

'Brink and I will follow. Over and out.'

He switched off the set, stood up and went to the front window, standing just far enough back to be in shadow. Across the clearing he could make out the men rising from among the thorn trees, beginning to move away towards the river. They'd be in for a shock when they met the reinforcements.

To one side of him the bodies were already beginning to hum with flies. From the other corner the snake still watched him impassively. It had done its work, and he would be sure to let it go. You always knew where you stood with a snake.

MARRINER THREW OUT the last two spikeboards just after they turned onto the short spur road leading to the reactor, and followed it with the last of the smoke bombs. The bevy of police cars following them promptly disappeared from sight. Belching steam, losing speed, grinding its way up the slight rise with its wheels flattened almost to their rims, the Saracen must have looked to the Pelindaba guards like some monstrous old railway engine that had run off its tracks. Younis, in the turret, fired a couple of short bursts over their heads, and then the wagon was banging its way through the flimsy mesh gates and heading up the slope in front of the reactor building. At the very moment it crested the ridge, its overheated engine finally seized.

There was a great clunking noise as the vehicle slithered to a halt, and the cursing of Brakpan as he tried to work the engine out of gear. The cab was filled with the stench of hot oil and burnt rubber.

Brakpan declutched a couple of times, letting the Saracen roll forward, and then it sprang out of gear and began freewheeling towards the barbed-wire fence. Lumbering slowly at first, it gained speed rapidly under the momentum of its ten-ton weight. But no power meant no power brakes, so that among the passengers the momentary relief of moving again was quickly overtaken by the knowledge that the vehicle was hurtling towards the fence at a terrifying speed, quite out of control.

FROM THE HELICOPTER, fifty feet above, Rendle saw the Saracen bowling past the reactor plant, in quite the opposite direction from the one he'd expected. Then the chopper made a steep banking turn to orbit the clearing in front of the farmhouse. He could see Blikkies waving them down. There was no sign of anyone else, though he'd caught sight of a line of troop carriers parked at the edge of the road about a mile away.

'Take her down, Jumper!'

Jumper eased the chopper down gracefully to the middle of the clearing, landing with scarcely a bump. As the rotors slowed Blikkies came running towards it, shielding his face from the dust storm.

'Out we go, Jumper.'

The pilot throttled back his engines, and he and the crewman resignedly unfastened their seatbelts. Rendle covered them with the Uzi gun until they had climbed out through the cockpit door and hopped to the ground, and then he followed. There was an uncannily peaceful air about the farm, like somewhere at the still centre of a hurricane.

'You made it, thank God!' Blikkies yelled. 'See any sign of the others?'

'They're just over there.' Rendle pointed to the hillside behind the house. 'But how they intend to get down, I don't know.'

THE SARACEN BROKE THROUGH the fence with a scream of tearing wire, uprooting the iron posts on either side of it. Brakpan was fighting to steer some kind of course through the thick screen of vegetation. The wagon mowed down the bushes and all but the toughest trees; these he tried to cannon off, to retard the downward plunge, wrenching the wheel this way and that, taking them in a lunatic slalom down the hill.

Suddenly the bushes parted in front of them and the farmhouse was right ahead and below, surrounded by its collection of junk. The Saracen lurched into an outcrop of rock, then cruised down the gentler slope to the right of the house. Losing speed, it rode across the edge of the clearing, dipped its nose into the Crocodile River, and stopped.

The back of the cab was a shambles. Marriner was the first to extract himself. Dropping to the riverbank, he saw Blikkies running towards them; in the background the great helicopter sat framed by the trees in a flood of sunshine.

'Come on, come on, we've got to move,' Blikkies said, urging the passengers out.

Marriner lifted Judith to her feet and Carver gave Nandi a steadying hand, but everyone's concern was really for Kumalo. He was the last to be helped out, Nandi at once going to his side. Whatever lingering effect the anaesthetic had had must have been shaken clean out of him in the last few minutes, for he stood upright without assistance and gazed around him. He was unsteady on his feet, but his eyes were clear and he was obviously alive to everything. Quite suddenly he gave a huge grin and said to Brakpan, 'Man, you are some driver!'

'Can we get going?' Blikkies demanded, not charmed by any of this.

They went in a shambling line towards the clearing. The helicopter's two crewmen stood watching them from one side, disconsolate, hostile, but not quite succeeding in hiding their curiosity. Rendle had climbed back into the helicopter and was out on the sill of the cockpit door, using a hatchet from the emergency kit to smash off the stubby little IFF aerial above the windscreen: without it the radar trackers would have trouble identifying the aircraft.

On Marriner's instructions the ten of them besides Rendle scurried one by one beneath the moving blades to the gun door on the port side, pulling themselves into the cabin, finding seats wherever they could. Marriner went last, and he had just scrambled through the doorway when he realised Judith wasn't with them. Judith was still outside, standing close to the cockpit, watching Rendle. As soon as he had dealt with the aerial he dropped to the ground and she ran forward and embraced him.

It was the kind of embrace that a woman could give only to a lover. There was something so perfectly ridiculous about the scene, and at the same time so logical, that Marriner supposed he should have seen it coming. Judith had at last found the justification that she needed for running away. She was running away with Rendle.

They separated, Rendle climbing into the cockpit and Judith running to the gun door. She avoided Marriner's eye as he helped her over the sill. Rendle too was embarrassed, making much of checking out the switches on the overhead panel. Then, after leaning out of the side window to shout something, maybe an apology, to the two airmen they were abandoning, he throttled up the two turbine engines, and the helicopter lifted. They were airborne, the clearing and the farmhouse falling away below them. A quarter of a mile along the riverbank, towards the road, they glimpsed a line of heavily armed policemen staring dumbfounded up at them.

IT WAS NINE FIFTEEN when the radio link to the farmhouse suddenly came back to life in Prinsloo's caravan. He talked into the headset with a curious lack of passion. 'Brink? Smit?'

'Neither, Colonel,' said a new, tense voice. 'Brink and Smit are dead. They've been dead for an hour or more. There's been a snake here, and a man with some sort of knife ...'

Prinsloo grunted. He wasn't hearing anything he hadn't guessed since the moment Brink and Smit—or whoever had been playing Smit—had gone off the air. He had been fooled, fair and square.

'And you know that they got away, of course?' the voice concluded nervously.

'I know they got away. Thank you.'

He dropped the headset and stared through the window, across the grounds of the clinic. He was exhausted, drained of anger. Kumalo was no longer his responsibility. He had never believed a thing like this could happen: a stolen helicopter, a stolen Saracen, a ragamuffin crew of troopies, who had slipped through their hands like so many eels. Oh, well, he didn't care any longer. Let them blow Kumalo out of the sky if that gave them any pleasure, and this time let them pick up the pieces themselves.

Chapter Seventeen

A little after ten o'clock the helicopter crossed the escarpment that marked the eastern edge of the Drakensberg range and the limit of the southern African plateau. The land dropped away ahead of them, a great rolling plain of deep, dark green bushveld studded with citrus groves, ideal terrain for the Puma's ground-hugging progress.

Back over the less friendly grasslands of the Highveld they'd had two close calls, both times with pairs of Mirage F1s that were clearly out to intercept them. The first had been near the town of Witbank, and Rendle had played cat and mouse among the six cooling towers of a big power station while the jets screamed back and forth, unable to fire their rockets for fear of an industrial disaster. The second pair had picked them up further east, and Rendle had dived into the deep gorge of the Komati River and plonked the Puma down between two high cliffs, simply waiting for the fighters to go away.

Now, slipping down from the escarpment, the wheels of the Puma practically brushing the flat tops of the acacias, they could breathe a little more easily. There were no air bases closer than Pretoria, and every mile they travelled took them further from the likelihood of aerial interception. There were still the Cactus missile bases clustered close to the Mozambique border, but in the meantime Swaziland lay before them.

IT TOOK THEM half an hour to cross the tiny country, the altitude of the land below falling all the time, until the flanks of the Lebombo Mountains rose before them, marking the eastern boundary of the kingdom and signalling the final drop to the coastal flats. There'd been no sign of any further pursuit, and they could reasonably conclude that the South African radar had lost track of them completely. Nor, apparently, was there any knowledge of their intrusion into Swazi airspace. They'd listened in to Air Traffic Control at Matsapha and heard no requests for identification. They were in Mozambique. They had made it.

Lincoln Kumalo sat just behind the cockpit. Rendle turned to give him a thumbs-up sign, and Kumalo roared the news back to the others. No proper conversation was possible in the helicopter, but in shouted snatches Marriner had told him as much as he could of the background to his rescue, the several ways in which it had nearly failed. Now he gave Marriner his big infectious grin and yelled, 'Home and dry?'

'I guess so.'

But one thing was still bothering Marriner. Their present bearing should bring them to the Indian ocean coast in fifteen minutes or so, close to the Ponta do Ouro lighthouse. When Rosenblatt had first mentioned the place, Marriner had wondered why the rendezvous had been arranged so far south, close once again to the South African border. He'd had no time to think about it since, but now it seemed almost nonsensical. A helicopter could land anywhere within reason. And that story Rosenblatt had repeated about the state of the roads was hard to believe. Unmade roads in these parts were uniformly awful. Why should the one from Ponta do Ouro be better or worse than any other?'

Another point: the South Africans kept their borders with Mozambique carefully guarded. Rendle said one of their Cactus missile batteries was stationed permanently in the area, somewhere near Kosi Bay on the North Natal coast. Having got themselves out of the lion's mouth, they seemed almost to be returning deliberately to tweak his whiskers.

He remembered something Rosenblatt had said. He turned to shout at Kumalo. 'I told you about Harry Makibani? Your people have got Harry under arrest. A man called Gumbi.'

'Lawrence Gumbi. I will have to see about this.'

'I think he'll be meeting us. Do you trust Gumbi?'

Kumalo chose his words carefully. 'He's an ambitious man, but very sound. I have no reason to distrust him. Why?'

'No reason I can explain.'

He couldn't explain it even to himself. It was not the internal feuding of the Congress leadership that concerned him, but the proximity of those

missiles. Come to think of it, there was no reason why they should expose themselves unnecessarily to danger from that quarter. He gave Rendle a nudge, and unobtrusively indicated what he wanted. The pilot nodded, altered the helicopter's course and put it on a heading to the northeast.

THEY WERE STILL FLYING very low, so they didn't see the ocean until they were half a mile from it, the sudden sweep of brilliant blue, the creamy surf and the fringe of palms straight off a travel poster.

The helicopter had reached the coastline eight miles north of where they were expected, and now Rendle turned south and flew parallel to it. The

shore was broken here and there by muddy lagoons, but was otherwise straight, the country just inland from it swampy and uninhabited.

Marriner had chosen this approach from the north because it made the Puma a far less tempting target for the missiles across the border. Although it would still bring them within the five-mile range of the Cactus rockets, it avoided crossing their path at a much closer distance. It meant the helicopter's radar would also give earlier warning if a missile should be launched at it.

'Not much chance of that,' Rendle had said. 'Flying at this height, we won't make a blip on their screens. Even if we did, they couldn't be sure it was us without a signal from our IFF antenna. They could be zapping some weekend pilot in his Cessna.'

Within two or three minutes he spotted the lighthouse through the smoky sea haze. A short distance this side of it a jumble of low pale buildings must certainly be the site of the rendezvous.

They flew on. Rendle gave a start. 'Will you look at those crazy bastards?'

Marriner peered forward and saw what he meant. Parked in the centre of the erstwhile holiday camp that Rosenblatt had described were six big olive-coloured trucks, with dozens of figures swarming round them. As if all this didn't make their presence obvious enough, there was also a flagpole at the edge of the site on which the gaudy colours of the People's Congress had been hoisted. They were perhaps a mile from the South African border, and they were advertising their presence like a circus.

'Back off for a minute,' Marriner said suddenly. 'Put us down somewhere. I want to think.'

The figures in the clearing had spotted the helicopter and some of them were waving. Rendle banked rapidly out over the sea and circled inland again, looking for a firm landing in the marshy ground. He found one, a patch of baked earth with broken fenceposts round it that might once have been a cattle kraal. He put the chopper down easily in the middle of it and looked at Marriner. 'Well? What are we getting ourselves into?'

'There's something so illogical about all that,' Marriner said, 'that there's got to be a good reason for it. They may be attracting attention to themselves, but they're also attracting it to us.'

'I don't follow, man. Spell it out.'

'Look, you say the South Africans can't tell this aircraft from any other on their radar. But they can certainly identify that roadshow. That would make it a fair bet to them that anything approaching that place from Swaziland is the helicopter they've been told to look out for.'

Rendle was watching him stonily. 'So if we'd come from the expected direction, we'd have got a Cactus up our backside?'

'I'm not saying it was *arranged* that way. I think somebody hoped it would happen.' He turned to Kumalo. 'Somebody who wouldn't mind seeing you out of the way, even if he wouldn't dare to eliminate you himself.'

'Are you accusing Lawrence Gumbi?' Kumalo asked. 'I hardly think you have any evidence for that.'

'I'd rather let you be the judge. All I know is that whoever arranged this state reception for you is either very crazy or very smart. All he'd need to know is that one of those missile batteries is within range of this spot and he could reckon on a fair chance of them downing you on the way in. Not his fault. Just the fortunes of war.'

'Well, we are safe now, and nothing can be proved. Maybe I'll ask Gumbi about it and see if it embarrasses him.'

Marriner was incredulous. 'What do you mean, "safe"? We're talking about a man who could be trying to kill you. Backed up by perhaps a hundred of his guerrilla fighters!'

'Not his, Mr Marriner,' said Kumalo, watching him calmly. 'Ours. I have nothing to fear from any Congress soldier, and I doubt if I have much to fear from Gumbi.'

'So why don't we just hop out and start walking?' said Rendle. 'Give this Mr Gumbi a nice surprise.'

Marriner glanced back at Kumalo. 'Are you up to walking half a mile or so?'

'Ten times round the exercise yard every day for twenty-five years.'

'OK.' Marriner called down the cabin to the others, and they started unbuckling their seatbelts, exchanging puzzled shrugs and frowns. He undid his own harness, climbed out between the seats and followed the others through the gun door, and in a minute they were all assembled at the edge of the kraal. 'What's happening?' Judith asked him.

'Let's get started,' Marriner said. 'I'll explain on the way.'

They set off in a line, picking their way through the waist-high bushes, Marriner telling Judith their doubts. The sun beat down on them fiercely. When they reached a gap in the vegetation they saw a crowd of Congress soldiers who'd been moving northwards along the edge of the beach, coming to see why the helicopter had turned away from the rendezvous and landed elsewhere. Now they swarmed up from the beach to greet Kumalo, stopping for a moment in awe and then closing in to surround and seize and hug him, breaking into nervous, excited laughter. The rest of the group came forward, and the black soldiers began grabbing the white ones and embracing them, too, and kissing Nandi and Judith, forming a rapturous milling throng round the newcomers, gabbling, laughing and cheering, until Kumalo raised a hand to silence them.

A tall, lean black man in olive-drab fatigues had appeared at the edge of the beach, twenty yards away. He stood there alone, as though he couldn't quite bring himself to join in the fun. His bearing was aloof and dignified; at another time it might have been quite commanding, but now it contrasted oddly with the expression on his face. To Marriner, and as surely to Kumalo, that expression said everything.

'Lawrence!' Kumalo called. 'Aren't you going to say hello?'

Lawrence Gumbi seemed to recollect himself. He managed a smile and walked forward. The soldiers round them parted silently, sensing something strange about this encounter, but Kumalo embraced Gumbi warmly as though nothing at all were the matter. He held him by the shoulders and looked him in the face.

'You seemed almost surprised to see me, Lawrence.'

'It has been a long time, Lincoln. I . . . could hardly believe you'd made it.'

'Maybe we nearly didn't. If it hadn't been for the wisdom of my friends here, choosing a different route to this place, there might have been a most unlucky accident at the last moment.' Kumalo paused. 'Maybe this wasn't such a good place to choose, so close to the frontier.'

Gumbi's eyes flicked away for an instant. 'Maybe it wasn't, Lincoln.'

'In fact, it was a bit foolish, Lawrence.'

'I agree, it was foolish. I ...' He stopped himself from saying more, offering some excuse that he knew wouldn't be believed. In the way they looked at each other now there was complete understanding, which seemed to reach out to the soldiers round them. Watching them exchanging uneasy glances, Marriner knew they sensed a choice confronting them, and he also knew which way they would choose. Kumalo had been right. Kumalo would only have to snap his fingers and they would kill Gumbi here and now.

But Kumalo clapped him on both shoulders instead, and grinned.

'All right, Lawrence, we all make mistakes. It's not good for us to punish each other for each and every one. We have a common enemy to fight. We bury our differences, we work together. We all have our own jobs to do and we don't become ambitious for ourselves. That's the worst mistake of all. Right, Lawrence?'

'Right, Lincoln.'

'Wait your turn, Lawrence. In time it will come.'

Now Gumbi could smile with genuine relief, and the feeling spread at once to those around them. The tension had gone. The black soldiers surged about Kumalo again, hoisted him to their shoulders and began carrying him along the footpath. Nandi still hovered anxiously by his side, and Marriner, Judith and the others, already half forgotten, traipsed along behind. Kumalo raised his fist in the Congress salute. The Leader had come home.

Epilogue

'He froze them,' said Harry. 'Joshua froze the funds. Hey, are you listening to me, man?'

Marriner had been only half listening. Through the open french windows he had caught sight of Judith and Rendle, in their borrowed bathing suits, crossing the lawn. They had just emerged from the back door of the house after what they called their siesta. It was Monday afternoon. The safe house was a crumbling colonial villa in the Polona district of Maputo, once the retreat of wealthy Portuguese *colonos*. The garden was a wilderness of overgrown tropical plants—oleander, frangipani, hibiscus—but it boasted a cracked old swimming-pool which Rendle had managed to half-fill with water from a hose. They were heading towards it now, arm in arm, talking and laughing softly, Judith pausing to plant a kiss on Rendle's shoulder.

Harry chuckled. 'Just imagine Josh, sitting in Switzerland like some South American general, with seven million dollars of other people's money in his hands. And dictating terms for releasing it.' The thought still gave Harry pleasure. He chuckled and leaned back contentedly in the rickety bamboo couch, sipping warm gin out of a teacup.

'So I'm sitting in that damned camp, nothing to do all day but worry about Lincoln, when I remember this loophole in the Congress constitution. I managed to smuggle a message out to Joshua. There he was, still holding in trust nearly all the money he'd raised after the Algiers conference. Seven million dollars, all in his own name.

'There's this provision that when the treasurer believes the proper voting procedure won't be followed on the disposal of funds he's entitled to freeze them. That means no income for the Congress. No money to feed and pay our soldiers, apart from anything else. We could have had a mutiny on our hands. Josh with all of it under his mattress, somewhere in Zurich—they didn't even know where to find him.'

They sat in the sparsely furnished drawing room, waiting for the car to the airport. After bustling around town all weekend Harry had finally turned up half an hour ago with the paperwork Marriner would need for his journey: emergency passport, exit visa, air tickets. This wasn't the kind of bustling he enjoyed. The glory-train of the People's Congress leadership, with Lincoln Kumalo at its head, had swept northwards to Lusaka within a day of its arrival, leaving Harry to tie up a lot of loose ends: running to and fro with papers, arguing with consular officials and bureaucrats. Getting Marriner out was no real problem, but the South Africans—Rendle and Judith staying here, the rest of the squad holed up in a villa of their own at Catembe—would need to be granted refugee status before they could move on. More red tape, even though the Mozambicans were making it as easy as they could.

All this had not improved Harry's temper. He leaned forward and poured himself some more gin.

'I had guessed that the three of them—Pahlani, Govender and Gumbi—were going to find a way to keep me and Josh out of circulation, and vote Lincoln out of office. So what Josh told them was that he was simply holding on to the money until Lincoln had been reinstated with full presidential powers. It was all in the rulebook. Well, more or less. Without the money the Congress would be helpless. Without Lincoln we'd be more than helpless. They could have both together, or neither. They began to see sense, after that. I wasn't to know that Gumbi was pulling a stroke of his own, but even he has fallen into line behind Lincoln, now.'

Marriner smiled. 'I remember you telling me once about your faith in the power of money.'

'That's right, Patrick. You and me, drinking gin like this, in Ireland, a lifetime ago. How does it feel to be rich?'

'It hasn't sunk in. I suppose that's what they all say.'

They heard a car draw up at the front, doors slam. It was going to be a long, zigzagging journey back to Europe for Marriner, avoiding exposure to unfriendly eyes. At least he could be thankful that the press hadn't picked up his name, the South African Government, with too much of its own to hide, having smothered all the details it could.

They stood up. They shook hands. He had said goodbye to Judith and Rendle earlier, and would only be disturbing their absorption in each other by doing it again. To his surprise, she had shown him a letter she was writing to her father: a first attempt at reconciliation, possibly the start of a friendship that would prosper better at a distance.

He took one more look at them, sitting on the edge of the pool, and felt a whisper of regret. Back home there would be the Widow Swanson, evenings by turf fires, days in the damp green fields, some contentment, some restlessness. And always the same faint flickering of unease at the sight of a strange car nosing down the avenue at Ballygarron.

PETER DRISCOLL

Born in London, Peter Driscoll spent the first twenty years of his life in South Africa, the setting for *Spearhead*. He went to school and university there, and absorbed the beauty and attraction of the country as well as its smouldering political and social tensions.

His career started as a journalist working on the *Rand Daily Mail*, then one of the country's leading newspapers. He later moved to London and worked for ITN for three-and-a-half years as a sub-editor and scriptwriter. 'Unfortunately, as I was not a reporter, I was not sent to all the glamorous and exciting places that one might expect to go while working for ITN,' he confesses, 'but I did gain plenty of experience of writing dramatic stories.'

In 1973 Peter Driscoll decided to concentrate on writing, and his second book, *The Wilby Conspiracy*, also set in South Africa, established him as an international best-selling author. *The Wilby Conspiracy* was made into a highly successful feature film, and Driscoll hopes that *Spearhead* will also be filmed. 'All the feelers are out—we just have to wait and see.'

The background for *Spearhead* was based very much on his own experience of the country and of the issues that are at the centre of today's news. 'I keep very closely in touch with the events that are taking place in South Africa. Even though I have not lived there for more than twenty years, I still feel deeply involved with the country and its people.'

Peter Driscoll is currently hard at work on his eighth novel, written in the peace and tranquillity of his home in County Wicklow, in Ireland, where he lives with his wife and family. The book, still in its early stages, will be about espionage in Europe and the USA. Readers can be sure that it will be full of action, suspense and excitement.

HUNTER'S MOON

A CONDENSATION OF THE BOOK BY

GARRY KILWORTH

ILLUSTRATED BY BOB BAMPTON

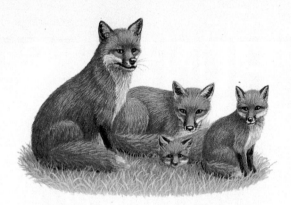

Tonight a hunter's moon rides high above
Trinity Wood. It shines on O-ha, the vixen,
and her mate, and on Gar, the badger, and on
a myriad other denizens of the countryside.
It also shines on O-ha's enemies: on Breaker,
lead hound of the local hunt, and on Sabre, the
vicious ridgeback at the manor house, who has
a score to settle with all foxes.

But the same moon glints on even more
dangerous enemies, who threaten the entire
world of Trinity Wood: the bulldozers and
concrete mixers of the men who are about to
turn it into a part of the encroaching town.

What will befall the creatures of the
countryside when these monsters start their
dreadful destruction? Who will run and who
will remain in a world where woodland paths
are changed to alleys, grassland to streets?

What will happen to O-ha and the cubs
she is expecting?

A masterpiece of suspense, as well as one of the
finest examples of nature writing of recent years.

PART ONE
The Foxes of Firstdark

Trinity Wood stood on a rise above a tidal river which wound its way over coastal flatlands. Its fox-spirits could tell you that it was an ancient knoll, its rocky ground untouched by the farmers who had closed round it since wolves had roamed the area. It was a dense place, grown to weakness in its centre where spindly oaks and blackthorns fought each other for light and space. Away from its heart there were small glades which encouraged bluebells and ferns, ground ivy and the occasional clump of cuckoopint. Among its inhabitants were wood pigeons, badgers, grey squirrels and foxes.

O-ha had not been born there but had moved in shortly after the dispersal period, when cubs leave their parents. She had found an old earth in the clay bank just inside the tree line. She had freshened it a little by scraping out the tunnel and chamber, but like most foxes was not fussy about the state of her home: it was simply a safe place to sleep, and the main priorities were that it remained warm and dry. O-ha was an untidy creature and any house-cleaning consisted of tossing rubbish outside the entrance. She was not unusual in this. Though personal cleanliness is important to foxes, the idea that one should spend time keeping the home tidy is dismissed with contempt.

The entrance to the earth was almond-shaped and around its roof arch was the strong protective root of a sturdy, squat oak tree. Its lowest branches were close to the ground, and on days when even the slightest breeze was blowing, the moving shadows of these boughs produced a camouflage effect which helped to disguise the earth's entrance. This, coupled with the way the exposed root twisted over and round the hole, meant that any unknowing observer would have to be at eye level with the opening to realise that there was a hole there at all.

To the other side of the earth's entrance was an alder which dripped bright berries in the autumn. Nailed to its trunk were the remnants of a barbed-wire fence, which O-ha found to be a very effective back-scratcher.

Since O-ha was an intelligent-looking vixen, with a glossy coat which varied between rust-red and grey, depending on the light, she was courted by at least three dog foxes. She chose a male her own age, a fox with humour in his eyes and a way of cocking his head to one side that turned her legs to willow wands.

'I admire you above all other vixens,' A-ran told her. 'You're bright, alert and . . . oh, dozens of other things. It would take too long to tell you all the reasons why you make me dizzy with excitement.'

When she gave him her decision, he showered her with autumn leaves in his joy. The sky was alive that day, with rushing clouds which swept shadows across the land and produced an ethereal half-light of ever-changing shades. They went out onto the windblown grasslands and his eyes danced with wild unusual pigments, which reflected the radiance around them.

In the warm damp grass, they tumbled and nipped each other, finding excitement in touching even though it was not a time for serious mating. They learned the intimate details of each other's bodies, the scratch-scars on O-ha's nose, the small 'v' that had been clipped from A-ran's right ear, both the result of hunting play with siblings. She thought the small white patch on his flank unusually attractive, and he remarked on the sleekness of her muzzle hair.

A-ran changed his name to A-ho to reflect her family name, as is traditional among foxes. It was a heady time for both of them, being young enough for most experiences to be great new discoveries.

'Do you love the smell of pine needles?' O-ha might say.

'Pine needles? Wonderful aroma. I'd go out of my way to get a good whiff of pine needles—and sap.'

'Oh yes, the sap too . . .'

And they would both marvel at their compatibility, how startlingly lucky it was that they had each found someone who liked the scent of pine needles, '. . . especially in springtime.'

Were there ever two foxes more suited to each other in the whole history of the world? Was there ever a pair whose opinions on life matched each other's so sharply, so precisely? Was there ever a more intelligent vixen, or a wiser dog fox, given that they were still quite young and willing to learn? Never, they agreed. Their parents, they told each other, were all right in their way, but somehow lacked the clear thinking and reasoned judgment which they themselves possessed.

That autumn was a magical time for the two new mates. There were golden scents in the air and hunting was good. They lived almost constantly in each other's company.

IT WAS MIDWINTER and the air was still, clean and sharp.

A-ho had been keeping close to her side for many days and his rising excitement was indicated by the way he carried his tail: high, like a bushy pennant. O-ha was keenly aware of her mate and was sometimes irritated by him as he persistently brushed against her, leaving her hardly enough room in the earth to move a paw. However, today she too was aware of a stirring of excitement in her body, and she knew that she was putting out a fragrance which had turned the brightness in his eyes to a hot fire.

Suddenly, she rose to her feet and went to the earth's exit, licked her nose, went through the rituals to test the wind for danger, then slipped outside. As always there were a thousand scents vying for her attention which her brain filtered automatically, so that the important ones received priority.

Although it was cold the sun shone down with winter hardness through the trees of Trinity Wood. She found a patch of grass and stood there, letting the weak rays warm her fur. A-ho was right behind her.

After a few moments he came up beside her and touched her flank with his forepaw. She could feel him trembling and an electric shiver went through her body. A-ho nuzzled her under her chin, and she nipped him sharply, to demonstrate her affection. He blazed like a high, hot fire on the grass, warming her with the red flames of his coat, ready to burn deep inside her body.

Suddenly he was behind her, and the skies turned crimson and the grass began to crackle beneath her. She let out a short yelp: he crooned once, and after a few seconds the world righted itself and she was able to look at her mate again. She studied his long, pointed muzzle, the handsome black-tipped ears, the russet coat. How lucky she was. A-ho lay on the damp grass, his narrow, foxy eyes drinking in her form. Then he let out a triple bark, and then a loud scream, before giving her his cocked-head look which he knew always endeared him to her.

'All right, tell the world,' she said, 'if you feel it's necessary. Personally, I don't. They can all see what a virile fellow you are.'

'It's traditional,' he remarked, casually.

Over the next three days they made love on several occasions and each time was as good as the last. The sky changed colour, and the air seemed to have promises hanging in it, like the lanterns of fruit which had hung in the autumn trees.

Yet Melloon, the fox name for the autumn wind, had long since departed, leaving bare trees dark with fungi, and bushes without berries to blood their branches. Sodden leaves covered the floor of Trinity Wood and there was great competition for meat amongst the predators: the owls, the hawks, the weasels. O-ha's diet was three-quarters meat, and she had to be sharp. On days when the ground was soft there were earthworms to be had, or she would steal winter cabbage from the *havnot*, the farmlands round Trinity Wood. Shortly after the mating season was over she found a fence full of *gubbins*, the fox word for animals killed and left by humans. These were old crows and stoats hung on fence wire. She cached some around the area, marked the place, then took one home to A-ho. He thanked her by licking her ear. Now that the mating was complete, there was no strain in their relationship.

Inside her, there were changes taking place. She looked forward to warmer weather and to Switter, the spring breeze. Many of the meadows round Trinity Wood were old grasslands and there were still hedgerows and ditches, necessary to birds, mammals and reptiles. The hedgeless landscape and sterilised new grasslands were moving in but had not yet overtaken the area round Trinity Wood.

The wood itself was an old-world mixture of coniferous and deciduous trees—yew, cedar, juniper, oak, beech, alder—not one of the man-made silent forests of sitka spruce, where pine needles suffocate undergrowth and insects and where the neat rows of trees are so close together that a rabbit could not squeeze between them.

Of course, O-ha and the other animals took Trinity Wood for granted, even though itinerant beasts brought warnings of an outside world that was being reshaped to suit the comfort and needs of those ugly bipeds whose hairless, featherless bodies were draped with loose-fitting cloth, and who showed their teeth even when they were not angry.

Not in our time, they said to themselves and to each other. *The woodlands and fields will not change in our lifetime.*

True, said the wigeon, whistling on the wind. And in a voice like two pebbles being struck together, the stonechat agreed.

The shrew, the grasshopper, the fox, the squirrel, the gregarious rooks and solitary crows; the shelduck that nest in old rabbit holes, the adder, the magpies, the winter balls of ants in hollow logs; the tree creeper, the nightjar, the hare and the rabbit; the badgers, the rafts of coots on the river . . . they all sang the same song: *Not in our time*.

FOR FOXES, THE WINDS are gods. They carry the scents and sounds necessary to fox awareness of all things: danger, food, rain, love, trees, earth, landscape. Each individual wind is a deity with a secret name, to be whispered by the rocks and trees, to be written on the surface of the rivers and lakes. More important than the sun or the moon, the wind is the breath of life. Somewhere, seasons out of time, is a mythical land known as *Heff*, where a shapeless form breathes through a series of hollow tree trunks. This is the palace of the winds.

The time was Ransheen, the white winter wind, when soft things had become brittle and the landscape had taken on sharp edges. Ransheen brought with her a belly full of flints and lungs that burned. The world was a block of stone with a frozen heart.

It was night and O-ha prepared for the ritual of leaving-the-earth with unhurried precision: an elaborate procedure which tested for dangers outside and ensured the secrecy of her earth's location. She licked her nose and poked it out into the cold path of Ransheen, getting her strength and direction. A thousand scents were out there, each one instantly recognisable. The smells of men and dogs were absent, however, and after some time O-ha gradually emerged from the earth to stand outside.

Around O-ha the trees of Trinity Wood were sighing in the moonlight. She moved her head from side to side, slowly; then made a swift dash to put ground between herself and her earth, through the edge of the thicket and out into the *hav*, the open heathland.

There was a hunter's moon, throwing its pale light over the landscape. When she was a cub, O-ha's mother had told her that the moon was the soul of the sun. In the beginning, not long after the world was formed, there had been no night or day: world-shapers like the great fox A-O, and the wolf Sen-Sen, had moved through the Firstdark using scent and sound, and had no need of light. However, the giant Groff, sent by humans to prepare the world for their invasion, had been instructed to provide light for the humans to hunt by. He plunged his hand deep into the earth and came up with a ball of fire. He called this molten ball the sun, but when he tossed it up into the sky he threw the sun so hard its soul became detached from its body. This ghost of the sun was called the moon, and followed a similar but separate path in its circuit of the world.

O-ha used the ancestral highway from Trinity Wood to Packhorse Field, where she knew she would find water. Her tread was delicate, and from time to time she paused to look over her shoulder, not to see, but to listen, for like all her kind she was unable to focus on a stationary object for more than a few seconds. She passed a cottage, using the ditch at the end of its long garden as cover. Her ears picked up the sound of a clock ticking in the bedroom of the house. Somewhere, out on the road that ran by the cottage—perhaps half a mile distant—a man was walking. His scent came to her on the back of Ransheen.

She lay still in the dark ditch. It was wise just to wait sometimes, if for no other reason than that some feeling had disturbed her. If the feeling said 'stay' then she stayed. Survival did not depend upon knowing everything, but on following instinct. Her thirst could wait.

Eventually she resumed her journey to the pond. O-ha was a very conventional fox, and even as she walked she carried out certain rituals. There was one set of these which was carried out religiously on all occasions: the marking. Almost subconsciously, O-ha marked certain areas of the highway with her urine, so that if A-ho came that way he would know she had recently been there.

AT ONE OF THE FOX byways O-ha heard a familiar tread, as delicate as her own, and smelled an odour which always sent a shiver of delight down her spine. She waited, poised, and soon another red fox came out of the tall white grasses.

'A-ho,' she said, 'I didn't hear you leave the earth. Why didn't you wake me?'

A-ho stopped and scratched his muscled body with the fluidity of a cat. 'Seemed a shame to disturb you.' He flicked his head. 'Been down to the orchard, looking for rats, but all the windfalls have gone. Nothing to get them from their holes. What about you?'

'Just going down to the pond for water.'

'Well, you be careful—in your condition . . .'

She was three weeks pregnant now and a warm glow was in her belly.

'I'll be all right.'

'Be careful,' repeated A-ho, and then he was gone, his dark coat moving towards their earth.

O-ha continued her trek through the moonlight. The man she had smelled earlier, out on the road, was now walking towards the animal highway. She could hear the crunch of his boots on the hard ground. Occasionally he lost his footing and barked softly.

O-ha slipped into the grasses and lay still, waiting for the man to pass. He came within a few feet of her, smelling strongly of smoke, and the other scents which he carried around him in a cloud showed that he was ill in the way that men she encountered in the early hours often were. His tread was unsteady, and once he fell over and lay still for a few moments. Then he growled softly and heaved himself to his feet, yapped again, and continued his meandering over the fields.

O-ha's encounters with humans were not infrequent, though it was rare for them to be aware of the meeting. Humans had the sharp eyes of a predator, but they had lost the instinct which went with such vision. She had decided that most humans were preoccupied with things which were outside the consideration of a fox. Why else would solitary men wear such strange expressions, and smell constantly of one kind of fear or another? And when there was more than one of them, they were usually so busy barking at each other that the world could turn upside-down and they would not notice. As for killing, humans sometimes killed neither for territorial reasons nor for food. There were times when they made a great spectacle of killing foxes, and there were times when they did it slyly, secretly, while no one was watching.

O-ha was no stranger to death, even to slaughter. She and A-ho had once entered a chicken coop and slaughtered the whole population. This was not bloodlust, but good husbandry: afterwards the pair of them had carried away and cached as many chickens as they were able, before the farmer arrived on the scene. O-ha understood about killing, so she did not think humans unnatural, only unreachable.

376

O-ha came to the pond and found there was a sheet of ice covering its surface. She knew she would have to lick away at the edge. First she muttered the ritual chants: *'Water, preserver of life, body of A-O the first fox of Firstdark, cleanse my spirit . . .'* Then, her senses tuned to the world around her, she licked steadily at the ice until she was satisfied. Never for a moment did she relax. She had to be constantly on the alert for any sound that spelled discord, for any smell that meant danger.

Her thirst satisfied, O-ha slipped away across the *havnot* until she reached the relative safety of the open *hav*. By this time dawn was beginning to creep across the fields. O-ha found a byway in the grass, following it towards the sun. When she had travelled about two hundred yards, she stopped and sniffed the air.

Meat! She could smell the heady scent of rabbit.

Her senses flamed as she turned from the byway into untracked country, a place where brambles wrestled with bryony and tall thickets of blackthorn sprouted from the cropped grass. A stoat, having changed its name and colour for the winter months to become the ermine, hissed and spat at her as she passed its labyrinth of tunnels. She was not hungry enough to tackle the ferocious little beast, and anyway, there was a promise of rabbit. O-ha knew of a warren near by, but this was a wounded or freshly dead creature.

Proceeding carefully, she eventually came to a covert of blackthorn, riddled with rabbit runs. At the entrance to one of these lay a rabbit, a line of blood round its throat. One of man's traps had caught the creature: a wire snare that strangled its victims to death. O-ha could see where the base of a blackthorn had been stripped of bark as the rabbit thrashed out with its hind legs.

O-ha moved forward slowly, her muzzle close to the ground. The first thing she did was to pass her shadow over the rabbit twice, in the ritual cleansing of carrion. Then she gripped the freshly dead rabbit in her jaws and tried to pull it away from the wire but, as expected, it held fast. Realising that it was impossible to free the meal from its trap, she satisfied herself by gnawing its underside. Her snout buried itself inside the rabbit as she fed and her belly welcomed the warm food.

When she had been feeding for some time, a sound came to her from the far side of the covert. Since her nostrils were clouded with the smell of blood, she could catch no scent. She stiffened, flattening herself to the ground. One thing she did know: it was not the tread of a human. It was a four-footed creature: a small dog, badger or fox.

She was not afraid of badgers, even though they are more powerful creatures than foxes, but a dog was another matter. Her breath quickened as she swiftly assessed the avenues of escape. Then the scent of fox filled her nostrils as a grizzled dog fox came round the blackthorn, licking its grey muzzle.

O-ha said, 'A-magyr! You startled me.'

The old dog fox eyed her belligerently. A-magyr had once been a *rangfar*: one of those itinerant foxes that wander the countryside, the gypsies of the fox world. Although he had now settled in the district, it was said he still had nothing but contempt for *ords*, the foxes that never move more than a mile from their parish.

'Startled?' he growled. 'Foxes shouldn't be startled. They should have their wits constantly about them. They should know the time ahead as well as the time past.' He shouldered her out of the way. 'Now, push off. I like the look of that rabbit.'

O-ha considered the situation. She had eaten most of the soft meat and breast. Only the head and legs remained untouched. But this was her rabbit. A-magyr was robbing her of her find, and he knew it.

She flattened her body against the ground in front of him, her ears against her head and her hindlegs as taut as springs.

A-magyr looked up, almost lazily. His eyes narrowed. 'What?' he said. 'Try me, would you? Go away, vixen, before you get hurt.'

O-ha bristled with frustration. She dearly wanted to fight, but she was concerned for her unborn cubs. It was wrong to put them at risk. She decided to back off, saying testily, 'Mind my cubs.'

He paused to eye her haughtily. 'Pregnant, eh? Couldn't care less.'

'Of course, you wouldn't know anything about cubs, would you?' she said. 'Was there ever an O-magyr in your life? They say no vixen would ever live with such a . . .'

She stopped when he turned to face her.

'Watch your mouth, *ord*,' he said. 'Don't think those cubs will prevent me teaching you a lesson. Respect your elders.'

A-magyr crossed his shadow back and forth over the meat, the way O-ha had done, then began to chew a hind leg. She watched him for a short while as he chewed the meat that was so precious during Ransheen, then she strolled away at a leisurely pace.

He called out to her, with his mouth full, 'Hunt on today. Heard the hounds this morning. Look to your tail, vixen.'

A hunt! A cold shiver went down her spine. She ought to thank A-magyr for the warning, but she wondered if this was his idea of a joke, to watch her running back to her earth while he finished the rabbit. The trouble was, she was thirsty again after the meal, and the pond was too far away. She considered other watering places.

O-ha carried with her ancient knowledge of all the water holes, soaks and hiding places in her parish. Most of this topographical knowledge was passed between generations—from mother to cubs—but some of it was retained through racial memory, from the time of Firstdark, when the world was formed. Foxes had been on the earth longer than many animals, certainly longer than those upstart humans, and had witnessed the birth of the world into its basic form. During Firstdark, foxes had fought great battles with other creatures, much larger than themselves, and the ancestors of O-ha had triumphed. Those first heroes and heroines still lived on, as the fox-spirits of the *hav*, and from time to time they appeared; you could not summon them, but they came to the spiritually oppressed when they felt their presence was deserved.

Survival, in any parish, depended upon the knowledge passed down from Firstdark, which was held in songs and chants. The mystery and magic of Firstdark were locked in fox memory. Walking through the tall grasses, now glistening with the melting frost, O-ha made her way to a depression a quarter of a mile from Trinity Wood, where water was often held in a natural cup of rock. The rock was one of the first objects struck by the morning sun and it was possible that there might be meltwater in the hollow. Once she had drunk, she intended to go to earth.

She stepped out with a determined stride. As she travelled along a ditch beneath a mossy bank, Ransheen brought a warning to her from upwind. She stiffened. Almost immediately, she heard the terrible sound of the hunting horn and the distant yelping of dogs.

'Up! Up! Get the red devils up!' the hounds were shouting in that dog dialect of theirs.

The mob was abroad.

O-ha was alarmed, but did not panic. The hunt was still a long way off. She could not even smell the horses yet. She could hear their hooves drumming against the hard turf, but they were still at a canter. No gallop had begun, which meant they had not picked up a scent.

She crossed from the bank to some trees, still walking in the shadows. A fox does not have the stamina nor the speed to beat foxhounds in a race across open country: the dogs are able to run long after a fox's heart has burst, or its legs collapsed beneath it. Given such odds in favour of the pursuer, it is surprising that so many foxes escape the pack, but they get away because they rely on wile and guile rather than speed. Foxes can leap fences, walk the edge of a plank with perfect balance, squeeze through holes, and use the odours of external things such as cars to disguise the trail. O-ha had ten times more resourcefulness than any hunting hound.

Just as she was about to enter a covert, there was a barking from downwind. A human on foot! He had seen her and was yapping excitedly to attract the distant riders. She saw the man wave his stick and point in her direction.

'Damn you,' she snapped. She caught a whiff of his odour, between the safety of her earth and herself.

Like the sound of a bloodthirsty beast itself, the horn was growing louder, and nearer.

THE CRIES OF THE HOUNDS filled the air, punctuated by the nightmarish sound of the hunting horn and the baying of the huntsmen.

O-ha's heart was racing now, as she zigzagged over the *hav*, hoping to find some hiding place where the hounds could not get at her. She had never witnessed the end of a hunt, but she had heard from those who had that the dogs would rip her to pieces and that her tail would be cut from her coat, to be wiped over the face of some human new to the gory business, smearing it with blood. It was one of those human rituals which went back to the time when the two-legged beasts came out of the sea of chaos: a ritual they had brought with them from the other side. O-ha was not the first fox to wonder what kind of creature it was that used the reeking, smoking blood of another animal for decoration.

She reached a ditch beside a road and immediately used it like a tunnel, hoping that the icy bottom would not hold her scent for long. Smaller mammals scattered out of her way as she travelled along: fear was abroad, and they caught it from her as she swept past them, scurrying away to their holes in an effort to rid themselves of the foul smell, which created such panic.

O-ha left the ditch as the hounds were milling around, trying to pick up her scent at the point where she had entered it. She waited for a few seconds, gathering her breath. She knew if she did not get a drink soon, her strength would ebb rapidly. Then she heard the hounds tumbling along the hedgerow, and knew her ruse had not worked.

Instead of crossing the field adjacent to the ditch, she travelled down the centre of the road for part of the way. Her instinct told her to do the unpredictable thing. Behind her, the hounds still shouted. 'This way! We've almost got the devil.' The riders were thundering alongside the road, knowing that the hard surface would damage their horses' legs with the jarring. It slowed them a little.

A car came round the bend and its driver, on seeing O-ha, skidded to a stop. O-ha hesitated for a few moments. She knew cars to be dangerous, because animals had been struck and killed by these machines; however, she knew from experience with tractors that the fumes which clouded them were able to mask an animal's scent.

The driver of the car was a female, staring at O-ha with a strange expression on her face. O-ha made a swift decision, and jumped up onto the bonnet of the car, ran across the roof, and down to the roadway on the other side. The car's fumes would help to scatter her own odours over the landscape.

She continued along the middle of the road, and a little later heard the sound of confused voices as the hounds milled round the car. The vehicle itself was trying to edge forward through the dogs, until another car came from the opposite direction and also became entangled with the hounds. Then the riders caught up with the pack and the car drivers began sounding their horns. O-ha gained valuable rest minutes as dogs, horses, people and machines tried to extract themselves from each other. Humans howled and the hounds cursed, shouting obscenities at the cars and their occupants, and swearing at the horses who threatened to trample them. But soon the hunting horn was sounded, the dogs were urged onwards with barks and whips, and they were in full pursuit again.

O-ha came to a roadside cottage, leaped up onto the fence and with remarkable poise travelled along it to the gate, where she jumped down into the garden. There was a stone bird-table in the middle of the small lawn. O-ha smelled the water and jumped, balancing precariously on the edge of the bowl. As she drank, the bird-table rocking under her weight, a small dog came round the corner and shouted, 'Ha, fox! Ha, fox!'

O-ha bared her teeth at the mutt and then leaped the fence with an agility that had the dog looking vexed and angry.

'Stupid beast,' she muttered to herself. The water had given her new heart and energy, but now the hunt was very near. A sudden noise behind her told her that she had been spotted by a huntsman who had unwittingly overtaken the pack, and the hounds were screaming now in a frenzy of excitement.

Too close, she thought, panting, as her heart hammered in her breast. They're getting too close. I'm going to be caught. Oh, A-ho! Oh, my poor cubs! How am I going to throw them off now?

She did a circuit now, crossing the road again, and set off over the fields. She ran and ran until her heart was bursting within her and her brain jangled. There was a thought in her head that she could lead the hounds on to where she had left A-magyr. He would have gone, but the rabbit would still be there. It might delay them long enough to enable her to get back to her earth.

She reached a field of cows and ran in and out of the animals, hoping their presence would help in throwing the scent, but the lead hound was only a dozen yards behind her. Now he was calling, 'I'm here, I'm here. Don't look back, fox. You're about to die. I am Breaker, lead hound of the hunt. Breaker will tear your throat, spill your fox blood. Breaker, Breaker, Breaker . . .'

The other hounds took up his cry behind him, screaming, 'Breaker, Breaker—follow him close! The kill is only a nose away!'

Waste your breath, she thought, but the misery and terror of death was on her, and she had to fight the pain in her body to force it onwards. While she still ran, there was hope. Many a fox had escaped at the last moment, through some fortuitous action.

The cows began running this way and that, slowing the riders but not the dogs. At the end of the field was an encampment of travellers' caravans, and she ran right through the centre, narrowly missing a sleeping lurcher dog. It leaped to its feet and was about to give chase, when it was bowled over by the impetuous Breaker.

The gypsies themselves cheered the fox through the encampment and even made an effort to prevent the hounds from following, until the huntsmen came up and began laying about them with riding crops. One or two fights broke out, but Breaker was still on her tail and she knew that most of the other hounds would follow his determined lead.

She reached the edge of a copse and just as she entered she heard a voice she knew well. 'Quick, up onto that branch. I'll take over.'

It was A-ho, her mate.

She needed little encouragement. She leaped from the ground up into the tree, and balanced there against the trunk.

A-ho showed himself briefly to Breaker, who came crashing into the undergrowth, and then the brave dog fox was away.

'Don't worry,' he called, 'I'm as fresh as a daisy. I'll get rid of this one, and see you at the earth.'

Oh, run, run, she thought, gasping for breath and hardly able to maintain her position on the branch. Several of the hounds began milling round the base of the tree, looking up at her, but on hearing Breaker's full-blooded, throaty cries, they continued the chase. The riders swept by, urging any slow hounds onwards, unaware that the quarry had changed and that a relay had taken place. Soon the sounds of the hunt drifted into the distance and she was able to think a little more clearly.

She was still terrified but not now for herself—for A-ho, her mate. Although his voice had been full of bravado, she had smelled his fear-sweat, and she was in an agony of apprehension for him. She told herself he was no fool: if anyone could outwit the hounds, it was A-ho. He was a clever fox who knew the tricks, knew the parish. He would have some idea in mind, and he would apply that, no matter how frightened he was. She told herself all this, as she waited for the tiredness to abate from her limbs, so that she could be on her way back to the earth.

Some time later, she jumped to the ground and padded to the top of a rise beyond the copse. She sniffed Ransheen for any scent of the hunt, but there was nothing. No sounds fell on her ears either, and she was beginning to feel that the nightmare was over. Around her, the world had returned to normal, as if there had never been a horde of barbarians on horseback sweeping across the countryside, intent on gorging their lust for blood.

As she approached Trinity Wood, there were warnings on the wind. She moved slowly and deliberately, until she heard the clink of metal on stones. She went no further. There were humans round her earth, digging. Sometimes, before or during a hunt, they filled in an earth to stop foxes from returning to relative safety. She imagined that was what was going on at the moment.

'Do your worst,' she said. 'A-ho and I will find another earth.' The home was just a hole in the ground and could be abandoned without regret. Winter was a difficult time to find another earth, but there were two of them to search.

She went back to the tall grasses, where she could lie without being seen. Although her poor eyesight did not permit her to observe the activity in detail, she could use her other senses to tell her what was going on. After a while she realised the digging was going on too long for the men to be filling in the earth. They were digging it *out*. The only reason they would bother to do that was if they believed there was a fox inside.

Her mouth went dry at the thought that A-ho was in the earth. Could he have returned so quickly? She realised with a sickening feeling that it was possible. And suddenly the chinking of metal against flint ceased, there was a moment of quiet, and then a great howl of delight went up from the men. O-ha stood up, careless of being seen, and witnessed A-ho being dragged from the remains of the earth by his tail. He dangled at the end of a strong-looking arm, trying to turn and bite the wrist. She could smell the fear in him.

Oh, A-ho! The odour of his terror almost drove her crazy. She ran back and forth in the grasses, knowing she was helpless to give him any kind of support. There was a vague thought that if she could get to the man who held him, he might have a chance, but it was against the nature of a wild thing to launch a direct attack on humans. Were she cornered, she might fling herself forward in desperation, but the instinct to run away was so powerful that it was all she could do to remain within listening distance. Finally she could stand it no longer and began to run, and at that moment she saw one of the men raise a spade above his head and swing downwards. Immediately afterwards there was a horrifying sound. It could have been a metal blade striking turf, except that O-ha knew it was not. No more sounds came from her mate after that. She smelled blood and slunk away, bile rising to her throat.

She spent the rest of the day in a daze of disbelief. The idea that A-ho was dead was such a terrible one that unconsciously she put up a great resistance to it. All day she lay in the grass, resting and chewing at frozen grassroots to satisfy her growing hunger. The rabbit seemed so far in the past, it might have been a week ago.

When evening came, she returned to Trinity Wood.

The earth was a scene of devastation. The tunnel had been torn open, clods of frozen turf lay scattered in all directions. There was a brown stain on the root of the oak. A hard cold lump formed in O-ha's stomach. At last she accepted what had happened, and grief flooded through her.

'A-ho!' she called frantically.

The wind soughed through the trees.

'A-ho, A-ho . . .'

She called and called, knowing that she would never receive an answer. The men had executed her mate. They had not even left his body, but had carried it off somewhere for their own purposes.

Then she had the wild thought that maybe he had escaped, wriggled out of their grasp. Perhaps he was hiding somewhere, waiting for her to return? Maybe A-ho was out looking for her, thinking that she had not returned because she had herself been caught?

'It's all right,' she called, out into the darkness, 'I'm alive. They didn't get me.'

She lay down and waited. All through the long night she waited, but when the dawn came she lapsed into despair, knowing that he had gone.

Then, as a red sky began to emerge above, a fox came to O-ha from out of the half-light: an insubstantial fox with a pure white flame hovering a few inches above its head. The flame did not flicker but burned steadily. An eternal flame. The fox-spirit paused by Trinity Wood, and then continued its journey.

O-ha climbed wearily to her feet and followed it, across the fields to the manor house beyond the farm. There, hanging by his neck from a piece of wire, was the shredded body of her mate A-ho. He swayed gently in Ransheen's unseen hands. They had left him on a fence, like a piece of *gubbins*, to warn all foxes that the gamekeepers of the manor house were people to be reckoned with.

'The hunt—he evaded the hunt. He was a clever fox, my A-ho,' said O-ha, to the fox-spirit.

Vacant eyes were turned on the vixen.

'Yes, he evaded the hunt. I think you are aware of what happened. He was seen by some stableboys, returning to earth, and they dug him up and killed him with spades. They brought him here, threw him to the hounds.'

'And his tail?'

'They took that first. They have a word for it. A brush. It's their word, not ours.'

O-ha stared at her mate, at the ragged fur that used to lie beside her own, full of warmth and vitality. Now it was an empty thing, covered in black, dried blood. Glazed empty orbs were in the place of those hot, bright eyes she was used to seeing, looking into her own. It was not A-ho. Nevertheless, she asked the fox-spirit, 'Can you get him down from there?'

'No. I have no power over physical matters. We are made only of mist and light, of dreams and visions, of songs and memory. You understand? I am the fox-spirit that leads the living to the dead. Another will come to guide your mate to the Perfect Here.'

O-ha watched as the cloud of mist scattered before her eyes, and the flame drifted away over the grasses.

O-ha then began the ritual for which she had been led to A-ho's corpse by the fox-spirit. She chanted sacred rhymes, and at the same time she traced symbols on the ground round the hanging body. To anyone but a fox these marks would be incomprehensible scratches in the dirt, but to *Vulpinae* they represent the four winds: Ransheen, the winter wind; Melloon, the autumn, Frashoon, the summer; and the most erratic and unpredictable, the crazy March wind Scresheen, who came during the month of birth and created turmoil amongst the trees. After this the ground was marked in a special way, which to humans would be nothing but an offensive smell. Then O-ha walked from the three corners of the trinity towards the body of her mate, but from Scresheen's corner she walked away from the carcass, drawing the unpredictable one away from the corpse, to allow the remaining trinity to attract the fox-spirits to where no humans reside. The Perfect Here is the fox's own parish, with all its familiar woods and fields, coverts and streams—but in the otherworld beyond death, a mystical shadow of a beloved landscape, without the terrors found in the world of the living.

A-ho was at peace, but O-ha was alone.

She took one last look at her erstwhile mate, and then made her way back to Trinity Wood. Outside the wood she took stock of her situation. She had no earth to go to and no mate to help her find another. She was homeless. All she had left was her cubs.

'It isn't enough,' she said fiercely, the pall of grief for her mate heavy on her spirit. Then the fear for her cubs came through. 'I have to have somewhere to rear my cubs.'

She first went looking for the mystic fox, A-konkon, famous for his wisdom. It was her hope that he could offer some practical advice on finding a new earth in the middle of winter. Instead, when she found him, he gave her a lecture on the spiritual joy of death. 'A-ho has undergone a release,' said A-konkon. 'He's happy where he is.'

'I know he's gone to a nice place,' she said. 'A better place than this—but I still feel terrible. He may be happy, but I feel bad.'

A-konkon looked her directly in the eyes and said, 'Grief is a complex thing. We do not grieve because someone is dead, but because they are no longer alive. They have left us.'

'You mean, I'm selfish.'

'There are all sorts of other emotions entangled with bereavement. We may feel guilty because we treated them badly at some time, or because we feel responsible for their death . . .'

O-ha nodded.

'. . . the fact is, we can't reach them any more, to talk to them about these things, so they're difficult to work through. The important thing is that although you believe A-ho has gone to a better land, you still have to work through this storm of emotions, to prise them out slowly, and get on with life.'

'Believe?' she contested hotly. 'I *know* he's gone to a better place. I saw the fox-spirit, remember.'

'*You* saw, no one else. If we believe in something strongly enough—which we all do about the Perfect Here—then isn't it possible that our brains, fevered by emotion, may produce what we want to know?'

'You mean, I had a hallucination?' She was getting very angry with A-konkon.

'It's possible. Anything's possible.'

385

'Thank you,' she said, coldly, 'for your *help*.'

'You're entirely welcome—I shan't expect payment for a couple of months, but once the weather turns and the hunting gets better . . . ?'

Before she left she asked A-konkon about finding a new earth, but he shrugged impatiently.

'Material needs are not my concern. I can help your soul, your mind, but not your body. Personally, I think an earth is an unnecessary luxury.'

Nevertheless, O-ha felt a little fortified. A-konkon had angered her with his useless words, and there is nothing like anger to oust other emotions. *He* might not need an earth, but in her condition, she certainly did. Later, it came to her that A-konkon might have said what he said on purpose, in order to redirect her anger. It had raised her out of her apathy and started her searching for a new home.

She decided he was a very wise fox, after all.

THERE WAS A STORM, with rain coming down like lead shot and battering the saplings, forcing them to bow low, as if the weight of the heavy, black bull-clouds was borne by their supple stems. Giant goat-gods fought in the heavens, their eyes flashing in terrible anger, their great skulls crashing together and shaking the skies. Through this driving rain, light and noise, O-ha stumbled around looking for a home.

For a whole day O-ha searched Trinity Wood. She found an earth on the north side, but it turned out to be occupied by a *stoad*, that is an elderly fox whose age entitled her to a certain respect and esteem. This one was a testy vixen who did not want a young parent-to-be invading her earth. She screeched at O-ha, telling her to find some other place.

'Have you no heart?' said O-ha. 'My mate has just been killed and our earth destroyed. I need somewhere to stay, just for a while.'

'No heart whatsoever,' snapped the *stoad*. 'I lost it a long while ago, and I don't remember the last time I had a mate, so you won't get any sympathy out of me on that score.'

O-ha was too weary and dispirited to fight with the *stoad* and she left, to wander the woods again. By the time the moon was high, she had found a large oak and was curled up in a hollow between the half-exposed roots. It was cold and damp, and she knew if she did not find shelter soon, she might put her unborn cubs in danger. The hard edge of winter was cutting into her like a blade.

The following morning she shook a light fall of snow from her fur and staggered to the edge of the wood. There she dug as well as she could in the humus, looking for earthworms to eat. She found a rotten log full of woodlice, which she devoured. Then she licked what moisture she could from the snow, before setting off again to search for a home.

The day seemed full of angles and sharp edges. The sky was a hard blue, even the sunlight seemed cold. O-ha's body trembled as she wandered in the *hav* beyond the wood, along the ditches and hedgerows.

Once, she came across another pair of foxes, O-lan and A-lon, but they told her there was no room in their earth. The vixen was pregnant, and would soon be having a litter.

'We'd like to help you,' said O-lan, 'but our earth is small. It's clay, and you know how hard clay gets in the winter. You can't scrape out a hole big enough to store an acorn, let alone a place big enough for another fox. Sorry, but there it is.'

As O-ha stumbled away, A-lon called after her, and she turned to face him. 'Listen,' he said, 'I've just remembered there's a colony of badgers on the south side of Trinity Wood—a large sett. Why don't you ask them if they'll take you in? It's a fairly common arrangement, you know, for badgers to share their homes with us. One of my brothers lives with badgers and gets on all right with them.'

'Thanks—thanks very much. I'll give them a try if nothing else turns up.'

'Well—good luck,' he said.

By the time evening came again, O-ha was still homeless. Being near to the south side of the wood, she searched for the entrance to the badgers' sett, and found a hole at the base of an elm. She went down into the darkness, and along a sixty-foot tunnel. The smell of badger was strong in her nostrils and she could hear them moving about in adjacent chambers. While she was not afraid of badgers, she felt insecure in one of their tunnels. She was by no means sure of a welcome.

She came to a point where the tunnel opened up into a chamber, and a voice cried, '*Feond oder freond?*' in harsh tones. Although it was dark in the sett, O-ha had a good mental picture of her surroundings, and knew she was confronted by a large, elderly male badger.

'Fox,' she said, not understanding the guttural tongue of the badger. 'I . . . I lost my earth. The humans destroyed it.'

'*Guman* destroy? Ah, I speak some fox. You lost, eh?'

'No—I was wondering, hoping, that you had some room? A spare chamber? I have nowhere to live.'

The badger grunted. 'Ah, we got plenty room. You want stay, eh? I ask the others. You wait here.'

There was a shuffling from the other side of the chamber and then silence. She waited for some time before there were sounds of the badger returning.

'Others say you stay—most say. You no bother us, eh? You keep yourself and no bother. I show you bed, top level.'

'That's very kind . . .' she began to say, but the badger merely said gruffly, 'Follow.'

The badger took her up to the second level, to a chamber which felt quite roomy and which had dry bedding on the floor. First she marked the chamber, under the disapproving eye of the badger, then she regarded the dry grass and leaves. She was not used to a bed, having a fox's ascetic nature, but this time she sank gratefully onto the leaves, her eyes closing almost as her head touched her paws. She heard the badger saying, 'You go out through top hole. No come through my hole no more, see . . . ' Then she was asleep.

ON WAKING NEXT MORNING, she stretched out a paw to touch A-ho. She wondered, sleepily, why she could not hear or smell him. Then bewilderment followed, as she failed to recognise anything about the dark chamber in which she found herself.

'A-ho?' she whispered, a little afraid. Where was he? Out hunting perhaps, hoping to surprise her with a rabbit or some other kind of food? Where was the scent of his marks? Why did the earth not smell of his warm, musty fur, his sleep-odours?

Then, at last, she remembered the events of two days ago: the hunt, and the fox-spirit leading her to her mate's torn body. The sense of loss was even more overwhelming than it had been the previous day and night, and the full impact of his death descended on her like a heavy coat, smothering her. The previous day she had woken in the wood and remembered that A-ho had gone but now, waking and forgetting he had gone, then to remember, was far worse. It was something she would do many times, for seasons out of time, and it would never cease to cause her spiritual torment.

With heavy heart she found the tunnel and was about to go along it when she recalled the badger's last words. She was not to use that way. There was a second, narrower, exit on the far side of the chamber and she found that this led to the surface within thirty feet, without entering any other chambers.

During the next few weeks, O-ha tried to have as little as possible to do with the badgers, simply because they preferred it that way. One night, however, when she had just returned to the sett after searching for food, the old badger who had first spoken to her came to her chamber. His name was Gar.

'I come to say how you are?' he said, settling down.

'I'm fine,' she said. 'A little lonely, but . . .'

'Sure, sure. This is bad thing that happen to your mate. *Guman*, huh!' He clicked his teeth to show what he thought of mankind. 'Once they send a dog down here—small-middle dog—I bite him—ha!' Gar bared his ferocious-looking incisors.

O-ha was impressed. 'You fought a dog?'

'Ya. Fight him and send him run. We badger very strong animal. We badger, long, long history. We no bother this men, but they all the time try kill badger. Many *guman* not hurt badger, but some . . . they kill.'

'Oh, we have a long history, too, and they bother us all the time. I don't know why.'

'You fox run fast, is why. They like run, *guman*—run, run, run, for no thing. Crazy animal, *guman*. Sometime they give us food, in the little field by house. Watch through window. Look, look, brock eat our food! What they think we do?' He grunted, to show his contempt. 'Gar not worry, though. Gar strong in here.' He indicated his chest. 'Men can take old Gar body, but not his soul. Soul belong to no one but Gar.'

O-ha liked Gar. He seemed to have found the something which foxes talked about and believed only existed in the spirit world, beyond death.

'What you should do,' said Gar, dreamily, 'is go for long journey. Things happen on long journey. Big hill, deep valley, fast, fast river—see all these things. World is big place.'

'I don't want to go on a journey,' she said. 'Boring as it may sound, this parish is large enough for me.'

'I understand,' said Gar. 'Listen, I hear you fox can copy other animal, like sheep, or bird. Is this true?'

O-ha said, 'We can mimic other creatures, yes.'

'Let me hear—you make bird sound.'

O-ha obliged by chirruping. Then she bleated plaintively, like a lamb calling for its mother.

'Ha, good. I heard this was true. Now we talk, find out about fox. You find out about badger. What you think, this *guman* not like fox because run fast, eh?'

'I was told as a young cub that humans have never liked us because we kill chickens.'

'What means is, fox kill chicken before *guman* kill chicken, is all. Everybody want eat chicken. Anyway,' Gar went on, 'they not all hate fox. No, no. I know fox live in *guman* place. They no kill him. Is only *guman* on horse—*guman* with gun—these hate fox.'

'That is the only kind I have met,' said O-ha grimly.

'Whole world full of other kind. You go on long journey—you see other kind.'

'I'd rather stay here,' she repeated.

Gar sighed. 'Well, I getting back now. Nice to talk. We do some more some time, eh?' She heard him get to his feet and shuffle out of the chamber, down the tunnel towards his own bed.

She slept after that, dreaming of humans, the secondary fear of foxes. The primary terror, the Unremembered Fear, was never dreamed. It lurked somewhere beyond even the subconscious, deeper than dreams could reach, for its terrible white eyes and white jaws marred a face even the bravest of the brave could not visualise without travelling to the borders of madness. Long ago it had been pushed down into the back of the mind, from where it could not be retrieved. Not until it showed its ugly visage in the land once again, and mercifully that had not happened for some time.

One evening, when she was out hunting, she came across an old disused shed in a copse not far from a human dwelling. She checked for footprints or recent signs that men had been there, but she found nothing to arouse her fears. Inside the shed were some metal implements, all rusting away and joined to the shed walls by the lacy traps set by spiders for their prey. There was a blackbird's nest tucked high up in one corner: a good indication that the place was not frequented by humans.

A fox likes complete security for her young, and it had been worrying O-ha for some time that she would be exposing her cubs to danger by having them in the badgers' sett. This shed might be a better place: the grass between the shed and the house, some three hundred yards distant, was high and had not been trampled, and it seemed as if the hut had not been visited for a long time. Another thing in its favour was that the door was still secure. She could only enter through the small, glassless window, which a dog would have difficulty getting through.

So she set her heart on using the shed. Until the time came, she would continue to live in the sett. It was convenient to be in a place where others could guard her stores of food, even if they did not realise they were doing it.

The days slid into weeks. Iron-grey skies were broken only by occasional weak sunlight, but rain and sleet lashed down quite often, washing the smaller creatures out of their homes, so hunting was not as difficult as it might have been. The humans stayed inside their houses when the rainstorms were sweeping across the land, and in any case, the ground was too wet to hold much of a scent.

One day, when Scresheen was screaming across the fields, snapping the branches off trees; when the hares were doing silly things out in the fields and weasels danced in front of stupefied rabbits; when hawks dropped out of nowhere on unsuspecting mice—on such a day, O-ha felt strange things happening inside her. She made a goodbye call on Gar.

'Where you going?' he asked, surprised.

'To see the world,' she said.

'Ha. Well, give it some kick from me,' he said.

'I will,' she said. 'And thank you for your kindness.'

'Pah. You look to them cubs, vixen. I see you some day. Gar see you when he nosing around that big old world, and you come back full of great things. Ha.'

She left the sett with a few misgivings, but these were soon dispelled when she reached the shed. There were no indications that anyone, dog or man, had been near it since she was there last. She jumped through the window and settled down on some old sacks in the corner to give birth to her cubs.

It was a painful business.

ONCE UPON A TIME there was no *hav* or *havnot* for the windwalking foxes. There was no *face*, which is the word for land covered in concrete and brick, and no *gerflan*, which is land not usually frequented by

390

humans, such as military ranges. For a long time after the Long Hot Wind shaped the world, the land was just the land, consisting of earth and sky and, after A-O, rivers and ponds. In those days, when the world was still warm underfoot, and the rocks were living things that moved ponderously over the landscape like giant snails, there were no humans. There were wolves, deer, tree martens, wildcats, but no men. There were forests then, stretching into infinity, and the universe was green from end to end.

When the first humans arrived they frightened the timid rocks and stones so profoundly that they froze in their tracks and never moved again. The new two-legged animals began cutting down the forests and clearing the land until it lay bare and cold under the moonwatch. All things became their prey. One by one the animals fell under the tyranny of man, some resisting, some too timid to put up a fight. The horses went down early, as did the dogs and cats. Many of the pigs held out for a long time in the remains of the forests, but they too were overcome eventually. The wolves, cousins of the foxes, refused to give ground and were exterminated. Foxes themselves changed to meet the new circumstances: they went underground and took to using the night instead of the day. They survived by wit and guile, by stealth and determination.

One of the reasons for the successful survival of the foxes was that they elected no leaders to be followed blindly into hopeless battles. They did not form packs or herds; each dog fox was his own leader, relying only on himself. They remained individuals, able to adapt to circumstances as external changes took place, and there was no spot which man could point to and say, 'That's where the foxes gather—we can wait there and ambush them.' The foxes took notice of, but did not worship, their ancestors, the fox-spirits of the Firstdark.

Since those times foxes have managed to keep to their solitary ways. They use many voices, from a cold bark to a banshee scream, to fool any listeners. They use the darkness as a cloak. They never rush or hurry, knowing that a cool, clear head and calculated movements are more likely to keep them alive.

All this, O-ha would tell her cubs once they had grown to an age where they could understand. There were four in the litter and she licked them clean with an air of contentment. They were hers and she was prepared to defend them to the death. On the first day, she managed to catch a rat that came into the hut, and at the bottom of the garden she found a sack of rotten potatoes which had been thrown onto a compost heap. But when this food ran out she knew she was facing a grave problem, with no dog fox to hunt for the family.

As it happened, she was seen from the window of the house by one of its occupants, and to her surprise food was left for her about halfway down the garden. Gar had mentioned this strange behaviour by some of the humans, and she could not believe her luck in having found such people. They did the same for the hedgehogs which were constantly rolling into balls on O-ha's approach. Had she been starving, she might have attempted to get at the creatures, but she knew from her days as a cub that hedgehogs were almost impenetrable.

When the cubs were eight days old, the food source suddenly disappeared. The house appeared empty and it seemed that the occupants had gone away. They had done so without realising how much O-ha relied upon their generosity, possibly thinking that they were merely supplementing her diet rather than keeping her alive. She was bereft of support and had to wander further afield in order to keep herself fed and her milk flowing.

The next human dwelling, beyond the small cottage, was a great manor house where the man who led the fox hunts lived. The cottage was in fact the gatehouse at the entrance to the long driveway which led to the manor. This was a large, foursquare, cold-looking dwelling of grey, stone blocks. The lawns around it were kept short and neat, and a box-garden enclosed a concrete lily pond. It was not a place which attracted foxes.

O-ha kept away from the manor in her short forays for food, but one night she was attracted to a gazebo at the bottom of the lawns. Some human had been there during the day and had left bacon sandwiches inside. She could smell the bacon from the safety of the unkempt grass, and eventually climbed the ivy-covered wall which encircled the estate. She walked quickly up the gazebo steps. After a quick look round to see that she had not been observed, she snatched up the package and began to chew.

At that moment a shape came hurtling out of the darkness: a huge hound with a savage face. O-ha's instincts were ahead of her heart, and although afterwards she felt it thumping in her chest, she was by that time on the roof of the gazebo and out of range of the hound's snapping jaws. Strangely enough, this giant beast from the Unplace—most definitely the largest dog she had ever seen in her life—was not shouting at her. Doubtless it did not want to attract human attention and have them spoil its fun. It tried to reach her by leaping high off the ground with its powerful hindlegs, but when it was apparent that she was too high to get at, the dog lay on the grass and watched her through narrowed eyes. The great bony head rested on massive paws, waiting for her to make her move.

O-ha quickly assessed her chances of escape.

'You can look round all you want,' said the dog, 'you don't stand a chance. I'm going to break your neck, fox.'

O-ha shivered. 'Why would you want to do that?' she asked, playing for time. 'I mean, we're both canines—cousins, in fact—we speak the same language. The only difference between us is . . .'

'That I live with men. That's more than a small difference, fox. I know what you think of dogs. We're the traitors, the weaklings, the slaves—you've got all sorts of names for us, haven't you? Well, let me tell you something. I would kill you even if you were one of my own kind—another ridgeback hound. I was trained to hunt lions in the hotlands beyond the sea. You know what a lion is, eh, bitch?'

Ridgeback? She had never heard of a ridgeback. She noticed a ridge of dark brown hairs running counter to the normal, backswept hair of his tawny coat. This strip of coarse hair obviously gave the breed its name.

'I'm a vixen,' she replied coldly.

'I don't care what you call yourself, you're dead meat. I enjoy killing. It's my reason for living. I'm not one of your namby-pamby foxhounds: I can snap a fence post in two with these jaws. I'm one of the world's biggest dogs and I have killed a human in my time, in that land I was telling you about . . . oh, you can look around while I'm talking, but don't think because I blow off at the mouth that I'm any less attentive.'

O-ha was beginning to get worried about her cubs. She had already left them too long and they would be cold, and mewling for her warm belly fur. Still, she did not show this. Instead, she sat on her haunches and began to scratch her ear with her hind leg, as if careless of his presence.

'I can stay up here all night,' she said.

'And I can stay down here just as long. I could of course yell for assistance, bring the men out here, but they'd only shoot you. That's too quick, and it wouldn't satisfy my craving, now would it? We'll see who weakens first. I've tracked a lion over several days, without sleep. It's the thrill of the kill, you see, for Sabre the ridgeback.'

'I'm not one of these lions,' she said. 'You may be trained to catch those, but you're not trained to catch foxes. We have our own ways of getting out of trouble.'

'I've seen jackals and hyenas, I know your kind. You're all the same, you skinny wild scavengers. You think you're clever, crafty, sly, but I know all the tricks, see. You're going to die, painfully, and that's that.'

'No,' she said, simply.

The baleful eyes were on hers. 'What do you mean—no?'

But she refused to answer. For a long while they just stared at each other, the night growing into itself. Gradually, the light went out in different rooms of the house as the occupants settled for the night. Finally the whole place was in darkness, save for one small room on the ground floor. O-ha remarked on it, hoping to distract the hound, but Sabre refused to turn his head.

'My master,' he said, 'in his study. Don't you worry about that, vixen.'

Then O-ha had an idea. She stood up on the roof of the gazebo and began screaming at the moon. Her voice went out, clear, cold and ugly—her banshee shriek.

'Quiet,' growled the hound. 'That won't do you any good.'

She continued to scream. Just as the hound was about to speak again, a

393

human bark came from the house. The dog instinctively turned towards the call from his master and in that instant O-ha was down from the gazebo and racing for her life, zigzagging across the stretch of grass between her and the undergrowth. The ridgeback was swift to follow, and twice he almost had her in his jaws, but she evaded the large beast by leaping sideways. She hit the tall grasses and brambles, jumping over high objects that he had to race round, until they reached a wall. With supreme effort and agility she managed to spring to the top and down the other side. The dog could not follow. She heard him calling, in a voice cold with rage, 'You haven't seen the last of me. I'll hunt you down, you skinny vixen.' The sounds faded into the distance, as she ran through the gatehouse garden, to reach her precious cubs. One final leap and she was through the window and inside the shed.

Two of the cubs were dead. When she nosed them over, they were cold to the touch. The others were barely alive. She set about trying to warm the two living cubs, without pausing to take out the dead ones. Seconds were vital.

She had not long settled on her brood when smells and sounds came to her which were unmistakable. The dog was leading his master to her hide-out, following her scent. She snatched up a cub in her mouth and leaped through the window just as the door was forced open on its rusty hinges.

O-ha ran into the wood, hearing the hound call after her; he was undoubtedly on a leash, or he would have followed.

'We've got them, vixen, wherever you are. Can you hear me? My master has crushed them under his boots. Can you hear me, vixen? Can you hear . . . ?'

An overwhelming despair rose within her.

The ridgeback had beaten her after all. The last cub had gone cold in her mouth. She could feel no pulse, no heartbeat against her lips. The dog could not have devised a more cruel punishment if he had sat for seasons, planning it.

She laid the cub down and screeched, 'You killed my cubs, but you failed to catch me. Your stupidity, even for a low-life dog, amazes me. I'll catch you sleeping one day and tear your throat out!'

She knew, of course, that such a dream was impossible, but it had its effect on the dog. She could hear the sounds of fury coming from the shed. O-ha picked up her dead cub and ran.

O-HA RETURNED to the badger colony two days later, prepared to make it her lifelong home. She was no longer interested in dog foxes, or litters, and her heart had hardened against life.

When she ran into Gar again, he said, 'Ha! The little fox. How was it, the world?'

'It was a cruel, terrible place,' she answered.

He nodded his badger head sagely. 'That so? That so? Some animals tell me this, but I think, is it so? This can be a cruel place here, if you look for cruel. When you go out again, you must look for different, not for same.'

'There won't be a next time,' she said bitterly. 'The world has taken all I ever had.'

For quite some time she thought about committing *ranz-san*—tearing open her stomach with her teeth—but something held her back, some thought that it would be regarded in *Heff* as wrong. So she did not resort to this last desperate act, available to foxes caught in savage metal gins, or snares, but not to foxes who were simply tired of living. It was not for the weary in spirit but for the sorely oppressed.

BACK AT THE MANOR HOUSE, Sabre was swearing vengeance. The ridgeback was furious at the little fox for thwarting his attempts to kill her. I'll remember that scent, he thought. I'll find that vixen again if it takes me a lifetime, and rip her from nose to tail. No one makes a fool of me and gets away with it. The dog will have its day. Thus the vow was taken, the promise made, which would end in death for one of the two antagonists. Unfortunately for O-ha, she had exposed the one weakness in Sabre's nature for which he hated himself—the deep-seated instinct to obey his master—and that he could never let pass. Hate for oneself is almost always transferred to some other creature, and in Sabre's case that creature was O-ha. In the hotlands, beneath a fierce sun, he had tracked lions, hunted down leopards, and (at his master's instigation) attacked and torn the throat out of a fugitive black man trying to return to his homelands. To be outwitted by an animal not much bigger than a cat was a terrible insult, which would not be forgotten.

PART TWO
Escape from Bedlam

The sign on Camio's cage said: American Red Fox. The back of this board was gnawed at the corner where he had cleaned his teeth on it, through the wire mesh. Camio had a coat of rich, dark red fur and he was, or had once been, bright-eyed and with a knowing look. He was a suburban creature, from a place with wide streets and houses with plenty of space round them. Most of the houses had had porches under which a fox could hide, could sleep away the day in the shade and could make an earth, providing there were no children. Human children, like foxes, enjoyed the musty, spidery atmosphere of the twilight world below the floorboards.

In that far-off place of his birth, Camio had lived on the small creatures that were to be found under the houses, and on the food humans threw away. He was a scavenger, not recognising any disgrace in so being. There were those who believed hunting was a more noble way of obtaining food, but most animals thought this a load of nonsense. To survive was the prime objective, and if this could be achieved by making use of man's wasteful ways, then so much the better.

Like many streetwise creatures, Camio was an audacious, impudent fox with a cocky walk. He was aware that he did not know it all, but there was no reason why the rest of the world should be enlightened as to that fact: he was happy to give the impression that there was nothing he could not handle, nothing to match his cunning. His vixen Roxina was not entirely taken in, but she allowed that he had a character of charm and strength. She would have been proud of the way he conducted himself in the zoo, he thought: with quiet dignity and reserve.

He lay on the floor of his prison, while visitors peered in at him. He ignored them all. Let the monkeys show off and get all the attention: he was not going to demean himself by cavorting all over the place just to hear humans bark. He would get fed whatever he did, whether it was lazing around on the floor, or snapping at the faces that peered through the mesh. He considered himself lucky that he was not a very unusual creature, so that visitors to his cage were small in number and tended to stay only briefly.

A keeper went by, leading two Alsatian dogs on leashes. These were two of the animals that helped guard the zoo at night. Camio saw a chance for a little sport.

'Morning, minions,' he drawled, 'how's the great brotherhood of slaves today?'

One of the Alsatians jerked on its lead, snapping at him. 'Keep your trap shut.'

'Yes,' said the other, 'at least we're out here in the fresh air.'

'Fresh air? With all those humans stinking the atmosphere? You can keep it, cousin.'

'Don't call me *cousin*,' said the first dog, 'or I'll . . .' The rest of the sentence was choked off, as the keeper tugged on the lead.

'Convict,' snapped the second dog.

'Look who's talking,' replied Camio. 'The one on the end of a chain. But then you poor saps haven't got much choice, have you? Your ancestors made sure of that when they gave in to the domination of man.'

The dogs erupted into fury and were dragged away by their keeper, who barked at them and pulled on their chokechains.

Camio scratched his ear in a show of contempt. 'German shepherd dogs? Killers. They should be behind bars, not me. I never bothered a human in my life . . .' He grumbled away to himself until his meal was delivered. The truth was, Camio was going a little crazy. The zoo around him was like an asylum for mentally disturbed animals. If they weren't crazy when they came in, it was not long before they were.

In their wild state, the carnivores only came into contact with the herbivores when they were hungry and needed a kill. Then their hunting modes came into operation, and all the small chemical changes and mechanisms required for speed, agility and single-minded sense of purpose were triggered into action. On the other hand, when the grazing animals smelled a hunter, their hearts began to pump adrenalin and their minds flashed through possible escape routes.

In the zoo, they found themselves only yards from each other. Prey could smell predator, hunter could smell quarry. Their bodily juices ran wild, sending waves of panic through the grazers, and frenzy to the brains of the hunters. The leopard could scent the antelope, the lion the wildebeest. They were all too close to each other to allow any respite.

A thousand animals were crammed into less than a square mile; a thousand animals, one half of which were going crazy trying to get at the other half, and that second half going insane with fear. And there were other ways to go insane besides having your instincts tinkered with. You could lose your mind quite easily in a place where the scenery remained the same—four walls and a set of bars—and where nothing happened from one day to the next; where three strides took you to the edge of your world and another three strides took you across it again.

For Camio, hopelessness was beginning to set in: despair had opened beneath him like a giant black pit, and he was in danger of falling into it. Only a spark of his former self remained, which he kept alive by baiting the Alsatians, or snapping at the visitors.

That night, after the visitors had gone, he paced the cage, grumbling to himself. At one point in his turn, he knocked the cage door, which rattled loudly. For a moment this did not register, but then he thought, Something's not right. The door did not rattle when fastened securely.

He threw his body against the door. It rattled once more, and jiggered itself open, just half an inch.

Camio had been locked up for so long, he was not completely aware of what this meant. But then he hooked a paw behind the metal edge of the door and it swung inwards. He needed no more convincing: the keeper had forgotten to lock the cage door and the way was open. In the next moment he was padding quietly between the cages of other animals, his tread wary and primed for danger. It was all coming back to him now, his strong sense of survival.

A wolf called to him as he passed, 'Hey, cousin. Let me out.'

Camio paused, but then said, 'I'm sorry. I don't know how. I would if I could, but the way they work those locks is a mystery to me. You need fingers for such things. I'm sorry.'

The wolf looked disappointed, but shrugged.

'That's all right, cousin.' Her eyes took on a glazed look and she slipped back into her former state of hopelessness.

Camio continued to the inner wall of the zoo. Although he was out of his cage, he was far from free. There was a high wall round the zoo, beyond which was an empty area patrolled by dogs. The Alsatians were there to prevent people from entering the zoo and stealing rare creatures, rather than to stop animals from getting out; but Camio knew they would not hesitate to attack him if they saw him.

Camio managed to get on top of the high wall by running along the banked rock of the bear pit and up to the goat pinnacles above. There was a fence on top of this outcrop of rock which it took three tries to leap. The last time, he managed to get over, but not without cutting his underside on the sharp wire. The wound was not deep, however, and certainly not bad enough to keep him from going on.

Even having made it to the far side of this wall, he was not yet out of the zoo. There was a chain-link fence to negotiate, within which roamed the Alsatians. Camio entered this region warily. When he was halfway across the space between the wall and the fence, he caught a warning on the night air. While he hesitated, the two dogs that he had baited that day came hurtling round the corner, in a state of excitement. Then Camio saw that there were some humans close to the fence, eating sweet-smelling cooked meat skewered on sticks. They were noisy juveniles, covered in leather and chains. Camio slipped into the shadows and waited with a beating heart.

The Alsatians threw themselves at the fence, shouting insanely at the group of young humans, who at first backed off, startled. Then, when they saw that the dogs could not get at them, they began teasing the Alsatians with pieces of meat, driving the dogs into a frenzy.

Eventually, the juveniles tired of baiting the Alsatians and walked off down the street. Still the dogs foamed at the mouth, screaming after these ugly humans, until at last they walked grumbling away from the fence and moved towards Camio's hiding place.

The fox held his breath. The smell of the spicy meat was still in the air, but if the dogs came any closer even they would not be able to miss his scent.

One of the Alsatians stopped to scratch behind his ear.

'Come on, come on,' growled the other.

'Wait a bit . . .' He sniffed. 'Can you smell anything?' he said.

'Can I smell anything?' said the other, the sentence dripping with sarcasm. 'Only cooked steak, that's all.'

'No.' The first Alsatian's head snapped up. 'Fox! I can smell fox!'

It was time for Camio to move.

He dashed forward out of the shadows and leaped at the fence. Both dogs came at his flank, but by halting and swerving, Camio managed to avoid the snapping jaws. The little fox hit the chain-link fence about halfway up, his paws scrambling to obtain a purchase. He slipped. He fell on one of the dogs below, rolling off its back. There were canine teeth on his hind leg, trying to get a firm grip. He wrenched his leg free and rolled over just as a second set of jaws went for his abdomen.

Gasping for breath, Camio ran again for the fence. This time the two dogs came at him from different directions. He swerved and turned, and they crashed into one another. The fox saw his chance and, running full circle, used their backs as a launching pad. He took off from their tangled bodies.

It was a supreme jump, and Camio's front paws caught on the top of the fence. He hung there suspended for a moment, and almost fell backwards. Below him, the two dogs were jumping, snarling and snapping at his hindquarters. He could feel their hot breath on his fur.

Employing the last of his reserves, and with a tremendous effort, he managed to scramble to the top of the fence. He fell to the ground on the other side, hurting his right forepaw, and the Alsatians hurled themselves at the chain-link fence in fury, their eyes blazing hatred. Camio was triumphant.

'You brainless brutes, you've let me get away. Maybe they'll put you in my cage, to take my place?' he said. Then he realised he was now in a street, with traffic roaring past and people hurrying along the pavements. He took to his paws, limping along the edge of the road, hoping to find a place where there were fewer human beings.

He need not have worried overmuch: city people are notoriously blind. They have set purposes and walk with glazed eyes from one place to the next. Those who noticed him at all took him for a stray dog and barely glanced at him; a news vendor pointed to him and barked something, but it was not a sound of alarm, merely of curiosity.

Camio instinctively made his way down to the river that ran through the centre of the city. There he found a place under one of the bridges where he could rest his injured leg and lick his belly wounds. He was very pleased with himself. Now that he had escaped he would stay out; since he was only a fox, the zoo would simply set about getting some other poor creature to take his place in the cage. He was lucky. He was neither rare, nor valuable, nor dangerous to humans. He was just another fox.

Camio was not unused to city life: in his former homeland he had lived on the outskirts of a city. He knew enough to stay off the road whenever possible, and that city people were not as dangerous as humans out in the country, because if they did carry guns it was to shoot each other, and not the foxes that robbed their rubbish bins. There were dogs, but most of them were on leads and those that were not could be evaded very easily. The most dangerous thing about the city was the road and its traffic.

Camio stayed under the bridge the whole of that night, watching the boats slide by in the dark. The air stank with the fumes of engines, but at least there was no jaguar pacing up and down a few feet away, swearing under its breath that it was going to kill every living thing in existence once it got out; there was no poor creature keeping him awake with pitiful cries for freedom. The air stank, but it could be borne.

The next morning Camio's leg felt better. Traffic had begun thundering over the bridge in earnest, and humans were clip-clopping in that city-hurry way of theirs, and he rested until midday before venturing out. The tide had ebbed and the river had retreated a little, so he went down onto the mud and chased a seagull, mostly for fun. There were bits of food in the mud too, which kept him interested until the evening. He enjoyed a day of running around in freedom, getting the strength back into his bad leg on the soft mud and generally having a fine time of it. By the time it got dark, he was ready for the streets again. He followed his nose to a restaurant and went round the alley at the back where the dustbins were.

Each of the bins had a lid, fastened securely, so he had to wait in the shadows until eventually someone came out of the back of the restaurant and opened a bin, tossing stuff inside. The lid was thrown back on casually, and Camio went forward as soon as it was safe and nosed the lid off. It clattered to the ground and he leaped into the bin, gobbling down the mess inside. Then he heard barking, and before he could escape the lid was slammed back on again and jammed tight. He pushed with his head, but it would not move. He contented himself with eating his fill for a while, but eventually realised he would have to wait until someone came to put more scraps in the bin before he could get out.

They came all right: he heard them. But they went to other bins, leaving his alone. Once, someone tried to open it, but the last person had obviously done a good job, because it would not shift. He was trapped inside until something else happened.

It was a long, tiresome wait. Camio used it to dream of better places, of his lost mate, of new freedoms and exciting times ahead.

CAMIO WAS WOKEN by the clatter of bins and the grinding sound of something mechanical. From within the bin the noises were terrifying and for a few seconds he tried to gnaw his way through this metal prison. Then the bin moved and the lid was raised. Camio sprang out into the daylight, narrowly missing a human face; there was a startled bark and the bin was dropped. He did not wait to see the results of his sudden appearance, but raced away down the alley and out into another street.

Spurred on by panic, without thinking, he ran out into the road. He felt something strike his shoulder with great force and went spinning into the gutter. His mind whirled with dizziness and when he tried to get to his feet, he fell over again. Around him were the muted barks of humans, and eventually he felt someone lifting him. Although the hands were gentle, he tried to bite them. Then he was aware of being placed on a soft surface and shortly afterwards there was a sensation of motion.

Gradually his senses came back to him, and he was able to lift his head. He was in a small room with a human being. The human was facing the front, looking through one of the windows that surrounded them. Beyond the window, to Camio's left, the world was racing by in a blur of light and dark. The sensation brought back the giddy feeling, and he lay back again, feeling sick. The human in front glanced back once or twice and Camio could see the black round its eyes and the red lips. From studying them in his zoo days, he knew this was the female of the species, since the human young were always more attached to them. He knew that females, providing they were not keepers, were often a soft touch; though some females tried to disguise themselves by wearing the coats of other creatures, such as minks. That kind were unpredictable and Camio was glad to see that this female had adopted no such affectation.

Finally, the motion ceased and the female turned right round in its seat to look at him. He snarled into the painted face, and the human opened a door and jumped out, closing it before Camio could follow. For the next few seconds he tore round the inside of his new prison, trying to find a way out. Then he became aware of someone other than the female looking at him through the window. He recognised the human type, well known to him at the zoo, by the white coat: it was one of those torturers who stuck needles into you, or forced pellets down your throat which sent you to sleep. They did that when they wanted to take you some-where—and he knew where he would be going now: back to the zoo.

But the white torturer was gesturing at the female, and unbelievably the door was opened and the way left clear for him to escape. He quickly hopped down onto the pavement, to walk away in a dignified manner. No one chased him and when he looked back the female was waving an arm at him.

'Weird,' he said to himself. 'First they capture you and carry you off'— he could see now that his 'prison' had been a car—'and then they let you go.' There was no fathoming such behaviour and he did not try. He had long since given up trying to understand humans. They were all unpredictable, fur coats or not.

He walked the length of the street and found an area with a tall boarded fence round it. There was a small gap in the boards, through which he squeezed his pliable body, and he found himself standing on the edge of a great square hole. Inside the hole and round its edge were huge mechanical devices, all lying idle. Not a human in sight. He heaved a sigh of relief, and walked down an earth ramp into the hole.

There were puddles down there, one of which he drank from, satisfying his thirst. Then he put his nose to the wind and scented a fellow fox: a female. Following the scent, he came across a vixen who was lying alseep on a pile of rags. She woke when he nosed her.

'Hello,' he said.

She opened one eye, and replied, 'Hello yourself. What do you want?'

He was taken aback for a moment, expecting a more friendly reply, but then he was a stranger in this place. Of course the locals would be suspicious of uninvited foxes. 'Nothing really—it's just that I haven't talked to another fox in a long while.'

'Really?' she yawned. 'And you woke me up for that?'

'Look, I've been out of circulation. Humans trapped me a long while ago, took me on a long journey, stuck me in a cage to be gawped at. I haven't contacted another fox for . . . I don't know how long. What gives around here? Where are all the coyotes and raccoons?'

She was awake now and looking at him strangely. 'Coy-what? Raccoons? I don't know what you're blabbering about. I came in here to get a rest—go and look for your raccoons somewhere else.'

'I'm not looking for them—I just thought . . . look, what is this place? Why aren't there any humans here?' He gestured with his nose at their surroundings. Clearly men were working to build something over the great square pit. In which case, where were they?

'Part-time *gerflan*,' she said. 'You don't get humans in here all the time. They leave the place empty at nights, and every seventh day for some reason. Don't ask me why, because on the other days the place is crawling with them, but every seventh day—empty. Now, can I have some peace?'

'*Gerflan*? That's a new one on me. I'm obviously a long way from home. Are there more places like this?'

'Lots of them, in this part of the city. Places where they put their cars on five days that are almost empty on days six and seven . . ." She seemed to be enjoying the conversation, now that it appeared she was teaching a green fox about the ways and wiles of the city. 'You from the country?' she asked. 'You have a strange way of talking. I've never heard anyone talk like you. And your fur—it's darker than . . . you're not from round here, are you?'

'I don't know. I mean, I know I'm not from here, but I'm not sure quite where I am from—in relation to this city.'

She rose lazily to her feet, staring at him. 'You got a mate?' she asked.

'Not at the moment,' said Camio. He studied her carefully. She was meaty and middle-aged, and her coat was ragged. He also noticed that her mouth and teeth were stained yellow.

'Neither have I. Last one ran off . . .' she muttered. 'Tends to be a bit like that in the *face*. In the country we used to find a mate and stick with him, but here relationships are not as stable. I like the look of you . . .'

'Thanks,' said Camio, feeling uncomfortable for some reason. This vixen was a little too sharp-featured and cynical for him. Maybe he was old-fashioned, but he preferred foxes that were less jaded. His own mate had escaped the net that had caught him, back home, but she had not been as knowing as this one. She had just been bright and alert.

'You going to hang around for a while?'

'For the day at least. I want to learn a little more about where I am and what the rules are.'

'I know what you mean.' She came up beside him and settled down so that they were touching. They lay like that for about two hours, each warming the other.

'You know,' he said dreamily, as they lay there, 'I once heard of a land—the Land of the Lions—where the trees are tall and wide at the top, and the sky is big and always blue. The air is full of mountains and dust, and there's hardly a human to be seen. It's a lazy land, but there's excitement around every bush—the jackals said you could smell the excitement in the atmosphere . . .'

'The what?'

'The . . . oh, never mind. You wouldn't understand unless you'd been where I have. And they all go mad. So would I if I'd been taken from such a wonderful place—a place where you can run and run and never reach a town or city. I'd like that, I think, though food's easier to get in places where the humans collect like ants—'

'The *face*,' she said, breaking his reverie. 'Talking of food, let's go and get something to eat.' She got up and walked languidly towards the hole in the fence, saying, 'My name's O-tasso by the way. What's yours?'

'Camio,' he replied.

'A-camio?'

'No—just Camio.'

She turned and looked at him closely.

'Funny name. Where did you say you were from?'

'The country,' he said, not wanting to get into one of those confusing conversations again. 'Now, where do we eat? I had a bad experience last night, I got trapped in a bin. I don't want that to happen again.'

She bared her teeth. 'No, stealing from bins is easy. We'll have some fun, you and me. There's a place not far from here where humans collect hot food and carry it home. We'll go there . . .'

She slipped out into the street and Camio followed her, his stomach doing flip-flops at the thought of warm food. He followed her to a cobbled street with posts at each end. In the middle of this small street was a takeaway restaurant. Camio knew of such places from home: they often had delicious hamburgers covered in sauce.

This place smelled different from others he had known, though. The scents were sharp and spicy and the meals were carried out in shiny metal-foil containers. O-tasso motioned for him to crouch down in the shadows of the shop doorway, while she did the same.

'Hot, hot, hot . . .' she kept muttering. 'Deliciously hot.'

'Are we going round the back?' he whispered, but she glared at him, indicating that he should be quiet.

Behind the glass-fronted takeaway Camio could see several brown-skinned humans hard at work, the steam billowing round them like hot mist. Of course, Camio could not focus on these things for very long, and he concentrated on the smells, which were among the most exotic

404

and pungent he had ever experienced.

Still O-tasso waited, as couples and threes went into the takeaway and came out laden with goods. Then, finally, a single human went in on its own, and O-tasso stiffened.

'OK,' she said, 'this is it. I'll make the snatch and you act as decoy. When I say *now*, you follow me out . . .' She stopped, seeing the man leave the restaurant.

'Now!'

She flew forward with amazing speed, and instinctively Camio followed, though he had no idea what was going on.

As if she was moon-crazy, O-tasso ran straight at the human, leaped into the air, snatched the package out of his hand with her teeth, and hurried away, down the alley, leaving Camio running in her wake.

The human gave out a sharp bark and kicked at Camio, just catching his flank, but not hard enough to bowl him over. Then he gave chase, as two other people came out of the restaurant and joined him. O-tasso was nowhere to be seen.

With his heart thumping in his throat, Camio wheeled round a corner and eventually evaded his pursuers. Then he found his way back to the boarded place with the hole behind it. A spicy aroma was in the air: in the pit below, O-tasso was wolfing down the contents of the box.

'Come on,' she said, as he approached her, 'I've left you half.'

This was not quite true. When he looked into the box only about three mouthfuls remained, but these he was determined to have, since he had risked his life to get them. He took a mouthful of the yellow-juiced, greasy-looking slops in the bottom of the shiny box.

Hot! Hot! Hot! Not only did it burn his sensitive mouth, throat and gullet, but the stuff numbed his taste buds with an eloquence of spicy fire which had his eyeballs starting out of his head and water pouring from the sockets.

'*Haaa!*' he cried.

O-tasso nodded. 'Wonderful, isn't it?' Camio ran to the nearest puddle and drank a bellyful of water before returning, to find that she had finished off what was left in the bottom of the box.

'Sorry,' she said, as if she had just noticed what she had done. 'We'll go out to another one. This time you can make the snatch and I'll be the decoy. We make a good team, don't we?'

'What is that stuff?' he asked huskily.

'Oh, this is the real thing. You have to get it fresh from their hands or it's not the same. The waste they throw out at the back goes cold very quickly. Hot, eh? I love it. I won't eat anything else now. Mind you,' she said reflectively, 'it plays the devil with your guts, but you get used to that after a while. It's the hot spices, you see.'

Camio was beginning to see why her mate had gone off with another vixen. This one was obviously as mad as a weasel with a worm in its brain, and was hooked on food that would burn through solid stone. He would not call himself a coward, but if he did something brave there had to be a reward at the end of it, not a punishment.

'I think I've had enough,' he said. 'Ate very well last night.'

She looked disappointed, but settled down on the rags again.

'All right. Wake me up when the men come. Once they start those machines there's no rest for the wicked. You'll soon get used to life in the *face*, Camio, and I'll teach you all I know. When we have our first litter, you'll have to go out and get the food on your own, you know. The real thing—or nothing.'

'Right,' he said. 'The real thing.'

Once she was asleep, he slipped away quietly, thinking that city life was not as agreeable as life in the suburbs. He would have to find a way of getting further out, on the edge, where food was cooler.

He trotted through the evening streets, occasionally coming across another fox or a cat, but very few humans. The city was very different from the suburbs on this, the seventh day. In the suburbs humans would be out washing their cars or weeding the garden, going into the churches —which were safe, empty hiding places on most other days—or visiting other houses. But it seemed that on the seventh day in the city everyone went underground, which was all right with Camio.

The thing to do, he mused, was to find another one of those *gerflans*. He liked the idea of places where humans came only infrequently and in small numbers. They had had such areas back home, of course, like the railroads, but foxes there did not have special words for such places. There was just *safe* and *unsafe*. 'Is it safe?' was all a fox would ask of a raccoon or coyote. And it was the one question which all wild urban creatures were obliged to answer, regardless of feuds or traditional wars between the species. You might battle to the death with the animal who posed the question, but only after you had informed him or her that it was safe from human intervention.

'Funny world,' he said to himself.

FOR THE THREE DAYS following his encounter with O-tasso, Camio went hungry. On the first day, his wanderings took him into a disused dockland, which was fine for avoiding the human race, but all other creatures had also vacated the area. Not even rats had remained on the stark, clean concrete. On the second day, he re-entered the area of tall, glassed buildings where men and women dashed from one doorway to another. They did not seem to eat the whole day long. On the third day, Camio was beginning to wish he had stayed with O-tasso, despite her penchant for hot food. He had walked into a poor district where the humans had hardly enough to feed themselves, let alone itinerant foxes. He found small scraps on the waste ground, but his stomach felt as if it had been turned inside-out and dragged along the ground.

That evening, walking past prone bundles of rags that had humans inside them, he went down an alley and found the heel end of a mouldy loaf. He was halfway through chewing it when he saw the corpse of a fox lying at the end of the alley. Camio went up to it and sniffed around it. Had it been any other dead animal, he could have eaten it. But it was a fox, and though he was almost starving, he could not bring himself to touch the corpse. There was a severity in the dead eye; staring into it, Camio found he was looking at himself. He was just a puff of wind away from the poor creature on the alley floor: his lungs were full of air, the other fox's empty, that was all. It worried him, coming face to face with his own mortality. Camio left the alley.

A few moments later he was vomiting the crust, and he recognised the smell of rat poison.

Later that night he stumbled across a railroad depot and met a friendly fox called A-lobo, who offered him some food from one of his caches. Camio was as grateful as any hungry animal could be on finding such generosity in a strange land. He thanked the dog fox profusely as he gobbled down the food.

A-lobo was a nervous, neurotic fox who had abandoned the streets for the relative safety of the *gerflan* which ran in long strips over the whole country. Of course, there were still vehicles to avoid, but you could hear them coming along the rails from a long way off: the metal vibrated and hummed. You learned, he told Camio, the busy times, when the tracks were in almost constant use, and the quiet times. There were mice and rats to be had, packets of sandwiches or half-eaten pies by the tracks, and though the scenery was a little boring, the smell of oil and grease made up for that.

'You like this stink?' said Camio. They were lying on the bank beneath the black cables that looped from post to post for as far as they could see.

'I adore it—ab-ab-absolutely adore it,' stuttered A-lobo. He filled his lungs, through his nose, to prove it. 'N-n-not stink—wonderful s-smell. And when they b-burn it in their fires—oh, sweet Perfect Here . . .'

A-lobo was not pretty to look at. He had once been struck by a train and the left side of his face was badly scarred, and he had lost an eye and an ear in the accident. He was very friendly though, and enjoyed teaching Camio all about the railroads (which he called 'railways') and life near the depot.

'Switter is here, so spring isn't far away. G-g-good to get rid of the cold w-weather.'

'Switter?'

'You know. S-small spring breezes.'

A train thundered by, interrupting their conversation. Sunlight flashed on its many windows, which had a dazzling, mesmerising effect on the foxes. The noise was overpowering, the smell of diesel oil blotted out any other scents, and their eyes were fixed on those blinding panes of glass.

When it had gone, A-lobo asked Camio if he had ever played 'the game'.

'Game? I haven't played games since I was a cub. Foxes don't have time for games, do they?'

'Th-this game is a li-li-little different. It adds a b-bit of spice to life. Otherwise, it's the same boring old th-thing—eating and sleeping. There's got to be more to life than eating and sleeping, hasn't there?'

'Well, I suppose so. When I was in the zoo I used to think that there should be. Out here, the excitement is in finding food, and a place to rest your head without fear of disturbance. Just staying alive is pretty exciting, isn't it?'

'N-no,' said A-lobo bluntly. 'It isn't.' He climbed to his feet and shook himself. 'Come on—I-I-I'll show you.'

He walked down to the rails, and Camio followed him curiously. A-lobo selected a spot in between the rails of one track, lying across the chunky gravel, his head on a wooden sleeper.

'Like this,' he said.

Camio went and lay beside his new friend. Perhaps A-lobo knew of some kind of creature, a rat perhaps, that travelled underneath the rails, and was waiting in ambush.

'What are we waiting for?' he whispered, after they had been lying there for some time.

'Sssshhhh.'

So Camio went quiet again. It was pleasant enough, between the rails, with the warm sun on their backs and the breezes passing overhead. He could almost drop off to sleep, except that a train might come along. He closed his eyes, and the sun ran warm fingers through his russet coat until even his fleas were dozing.

Camio woke with a start. The rails were rattling and jumping as if they were alive, and there was a noise in the near distance, which grew louder by the second. A train!

Camio jumped to his feet. 'Train coming!' he yelled.

As he leaped away he felt the slipstream of the monster blow him sideways, and the scream of its passage stunned him with its volume. His brain jangled with the roar and rush of wind and sound as he fell heavily on the hard earth between the rails and the grass verge. Just inches away, the railway train careered along the steel strips, its wheels singing a loud metallic death-song which hurt Camio's ears and drove terror into his heart. On it sped, invincible, immortal, irresistible, and noisier than a thousand foxes screaming their banshee screams in unison.

Then the train was gone.

Camio, still badly shaken, staggered to his feet and looked around him. A-lobo lay between the tracks as still as death. Poor A-lobo—how pathetic he looked, lying there on the sharp gravel, his nervous soul twitching its way through the useless body.

Suddenly, the corpse sat up!

'You're—you're alive!' said the amazed Camio. 'But the train—it went right over you.'

'Ahhh—that's—that's the game,' replied A-lobo in a voice like honey trickling from a fractured beehive. 'The *excitement*—wonderful, wasn't it? Every time I do it, I say to myself, this is it, this is the day you die, A-lobo. There's always the almost irresistible urge to run, but you have to resist it—to run is death. So you lie there, spinning steel on both sides and a rushing river of steel above you, knowing that if you move a muscle you will literally lose your head—so you lie there as still as stone until the sound recedes, and you know you've done it again. You've beaten fear. You've met it face to face in mortal combat and you have won—won, won, won!'

His face had a faraway look on it: during this speech A-lobo had not stuttered once and Camio noticed a confidence in the animal that had not been there before. Clearly 'the game' did something for A-lobo, but whatever it was, Camio could do without it.

'You almost got me killed,' he said, not without a little anger. 'You should have told me—given me the choice.'

'But you would have said no, and you would never have tried it. You might have liked it, but unless you try it you can't find that out, can you?'

'I don't have to jump into a fire to know I'm going to burn.'

A-lobo shook his head. 'I've heard that sort of argument before. It's not the same thing.' He paused, then asked tentatively, 'D-did you enjoy it?'

'Look, I jumped—the train almost hit me. No, this kind of foolishness is not for me.'

A-lobo shrugged, nodding his one-eyed, one-eared head. 'Well, I'm sorry about that. My mate did the same thing, the first time she tried it. She panicked and jumped, just before the train reached us, like you did.'

'So, she must have told you the same thing I have.'

'She didn't tell me anything. The train hit her. She's dead.'

Camio was too shocked to say anything.

The pair of them spent the rest of the day looking for sandwiches along the line. Towards nightfall, Camio said to A-lobo, 'I think I want to get away from here. Out of the city.'

'L-leave the *face*? Whatever for?' The stutter had returned.

'I'm not used to it. I think I want to get out a bit, on the edge of this *face* of yours. How far is it, do you know? Could I walk it in a night?'

A-lobo shook his battered head.

'I don't know. I've walked these r-r-rails all over, and I've never been where the buildings stop. Maybe you should jump a train.'

'Do what?'

'There are some t-trains with big open trucks with no people in them. If I take you to the place where they stop for the night, you can get inside one and wait until it halts again, out of the ci-city. I knew a fox who did it all the time . . .'

'Suppose I get caught?'

'I think you'll be all right. Th-these men don't carry guns or anything. They m-m-might chase you, but they won't catch you on foot.'

That night A-lobo took him along to the depot where trains were lying idle, waiting for the morning before moving off to places unknown.

They found a suitable truck, with straw in the corner for him to lie underneath, and then they said goodbye.

'Y-you think we'll see each other again?' asked A-lobo.

'It's doubtful, isn't it? Anyway, you'll be dead soon—knocked down by a train.'

A-lobo shook his head firmly. 'No. Not that. Probably the mange, or someone coming up on my deaf side, without me knowing. At l-least I'll go with the smell of the railways in my nostrils.'

'If that's what you want . . .'

'Yes—I'm a railway fox. You—you're one of the strangest I've ever met. But you're a good fox, Camio.'

'Thanks. Keep your head down for me, A-lobo . . .'

And with those parting words, he leaped up into the car and buried himself beneath the sweet-smelling straw, ready for his journey. He would have been lying to himself if he had said that he was not afraid, but there was something of the excitement that A-lobo found in his 'game' rushing through his veins. It was to do with reaching out into the unknown. When he had been with his mate, in the old country, he had definitely been a *stayner*—but now he had done some travelling, there was no reason why he should not become a *longtrekker* like his father.

He was thinking about it when they slid the doors shut, leaving him in darkness. After a while the train began to move off.

PART THREE
The Coming of the Stranger

Spring had arrived on the back of Switter, the breeze carrier, and there were births all round the badger sett: in the bushes, on the ground, under the earth. In the trees of Trinity Wood eggs were cracking, and the urgent cheeping of newborn birds mingled with the mewling of young mammals.

O-ha might have resented the coming of spring, but in fact she was happy to smell the apple and cherry blossom, and did not mind the sounds of the young that filled the air. Her heart was still heavy for her mate and her cubs, but she contented herself with sitting once a day in the traditional pose of the mourner, her forelegs crossed and her tail straight out and flat against the ground. Gar realised that his friend was still grieving, and came to visit her as often as his solitary temperament would allow.

One evening they were sitting in her chamber, remarking on the freshness of the world outside: how clear the streams were in the spring, and how good the soil smelled. Neither foxes nor badgers are much interested in the way the world decks itself out visually, but they love the clarity and the aromas of new growth.

'You see the *gaers*—the "grass" you call it—how sweet it is coming to the tongue at this time? Eh?'

'Yes, this is a good season. I like it very much,' O-ha replied.

'So,' Gar said, 'you were telling me from this spirit-time of foxes— what you call it?'

'The Firstdark.'

'Ya—that the thing. We badger have something like, when first two badgers who live on world make love—come ten thousand badgers from this mating, all one time. Some badger not grow and these become weasel, otter and stoat, who are cousins of Gar . . . so, the Firstdark very like same badger, I think?'

'It sounds like the same. Our Great Ancestor is A-O, who was both male and female in one, and who gave birth to A-wan and O-won, before changing into a great lake of water. Because it could not breathe under the water, the land rose up from underneath to get to the air, and A-O was split into many parts, which are now our ponds and streams, our lakes and rivers. It is A-O we drink to cleanse our souls, and A-O who washes our coats, to cleanse our bodies.

'A-wan and O-won were giants, left by their mother-father to fight for a place in the new world. They battled with the rocks and stones, who wanted to cover the ground so that they could sun themselves for eternity. A-wan gathered up all the stones in his mouth, and spat them out into a great pile. O-won did the same with the rocks. Then they both turned their backs on the piles and sprayed them with earth, using their paws to dig. Soon the trees marched into the land and covered the new hills, one of which we live on now, the other is on the far side of the river, beyond the marshes . . .'

'I know it—I know it,' said Gar. 'Go on.'

'Next, the two giant cubs fought with the wolves and'—she was about to say 'badgers' but changed her mind quickly—'dogs and other beasts, for a right to live in the world. In those days foxes lived out in the woodlands and grasslands, and only had to come down underground with the badgers and rabbits when men started to hunt us with dogs. We have lived underground for so long now, we're used to it.'

The pair of them continued to exchange stories until well into the night, after which O-ha went out to find food. She went into the *havnot*, chased and caught a rabbit, and satisfied her hunger.

When she was returning to the sett, just as the dawn rays were striking the topmost whips of a crack willow, a distant rumble made O-ha halt in her tracks. She was using the main highway from the farm to Trinity Wood, and the sound seemed to be coming from the village. She licked her nose and tested Switter, but the breeze was too light to carry scents very far. The sound was of heavy machines, louder than tractors or any of the farm equipment. Something was happening in her parish which was out of the ordinary. She decided to investigate.

O-ha took one of the byways across the *hav* to a network of dry-stone walls which enclosed the *havnot* in that area. She travelled along the top of these walls and reached the remains of an old windmill, of which only the stone tower remained. Climbing quickly to the top, she looked out towards the sound.

Her poor eyesight defeated her because she was looking directly into the morning sun, and she could only see a haze of light sparkling on some objects in the distance. Just as she was about to go down, a jay landed on the far side of the tower, eyeing her suspiciously.

'You know what's going on over there?' O-ha asked.

'*Bitte?*' said the jay. '*Ich verstehe nicht.*'

'The noise over there—the machines—what are they for?'

'*Was? Oh, fur ausgraben.*'

Then the bird flew off, still keeping a wary eye on this fox which asked so many questions. O-ha saw the flash of blue on its wing as it dipped down and disappeared near to the place where the shiny vehicles were rumbling along. The *Corvidae*—the jays, magpies, rooks, crows, jackdaws and ravens—appeared to be a sinister lot, full of intrigue, but they knew what was going on and they were harmless enough. The birds to watch were the gulls—now there was a vicious lot of villains and thieves! The bird world had a saying: Sooner trust a housecat than a seagull.

What did *ausgraben* mean? Well, there was only one way to find out. She climbed back down from the tower and went to find Gar. She tracked him down in his chamber and refused to be put off by his gruff manner. 'Do you know the language of the *Corvidae*?' she asked.

'What—eh? Oh, little. Crows, eh? What crows?'

'Look, this is important, Gar, or I wouldn't disturb you. There are some machines coming down the road—big ones by the sound of them— and a jay told me they are for owsgrabben, or something like that. What does it mean?'

'Oh, you meaning *ausgraben*—what we badger do, and fox. It means to dig—to dig up land. Now, you go away like nice fox, eh?'

'To dig up the ground?' O-ha persisted. 'But they didn't sound like farm machines.'

'No? Then maybe, to make road, eh? Dig road, or make house?'

'Houses?' A cold shiver went through her. 'You mean, they're going to put some *face* around here? I don't like this, Gar. I don't like it at all.'

412

'But what you going to do, eh?' Gar sounded irritable. 'You can do nothing—nothing is what you can do. The humans build house, they build house. Who can stop them? Anyway, they not come here, in the wood. Too much work, chop, chop down tree. They maybe put up new farm—old one falling down anyway. You see—no worries. Now, Gar will be alone . . .'

But it was to be more than just a farm. Over the next few weeks the machines were all over the landscape. They chugged and hummed, they clattered and scraped. Flints saw the light of day for the first time and clumps of chalk appeared like the backs of giant white fish swimming through the clay. Soon a pattern of roadways began to form round Trinity Wood, marked off by posts and string, with coloured flags hanging from loops.

Crouched at the edge of her covert, O-ha felt the tremors drumming through the clay and wondered why the earth did not scream out in agony as its green skin was flayed open to reveal the raw, brown flesh beneath. The machines were like brittle, giant predators, tearing apart a live creature. Heavy, shovel-nosed, jerky brutes crushed the bushes and shrubs to pulp, and herded the trees before them until they cracked and splintered like old bones. The swiftness of the destruction astounded the vixen, who clung to her own patch of grass, bracken and trees, afraid that she might wake one evening to find her home-place bared to the dark, churned clay. And everywhere there was the smell of men and machines, the sound of destruction.

There were men all over the place. It was almost impossible to avoid being seen, especially since the lights never went out, but to O-ha's surprise these new men seemed quite delighted by the sight of her. Whenever she was spotted slinking past their little encampments they would point to her and exclaim, and their barking had none of the animosity or bloodlust in it that she was used to detecting.

Still, it was a troubled time for her and the badgers. Each day they expected an invasion of the woodland, which never came. O-lan and A-lon had to move out of their earth in the ditch beyond Trinity Wood, but they made themselves another by digging out O-ha's old earth: something she had been intending to do herself, now that the ground was soft. The other animals that had lived on the *hav* either set out looking for pastures new (the rabbits did this, and a few others), or they moved into Trinity Wood. There was a concentration of animals in the ten acres of woodland which had everyone confused for some time, and some territorial fights occurred which resulted either in the shrinking of an animal's hunting zone or the expulsion of the newcomer. Occasionally an immigrant would get the better of a long-standing resident, but that was seldom, since the established members of the woods felt they had right on their side and fought to keep their ground with a ferocity which could not often be matched by newcomers. By midsummer, with its warm wind, Frashoon, most of the battles had been fought and settled, and there was only the activity around the wood to worry about.

'Things will change,' said Gar. 'Ya, things will change round here.'

'Will you and the other badgers move on?' asked O-ha.

'We wait—we stay for a while to see what happens. What about you?'

'I have nowhere else to go. I must make the best of it.'

O-ha got used to the new face of the landscape fairly quickly. Although many points of reference had changed, and there were new landmarks to learn, it did not take very long before these were in her head. One thing was certain, there were plenty of earthworms to be had.

The new landscape played havoc with the ancestral highways, of course. On one of her walks, O-ha found that a new road had cut across one of the animal highways. She did not hesitate to cross the road, even though vehicles were now moving along it. Her highway had been there for thousands of seasons. Why should she change direction simply because humans had decided to lay tarmac across the country?

Another time, she came across a badger glaring up at a new wall: again, the wall had been built right across an animal pathway. The badger could have gone round it, but it stubbornly refused to do so. Instead, it sat there calling down all kinds of terrible events on the heads of these humans who had had the audacity to block its path.

She told Gar this, and the elderly badger said thoughtfully, 'If we go round things every time *guman* build it, we change highways every day. Best to ignore. Some seasons go by, then all things change again.'

Despite the invasion of the countryside, and the displacement of thousands of insects, birds and mammals, life in Trinity Wood tried to move into summer much the same as always. The froghoppers left their 'cuckoo spit' on the hedges that remained intact; the woodbine and the honeysuckle drugged the moths with their heady perfumes; in amongst the many different grasses of the *havnot* grew the common herbs: yarrow, ribwort, plantain, dandelion and chicory. Mother shrews led their strings of babies through tunnels in the grass, each one holding on to the tail of the next with the smallest, at the end, being dragged and bumped along, as the mother hurried from one place to the next. Otters cruised the rivers and inlets of the wetlands, and kingfishers flashed like blue darts along the banks of streams.

Life and death went on in the old ways where the ground remained untouched by the digging machines, but gradually the process of stripping the land forced more and more creatures to abandon the area. Soon the population of Trinity Wood was a fraction of what it had been the previous summer. Many species would never be seen there again.

A HOT SUMMER SUN lay heavy on the fields, like a huge invisible weight pressing evenly on the land. Flies buzzed over ditches whose marrow was dry and brittle. Animals that were out on business constantly blew hot air through their nostrils, to rid themselves of the feeling that there were cobwebs up there. The earth was parched and crisp as old reeds.

Over the dusty stretch of *hav* between the building site and the manor house came a red fox, a fox that appeared just a little different from the others which lived in the area: a dark fox with a jaunty step and high head. He walked as if he knew the whole earth intimately and no place was strange to him. Those animals that noticed him might have thought that he was a *rangfar*, an itinerant fox, but on closer inspection they would have seen that he stared about him keenly, gathering impressions. He was in fact seeking a place to stay, for Camio was not a *rangfar* or, in his own idiom, *longtrekker*, by choice, only by circumstance. In his heart he was a fox who wanted to make his mark on a square mile of land and say, 'This is my parish. Here I shall live, and die.'

Camio passed by the large manor house, which was just outside an area being devastated by men in shirtsleeves and hard hats. There was a set of wrought iron gates at the beginning of the driveway, behind which paced a dog as large as a tiger. Camio stopped and regarded this beast, the like of which he had never seen. It was a giant among dogs, and on seeing Camio its jaw slavered and a sound came rumbling up from the depths of its muscle-ridged belly. Camio decided that he had seen enough and slipped away into the hedgerow as the monster threw itself at the gates.

Camio was no coward, but there was no sense in antagonising such an enormous beast: to face such a monster would have been like a cat meeting with a lion. He slipped through the workmen, as they toiled on the grounds surrounding the wood, and entered the coolness of a covert on the north side. No sooner was he within the woodland's shade than he encountered an elderly dog fox, who barred his way. Camio sighed. He knew that he was trespassing, and that he was going to have to turn round or fight. Normally he would have respected another fox's area, but he only wanted to pass through unmolested—the code of right of passage—and he had come a long, hot way.

They regarded each other for some time before Camio broke the silence. 'Is there a problem?' he asked.

'There might be. It depends on where you think you're going.'

Camio said, 'You have a name, I presume? Mine is Camio.'

'They call me A-magyr. I'm the toughest fox in the parish, and one of the oldest—as strong and hard as any you're likely to meet.'

Though grizzled, he did indeed look like a gritty, mean character and a nasty opponent in a fight. But Camio did not like to be told what to do by one of his own kind. He certainly was not going to lie back submissively with his paws in the air just because this local dog fox wanted to add another victory to his list. 'So,' said Camio, 'you want to stand here all day, or are you going to let me pass? I'm reasonably patient, but I've come a long way and I need a place to rest.'

'What's wrong with where you're standing?' asked A-magyr.

'What's wrong with it is I didn't choose it. I'm a peaceful type of fox, but I like to pick my own bed.'

A-magyr narrowed his eyes. 'No one has spoken to me like that for a long time. I could chew you up and spit you out.'

Camio shrugged, and then crouched, ready to spring. 'Right, let's see you do it, A-mouthy—I'm ready if you are. I came into this wood seeking nothing but friendship, but if I have to fight, I will.'

A-magyr made a rush at him, but Camio leaped neatly aside, turning in the air so that he faced his opponent again.

'That's a clever trick,' snapped A-magyr, 'but it won't work twice.' He made another dash. This time Camio jumped while keeping his head towards his combatant, managing to nip A-magyr on the haunch as he passed.

A look of disbelief and pain crossed A-magyr's face.

'I've killed foxes who . . .' A-magyr began, but Camio interrupted him. 'Swallow it,' he said, 'the time for talking is over.'

A-magyr bristled, sinking low into his legs, so that his body arched downwards. He did indeed look a formidable opponent, with his head low and teeth bared, his ears flat against his skull and his eyes burning ferociously at Camio. Camio stared back, snapping at the air in front of A-magyr's face, daring the old dog fox to make another move.

'I'll tear you . . .' began A-magyr, but this time he knew he had lost ground just by opening his mouth. Inside a split second, Camio was astride his opponent and the other was on his back, paws in the air, staring at the savage face which looked down into his eyes. Camio's teeth were bared back to the gum and hovered over the neck of his adversary. A-magyr slowly turned his head away, exposing his throat. Now both his jugular and belly were open for the teeth to tear.

However, Camio did not go for A-magyr's throat. Foxes do occasionally fight to the death, but more often, once they have gained the upper hand, they allow a retreat to take place. A-magyr had been broken, his spirit crushed, and the fact that they both knew this was enough. The battle was over. The loser slunk away. This is not to say there would be no more fights between them, but A-magyr would have to have a very good reason for attempting the same thing twice.

The newcomer heaved a sigh of relief. Camio was weary of the city and the so-called 'suburbs' which seemed as dense and limitless as the city itself. He was also sick of trains and travelling. It was time to put his paw-print on a piece of clay and say, 'I'm not moving from here!'

Camio entered the depths of the wood and found a place to lie, in the half-exposed roots of an old oak. He sank wearily to the earth and there he rested until the evening.

Camio woke as a sun the colour of drying blood threw dark lanes through the woodlands. He climbed to his feet and drank some murky water from a hollow in a rotten tree. He opened the bark with his teeth and found bugs beneath, which he ate quickly. Then he cleaned some of the dust from his coat, and decided to explore.

He found a fox's earth at one point, but the occupants were out and he did not wish to violate a home without being invited. As he was leaving the spot, on the edge of the wood, a vixen came out of the trees and took a brief look up into the night sky, before noticing he was there. Camio studied her. She was, he decided, a mature but attractive creature—very attractive—and he found himself walking towards her, wondering what to say. For once in his life he felt tongue-tied, and his conversation seemed buried at the back of his throat.

The vixen glanced at him and then made to leave the place.

'Wait,' said Camio quickly. 'Could we—talk?'

She stopped, but remained on all fours, as if still prepared to leave within the moment.

'Talk?' she said. 'About what?'

'Well, I'm a stranger round here . . .'

'I know that.'

'. . . and I wondered if you could give me some information, about the lie of the land, that sort of thing. I recently escaped from a zoo and I'm a little lost.'

'A zoo? I don't know what a zoo is.'

'It's a place where they lock animals in cages—like chickens, you know?—so that humans can come and look at them without being bitten. Not a very pleasant place, if you happen to be in it rather than visiting. However, I got out, and here I am.'

'What's all this got to do with me?' She seemed very haughty and superior, and for the first time in his life Camio worried that there might be something inferior about the background of suburban foxes who lived off the contents of trash cans.

'Well, nothing I suppose . . .' A flash of inspiration came to him. '. . . unless you have a regard for hospitality? I'm a strange fox in a strange land, and I need help.'

She looked a little contrite at this, but impatience still showed on her face. 'I can hardly help you if you don't tell me your problem.'

Before he could stop himself the words came out all of a rush, tumbling over each other like torrents of water, and even before he had finished he could see by the coldness in her eyes that he had made a terrible mistake. He had been too rash, too impetuous.

'I need a home, and a vixen to share that home. I'm tired of wandering, I want to settle down, have a family, be a father fox with a mate again . . . I know how this must sound, since we don't know each other, but I'm not a fox to hold back my feelings. I saw you, with the dying sunlight behind you, and you looked so—so beautiful.' He plunged into desperation as her look formed droplets of ice in the air between

them. 'You have such delicate lines. Your scent is like a drug to me—it makes my head spin. And your voice! A thousand nightingales—'

'You want to be a father fox, *again?*' The haughty look was redoubled. 'The trouble with you *rangfars* . . .'

'We what?'

'. . . you travellers, or whatever you like to call yourselves. You think you can walk into a parish and make up to any female that takes your fancy. No doubt you have dozens of so-called mates, all over the country! Well, let me tell you that I am one vixen who does not find you attractive, whatever your name is, and I don't wish to share my home or my life with someone who just walks out of nowhere and will no doubt go back there twice as fast, once the business has been done.'

She turned abruptly on her heel and began to walk off, when he shouted, 'Camio.'

She turned again, as if he had yelled a common insult. 'What?'

'My name—it's Camio. And I think that's one of the most magnificent speeches I've ever heard. I'm just sorry I had to be at the sharp end of it. Listen, I'm not a *rangfar*, or whatever you call it—we say *longtrekker* back home. I'm just an ordinary fox in extraordinary circumstances. I was captured, drugged, and put in a cage. I don't know where my home is, but believe me, if I did I would go there in an instant. I've tried city life, and it doesn't suit me. So I came out here, on the train, and here I'm going to stay. I've already had to thrash one of your local foxes, someone called A-magyr, in order to enter the wood.'

'Where did you get a name like "Camio"?' the vixen asked curiously.

'I told you, I'm not from around here.'

'But so far as I know, foxes all over the country take a letter from A-O, depending on their sex.'

'Then I don't come from this country. Don't ask me how I got here, because I don't know. Some say we were flown through the air, inside a man-made bird called an aeroplane, but I'm not sure that's true.'

'And you beat A-magyr?'

She regarded him for a little while longer as they stood several yards apart in the gloaming. Her attitude was less superior than it had been, but she still maintained a certain poise, so that he felt he could not approach her without desecrating holy ground, or violating some sacred trust. He did not understand why this should be so, but it was, and he knew he wanted her very badly. He wanted to call this high-minded, proud vixen, with an obviously impeccable lineage, his own.

His mind was a turmoil of passion, which he kept under control with difficulty. He knew they could not mate: it was not her time. But the very thought of it sent his brain into a spin.

'What do you want to know?' she asked, her tone softer.

'I've said—do you have a mate?'

'No, and I've no wish for one. My mate was killed by the hounds, some time ago. You may want to start again, Camio, but I've no wish to. I intend to enter my old age as a female *stoad*.'

He thrilled to hear her say his name, but answered in a steady voice. 'I'm sorry about your mate. It wasn't that big hound down at the great house? I saw him as I came by.'

Her back bristled, but she said, 'No, not Sabre. He has other things to answer for. Now, I must go.'

She turned again, and walked away into the wood. Camio watched her, then did a little dance on the grass in the moonlight. No mate. She has no mate, he kept telling himself, over and over again. He stared down the slope from the wood, into the surrounding area. And what have we here? A town being built, by the looks of it. A new town. Well, well. A nice suburban area, with new houses and new restaurants. A local bully whom he had thrashed, and a lovely vixen without a mate. How could anything be better? And if this snooty vixen did not like him now, because she had lived the country life—this madam of the woodlands, with her high nose and dainty step, and rows of ancestors steeped in culture—if she would not take notice of him now, she would do soon. He was a fox who knew how to survive in the streets, amongst the bricks and mortar, the fast vehicles, the sewers, alleys, and rooftops—yes, rooftops, where foxes glided from one building to the next, unseen by those in the street. He knew this man-made jungle, its whys and wherefores. She might know where to find a tree fungus, but she would not know the mushrooms and toadstools that grew at the base of gravestones, or under wrecked cars at the breaker's yard. She could climb a tree, but could she climb a garage, walk the length of a gutter some thirty feet off the ground?

I've got a chance, he told himself. I've got a chance to make this place my home.

GAR AND O-HA were sitting outside the sett, amid the wild flowers on the edge of Trinity Wood, lazing in the hot noonday summer's sun. Gar was watching a bee making crazy flight patterns in the air, flying from bloom to bloom. It was one of those days when foxes emptied their heads of care and allowed Frashoon to ruffle their coats with warm fingers; days when they dreamed of their own *sowander*—holy death-place—where their spirits would rest for ever in the Perfect Here. It was one of those days when the minds of badgers turn to philosophy and invention.

O-ha had learned that badgers were wonderful creatures for thinking up great truths by which others could live their lives, but forgot them the moment the mood passed. Badgers were marvellous inventors of the most delicate, intricate devices, but never got around to making any of them, either because their paws were inadequate for the task, or, most likely, because they lost interest. O-ha had no patience with this side of badgers. They seemed to her to be dreamers and storytellers, whose great minds were of little use because they had not the tools nor the determination to carry the schemes through. She said this to Gar.

'Ha,' he said, watching the bee through narrowed eyes. 'Importance of dreams is not in using—importance is in having. You think dreams must be real—all wrong, all wrong. Reality is feeding body—finding food for keep alive. Dreams feed spirit. Soul need food same as body, and dreams, philosophies, stories, creations, all food for spirit, see?' He pointed to some scratches in the dust, where earlier he had tried to show her an invention he had just thought up for getting honey out of hives without disturbing the bees. 'Here is wonderful idea, full of sticks that move against each other, stones that swing. I see it all, up here.' He nodded his head. 'How it work, push, pull, swing, honey in paw, bees all happy. It fill me with delight, to see this picture in my head, but if I try to make, it becomes something else. No longer dream, but something of the world. Inside is best. Once come outside, then something lost to spirit.'

'But think how useful it would be.'

'Useful, yes, but badger not care for useful unless necessary for life to go on. Badger not want to lose dream just for sake of useful. See?'

She sighed. 'No, I'm afraid I don't, but it doesn't matter. You are what you are. I'm different. I don't suppose we can change one another. I wish I could invent things. I would build something to catch those hounds—Breaker and Sabre. And then . . . my dream is full of blood and satisfaction.'

The badger shook his big head. 'I think that is nightmare, not dream. Blood and satisfaction not go together well, not well at all.'

He went back to studying the bee, slowly slipping into his solitary mood.

Out of the trees, further down the wood, came another fox. It was O-lan, one of the 'perfect pair'. O-ha called them that because they never seemed to argue or fight, never crossed one another in talk, and professed to live in bliss. The boring, perfect couple, she thought to herself, rather maliciously.

Gar retreated into his hole when he saw the other vixen, and O-lan greeted O-ha and flopped down beside her.

There was a long period of silence, but O-ha suspected that a favour was about to be asked: O-lan's expression was one of uninterest, and that always made O-ha suspicious.

'Well?' she said at last, unable to contain her impatience, 'what have you come to talk about?'

O-lan turned an innocent-looking face on her acquaintance.

'Why,' she said, wide-eyed, 'I just thought I'd come for a chat. You know how much I like chatting with you, O-ha. How are you getting along? Isn't it time you moved out of that badgers' sett and into your own earth again? It can't be good for you, living with those grumpy creatures—they're always so sullen and unsociable.'

'They are in fact very nice animals—placid and self-contained. They just look dour, that's all.'

'Really?' O-lan flicked an ear. 'Well, you know them better than anyone, I suppose.' She looked down at the devastation of the land round the wood. 'Just look at the *hav*,' she said. 'All our fine fields, and the heath, all gone.'

There were half-built houses below now, and streets were beginning to form networks in the churned clay and mud. It seemed that the builders were determined to get some people in the new town before the winter arrived, and they worked night and day. Trinity Wood had not been touched, but there were rumours that it would be drastically pruned: the new fox, Camio, was saying the wood might become a park—a place where humans would walk their dogs and put up devices for their young to play on. But probably, he said, a lot of the old wood might remain untouched, as humans liked to think they had a wild wood in the middle of their town: somewhere they could go to find a little natural life.

Camio seemed a bit of a know-all to O-ha, and she was inclined to treat the hearsay (she had not spoken to the animal since that night he had accosted her on the edge of the wood) as dubious information. He probably thought he knew what he was talking about, she decided generously, but there was every reason to suppose he was mistaken. No one had approached Trinity Wood, and she had never heard of a garden, for that was what a park seemed to be, which was for the use of all. Gardens were private things, attached to individual houses. No, this impertinent new fox had got it all wrong.

'Yes, it's very sad,' replied O-ha. 'We're losing our ancestral highways, our hide-outs, and many of our soaks and water holes.'

O-lan nodded. 'Still, it's very exciting. All that hustle and bustle going on down there—and Camio says that when it's finished, it'll be easier to get food than in the countryside. They waste so much, those humans. It won't be like the farmers, or the country people, who use their scraps on the pigs and chickens.'

'Camio, Camio, I'm sick of hearing that fox's name,' snapped O-ha. 'He doesn't know everything. He just thinks he does.'

O-lan's eyes opened wider in surprise.

'He doesn't pretend to know everything, O-ha. He's just giving us the benefit of his experience. He's lived in a town, after all.'

'So he says,' sniffed O-ha.

'My goodness, O-ha, you have got a down on him, haven't you? And he speaks nothing but good of you.'

'Does he?' she said quickly, suppressing a flicker of feeling deep inside her breast.

'Yes, he does—and I think you would do well to take notice of that. You've been too long on your own.'

'Oh, I understand. We're matchmaking are we, O-lan? Getting poor

O-ha, the pitiful, lonely vixen, a new mate? Well, I do very well on my own, thank you. It's less troublesome and I'm fond of not having any responsibilities. All right?'

'Yes, of course. We know a vixen can manage very well by herself. But what about cubs, O-ha? Don't you want a family? It's delightful . . .'

'I'm sure it is,' snapped O-ha, 'but I've no time for such things. I'm not interested in dog foxes, cubs, or anything else.'

O-lan rose to her feet, looking sad. 'Oh well, you know your own mind best. I'd better get back to my litter. I've been teaching them how to hunt and they're doing very well, but they're saying they'll have no need to hunt once the town is there. They'll just pick things up in the streets.'

'These new foxes don't realise the harm they're doing,' O-ha burst out. 'They don't realise we have a history, a culture, behind us, which is thousands of seasons old. Hunting skills will always be needed. I for one am not going to let such things drift away from me.'

O-lan blinked. 'Camio is as good a hunter as anyone I've seen, O-ha, and he certainly doesn't advocate that we ignore all our old ways. It's the cubs, that's all: when they reach a certain age, they think we can't teach them anything.'

'I still think that there are bad influences around which need to be curbed.'

'If you say so.' With that, O-lan left her to herself.

The following day there was a hunt. When O-ha heard the horn, the shouts of the hounds, she froze in her chamber. Gar went to the entrance to the sett and poked his nose out, and came down later with the news that there had been great battles outside: other humans had come to interfere with the hunt, spraying things on the ground to confuse the hounds, and generally causing consternation amongst the riders. Some of the huntsmen beat the interferers with riding whips, and then the workmen got angry with the horseriders for knocking down their makeshift fences, and helped the newcomers to turn them back.

'Such happenings!' he cried excitedly. 'Such anger! I never saw such glorious things. And the dogs—they ran this way, that way, sniffing, screaming in frustration. It was good to see this—you should see this happenings, O-ha.'

She lifted her head from her paws. 'I—I was afraid. Poor A-ho—it was as if it were happening all over again.'

Gar at once became tender, realising that she had relived her old ordeal. 'Oh, ya, I see. Well, never mind. I think we get no more hunts in this place now.'

He left her then. Later she went up to the surface, to look around. The workmen below were preparing to leave for the night, locking up their site sheds and leaving their great machines silent.

The moon came out, a hazy light in the heavens, and O-ha made her way to the farm, picking her way carefully between the digging machines which smelled strongly of steel. As she approached the farmhouse she was aware of a dog sitting outside his kennel, a chain attached to his collar. He looked miserable and dejected, and despite her hatred of dogs she felt sorry for him. She could not imagine anything worse than being restricted to a few square feet of ground. How had Camio stood it? She would have killed herself—ritual suicide, *ranz-san*—rather than submit to such terrible treatment. He must have had a high survival instinct. There was a saying that 'Foxes know no tomorrows': it was only the present that counted.

She crouched by one of the barns and stared at the dog, whose large mournful head looked up at the moon. He seemed familiar.

Suddenly the hound smelled her, and turned his head. O-ha prepared to flee, thinking that his yelling would have the farmer running out with a gun, but the dog did not cry out. Instead, he called softly, 'Is that a fox out there?'

Without thinking, she replied, 'Yes.'

'Ah.' He placed his head on his paws with a sigh.

'Why don't you yell for your master?' O-ha asked curiously. 'I've come to steal chickens.'

'Get on with it, then. I'll start yelling once you attack the chickens, if I feel like it. Right now I'm in two minds.'

She was amazed at this talk. 'But you're a farm dog. You're supposed to protect the place.'

He snorted then, through his cavernous nostrils. 'Farm dog? I'm no farm dog. I'm a hound, a hunting hound. I've run down more foxes than you've caught chickens. I've broken them—broken their necks . . .'

'Breaker!' she breathed.

His head came up again. 'Yes, that's my name. How do you know my name, fox? Famous, is it?'

'You killed my mate,' she snapped, 'towards the end of winter. You chased me along a road to the wood, then my mate took over and you killed him.'

'Not me. I've not caught a fox for a long time. That's why I'm here.' He looked round him in disgust. 'This is my punishment, to be trussed up, chained. You must be feeling good, seeing me like this, when I was once a hero of the pack. It must make you feel good.'

O-ha remembered then that A-ho had not been caught by the pack, but killed by stableboys and then thrown to the hounds.

'No, I don't feel good. I still hate you, but I don't like seeing any animal chained . . .'

He sighed. 'Well, don't go near the chickens or the ducks, or I'll have to make a row. I suppose I still have a little honour left. And don't come near me. I'm a trained killer. I'll have your neck.'

'I know,' she said.

She drifted round the farm, finding some *gubbins* out at the back, hanging on the fence. The cows watched her silently as she crossed her shadow over it twice, then ripped it from its wire. Then she performed the ritual chants and drank her fill from the pond.

O-ha left the farm and, for the first time since his death, visited the *sowander* of her old mate. Several times she passed by the spot where he had died, imbibing the spirit of the place; she told herself she was there to pay her respects to A-ho, but deep down there was also a subconscious desire to obtain his approval for something—for someone. The face she put to the world was strong and unyielding, but inside she was very lonely. So the messages went out from her heart to her erstwhile mate, hoping for some guidance from him: some sign which might tell her whether he approved of what she wanted.

Nothing happened. It is the living who must make the decisions on their own lives. She went home desperately disappointed, but refusing to admit it to herself. 'A-ho knows how I feel,' she told herself, 'that's the only important thing.'

That night, O-ha had a dream. It was a dream in which fear rattled in her throat, and her legs were weak with terror.

She dreamed she was in a bright place and struggling to walk. Suddenly, black bars fell across the ground . . .

THE SUMMER ENDED and Melloon, the autumn wind, was sweeping across the landscape like a grand, shaggy fox. The river began to gather more scarlet hues upon its surface during twilights, and ripe fruit and nuts fell to the earth. Around Trinity Wood the first occupants were moving into the town's new dwellings, though many roads were still unmade and dozens of houses were still empty shells. The evacuation of the animals had continued throughout the warm months, but some animals were determined not to recognise the human invasion. Prominent amongst these was A-konkon, visionary, mystic among foxes.

'A-kon' had been born on the far side of the river, in the crypt of a church; the repetitive syllable was added to his name at three months old when it was realised by his mother that he had special powers. It was said that A-konkon was able to recognise as many colours as humans themselves, the result of lying as a cub beneath the great stained-glass window that arched above the altar, soaking up the brilliant hues projected by the sun onto the stone floor. During his childhood he had also imbibed much that was sacred to humankind, listening from the crypt below while their services went on overhead, and falling into a trance under the murmurings and organ music which came from above.

After his parents had left their breeding earth in the church, A-konkon still returned to ponder over the symbol of the cross. His presence was tolerated by the humans, who had known of his mother's breeding earth and had not interfered with it. The ancient stones of the building whispered secrets to the fox, and some gleanings of intelligence penetrated his mystic consciousness.

'There is something which is denied us,' he told other foxes, 'because man does not believe we have a spirit, a soul. I cannot tell you what it is, not knowing human language, but I know it is important. A-O was not the first in the world, that much I can tell you.'

Such heresy was not popular amongst the common foxes. A-konkon was considered mad, and for many seasons was regarded as an outcast. However, he continued to preach obscure theories about a superior Being under whose judgment all would eventually fall. A-konkon believed utterly in the purity of the soil and all things that sprang from it, except the works of man. These, he said, were a blasphemy and false in the eyes of nature.

'A fox's life should be based on the doctrine of asceticism,' he told those who would listen. 'A fox should practise frugality, austerity, and learn to do without such bodily comforts as warmth, food and shelter. A fox should deny himself material things . . .' He also told them that they should sleep in the open, even during the most inclement weather, and never, ever, soil their bodies with the food of humans.

'The impurities in such foul waste will stain your souls, and you will be denied access to those grasslands and coverts beyond death, the Perfect Here, and be left to wander, deaf and blind, through the muddy wastelands of the Unplace. Foxes of the Earth, go forth and gather seeds from the wind in your coats. Let the burrs from the bushes tangle your fur. Collect twigs in the beautiful rust of your brows, the white of your bibs, and know you are nature's children. You are the salt in the wound of man, because you have not knelt before him. Your tail flying above the grass is man's failure to subdue all to his way. You are nature's blessed creatures, full and happy. Go forth and roll in the wet clay, let the mud of the ancients cling to your fur, and know that you are foxes!'

If nothing else, A-konkon gave his followers a positive image of themselves. He told them they were not sly, sneaking creatures to slink over the world, but proud, keen hunters who could outwit even the most intelligent of all animals, the name-caller, man.

The fox-mystic was also a herbalist who prescribed remedies for fox maladies and advocated the eating of herbs as clarifiers, purgatives and energisers. He would help ailing foxes when he could and proved to be a very able physician.

But most of the time A-konkon slept in the snow and ice alone, and was despised for his rejection of the easy pickings to be found in and around human habitations. When others challenged his teachings with the objection that weaker foxes might die when exposed to Ransheen's savage breath for days on end, he replied that death should be accepted as a reward. Death was not a failure of the body and soul, but a victory over life.

426

One morning just after the rain had ceased Camio sat talking to A-lon about A-konkon.

'I admire him,' said Camio, 'but I cannot agree with him about the "human obscenity" thing. There are humans and humans, some good, some bad. They're animals too, and entitled to live in the world.'

'Live, yes,' replied A-lon, 'but not claim most of it for themselves, even areas they don't use. And you must admit, some of that food they throw away does terrible things to the gut.'

'Only if you're not used to it.'

At that moment a vixen walked out of the trees, on her way back to her home. 'Hello,' Camio called eagerly. 'How are you?'

O-ha looked up, though she had obviously smelled and heard the other two foxes from some way off. She followed her nose and came up beside them. 'I'm very well—thank you for asking.'

'We—we were just talking about A-konkon, weren't we, A-lon? About his ideas . . .'

'Oh,' said O-ha, 'you wouldn't agree with him, of course, coming as you do from another land.'

Camio did not want to antagonise her, so he said, 'Well, I'm not sure.'

'What about dogs?' she asked. 'A-konkon maintains that dogs are no longer true animals, that every vestige of purity has been drained from them and that they have become something other than real creatures, something apart from nature.'

'Bit strong, I would have thought,' said A-lon, bravely.

O-ha said, 'Oh, you think so? Well, I know one that isn't natural.'

'Sabre,' said Camio, 'the ridgeback at the manor house.'

O-ha drew herself up. 'Yes, Sabre, and if my mate were alive he would have found some way to repay that beast for the death of our cubs . . .'

'Oh, come on, O-ha,' A-lon interrupted. 'What could a fox do against such a creature?'

Camio said quietly, 'He killed your cubs?'

'He was responsible for their death, and I'm sorry there's not a fox around with enough courage to put an end to him. We all know our strength is limited, but there have been foxes with enough art to get round that drawback. Clever foxes . . .'

'Like your A-ho?' said Camio.

'I think so.'

Camio seemed to slip into a reverie at that point, staring out across the fields, towards some distant place which could not be seen. O-ha suddenly felt guilty for baiting him. Why she should feel angry with this dog fox who had wandered into her life she was at a loss to explain, but she could not seem to help herself.

He turned to her now. 'If someone were to destroy this beast for you, no doubt you'd be eternally grateful?'

'Of course,' said O-ha, stiffly.

'I see,' said Camio. He looked rather grim. 'Well, you two, I'd better be on my way. I'll see you soon.'

With that he walked down the slope, towards the river, which sparkled in the morning sunlight.

FOR A WHILE there was silence between A-lon and O-ha. Then A-lon said, 'I think that was the most despicable thing you've ever done, O-ha. I used to admire you for the way you conducted yourself after the death of your mate. But that was really low.'

O-ha looked at him in surprise. 'I'm sorry, I don't understand.'

There was condemnation in A-lon's features. 'You don't understand? Let me enlighten you, then. You've just sent a good dog fox to his death. He's almost certainly on his way down to the manor now, to try and kill Sabre. And all to satisfy this bloodlust of yours, which you nurture like a litter of cubs. I don't want to have any more to do with you.'

O-ha faltered, 'He—he wouldn't do that.'

'Why not? It's the only hope you've ever given him. I've seen vixens plant themselves in his path, and he's ignored them, hoping that one day you'll change your mind and accept him for what he is. Your bitterness will be his death, though.'

She felt confusion whirling in her brain. 'I still don't know what you're talking about,' she said. 'Camio won't go to Sabre. Why should he?'

A-lon shook his head impatiently. 'You're not trying to tell me that Camio hasn't asked you to become his mate?'

O-ha shuffled uncomfortably. 'Well, yes, but I expect he's asked every available vixen at some time or another, he's that type of fox. You can see that he'd make up to females at the least opportunity. One can't take flatterers seriously.'

'Sometimes you exasperate me beyond reason, O-ha. Let me tell you something about this Camio: to my certain knowledge he hasn't "made up" to another vixen in the region once. All he ever talks about is you. In fact he's quite boring about you. And because of his feelings for you Camio has gone to fight Sabre, and good as he is, he can't win.'

A chill went along O-ha's spine. Was it possible that Camio found her so attractive that he would die for her? Foxes didn't do such things.

Then she remembered A-ho, and she knew that she herself would have sacrificed her own life for her cubs, if that would have saved them. This was serious. She had done a very silly thing.

'We must stop him, A-lon. We must stop him.'

'Too late for that. I couldn't catch him, and neither could you. I hope you're satisfied.'

With that, the dog fox walked away, leaving O-ha feeling miserable. A-lon was right, it had been a terrible thing to do. Her mind had been twisted by all that hatred and now it might lead to the death of a fox she . . . yes, it was time to stop lying to herself, she admired greatly. He had been through terrible adversity and had survived. Not only survived, but was balanced and kind. A little rough round the edges, but nevertheless—'Oh, no!' she cried. 'What have I done?'

There was only one thing to do: she had to go to the manor house. She set off at a fast pace in the direction taken by Camio.

CAMIO, IN THE MEANTIME, had gone not to the manor but to seek out A-konkon. He wanted to speak to this prophet amongst foxes, to try to understand the vixen he wanted so much. If he could not receive any insight into her complex attitude towards him, he would abandon all attempts to win her.

Why, for instance, was she trying to bait him? He could not think she was serious about asking any fox to go down and fight Sabre: it was like asking a hedgehog to attack a wolf. Yet she had thrown this challenge down at his feet. He wanted to understand why she did these things.

'You come asking for information I cannot give,' A-konkon said to Camio. 'One animal can never fully understand another—we are all different and react differently to different circumstances. My advice to you is to become celibate—a state in which I have kept myself since birth. Unions soil the soul . . .'

'But there would be no new foxes born, if everyone felt like that,' said Camio despondently.

'You talk as if continuation of the species is a necessary thing. The world will still be here when we've gone. It isn't necessary for a single fox to inhabit the earth to ensure that the sun rises in the morning.'

Camio did not agree with this, but there was something about A-konkon which deflected argument.

'To me, the most noble creature on the whole earth is the snake,' A-konkon continued. 'It is closer to the soil than any other beast.'

'Except the worm,' interrupted Camio, unable to help himself.

'The worm,' spat A-konkon, 'burrows through gardens desecrated by humankind. Only the snake remains aloof and for this reason is hated and feared by humans.'

'And because its bite is poisonous,' said Camio.

'That too,' replied A-konkon, after a long stare, 'but that is its defence against the poisonous nature of man. The *nagas*, the snake, has its spiritual homeland under the earth, which is kept holy by denying access to humans or any of their minions. Ever since man split the tongue of the snake by planting sharp grasses where the serpents lick the dew, *nagas* has kept distant from him and managed to remain pure in spirit. *Nagas* alone shall inherit the earth, because he has separated himself from the poisonous odour of humankind, the stink of people whose houses and machines breathe foul gases into the air, whose waste pollutes the waters of A-O and whose bark wounds the ears of all those who have to suffer its sound.'

'I once knew a keeper that I quite liked,' said Camio, reflectively. 'She had one of the softest barks I have ever heard, quite pleasant to the ear. And despite my snapping at her on several occasions, she showed nothing but kindness to me.'

'Did she open your cage and point the way to freedom?'

'No, but I've heard there are those that do.'

A-konkon sighed deeply. 'I'm afraid you are lost to me, Camio,' he said. 'You've been tarnished by your experiences in the world of men. I can do nothing to save you'—a glazed look came over A-konkon's features—'just as you can do nothing to save the vixen, O-ha.'

Camio jerked upright. 'What do you mean by that?'

A-konkon's voice was far away, as if he were somewhere in the back of his own mind. 'She is walking into the jaws of death,' he murmured, 'the slavering jaws of death.' His eyes seemed to focus once more. 'I saw her just before you came to visit me. She was heading towards the manor house, and she exuded an odour of fear and apprehension. I think she has gone . . . gone . . .'

Camio jumped to his feet. 'Damn your red hair, why didn't you tell me before?'

He left the mystic to his mutterings, running at full speed towards the place where she had gone.

THERE WAS A STRONG SCENT of humans at the manor house, and O-ha skirted the lawn, using the shrubbery directly in front of the building. She entered an area of low, squared hedges not much higher than herself, planted in rectangles. Some of the individual bushes had been cut into the shapes of animals: there was a cockerel and a peacock, but no fox.

Several pieces of white furniture had been set out on the lawn, and the growling of humans could be heard coming from within the house. Sabre was nowhere to be seen. Neither was Camio, and O-ha began to wonder whether A-lon had been right. She was about to sneak away, when some glass-panelled doors opened and humans spilled out onto the lawn. There was a smell of burning, and smoke wafted from several of the humans' faces. O-ha wrinkled her nose as the stink of human sweat, mingled with the frightening odour of fire, reached her sensitive nostrils. She flattened herself against the ground.

They sat on the furniture, barking at one another, and the clinking of glass added further sounds to the confusion. O-ha's poor eyesight gave her only an impression of colours, predominantly white. Then another odour came to her, which made her heart patter faster in her breast.

Sabre was amongst them: his scent was one she would never forget, and she judged that he was not more than a short run away from her. Then a head jerked up from the lawn, its nose high, as if sniffing the wind. Yes, he was there, lying full length on the short grass, and from the signals he was putting out she knew he was aware of an intruder. This was no pampered pet, but a killer with a nose for blood.

She quickly assessed the situation and her chances of escape. She could run, now, before he really knew what was happening, but the humans would surely catch sight of her and might give chase too. Was it possible that one of them had a gun? Unlikely. Their clothing had a different smell when they were out hunting, and their voices were different too, their barks coming out in a taut staccato rhythm. Were there any other dogs? She could not smell any and certainly Sabre was not paying attention to anyone but himself. So, only Sabre to deal with.

Only Sabre? She had got away from the ridgeback once, but could she hope to do it again? The wall at the bottom of the garden was a good long run: even if she took him by surprise it was doubtful she would get halfway there without having her back broken. So, she had to stay where she was and hope to remain downwind of her adversary.

For some time the human sounds continued unabated. Then something began, further out on the lawn. Some sticks were pushed into the ground and the humans began throwing a leather ball and hitting it with a flat piece of willow. O-ha had seen this kind of activity before, and knew how engrossed humans became in such things. Sabre, too, would have his attention taken up by this game. Dogs had lived with humans so long they enjoyed the same sorts of games, and would race after sticks or balls thrown into the air.

Sure enough, Sabre went running after the ball, but one of the humans barked orders at him and he had to return to the same spot as before. Once more O-ha was amazed at the size and speed of the ridgeback. He was a giant among dogs.

The sound of the ball being struck, and the excited barks of the humans, continued for a while. Then the wind began to change direction, and the dog got a whiff of fox. His head went up, first one way, then it jerked the other. O-ha wondered what was happening. Sabre was on his feet, his head whipping backwards and forwards as if he were not sure in which direction his quarry lay. The master barked at him, but the dog refused to obey. He came trotting towards the shrubbery, his eyes narrowed, then stopped and went the other way, towards a flowerbed.

Then O-ha realised what was happening. She had now caught a scent of fox herself, and knew that Camio was in the flowerbed on the far side of the lawn. It was time to flee, while Sabre was confused.

She came out of the shrubs running, and headed straight for the game in progress in the middle of the lawn. Camio had seen her break and went at the same time, running parallel to her.

'Go, vixen, go!' he yelled. 'Head for the humans. Confuse the dog.'

'Exactly what I was doing,' she snapped through clenched teeth. She ran right through the middle of the players, who barked and howled at her, some of them mesmerised, others looking for objects to throw.

A boot struck her side, but not hard enough to put her off course. A quick glance told her the dog was almost on her. His teeth were bared to the gums and his eyes were demonic, his determination evident in the way he remained silent, intent only on running down his prey.

Camio came rushing in at the ridgeback from the side, distracting him, and he turned his head for an instant, trying to make up his mind which one to go for. At that moment the sky overhead suddenly went black, the air was full of sound: the clamour was appalling and even the foxes looked up for an instant. A noisy, dark sheet was moving over the sky. The dog, unused to such a strange phenomenon, looked for too long, and stumbled.

The two foxes, quick to take advantage, increased their speed and reached the wall almost together. The dog recovered, and went for Camio, who was closer, but the American Red was at the foot of an oak, and within a moment was up in its branches and jumping for the wall. He ran along the top in the opposite direction from O-ha, with the dog following him. Now the hound was screaming threats, but it knew it was beaten. O-ha took two leaps at the wall before she finally scrambled over the top and down to the other side. She ran on until she reached the building sites. There she waited for Camio.

When he arrived he began to remonstrate with her. 'What on earth made you go to the manor?' he said. 'You were almost caught.'

'I might ask you the same thing.'

'I came to rescue you.'

'Well, it wasn't necessary. I'm quite capable of looking after myself, thank you.' She faltered. 'I—I was told you had gone to the manor first.'

'Now you know that's not true. I was with A-konkon when he told me he'd seen you heading in that direction. I guessed you were going down to try to even the score with Sabre. Listen, you have to forget that hound. There's not a fox on earth that could kill such a creature. It's too big and fierce, and it's not worth it.'

She sniffed. 'Well, I couldn't expect you to fight my battles for me, that's obvious. It's a good job the geese arrived when they did.'

'Me? Have a go at the beast? You must be mad. Next time you get such a crazy idea into your head, I suggest you go down to the pond at the farm and stick your head into the water—wash it clean of such thoughts.' Exhausted, Camio walked away towards the wood.

Overhead the geese, some two hundred thousand of them, were honking away at each other, their beating wings filling the air with sound. They came down from the north every winter to spend the cold months on the mud flats of the estuary. They were, fortunately, unusually early.

O-ha went to the top of the ridge and watched the large birds landing on the fields adjacent to the river. They were all talking to each other, milling around in their multitudes, an occasional head winding up above the crowd looking for a friend or relative missing since the flight began. 'Has so-and-so made it?' they would be saying. 'I saw her start out, but

lost her when I took the lead. Oh, yes, there she is, with whatsisname!'
Tired wings, aching muscles, relieved hearts: they were all down there on
the mud.

O-ha watched the birds for a long time, wondering what it must be like
to set out on such an arduous journey: what fortitude was required in
such an enterprise. Then she thought about Camio: he had saved her life
and yet she could not bring herself to thank him.

HUMILIATION! IF SABRE could have wept tears of frustration he would
have done so. To have been outwitted by that vixen once was bad
enough, but a second time . . . unthinkable. Yet, she had done it. It was
as if she were deliberately mocking him. Why had she come to the
manor? To make him look ridiculous, of course. The walls that
imprisoned him were barriers that would have to be breached. He would
get out one day—one day soon—and go looking for that vixen and her
mate.

The male guests at the house had taunted his master (he knew the
whining note of such barks!) and Sabre, in turn, had received a thrashing
for coming back without a kill. He knew he deserved the stick his master
had administered, shamed by his ineptitude.

Sabre paced the wall round the estate. He found a place where the
mortar was crumbling, and scratched at it with his claws. It fell away as
dust.

There was a bark from the house. His master. He would have to go.
But he would come back here, to this spot in the wall, and work on those
bricks until there was a gap large enough to let him escape. Then he
would go looking for this vixen, this blight on his honour, and crush her
skull in his jaws. It might take a season, perhaps more, but he would,
eventually, taste her blood.

Domesticated canines had suffered the gibes and jeers of wild
creatures for too long, simply because of the relationship dogs had with
humans. It was time for dogs to reassert themselves and show their
cousins that they had not been tamed beyond redemption: that there
were hounds whose honour was unbesmirched. Sabre had a pride in his
ancestry. He recalled being taught the 'middle history' of dogs: a time
when men and their hounds were much closer in spirit as well as in body.
In those days, hounds used to lie under the table while dinner was in
progress and receive choice bones from the hands of their masters. And
man and dog would hunt in the forests together, for the boar and the wolf.

Sabre wanted a return to those old times, when dogs were valued not
for sentimental reasons but because of their ability to track and hunt. He
could not afford to let an insignificant creature like a fox bring ridicule
upon his head. He had to be the epitome of houndhood: noble, strong,
revered, unsullied, merciless.

It was essential to kill the vixen.

PART FOUR
The Unremembered Fear

It was winter, and Ransheen blew through the streets of the new town finding fresh directions: being deflected down alleys, into courtyards and round squares. Although the finished buildings were new they had a period design, with cobbled precincts round the central square; there was even a mock horse trough for the birds to drink from, though of course the foxes used it as well. The animals found the inhabitants to be generous. Saucers of bread and milk were left out for hedgehogs (who would have preferred cat food) and the birds grew plump and lazy. Earths were dug in various places: some within a few feet of a human dwelling. One fox even had its earth in the utility room of a house which owned a cat and a dog, and used the cat flap to enter and leave the premises. The owners of the house knew it was there, of course, but tolerated its presence for reasons known only to themselves. Another vixen lived in the boiler room of a school and managed to chew through a water pipe while cleaning her teeth. Instead of chasing her away, the school authorities had the pipes sheathed. It seemed that having a fox in the grounds was sometimes regarded as a status symbol amongst the human occupants.

Trinity Wood was indeed landscaped at the south end, with devices for children to play on, and asphalt walks. Exotic trees and flowers were planted, and the wild creatures were pushed into an even tighter area.

Luckily the sett was not interfered with, since the authorities wanted to retain what wild life there was remaining in the wood. Food, however, was a problem. Many of the hunting areas had disappeared, and O-ha had to go down into the streets to find food. Under Camio's guidance she learned quickly where to go and at what time.

Camio had said it would be easy, but he had reckoned without the great numbers of creatures that would be dependent on the town. Most of them had not the skills necessary to live in the streets and the town itself was only partially built and would take some time to flourish. It was the next generation of creatures who would find life easy, when their numbers had settled to acceptable levels for the food available. Until that time survival would continue to be difficult for those without a sound knowledge of street life.

O-ha still maintained a rather aloof attitude towards the dog fox, but was gradually relenting. They would walk together through the half-finished streets discussing the differences in their cultural backgrounds.

'So you don't know about A-O?' she asked him, as they skirted the main square one evening, heading for a bin outside a takeaway which had closed for the night.

434

'It's not that I don't know, but I was taught that Menxito was the first fox, also of dual sexuality I might add, so there's a common link there.'

'But that's wrong—A-O . . .'

'Look, there's no right or wrong about it. It's just a fox by another name.' Suddenly, he turned to look at her intently. 'Isn't it about time we set up an earth together?' he said, bluntly.

'I don't know what you mean.'

'You know very well what I mean. I want us to live together, have a litter. Your time isn't very far away. Don't you like me?'

She stared at the ground. 'Of course I like you. But you're so different from me. I'm—I'm still not sure about you.'

'What's there to be sure of? I'm a fox, you're a fox. I've lived with a mate before—I told you. But I shall never see her again and no doubt, if she's still alive, she's found another. You're the one I want now.'

'You can't have me just because you want me.'

'I know that. That's why I'm asking. Look, I'm not one of your promiscuous foxes. I won't leave you in the lurch once the cubs are born. How can I convince you of that?'

'If—if I came to you, it would have to be for always. I've lost one litter because there was no dog fox to feed me while I kept the cubs warm. I couldn't bear it to happen again.'

His eyes were suddenly very bright and she warmed to him.

'Look,' he said, 'I respect your memories of A-ho, but nothing can bring him back to life. I'm sure he was a good mate, none better, because I can't imagine you choosing anyone that wasn't.'

She made a snorting sound. 'That's a little immodest, since it's now clear I've chosen you.'

He looked hard at her. 'You mean it? You will come to me?'

'Yes. Just don't let me down.'

'Let you down? Not in a million seasons! The winds will stop blowing before I do such a terrible thing. Now, we must choose a suitable earth. You must leave the sett, of course. I've seen an old house on the edge of—what do you call it—the *face*. There's an orchard at the back which has been neglected. The female human that lives there is very old, and no one comes to do the garden. We could live under the shed at the bottom. How do you feel about that?'

'Sounds quite good. But I must see it first.'

'We'll go tonight.'

They rummaged in a bin, finding some waste food, before he took her to the place he had found. When O-ha saw where it was, her heart turned over. It was the gatehouse to the manor where she had lost her previous litter. She said nothing to Camio, however, and showed delight in his choice of location. The manor house itself was near enough to concern O-ha, but Camio took her on a tour of the wall and showed her that Sabre's kingdom was completely enclosed and the barbarian was a

435

prisoner of his own world. She reluctantly accepted this reassurance.

Life was good once again. There was a space beneath the shed, suitable for an earth. The trees in the orchard would certainly show fruit the next summer. There were apples, pears and greengages laid out in rows a little too neat for his taste, but it suited her fine.

The next day she visited the sett for the last time. She found Gar in a grumpy mood, but when he heard she was leaving he stayed to talk to her. 'Ha, you go. I miss you, fox—most strong I miss you. We talk good together, eh? Well, you go—make nice little foxes—come see badger some time, with little fluffy foxes. We made good friends, ya? Good, good.'

Apart from having to leave Gar, O-ha was not sorry to move out of the sett. Badgers were noisy creatures, always chattering and snuffling and disturbing her. She was ready for a new life.

When she got back to the earth in the orchard, she spent some time sanctifying the new home with various rituals performed around the entrance and inside. Camio watched her, mystified by all the to-ing and fro-ing, the chanting, the spirals scratched in the dust. When it was over, he said, 'Is that it? Are we safe from mad spirits and tree ghosts?'

'You be careful what you say about tree ghosts,' she replied, while marking the posts round the garden with her scent.

When they were settled in for their first rest, side by side, she said sleepily, 'You must change your name now, to A-ho.'

'What?' His head jerked up. 'I'll do no such thing. My name is Camio.'

'But it's traditional. The dog fox takes its name from the vixen, and since my name is O-ha, you have to be . . .'

'That's a stupid tradition. No, I won't do it.'

'I suppose you expect me to change my name to reflect yours?'

'You keep your own name and I'll keep mine. I see no reason to change either of them.'

'But the other vixens—they won't know you're my fox.'

'Good thing too, smacks of ownership. Look, I couldn't care less about other vixens, or dog foxes, or anyone but us. We know we belong to each other. I know you like all this tradition, but I find it all a bit too tight, too constricting. I'm afraid it's something about me you'll have to put up with.'

She went back to the entrance to the earth.

'There—I knew it was a mistake. We are different.'

'But this is just a little thing.'

'If it's so little, then why not do as I ask? After all, this is my country, not yours. You should go by the customs here, not try to import your own ways and change us.'

Camio looked very hurt, and crossed his forepaws.

'A-ho, A-ho,' he repeated to himself. 'I'll never get used to it. It's not me at all.' He looked into her eyes, which were glowing in the near dark.

'I'm not him, you know. You can't make me into him. If you try, it'll only bring us both grief. I'm me, Camio, the fox from another land. A-ho is dead and wandering the woodlands of the Perfect Here.'

She suddenly saw the logic of his reasoning. She still dreamed of her previous mate, and those dreams would become confused with reality if she could not clearly differentiate between past and present.

'You're right. A-ho is A-ho, you are not him. I'll call you A-camio.'

'No, not even that. I'll just be Camio. You can be O-camia, if you like.'

'I certainly don't like, thank you. It seems we're to share an earth without belonging to each other in the eyes of the world. So be it, if that's how it must be. A-konkon will have a fit when he finds out. If you think I'm a traditionalist, wait until you hear what he has to say about such unorthodox pairings. Well, I don't suppose it'll make any difference to the way we feel about each other. Let's get some rest.'

They marked each other and then lay down together, touching.

WHEN HER TIME CAME, O-ha was surprised how good it was with a fox other than A-ho. Camio was just as sensitive and considerate to her needs, and spent a long time gently nipping her flanks with his teeth before the actual act, which after all only lasted seconds. When it was over, Camio let out a triple bark and a scream, and she thought, Some things never change. Then they lay contented, side by side, touching just enough to know the other was there.

In the world around them winter set in. Frost made the grasses crisp underfoot, and the soil became solid and impossible to dig. Insects disappeared from the face of the world. Water was hard to find.

O-ha taught Camio the rituals of leaving and entering the earth, which after all, she said, were insurance against discovery. Camio wanted to please her, and also ensure that his future cubs had a home which was not likely to be attacked, so he learned her ways.

Midwinter came, and with it heavy falls of snow. One night, Camio left the earth, only to come back a little while later without any food. His eyes were full of anxiety and O-ha knew that something terrible had happened.

'What is it?' she asked. 'Tell me what it is.'

'Keep calm,' he replied. 'We have got to get out—go away—as quickly as we can. There are men abroad with guns, all through the town, and out in the countryside, too. They're shooting anything that moves, especially foxes.'

Her heart felt leaden and heavy in her breast. 'Why us?'

'It was A-konkon, damn his soul to oblivion,' said Camio with great feeling. 'We must get out—get you to a safe place . . .'

'A-konkon? But what could he have possibly done to bring the humans down on us like this?'

'He committed *ranz-san*, in the main square. Tore his own stomach out and died in front of a dozen people. How could humans understand? He did it as a protest, against the decadent life we are leading here, as he called it. A protest!'

'But what was it they thought?'

'As soon as I heard what had happened I guessed. The humans are scared out of their wits, frightened for their young. And when humans get like that, they'll destroy anything and everything.'

'You still haven't told me—I still don't understand.'

'The Shadow-with-a-thousand-names. The White Mask of Terror. *Now* do you understand? They think A-konkon died the death of the Foaming Mouth. They're killing dogs out there, as well as foxes. Dogs, cats, everything.'

'But . . .' O-ha faltered, reaching deep down into her mind for the Unremembered Fear, deep down into the black well where it had been laid long ago by her ancestors. 'But we haven't had such a thing here for—for seasons out of time.'

'Well, I've seen it, in my old country. And it's not here. They only think it is—but that's enough. They'll kill and kill until there's nothing left to shoot. Or until reason returns to them once again. At least they're not using dogs to hunt us down. They daren't. We must go.'

O-ha followed him to the entrance to the earth. For once she did not complain when he failed to observe the rituals.

THE FOX-SPIRITS from the Firstdark, who know all things, said there had not been so many abroad with death on their minds since the infamous days of Herod and the mass murder of human babes. There were shadows moving across the land and the night was full of thunder and fire. All the animals along the coast caught the smell of terror and either froze or ran. Blood fell on the snow like warm rain, and the land choked on its own fear.

For Camio and O-ha, the flight from the *face* began with a hazardous journey through the streets. There were men everywhere, in cars and on foot, and each corner was a potential deathtrap. The rust-coloured foxes moved against a backdrop of red brick walls, and slipped down dark alleys, over the fences of gardens, across low rooftops. The snow showed their tracks, however, and they had to be away from the town before the morning light.

Whenever the smell of man was strong, or the sounds of his boots crunched on snow, they found a hiding place: rubbish bins or a shed, or under a car—anywhere, especially if the hidey-hole was small. Camio knew that humans often mistake a fox's size, thinking it to be as large as a medium-sized dog, whereas it is only a little larger than a cat, and can squeeze into spaces which look too narrow to take a man's fist. Once, a pair of legs passed by them only inches away from their noses.

They found a manhole cover off a sewer, in the part of the town where building was in progress, and travelled along the pipes beneath. Even under the ground they could hear the reports of the guns, and boots thumping the snowcovered concrete above. There were other animals in the sewer pipes, quaking with fear, frozen to the spot. Camio ignored these creatures, mostly smaller mammals.

At one point, O-ha said, 'Why don't we stop here?'

'Because we'll have to go out for food some time,' he answered, 'and they'll be waiting for us. You'll see. They won't stop tomorrow, or the next day. This thing will go on for at least a week or two. We have to go somewhere and let the time pass.'

Once they reached the point where they had to abandon the sewers, they made a dash across a building site. A shotgun opened up on them, but the user was inexperienced and the lead pellets went high. The man howled to his companions, and raced after the two foxes, trying to reload his weapon at the same time. O-ha turned on the human when he got too close, and even in the poor light she could see his face turn pale as he skidded to a halt, dropping the cartridges. As he bent to pick them up, the foxes continued their flight into the darkness.

They reached the edge of town, but there were watchfires ringing the *face* and gun-carrying silhouettes moved across them, walking along the highways. Camio quickly realised that these figures were to keep foxes out, rather than to stop them getting away, but they would shoot anyway, if they saw something slinking through their lines.

Now O-ha took the lead through the forest of men. She used her nose, while running parallel to the lines, and finally came across some humans whose attention was on the bottle they were passing round, rather than the night. The group was huddled round a fire in an oil drum and barked loudly, warming their hands. She and Camio crept past, low to the ground, their belly hairs touching the snow, on the side of the fire where the men were shoulder to shoulder and blocking the light from the white ground.

Once they were through the lines it was ploughed fields, the furrows rigid beneath the snow and difficult to negotiate when walking crossways to them. When they reached a ditch, they lay in the bottom for some time, gathering their strength again.

'I'm not sure where we are,' O-ha said to Camio. 'I've never been this far from home before.'

'It doesn't matter for the moment,' he replied. 'We're out of the town at least. Just think of the creatures in Trinity Wood. That's the first place the humans will have gone, and it's ringed by the town.'

O-ha thought of Gar, the 'perfect pair', and others . . .

When morning came they were aware that they were being tracked, and set off again at a fast pace over the fields. They tried all the tricks: climbing trees and running along a branch, hoping to break the line of spoor; travelling along ice in ditches; balancing on the edges of fences. Still they could not shake off their pursuers. A farmhouse was circumnavigated with caution. Finally, they came to a railway track.

'Quick, they're not far behind,' said Camio. 'Up on the track.'

O-ha followed him, wondering what he had in mind. Camio ran along the steel rail for quite a distance, before dropping between the tracks and flattening himself against the gravel. O-ha copied him.

Shortly afterwards, the barks of men could be heard, and she was aware of some confusion amongst them. They had lost the trail at the point where the two foxes had climbed the embankment, and were searching the snow for their tracks.

There was a loud report, which almost had O-ha bolting, followed by a strong smell of cordite. One of the men had fired his gun, hoping to flush the foxes from their hide-out. It had almost worked. Then the rails began to vibrate and hum, and O-ha was almost beside herself with fright.

'Stay here,' whispered Camio. 'Don't move a muscle. You'll be all right, I promise. I know what I'm talking about. The train is coming, but it'll pass over us. We won't be hurt. Stay, stay . . .' His voice was calm and gentle, with only a trace of apprehension behind it.

The vibration increased to a rumble. A machine was hurtling down on them at tremendous speed and O-ha was convinced they were going to die. She could not understand why Camio did not bolt, but she trusted his judgment, waiting for a move from him before she went herself.

The noise was excruciating. They were entombed in living steel that screamed around them. She thought it would last for ever. Then it was over, just as suddenly as it had begun, and all she was left with was a ringing in her ears and a pumping heart.

They lay there together for a long time. Ransheen whistled over their bodies, lifting their fur, and when he was sure there was no scent or sound of man, Camio lifted his head.

'I think we'd better be getting on. They've left. That was some experience, wasn't it?'

O-ha looked at him in surprise. 'You talk as if you've never done it before.'

He flicked his head. 'I haven't—not quite. I almost did it once, but my courage failed me at the last moment. Nearly got killed. A city fox taught me that there was no problem, provided you keep your head down and remain quite still. I was worried for you. I prayed you wouldn't panic. You were very brave, extremely brave . . .'

'So,' she said, not without a trace of condescension, 'you actually jumped clear the first time you did it?'

'I'm afraid so. It's a horrible experience. I don't think I have your courage.'

He was so magnanimous in his praise, that she confessed shame-facedly, 'I was scared.'

440

'I expect you were—you'd be very foolish not to be—but the important thing is, you didn't let that fear rule your head. Come on, let's get out of here. Which is the best way to go?'

'I think if we head towards the sun, following the rails, we should reach the marshes of the estuary. Perhaps we can hide there until all this has been forgotten?'

So the pair of them began walking, keeping their noses to the wind. By midday they had reached a point where the ridge dropped down gently towards the creeks and salt flats of the estuary, and they left the railway. Several trains passed them while they were walking, and O-ha marvelled that she had ever allowed one to hurtle over her prone body.

When they reached the flats of the wetlands, the tide was out, leaving only thin slivers of water running between the banks of the river and its inlets. Here were several square miles of marsh samphire, bladderwrack and seablite, with eelgrass flowering just below the water. Here the sharp sound of the wading birds mingled with the deep honking of the brent geese, gulls robbed and scavenged, and graceful, dagger-faced herons went on lonely dawn patrols, looking for meals in shallow pools. These were the saltings, the marshes, where wrecks of rotting vessels appeared to be climbing from the sludge like corpses rising from their graves on the day of salvation.

The pair of foxes travelled along, hidden by the dykes that protected the land round the creeks. There were dozens of new smells that took time to assess and store in their olfactory memories for future reference. They found a place to cross to an ancient wreck on an island of sea poa grass. The hulk was cold and damp, but there was a space in what was left of the cabin which seemed to remain clear of the water when the tide was in. This they decided to make their home for the winter months, until the Unremembered Fear faded from the minds of humankind.

The first time O-ha went out hunting she found a group of seagulls that refused to fly away when she caught one of their kind. The red mist clouded her brain for an instant, and she had the urge to kill wantonly. But her experience of the last few days had somehow penetrated beyond that drive to kill for the sake of killing. Something akin to sympathy for the birds entered her emotions—a feeling which was strange to her, since her emotional mechanism was geared to survival, and survival meant obtaining food when and where it was available. She took only the quarry she had first caught. It was not something she spoke to Camio about, because she could not explain it even to herself. She just knew that out there in the river mists something unusual had happened to her.

When the tides came in most of the boat was covered, leaving only a small space in the cabin for the two foxes to huddle together. They suffered a great deal. The shellfish that they cracked open left their stomachs sore, and the cold was bitter. Ransheen came across the marshes like a well-honed scythe, ready to cut down anything taller than a blade of grass. The alluvium of the estuary stuck to their paws and froze between their pads, so that they had to dig it out with their teeth. There were dens of hibernating adders in the grasses on the top of the dykes, and the foxes trod warily round them.

O-ha and Camio hunted on the network of raised areas which were sometimes islands, at high tide. Come spring there would be eggs and elvers, spawn and spanworms aplenty. But until that time, the pair had to make do with what they could find in the mud, or flying above it. They occasionally caught an unlucky bird, but lived mostly on shellfish: crabs, shrimps, worms and roots. Most of all, O-ha missed the succulent chanterelle fungus and wood blewit, which she loved, and the insects to be found in the rotten logs of Trinity Wood.

EACH DAY WAS TAKEN as it came, and visits by man were rare. When humans were abroad the geese set up such a clamour that it was known for miles around, and the foxes were warned well in advance. And there was a certain feeling of security which came from being surrounded by mud or water, especially in the winter. At least the exposed creeks, with their merciless winds and unerring drabness, ensured that humans kept their distance.

One evening, after she had been out hunting, O-ha returned to find the smell of dog clinging to the wind. The odour came from the direction of the dyke, and was persistent.

O-ha leaped down through the hole into the dank interior of the hulk. Camio was there, asleep, and she woke him and asked him if he could smell the enemy. He licked his nose, sniffed the air for a few moments, and then confirmed her suspicions.

'Dog, most definitely. But what would an unaccompanied dog be doing out here in the marshes? Lost?'

'I suppose so,' she replied. 'There's no human scent, so it must be. Perhaps it's hurt—lying there injured? Do you think we need to worry?'

Camio suggested they stay where they were for the rest of the night, just to be sure. She laid her head across his shoulders and tried to sleep, but during the night both animals were woken by a whining from the dyke: a pitiful sound which filled them with a feeling of despondency.

When morning came they saw a movement on the dyke. It was indeed a dog and O-ha recognised him immediately: Breaker, the old hunting hound. He looked half-starved, and misery seemed to have hammered his features flat. Then, suddenly, he seemed to see the boat for the first time, half hidden by reeds and partly submerged in the mud. He began to make his way towards it, sinking in the sludge up to his belly. As he began to approach the boat, O-ha started to get alarmed.

'He's coming here,' she whispered. 'What are we going to do?'

'Hey,' Camio called. 'You, dog. What do you want?'

Breaker paused in the act of climbing an overhanging bank, and looked at the boat. 'Fox? I smelled you around here, a day ago. I still have a good nose, even though they've thrown me away like a piece of rubbish. Look, I'm nearly done in. Need a place to rest. I'm coming into the boat.'

'You are?' said O-ha, her instincts telling her to bolt.

'I'm coming into the boat, but I promise I won't attack you. You understand?'

Camio snorted. 'You promise you won't attack us? I think you've got it the wrong way round, my friend. You're in a very vulnerable position out there, on the soft mud. There are two of us, and only one of you . . .'

Breaker had another go at the bank, slipping back down again, but at the same time saying, 'You think you could take a hunting hound? No way. I've broken more foxes in half than you have hairs on your tail . . . But I promise I won't hurt you.'

They watched him while he struggled. Breaker did not look as if he could damage a soft-shelled crab in his present condition, let alone a fox. Finally, he managed to crawl up the bank and into the bottom of the wreck. There he found some scraps of food which the foxes had cached, and chewed the salty pieces, swallowing them with obvious distaste.

'Muck,' he kept muttering to himself. 'Not a decent piece of meat amongst it.'

'Listen to him,' said Camio. 'He scorns the fare of outlaws, but he doesn't ask whether it can be spared, does he? Maybe you can hunt for yourself next time?'

Breaker growled. 'You be careful what you say to me, or I'll have your skin, Reynard.'

'We don't like that name,' snarled Camio, nipping the dog's nose with his sharp teeth.

'Hey!' said the hound, his eyes watering. 'There's no need for that. If you're not careful I'll have to break your back. I'll overlook it this time.'

The exhausted dog licked his nose with such a feeble effort that the foxes could see he was almost finished. His eyes told them he might not live through the day, and despite all his brashness and bravado he was as weak as a kitten with no promise of its mother's milk.

O-ha said, 'Let him alone, Camio. He can't do anything to us. We might as well go out and hunt, while the tide's still on the ebb. Come on.'

While they were out hunting it rained heavily, and they knew they would have drinking water waiting for them back at the boat. They found three geese which had been shot by hunters, probably in mistake for foxes, dogs or badgers—which told them the Unremembered Fear was still abroad. They cached one amongst the reeds, and then took one each back to the wreck, pulling them by the neck across the mud.

When they got back to the boat they found Breaker still alive, drinking rainwater. He looked starved, his rib cage showing through his skin like a row of iron hoops, and he watched hungrily as the two foxes tore away at the geese, eating their fill. When O-ha and Camio had swallowed all they needed, and had left the carcasses in the bottom of the boat, the dog approached the meat and began chewing. O-ha thought about protesting, but she was full and had little interest in the meat now, so she let the hound eat. Afterwards he seemed a little more alive, and found himself a beam on which to lie while the tide swirled into the hull.

O-ha's feelings over sharing her hide-out with a dog confused her. Each time she woke and smelled the dog's presence, a panic began in her breast which was difficult to suppress. She found the odour unpleasant and offensive, especially when it mingled with the scent of her Camio.

Yet when Ransheen blew through the holes in the hull and took the dog's scent away from her, she was able to view him with a more dispassionate eye. What she saw was a hound whose spirit was broken, but who was too stubborn to admit that he was finished as a hunter. When he mumbled about past glories, she felt pity rather than scorn. Breaker had placed his faith in a faithless master, had carried out that master's bidding, and when his body began to fail had been tossed aside. It made his whole existence a lie, and he retaliated with falsehoods.

'My master admired me above all the hounds he had ever known. I was given the choicest cuts of meat, the best accommodation. I deserved it, of course: I was the best. My master cried the day I left the pack for the farm. But he knew I was a working dog and guarding the farm was a very important job. They value me tremendously at the farm . . .'

Had Breaker stuck with his story they might have believed him, but sometimes he cursed his old master with savage oaths. Occasionally he spoke of his detestation of the farm and its occupants. Once in a while he even swore at himself and mouthed contempt for his condition.

When darkness came one evening, Camio said to the dog, 'What made you come out here? Did you get lost?' and then they got something like the truth from him.

'Hounds like me don't get lost, Reynard,' said the dog, but without malice in his voice this time. 'I know this countryside backwards. No, I escaped.'

O-ha said, 'Escaped? From what?'

'You remember the chain, vixen? You're the fox that came to the farm one night—I never forget a scent. That damn chain. I'm used to running free, with the wind in my coat and the scent of the earth in my nostrils . . . you foxes can understand that. I nearly went crazy at that farm, stuck on the end of a chain, with seven paces of ground.'

'I can understand that,' said Camio, sleepily.

'So what happened?' O-ha asked Breaker.

'One night I slipped the collar and I was free. I ran through the fields and woods, chased anything that moved. Then in the morning I went home. I never intended to stay away. My masters are my masters, no question. I just wanted a little freedom.'

444

'And?'

'They were waiting for me with guns. They were going to shoot me. Me, Breaker, the foxhound—blast me like a common wild animal.'

'I see,' said Camio. 'They thought you might have come into contact with the White Mask.'

'White Mask? Why mince words? Rabies. They were scared I'd caught rabies and they weren't taking any chances.'

'They didn't trust you any more,' said Camio.

'I could smell the fear in them. Their mouths were barking softly— "Come on, Breaker. Good boy, Breaker. Come and get the nice juicy bone we've got for you." I was used to seeing guns, and they held them casually enough, under one arm, but the tenseness was there, ready to jump the weapon level and blow me to pieces once I got within range. I pretended to approach them with joy—you know, tongue lolling out, lazy, rolling gait—but the closer I got the more agitated they became, and finally one of the guns came up and I ran. I was out of range. Since then I've been wandering, avoiding them whenever they appeared.'

O-ha became alarmed.

'You don't think they followed you here, do you?'

'Not a chance. Humans are useless at tracking without dogs to help them, you know that, Reynard. Those farm boys can't smell a dead rat until it's ten days old.'

'Well, it's time we all got some sleep,' said Camio. 'If you've any ideas about trying to reach us during the night, forget it. You'd drop into the freezing water and, in your state, drown very quickly.'

'Don't worry,' said Breaker. 'I couldn't care less about a pair of tatty-looking reynards when none of my pals is here to watch me break their backs. You can sleep in peace.'

'Thanks for nothing,' said Camio, and O-ha felt him snuggle up closer to her, to keep her from the night frost.

IN THE BEGINNING, that time which all the canid mythology shared, after the Firstdark, the wolves ruled the forests. They were swift to organise themselves into packs, with leaders, and quickly parcelled out areas of land for the separate packs. While the foxes were able to remain in these territories by virtue of their ability to ghost past the packs one at a time or in small groups, the dogs were driven out onto the unsheltered plains, where the horses grazed in their herds. The dogs, too, found security in forming themselves into packs, but being weaker than wolves were unable to match the grey ones in battle. The dogs bitterly resented wolves, who had the choice hunting grounds, and were forced to wrest a meagre existence from the treeless wastes.

Some time after the Firstdark the dogs, who were now close to starvation, set aside their individual differences and gathered on the great central plains to form a single mighty pack that would sweep the wolves from the forests and into the sea. In hound mythology, this was called the Season of the Dog. All quarrels and arguments between separate packs were put aside and Skellion Broadjaw, the leader chosen as king-hound in the coming battle, coined the saying which was to be their watchword: I am against my brother dog, but my brother dog and I are against our cousin wolf. In this way their petty jealousies could be contained without being dismissed.

During this time the foxes merely looked on, and no doubt hoped that their two major rivals in hunting would wipe each other out.

At first, the dogs were extremely successful. They swept across the countryside, driving out the smaller wolf packs onto the plains where the horses grazed. The horses were no friends of the wolves, and welcomed the opportunity of battering down these grey shapes from the forest. Skellion Broadjaw was universally regarded as one of the greatest chiefs of all time.

The wolves were in a state of panic. They suffered a terrible defeat at the Place of the Swamps, when they gathered together a mighty pack on the edge of the eastern wetlands. The scouting dog packs in the area had watched the wolves gathering in some dismay, as Skellion Broadjaw and the main army was two days' run from that place and the wolves outnumbered them ten to one. They sent a runner to Skellion Broadjaw, and prepared to try to hold off the wolves until the main army arrived. Meanwhile, the wolves, aware that they were watched only by a few small packs of dogs, from the ridge above the swamps, set about choosing leaders and organising strategy and tactics.

However, about noon on the second day, the dogs noticed there was some confusion below. More wolf packs had arrived and had swelled the numbers to such an extent that they were jostling each other for room on the firm ground. The wolf leaders had thought that with the marshland on three sides of them, they would be protected flank and rear, and would need to worry only about their front. As the sun reached its peak a dog named Zerfuss trod on a thorn and let out a high-pitched cry of pain. In their excited state, most of the dogs on the ridge misinterpreted his yell as a command to charge, and began running full pelt down the slope towards the wolves. The dogs were channelled into a narrow dip between two spurs and, unable to control their speed on the steep slope, they hit the wolves in a solid wedge of bodies, driving the grey ones backwards and to either side. Thousands of wolves found themselves floundering in the mire and sinking to their deaths, while many others attempted a retreat across any firm ground the marshes had to offer.

It was a great victory for the dogs, and when Skellion Broadjaw arrived celebrations were in progress. He decided that the final great battle should take place on a promontory north of a wide river. Skellion Broadjaw's forces now outnumbered the wolves by almost twenty to one.

The evening before the fight was to take place a messenger came from the wolf camp, saying that Shesta, the great wolf warrior-priestess, had offered to fight any warrior of the dogs' choice in single combat and the winner of this fight would carry the day. In this way much bloodshed could be avoided.

By this time the praise of his troops had gone to the head of Skellion Broadjaw—they called him the Invincible One, the Dogday Warrior of Ten Lives, Hound Magnificent—and his vanity was so swelled that he believed no animal on earth could defeat him. He informed the messenger, 'Tell the bitch I'll meet her at One Tree Hill, at dawn tomorrow.'

So, at the place of the single tree, Skellion Broadjaw met his death under the savage teeth of Shesta, the warrior-priestess. She tore him from throat to groin and ate his heart before thousands of dismayed dogs and crooning wolves. The dogs immediately began accusing each other, and were routed by the triumphant wolves who took advantage of their disarray. In the end, they were beaten by their own character.

Skellion Broadjaw's body was dragged by the wolves into the forest and buried under the roots of an unnamed tree. To this day, when a dog sees a tree he will piss on its trunk, hoping to desecrate Skellion's monument, wherever it may be.

These battles had left the wolf population severely depleted, however, and against their better judgment they became allies with the boars of the forest, whose tusks took many a dog life. This was the time when the giant *Groff*, the agent of the humans, came down from the white-peaked mountains to gather allies and pave the way for the humans. The first animals he won over were the cats, who saw an easy way of life ahead of them if these tool-handed creatures called men were allowed to establish themselves in the world. They told the agent of men that they would help him, provided they were allowed to retain a certain autonomy once the humans were in the land.

'We will work with man, but not under him,' said the she-cat Callissimmini. 'There will be no question of a master-slave relationship. We own our own selves. We have nothing but contempt for all other creatures, and that includes you and your clients. I hope we understand one another?'

Groff accepted this proposal, but when he went to the dogs he told them that the cats had capitulated unconditionally, and the dogs were tricked into complete submission. To this day the dogs maintain they were misled by the cats.

So under the guidance of cats and dogs, men came up from the ocean of darkness with spears and bows, and began to hunt and kill the wolves and boars. The dogs rejoiced in victory at last, acting as trackers and scouts for the men, and leading them to their deadly enemies. The dogs were even willing to drag the machines of men over the snow when

horses could not serve. The horses themselves went down hard. They fought against humans but eventually succumbed and were yoked to the plough and the cart, suffered the indignity of having men on their backs, and finally became as much a part of man's progress as the dogs themselves.

O-HA AND CAMIO had listened to Breaker's story with interest. However, they pointed out to him that their own stories of the past, though tinged with certain similarities, differed from those of dog mythology. In fact, O-ha's version of how things began was different from Camio's, and the two of them were arguing well into the night about the names of various fox heroes and heroines, and who was responsible for what, and where the winds came from.

448

In the end, Camio said, 'It doesn't really matter whether this was that, or that was this—what is important is the similarities, not the differences. I know I was born a long way from here—how far is impossible for any of us to guess—yet the same tales of the world's beginning are told in that place. Yes, there's a difference of opinion as to names and places, but think of it! How much alike we all are.'

With that he fell asleep and O-ha followed his example not long afterwards.

SHE DREAMED. She dreamed she was in a bright place and struggling to walk. Suddenly, black bars fell across the ground. They were like the iron rods of a cage at the zoo, once described to her by Camio. And then she was . . .

O-HA FELT LIKE a ripe autumn plum, ready to split down the middle: there was a warm mellowness in her spirit. She had not told Camio that she was pregnant but her condition was now obvious to both him and the hound. The dog fox had said nothing, waiting for her to open the subject. The problem was, she felt insecure once more, and wanted no one around at the birth. Since the death of her first litter, she trusted no one, not even the father of her cubs. It was not a feeling she liked, and she hated herself for harbouring such disloyal misgivings towards her present mate, but she could not help herself.

She kept thinking of A-ho—of his gentle passion for her, of his sacrifice—and at that moment it did not seem right that Camio was the father of her cubs.

She watched the brent geese getting ready to fly back to the land where they spent their summers, far to the north. The hunters and fishermen would soon be swarming over the marshland, and she realised it was time to leave the marshes and go back to the town.

Breaker asked, 'You'll be leaving here soon?'

'Yes,' she replied, 'soon.'

'We can all go back now. They'll have found out that there was no rabies. That fox you told me about—A-konkon—they'll know by now that he did not die of the White Mask.'

'I suppose so.'

'I'm a lot stronger now,' Breaker said. 'I think I can make it back to the farm.'

'Good. You can be there to kill more foxes when they raid the farm for chickens.'

'It's what I'm there for—to protect the place.'

'I suppose so.'

Then Breaker said, 'Don't come to the farm any more. If you come, either of you, I won't be able to do my job.'

It was the closest he ever came to thanking her for keeping him alive. He was telling her that he would not attack her, or Camio, if they crossed his path. She was astounded by his confession. A dog, a hunting hound, had made a pact with two foxes.

Camio returned a little later and they talked about going back to the town. He agreed that they should set off before dawn.

So, in the early hours, they swam across the river. They went across country to the railway embankment and followed it to the point where the *havnot* lay between them and the *face*. There was no suitable place for an earth on the farmland, so eventually they entered the town and began to search.

There was the beginnings of a scrapyard on the edge of town, where already there were several wrecks of cars, and other discarded items. It seemed a safe enough place for the time being. Camio and O-ha chose a suitable car in which to set up home, and marked the territory together.

450

'If we find too many humans coming here,' said Camio, 'I'll look for somewhere else.'

'That's fine,' she said. Then, 'Camio—I—feel very strange at the moment. Old memories keep interfering with what's happening now . . . I'm sorry if—I can't explain it.'

He looked away from her. 'Well, we'll see how things go. When are the cubs due?'

It was the first time her pregnancy had been mentioned between them, and she felt guilty that it was Camio who had spoken of the forthcoming birth first.

'Soon,' she said.

'I won't let you down, you know. If you're thinking that I'll go out and not come back one day, you're wrong. I like the idea that I've got responsibilities.'

Her guilt almost crushed her on hearing these words. He was such a thoughtful mate. Why couldn't she have the same feelings for him as she had had for A-ho? It was so stupid, dreaming about what might have been, when a good life lay ahead of her. She wanted to be fair to Camio and give him all she had to offer, but there was still something holding her back.

'It's—it's not that exactly.'

'No? Well, whatever it is, I am reliable, and I'll prove that to you in time. Only death will keep me from you and the cubs now . . .'

'Don't say that.' The thought that he might get killed before the cubs were born filled her with panic. And suddenly she realised that it was not just the cubs she cared for—it was him. She did not want to lose Camio. He was part of her now. They were linked by their cubs: those little lumps that squirmed around in her body, making her feel warm and motherly.

'Don't talk about death while I have our life within me. I'll be all right, I promise. Vixens get funny dreams when they're having cubs. I'm feeling too protective towards the litter and I'm afraid I look on everything as a threat towards them.'

'Even me?' He looked surprised, and desperately hurt.

'Perhaps. I don't know—I'm not really myself at the moment. Will you be patient with me?'

'Of course I'll be patient.' He still sounded upset and his scent was strange. 'Now I've got to go out and get food for us. I'll be back before noon.' With that he left her.

O-ha felt dreadful for some time after he had gone, but then the men who owned the scrapyard came and began clattering around on the edge of the heap. The car the foxes had chosen as an earth was in the centre, under a pile of other scrap, so she felt quite safe. There were only small tunnels through the jagged metal, which no man could crawl along.

Camio came back later, with some old scraps of meat wrapped in paper and a half-full carton of yoghurt. She could see he had had difficulty in carrying the items and thanked him.

'The curdled milk stuff is for you,' he said, 'and the cubs.'

WITH MARCH, SCRESHEEN came screaming through the torn metal and whistling insane tunes along the open ends of pipes. One night, when Camio came back to the earth, O-ha told him he could not enter. He had to remain outside until she called him. He began pacing up and down the tunnels, waiting.

The cubs were born in the early hours of the morning: three little mewling blind and deaf blobs, covered in short black fur. O-ha cleaned them and warmed them in the cavity of her belly fur. Camio, once he was allowed back in the earth, sat by, looking on with a kind of wonderment. He said nothing: he just let O-ha get on with what she had to do. Later, when they were suckling, he came and looked at them more closely, nudging the smallest with his nose. O-ha snarled at him, baring her teeth savagely. He took the hint.

He backed off, saying sadly, 'Looks like a runt,' and indeed before the day was over that particular cub was dead. He took it out and put it well away from the earth. He carried out the last rites, scratching and marking the ground as instructed by O-ha, then left the rest to the fox-spirits.

The remaining two cubs looked strong enough, and weathered their first night without harm.

Camio spent most of his time outside the earth, looking for food, always announcing his arrival before entering. He knew that she would be very tense and unpredictable for a while after the birth and he took his treatment in a subdued manner.

There were times when O-ha realised he was a bit jealous of the attention the cubs were receiving. There was little she could do about this. She was still cautious when he was around, and Camio made no comment on her behaviour, simply letting things ride.

The cubs grew stronger by the day. After fourteen days they could see and hear; their eyes were bright blue sparks in their faces and they started at sharp sounds. They began crawling round inside the earth, very shakily. Occasionally O-ha got up and retrieved one before it fell out of the vehicle, but as time went on she fought a losing battle with them. They ignored her calls and only came when hungry.

During this time she talked to them, about their history, their religion, the water holes and soaks (though many of the old parish watering places had disappeared and Camio had to tell her where the new ones were), and the topography of the land. She called the cubs O-mitz and A-cam; the male had darker markings than O-mitz, who sported a thin white streak through her fur on the right side of her brow.

At first the youngsters just mewled and squeaked, but gradually they picked up words from both parents. During this time O-ha and Camio

452

became close again, talking more than they had ever done, and a mellow feeling grew between them.

'This is a good thing we've done, Camio,' O-ha said one evening, while the cubs were gambolling just outside the earth. The faces of the little ones had changed from being stubby, with short, round-tipped ears, and were becoming elongated, with pointed ears. Their tails had begun to bush.

'They don't stay young for very long, do they?' Camio sighed.

'We can't hold them back. I'd like to, of course, but it's not possible.'

Outside, the cubs grew boisterous.

'You run away,' shouted O-mitz, 'and I'll chase you and jump on you! Wait until I can hide behind that thing there . . .'

There was a squeal from her a moment later.

'Oh, that's not fair, A-cam. You were sneaking up behind.'

'Surely that's what it's all about, O-mitz? Sneaking up—pouncing!'

They fought mock fights, they argued incessantly, they roughed and tumbled each other for hours on end. Once, A-cam fell down a shaft that was really an upended pipe. It took hours for Camio and O-ha to discover how to push the pipe over and release their cub. This close encounter with death—for A-cam would have starved if he had not been rescued—brought the two adults even closer together. It called to mind the fact that though they hunted and killed prey every day, death was doing the same, stalking them.

'WHO WERE YOUR PARENTS?' O-mitz asked her mother one day. The little chocolate-coloured vixen cub had just begun to moult, and patches of orange fur were visible on her face.

'My parents?' said O-ha. 'Well, they were a pair who lived to the north of Trinity Wood—the place that is now a human parkland. In those days there was *hav* all round us, and the country was open and free.'

'I like the town,' said O-mitz. 'Camio tells me about the streets and houses.'

Camio was listening. 'This is where they have to live, at least to begin with,' he told O-ha. 'Not much point in telling them what was—they need to know what is.'

'Go on, O-ha,' O-mitz cried. 'Your parents?'

'My mother was killed by a tractor which ran over her while she lay asleep. It was an accident. My father went away somewhere after that. Nothing much more to tell.'

'My parents,' said Camio, 'were giants . . .'

'Don't tell them lies,' said O-ha, shortly.

He looked contrite. 'My parents were not giants,' he continued. 'They were not as tall as oak trees, and my mother didn't have hair as red as the sunset we saw last night. My father did not wrestle with bears and win, and he didn't jump wide canyons where rivers flowed far below . . .'

453

however,' he went on, 'they did have silver hairs on their rumps, just as I do, and you probably will.'

'Why hasn't O-ha got silver hairs?' A-cam asked.

'She has, only you can't see them so well on her, because my coat is darker. My father was a black fox and you could see the silver hairs in his coat shining . . .'

'Camio!' said O-ha. 'A black fox?'

'It's true,' he said, indignantly. 'My mother was a red fox and my father was a black fox. That's why my coat is so dark. The trouble with you provincial vixens is that you think the world begins and ends with your own parish. There are all kinds of foxes out there: bat-eared foxes with lugs the size of my bib; arctic foxes, white as the snow; desert foxes, fennec foxes—we're the best, I hasten to add.'

'Really?' O-ha said, secretly impressed.

'Yes, really,' he replied. 'There are still wolves in certain parts of the world, too. Where I come from they still have the timber wolf. Man hasn't wiped them out entirely.'

'You've met one of these wolves?' she said.

'No, not exactly, but they're talked about. And I've seen them, in the zoo,' he finished, triumphantly.

'What's a zoo?' asked A-cam, trying to bite O-mitz's tail.

'A place where they lock animals up and leave them to die,' Camio replied brutally.

That night, when the cubs were asleep, O-ha snuggled up close to Camio and whispered, 'It's all right now.'

'What's all right?'

'We are,' she said.

Somehow, without feeling any disloyalty towards A-ho, she had come to be glad it was Camio lying beside her, the father of her cubs. He was a good mate and a dependable parent. She told him so.

After that she lay there, thinking about her young ones, wanting to protect them, for ever, from all the terrible things in life, wanting to keep them as they were, innocent and happy, and never let them go out into a world of harsh reality.

The impossible dream of all mothers.

THE SKILLS OF THE CUBS improved as the summer wind, Frashoon, began to move Switter aside. They began bringing home small prey as well as beetles and woodlice, and learned to cache much of this extra food in places around the scrapyard.

O-ha and Camio grew more comfortable towards one another. It was difficult for O-ha to remember a time when Camio had not been there, with his dry witticisms, his soft drawl and his warm body. Most of all she valued the one thing she had believed he lacked—reliability. She now knew that Camio stood as firm as an oak tree when it came to his family.

He was fiercely loyal to her, and would have stood in the way of mighty machines if they threatened her or his cubs. She knew that if she were ever lost, he would spend a lifetime looking for her, and if she were ever sick, he would stay by her side until death took her off or she got well.

She realised how lucky she was to have had two mates in her life, both of whom would have died for her.

The cub A-cam was a little reckless at times, but he had none of the stubbornness of O-mitz. He was a playful, all-round fox, with no quirky corners to his character: when he was not playing or hunting beetles, he would lie and sun himself on a warm piece of scrap metal. Uncomplicated, he was his mother's favourite, though his father thought him a little too staid. He wanted to impress his father, and boasted that one day he was going on an adventure which would make him famous among foxes. Then Camio would have to take notice of him. O-ha heard this remark and was concerned about her cub for a while. Then she thought, It's just young talk, not serious. Nevertheless, she determined to have a word with Camio, to see if he could reassure A-cam that his father respected him without any silly adventures.

ONE DAY, A CAT wandered into the yard. It was a big bruiser, a black-and-white tom with a face like a flattened tin can. A-cam saw his chance for fame. The cat looked fat, old and slow, and he thought he could run rings round this creature with his newly acquired evasion tactics.

'I'm going to show Camio how much I've learned,' he told O-mitz. 'Watch me taunt this cat!'

O-mitz cried, 'Don't do it, A-cam. You'll be killed!'

'Killed?' said A-cam. 'Me?'

Until that moment he had been half joking about the cat, but now he was determined to go through with it. He walked towards the beast, which was sunning itself on a patch of earth. As he got closer, A-cam could see just how big the tom was, and he began to quake inside. However, he was aware of O-mitz's round frightened eyes on him.

A-cam stopped outside what he reckoned was the cat's pounce limit. 'Cat,' he said, 'you're a fat, lazy piece of mangy fur, not worth a second glance, but I challenge you to mortal combat.'

The cat opened one eye. It looked as if it had seen battles galore and an aeon of decadence. Cynicism ran deep in its veins.

'*Pissenlit!*' said the monster.

A-cam gave the cat a withering stare. 'And what's that supposed to mean?'

To his shock, for he was convinced that cats never learned any language but their own, he received a reply.

'It means that you are a fluffy bunch of seeds—and I can blow you away with one puff. Go away, before I fill my lungs with air.'

'You—you speak . . .'

'I speak with the tongues of dogs and of foxes. What? Did you think that cats and dogs who live under the same roof never talk to each other? Go away, ball of fluff, before your parents catch you. I should hate to have to move out of the sun to fight one of them.'

A-cam suddenly saw himself through the cat's eyes. A tender little animal with fluffy fur, still covered in cub fat.

'I'd—I'd better go, then. I don't suppose you would care just to turn round and walk off, would you? My sister is watching from that tangle of scrap over there.'

'So that's what it's all about?' The tom yawned, revealing some very frightening teeth and a cavernous mouth. 'No, I wouldn't.'

'Oh, well . . .' said A-cam, dismayed. He was about to turn away from the cat, when the beast suddenly yelled, 'Oh no, fox! I can't fight an animal as ferocious as you. Please leave me alone. I won't harm any of your family.' The creature's voice made A-cam's fur stand on end.

Then, in a much softer tone, the tom said, 'How was that, *pissenlit*? Good enough to send you back a hero? Turn round now.'

A-cam did as he was told, marching back to O-mitz.

'What did you say to it?' she whispered.

'I just told him to watch himself, if he was coming into our yard,' replied A-cam. It was a long time before his heartbeat returned to normal.

CAMIO LEFT THE EARTH one day after scrupulously observing the leaving-the-earth ritual, since now that the cubs were around O-ha had become stricter than ever about such things. He wanted to be out of the way when she lectured the young on 'the right way' to mark, drink water, eat various kinds of food, enter and leave the earth, and the rites for the dead. True, he paid lip service to these observances, but he was becoming a little bored with the repetition of chants, rhymes and songs.

'Can't see what the fuss is about . . .' he muttered as he walked along the fox highway through the *face*, which crossed seventeen back gardens, a factory yard, a bridge, three alleys and two sets of garage rooftops, and ended up at the entrance to Trinity Parklands.

He paused at the gates. Inside there were human children playing on the apparatus, yipping away in shrill voices. He slipped into the shrubbery which ran round the edge, using it as a shield, to travel to the wooded part: enjoying the soft feel and aroma of the peat-bark beneath his feet. It was his intention to try to confirm some information which had come his way: he wanted to find out if Gar the badger was still alive. O-ha had spoken of him often and he wanted to surprise her with the good news. Of course, if the old grouch was dead, then Camio would keep it to himself for a while.

O-lan and A-lon were both dead, he knew. They had been shot in the early hours of that morning when the Unremembered Fear was abroad.

Many other animals had met their deaths that night, some of them mistaken for carriers when they were immune from the disease. A-magyr was missing, believed dead, though he could have gone on one of his famous walkabouts. Camio doubted if the old fox had escaped.

Camio travelled through the woodland, avoiding the human paths, sniffing for marks and trails, until he came upon a fox earth. There was litter all round the entrance, and he stood amongst this and cried out, 'Anyone there?'

Shortly afterwards a dog fox poked its nose out.

'What do you want?' he said, brusquely. Camio guessed he had a mate inside the earth and was suspicious of another dog fox calling.

'No need to be unfriendly, I've already got a mate, if that's what you're worried about. I'm looking for a badger—big old gruff one by the name of Gar. Do you happen to know if he's still around these parts?'

The dog fox emerged from the earth's entrance, looking a little less aggressive. 'Don't know the names of any badgers—we are newcomers to the parish—but I think there's some of them living in the roots of an old blackthorn just south of here.'

Camio thanked him and followed his directions. When he reached the sett, he found the main entrance and called down.

'Is this the home of Gar?'

There was no answer.

He tried again. 'Who lives here? I'm looking for Gar. Is that the name of the occupant?'

There was a rustling from behind him and a gruff voice said, 'Ha, fox. *Hider*—come hither.'

Camio turned to see an old, cross-looking badger standing under an ash tree. 'Are you Gar? I think you are. I saw you once, when O-ha was living with you.'

The darkness lifted from the badger's brow.

'Oh-ha? The little fox. You know her? Eh? Speak, fox.'

'I am O-ha's mate, Camio.'

A sparkle came into the badger's eyes. 'She's alive?'

Camio nodded. 'We have cubs, two of them, down in the *face*.'

'Well, well,' gargled the old badger. 'Cubs too, eh? Ha! Is good. Come, come . . .' He waddled towards his sett. 'We talk together, fox.'

Camio followed him down to a chamber where there were some rushes on the floor. When they had both settled, Gar motioned for him to proceed with his story, and he told the badger all that had happened since O-ha and he had left the wood. The badger nodded approval in places, or clucked softly to himself when Camio touched on times where they were in danger. When he had finished the big black-and-white skull nodded thoughtfully.

'So, she is well—is all turned out for good. And this Breaker?' He shook his head. 'Hard to imagine this hound living with foxes. World is

457

strange place, fox. So, you get from here that night—me, too, but alone. My sett-others, all killed.'

'I'm sorry,' said Camio. 'That stupid fox . . .'

'Yes. I hear this and am very angry then, but now . . .' He shrugged. 'I am old badger. Things get little dim in my head.'

'You've got many seasons yet,' said Camio politely, 'but how did you escape that night?'

'Ha, that is good story. That night . . .' He paused for effect, settling down onto his haunches, which Camio had noticed were swollen with arthritis. 'That night, Gar out hunting—out in cold snow. I hear guns go "bang, bang, bang", and think to myself, Gar, something happen down there. Then I smell men coming from town. I smell the fear.

'I feel the terror in this heart and I freeze, still, like rock. I think, If Gar stays still, man pass by. But then I see lights on snow, and gun fires in wood. Then I know I am to die. These men not play sport. Too many men. Too many guns. Too much fear.

'I run to edge of wood and there . . . there I see bright star crossing the sky. It makes noise like this,' he growled softly in the back of his throat, 'and flash on, flash off. On, off, on, off . . .' His voice drifted, but was pulled back again. '"Gar" I say to myself, "this is sign. You follow this grumble star that makes brilliant on-off." So I go same direction, even though it lead me down, into far side of town. Then I find this hole in ground—in street—where iron cover gone. Houses all dark. No people yet. I go under, into dark, and follow tunnels. Stay there for long, long time. *Guman* not find Gar.'

Gar went on to explain that he lived in the sewers, which were not at that time in operation, until they began to complete the buildings. Then he thought it was time to get out, before the drains were put to use and he was drowned or 'stinked to death'. He poked his head out of the hole one morning and shambled back to his sett.

Gar finished his story looking dreamily into space, and Camio had to make a noise to let the badger know he was still there.

'So,' said Gar, 'you and O-ha are well, yes? We have lived through such changes . . . All the old ways are gone.'

Camio slipped away after that, with a quiet farewell, and the badger fell asleep before the fox was even out of the sett. Camio suspected that the old badger had not got very long to live. Still, he had had a long life, and would probably not be sorry to go.

When Camio got back to the scrapyard O-ha was looking weary. The cubs had no doubt had another boisterous day. Her tail looked in a very sorry state where they had pulled out pieces of fur in their playfulness.

'You indulge those cubs too much,' he said, looking down fondly on the sleeping bundles.

'Perhaps,' she replied. 'Where have you been all day?'

'Ah. Now, there's a thing. I heard that an old friend of yours was still living in Trinity. Went to visit him.'

'An old friend?'

'Gar, the badger,' he said.

Her eyes shone. 'Gar? Still alive? He escaped that dreadful time?'

'Yes, indeed,' said Camio. 'He's a nice old thing, isn't he? I thought you said he was bad-tempered.'

'Well, he can be. I expect you caught him on one of his good days.'

'Anyway, he was delighted to hear about you. If you weren't so desperately attached to me, I might have been jealous. From the way he spoke, anyone would have thought you were responsible for the sun rising and setting each day. He thinks you're very special, doesn't he?'

This seemed to please her. 'We did get on rather well together,' she said. 'I suppose there are those who like to be needed—and he was there when I needed someone to talk to, someone strong.'

'Oh, he's a strong old character, all right. A lot of authority there. Told me to look after you or I would answer to him. I found respect creeping into my voice when I spoke to him. Not many animals do that to me, I can tell you.'

She lay with her head on her paws for a while, obviously musing over the news. 'Funny old Gar,' she said. 'I must try to get to see him one of these days, once the cubs are off our hands . . .'

PART FIVE

Terror in the Streets

Frashoon, and the cubs were half grown. They played outside in the scrapyard, when the men were not present, gambolling and fighting in the dust. They tracked spiders and pounced on them. They jumped for butterflies. They stalked each other and practised their hunting skills. When they rested they did not go back into the breeding earth, but found a hole somewhere under the junk and slept away from the adults. They had begun to forage for themselves round the nearby houses, and there were narrow escapes, but this was all part of the learning process. They remained near to their parents' earth, but were no longer part of it.

Of course, O-ha and Camio still talked to their cubs, advised them, instructed them, and were anxious over their welfare.

O-mitz announced that she was dropping the O to her name.

'It's so old fashioned,' she told her distressed mother. 'Mitz sounds much better. I feel like a Mitz. All these silly distinctions between the sexes. Ask any of the foxes my age—they'll tell you they don't want all that labelling stuff.'

A-cam said he was quite happy with his name as it was. 'Don't see any point in changing it,' he said. 'That's just another one of O-mitz's silly affectations.'

'A-cam is just too lazy to make any effort at individuality,' Mitz retorted bluntly.

So, personalities were developing—perhaps not in the way that O-ha might have wished, but then most mothers are slightly bewildered by the fact that their young do not follow the paths imagined for them at birth. It was not that she wanted copies of herself so much as shining versions of her ideal fox. Camio seemed quite happy with them, but then (she told herself) he was a foreigner anyway and had some strange ideas about the role of foxes in the world. She wanted her cubs to be conventional.

One of O-ha's strongest warnings was to stay away from the manor house on the edge of town. She repeated this so often, and with such force, that the inevitable happened: the cubs were intrigued, and the two of them went there to find out what unspeakable horrors lay behind the wall that surrounded the gardens.

MITZ AND A-CAM approached the wall of the manor house. Between the brickwork and the road was a greensward of uncut grass. The two foxes were able to slip through the grass, remaining hidden from the cars that flashed along the road. All along the wall was a cloak of ivy which the two foxes used to scramble to the top. Once there, they travelled its length, peering down into the gardens, hoping to catch sight of the giant dog they had been threatened with as youngsters.

'I don't think there is such a dog,' said A-cam. 'I think O-ha made him up, just to scare us into doing as we were told.'

The little vixen shook her head. 'No, I heard Camio talk about him too, and anyway, O-ha doesn't tell lies—you know that.'

'Well, where is he then? Shall we just drop down inside and have a look round? There might be some juicy frogs in that pond over there.'

Mitz tested the air for dog scent and listened hard, but could detect nothing unusual. Frashoon was veering off in a funny direction though, due to the concave shape of the wall, and she was not sure which was upwind and which was downwind.

'No,' said Mitz. 'That's not a good idea at all. You stay up here.'

Just as she said this, A-cam stepped out onto the branch of a tree growing on the garden side of the wall, and walked along it to its trunk. He dropped down to a lower bough. Then he called to Mitz. 'See, I told you there was nothing to worry about . . .'

Just then a blur of brown caught Mitz's eye as something hurtled through the bushes. At the same time the scent of hound hit her nostrils.

'A-cam!' she screamed.

A-cam must already have caught the dog's smell, because he was in the act of jumping back up to the higher branch when the hound launched himself from the ground, his wide jaws slavering. There was a horrible *snacking* sound as the ridgeback's teeth cracked together. A-cam let out a yell. For a moment, Mitz was unsure what was happening.

The dog fox's forepaws caught on the upper bough and he hung there precariously as the hound crashed back into the bracken surrounding the bottom of the tree. There was blood pouring from A-cam's hindquarters, and Mitz saw with horror that his tail had gone, bitten off at the base.

'Hang on!' she cried, trying to keep the terror out of her voice. 'Oh— get up, get up, A-cam!'

A-cam's face was twisted with effort and the agony of his injury. His back legs scrabbled at air, trying to get a purchase on something to help him haul himself up. For a moment he dangled there, his front legs hooked over the branch, his body hanging.

Below, Sabre was back on his feet, the bloodied tail still in his mouth. He shook his prize as furiously as if it had been a dead rat, and spat it out. Then he retreated, to give himself a run up, in order to spring from the ground again.

Mitz ran out along the branch and gripped A-cam by the ruff, and he managed to get one of his hind legs over the bough. By the time the hound came thundering back, the two foxes were on top of the wall, though A-cam was very distressed, with blood gushing from his wound. He fell, rather than jumped, down to the greensward. There he lay panting, tongue lolling out, the grass behind him stained scarlet.

'A-cam,' said Mitz, 'what shall I do? Shall I go for O-ha and Camio?'

From the other side of the wall came the sound of taunts and gibes. Sabre knew they were there, and in trouble.

'I've got your brush, fox,' he called. 'Going to give it to the chickens to pick clean.'

'Please, try to get up,' begged Mitz.

A-cam dragged himself to his feet. But then he staggered a few paces to the edge of the greensward, and next walked dizzily into the road.

Mitz cried, 'Come off there, you'll be hit . . .'

There were several cars going along the road. One of them swerved to avoid him, narrowly missing running him over. The vehicle behind this one, however, screeched to a halt.

Mitz crouched in the grass, hoping that she had not been seen, as a door opened and a human emerged, barking to someone else inside the vehicle. It was a male and he marched over to where A-cam lay panting on the tarmac. Hands reached down and A-cam snarled, 'Don't—don't you touch me, you . . .'

But the cub was too weak to move, and the human went back to the car, put on thick gloves, and then quickly picked A-cam up, putting him in the boot of the vehicle. The man got back into the car and drove off along the road. Soon, it was gone.

'A-cam,' whispered Mitz.

She was shocked at how quickly it had all happened. One moment they were playing a searching game, the next A-cam was mortally wounded and had been abducted by a human. Now she had to go back to her mother and tell her that one of her cubs had gone, probably for ever.

O-HA'S GRIEF at the loss of her cub was almost more than she could bear. Over the next few evenings she lay outside the earth, waiting for the fox-spirit to come, to lead her to the body of her dog cub. Part of her hoped it would never appear, but since it seemed certain that he was dead, she desperately wanted to perform the last rites over his body. Once again, waves of hatred went out towards the hound at the manor house.

Camio, too, was devastated. Of the two cubs, A-cam had been his secret favourite, since he shared much with his father: he was idle, but lovable, and though there was a restlessness in his nature which meant that he would eventually have left his parents for a life on the road, Camio felt that part of him would always have been with the cub.

Mitz wailed constantly, believing that it was her fault that her brother had been taken. 'It was me that persuaded him to go to the manor house,' she whispered to Camio. 'He wouldn't have gone if I hadn't suggested it. Why am I so stupid?'

'You're not stupid, Mitz. You're still a cub. It's not your fault, but mine,' he said. 'I should have explained more. You see, that dog at the manor has already been responsible for a lot of grief in your mother's life. He nearly caught the pair of us, once, when we got our messages crossed and each of us went there to save the other . . .'

'You and O-ha?' said Mitz, wide-eyed.

'Oh, yes. We're quite capable of doing stupid things too, you know. Just because we're fully grown doesn't mean we know all there is to know, or follow our own good advice. Now, you have a life to lead. I want you to put this out of your mind as quickly as you can, because survival is tough enough, without bearing the weight of past mistakes on your shoulders. Look to the future, little one.'

'I'll try,' she said.

THE SUMMER MOVED ON and Mitz grew stronger. By the time Melloon was blowing across the land, the dispersal began in earnest in all the fox earths. It would soon be time for Mitz to seek a mate.

Camio had a serious chat with the little vixen, who was not entirely happy about going away from them.

'I don't want to go out there,' she said.

'But you've slept outside for months now,' replied Camio.

'That's different. Once I leave here I'll be grown up. I'll have to hunt for all my food, won't I?'

'That's true, but you're a good hunter and scavenger. You feed yourself already. Just make sure you cache your finds in a safe place, for the lean periods, and always get plenty of vegetables. You'll be all right, I have no worries about you. Tough as they come.'

'I don't want a mate yet,' she said, firmly.

'Well, that's up to you. Chase the dog foxes away, if you want to stay on your own. We're scared of you vixens, you know. All you have to do is bare your teeth and say no.'

'I will—for the moment, anyway.'

'You'll always be welcome here, you know that.'

'When must I go?' asked the little vixen.

'It would be proper to leave us quite soon now. I suggest you look round for a suitable earth within the next few days. If you really don't want to leave, of course you must stay, but you can't know what's best unless you have a look at the outside world and give it a try.'

So, the lead up to the dispersal had begun. Both O-ha and Camio felt sad about it. Cubs often left home never to be seen again.

'It'll be quiet round here, won't it?' said O-ha.

'It'll be very different, that's for sure,' replied Camio.

'I'll hate it, won't you?'

'Yes,' he said, simply.

AT THIS TIME Camio and O-ha began to talk about moving to another earth, away from the close proximity of men. Camio was concerned that the scrapyard was growing too large and that there would soon be an Alsatian or a Doberman to guard the place. Already there was a night watchman in attendance. Apart from that, it was usual to move from the breeding earth once the dispersal of the cubs had taken place.

'Well, you know the *face* better than I do,' said O-ha. 'Where shall we start looking?'

'I've heard that the railway is coming to the town. We could make an earth on the embankment, in the *gerflan*.'

'After that story you told me about the fox you met before you came here? Is it wise?'

Camio shook his head. 'That was different. It won't be anything like that. There'll be wild flowers, bushes, tall grass—all the things you like. We won't be bothered, because it'll be *gerflan*. The only thing is, we'll have to get used to the noise of the trains.'

O-ha looked dubious.

'After a while you hardly notice them. You can sit there, watching the carriages full of humans go by, knowing they can't touch you. And you like the railway tracks, you told me so. You can sit and look at the strips of steel if you want to, or you can laze around catching butterflies all day. Or even practise all those rituals you're so fond of.'

'One doesn't practise rituals,' she huffed, 'not in the way you mean. Rituals are there to be observed. What will we eat?'

'We can still scavenge around the town, and make our caches on the bank, where only we can get at them. There'll be rats and mice too, and of course, worms.'

'You make it all sound so idyllic.'

'Well, I'm going out now, to scout around where the work is in progress. What do you want to do?'

'I think I'll wait here, in case O-mitz comes back . . . or A-cam,' she said.

Camio left her then, and went out into the night streets. His heart was heavy at the mention of their missing cub, and he knew she was still grieving, but there was nothing he could do about it. He could search—he had searched—but the world is a big place. If A-cam were still alive, he might be many days' journey from the scrapyard.

Camio padded down the empty main precinct of the town, a cobbled street lined with shops on both sides. He passed another dog fox with barely a nod. Territories in the town were difficult to define and there were places round the takeaways and restaurants that were considered neutral ground, outside the patches that foxes defended as their 'own'. Chance encounters were reasonably common in the *face*, and foxes were inclined to relax their territorial attitudes.

Camio passed under a streetlamp, and slipped down an alley. There was a human asleep on some cardboard boxes, exuding those fumes which made foxes gag. These creatures on the borderland of human society often made a lot of noise and shouted at foxes if they came too close, but in general they were harmless and seemed incapable of giving chase, so Camio did not pause in his stride. He went up and over a fence at the end into a garden where he almost trod on a hedgehog which had rolled into a spiny ball. There was a saucer of bread and milk nearby which had been left out for the little creature; Camio took a few laps of the milk and then carried on down the side of the building and out into the next street. One or two cars were still humming along the tarmac, their blinding headlights sweeping the darkness away before them. Camio crossed quickly, keeping his head down. He knew too well that those bright beams could hypnotise an animal into rigidity, and he had no wish to be squashed into *gubbins* on the road.

There was a wind blowing up from the marshes beyond the town, and the tangy salt smell reminded Camio of the months he and O-ha had spent in the old wreck. They had never encountered the hound, Breaker, since that time, and he wondered whether the dog was now dead.

Suddenly, as the thought of 'dog' entered his mind, he stopped, and sniffed. There was something else caught up in Melloon besides the scent of salt—something sinister, which triggered alarms in his nervous system. Had this happened before? What was so familiar yet at the same time strange and disturbing? Camio shrugged. Perhaps he was being over-cautious? There was a smell of dog, certainly, but in the *face* there were many pet dogs around, leaving their marks on posts and in the gutter. It would have taken a hundred days of rain to wash away such odours.

Just then there was a cry from several streets away, followed by a chirruping sound. Two foxes were calling to one another. Was there anything sinister in that? Silence. He waited for a while, to see if anything further would be said. Then came a word, full of fox-fear, which made his fur stand on end.

'*Dog!*'

Why such a call? There were several strays in the town, but town dogs were seldom dangerous. They hadn't the wit, nor the will, to catch a fox. So, why the—

'*The dog is abroad!*'

A long, chilling sound rang out over the rooftops, through the streets. It was the call of a hound: a hound in full cry. The call rang out again, and then the shout of a fox.

'*Look out! Sabre is loose!*'

Sabre! The ridgeback was in the streets! It must have found a way out of the walled garden, and now it was hunting its favourite prey in the streets of the town.

Camio realised that he and his family were in great danger. Sabre was familiar with his and O-ha's scents; the smell of them would be imprinted in his brain, and he would only have to catch a whiff to be on their trail. All foxes were Sabre's prey, but those who had outwitted the beast would surely be top of the death list: he would be searching the highways for the foxes who had made him look a fool in front of his master.

465

Camio began to retrace his steps, and all the while the fearful cries rose around him, filling the night air. Dogs in their houses began to take up the call too, some of them yelling, *'Give it to them, Sabre!'* Lights went on and humans started barking at their dogs, and then at each other. Then suddenly there was a terrible scream and the whole town went quiet, listening. The sound of cracking bone followed, after which a voice full of triumph, in the rich timbre of the ridgeback, crooned out the words, *'A fox is dead!'*

Pandemonium broke out and Camio hurried on, concentrating on finding the shortest route back to the scrapyard. He followed his own instincts and cut a path over garages, sheds and gardens, careless of any other known dogs in the area. He was moving too swiftly to be caught.

When he arrived back at the yard he went straight to the earth, where he found to his relief that O-ha was waiting. 'What's happened?' she said. 'What's the matter? Is it the Unremembered Fear?'

'Nothing so pleasant,' he said, once he had got his breath. 'Sabre's out. He's loose in the streets.'

O-ha sank to the ground. 'Oh, my poor Mitz!' she whispered.

A tingling sensation went down Camio's spine. Of course, Mitz was out looking for an earth! Camio remembered the horrible death scream of a fox having its neck broken and tried to convince himself that the voice had belonged to an adult fox.

'I must go back,' he said, 'to look for her.'

'*No!*' said O-ha violently. 'I don't want to lose you too. We can have more cubs . . .'

'You don't mean that, I know,' he replied gently. 'I realise you're afraid for me, but you needn't be. I've faced worse dangers than Sabre—I outwitted two Alsatians to escape from the zoo.'

'Sabre *eats* Alsatians.'

'He won't get me, I can assure you of that. And I have to go, O-ha—she's my cub too.'

'I'm coming with you.'

Camio did not reply for a few moments, thinking that Sabre would only have to catch a whiff of her scent and she would be in terrible danger. However, he realised that she was as entitled to search for her cub as he was, and the big dog had not got her yet, despite two attempts.

'Fair enough. But we have to keep together, unless we come up against him, in which case we immediately split up, the way we did in the manor garden. That way confuses him. All right?'

'You don't have to tell me.'

'No, I don't. Just wanted to have things clear between us,' said Camio. 'Let's go then. We'll try the area near the centre of the *face*. Keep your nose to the wind and your ears tuned . . .'

With that, the pair of them left the earth. For once, O-ha forgot to observe the rituals.

They travelled to the middle of the town swiftly but cautiously. There was still an uproar in progress, but the barking humans were gradually winning their battle for silence. They came to a street which stank of Sabre residue. The body of a fox lay under the light from the lamps. It was twisted into an unnatural position and they could smell the deadness about it as they approached. It was a juvenile, but when they got closer they were relieved to smell that it was not Mitz. They looked about them nervously, wondering whether the hound from the Unplace was lurking in the shadows, waiting to pounce.

'It's just a youngster,' said O-ha, sadly, still sniffing the corpse.

'Let's get on,' replied Camio.

They began a systematic search of the town, weaving through streets and gardens, alleys and yards, but found no trace of their cub. Always, somewhere around them, they sensed the presence of that great hound.

At one point, O-ha stopped suddenly, stiff in her tracks.

'What's the matter?' whispered Camio, but even before the final word was out, he had caught the scent too.

'Quick, up on that roof!'

O-ha leaped up onto the roof of a car parked outside a garage, then onto the roof of the garage itself. Camio was close behind her. They found the shadow where the garage roof joined the wall of the house, and lay there, their hearts pounding as they pressed against each other.

Down at the far end of the street, in the light of a lamp, Sabre was standing. They could see him lifting his nose to the breeze, but they were upwind of him, his scent coming to them quite strongly.

The great hound stood staring down the street. Then he began to walk along it, sniffing at the fence posts and the bases of the garden walls. Camio held his breath. If Sabre reached the point where they had left the street, he would locate them for sure. Then he would follow, using the car as a launching platform.

Camio thought, If he gets this far, I'll have a go. I'll have the advantage. The dog won't be able to keep his footing on the roof. Perhaps I'll be able to get to his throat before he can get to mine. The American fox was calm by this time. He knew that he would have to stand and fight. Once that decision had been made, the terror went out of him, to be replaced by that heightened feeling of controlled fear that would quicken his actions and clear his brain.

The ridgeback came closer. Under the light of the streetlamps Camio could see the ridged muscles on the great hound's back. Closer. Closer. Until the foxes were sure he must have caught their scent.

The dog stopped. It looked up, turned its head. And then, suddenly, something streaked across the end of the street, running for its life. Camio caught the strong scent of cat. Sabre was off in pursuit, a thin growl in the back of his monstrous throat.

Once he was round the corner, the foxes leaped down from their hiding place and took the opposite direction. They carried on the search but they had had a bad fright and their attention was not completely on the task they had set themselves.

Eventually, they felt that they had covered all the ground they could, so they made their way back to their earth, hoping that Mitz would be there waiting for them.

She was not.

THAT NIGHT, O-HA had the dream, the recurring nightmare. She dreamed she was in a bright place and struggling to walk. Suddenly, black bars fell across the ground. They were like the iron rods of a cage, once described to her by Camio. Then she was being chased, and she sank to her shoulders in snow, which hampered her escape. Finally, the shadow of her pursuer fell across her path and she looked up to see . . .

IN THE MORNING Sabre found a resting place in one of the newly built houses whose occupants had not yet arrived. He was feeling disappointed. Having got that juvenile fox, he had been hoping it was one of the vixen's young, but her scent was nowhere on the creature. That was a shame. One, Sabre would have considered the killing as part repayment for his humiliation, and two, she might have come looking for the youngster.

Having escaped through the hole he had been digging for such a long time, Sabre was determined to stay out until he caught the vixen. She would not escape him now. Tomorrow he would take up the search again, and let the vixen beware.

MITZ WAS HAVING a great deal of trouble in her search for an earth. Because she did not know the *face* as well as Camio, she found she was continually transgressing territorial rights: she had been snarled, spat and shouted at, and was quickly learning that she should take serious note of 'marked' areas. The trouble was, the streets were full of stale scents, especially those of dogs, and the under and over layers of odours became confusing. Even though much of the town was still under construction, there were foxes in almost every part of it, and though cats did not bother her a great deal, they too seemed to resent her presence. Being still a juvenile, she was wary of some of the big tomcats, with bellies that brushed the ground and faces like battered tin cans. They seldom ran from her, once they saw she was not an adult, and their eyes would glint, their faces would contort into devilish features and their fur would rise, making them look twice their actual size.

'*Peau-Rouge!*' they would hiss. '*Sauvage!*'

Although she did not understand these words, she guessed they were not complimentary.

In the middle of the night there was a commotion in the town, but Mitz was too intent on finding a new home to take much notice of it. She thought she caught her father's scent on the breeze once or twice, and wondered if he was out scavenging for food. It would have been nice to come across him, but somehow their paths never met.

She found a half-eaten package of fish and chips in the gutter and swallowed over three-quarters of it before a human came along the street and she had to leave. Once she was almost struck by a car that came sliding round a corner and caught her in the middle of the road.

On the edge of town there were partially built houses and she was tempted to make an earth in one of these, but some instinct told her that such places would be alive with humans during the day, and she resisted the temptation. It was there that a mouse panicked and ran out, under her nose, from beneath a pile of bricks. It was only a length away from her when an owl swooped down silently from out of the night and snatched the creature from the ground in its talons. It happened so fast she hardly had time to blink, and the bird left a hoot in its wake, as if to say, 'You're not quick enough, vixen! This is the big wide world and we're all out here competing with one another.'

Discouraged, she finally came to a street where the houses had been occupied but the gardens were still unestablished. It was as she entered this long dark road that a faint scent of dog came to her. She stopped and stiffened. She had smelled that scent before! Where? There was an underlying whiff of chase-and-kill attached to the main odour of the hound and though she had never been the quarry in a hunt, her racial memory sent needle-sharp warnings to her brain. There was a dog in the area which was out looking for creatures to kill.

A large shadow crossed the bottom of the street and drifted into the blackness at the base of a wall. Luckily Mitz was downwind and her scent was blowing away from her, but she caught the full force of the other creature's smell and recognised it. She knew the owner of that huge shadowy form—it was Sabre, the ridgeback.

All caution left her and the fear that rippled through her small body took control. At that moment, a door opened into the street and she dashed forward into the blaze of light which seemed her only escape from the terrible beast that stalked the streets. There was a screech from the human as she ran between a pair of legs, but this was a minor consideration when the alternative was being ripped from throat to tail.

Blinded by the light, she ran round in circles for a while before finding a solid object under which to hide. There she crouched, her heart beating fast, and waited. The smells were overwhelming and if she had not been frozen into immobility Mitz might have gone berserk.

But nothing happened, apart from some muted excited barking from the owners of the property she had invaded. They quietly shut the door of the room she was in and went away. There followed some whirring sounds and more growling noises from the humans. Then there was a long wait during which Mitz got her breath back and began to consider.

At first she thought, As soon as that door opens, I'm going through. But then she remembered that Sabre might still be in the street and it did not seem like a good idea any more. Nothing to do then, but wait.

After some while she heard a car stop outside the house. Then the front door to the house was opened and there were barks and growls coming from the hallway. Finally, the door to the room was gently opened. A tall human male with black fur on his face entered the room, closing the door behind him. For a moment the man stood still, allowing his scent to fill the room. When he moved again, Mitz noticed that he had something in his hand: a short pole with a loop at the end. She did not like the look of that pole, and snarled at him.

All the while he was in the room he was growling softly at her and, surprisingly, they were not menacing sounds. She sensed he was trying to communicate with her. This was deeply suspicious. Men were out to get you, and that was that. Well, if this one so much as placed a toe within biting distance he was going to find it missing shortly afterwards.

Ever so cautiously, the man came down to eye level with her and extended the pole with the loop, so that it was before her nose. She snapped at it, biting the loop of wire. It was hastily retrieved.

Next, the man barked and someone opened the door. Mitz's attention was distracted for a moment, and in that second the loop was round her neck. She tried to back off, quickly, but the noose tightened.

O-ha had told Mitz about snares that were laid on fox highways and byways, and strangled animals to death. Sometimes the choking was so agonisingly slow that it was better to commit *ranz-san*, and cheat the snare of its ugly job. Mitz now desperately thrashed around on the end of the pole, expecting the noose to begin its work of choking her.

It did not. There was some sort of catch which prevented the loop from closing any further than the approximate girth of her throat. Then strong hands were on her, lifting her up. She tried to snap at them but they were gloved and out of reach. The noose was removed by the trembling hands of the householder and a cage brought forward. Mitz was thrust gently inside and the exit was locked. She knew then what was going to happen to her. Her father had told her enough tales about cages . . . She was going to the zoo.

As she was carried out of the house by the man with fur on his face, she felt thoroughly miserable. She had escaped from the killer, Sabre, but now she was going to spend the rest of her life locked up in a small room, to be peered at by little humans with sticky faces. It would have been better to throw herself into the jaws of the ridgeback. Such an end was less distressing and certainly much quicker.

In the back of the vehicle she was bumped and jostled along, the movement making her spread her legs and flatten herself against the bottom of the cage. The man seemed to be aware of her distress and

471

continually rumbled sounds at her in a deep, rich voice. The entire journey was stressful, but although she whined a couple of times she did not disgrace herself by screaming for freedom. The thing to do, she had been told by Camio, was to watch and wait. 'The quieter you stay,' he had told his cubs, 'the more they trust you. Pretty soon, they hardly notice you're there, and that's when they make mistakes.'

Eventually, the vehicle drew to a halt and the back was opened. Sweet smells flowed into Mitz's nostrils, of apples, pears and plums, and she could hear only the wind soughing through the branches of the trees. They were in the country somewhere. The cage was lifted out and Mitz was carried along a path to a house with a roof of dried reeds. The man barked at someone as they approached the door and it was opened to reveal a female human and—her heart skipped a beat—a giant dog! Despite her resolve to remain calm, she drew back in the cage and snarled at the hound.

It gave her a mournful look. 'What are you getting so upset about?' it asked, not unkindly.

No dog had ever spoken to her in this way before, almost as an equal, and she was rather taken aback. All the stories her mother had told her about the slaves of men emphasised that they were foul creatures who would attack foxes without provocation.

Her cage was placed down on some paper and the man left the room. The dog continued to regard her with a sad expression.

'I'm Betsy,' said the hound. 'I take it you have a name?'

'Why are you talking to me?' asked Mitz. 'I don't understand what's happening here. Is this a zoo?'

'Zoo? Whatever gave you that idea? This is a cottage. Haven't you ever seen a cottage before?'

'I'm only young. I haven't even left my parents' earth yet—not properly. What kind of dog are you? You're not a ridgeback, are you?'

'Well, there you've got me. I've never heard of a ridgeback. I'm a St Bernard,' Betsy said. 'They have the reputation of saving humans in distress. Never done it myself, of course. No one gets lost round here.'

'Do you normally chat to foxes like this? The only dogs I know spend all their time chasing us.'

'Ah, well, that's because this is an unusual household. Lots of foxes get brought here. Him, my master, he brings them.'

Mitz was almost afraid to ask what for. It was her understanding that when men trapped wild animals like herself, it was either to kill them because they were considered pests, or because they wanted them for food. Then she recalled an even more chilling reason. Sometimes, especially with furry animals like foxes, they skinned them and turned their coats into human clothes. Did they kill you first? She hoped so.

'What does your master bring us here for?' she asked the St Bernard, bluntly. 'Skinning?'

'Not usually,' said Betsy. 'In fact I can't think of one single fox that he's skinned.'

'Then what am I here for?'

'To look at.'

'To look at? Then this is a zoo.'

'No, it isn't,' said Betsy, patiently. 'Look, for some reason—lord knows why—this man of mine likes to catch foxes and look at them. I think it must be the result of some kind of brain damage when he was a puppy, because I don't know any other humans that do this and his own friends think he's crackers. Anyway, little fox, you can rest assured that no harm will come to you while you're here. All he wants to do is look at you: almost every day we go out somewhere and look at foxes and we follow them wherever they lead us. And she's always stroking you lot, as if you were dogs. Both mad, but I wouldn't change them, you know. They're nice people in a peculiar way.'

'And you? You won't hurt me?'

Betsy looked offended.

'Of course not. What do you take me for? I've never hurt anyone in my life. Why, only the other day we had an intruder in here, and I was the first one under the bed.'

The man re-entered the room, while the woman stood behind him in the doorway. There was a perfumed odour wafting from her, and Mitz wondered whether she had rubbed herself all over with wild-flower blossoms to get such a smell.

'Ah, look,' said Betsy, 'he's brought you a dish of water. Trying to make friends with you. Take my advice and play hard to get at first. It pleases them more when they have to work to get you to trust them. I know that sounds silly, but it's true.'

The man barked at Betsy and she got up and lumbered to the other side of the room. Then the front of the cage was lifted gingerly and the water dish pushed inside.

Mitz eyed it for a moment, and then said the ritual chant: *'Water, preserver of life, body of A-O the first fox of Firstdark, cleanse my spirit as well as my limbs, my torso, my head. Water, clarify my soul, my sensations, my senses. All.'*

The man got very excited at this and barked at the woman, who nodded and showed her teeth.

'That's it,' said Betsy, before the man could shut her up. 'Play hard to get. Do a bit more of that rigmarole. It gets them going, it really does.'

But the ritual was over, and Mitz was thirsty. She drank gratefully.

LATER, MITZ WAS TAKEN out of the back of the house and put into a much larger cage, similar, she imagined, to those Camio had described as being part of the zoo. There she was left for the rest of the night, with a plate of meat mixed with some sort of vegetable.

There was hay on the bottom of the cage and after eating the food she lay on this, feeling quite miserable. The dog had told her that she would not be harmed, but how much could she trust the St Bernard? Betsy was, after all, one of the minions of the oldest enemies of foxes.

Mitz settled down with her head on her front paws. She could hear a brook gurgling somewhere at the bottom of the man's garden and when she listened very hard she could hear sounds of activity coming from that direction. There was a creature at work down there, and she wondered if it might be able to speak *Canidae*. She began to bemoan her fate, loudly, to anyone who might be listening.

THE SOUNDS THAT MITZ could hear were in fact coming from an otter's holt in the bank of the brook. There, a bitch and a dog otter were feeding their cubs on a rock, known as an *altar*, worn smooth by generations of use. The dog otter, whose name was Stigand, was familiar with the pair who lived in the house: over the course of a year the otters and humans had reached an understanding with each other. Stigand and his partner, Sona, would often accept fish from the humans for, unlike foxes, their kind had no reason to hate the two-legged beasts that took little notice of territorial markings. Otters are members of the *Mustelidae* family, which includes badgers, and Stigand often spoke to his black-and-white cousins, some of whom had a sett out in the field close to the brook. There was a pair of foxes living in the same sett and the badgers would often slip *Canidae* into their conversation to impress visitors: consequently, Stigand had picked up a certain amount of the foxes' tongue, which he augmented in discussions with the dog, Betsy.

When he heard the fox cub calling, he said to Sona, 'Sounds like he's grabbed another fox. We shan't get any rest if she keeps that up.'

'Poor creature's probably frightened. How would you like to be locked up in a cage?'

'Well, of course I wouldn't,' replied Stigand, 'but Betsy must have told her that there's nothing to worry about.'

'Perhaps Betsy wasn't around when the cub arrived? Sometimes they lock her away, thinking she's going to frighten any fox they bring in.'

'True. True.' Stigand began to play with one of his own cubs, knocking her off the *altar* into the water. The cub squeaked with delight. The fox in the cage became louder in her complaints. Stigand sighed. 'I'll go and have a word with her.'

He slipped from the *altar* into the cool water of the stream and swam to the bank. Once on dry land, he waddled the length of the garden to where the cage stood, and peered at the little fox that was whining in the corner. Then he gathered together his command of *Canidae*. He prided himself on being fairly adept at languages, and refused to punctuate his speech with words of his own tongue. What came out was rather stilted, rather precise, but perfectly correct.

'Hello, smallish fox,' he said. 'You make quite a clamorous noise for one of such as your dimensions.'

Mitz had never seen an otter before, but her education had been good and her mother had provided her with descriptions of every animal she might ever encounter within her own land. She stopped yelling and regarded the chocolate-brown creature for a moment, thinking how smooth and sleek it looked in the moonlight.

'Better,' said the otter. 'Better that you should fall to quietness on this wonderfully still night, with the stars like stipple on a silvery trout.'

'Who are you?' she asked.

'My name is Stigand. *Stig-and.*' He pronounced it very precisely, in order that there should be no mistakes. 'I have my holt not far from this region and your complaints have been borne by the wind to my sensitive ears. Might I comprehend your own title?'

Mitz struggled with the sense of this speech which seemed to become more convoluted with each sentence. 'My title? Oh, my name. Mitz.'

'And you are almost young, I think?'

'Almost, yes. I'm just about to leave the earth. At least,' she sighed, 'I was before this human abducted me.'

'Ah. Now, I have undertaken my journey to inform you that this human is not dangerous. I think the dog might have said something?'

'Yes, she did, but you can't trust dogs . . .'

'Not in the typical course of history, that is true,' replied Stigand, 'but here the dog is like the pair with which it cohabits—soft as summer mud to its very soul. The dog can be trusted. The humans can be trusted. Is it certain that we shall now entertain silence?'

'I suppose so,' said Mitz.

'Good,' said the otter, and turned to go but then, seemingly as an afterthought, it asked, 'My fox talk. You find it well founded in excellence?'

'You speak it very well,' replied Mitz, politely.

The otter nodded. 'Otters have this gift. Goodbye, smallish fox.'

'Goodbye, Stigand.'

So Mitz spent the rest of the night in quiet contemplation of the world beyond the cage. She heard the hooting of an owl, and the rustlings of the small creatures in the grasslands. With the early morning came a mist that wound itself round the fruit trees in the garden and clung to the bushes. The day drifted in and spiders' webs trembled at its coming, the dew sparkling as the sun shone through the drops. Mitz fell asleep just as the household began to stir, and she dreamed of her home, of her mother and father, and the dream was full of anxiety.

She was woken by the man who came to give her water and food. Then he sat with her for a long time, having gradually edged himself inside the cage. He made crooning noises the whole time and slowly reached out and touched her once or twice. She watched his hand warily, but did not snap or bite. Eventually he took her up in his arms and stroked her, though she remained stiff and unyielding. It was true that his touch was sure and firm, and if she had to be handled she preferred such a grip. The man knew what he was doing.

Betsy came out into the garden a little later and when the man saw that the two animals were not going to attack each other, he allowed the dog to go up to the cage.

'How did you spend your night?' said Betsy.

'How do you think? Would you like to be locked up in a strange place?'

'No, I wouldn't, but you couldn't be in better hands. He'll probably let you go today or tomorrow.'

Mitz sat up immediately. 'Are you sure? I mean, how do you know?'

'Oh, he never keeps you foxes for very long.'

Mitz was relieved. 'I think I believe you,' she said. 'There was an otter here last night . . .'

'Oh, Sona? Or was it Stigand?'

'Stigand. Rather pompous, but friendly. He said I should trust you. Since he had nothing to lose by telling me that, except a peaceful night, I decided he was right. My parents will never believe this—me, making friends with a dog. They're a little prejudiced, you know. I suppose most of the older generation are . . .'

'Well, you can't blame them. We've been at each other's throats for centuries—ever since men started using us for hunting foxes. Fortunately all that is changing. Some humans find the idea of hunting abominable and try to disrupt it when they see it happening. There will always be some who will never accept you—but that's the way of the world.'

At that point, Betsy was pulled away, since they had been talking to each other for several minutes and the man never seemed sure whether or not their conversations were friendly.

There were continued efforts on the part of the humans to gain Mitz's friendship, and she finally found out the reason. As she was being fondled and stroked, a collar was slipped over her head and fastened. She was angry. What were they trying to do to her? Dogs wore collars, and very occasionally cats, but these were domestic beasts, and the collar was to foxes the mark of a slave. She tried to get it off with her hind legs, but it was quite secure. Unlike those leather collars she had seen on dogs, the one she was wearing was quite thick in places, and had a little strip of steel on the side. Betsy came over to look at her.

'Very smart,' said the dog. 'Such a nice shape, too.'

'What are they trying to do to me?' growled Mitz. 'If they try to put a leash on this thing . . .'

'They won't,' said Betsy. 'It's not that kind of collar. He has a device which somehow connects with the collar you're wearing. When he sets you loose, he wants to be able to track you—find out where you go.'

'Spies!' Mitz snapped. 'You mean they want me to lead them to my family, so they can annihilate us all in one go. Well, they won't get that out of me. I shall walk in the opposite direction.'

Betsy shook her head. 'No, no. You don't understand. All he wants to do is look at you. He watches, scratches marks on a piece of paper, or growls into another of his devices—nothing else. He just wants to find out all about foxes. My guess is, once he knows what you're all about, he'll inform his pack leaders and there will be a greater understanding between humans and foxes. That can't be bad, can it?'

Once again, Mitz suspected Betsy of being an agent of the man and his tricks. But then, why had the otter bothered to soothe her qualms? The man fed the otters, of course, but she doubted if they needed such handouts. They were perfectly capable of catching their own fish. In fact O-ha had told her that they were better at it than men themselves.

So, what was she to think? The collar was uncomfortable, but not unbearable. It was merely an irritant. If she could just be sure that this was not a trick to discover where the fox hide-outs were situated. Men had wiped out the wolves because they had known where to find them. But men knew foxes well enough to realise that they worked in family cells and colonies.

'How will he get his collar back, if he lets me go?' she asked Betsy.

'Don't suppose he'll want it back. If he does, he'll just find you and take it, without any fuss. You worry too much. What you should do now is just accept it, forget about it, and once you're free and you see him sneaking around out of the corner of your eye, or catch a whiff of his scent, then just ignore it.'

'There's not much privacy in this world, is there?' grumbled Mitz.

'Lord, no,' said Betsy, 'not where humans are concerned. They say cats are curious, but to my mind they don't come anywhere near humans in that respect. Some humans want to know anything and everything. They're the best kind though. Those that don't seem to fill their time destroying things. My advice to you is, don't worry. You can spend your life worrying, and it's not worth it.'

With that the big hound lumbered off towards the house. Mitz was left to an autumnal afternoon, full of wasps feeding on ripe fruit and the sound of crows out in the *havnot* beyond the stream. Captivity was getting on her nerves and she wanted to be back with her own kind.

MITZ FUSSED OVER the collar for a long time, trying to force it over her head with her hindlegs. But it was fastened very firmly, and in the end she decided to accept it for the time being. She realised that if she took it off now, the man would only replace it anyway.

In the early part of the evening the man came out of the cottage carrying a box with a metal rod sticking out of the top. From the way he played with it and kept staring in her direction, she guessed this was the device which Betsy had told her about, for tracking her once she had been set free. Then she was given another meal at which Betsy was allowed to be present. The dog chatted to her while she ate.

'He's going to let you go, now.'

Mitz said, 'But I don't know where I am. I feel I'm a long way from home and I'm not sure if I can find my way back again.'

Betsy shook her mournful head. 'Oh, he won't do that to you. He'll take you to the spot where he found you and let you go there.'

'Not back to the human's house?'

'No, he'll let you go somewhere outside, near to the house. I've seen it all before.'

Once it was dark, Mitz was encouraged to go into the small carrying cage again. She resisted this, not because she did not trust the man, but because she hated being confined in a small space; however, she eventually entered it, and tried to keep calm as she was carried to the vehicle. Betsy was there too, clambering onto the seat next to the man and sitting up like a human to stare out of the front window.

'Doesn't this frighten you?' said Mitz, as the vehicle roared and the funny sensation began again in her stomach.

Betsy said, 'No, I like it. I suppose when you've been driven around since a puppy, you get to enjoy it. I find it quite exhilarating.'

'Oh, it's exhilarating all right,' said Mitz. 'It's just that I think my stomach has difficulty in keeping up with the rest of my body. It keeps dropping behind a little.'

'Just try to relax and enjoy the ride. You won't get many of these in your life, I can tell you.'

'That's the best news I've heard today,' replied Mitz, firmly.

Lights flowed by outside the vehicle and Mitz crouched in the bottom of the cage until the ordeal was over and the car stopped. She was taken out of the back and saw that she was in the street where she had been shadowed by the ridgeback. A shudder went through her as she remembered that he might still be around.

She called to Betsy, 'There's a huge dog loose—a hound called Sabre. He'll kill me if he catches me.'

'Don't worry,' shouted Betsy. 'We'll be following you on foot. I won't let him touch you.'

'You'd protect me? Against one of your own kind?'

'Listen, don't put me in the same category as that creature. I know that manor dog. He's despised by everyone who knows him. Thinks he's king of the neighbourhood, but I could give him a walloping.'

Mitz doubted that, but she was relieved that she would have some company. Then the man barked at Betsy and the bitch told Mitz that she had been ordered to keep quiet.

'I suggest we do as he says,' she added.

Mitz was then released, and immediately began walking along the street. She glanced back once, to see the man and his dog following at a distance. At each corner she paused and studied the dark shadows thrown by the streetlamps. Out of any one of these the giant beast might hurtle and fall upon her with his terrible jaws.

She took the shortest route back to the scrapyard, her heart pattering all the time. She slipped through the hole in the fence, looking back one last time, to see that the man and his dog had stopped some distance behind. She gave a farewell cry to Betsy, and then traversed the tunnels through the jagged metal to the earth.

After the rituals, she entered, to find O-ha and Camio.

They had obviously smelled her scent before she confronted them. O-ha leaped forward and licked her daughter's face with such enthusiasm that Mitz felt she wouldn't need a wash for another season.

'You missed me then?' she said.

'Missed you?' cried Camio. 'Of course we missed you. What in the world did you think? You're our daughter.'

'Where have you been?' O-ha asked her. 'Tell us all about it.'

She told them her story, and they listened, fascinated.

'They let you go?' said Camio. 'That's amazing. I've never heard of that before in my life.'

'Yes,' she said, simply.

O-ha said, 'And you have to wear that slave ring round your neck? Shall we try to gnaw it off for you?'

'Earlier today I would have jumped at the chance of getting rid of it,' said Mitz, 'but I think I owe it to Betsy to keep it on for a while. I'm certain no harm will come to us because of it. She's quite a creature, Betsy. She told me she would defend me against Sabre.'

'Well, that's a little far-fetched,' said Camio. 'I wonder if it's true?'

'I'm sure it is.'

Her parents looked at each other dubiously, but Mitz knew, and that was all that mattered.

'Is Sabre still at large?' she asked her parents.

Camio nodded. 'We think so. It's best to remain here for a while. There are a few caches of food in the yard, so we needn't worry about eating. Water might be a problem, but I can smell rain coming.'

So the foxes settled down for another night of waiting. During the small hours there came the sound of raindrops hitting the metal above their heads, which grew to a thunderous drumming as the skies opened. Camio went out in the downpour and returned with some food, which the three of them ate in silence.

Towards dawn the rain stopped, and the ground smelled musty and dank. Camio and O-ha talked again of abandoning their earth. They discussed various places where they might search for a new one, and made some suggestions to Mitz as to where she might look. Camio was still in favour of the new railway embankment.

'We'll be among the first there,' he said. 'We can mark any posts in the area, to warn off others.' It was the same sort of discussion that would be going on in many fox homes at that time, where the parents were preparing to leave the breeding earth.

'So,' said Camio to Mitz, 'you'll be setting up your own home at last. I remember when you were a little fluffy thing with a short pointy tail.'

'Oh, Camio,' she said, 'not "I remember when" again.'

Camio took no notice of this.

'. . . you used to play with an old bone, outside in the scrapyard, you and A-cam. I used to watch you both and wonder, was I ever like that.'

'Of course you were,' said O-ha. 'We all were.'

Camio continued. 'I would watch you chasing beetles, or even bits of paper floating by in the wind. Clever little cubs, you were. I was so proud of you. Still am, of course.'

'Were you?' said Mitz. 'You didn't seem to be. You were forever telling us off.'

'Oh, I know I was a bit hard on you, when it came to discipline, but your mother let you get away with murder. I remember when her teats were sore and bleeding because you cubs wouldn't leave her alone—you were always hungry. Still, those days are gone—the stalking and pouncing is for real now. You have to feed yourself.'

'You sound really old,' O-ha told him.

'I'm not old, I'm just a family fox reminiscing. What's the point of having all these memories if you can't talk about them once in a while?'

'Those aren't all memories, Camio,' said Mitz. 'They're pictures you make in your head. I know there's some truth there, but you embellish everything. When you told us about your fight with A-magyr, you said it was over O-ha—that it was a battle to the death, the prize being our mother. When O-ha told us about it, it sounded very different.'

Camio shifted his position. 'Quite right, too. What's the point of having a memory if you can't make a decent story out of it? Anyone can remember things. It takes a special talent to make that memory interesting to others. Why, I recall the time your mother and I . . .'

IN THIS WAY, THEY PASSED the night, waiting, and hoping that the dark hours would not be interrupted by some terrible event. Each of them knew the danger they were in with the ridgeback still abroad.

When the sun was up, Camio decided to reconnoitre the area for signs of Sabre. Mitz and O-ha were asleep, so he left the earth quietly and worked his way through the elaborate system of tunnels under the mountain of scrap. Here and there were open pockets, like caverns, but for the most part the channels were narrow enough only to allow passage to creatures the size of cats or foxes. On reaching the edge, Camio spent a long time just listening and sniffing the air, making absolutely certain that no danger lay near the scrapyard. There were few humans about, since it was early morning and not many had risen from their beds.

He went cautiously out into the *face* and found the streets remarkably clear of other animals. That could mean that Sabre had been caught by his owners, but quietly so that no one knew he had gone. Or it could mean that he was still out there somewhere and all the other creatures were still in hiding. There were one or two cats around but it was no use asking them—even if they spoke fox they would not necessarily tell him the truth. Camio did try one dog, a nervous terrier, smaller than himself, and received the answer, 'O horror! O horror!' and then the dog ran away, leaving him more puzzled than he had been before. He guessed that the ridgeback was just as terrible to smaller dogs as he was to foxes, and that the question had stirred fear in the terrier's heart.

Someone had left a black rubbish bag outside and Camio tore this open to find some scraps inside. If he could feed himself out here there would be more for the other two back at the yard. Then, when the sun was beginning to climb higher in the sky and more people were in the streets, Camio felt it was time to find another way of searching the area. He was crouching in a garden when he heard a sound with which he was reasonably familiar. It was the deliberate ringing of a bell, accompanied by a gruff human barking. A vehicle was moving slowly along the road: an open truck with junk in the back.

Camio waited until the truck was alongside the garden in which he was hiding and then ran out and jumped into the back. There he found some old coats, which he crept underneath. There were many smells wafting from the junk, which he knew would mask his own scent, so that he could travel the streets in safety. However, it meant that he himself could not use his nose and would have to rely on his poor eyesight to scan the streets for the ridgeback.

From time to time the vehicle stopped and something was tossed into the back. But then the swarthy human who was in charge of the truck dropped the tailgate and began moving the junk around. Camio quickly jumped down into the street; some barking ensued, but Camio knew he would not be attacked by the man. He trotted off down an alley.

Disheartened, Camio began to make his way back to the earth. He was naturally still very cautious and as he got closer to home he recognised a figure at the end of a street. It was Mitz. He walked up to her.

'What are you doing out?' he cried.

'I was worried about you. When I woke up O-ha had gone too. I got lonely.'

'Your mother's probably still in the scrapyard, looking for a cache of food. Come on, let's get back. That dog . . .' Suddenly, as if his words had conjured his enemy into being, he caught the whiff of his scent. He saw Mitz stiffen and realised she had noticed it too.

'He's around here somewhere,' she whispered.

The two foxes melted off the street, into the shadows. They were about two roads from the scrapyard. Camio led the way behind an old fence, past some vegetable allotments, and they worked their way through the grasses to a hole in the fence. Camio peered out through the hole, sniffing the air. It still had a faint scent of the ridgeback.

'We'd better make a dash for it,' he told Mitz. 'You go first. Head for that narrow street over there and follow it through to the scrapyard. You have two corners to pass. Don't look down the side streets, just run for all you're worth. I'll be right behind you.'

Mitz did as she was told, streaking over the main road, with Camio behind her. They reached the first corner without incident. It was when they passed the second that they knew Sabre was behind them.

A car came round the corner and passed the two foxes.

Hit the dog! thought Camio. Please hit the dog!

But his prayers went unanswered, because a moment later a yell came from just behind him. 'I know you foxes. I know both of you.' His strong body odour was in the air. 'You're dead! I'm going to gut you, one at a time—rip open your bellies and let the insides out.'

'Keep running!' shouted Camio.

The dog was trying to frighten them, for a scared animal will often freeze in its tracks. Camio could almost feel the hot breath of the beast on his hindquarters. His head was jangling with the terror of being torn limb from limb.

'You know you're dead, fox. You can feel my teeth at your throat. Blood spurting over the ground . . .'

An elderly human stood like a statue, shopping bag in hand, gawping. Two human children on wheeled boards, unaware of the drama, had their eyes on their task. Mitz almost bowled one over as she ran between them. There were squeals in the foxes' wake.

None of this had slowed the ridgeback. 'This is it, fox! Time to die!'

The dog was right. A few more steps and he would have one of them. Camio wondered whether to turn and face the dog now, but as always there was a faint hope that something might turn up, something might . . .

Suddenly, a blur of brown and white flashed behind the running fox. Out of the corner of his eye Camio caught sight of a huge mound of hair; his nose snatched at the smell of a strange dog; his ears captured the double sounds of heavy breathing. What was this?

Camio heard the angry shout, 'Out of the way, you stupid . . .'

The foxes kept going, but just before the yard Camio glanced over his shoulder. What he saw pulled him up short. Mitz had stopped too.

Standing in the middle of the street, barring the ridgeback's path, was another giant dog.

'It's Betsy,' said Mitz in excitement. 'You know, that dog I told you about! And there's the man!'

'You stupid bitch!' screamed the ridgeback, his anger making the hair

482

on his back bristle. 'They'll get away. What are you? A fox-lover bitch?'

A human stepped onto the street. He moved towards the ridgeback, who was still screaming at Betsy. The St Bernard stayed where she was, looking bulky and immovable. The foxes heard her say, 'Well, I am a bitch, though I suppose you've seen so few of us in your time you don't recognise one. Never been with one of us, I suppose? Can't imagine any of us wanting you.'

'I'll gut you . . .' snarled Sabre.

Betsy glanced behind at Camio and Mitz, and then, turning back, nodded. 'I'm sorry to hear that.'

'You will be. You will be.'

But by this time the man was closing in on the ridgeback. He held a stick in front of him like a bar, one hand on each end of it. He held it horizontally, as if offering the middle of it for the hound to bite. Camio had seen this method of keeping a dog at bay back home.

Sabre leaped forward and gripped the thick pole in his massive jaws, tearing at it. Bits of chewed wood fell to the ground.

The man barked: a firm clear bark. Camio could hear the confidence, the absolute lack of fear in that voice. It was a stern command and a warning. The command was repeated. Sabre stopped attacking the pole.

No doubt he was coming to his senses and realising that if he actually inflicted a serious wound on this human, the sentence would be death.

The ridgeback ran off, away from the scene.

Betsy scratched behind her ear, a sure sign to Camio that she had been scared. He wanted to go up and thank the bitch for helping them escape, but it was an unnatural action and in the end he nosed Mitz towards the scrapyard and followed her in.

'Good old Betsy. Did you see that? She's got courage, that dog.'

'She's very brave,' agreed Camio.

'They were following me,' said Mitz proudly. 'They were tracking me by my collar. Now you see why I didn't want you to gnaw it off?'

'Indeed I do,' said Camio, gravely.

O-ha had gone frantic waiting for them back in the earth. She gave her daughter a scolding, after which there was a cooling-off period for all concerned. Then they recounted the story to her.

Reports came to them later, of Sabre rampaging through the *face*. It seemed that nowhere was safe: while the hound was running loose, no real hunting could be done, nor gathering of discarded human fodder outside restaurants. Stores were beginning to run out.

'We'll give them one more day to catch him,' said Camio, 'and then I have to go out again to hunt. I'm sick of being trapped in this place.'

O-ha said, 'Hasn't today taught you anything?'

'Yes,' he replied, 'today has taught me to be more cautious. Today I ran when I should have sneaked over the rooftops and under the fences. I'll be more careful in future.'

She nodded. 'You're right, I suppose. We can't stay in here for ever.'

That night, as Mitz dreamed fox dreams of her cubhood, she was woken by some instinct which told her that she had heard a sound amongst the scrap. She listened hard. Since the winds in the tunnels of junk could not be trusted to bring her a scent, she waited, her heart pounding softly. In the dimness she could see that her mother's eyes were open, and her father was lifting his head, cocking it to one side.

'Is it he?' whispered Mitz. 'Is it?'

There was no answering sound from either of her parents, only a warning from O-ha's eyes, which narrowed very slightly. Mitz waited silently, licking her lips.

Then she smelled the familiar scent. It came drifting down the main tunnel and into the earth. She could hear scrabbling sounds out in the scrapyard where an animal was slipping as quietly as possible along the metalways. She smelled the scent and wondered whether her parents had caught it too.

Camio remained by the exit, ready.

PART SIX
The Time of the Dispersal

Inside the boot of the car it was dark. Although he was lying on something soft, A-cam felt himself being bumped and tossed, and his bleeding tail-stump was extremely painful. He reflected miserably on his captive state, but determined that he would not go down easily. His parents had always taught him to fight until the last of his strength ebbed.

He set to work to try to gnaw his way out of the boot, starting with the fabric lining. He was just starting to make good progress when the feeling of motion ceased abruptly and the prison door was flung open. The man with the thick gloves on reached inside and grabbed him, and A-cam tried again to bite his attacker.

He was then carried through a door and into a room full of humans holding other animals, mostly dogs and cats. Pandemonium ensued. Dogs were shouting and straining at leashes; cats were crying and spitting, their fur on end, and a white rabbit, its eyes bulging, had shrunk to the back of its box and was trying to bury itself in the plywood panelling. A-cam was hurriedly carried out again and round to the rear of the building. Then another door was opened and he was in a room with another human: a woman wearing a white coat. Without any regard for his dignity, he was stretched out on a table and his rear end inspected.

'Let me bleed to death in peace,' he yelled.

They growled back at him in strangely sympathetic voices, and to his bewilderment they began to run hands through his fur, the growls softer and less alarming. White fluff was applied to his wound, followed swiftly by a stinging sensation. Finally, some sweet-smelling paste was applied to the injury and then he was held tightly while the two humans barked at each other.

A little while later he found himself in the back of the car again and the sense of motion returned. This time the journey was a much longer one. The pain in his rear had dulled somewhat and he was able to fall asleep. When he woke the vehicle had stopped, and the boot was flung open again.

The daylight hurt his eyes but he sat up and sniffed. Country smells hit his nostrils, overpowering the petrol and oil. The human gingerly lifted A-cam out and placed him on some grass. As A-cam staggered away, the car door slammed and the vehicle roared away.

Still very unsteady on his feet, the little fox made his way across some *havnot* to a spinney on the far side of a field of shire horses. Then he lay down in the fallen leaves to recover his strength, allowing other leaves to float down upon him. In the meantime, he chewed grass.

Night came and the leaves continued to cover his body. He could smell chestnuts all round him, and only had to nose a little to find some. He crunched them and swallowed. They tasted good. Soon, the edge had been taken off his hunger.

A-cam inspected his tail-stub as well as he was able. The pain was bearable. But when he tried to walk around he found that the loss of his tail had impaired his balance: the best he could manage was a lopsided stagger. He hoped it would not take long to adapt.

The next thing was to find some water. He sniffed the air and followed his nose round the copse, licking puddles from root hollows. The spinney was a delightfully dark and dank-smelling place, with rotten logs, balls of ants and thousands of woodlice. There were tree fungi low enough to gobble while still standing on the ground, and edible toadstools round the base of the trees. Pigeons made a racket in the treetops when he passed beneath a roosting bough, but apart from that it was a quiet place, with spongy humus for a floor, and lots of small holes which held interesting meals.

A-cam had absolutely no idea where he was.

The humans, though they had been kind to him, had dumped him far from home. No doubt their intentions had been good. They had found a wild creature and had returned it to the wilderness, not realising that he was a town fox, born and bred.

So, where did he go from here?

He spent the whole of the next day resting in the wood. The owners of the horses came, took them away for the day (allowing A-cam to drink at their field trough) and then brought them back in the evening. A party of human walkers went through the copse and caught a glimpse of him lying amongst the leaves. They stopped to twitter to each other, pointing at him as though he was not aware of their presence, and then tiptoed away.

Evening came, and A-cam was back on his feet. At the corner of the wood a partridge whirred out of hiding but A-cam was too slow to catch it. At the bottom of the hill on which the trees stood there was a farm. He crept under a fence and found an area where chickens roamed. He was just about to chase them when he discovered some eggs in the grass. Still feeling weak, he settled for the eggs, which was just as well because not long after a dog came out and A-cam only just managed to slip back under the fence in time.

He struck out across country, often faltering because of lack of balance and dizziness. He realised that he had become a *rangfar*, without intending to, and he wondered if it happened to many foxes that way. Perhaps few of them started out on the road from choice, but once they had, they got a taste for travel. He could see why it was attractive. Each hour brought a different perspective to the land. There were ploughed, empty fields; coverts and woods; rolling pastureland and hilly steeps. The world had opened up before him. So far, he had not run into any humans. He felt it possible that one could walk and walk and not run out of *hav* or *havnot*.

Once, he caught the smell of another dog fox and paused to sniff the breeze, wondering where the creature was hiding. A voice from a bramble bush said, 'Keep walking,' in a casual but firm tone, and he realised that he was probably crossing parishes with established hunting rights for local foxes. They did not mind him passing so long as he was out of the area quickly, but apart from snapping up the odd field mouse or shrew, he was not going to be allowed to hunt.

That morning he reached a rise from beyond which came a constant rumble, like deep, rolling thunder, muffled by an earth bank. He went to the top of this escarpment and looked down in wonder on a roadway which was thick with fast vehicles; two roadways in fact, running parallel, each with three lanes of traffic. He wanted none of that. He could see the crows taking advantage of *gubbins*, but it looked an extremely dangerous business, dashing out and grabbing the remains of some creature that had refused to acknowledge that its ancient highway had been severed by an impassable river of traffic. He turned from this madness on wheels and retraced his steps for some way.

When night came he continued his journey, striking out southwards. He found a quiet road and travelled along the verge, ignoring the cars that flashed past him occasionally. When he eventually reached a village he passed through it without encountering any other foxes, or indeed dogs. Some instinct told him he was moving in the right direction.

As the sun cast its first rays across the countryside, he came to a cottage with a small shed in its garden. The roof of the shed looked warm and inviting and he jumped up onto the wall, and thence to the top of the shed. There he fell asleep in the soft warmth of the autumn sun.

He was woken abruptly by rain, which fell in torrents. It was around noon and he shook himself and climbed down from the shed, back to the edge of the road. There was a deep ditch running beside the road and he slipped down into this gully and walked along it, snapping up beetles and whatever came into his path. With the wet came the cold, and he shivered constantly as he walked, a fever coming over him which made him giddy. The downpour became torrential and hampered A-cam's progress as it splashed up from the ground, constantly spraying his face, getting in his eyes and nostrils. The only recognisable smells were those of musty, churned earth and wet grass. Visibility was down to a nose.

A-cam decided to leave the highway. He found a wood in the middle of some *havnot* and spent the rest of the day there.

That night, when he woke, he found the rain had stopped. There was the smell of rotting crab apples nearby, and he made for these, but overriding this odour was the scent of foxes. Not just one or two foxes, but hundreds, perhaps thousands of them. This was both alarming and puzzling. He could not think why so many of his kind had gathered together in one place. Was it a meeting of some sort? If so, it was unprecedented. Foxes prided themselves on the fact that they were not pack or herd creatures. They might live in small groups of four or five, but these groups never gathered in one spot. It was too dangerous.

A-cam ate his fill of crab apples and then walked to the edge of the wood. He looked down the slope. At the bottom was a large piece of land surrounded by a high, chain-link fence. Beyond this were some long wooden huts. They looked ominously dark and A-cam felt a chill of apprehension go through him. The place below stank of evil.

Yet this was where the scent of the foxes was coming from. Was it a zoo, like the one his father had told him about? But zoos were not full of foxes—the whole idea was to have lots of different animals and birds which the humans could come and stare at. Perhaps it was a kind of prison, where they took foxes before killing them? That too seemed unlikely. Men were more fond of shooting or running down foxes with dogs in their own environment. There seemed to be more excitement from the chase and kill that way.

A-cam gave up on his speculations and was about to turn away when he saw a chain of lights moving across the distant landscape. After a while he realised what it was and became excited: it was a train, racing along a track. He knew that a railway track passed quite close to his own home, and though he knew from his father that there was more than one of these steel roadways running across the land, he considered it a strong possibility that this was his way home. Here was the first landmark that might help him get back to his parents again.

However, to reach the railway he had to cross through that fenced-in piece of *havnot*, which was not a comforting thought. He did not want to end up in one of those huts with all the other inmates, whatever the reason why they were held there. He decided to spend the night in the wood and go down later to inspect the fence. He would be able to find a way through, he had no doubt. Foxes, when they have to, can squeeze through a pinhole.

A-CAM'S FEVER took a strong hold on him during the night and by the time dawn came he no longer felt able to go down to the fence. Besides, a group of travellers had arrived with the rising of the sun and their caravan encampment was between him and his goal. He watched through narrowed eyes as lurcher dogs strolled round the camp below, sniffing at anything that they came across. These were very dangerous animals to a fox: they had the savagery of an Alsatian and the speed of a greyhound. They were lean, whippet-like crossbreeds, trained to hunt hares and rabbits, but they would undoubtedly settle for a fox if one broke cover. A-cam hoped the travellers would not stay long.

During that day he watched the activity below. There was much coming and going: children running and screaming in play; rattling, rusty old vehicles arriving and leaving; knotted, swarthy men banging away at old metal; dark women stringing up lines of wet, grey clothes; radios blaring out at full volume. Then men in flat hats arrived in a black-and-white car. The hard, dusty men began barking with the soft-cheeked ones in hats, who stood with their hands on their hips and looked everywhere but into the flashing eyes before them. Finally, the black-and-white car drove away and the camp returned to its normal activities.

That evening there was music, which A-cam enjoyed. He listened to the wailing, dancing sounds that came from the stringed device which the traveller tucked under his chin. When birds made sounds like that, it was usually to warn others away from their territory. A-cam wondered if these humans were sending signals to the flat-capped ones, saying, *Keep away, this is our hunting ground*.

Light from an open bonfire caught the children's faces and the swirling clothes of the women as they sat or moved around the camp. Later, overriding the odour of mansweat and diesel fumes, came the smell of cooked food. A-cam's saliva flowed and his stomach churned. His fever was easing now and his nose was once more wet and sensitive, a useful tool. Without it, he was like a blind hawk.

He toured the copse, looking for worms and beetles. There were fungi to be had, and crab apples, and sloes. A-cam ate his fill and then settled back to sleep again.

When morning came, the travellers had moved on. Where they had been was a sea of rubbish: paper stuck to the chain-link fence, and cans, bottles and plastic cartons littered the ground. It seemed that these people could conjure rubbish from beneath the turf, for surely they could not have produced such an amount of waste in just one day?

A-cam went down the hill and inspected the fence. Moving along it he found a place where he could dig, and burrowed underneath the wire. Once he was on the other side, he became wary. There might be dogs guarding the place.

He trotted quickly across to the first long hut. Since the dwellings were raised off the ground, he intended to go underneath them to the other side, walking quickly from hut to hut. He would not run. He had been trained by his parents not to run except in a dire emergency, as running creatures only attract attention.

Once under the huts, A-cam was sure they contained foxes. Also there was a chilling sense of passing near to a thousand *sowanders*. Many foxes had died in this place and the atmosphere was one of terror that had been suppressed by hopelessness and despair.

The scents were overpowering. Under the third hut he found a small knothole and he whispered curiously, 'Who's there? Can anybody hear me?' Then he put his ear to the hole through which bits of dirty straw were poking. He could hear breathing from above, and a shuffling. Then a faltering voice said, 'Is—is that a fox-spirit?'

'No,' he said, 'I'm a real fox. I was just passing by. Who are you? What's your name?'

'O-sollo,' came the reply. 'What are you doing out there? Have you escaped? How did you get out?'

'I didn't get out—I've never been in. What is this place?'

There was a long silence, then she answered uncertainly, 'This is a place where they keep foxes.'

'What for?' he asked.

'What for? The disappeared ones could tell you better than I, except that they're never likely to come back.'

The 'disappeared ones'? What did that mean? 'Listen, can you help us escape?' the voice went on. 'My sister and I are in a cage above your head. Only this wooden floor stands between us and freedom.'

A-cam paused. He knew he was in great danger. If foxes were kept caged in long dark huts, it meant that humans would go to enormous lengths to keep them there. What did it all mean? His instinct told him to get away from the place as fast as he could, but the voice above had aroused something within him which he might have recognised had he had the time to think about it.

Then he remembered something his father had told him. There were places called fox farms, where foxes were bred and then taken away . . . nobody knew what happened to them, but it was easy to guess; foxes are not stupid. They had seen their skins used as clothes: wrapped round ladies who smelled as if they had taken an overdose of violets. The 'disappeared ones' were taken away, killed and skinned.

He studied the planks above his head. They looked formidable. What he should be doing was trotting on towards the railway line.

'O-sollo,' he said. 'I would like to help you, but I don't see how.'

'One of the boards is rotten,' she whispered. 'We've been wetting on it ever since we've been here, always in the same place. If you could gnaw from your side . . .'

He sniffed around the area and found the plank that smelled. He pushed his nose against it. The wood was soft. But how to get his teeth to it? The planks were flat. There was nowhere to get a grip.

Then he thought of something. 'I've got an idea,' he said, proudly. 'Give me a few moments.'

'You won't be sorry,' she whispered back. 'I'm a vixen of rare beauty.' Then she added, modestly, 'We all are in here. But you'll . . . you'll have a mate to treasure . . . if you want one.'

A-cam turned round and began digging with his hind legs, until he had piled earth up under the softened plank. When he had got it high enough, he squeezed his body between the mound and the plank, and then arched his back, pressing down with his four legs. To his intense delight the plank began to move, bending upwards. It was indeed rotten, the wood like sodden cardboard.

'All right,' came a voice from above, 'we can get at it now.'

Above him the two vixens tore at the pulpy wood, pulling it away in great chunks until there was a hole half the size of a man's head. In the meantime, A-cam slipped to the edge of the hut and sniffed Melloon. There were no dangerous scents abroad. He came back as the second vixen was forcing her way through the hole.

When both were safely out, A-cam said, 'We must make for the railway. It's *gerflan* for a start, and they'll have difficulty following us. Also, I need it, to guide me home. Which one of you is O-sollo?' he added, staring at the twins.

'I am,' said the one with the darker ears. 'This is O-fall.'

'Right. Let's go then. Move from hut to hut until we come to the last one, then I'll go out, dig us a hole under the fence, and we'll be free.'

'Free,' breathed O-fall, speaking for the first time.

They did as instructed, slipping from one hut to another, but just as they came to the last a human barking went up. The foxes in the huts, who until now had been silent, took up the cry, and began shouting to one another. The noise was appalling.

What to do? Remain where they were? A-cam put the suggestion to the other two.

'No,' said O-fall, firmly. 'The first thing they'll do is search the grounds. We have to get out.'

'Will they use dogs?' asked A-cam.

'And ruin these beautiful furs?' replied O-sollo. 'That's one advantage we've got. We're valuable.'

A-cam heaved a sigh of relief. 'Good. Now for that fence . . .'

Without waiting to think about it, he trotted over to the fence and found some soft earth. He dug like fury and then shouted to the two vixens, 'Come on!' At that moment, he saw a man running from behind the huts with a gun in his hands.

'*Come on!*'

O-sollo was through and O-fall had her head on the other side when the first bullet zinged off the wire, just above her head.

'Keep going,' yelled A-cam.

She was through in an instant, A-cam right behind her. Another shot raised some turf an inch from his nose. The two vixens were already running into the shrubland beyond the fence. He followed them, zigzagging. He heard another shot, but did not know where it hit.

Maybe he got me, thought A-cam, and I won't feel it until I stop.

He scrambled under a bush and waited until he got his breath back, then he called, 'Are you two all right?'

'Yes,' called O-sollo.

'Let's go again. Make for the railway and get down on the other side of the tracks.'

The three of them slunk quickly through the shrubs, up the railway bank and down the other side. A-cam kept them on the move for a mile before he let them stop and rest. Then they sat down beside the track, to get their breath back.

Suddenly, O-sollo cried out.

'What is it?' asked A-cam, alarmed. 'Were you hit?'

'No,' she cried. 'It's you! The man shot your tail off!'

A-cam sank to the ground in relief.

'Oh, that. Don't worry about that. I lost my tail a few days ago—to a dog the size of one of your huts. That's no exaggeration either. He's a monster. Why are you staring at me like that, O-sollo?'

'You've lost your tail,' she said sadly.

'If you don't want him, I'll have him,' said O-fall, quickly.

'Don't be silly,' said her sister, 'of course I want him. He's my rescuer. I just think it's sad, that's all. Anyway, there's nothing to stop us all living together, in one earth. Is there?'

'I've always wanted to live in an earth,' sighed O-fall. 'They spoke about these things in the compound, but none of us had ever seen one. We were born there, you see. And we would have died there. What . . . what's an earth look like?'

'Look like?' A-cam scratched his haunch against a bush. 'Depends where it is. The only one I know—my parents' breeding earth—was an old car hulk in the middle of a scrapyard. Traditionally, I suppose, they're dug out of the ground, under the root of some tree. But I've heard of foxes who live under the floorboards of houses.'

'I would like a traditional earth,' said O-sollo, firmly.

'Me too,' O-fall agreed.

'In that case, we'll dig ourselves an earth, just as soon as we find a suitable place.'

They walked on for some miles, along the railway embankment, until they came to a wooded area that spilled down onto the track. A-cam spent a long time sniffing round the area, checking for other foxes' marker posts. When he found none, he concluded that they could make their home in that place. All three foxes were exhausted by this time and they went up into the wood and found a place to rest for the night.

The two vixens had never hunted and were anxious to learn from A-cam. He talked to them about it, saying that he was no expert—not like his mother, who could track anything over the poorest ground—but he would pass on what he had learned from her. He would also teach them about berries, roots, worms, insects, fungi, and all things edible, just as his mother had taught him.

'Did your father teach you nothing?' asked O-fall.

'Camio? Yes, but about town living. He was not such a good hunter as O-ha, but he was a better scavenger. He once told me he had taken a meal out of a man's hand on the run. He's very good at that sort of thing. He's good at storytelling too.'

'So,' said O-sollo, 'your parents sound like good foxes. But now we are on our own. I think we're a few seasons older than you, A-cam, but because we've been locked up since birth we're going to be a bit of a burden for a while. We'll learn quickly, though. I don't want to be dependent on a dog fox for my food, even if he is my mate.'

'My mate . . .' A-cam said, remembering. It sounded good. How proud of him his parents would be. He had found himself a mate, a very pretty mate. One of rare beauty.

A-cam lay awake, long after the vixens were asleep, thinking about what he had said to them. He had been bragging a little and was not as confident as he pretended. Yes, O-ha had taught him a great deal about living off the countryside, but in theory rather than in practice. Now, during autumn, there was a wide choice. But what about when food got scarce, in midwinter, when they had to take anything they could find? And what if he turned out to be a poor hunter, unable to catch rabbits or birds? What if all three of them were useless at living in the wild?

These questions churned around in his brain as he lay awake. He decided that, once he had set up some caches around the place, he would visit his parents. They would be able to advise him further.

A-CAM MADE THE JOURNEY, following the railway track, coping with hardship the way an adult fox would. Now he had responsibilities and he had begun to take himself seriously. He learned about the trains and when they were likely to come along, leaving the track at those times and hiding in the grass on the embankment. He met other foxes, but treated their territory with respect and received nothing but respect in return. One or two dogs were encountered, but he used his skills to advantage. He was no coward, but did not court danger unnecessarily: only fools stayed and fought when there was a chance to run. He was a fox: crafty, subtle, furtive, stealthy, secretive. He slid in and out of danger, as lean and unobtrusive as a shadow, and his enemies caught only a glimpse of him out of the corner of their eyes, if they saw him at all. He sought the corners, the hidey-holes, thickets of blackthorn, deep ditches. He learned how to travel without causing a fuss amongst the birds and he rested lightly, ready to spring to his feet, so that an enemy would remain wondering about the flash of red seen only for a second, before it was gone.

A-cam arrived in the town to find a strangeness in the atmosphere. There was danger about but he did not wait to discover its meaning: he had come to see his parents and that he would do.

He reached the scrapyard without mishap and entered one of the tunnels. The mountain of junk had changed shape since he had last been there and he had a little difficulty in locating the main highway, but once he found it, he went straight to the earth. His heart was beating fast with the anticipation of seeing his family again. On the journey he had not stopped to think about the meeting, but now that it was imminent it was difficult to contain his joy and he covered the last few yards at a rush.

Camio had been waiting at the entrance and they fell on one another in a storm of happiness.

'I'm home! I'm home!' cried A-cam, and his mother and sister leaped on him and covered him in nips and licks, so that when they were eventually persuaded to back off, his coat was quite damp. He shook himself, still bursting with pride and joy.

O-ha groaned at the stump where his tail used to be, but A-cam shrugged it off.

'Mitz!' he said, noticing her collar.

She knew what he was going to ask and said, 'Later, let's hear your story first.'

He proceeded to tell them about his adventures, beginning by telling them they should call him A-salla now, since he was mated to a vixen of rare beauty, called O-sollo.

PART SEVEN
The Palace of the Winds

'A vixen of rare beauty?' repeated O-ha, as A-cam neared the end of his tale. She regarded her son with approving eyes. He seemed to have landed on his feet, albeit without a tail.

'Well, no more beautiful than yourself . . . or Mitz . . .' stumbled A-cam in an attempt at diplomacy.

'Now you're spoiling it,' said Mitz. 'You shouldn't be so eager to please us all. I have this vision of a vixen with a soft, velvety coat that shines in the sun—a light frame and a high, pert head, with deep brown eyes . . . a fox to put a hunter's moon to shame.'

'Yes, yes, that's her exactly,' said A-cam, excitedly.

'Well, then, I shall always think of you as rescuing a vixen of rare beauty from the clutches of certain death.'

Camio interrupted. 'You were telling us, A-cam, about your inability to put into practice your mother's teaching.'

A-cam looked at his father with a hurt expression. 'No, that's not true. I was saying that I thought we might not manage. As it turned out, we got along very well. Of course, there's Ransheen to contend with yet—the time of scarcity. But we've learned an awful lot in just a short time. And though I'm not as good at hunting as the other two have become—O-fall is best—I can catch most things. O-fall will probably not be with us for long, anyway. There's a dog fox in the area interested in her.'

'I was wondering about that,' said Camio. 'I mean, two mates. It doesn't work, you know.'

A-cam said, 'I never intended to have two mates. That's not how we manage things at all. O-fall's staying because she has nowhere else to go at the moment. We'll survive, don't you worry.'

'I'm sure you will,' said O-ha. 'I'm very proud of you.'

A-cam nodded. Then he cried, 'Sister! What about this collar you're wearing? Were you caught? What's it for? You look like a dog.'

'I don't need to be told that, thank you. I had an adventure too, just like you. Well, quite different, actually. I was captured by a human and taken to a house, met a friendly bitch called Betsy, had a conversation with an otter and then this collar was put on my neck. The man who captured me uses it to track me, wherever I go.'

'Don't you mind that?' said the wide-eyed dog fox.

'Not really. The human doesn't intend me any harm, and it's a good thing to be tracked at the moment, with that killer dog loose. We've been rescued once already.'

'Yes, I heard rumours about Sabre as I came across the *face*. Having lost my tail to that beast, I have no wish to offer him the other end. Can't something be done?'

Camio replied, 'He'll be caught soon. He can't survive without raiding dustbins and he's no slinking fox, to do such things silently. I expect they'll get him before long.'

'I hope so,' said A-cam. 'I have to get back to my mate. I need to reach the railway track, so that I can follow it along to my earth. You must come and visit me, all of you.'

They all nodded, knowing that it would never happen. It was right that A-cam had returned to the breeding earth to inform his parents of his success in finding a mate and establishing his own home, but foxes are not like humans, who make regular visits. A-cam had left the earth. He was now a fox with his own responsibilities. He would soon have his own young to feed.

They continued to exchange news for some time, when suddenly there was a barking from beyond the yard. Some humans were getting upset about something. The noise of a chase came to their ears: the panting of an animal, the sound of running feet. O-ha was the first to catch the scent. 'Sabre! He's in the yard!' she whispered.

The two cubs crouched instinctively and began backing into the rear of the earth. Camio bristled, baring his teeth.

Next came the sounds of a creature forcing its way along the tunnel to their earth. The tunnel was wide at its opening and became narrower towards the centre of the heap of scrap, where the car body was situated.

'I can smell you in there!' called the dog. 'One, two, three, four—I can smell you. This time! This time!'

O-ha's blood went cold at the sound of the voice. Her stomach was in her mouth. She was sick, sick of running from this deviant hound that would never let them rest. Fear was there, but also a bitter hatred for one who would never let her or her family alone. If only she were larger, more powerful! She would give anything just for a chance to win.

Scrap metal moved around the car's shell, as the dog shouldered his way through. They could hear his exertions as he squirmed and pushed his way onwards, towards them.

'I can smell you, vixen. This time I've got you, all of you. No St Bernard bitches to protect you now. No do-gooder humans in here, just us. My teeth ache to sink into your skull. I'll crush it like a rotten apple. I'll spread your brains from here to Trinity.'

The foxes said nothing to each other. There was no other way out. The two adults positioned themselves at the entrance to the earth.

There were further sounds coming from Sabre now, grunting and swearing, as he continued to heave his bulk through the scrap. The whole heap moved as if an earthquake were in progress, cooking stoves grinding against rusty bedframes, empty oil drums rolling across the mountain of scrap, freezers shifting before Sabre's immense strength.

'My head,' gasped the hound, 'my head swims with the sweet taste of blood. I am near—I am so near. I can smell the blood in my nostrils. I'll have you twitching, this way, that way. I'll have you . . .'

They could see his eyes now, blazing in demented triumph. The jaws opened wide, foam round the lips of his mouth. The veins on his neck stood out like thick cords as he forced himself, inch by inch, closer to the foxes. At the rear of the earth the two terrified juveniles were trying to squeeze through a hole in the back hardly big enough for a kitten.

Men were on top of the scrapheap now, trying to get at the hound, unaware that the dog was after a family of foxes.

Sabre gave one last heave and brought himself within a nose of Camio and O-ha. This last jerk loosened a bale of barbed wire which had been balanced on top of the scrap. It fell on the dog, who was stretching his whole frame to get at the foxes. His forelegs were caught in the mesh and ripped open by the barbs. His head and throat were scissored by two strands which closed every time he tried to move forward.

A bellow of frustration came from his mouth. 'I—*will*—get—'

With a supreme effort he launched himself forward, only to bring the roof of scrap metal crashing onto him. The whole heap of scrap heaved, swayed, and began rolling like a rockslide. A hole opened above the foxes' earth, through which the blue sky was visible. Everything was moving, twisting, turning. Nothing had stability.

'Once—more—'

The hole in the scrap widened. One by one, the four foxes bolted through this exit, avoiding the men balanced precariously on top of the scrap. They skipped round obstacles and made their escape, with the hound's muffled words in their ears: 'I'll—get—you!'

As they raced for the street, a man with fur on his face and a box on his back waved them on with encouraging barks. When one of the humans from the manor gave chase, the man who was Betsy's master barred the way, allowing the foxes time to escape.

THEY GATHERED on the edge of town.

'Well,' said A-cam to his parents, 'I'll be on my way.'

They said their goodbyes in the way that foxes do, very formally, with little outward show of emotion. Inside, however, O-ha was awash with sentiment. She knew she would not see her cub again, and she felt as though a piece of herself had come adrift and was floating away from her. Camio, too, despite his serious expression, must be feeling something.

A-cam left, and Camio suggested that they find a temporary earth until they set up their permanent one on the embankment.

Mitz said to her mother, 'If it's all right with you two, I shan't look for an earth yet. I'll stay with you for a while. It's not that I'm not ready to leave home, but I want a year without cubs. If I set up an earth with a dog fox, I shan't be able to resist having cubs, in spite of my feelings now.'

'Well,' said O-ha, 'when the time comes to mate, you'll know.'

MELLOON BEGAN TO BLOW herself out, and Ransheen sharpened her teeth, ready to savage the landscape. The owls sharpened their claws too, honed their beaks and, like most carnivores, prepared themselves for a hard time. Those animals that wished to sleep the winter away, like the hedgehog, went into hibernation, a dangerous state. The creature is physically vulnerable and its body mechanisms fall to such a slow tick-over that they sometimes stop altogether. Animals in hibernation are so close to death, they can look over the edge and see what it's like on the other side.

They moved to an earth on the embankment of the railway loop that was in the process of being built to accommodate the town. At first there were quite a few humans around, working on the rails, but they had no time to bother foxes and were even quite pleased to see them.

The frost crackled across the land, covering tree stumps in hard white crystals, turning them into gravestones. Brambles became thick wire with hooks that caught the coat. Ice grew in thin layers that formed thicker wedges, until water was scarce.

The town continued to expand and food became easier to find, in the bins outside houses and restaurants. Foxes and kestrels fed well, if not on the waste food itself then on the rats and mice that arrived to cohabit with the humans. Of course, most humans did not realise the rodents were there, since they kept a low profile, but the foxes did.

O-ha was more at home on the embankment than she had been in the scrapyard. She was still a rural fox at heart (a rustic, Camio called her in play) and disliked and distrusted the town. The *gerflan* on which she lived was a compromise: something between *face* and *hav*. She did not like eating worms out of the gutters in the street, she preferred to dig them out of the ground; slugs and snails, too, were somehow more tasty from a leaf than they were from a wall.

From her hole in the long grass at the top of the bank she watched the bright steel rails being laid. They looked magnificent. She admired their clean, straight dimensions. There was great beauty in a strip of steel, she decided. It looked cold, hard and efficient, just as a fox should be. The soul of a living fox, she decided, should be modelled on a steel rail. It should shine, but it should be immune from injury, devoid of anything but stark, capable toughness. This was the ascetic fox coming out in her. In fact she was a warm creature inside, and Camio frequently told her that just because she did not like soft beds it did not mean she had a hard soul. But some deep teaching from somewhere, perhaps her parents, had left O-ha feeling it was wrong to be emotional.

Over the next month the high, dark winds without names rushed heavy clouds over the land. The mating period came round, but a sudden fall of snow trapped Camio on the far side of town. He struggled to reach home, but it was three days before he reached the earth on the *gerflan*, and by that time O-ha's desire was waning. She was irritable with Camio for not being around at the right time, and when the mating finally took place, the oestrus was over. There would be no cubs.

The men finished work on the railway and the trains began to use the loop. At first O-ha thought she would never get used to the noise, but gradually the trains seemed to become quieter, until she had to concentrate to hear them at all. Of a night-time, she would enjoy lying side by side with Camio, staring down at the trains going by, all lit up. She wondered what the fox-spirits of the Firstdark thought about these modern times, when humans hurtled from one place to another inside glass boxes. After all, they had known the earth when it was young, when there were no machines at all and men ran naked through the forests, killing things with sticks and stones instead of guns. The fox-spirits had seen a lot of changes and would probably see more. No doubt they would be there to witness the end of the world when it came.

Fox mythology said that one day all the waters would rise up and reshape themselves into A-O's ancient fox-form, which was like an ordinary fox only a thousand times larger and with eyes so full of severe compassion that no mortal could look directly into them. A-O would then begin swallowing the sun, moon and earth, in that order. In this way, the ghosts of all dead foxes would become part of A-O.

So, contemplating her immortal state, O-ha daydreamed. It was only when she slept that the nightmares came, of black bars falling across a wide bright field of snow, the chase, and then . . . finally, the shadow of her pursuer fell across her path. Now, in her dream, she looked up to see the shape that cast the shadow—or was it the shadow that cast the shape? She was confused. Was the thing above her head or below her feet?

She woke, whining pitifully in her distress.

IT WAS RANSHEEN and the world turned to bone. The sky had moved down onto the land. Shapes were lost to sight, even in open spaces, and scents and sounds were whisked away by blizzards, upwards, to be buried in the grey above.

Life had become hard for the creatures of the *face*, since heavy snowfalls had brought the town to a standstill. Restaurants had closed temporarily, few people ventured out, and the foxes who relied on waste food found the sources had disappeared. O-ha, Camio and Mitz became thin, wasted creatures. Their bellies pinched tight beneath their fur and their eyes burned dimly from the depths of hollow sockets. Any scrap which even had the appearance of food was hastily devoured. Camio ate some unidentifiable piece of rubbish and became ill, lying close to death on the floor of their earth.

O-ha decided to raid the farmhouse on the edge of the *face*. It was during such weather that farmers forgot to lock up the chicken coop, or failed to shut the barn door on stored vegetables. The three foxes were so desperately hungry that she knew she had to risk the journey, even in such appalling conditions.

Camio, from his sickbed, tried to dissuade her from the trip.

'Why don't you wait a little longer? Perhaps the blizzard will clear up soon?'

'Perhaps it won't,' she said, emphatically. 'It's no good—I'm going, and that's that. If we don't get something to eat, we'll die anyway.'

'It's a bad time,' was all he added.

'Mitz will look after you,' said O-ha. 'She's outside now, getting some ice for you to lick. I wish we could find you some grass, but it's buried deep under the snow . . .'

'I shall be all right. Don't worry about me.' He did not look all right. He lay full length on his side, panting, his ribs sticking through his ragged fur like small wire hoops. O-ha was frightened to nuzzle him since the skin looked so taut it might split open.

Mitz came in then with an icicle in her mouth. She dropped it in front of Camio, then flopped down beside him.

'There,' she said breathlessly. 'That's as clear a piece of ice as you'll ever see. Where are you going, O-ha?'

'Out. I have to look for food. You see to Camio. I won't be long.'

She knew that Mitz thought she was going to search locally, so she hurried out of the earth before the vixen discovered that she was going on a much longer journey. She would have insisted on going with her.

O-ha struggled through the shoulder-high snow, ploughing forward with effort. Snow got into her mouth and nostrils, and the going was hard, but she was determined to make it to the point where the streets sloped upwards to Trinity Parklands before she had a rest.

Her legs quickly became tired but she forced them to carry on. When she fell into the deeper drifts, she burrowed her way through. There was a terrible pain in her stomach which she knew was echoed inside Camio and Mitz. Her head felt light, however, and not quite part of her. She forced herself to think of things other than her own agony.

Mitz! She had started calling her daughter Mitz, finally giving in and dropping the prefix. How is she ever going to get a mate? thought O-ha. She'll meet a dog fox, tell him her name, and he'll think . . . well, there was no reasoning what he would think. Still, the vixen was grown now. At least the collar had gone, slipped off when Mitz lost weight and her face had been pared down by lack of food. That collar had been enough in itself to turn any dog fox's thoughts away from her daughter.

She forced herself to think these thoughts, to keep her mind from her hunger and waning strength. There were pictures at the back of her mind, of foxes lying dead in the snow, fallen never to rise again. Well, it was as good a death as any. She had had a good life—some tragedy, admittedly, but what vixen got through the seasons she had seen without tragedy of some kind?

She found herself in a tunnel of snow and followed it to the end, emerging at the foot of the slope that led to Trinity. She began climbing the slippery street, her paws skidding on the ice the cars had formed from the packed snow. The blizzard increased in strength, and Ransheen threatened to throw O-ha back down the slope like a rag. If there were scents in the air, she could not smell them, and any sounds were lost in a banshee howling. These were dangerous conditions for a wild creature.

She reached the gates to the parkland and wearily settled down for a rest. It would have been easy, so easy, just to sleep where she lay and never wake up. But there were others relying on her. She had to force herself back onto her legs, and continue.

O-ha entered the woods, and once in the trees the going was a little easier. The woodland kept out a lot of the blizzard. She passed a small depression at the bottom of a tree. Gar's sett. But though she had not seen the badger for a long while, this was no time to go visiting. She promised herself she would visit Gar in the summer.

There was a hole in the snowscape ahead of her. Almost immediately she caught the scent of ermine and nosed it out. The creature was lying still, white on white, having given up its life to the winter. She made a swift meal of it, the meat giving her the energy she needed to make that long trek down through the edge of the *face* to the farm on the far side. She felt guilty, but there was little enough for one, let alone three. O-ha needed the strength to return.

Just as she finished her meal, the blizzard drifted away and the skies began to clear. O-ha was stunned at how quickly the blueness took over from the grey. It was as if the sky were in sheets and someone had pulled away the bottom one to reveal a complete contrast.

A few moments later the sun came out and the shadows of the trees fell in black bars across the glinting snow.

Black bars on white.

A chill went through O-ha as she took in the strange, uniform pattern of the shadows: they played across her mind like a tune. She was mesmerised by them. The scene was quite familiar. The trees, the clear day, the white world, and the black shadows like bars . . . something ran through her mind, a dark shape, tripping between the bars, in the sunlight, in the shadow, running fearful as if in a dream. Over and over played the tune, and she knew it so well because she had seen it night after night in her restless sleep . . . running like a dream, through a dream, and it was *her* and she was the dream.

She looked round quickly as a scent came to her from the direction of the parkland. There were two silhouettes there: a man in a heavy coat and hat, and a dog. The hound was tall and red in the light of the sun, his big-boned skull full of brute strength.

Then the image blurred as she failed to focus on the still scene. It had been enough, that one glimpse, accompanied by the odour. O-ha knew who that couple were. *Sabre and his master!*

Had he seen her? She waited, her heart beating fast, crouched in the snow. She was aware of her own red coat against the white landscape. The figures were upwind, but if the man had even mediocre eyesight he would see her. Then the wind changed direction, and though it did not blow directly towards O-ha's enemy, it swirled around the trees, carrying her scent with it. Ransheen, she thought, you traitor!

She looked towards the man and the dog. The hound's head jerked up, quickly. It stood, almost as high as the man's chest, and its head swivelled, scanning the countryside. Then the head stopped moving.

'Fox!' she heard Sabre shout, the word muffled by the snow.

Was it her? Had he seen her? Perhaps there was another fox? Better to freeze, remain still, just in case, just to be sure.

Sabre began pulling on the leash. The man jerked the dog's head back, snarling at him. The dog began straining, pulling his master towards the edge of the wood. He was heading straight for the spot where O-ha crouched. She broke cover and began to run, wading through the belly-high snow. The dog began running too, and the man was jerked off his feet and dragged for a while, his body cutting a furrow through the snow. Then the lead was released with a harsh scream of anger. A hat went blowing away, across the field.

O-ha knew the situation was desperate. She was afraid, it was true, but not terror-stricken, the way she had been in her dream. She had a job to do, which was to escape. She went through the snow in a series of leaps, as if she were jumping hurdles. It was a slow business, and she could sense the long-legged hound gaining on her, not hampered, as she was, by the deep drifts. Where he could not remain clear he would force his way through. Sabre was well fed and immensely strong.

Once she reached the road, she ran, skidding a little, on the hardpacked snow. A slow vehicle came towards her, shunting its way amid clouds of steam, in the same channel between the walls of snow. She was not going to give way and at the last moment the driver saw her and swerved instinctively, burying the front of his car in a drift.

She ran on, a quick glance behind her telling her that the dog was closing in.

Now he began the traditional taunting that hounds love during a chase.

'Skinny vixen! I'm going to break every bone in your body. You'll live long enough to feel me cracking open your skull. I'll colour the snow with your blood and brains.'

A young human came round a corner and Sabre struck him, sending the youth flying into the road. The boy went sliding along the ice and hit his shoulder hard against the kerbstone. The glassy surface took the dog's legs away from him too, but he soon regained control and continued the chase, ignoring the shrieking of the human he had hurt.

The streets ended and the lane to the farm came in sight. Why she was running towards this place, O-ha had no idea. It just seemed right. It was the way it had happened in her dream.

She knew that Sabre would catch her before she went through the gate. He was inches behind her now, his teeth snapping at her hind legs, trying to bring her down.

She skipped sideways, and rolled over onto her back. The dog followed her movements, his savage jaws going for her exposed belly. She waited for the pain of the strike.

'Gagggaaah!' The dog's head was pulled up short just a fraction from its target, and he crashed down heavily on his back. O-ha was up in a second and continued to run. A quick glance behind her told her he was back on his feet. His trailing leash had caught on a post and had jerked him off his legs, but he was back up now and straining to move forwards. The rotten post cracked at the bottom, and Sabre dragged it along with him for several yards before the lead fell free of it.

O-ha had gained about twenty yards, but she knew the dog would soon recover this distance. Much of the snow had been cleared from round the farm and while she found it easier to run, so did Sabre.

'Thought you had me, eh?' he shouted. 'Deathday is here. You have no hope of escape. Nothing will stop me from killing you now. Not walls, not people, nothing. I'll kill anything and anyone who gets in the way.'

She ran down the long driveway to the farmhouse, and past the whitewashed building, her breath labouring in her chest. Sparrows on the snow scattered with cries of terror frozen in their throats, as she ran between them. Sabre was very close again. He too was breathing heavily, his exhalations filling the air round his head with sprigs of steam. She could smell his scent now, the odour heavy in her nostrils. His great paws drummed on the snowpacked earth, just a few yards behind her.

She ran between the barn and the house, thinking to head across open fields again. If they had been ploughed up and left fallow, ready for spring planting, then the hard-edged furrows might slow the dog up. If there were a tree out there! But there were only low hedgerows.

There was a snapping at her heels and she half twisted in her run, to bite back. Death was only a second away. He was almost on her. One more yard . . .

Something flashed between her and the hound and Sabre went tumbling, somersaulting onto his back. He had tripped over a taut chain. Blood came from deep jagged gashes in his forelegs. He screamed an oath. On the other end of the chain was Breaker, the old foxhound. Breaker yelled something at O-ha and then threw himself on top of the ridgeback. It was no match. There was a very brief struggle, which gave O-ha a few more yards, before Breaker was thrown aside. The foxhound struck the side of his kennel and lay still.

'Stupid traitor!' screamed the ridgeback.

Now the dog was limping, though his wounds did not seem to slow him down. His determination was evident in his whole demeanour.

'This time,' he was saying, 'this time, fox, I will have your throat. I can taste it—taste it . . .'

O-ha ran round behind the back of the barn, looking for a shed to climb, but all the buildings were too high. She ran inside the barn and in and out of the machinery, hoping Sabre might be skewered on some of the blades, but he stayed by the door, getting his breath back, knowing it was the only way out.

'I've got you, fox—the vixen that's given me so much trouble, all these seasons . . .'

She crouched behind a tractor.

'And you . . .' she gasped, gulping air, 'you've never let me or my family rest. You killed my first-born litter. You hurt my cub, bit off his tail, and now you're going to kill me.'

For answer the hound began to move towards her. She waited until he was almost up to the tractor and then dashed round to the other side. His jaws clashed together, caught her ear, held on.

O-ha thrashed around, twisting, turning, trying to loosen the dog's hold on her ear. She clawed at his eyes with her back legs, scratching deep grooves in the dog's snout. Still he held on to her. She could feel him trying to get a firmer grip on her head and knew that if those jaws closed on her skull, they would crush it instantly. Her blood mingled with his.

Finally, her ear tore away from her head, and she found herself running again, out into the open. Her strength was all but gone now, and the dog was still on her tail, despite his wounds.

She raced across the yard towards the pond. She was fading fast and the ridgeback would soon be on her. He slipped over a couple of times where the tractor had churned up the mud and it had frozen beneath the snow, but these were just minor hindrances to the dog. He knew he had her now. She was staggering, dripping blood from her torn ear.

When she reached the pond, she was down to a tottering walk. The mist of imminent death had fallen over her eyes. She was numb from head to tail, feeling only regret that she had failed Camio. If she did not return to the earth with food, he would surely die too. Sabre had managed to destroy both of them, just as he always promised he would.

She staggered unsteadily onto the ice. Sabre followed, sure of his quarry. This was the final confrontation.

The ridgeback cried, 'At last . . .'

Then O-ha heard the loud *crack!* of the ice breaking.

She turned, and saw him go through. The huge dog disappeared into a jagged hole, the black water sucking him down. For a few moments there was just a swirling. Then his head came up, once, the mouth open, the front paws scrabbling frantically at the broken ice. It snapped off, in plates. The subzero temperature of the water froze the dog's muscles to a standstill. He slipped away under the surface again. As his head disappeared, his eyes were on her, still full of cold hatred.

She waited a long time, hardly daring to believe what had happened. Her heart was still thumping in her breast. Her legs were still taut, ready to run, in case the hound emerged roaring from that black hole, and fell on her like the devil he was.

There was silence.

When she eventually gathered enough strength and courage to investigate she went as close to the hole as she dared. His body was floating gently under the ice. She could still see his eyes, the dead eyes staring up at her. They had lost their look of hatred. Then the body rolled over, slowly, and she caught a glimpse of the dark ridge of hair running down its back, before it sank out of sight.

She walked back to where Breaker lay. He lifted his head as she approached. 'He's dead,' she said, simply.

Breaker coughed. 'So am I, I think.'

'Thank you, Breaker.'

'How did he die? You tear his throat out?'

'No, he fell through the ice. He drowned.'

Breaker coughed again, then said, 'Serves him right. Arrogant swine. You'd better get out of here, vixen . . .'

'But you're bleeding.'

His left flank was seeping blood.

'Someone will come out of the farmhouse soon. They'll find me, and it'll just be a visit to the vet—'

It looked like a death wound to her.

'Goodbye, Breaker. We were enemies once . . .'

'We still are,' he gasped. 'I just repaid a favour. Now get out of here, you red devil, before I break your back.'

'Oh, Breaker, you poor, proud old dog. Don't you know we're friends? It happens, you know. It's not your fault that a fox has grown to like you, or that you saved a fox's life, and she's indebted to you.'

'You're right,' he murmured, 'about me being old. Fifty-six seasons have passed. Fifty-six. And now I'm tired. I want to close my eyes and die in peace.'

And he did. His eyes closed and he was dead.

She left him then, his blood turning the snow red, and went out into the fields. There she found some rotting turnips. She ate her fill, then took one in her teeth, carrying it on the long journey back to the earth. When she got there she found that Mitz had been out after the storm, found an open kitchen door and run in and snatched some bacon. Mitz was good at that: better than her mother. Mitz had been in houses and knew how to cope with it, in an emergency.

Camio looked as if he were recovering already.

He coughed. 'You brought a turnip—well done,' he said. 'Any trouble out there?'

'No,' she lied, snuggling up next to his warm, furry body. 'It's a white, peaceful world, with hardly anyone about.'

Mitz cried, 'O-ha! Your ear!'

'Oh, that? A little tussle with an ermine.'

'But your ear . . .'

'Be quiet, Mitz,' said O-ha. 'Camio's not well.'

That storm was the worst of the winter. Once it had blown itself out, they were well on their way to Scresheen. There were no cubs on the way, which gave O-ha time to appreciate the change in the seasons, without being so preoccupied with her young. It was a good time.

O-HA'S WOUND HEALED. She was too advanced an age for other foxes to give her some silly nickname like 'one-ear', but she found herself cocking her head to one side in order to listen to the world. Camio, fully recovered, said it made her look endearing.

That winter had aged both foxes. O-ha and Camio recognised that the flush of youth had gone from them. They were no longer regarded as a young pair. They were mature foxes, who knew the tricks, who knew the old ways and the new.

Camio learned of Sabre's death, but said nothing to O-ha. He guessed she wanted it out of her head for ever. They had many long talks about the past, but they concerned the good times they had shared, not the terrors. There were still plenty of those around, even with the giant hound gone to the Unplace.

SEASON DRIFTED INTO SEASON and the town expanded. O-ha and Camio had two more litters: some of the cubs survived, some did not. Those that did grow to adulthood had their own litters which dispersed and carried the blood of the original pair into new regions.

O-ha and Camio remained on the embankment of the railway, changing their earth at the appropriate times. The days of harassment were over for the pair and they came to that contentment which is rare and golden.

Mitz lived close by and they saw her occasionally. She had had her own cubs, whom the older pair recognised by their markings. They were town foxes and their education had been appropriate to their environment. Knowledge of the ancient highways and water holes, passed on to O-ha through many generations, had no significance to the new foxes: the land had changed, and they were foxes of the *face*. There were new maps in the minds of the new foxes and the world was a different place. No better or worse than when O-ha was a cub—just different. She did not necessarily like the changes, of course, because she had pleasant pictures in her head of the times when she was a cub herself, chasing butterflies over the *hav* and wrestling with her brothers and sisters in the tall grass on the slopes below Trinity Wood.

A-salla sent word, from time to time; the news was easy to verify since all they had to ask was, 'Did this fox have anything unusual about him?' and wait for the reply, 'Yes, he had no tail.'

The time was Ransheen and the cold hard streets were thick with snow and ice. O-ha remembered when she had first encountered snow. She had been with A-ho then and had been halfway through the leaving-the-earth ritual, her nose poking outside, when something fluffy and cold landed on the tip. Then she'd remembered what her mother had told her about the winter white, and gathering her courage together, had gone outside. She had been astounded at the change in the world. The whole landscape was covered in a blinding, soft fur. Each footstep she had taken had been an adventure, and all ways had been hidden beneath the albino coat that had descended from the sky.

There was no magic in snow now, though. It was merely a nuisance, since it hid any *gubbins* on the roads, or food that had been tossed away by humans the night before.

'Did you ever have snow where you came from?' she asked Camio, as she was steeling herself to leave the earth. A train rumbled by below them, making the earth vibrate a little. She had grown used to the giant metal snakes now: there was a certain comfort and security in the regular passing of trains. The noise was reassuring somehow, as if it meant that the world was still working properly.

'Snow? If we did, I don't remember it. But then it seems seasons out of time since I was in that land. Things get a little fuzzy. I don't think my life began until I met you.'

She did not know whether he was saying this to please her or not, but she liked it. She knew she was very special to him: that she was his vixen, but she also knew that he had memories of another fox, as she did of A-ho. If they were warm, then so much the better, but the fact that he did not parade these memories before her proved him a caring old dog fox who spared her meaningless comparisons.

'I think I'll go out soon,' she said.

She was feeling peculiar. A little tired. She suddenly had the urge to go up to Trinity Parklands and see if Gar was still around. She would like to have seen Gar one last time, before either of them . . . before something happened. Just a little weariness in her bones, that was all. It would pass off, once she started walking.

'I might go to the top of the town,' she said. 'I want to see the trees.'

'As you wish. I think I'll rest a little longer.'

O-ha carried out the rituals and then walked swiftly to the top of the embankment, under the fence, and onto the path. Ransheen swirled top-snow round her. It was bitterly cold, with a sheet of ice under the snow. Most of the humans remained in their houses and the streets were almost empty. A dog passed by on the other side, only giving her the slightest of glances. Most of the town dogs were used to foxes now—it was only excitable breeds like setters or boxers that bothered to chase them. They never caught her, of course. In the *face* there were many places to hide, many fences and walls to leap which could not be jumped by dogs. Gone were those terrible days of hound packs and thundering hooves.

As she walked along the street, close to the red brick walls, the sun came out and icicles hanging from the eaves of the houses began to sparkle with frostfire. And then, strangely, they began to jingle.

She stopped and listened. It was as if Ransheen were running her fingers along the lines of ice cones, sounding their individual notes for her benefit. She wondered what it meant.

Then, just as suddenly, the music stopped.

She stood there, bemused by the experience. The dog she had passed went round a corner without pausing in his stride. Clearly he had not heard the phenomenon. Thus, she deduced, it had to be a mystical happening, relevant perhaps only to herself.

She crossed an empty cobbled square and pigeons rose in a flock, scattering before her. Strange that there were no humans abroad.

The tired feeling she had had on waking that morning increased in intensity, until her eyelids drooped and her step began to falter. There was a pain in her breast now, like a dull ache, which seemed both near and far to her. She tried to reach the pain with her mind but it was elusive. She thought it had something to say to her, if only she could make contact with it.

There was no noise, no sound now. Even Ransheen had stopped screaming at the corners. Everywhere, there was a deathly stillness, a silence which hurt her ears. The street before her had opened up into a wide avenue, with snowcovered trees and tall houses on either side. She felt terribly cold.

She stopped, and lay down full length in the snow. It melted beneath her and the thaw miraculously spread, moving outwards from her body. As the snow disappeared from the *face*, so the warmth returned to her body and the pain began to disappear. Soon the world was a summer place and she felt no reason to move.

She waited, patiently.

She waited, and time passed without passing. She waited through moments that no longer followed, but overlaid each other. She waited for a long time that was not time at all.

While she lay there in her warmth, the streets melted like the snow and the buildings dribbled away to nothing. Grasslands replaced the concrete. Coverts of blackthorn sprang up around her. The land became full and sweetsmelling.

She was at the head of a wide valley which she had never seen before, but which was familiar to her. In the distance there was movement. A fox came through the bracken: a fox with a pure white flame hovering over its head. It walked towards her slowly. When the fox-spirit reached her it told her to rise and follow it down the valley.

'What is it?' she asked. 'Has Camio died? Are you taking me to his body, so that I can send him to you?'

'I am not the fox who leads the living to the dead. I am the fox who leads the dead to the Perfect There.' There was a pause. 'Your living mate has been here. He found you in the snow. He has done what you would have wished him to do.'

'Oh,' she said, realising now what had happened. 'He gave me my last rites.'

'Yes.'

She began to follow the fox-spirit down the long valley, thinking, the

508

Perfect There? But of course, she had now crossed over!

'Would it,' she asked, looking into the vacant eyes of her guide, 'have made any difference if no one had found my body?'

'You might have had to wait longer, that is all. I would have had to search for you, over the timeless wastes between life and death, but I would have found you, eventually.'

'So all the rituals—they weren't of any real use?'

The fox-spirit replied, 'They were of use to *you.*'

She acknowledged this. 'That's true. I needed them, once.'

Finally they came to Trinity Wood, with all its old scents and sounds, all its old highways and paths, its soaks and water holes. Down at the end of the valley, shining like polished redwood, stood a tall, wide structure made of hollow tree trunks. It was magnificent. The trunks were of varying girths and heights and were joined together to form a concave wall which spanned the whole width of the valley. In each trunk was a series of holes, all of different sizes, and from these orifices came the notes of many winds and breezes. The giant pipes were blowing now.

'The Palace of the Winds,' explained the fox-spirit.

'So that's where *Heff* is. So close to my covert. It's very beautiful. I wonder why I never saw it before?'

'Because you weren't looking for it.'

At that moment, Gar came out of the trees, ambling down to meet her. She gave a shout of delight.

'I was coming to see you,' she said, 'and here you are.'

'Oh, ya. Here I am, here I am,' he rumbled.

'But,' she was confused, 'why are you here? With the foxes?'

'I am here and I am somewhere else,' he said. 'You are here, and you are somewhere else. What place must the soul stay? No one place. It is everywhere. I knew it all along. Here you are and here am I. So, and others . . .'

And the others came out of the covert to meet her, among them the one she had most hoped to see.

CAMIO WENT SADLY back to the earth after carrying out the ritual for the dead around the body of his O-ha. He had been a sceptic for most of his life regarding life after death, but now he had seen a creature with a flame over its head and things were not the same. More importantly, he found it impossible to believe that he would never find O-ha again. Her scent was still strong in his nostrils, and he knew that it would linger there for the rest of his life. They had done so much together. They had a history which went back so many seasons. Surely that couldn't be wiped out by something so negative as *not life*? The flesh had gone cold and still, but the rest still existed, somewhere.

So perhaps he could believe that she was in the place she called the Perfect Here? If that was so, A-ho, her former mate, would be there to greet her. Camio wondered if he ought to feel jealous, but could only be glad that she would not be lonely in the valley of death. He and A-ho might even like each other. Camio could not imagine that such earthly feelings as jealousy still survived in the spirit pure.

Later that day, he went to find his daughter's earth on another section of the embankment, and called her outside so that the other occupants would not feel he was invading the family home.

'I thought you ought to know, your mother is dead.'

Mitz stood there for a while, and then nodded.

'You'd better go back, Camio. Get out of the snow. It's a very cold day.'

'I hadn't noticed,' he said. 'I suppose you're right.'

He started to walk away, when she called, 'Father!'

He turned. Foxes seldom used titles for each other and Mitz had called him Camio for as long as she had been his cub.

'Yes?'

'I'll miss her too, you know. You're not alone in the way that you feel. She's gone to a good place.'

'I hope so,' he said. 'I keep telling myself the same thing.'

He left her then. She was too much like her mother and it hurt him to look at her. Walking along the embankment, he wondered how he was going to spend the hours. He glanced up at the white, swirling skies, not finding an answer.

When he entered the earth—their earth—he was amazed at how large and empty it appeared to be. When she was alive it seemed there was hardly room to move in there, without touching each other. Now, every sound he made echoed in the stillness. He would surely have to move, make himself a new home. Somewhere smaller, where he could closet his memories.

Mitz was wrong, of course. He *was* alone in his feelings. Mitz would miss a mother, but the seasons would still turn for his daughter.

As far as Camio was concerned, O-ha had taken the seasons with her.

GARRY KILWORTH

Garry Kilworth could be described in fox terms as a *longtrekker* or *rangfar*, having led a very nomadic life in many different parts of the British Isles and the world. This wandering lifestyle may be due to his part-gypsy blood, but is more probably due to his father being in the RAF.

The Kilworth family moved about so often that by the time Garry left school, with no qualifications, he had attended over twenty schools.

At fifteen he was sent to RAF Cosford, an RAF Technical College, and was signed up for fifteen years to serve as a communications operator and later a cryptographer. He was posted to Singapore at seventeen and then to Gan, in the Maldive Islands, where he spent his time exploring the coral reef, writing poetry, and educating himself by reading at least one book every two days. 'Towards the end of my year on Gan I began to write stories,' Garry recalls. 'I had always written *something* but I was beginning to take writing a little more seriously.'

It was in 1974 that he entered the Gollancz/Sunday Times Short Story Competition with a tale entitled *Let's Go To Golgotha!* and on the day he left the RAF he learned that he had won.

After working for a number of years for Cable and Wireless, Garry Kilworth went to King's College, London, to study for an honours degree in English. He graduated in 1985, having written a successful novel entitled *Witchwater Country* while at college.

It was after he and his wife, Annette, moved to a cottage in two acres of ground in the village of Ashingdon, Essex, that his interest in foxes began. Having lived in a town for ten years they found that foxes kept them awake at nights, with their banshee howling and twittering. In the winter of '86 some cubs were born in his garden. 'We used to watch them gambolling with their parents,' he recalls, 'only reluctantly getting out of the way of vehicles.' Scenes such as this became the basis and inspiration for *Hunter's Moon*.

Garry Kilworth has been married to Annette for twenty-seven years, has two grown-up children and is a grandfather. He is currently living and writing in Hong Kong—for ever a *longtrekker*!